"VALDEN!" KUSAC SHOUTED....

At that precise moment, the barrier on both tunnels broke open with a roar that deafened them all.

Kusac barely had time to launch himself backward, not for Valden, but for the Prince, then the wall of water engulfed them all.

As the water hit him, it flung him forward into Zsurtul, allowing him to grab hold of the young Emperor and lock him tight against his body. He felt another body hit them both—Zhalmo—and cling onto Zsurtul from behind as the force of the water tossed them. Briefly, he wondered if Valden was safe, then he was slammed against a boulder, bent around it, and was swept away again.

All it needed was a crack in the visor, and any one of them would be dead. He tightened his grip on the Prince as the water surged between them, threatening to drag them apart as it sucked them backward, swirling them about until they were once again slammed into a solid surface.

This time, his head hit the back of his helmet with enough force to stun him. He felt his grip on Zsurtul begin to relax and gave a low moan of pain as nausea swept over him.

Someone was saying something, but the cries of fear and distress from the others were drowning it out.

DAW Books
is proud to present
LISANNE NORMAN'S
SHOLAN ALLIANCE Novels:

LISANNE NORMAN

SHADES OF GRAY

A SHOLAN ALLIANCE NOVEL

DAW BOOKS, INC.

DONALD A. WOLLHEIM, FOUNDER

375 Hudson Street, New York, NY 10014

ELIZABETH R. WOLLHEIM

SHEILA E. GILBERT

PUBLISHERS

www.dawbooks.com

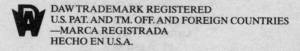

To Sheila, for having enough belief in me to let me have the time I needed to settle down in the USA and finish this novel.

And to Marsha, for núdging me just enough to make me keep at it, even when I found it almost impossible to concentrate with all the post-moving to a new country chaos going on around me.

And to Kai and Jackie for being just who they are, my family.

THANKS AND SPECIAL MENTIONS

My first thank you is to my readers for waiting patiently for this novel. Moving to the USA and starting a new life out here took more out of me than I thought it would, and it is taking longer than I expected to settle in with a place to live and a job. So my first thanks are to you for your patience.

My next is to Sheila, my editor, for her patience too. I don't know what I'd have done had it not been for you and Marsha. Love you both.

Now my thanks for help in planning this novel go to several very important groups of people. First is a group of friends who want only their Sholan names mentioned. They helped me with all the military tactics I needed to know, and one, Chayak, even ran a role playing game with the others of my plot to retake the City and Palace to see if it worked. It did. They are: Brandon Jasper and Koshan, Dyaku, Rhyart, and Nezzoh. Thank you, guys, for all you did, and do.

John Van Stry and John Quadling also helped with military scenes. John and Gina Quadling helped design my MUTAC as a fighting machine, and Jerenn drew it for me. Jerenn and M'Nar, both fan club members, also helped work out how it would operate and move. Mapping help came from the Traveller Role Players, and the Campaign Cartographer people. Helping me design the City and Palace of Light were VAIA from the Pharaoh city building game forum, John Van Stry, and Rachel McDonald. More help came from the Tour Egypt web site builder who sent me extra stills of the city of Aketaten—Pharaoh Akhenaten's desert city to his solar god, the Aten. Yes, the Valtegans' architecture is based on the Ancient Egyptians.

Thanks also to Bailey A. Buchanan for all kinds of help.

Special mention to Jerenn for drawing the MUTAC for me as his design is the one used by my talented artist for his rendering of it.

Finally, but not least, many thanks go to fellow DAW author and Anglo Saxon and Celtic Historian, Kari Sperring, for all her help with what is actually known about the British legends of Merlin and the Druids. The observatory legend fitted in beautifully, thank you, Kari, as did the story of Gwenhifer and her evil sister.

Once again, thank you all for your help.

Thank you each one.

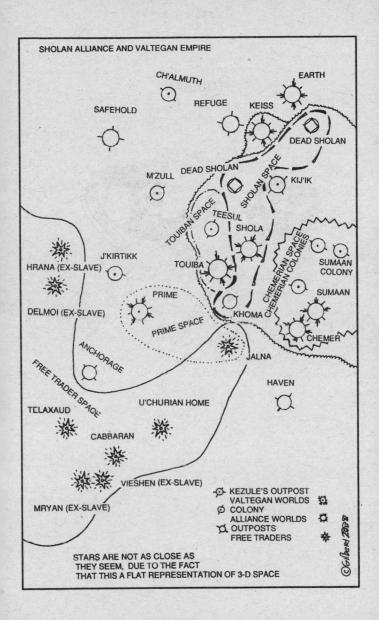

SHOLAN ALLIANCE AND VALTEGAN EMPIRE

CH'ALMUTH

EARTH

SAFEHOLD

REFUGE

KEISS

DEAD SHOLAN

DEAD SHOLAN

SHOLAN SPACE

M'ZULL

KIJ'IK

TOUIBAN SPACE

TEESUL

SHOLA

CHEMERIAN SPACE

CHEMERIAN COLONIES

J'KIRTIKK

TOUIBA

SUMAAN
COLONY

HRANA (EX-SLAVE)

PRIME

SUMAAN

DELMOI (EX-SLAVE)

PRIME SPACE

KHOMA

CHEMER

ANCHORAGE

JALNA

FREE TRADER SPACE

HAVEN

TELAXAUD

U'CHURIAN HOME

CABBARAN

VIESHEN (EX-SLAVE)

MRYAN (EX-SLAVE)

- KEZULE'S OUTPOST
  VALTEGAN WORLDS
- COLONY
  ALLIANCE WORLDS
- OUTPOSTS
  FREE TRADERS

©Gilbert 2003

STARS ARE NOT AS CLOSE AS
THEY SEEM, DUE TO THE FACT
THAT THIS A FLAT REPRESENTATION
OF 3-D SPACE

TOUIBAN

CABBARAN

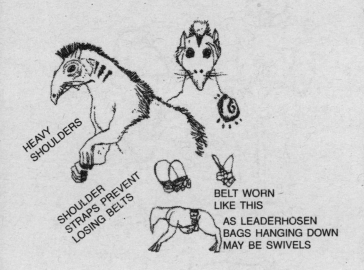

HEAVY SHOULDERS

SHOULDER STRAPS PREVENT LOSING BELTS

BELT WORN LIKE THIS

AS LEADERHOSEN BAGS HANGING DOWN MAY BE SWIVELS

PRIME ENCOUNTER SUIT

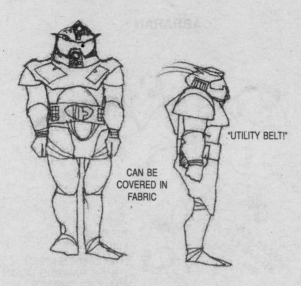

CAN BE
COVERED IN
FABRIC

."UTILITY BELT!"

IF CRESTED
EXTRA ROOM FOR
SUPPORT EQU.

CHAPTER 1

A WARNING tone followed by a burst of complex trilling speech through the conference suite's comm took Kaid's attention away from the scaled holo image of the City of Light they were studying.

Toueesut, leader of the Touibans quartered on Kusac's estate, frowned, his mobile eyebrows meeting over his deep-set eyes in a single bushy line. He replied in what for him was a terse, and short, burst of the same singsong language before looking around them, his expression grim.

"We must go. The Prime Prince and the children are causing a serious incident on the emergency Bridge."

The Sholan's ears flicked back into invisibility. "What?" Kaid asked incredulously as he got hurriedly to his feet. "There must be some mistake."

"None. We must go there instantly and resolve it."

"What's he doing there in the first place?" demanded Carrie, the only Human present, as she followed them out into the corridor. "And why has he taken the cubs with him? How did he even know where it was?"

"We will have to be asking him, Carrie," said the small alien, looking up at her. "It seems they have been using their mental powers on our soldiers to gain access and to guard themselves from interference."

"I'll be tanning some hides tonight," said Garras grimly, pacing along beside them as the other Sholans followed. "A warship is no place for childish pranks; Prince Zsurtul should know this. And where's the youngling, Valden? And Tanjo? He's their tutor, they should be with him!"

"I sent Tanjo to rest. He was up half the night with the cubs because they ate too many cookies," said Carrie. "I should have known better than to leave Valden in charge of them!"

Toueesut stopped at an elevator. "This is no prank. Prince Zsurtul has routed communications there from the main Bridge and is transmitting a message even as we speak."

Kaid could feel every hair across his shoulders and down his spine start to prickle in dread as his ears, which had raised themselves to their usual upright position, sank again.

"I can't reach any of them mentally," said Carrie as the elevator door slid open. "They've totally blanked the area. It's as if there were psi dampers there."

"Once a Valtegan, always a Valtegan," muttered Rezac as they piled in. "He's reverting to type now he's their Emperor-elect."

"No!" said Carrie sharply. "He's a Prime, you know that. There has to be a rational explanation for this."

"By Vartra's bones, there had better be," swore Kaid as they surged downward into the bowels of the Touiban battle-ship. His blood ran cold at the thought that they'd been harboring a snake in their midst all these months.

He hasn't turned on us, Tallinu, you know he hasn't, Carrie sent to Kaid as she rested her hand reassuringly on his arm.

I hope you're right, because if he and they combined can bring the Tooshu *to her knees like this, the Gods alone know how we're going to stop them!*

Armed and armored Touibans, their mustaches bristling, waited to escort them past the obviously hastily erected force field bunkers at every corridor junction and iris. As they walked, Toueesut conversed rapidly in his trilling voice with their escort. They rounded a corner and came face-to-face with a group of four unarmored Touibans standing with weapons drawn. Their escort halted.

"They'll let no one pass beyond here," said Toueesut.

"This is ridiculous," said Garras angrily. "How dare that young krolla involve our cubs like this!" As he started forward, Carrie grabbed his arm and held him back.

"There has to be a good reason for this *because* he's involved the cubs," she said, looking at them all one by one. "Before anyone gets hurt, we have to think this through."

"You may enter," said a voice from behind her in very badly pronounced Sholan.

Swinging round, she faced the four impassive Touibans. "Just me?" *They're being mentally controlled*, she sent to the others.

"And Kaid."

"Let these people go immediately," said Kaid, tail lashing from side to side in a show of anger. "What you're doing is wrong."

"Soon. We must finish this first," said one of the Touibans, his face blank and emotionless. "No harm is intended to anyone."

With a low rumble of anger, Kaid, followed by Carrie, approached them. "The rest of you stay where you are," he said over his shoulder. "That's an order."

Walking like a broken toy, the small alien turned and lurched alongside them until they came to a reinforced air lock. They stepped through it into an area unlike any they'd been in so far. Gone were the bright colors on walls and flooring so loved by their hosts; instead everything was a dull, uniform gray. Manual fire extinguishers were set every few feet, in addition to those in the upper walls and ceilings. The place was psychically dead as a morgue, and he didn't like it.

"They're here," they heard the cub Gaylla's voice say as their escort suddenly stopped in front of a doorway and barred their way. "Are you finished yet?"

"In a minute," Zsurtul said quietly before lapsing into a torrent of Valtegan.

Straining his ears forward, Kaid tried to make out what the Prince was saying.

Carrie shook her head helplessly when he looked at her. "It's a different dialect, and he's speaking too fast," she whispered.

"I'm finished. You can release our guards and let the Lieges in now," said Zsurtul. "Thank you for your help."

Suddenly, the psychic null zone vanished, and the guard beside them dropped his firearm and staggered against the wall.

Automatically Kaid reached out to catch him, murmuring a few comforting phrases before ordering him to rejoin his people. As he did, he sensed Zsurtul coming out of the Bridge a few feet away, followed by Valden and all five of the young Sholan cubs.

"This had better be good," Kaid snarled, letting his canines show even as he watched the way the cubs formed a defensive circle around the young Prime, and noticed that Zsurtul had aged almost overnight.

Valden was left facing them, his jaw set in a firm line of determination. "It's not what you think," he began.

"How the hell could you know what I'm thinking?" demanded Kaid.

"I asked to see the recording General Kezule sent of the usurper K'hedduk's broadcast," said Zsurtul. His eyes closed briefly before he continued. "When I saw the head of my father and the others from the Royal Court that he'd killed, I remembered that before I left for Shola, he gave me the access codes for the Palace and the fleet, in case . . ." He ground to a halt, his large green eyes blinking rapidly.

Against his side, Gaylla pressed herself closer to him, slipping her small furred hand into his where it hung loosely by his side.

"I had to act immediately," he continued, his voice firming again. "Before K'hedduk got into the system and changed the codes. I salvaged enough to contact the M'zullians and tell them there had been delays in K'hedduk's plan and not to send reinforcements for another six weeks." His brow creased as he looked from Kaid to Carrie and back. "Six weeks will be long enough for us to retake the Palace, won't it? Maybe I should have said two months."

"Six weeks will be fine," said Kaid weakly, feeling the bottom drop out of his world in shock.

"You didn't tell them . . ." began Carrie.

Zsurtul gave her a pained look. "Carrie, I'm not a fool. I didn't let them know who I was."

Dhyshac wormed his way to the front of their little group. "You can see why we had to help him, Father. There was no time to argue with everyone about it. As it was, Zsurtul was just in time."

Gathering his scattered wits, Kaid scowled at them all. "That doesn't excuse the liberties you took. Manipulating another person's mind is a criminal offense," he said, deciding not to mince his words. "Valden, you know that, you should have stopped them. Our Psychic Talent gives us power, but it also requires us to use it responsibly or face the consequences, and believe me, you will *all* face the consequences!"

"It was my idea," said Gaylla, moving even closer to the Prince, if it were possible. "They won't take my Talent away, will they?" Her eyes began to fill with tears. "I was very careful of my soldier. I only did it 'cos I know it's important to stop people being hurt."

"Gaylla's not to blame," said Dhyshac, lifting his chin. "It was me who organized it. If anyone's to be punished, it should be me."

Kaid was hard pressed to keep his face straight as he watched the unconscious signs of his son's anxiety—the ears lying flat against his head and the nervous twitching of his tail—vying with his obvious attempts at bravery.

"I take full responsibility . . ." began Valden.

"Mine is the responsibility," insisted Zsurtul, speaking over the top of the young male.

"I'll take all that into consideration," Kaid said roughly. "No one is going to have his or her Talent removed, but you all have some apologizing to do, and you must make amends to the Touiban soldiers, not to mention to Toueesut and the Captain of the *Tooshu*!"

"A week helping prepare vegetables in the kitchens is definitely in order," said Carrie sternly, pointing in the direction they'd come. "Go there right now, after you've apologized!"

"Yes, Liegena," the cubs mumbled, beginning to sidle abjectly past her.

Kaid kept his eyes on Zsurtul, gauging him carefully with his mind as well as his other senses, waiting to see what he'd do next, but the Prince remained silent, standing with his back straight, offering no excuses and no more explanations. He met Kaid's eyes, though his normally sand-tinted green skin was paler than usual.

"Apart from buying us some much-needed time, what else were you able to achieve?" he asked quietly.

"I changed the main offworld comm frequency," Zsurtul said. "The M'zullians and K'hedduk will be unable to reach each other on the old one. Their messages will come directly here for us to intercept."

"Does that include the fleet orbiting round K'oish'ik?"

Zsurtul shook his head. "No, I left that alone so as not to arouse suspicion, but I changed the codes, so even if K'hedduk discovers them, he can't access them. I could do nothing about the City or Palace defenses, he'd already changed those codes, but we do have control over the internal systems like power, water, and communications within the Palace."

"We have?" Kaid began to smile. "Won't K'hedduk suspect someone's been tampering?"

"No. He'll assume my father changed the codes before . . ." His voice broke on his final word.

"He'll assume your father forgot to pass on the new codes," Kaid finished for him.

"I should go and apologize now," he said quietly. "It isn't fair that the cubs should face the Touibans' anger alone."

Kaid stood aside for him to pass, calling out to him just before he rounded the corner.

"Next time, Prince Zsurtul, please have the courtesy to let us know what you plan to do beforehand. When you're finished, I'll expect you to join us in the conference room for a full debriefing. It's time you became part of the planning team."

"He did good, even if he went about it the wrong way," said Carrie, putting her arm through Kaid's as they began to walk back to Toueesut. "Six weeks! I can't believe he managed to talk both sides into that!"

"He did do good," Kaid agreed. "He's not a child anymore. I have a feeling his mother has more Warrior-caste ancestry in her than anyone reckoned for."

"I think his father knew that. Why else would he want his son trained by us? If we can know our genetic matches and form Leska Links with them, who's to know the Primes can't tell theirs?"

"The Primes aren't telepathic, Carrie."

When she replied with a small grunt, he said again, "They aren't telepathic."

Toueesut came forward. "I think perhaps you may be wrong about the Prince. Sensing what was going on I was through the harmonics we use, and to me it is obvious that he has sensitivity. Perhaps he is even empathic, like many of your Brothers and Sisters. Long have I been thinking this, and now I feel I am right."

"Empathic?" echoed Carrie. "That's not possible . . . is it?"

"Who knows?" said Toueesut, spreading his calloused hands. "These Primes are the Intellectual caste, more intelligent than others; it is possible it may have developed over time. I will make peace with my Captain over this. A feeling I have the young Prince felt compelled to act now. Among us are a very few who have sensings of future events . . ." Toueesut shrugged expressively and left the rest unsaid.

"He's lived with us, worked with us. If he had any psi abilities, surely we'd have sensed them by now," said Carrie, her tone doubtful

"Perhaps you're right," said Kaid. "We didn't even guess about Toueesut and his people. Maybe whatever he has doesn't work the same way our abilities do; perhaps it's more like the Touibans'. He did say he had a bad feeling about returning home when he asked to stay on with us."

"Well, there's one way to find out. Test him," said Carrie.

"No. He's going through enough right now."

"We need to know," Carrie insisted.

"Ask the little ones," suggested Toueesut as they all began to move down the corridor again. "If anyone knows, they will."

Kij'ik, Command Level Briefing room

"Is he purposely keeping me waiting?"

Kezule glanced away from the Brotherhood logo on his comm screen toward the black-pelted Sholan sprawled uncomfortably on the sofa on the other side of his office.

"No," said Kusac, wincing visibly as he sat up. "Master Rhyaz doesn't stay in his office all day; he's usually out and about with the students. He is the leader of the Warrior side of our Order. They'll have to page him for you. You do realize he was in charge of interrogating you when you were on Shola, don't you?"

"I haven't a problem with that. Maybe he'll be conveniently unavailable," grunted the Valtegan, checking the screen yet again. Already he wasn't enjoying this novel experience of asking for help, but he intended to retain the initiative.

"He'll answer you personally. Whatever else he is, Rhyaz is no moral coward."

Something in the other's tone made Kezule look back at him. There was obviously unfinished business between Kusac and this Brotherhood Leader.

"You should still be in the sick bay, or at least resting in your quarters," he said abruptly, the skin around his eyes creasing as he frowned. "My wife, Zayshul, said Dzaou had sliced up your side and arms pretty well, and I know your injured leg took a pounding in that fight."

"I'm fine," Kusac replied, his mobile upright ears flicking in what Kezule recognized as mild annoyance. "Just beginning to stiffen up, that's all. You know Dzaou was bucking my authority from the get-go. Our fight was long overdue."

Kezule grunted his disbelief and turned back to the comm just as the warning tone sounded for his incoming call. The screen changed to show a brown-pelted Sholan male dressed in a purple-edged gray robe.

"General Kezule, I'm Commander Rhyaz, Guild Master of the Warriors in the Brotherhood of Vartra. My colleague L'Seuli, leader of our Haven Outpost, said you'd be contacting me."

"We've met," said Kezule shortly, eyes narrowing as he remembered the male who'd been one of his more aggressive interrogators when he'd been a prisoner on Shola.

"So we have. You have a hard head, as I remember. I broke one of my fingers on it."

"Did you now?" The corners of Kezule's wide mouth twitched slightly in an involuntary smile. Kusac was right: Rhyaz was meeting him head-on, with no apologies. "Maybe there's some justice in the universe after all," he murmured sotto voce.

"I'm told this new emperor is K'hedduk, leader of the Directorate," said Rhyaz, ignoring the comment.

"He's also the younger brother of the M'zullian Emperor. It's imperative that he be removed from the Throne of Light as soon as possible," said Kezule, "before reinforcements arrive."

"Surely he's preempting his own ruler? Won't that destabilize M'zull—and be to our advantage?" said Rhyaz blandly.

"I'm aware of his intercepted messages to his generals, Commander," said Kezule. "We both know that by now there's likely been a coup on M'zull. By taking the throne, K'hedduk has reunified two of the remaining three worlds—

and he believes Ch'almuth is a ripe fruit waiting for him to pluck at his leisure. We must take back the Palace and put Prince—Emperor Zsurtul," he corrected himself, "on his rightful throne."

Rhyaz glanced at some printouts beside him. "That shouldn't be too difficult, Kezule, looking at the data you sent us on the Palace. It isn't that large, only about the size of Ranz, if you include the City around it. If we can get our destroyer in close enough . . ."

"The Palace cannot be destroyed," Kezule interrupted. "Both it and the throne have a deeply religious significance to us. Unless he's crowned on the Throne of Light, Zsurtul will never be accepted by the Primes as Emperor. Then there's the civilian population . . . I want as little collateral damage as possible."

He watched Rhyaz raise an eye ridge, but the Sholan Commander said nothing.

"We're looking at a combined air and land assault, Rhyaz," he continued, using the Brotherhood Warrior Leader's name for the first time.

"That complicates matters. We need to get past the craft guarding your world, K'oish'ik. When we do, our ship does have drop capabilities and ancillary fighters. I'll contact Commander L'Seuli, and we'll draft a battle plan. You can liaise with him when he rendezvouses with you."

"I think you misunderstand me, Commander." Kezule forced himself to keep his voice soft. "While I'm willing to consider your suggestions, I'll be leading this mission jointly with Captain Aldatan. Your warriors will be assisting us."

Again Rhyaz raised his eye ridge. "Able though the Captain is, he's hardly an appropriate choice. He lacks . . ."

"He knows my Primes," interrupted Kezule. "He's worked with them here for these past five months—they trust each other. With respect, they don't know any other Sholans apart from him and his crew."

The Sholan pursued his point. "Captain Aldatan lacks the necessary experience and seniority . . ."

"It's not negotiable—if your Brotherhood wants first chance at more Prime technology," he interrupted bluntly. "Frankly, I didn't expect you to be so hypocritical, considering the circumstances surrounding Kusac's departure for here."

Rhyaz regarded him silently, but Kezule could see the traces of the other's anger by the slight narrowing of his eyes and in the way his ears flared fractionally. He hadn't liked that—or expected it. Good, he might need the help Rhyaz could provide, but he'd be damned if he'd let him think he was taking over this mission.

"Very well," Rhyaz agreed, his tone icy. "However, I can speak only for the Brotherhood, not for Shola or the Alliance."

"Understood. I need our Emperor-elect brought here to my Outpost, Kij'ik. He'll be safe here with my family until we've retaken K'oish'ik."

"That's beyond my ability to do. We don't have access to the Prince . . . Emperor Zsurtul."

"Then I suggest you get it," said Kezule sharply, leaning forward. "His place is with his people. He cannot be crowned anywhere but on K'oish'ik, I thought I made that clear."

"It's out of my hands, General," said Rhyaz, his slight smile ironic. "The last I heard about him, your Emperor was staying on Captain Aldatan's estate. It's likely Governor Nesul has requested that he be relocated in secure quarters at the Palace."

"If you believe I'll tolerate him being held to ransom," began Kezule, his crest rising in anger. . . .

"I don't, and neither would we," interrupted Rhyaz coldly. "In that unlikely event, I assure you, he'll be liberated by our personnel."

Kezule searched the Sholan face on the comm screen, then took a deep breath. "I hope you understand that Zsurtul is all that stands between me and a job I swore not to take. I left K'oish'ik for that reason," he said softly. "Zsurtul is in no danger from me. I'll stay only long enough to see him crowned and surrounded by trustworthy advisers; then I plan to return here to Kij'ik."

"I believe you," said Rhyaz, surprising him. "However, it may be necessary for you to remain with the young Emperor during the inevitable M'zullian crisis. As you no doubt know, all Primes are too light in color to be able to negotiate with the M'zullians. Only you have the same skin tones as they and can therefore be seen as an equal."

Kezule frowned. He didn't want to remain tied to the Court for a moment longer than it took to get Zsurtul onto the throne. "We'll see," he said abruptly. "If we didn't need their bloodlines, I'd advise the Alliance to destroy M'zull and everyone on it."

"Genocide isn't an option, General," said Rhyaz. "No matter how tempting, even if we had the means."

Kezule grunted. He'd expected no other answer from the Sholan; they didn't have the stomach for such drastic solutions.

"Tell him to send the MUTAC," said Kusac suddenly, keeping his voice low enough so only Kezule could hear him.

Without batting an eye, Kezule said, "Send the MUTAC, Rhyaz. It's essential to our plan."

Rhyaz's expression froze momentarily. "So Captain Aldatan is beside you," he said softly. "Then he should have told you we considered it a failed experiment."

"Nevertheless, send it," repeated Kezule, keeping his eyes fixed on the Commander.

Rhyaz shrugged. "If you wish, though it will do you little good."

"How long until your people arrive here?"

"Kaid Tallinu and his team should be with you in three days, Commander L'Seuli and our destroyer in six, since they have to come from our Haven outpost. As I said, as well as thirty fighters, it carries five hundred drop pods for our armored Brothers and Sisters acting as ground forces."

"That should be more than enough. The Palace isn't that large, and by our reckoning, K'hedduk has just under three hundred and fifty people capable of fighting. The City and the rest of K'oish'ik can be discounted—it's in an advanced state of urban decay."

Rhyaz gave him a measured look and, choosing his words with obvious care, said, "It would be a tragedy if the Intellectual caste was lost to your species' gene pool, Kezule."

"What do you think I've been doing on Kij'ik, with Captain Aldatan's help," said Kezule shortly, reaching out to disconnect the call. "I'll see your Commander L'Seuli in six days."

Kusac waited until Kezule leaned back in his chair before speaking. "The MUTAC is a multi-terrain attack carrier. It carries only a pilot, but it has a very basic cargo area that would hold one injured person."

"Rhyaz said it was a failed experiment."

He spread his hands expressively, wondering what had prompted him to ask for it. "Depends on your point of view. It will look terrifying when it bounds into a battle."

"Bounds?"

"It's shaped like us, but it walks—or runs—on all fours. It has jets on each leg and can be used in a HALO drop. Armaments are explosive and guided missiles, and there's a top-mounted beam weapon. It's capable of standing upright and using its clawed feet to pull down structures. All in all, it's a useful piece of hardware, designed more for backup and inspiring terror than heavy fighting."

"How many of these have you?" asked Kezule, obviously intensely interested.

"Only the one. It's a Brotherhood prototype made when I was staying at Stronghold. It proved to be somewhat difficult to control with the levers and gears used to operate it."

"Then why . . ."

"For the look of it, Kezule, and the thought that maybe, since we know Kaid is with the Touibans, they may be able to find a way to adapt it for us. Forget that for the moment; we can't wait six days for Rhyaz to get here. K'hedduk's been in power now for nearly two weeks. Every day that passes he's digging himself in deeper."

"I know, but we have no choice. We don't have nearly enough people to mount an assault ourselves."

"We can, with the right plan."

"I'm calling a briefing in an hour, in the room across the corridor. We'll discuss plans then," said Kezule tiredly.

"You've met L'Seuli too," said Kusac, getting stiffly to his feet.

Kezule glanced over at him again.

"During your captivity, he acted out the reasonable soldier routine when they thought you were cooperating," Kusac elaborated. "And head of the Sholan Forces is General Raiban— she took you into custody at the edges of the desert when we brought you forward in time."

A hiss of anger greeted his disclosure.

"You were an extremely high-level captive then, Kezule," he said with an almost feral grin of amusement.

"Stop trying to manipulate me, Kusac; you've made your point," the Valtegan said. "I have no option but to ask for Sholan help."

"The Brotherhood's, yes. Shola's—no. Don't ask for military help. Call Shola, but ask for aid from the Alliance in rebuilding K'oish'ik. You'll need it when you realize your social engineering program can be realistically continued only on your home world."

"K'oish'ik isn't *my* home world," Kezule snapped. "I was hatched on an outpost world. Stop reading my mind, Kusac!"

"I'm not," he said mildly, leaning against the sofa for support. His body ached now that the analgesics Zayshul had given him after his fight with Dzaou were beginning to wear off. "It's obvious Zsurtul needs more than just a city, no matter how holy, to sustain him and his people. That world needs rebuilding, and you have an excellent beginning here. You've known all along that at some point you'd have to leave here for a planet."

"One day," Kezule admitted grudgingly.

"Dare to be truly different from the rest of your caste, Kezule, and give your people a positive legacy," said Kusac softly.

Kezule stared unblinkingly at him for the space of several heartbeats before looking away. "Will I have to speak to this Raiban female when I call Shola?" he asked instead.

"No, you'll be put through to one of the Governor's aides, then to Nesul himself. General Raiban takes her orders from the ruling Council of Shola and of the Alliance. We're not ruled by the military, thank Vartra! I need to speak to my son now, Kezule. I'll see you at the briefing in an hour," he said, pushing himself upright and limping toward the door.

"Bring Lieutenant Banner with you," Kezule called out after him as he stepped out into the corridor.

Kusac's quarters

"We need to have a serious talk, Shaidan," Kusac said, shivering slightly as he ushered his son into the lounge area of his quarters. He checked the thermostat, surprised to find it at the usual temperature; he hoped he wasn't developing a fever. "Would you like a drink? A fruit juice or something hot?"

he asked, before heading for the dispensing unit by the meal bar.

"A keffa, please," the cub said, trotting over to the sofa and easy chairs. "Is something wrong, Father? I can't sense your mind at all."

"I'm just marshaling my thoughts," he said, grabbing two mugs and sticking one on the dispenser pad. He programmed in a coffee for himself and a keffa for his son.

Behind his strong mental shielding, as he was now, he could only just sense Shaidan's mind. "It's not been easy for you, I know. From the beginning, you were thrust into the midst of an adult world. Just how much you've been aware of, I'm not completely sure, but it's time you learned some of the truths and reasons behind what's been happening around you."

He found his son's silence unnerving. Picking up the two mugs, he went over to join him.

Shaidan was sitting curled up in one of the easy chairs, his posture one of confusion and self-protection. Kusac sighed. As usual, he wasn't handling this well, he realized as he placed the mugs on the low table and took a seat on the sofa opposite the cub. He lowered his shielding slightly in an effort to get closer to his son.

Head now bowed, Shaidan seemed to shrink even farther into the chair, his tail tip twitching erratically in obvious distress.

"You're going to send me away as soon as they arrive, aren't you?" the cub said finally, looking up, his eyes glinting with unshed tears.

"Absolutely not!" Kusac said firmly, holding his hand out in invitation to the cub. "You're my son; you'll stay with me until I can take you home myself."

Shaidan blinked furiously, obviously determined not to cry. "You promise you won't make me go with strangers?"

"I swear it. Come here," Kusac urged, reaching his hand out farther toward him, remembering that though his son was physically ten years old, he'd been "born" less than a year ago as a result of the Directorate's illegal genetic experiments. "I swear that while I still draw breath, you will never be sent to strangers."

Shaidan slid off his chair and, taking his father's hand, allowed himself to be pulled up beside him on the sofa. "Then why are you so worried?" he asked.

"I have some difficult things to tell you," Kusac said, bracing himself mentally as he tucked his arm around his son. "You've been told about how the Directorate created you, but they didn't just steal genetic material from myself and . . . Carrie," he began, wishing it weren't still so difficult to talk about her. "They also stole from Doctor Zayshul and combined it with ours to make you. As well as being a Human/Sholan hybrid like your sisters, you're also a very little part Prime."

"Why?" Shaidan asked after a small silence. "Why would they want me to be part Prime?"

"I don't know," he said, raising his hand to gently stroke his son's head. "Don't worry," he reassured him. "It won't make you look any different from how you do now. But like your hybrid genes, the Prime ones will be passed on to your own cubs one day. Doctor Zayshul is working on finding out how else it may affect you, and as soon as she knows, she'll tell us." He hesitated. "There's something else you should know . . ."

"About you and the Doctor?" asked Shaidan, burrowing closer to his side. "The other Sholan told me, but I could smell the scent marker anyway."

"The Sholan in gray?" Kusac asked, trying to keep the sharpness out of his voice. "Do you know his name? Was it Vartra?" He'd long suspected it was Him, the Sholan Warrior Entity of Peace.

Shaidan nodded, snuggling even closer to him and wrapping an arm across his lap. "That's what he said he was called. He said he couldn't come to you any more, so he came to me instead."

Kusac filed the information away for later. Now he had to finish telling Shaidan about him and Zayshul. Within days, Kaid and Carrie would arrive and expect explanations he wasn't yet ready to give. The only thing that could protect his son from all the gossip and allegations that would shortly be flying around was the truth.

"What you don't know is that the Doctor was forced, against her will, by the Directorate, to put the marker on me and that it was impossible for either of us to ignore it."

"Is that why you and she quarreled a lot?" Shaidan asked in a muffled voice. "Why did the General make you return when he knew about the marker?"

"He needed my help, Shaidan. That was more important to him than anything else."

"He shouldn't have made you come back by keeping me. That was wrong."

"It was, but sometimes desperate people have to do desperate things when they need help," he said, responding to the underlying anger in his son's voice by gently touching the edges of his mind. "As for you being here, I wouldn't have been able to send you home with the other cubs anyway, I'd have kept you with me so we could get to know each other better. I want you to know that matters between the General and myself are now resolved, peacefully. We're not exactly friends, but we are allies, on the same side now."

He sensed the small growl of disagreement just before Shaidan uttered it.

"Pay close attention to me on this, Shaidan," he said, putting his hand under his cub's chin and lifting it so they were face-to-face. "You will be polite to him at all times, is that understood?"

"But he punished you—let you die!" the cub exclaimed, outraged, as he struggled to sit up.

"Shaidan! That's enough," Kusac said firmly, tightening his arm round him. "You've no idea how sorry I am that because of your telepathic abilities, you've been exposed to adult matters, but it happened, and it's over now. Trust me, you haven't the experience yet to judge the rights and wrongs of the situation."

The cub muttered something so low he couldn't catch the words.

"Do you understand me, Shaidan?" he demanded, taking hold of his son's mutinous chin again.

"I understand you, Father," the cub mumbled, giving up trying to pull away from him.

"It must end now, Shaidan. Kezule and I have learned to respect each other." He smiled briefly, letting him go to ruffle the hair between his ears. "It may be a grudging respect, but it's real. More, we trust each other now."

"Then why did he let you die?" the cub blurted out.

Kusac sighed, and held Shaidan close again, pulling him onto his lap this time, wincing as the claw wounds down his side pulled. "He didn't know that would happen. It was part of my healing process. No one realized how weak I actually was. I know you saved me, but Kezule did have the Doctor nearby on purpose. No one was expecting me to go into such a deep trance that I slipped into death." He fell silent, resting his head on Shaidan's.

"What was it like?"

"Unpleasant," he said, wincing at the memory. "Full of regrets, not at all what I expected. When you reached for me, your fear triggered a response called a gestalt. That's a special mental bond that exists only between Humans and Sholans who are mind linked. And because you and I were mentally linked, your cry for help was answered automatically by Carrie and your Triad father, Kaid. Ours is a special relationship," he said, forcing the words out. "It only exists among the Humans and Sholans of our Clan. You'll meet them soon . . . in three days to be exact."

"Carrie—is she the Human?"

"Yes. She's the one you saw in your memories, the hairless one like, but unlike, the Doctor."

Shaidan pulled away from him and sat up, regarding him thoughtfully. "What about the Doctor?"

"That's my private concern," he said firmly, trying to meet Shaidan's gaze steadily. "You will not worry about that."

The cub nodded slowly. "Can you show Carrie to me?" he asked, eyes lighting up with enthusiasm.

Opening his mouth to say no, he found himself saying, "Why not?" Leaning down, he touched his forehead to Shaidan's, and as he reached through his mental shields, he began constructing the image of Carrie to project to his son.

She was small, reaching barely to his shoulders—he could rest his chin on top of her head when he held her. Her long hair, the color of sunshine, was softer than any hair he'd ever touched before or since. Her fringe usually covered her eyebrows, and below them were dark brown eyes, ringed with amber—eyes that suddenly narrowed to the slitted pupils of a Sholan.

Sholan eyes, he heard his son think.

Yes. The night she defied her father to be with me, she changed herself briefly into a Sholan. When she changed back, her eyes remained like ours. Gods, remembering her consciously for the first time since he'd arrived here—what they'd shared and lost—hurt so much! And Kaid . . . It all came flooding back. Her scent, the feel of her skin, the sound of her voice, and his. Abruptly he pulled back from his son, shutting down the Link in fear the cub would pick that up too.

"You love them very much."

"Yes," he said, his voice low with emotion. "Yes, I do."

He closed his eyes briefly, realizing he should have known they were so inextricably bound into his life that he'd be unable to separate them for his son. It was several minutes before he was able to continue.

"So among special people, Shaidan, you're even more special. At the moment only the Doctor and we know about this. For now, I don't want you to mention this to anyone. I intend to tell the others myself, in person."

"Do we have to? I'd sooner no one else knew," Shaidan said very quietly.

"Yes, we do. There's nothing shameful about your heritage. Doctor Zayshul is a brave female—she's saved my life several times, and at great risk to herself. Be proud of what as well as who you are. I am."

"Are you?" Shaidan searched his father's face, his voice as troubled as his expression.

"Of course I am! When I think of how you fought against the Directorate programming and had the courage to Link to me when I had died . . . It was a shock when I first found out about you, but no more than it was for you, I'm sure," he said, leaning forward to touch the tip of his tongue to his son's nose in an intimate, loving gesture. "You are my son, I love you, and you belong with me and your family."

He watched the tension drop away from Shaidan as the cub relaxed, finally, against him.

"I wasn't brave at all. I was so scared of losing you, that's why I did what Vartra told me to do."

"True bravery is being scared and doing it anyway," he said. "And I'm sorry, but it's going to be a bit longer before we can leave here and go home. Do you know about the new Emperor on the Prime world?"

"It's all they're talking and thinking about now."

"Not all Valtegans are like the Primes. There are those called the M'zullians, who look like Kezule but are extremely aggressive and warlike. The new Emperor is from their world, and Kezule and I have to lead his people, with help from the Sholan Brotherhood that my crew and I belong to, to retake the throne for the rightful Emperor, Prince Zsurtul. Don't worry too much," he said quickly, feeling Shaidan stiffen again. "It won't be a long mission, and you'll be in no danger. You'll stay here with Doctor Zayshul and the General's daughter."

"What if something happens to you?"

"It won't."

"You don't know that."

"No, I don't, but it's my job, Shaidan. It's what we all do in the Brotherhood. Banner and I have to go to a briefing, so M'kou will be coming for you shortly. If it goes on too late, Jayza will collect you from the nursery and wait here with you until I return."

"Have we time for a game of squares first?"

He checked his wrist comm. "Just about. Go fetch the pieces."

They'd almost finished when M'kou, chief among Kezule's many laboratory bred sons and daughters, arrived to take Shaidan down to join the other children.

M'kou picked his moment carefully, waiting until he and Shaidan were alone in the elevator before asking the question that had puzzled him for days.

"Shaidan, the day after your father was shot, when you and I were alone in the medic's room, what happened?"

Startled, the cub looked up at him. "Excuse me?"

"I saw something . . . a dark shape, like a shadow, pick you up."

Shaidan looked down at the floor. "I was scared for my father," he mumbled. "I don't remember."

"Something, or someone, picked you up, I'm sure of it. You even spoke to it," M'kou insisted gently.

"I don't remember." The words were more distinct this time.

"There must be something you remember," said M'kou persuasively.

The cub looked up again. "I felt my father dying. I followed his mind and helped him come back, all right? It scared me a lot, and I don't *want* to remember it." The childish voice cracked, betraying that fear only too audibly. "You'll have to ask my father about the Sholan—he knows him."

M'kou was instantly contrite, reaching out to put a comforting hand on his shoulder. "I'm sorry, Shaidan. You can understand I had problems believing what I'd seen," he said as the elevator drew to a halt.

"I don't know what you saw. My mind was Linked with my father's," said Shaidan stubbornly.

As the door began to open, the cub wriggled out from under his grasp, darted through the gap, and ran on ahead of him to the nursery.

M'kou followed more slowly, wondering if what he'd seen had been a manifestation of the mental Link between the child and his father or something very different. It seemed that he'd now have to ask Kusac.

Briefing room

M'kou had just finished his presentation of up-to-date intel from the Prime system when suddenly Kusac was aware of Kaid's presence at the edges of his mental shielding—extremely distant, to be sure, but unmistakably him. He rose to his feet so abruptly that the chair fell over behind him, drawing everyone's eyes to him.

"Is something wrong, Captain?" asked Kezule.

"No," he said, ignoring the fallen chair and limping toward the exit. "I need some air, that's all." His hand was on the opening plate just as the buzz indicating an incoming transmission sounded. As the door slid shut behind him, he heard Shezhul telling the General it was Kaid Tallinu.

Giving Kusac's retreating back a curious glance, Kezule said, "Route it through to here, please." Had Kusac known the call was coming, he wondered, and if so, why had he left so abruptly? He'd no more time for speculation as he turned round to face the large comm screen behind him.

After carefully polite greetings had been exchanged, Kezule introduced him to those present, pausing briefly when he came to Banner. The tan-colored Sholan on the screen merely nodded his recognition.

"I'm glad you called," Kezule said. "We have another matter that will shortly need our attention. Ch'almuth, the remaining Valtegan world, has been raided by the M'zullians every five years for breeding stock. This time, they asked for our help. Since there is no way I have the resources needed to take on M'zull, I was reluctant to do anything that would result in further action against the peaceful Ch'almuthians. We ambushed their craft when it landed, overpowered the M'zullians on board, and after rigging it to look as though some natural catastrophe had affected them in jump space, sent the ship back."

Kaid raised an appreciative eye ridge. "Very resourceful," he murmured. "However, they will return."

"Yes. By my reckoning we have four to five weeks before they do. By then, we need to have found a more permanent solution, or at least send them back knowing that the cost of returning will be too great."

"Has Ch'almuth no defenses of its own? It seems unlikely that even the Valtegan agricultural world wouldn't be protected."

"They have an Orbital, and it was capable of defending them, but it's no longer in working order. It's beyond the ability of my engineers to repair, I'm afraid. We were able to patch up their weather control system so the ground control center could communicate with it again. They also now have access to two cruisers that we found berthed there. They are operational but badly needed repairs to the weapons systems. They're lending them to us for the time being."

While he spoke, Kezule noticed Kaid glance off to the side, one ear swiveling in that direction before it flicked in agreement.

"We may be able to help you," said Kaid as a hirsute, garish being joined him in the comm screen. "This is Toueesut, of the Touibans. We're on one of their ships right now, the *Couana*. As you may know, they are the Alliance tech specialists."

"Greetings, General Kezule. A pleasure it is to be meeting with you," the small alien trilled in his singsong voice.

Fascinated, Kezule studied him. He'd never had the opportunity to see a Touiban before. Humanoid in appearance, they had only a passing likeness to the Human males he'd seen. Dark, almost unkempt hair sprouted from the being's head above the deeply socketed eyes and grew beneath the flanged nose. The mustache was so mobile that it resembled a hairy caterpillar. What Kezule could see of his jacket was an intense blue, but it was almost completely covered in gold braid and intricate swirls of embroidery. Around his neck he wore dozens of gold chains, and his hands, when they came into view, were equally laden with rings in the same metal. This was the species Kusac had mentioned. How had he known Kaid was with them?

He realized that the Touiban had been speaking again and tore his attention back to what the small alien was saying.

"I do apologize," he began, feeling the blood rushing to his face in embarrassment before he could stop it.

"No matter, General. I was merely saying that we can be dispatching a small team to your Ch'almuth world to work on both the Orbital and the ships," said Toueesut with a large smile. "Hoping I am that my people are far more closely linked to yourself and the Prime world in the future."

"Thank you," he said. "The ships, however, arrived here a few hours ago."

"Then we will be working on them here; it's no matter to us. I will leave you now to continue your discussion with friend Kaid. When we arrive, we will be needing one or two of your people to come with us to Ch'almuth as we would not wish to earn their distrust by arriving without faces they are recognizing."

Taken aback by the continuous flow of words, Kezule blinked and managed a weak "Thank you," before Toueesut disappeared.

Kaid's grin of amusement at his discomfort over the Touiban was almost feral in its enjoyment, but he ignored it.

"I wouldn't worry; they affect everyone that way the first time," the Sholan said, with a purr of amusement the whole room could hear.

"Their aid will be very welcome," said Kezule stiffly. "If you can get their Orbital working, the Ch'almuthians are capable of defending themselves with that and the two cruisers. Their early-warning system is working so they do have at least one week's notice of any ships arriving in their system."

"You got my message on what young Zsurtul has done, didn't you?" Kaid asked abruptly, changing the topic.

"Yes. This six-weeks grace will be extremely useful—though we can't afford to wait that long before striking. Our new Emperor is more resourceful than I expected." Kezule emphasized the word Emperor.

"Agreed. Have you any intel on the City of Light defenses? Plans of the system would be extremely useful."

"I'll have them transmitted immediately," said Kezule. "The mission will be led by myself and Captain Aldatan jointly. I suggest that you hold your own briefing, then call me tomorrow at the same time and we can have a joint discussion."

"I don't think ..."

Kezule held up his hand. "I've already been through this with Commander Rhyaz. He's agreed that his people will work under myself and Captain Aldatan."

Kaid hesitated briefly. "Talking of Kusac, I don't see him there. I'd like to talk to him."

"The Captain stepped out of the room just before you called," said Kezule blandly. "He's not available right now, but I will pass on your message and ask him to contact you as soon as he can." Seeing the other's frown, he added, "Lieutenant Banner is here and can pass the message on to your ..." Here he hesitated, unsure of the complex relationships between Kusac, Kaid, and Carrie "... partner," he said finally.

"I'll tell the Captain," Banner confirmed. "You just missed him, sir, as the General said."

Kaid gave a brief nod of acceptance. "I'd also like the opportunity to speak to the Lieutenant privately when we're finished here."

"Of course. M'kou will show him to our comms room when we're done. Meanwhile, Commander Rhyaz informed me that our Prince has been staying on your estate. I need to talk to him."

"That's not possible, I'm afraid," said Kaid regretfully. "We're unable to contact our home from the *Couana*."

"I need to talk to him," insisted Kezule. "He is the Emperor-elect. He must be crowned on the Throne of Light or his ascension is meaningless to the Primes. For that, he'll have to leave Shola and come here. Whatever you think of me, I'm probably the only adviser to his late father who's still alive. Burn it, Kaid, if I wanted the Throne, I could have let that first coup go ahead or just taken the damned Throne for myself now! I have more of a claim to it than either of them!"

Kaid's eyes narrowed slightly, then he nodded once. "I'll see what can be done," he said.

"You Sholans were born suspicious," Kezule muttered, sitting back in his chair. "I'm done for now, Kaid. M'kou will take the Lieutenant to the comm room, we'll talk again at this time tomorrow. Transfer the call there, Shezhul," he said to his daughter.

Kusac, meanwhile, had gone across the corridor to the lab beyond the sick bay to see Zayshul.

"There's nothing wrong, is there?" she asked anxiously, turning round as he came in.

"No, I needed a break, that's all. Kezule's taking a call from Kaid, and I'm not ready to speak to him yet," he said, leaning against her bench.

The rainbow-hued skin around her eye sockets creased. "Why?"

"Many reasons, not least that when I left, I made sure matters between us were less than friendly so he wouldn't be tempted to follow me."

"Surely now he'll understand why," she said.

He shrugged his shoulders. "We need to talk properly tonight. Can you get away?"

"Of course." She hesitated, looking away from him, the light reflecting off her slightly textured pale green scalp. "Tell me about the knife wound you got from Dzaou during your Challenge fight," she said, lowering her voice.

"I told you at the time, it was shallow, just a slice," he said evasively.

"You know it wasn't. It was a stab wound, up near your armpit. I got a better look at it than you did, because of the angle. Yet when I came to stitch it, it had almost healed. We need to talk about that."

He shivered slightly, as if cold fingers were trailing down his spine, like a premonition, and suddenly knew he had to leave. "Later, then. In my suite. I'll ask Jayza or Banner to take Shaidan for an hour or so."

She nodded. "We should take the time together anyway because of the scent marker. I want to find out why it hasn't been affecting you the way it did when you were away on the trip to Ch'almuth."

Inwardly he cursed, but he reached out to touch her cheek with gentle fingertips.

"It's still there, I've just gotten better at controlling it," he said. If what he'd come to suspect in the last few hours since his fight to the death with Dzaou was true, there was no way he could tell her right now that he'd actually turned off the effects of her scent marker. One person who might know what had been done to him, and why, was K'hedduk, and now he was within reach.

The shiver swept through him again, diverting his attention. "Is it just me, or is it a little colder in here than usual?" he asked.

"I noticed it too," she agreed, leaning forward for her comm unit. "This is Doctor Zayshul in the Command Level lab. Would you check the heating in here, please? I think it may be faulty—it's getting cold."

"Will do, Doctor," came Zhalmo's voice.

"I hope everything is all right," she said, frowning.

"I'm sure it is," Kusac said, reaching out to smooth the skin on the top of her nose. That was where the first hint of the blues and purples that surrounded her eyes began, he found himself noticing. With a start, he drew back, mentally shaking himself. He shouldn't be thinking like this about her! He'd damped down his response to her scent, so what was making him behave like this?

"Nothing wrong with the temperature," Zhalmo's voice said from the hand comm. "I'm having the engineers check it out, though, just in case."

"Thanks," Zayshul said, switching the palm-sized unit off and putting it back on her bench.

"I have to go," he said abruptly, shivering again as vague memories of the nightmares of frozen wastes that he'd had the last few nights returned to him. "The meeting is about to start again. I'll be in my quarters after third meal."

"See you then," she agreed as he turned to leave.

Banner followed M'kou into the comm office with mixed feelings. Kaid was one of the very few people who'd earned more than his respect; he'd earned his allegiance. When he'd been asked, all those months ago, to keep an eye on Kusac during his recuperation after the ill-fated Jalna mission, his loyalties had been clear-cut. Now, six months down the line serving as Kusac's Second, they weren't.

"Strange how easy it is to slip into habits, isn't it, Lieutenant?" M'kou said, going over to the desk and keying the inset controls to bring the comm screen mounted on the right hand wall to life. "So many of those we follow today, on both the military and civilian sides, are due to Captain Aldatan."

Banner grunted noncommittally, waiting for the General's son to finish.

"Our people, all of them, even the Ch'almuthians, trust and respect him, you know. They like continuity. I believe continuity, especially in command, is vital."

Now M'kou had his full attention.

"Considering what we've all been through," continued the young Prime, "I believe it would be—unfortunate—if anything was said that might cast doubt on the Captain's ability to lead the mission to retake the Palace of Light with the General."

"What's that supposed to mean?" Banner demanded, a low rumble of anger underscoring his words. "Are you threatening me?"

M'kou looked genuinely shocked. "Far from it! I'm only trying to tell you how much faith and trust we have in you and your Captain."

"Trust! That's an alien concept to some of you." Banner bared his teeth in an almost silent snarl, taking a step closer to him. "I haven't forgotten the part you played in drugging our Captain and procuring a female . . ."

"Lieutenant," M'kou interrupted, coming out from behind the desk. "Doctor Zayshul has said more about this than you ever could. And when she was done yelling at the General and myself, she exacted a revenge on us I wouldn't wish on my worst enemy." He shuddered, obviously at the memory. "I have also apologized to your Captain, and we've made our peace with each other."

Taken aback at this outpouring, Banner looked skeptically at the younger male.

"What did she do?"

"That needn't concern you," M'kou replied, his pale green skin darkening in obvious embarrassment. "The whole incident, from start to finish, was contained. Only those directly involved—and you yourselves—are aware that anything happened, and none of them will ever discuss it. It's obvious you're about to give your report on your time here to the Captain's family and that it will, most likely, affect whether or not there is Sholan resistance to Captain Aldatan's leadership. I'm only asking that he not be deprived of the position he's earned because of his recent actions. Especially because our people trust him."

"That's Kezule talking."

"No, it isn't. I admire your Captain, Banner, and I hope that one day I'll possess the skills and self-restraint he's shown." M'kou moved past him, indicating the desk and comm. "I'll leave you to make your call. Please at least consider what I've said."

Banner watched him leave before taking his seat. He was thinking through what M'kou had said—and what he hadn't.

Kaid flicked an ear at him in greeting, his seemingly random slight finger movements enquiring whether Banner was alone or was being monitored.

"You look well," he said.

"We're all well," Banner replied, signaling that he was alone and the call wasn't being monitored as far as he knew. "We've been treated like members of the crew."

Briefing room, later

Kusac sat playing idly with his stylus, ignoring the flicking images of K'hedduk's ascension to the Throne of Light playing once more on the large screen behind Kezule, just as he'd automatically filtered out the sounds of the voices around him for the past hour. Back and forth the same arguments had gone among the same few people, principally Banner, Security head M'zynal, Captain Zhookoh, lately escaped with his crew from K'hedduk's takeover of K'oish'ik, and Kezule.

He was still aware of Kaid—and through him of Carrie—holding their own briefing and planning session on the *Tooshu.* Unlike his present company, they'd come up with a couple of good ideas but nothing yet that made a complete plan. He let his mind drift, adding their own pool of knowledge, taking Kaid's ideas and expanding on them, playing with various scenarios in his mind's eye.

Just as his eyelids began to droop, Banner dug him in the ribs with his elbow.

"Kusac!" he hissed.

With a jerk, he sat up to find all eyes on him.

"If you're not up to this meeting, Kusac," said Kezule, his

tone one of concern, "then go back to your quarters and rest.
I'm sure Banner can brief you later. It's only been a few hours
since your fight with Dzaou."

"I'm fine," he said shortly, deciding he'd had enough and it
was time for him to speak out. He leaned forward, searching
among the sheets of briefing documents they'd all been issued.
"I'm just tired of sitting here listening to the same arguments.
We can't wait for the *Couana* to get here. We need to act now,
not sit on our butts talking!"

"They'll be here in two days," said Banner.

"And it takes another three to reach the Prime world! Plus
none of you," he glared round the small group of Primes and
Banner, "have gotten even the germ of a workable plan yet!"
Grabbing hold of a couple of sheets, he eased himself to his
feet. "Well, I have."

Pushing his chair back, he limped around the conference
table to where Kezule sat watching him intently.

"Here's a plan, one that will work if we act now, before
K'hedduk digs himself deep into the Palace and gets its antiquated defenses up and running." He tossed the first sheet in
front of the General. "That's a schedule of shipping expected
at the Prime Orbital platform in the next few days. There's
only one, the U'Churian Rryuk family merchanter due in three
days. They're Warriors, and Clan allies of ours. I can contact
them and arrange a rendezvous. If I take a small team with
me, once we're on board and we've docked, they'll join us in
taking the Orbital. You said there's only a small crew there, all
Prime pacifists. Even if K'hedduk has sent any of his implanted
guards or the genetically modified warrior types up to supervise them, he's only got a total of three hundred and twenty. He
can't spare more than about five, maximum. The U'Churians
have a crew of seven, plus their four Cabbarans, and if I take
another four with me, we can easily handle them."

"What does that achieve?" demanded M'zynal. "What
about the *Kz'adul*, berthed there?"

"What about her?" he asked, rounding on the young
male, staggering slightly as he did so. "They're on alert, so
K'hedduk's few warriors won't leave her, and you know the
six thousand odd crewmembers will run for cover if they hear
a raised voice!"

"They're not quite that bad," murmured Kezule, hiding the
ghost of a smile behind his already raised hand.

"Captain, take my seat," said M'kou, getting to his feet and touching Kusac briefly on the arm.

Gratefully, he accepted it. "No one will be expecting us, M'zynal," he said. "If you've got soporific gas canisters, we can use them. In our battle suits, we'll be well protected."

"Battle suits?" echoed Banner. "What battle suits? We don't have any with us."

"We've eight," said Kusac, glancing across at him. "But they're in my cabin on the *Venture*. The Primes installed a concealed armory there with the suits and a selection of munitions. As for what taking the Orbital will achieve, their weather is controlled from there, isn't it? If I can take a couple of civilian engineers from here, they can create havoc on the world below. Meanwhile, we can contact the *Kz'adul* on one of the channels all ships use for unofficial ship-to-ship and ship-to-shore chat and get some of the friendlies to let us on board and point us in the direction of K'hedduk's people."

"Be a helluva lot easier if we had the shutdown codes," muttered Zhookoh.

"Shutdown codes?" asked Kezule, looking across at him.

"The Emperor had codes he could use to shut down each ship in case of a coup. Leave 'em dead in the water," explained Zhookoh. "It's new. Ironically, we had it brought in because of K'hedduk."

"We'd still have to deal with his genetically enhanced warriors at some point," said Kezule, thoughtfully stroking his chin. "The idea has good points, Kusac, but if we start tampering with the weather, K'hedduk will know something is wrong on the Orbital, even if the crew keep in regular touch."

Kusac pushed his second sheet in front of Kezule. "That's where the asteroid belt around one of your outer planets comes in," he said. "I assume that, like the *Kz'adul*, you have traction beams on your modern ships?"

"Yes, but you're not seriously suggesting what I think, are you?" asked Kezule, sitting up to study the photograph, suddenly all attention.

"I am. Send the *N'zishok* and *Mazzu* out to collect a few thousand of them, including some larger ones. Single out those, put them at the front and attach remote detonation charges on them in case we need to blow them, then tow them close to K'oish'ik and let 'em go so they start heading toward it. If that doesn't get the other three ships heading out to stop them, I don't know what will. Meanwhile . . ."

"Meanwhile," continued Kezule, "the small ones can't be stopped, and as they hit the atmosphere and burn up, it gives us the cover to launch our drop pod assault! If we get the angle right, they'll even think the Orbital has been hit, which would account for the weather fluctuations. I like it, Kusac, but if K'hedduk's got the Palace gun turrets working, to say nothing of the force field, it could turn into a bloodbath for us."

"The HALO drop isn't the main plan," said Kusac, sitting back and carefully easing his injured leg out in front of him. The healing wound was beginning to ache—and itch—again. He'd taken more of a beating from the late and unlamented Dzaou than he wanted to admit, even to himself.

Kezule looked at him over the top of the photo, one eye ridge raised questioningly.

"My team is," he said. This was where his plan differed substantially from Kaid's. "We go down on the shuttle and infiltrate the tunnel systems, making our way along them to the main Control Room under the Palace. Once there, we can work from inside to turn the defenses off or use them against K'hedduk. All your people have to do is create enough of a diversion to pull all K'hedduk's warriors to the defense perimeter, by the force field relay towers. You're the General, Kezule, you do what you do best—blend us all into one attack force."

"If we fail, then the HALO team will be the main plan," said Banner thoughtfully.

"HALO?" queried M'kou.

"High Altitude, Low Orbit insertion of troops or craft," said Kusac.

Kezule studied the maps thoughtfully, then turned on the holo display. Instantly a 3-D image of the City and the Palace, showing every level, coalesced about six inches above the conference table.

Tapping a series of buttons set into the keypad in front of him, he rotated the image, then stilled it, decreasing the amount of detail until the bare minimum of the tunnels, the underground control complex, and the Palace above it remained.

"To go in without more intel, especially now we have six weeks, would be foolish," said M'zynal.

"We don't have . . ." began Kusac and Kezule in unison, both stopping when they realized the other was also speaking.

As Kusac deferred to him, with the ghost of a smile, Kezule continued. "We don't have six weeks, and we don't need more intel. What our young Emperor is managing to get for us is enough." He glanced back to Kusac. "You realize that the City is built on a hill comprised of sand and limestone?"

"It's porous, I know. How else could the tunnels have originated or been so easily expanded to your ancestors' purpose?"

"It also means that if we create the electrical storms, we disrupt communications between the Orbital and the ships, and those tunnels will be flooded."

"Our battle suits can handle that," he said confidently.

"We set traps in the tunnels," said Zhookoh. "Some of them will still be active despite flooding."

"Then I'll take a couple of you with me to deactivate them," Kusac said more calmly than he felt. He sensed Zayshul bringing analgesics for him and began to swear under his breath, knowing she'd picked up his discomfort. Drawing attention to the pain he was still suffering was not something he wanted right now.

"With respect, Captain," said M'zynal, as the General's wife entered and went over to him, wordlessly handing him a charged hypo. "I don't think you're yet fit to go on such a mission, let alone lead it."

With little grace, he accepted the hypo, but he stuffed it into one of his belt retainers. "I'm fit. The armor is powered anyway. It takes very little effort to move in it." He shot the Doctor a glance that dared her to say anything, but she left without a word. "Besides, we should meet very little resistance."

"Your plan is good," said Kezule, turning the holo image round slowly to study it again from every angle. "I can see only one major flaw. Only Zsurtul can turn off the Orbital's safety devices and operate the Command Center. It needs to take a retinal scan from him."

"I planned on including him with my team. He's with Kaid on the Touiban ship."

Exclamations of disbelief, ignored by both Kezule and Kusac, rippled round the table.

"Yet you don't want to wait for the *Couana* to arrive," said Kezule.

"The *Couana's* on their battleship, the *Tooshu*, right now. They plan to leave it at the outer limits of the Prime system. We tell them to include Prince Zsurtul, then make for K'oish'ik, not here," he said. "They wait out of scanner range, possibly masked by one of your ships using its chameleon shielding, for a signal from us saying we've taken the Orbital. Meanwhile, the rest of the Prime fleet will be picking up the asteroids on their sensors, and, hopefully, they'll be moving away from the planet to intercept them."

"That should draw at least the two smaller cruisers away from K'oish'ik," said M'kou thoughtfully.

"Then Zsurtul contacts the *Kz'adul* on the private frequency I mentioned and finds out for us what the situation there is like. It may be that the crew can isolate any of K'hedduk's people they have on board without violence and take back control of the ship," said Kusac. "If not, we do it. I'm sure they can manage to conceal us docking with them. Finally, the *Couana* joins us on the Orbital, and Zsurtul deactivates the safety features. The regular crew can then take over from him, creating massive electrical storms and leaving him free to go downside with me."

"If those on the Orbital or the *Kz'adul* are members of the implanted Palace Guard, then they can be rendered unconscious without a shot being fired," M'kou reminded. "All we need is a remote tuned to their frequency, and we know that."

"That's true," agreed Kezule. "If you have fifteen people when you land on K'oish'ik . . ."

"Too many," interrupted Kusac. "Ten, maximum, including the Prince. Surely six of your commandos can ensure Zsurtul's safety in a battle suit?"

"Of course."

"Six?" Banner asked sharply. "That means no other Sholans."

"I want you to stay with Kezule and lead one of the HALO units with the rest of our crew," Kusac said, shifting slightly in his seat in an effort to ease the still-increasing pain.

"No," his Second said flatly. "I'm coming with you."

Kusac locked eyes with him until Banner looked away. "I'll take Khadui with me," he compromised. "You and Jayza will be with Kezule and our people from the *Couana*."

Kezule switched off the holo image and, pushing his chair back, stood up. "We're going with this idea. It's time for the evening meal. Take a break, discuss it among yourselves, and be back here in two hours to thrash out the finer details."

As everyone began to get to their feet, Kezule held Kusac back. "Stay," he said. "We need to talk privately. M'kou, have meals brought here for the two of us."

"Yes, General."

"Take the damned analgesic," said Kezule when they were alone. "I'd be as bad as you in the same circumstances, but that doesn't make you right."

Kusac gave a low rumble of annoyance, but he followed Kezule's advice, pushing his tunic aside and pressing the hypo against his thigh more vigorously than he intended.

"You're avoiding your family."

"I'm trying to get this job done as quickly as possible," he said, wincing. He concentrated on stowing away the empty hypo. Already he could feel the drug coursing through his system, dulling the pain from the still-healing blaster wound in his upper thigh, and the cut in his side where Dzaou's knife had stabbed him clear up to the hilt yet somehow left virtually no wound.

"The young Emperor is our only hope, Kusac," said Kezule, changing the topic abruptly. "I won't have him put needlessly at risk."

"Then we've little chance on our own of retaking the Palace. You might as well destroy it and start again." He heard the bite in his tone and, ears tilting slightly, opened his mouth to apologize.

"Forget it," said Kezule, with a gesture of dismissal. "Has the analgesic cut in yet? Fighting Dzaou like that in your condition was foolish."

"I know it was, but I had no choice," he said, frowning as a wave of dizziness swept over him, and he realized he was having to force his eyes to focus on the General.

"Destroying the Palace isn't an option; neither is losing Zsurtul. I have no intention of ruling. I'll stay and help him if he wants me to, but that's all."

"You'll leave Kij'ik and all you fought so hard to build?" Kusac asked, realizing, as a false sense of warmth and well-being began to steal through him that Zayshul had laced the drug with a sedative. He sat up, trying to fight off the effects.

"Of course not!" said Kezule, offended. "I intended to convince Zsurtul to continue my plan, but on K'oish'ik. We have more than enough land to accommodate as many

Ch'almuthians as want to leave their world to escape the M'zullian raids. As for Kij'ik, I'll have it towed into the Prime system and manned as a defensive outpost."

Kezule stopped, and leaned closer to him. "What's wrong?" he demanded.

"Your wife put a sedative in the hypo as well as an analgesic," he said, blinking owlishly as he grasped the arm of his chair.

Kezule swore and reached for a drinking bowl and the jug of water nearby. "I can't have you falling asleep on me," he said, pouring Kusac a drink. "We need to refine that plan of yours!" He held the bowl out, helping him to hold it steady. "This is important, Kusac. What did you do when you went into that healing trance? I don't mean your own mental disciplines, did you do anything else?"

"Like what?" he asked, taking a couple of mouthfuls and then pushing the bowl aside. "That won't help, the drug's in my blood, not my gut!"

"You used biofeedback, didn't you? You obviously know about our Warrior glands because of the drug your people developed. Have you got the same kind of glands?"

"We're not Valtegans," he muttered, slumping back in his seat. He knew he needed to rest, but dammit, not now!

Kezule spun his chair round and, taking him by the shoulders, shook him several times.

"Concentrate, Kusac! You've been changed, made partly Valtegan, how I don't know, maybe by that damned scent marker! Have *you* got those glands? If you have, I can tell you how to use them."

"Yes," he said, forcing his eyes open when his head finally stopped moving. "Yes, I have them . . ."

"Then reach inside for them, tell yourself you need to be alert, trigger the gland that produces adrenaline, and . . ."

"All right," he mumbled, reaching mentally inside himself. "I know what to do. It took me by surprise, that's all."

"You can't afford to be taken by surprise," said Kezule grimly. "You have to remember, and practice, until it becomes second nature—just as using your mental powers is."

A surge of energy flowed through his limbs, chasing the lethargy before it, then it hit his brain. He shuddered, grasping the arms of the chair tightly as his senses reeled. When it stopped, he found all traces of the sedative were gone. Startled, he stared at Kezule.

"That was fast even by my standards," said Kezule dryly. "One of us should have a word with Zayshul about this incident, both about her using the sedative and about how you overcame it."

"She's your . . ."

"Don't—go there," said Kezule coldly, sitting back in his chair. "For now, we're all in a situation we didn't choose— we'll make the best of it. I would have thought you'd have sensed what she was planning."

"She hid it. I was distracted by the pain, and I shouldn't have been," Kusac said, equally coldly, more annoyed with himself than her. "I won't let it happen again."

"Are you sure you're fit enough to handle a mission like this?" asked Kezule, his voice returning to normal. "It's no disgrace if you aren't, considering your injuries."

"They're healing," he said shortly. They were, and still far faster than was normal.

"I'm aware of that."

"I have three days. By then, I'll be more than fit to handle it. As I said, our battle suits are powered."

"What specs?"

He turned his mind inward, looking where his and Kaid's shared memories were stored. A moment later he had the information. "They make use of servomotors and gravity dampers to assist movement, giving us the ability to hit a top speed of thirty miles an hour for short bursts and the ability to jump two to three times higher than normal. Weapons are an energy rifle and pistol and an OC—oscillating—sword. There's a refractive paint on the suits that renders them all but invisible in low light."

"Sword?" Kezule looked faintly incredulous.

Kusac grinned widely, showing off the white canines against the black of his pelt. "Useful for close quarters or when the energy packs run out. The MUTAC is similarly equipped on its jointed tail."

"I'll take your word for it," he murmured. "And they'll stand immersion in flooded tunnels?"

Kusac nodded as he got to his feet. "They come with their own air supply. One that lasts three hours. I should join the others for third meal now. Jayza will have brought Shaidan up to the mess."

"I ordered meals to be brought here for us. You can call Jayza and get him to bring your son here, if you like."

Kusac hesitated for a moment, then shook his head. "I appreciate the thought, but I've been separated from my crew for too long. They need to spend time with me. Plus I have to call the Rryuk ship now. And, Kezule, I'd prefer it if you didn't tell Kaid about this mission until after I've left to meet up with them."

Kezule nodded, giving Kusac a curious glance, but he said nothing.

When he'd left, Kezule called his son and canceled the meal arrangements.

"I'll eat with you, if you like," M'kou offered. "I'd like a word in private with you."

"Very well," he said.

M'kou put his tray down on the table and set his father's plate in front of him.

"Thank you," said Kezule, picking up his fork. "What was it you wanted to talk about?"

M'kou sat down in his chair and gripped the arms to move himself closer to the table. "What the . . ." he began, lifting his left hand to look at the chair arm.

Kezule glanced over and froze, fork halfway to his mouth.

"How did that happen?" his son asked, tentatively putting his finger into one of the depressions. "They're his fingerprints. It looks as if they're melted into the arm."

"I can see that," said Kezule acerbically, putting his fork back on his plate and leaning closer. "Move your hand out of the way."

M'kou did as he was asked and turned to examine the other chair arm, but it was unmarked. "How did that happen?"

"I have no idea," said Kezule, probing the marks with his claw tip. "There's been nothing hot enough to cause that in here." The marks were deep, each one with the imprint of a claw tip just above it, as if caused by a hand gripping the arm tightly when the surface had been hot and plastic.

"Only Kusac and I have used this chair," said M'kou, "and those don't fit any Prime hand."

"They're Kusac's, no doubt of that," said Kezule with a sigh, sitting up. "More damned anomalies. You've read up on their psi abilities—have they any that could have caused this?"

"Not to my knowledge," said M'kou, cautiously taking hold of the arm again and pulling his chair closer to the table. "But they haven't been very forthcoming on their psi capabilities with us. And Kusac is different anyway, because he lost his original abilities. Banner told me they only returned after a surgical procedure was performed on him to restore them. Actually, it was about the Captain I wanted to talk."

"What's concerning you now?" Kezule asked, beginning to eat.

"Is he fit to lead a team through the tunnels?"

"Not yet, but I believe he will be in three days' time."

"I'd better accompany him to make sure."

Kezule glared at his son. "You'll stay here and look after Kij'ik and the children," he said forcefully. "Your Warrior glands have been destroyed, you no longer have the ability to use biofeedback. I'll not have you putting yourself in danger."

"I'm not staying here," said M'kou stubbornly.

"It's an order," interrupted Kezule. "It's not open to discussion. And have that chair stowed in my office after you've finished eating."

CHAPTER 2

BY the time Kusac had called the Rryuk Clan's ship and made his way up to the Officers' level, he realized the stupidity of trying to make it to the mess and instead limped painfully along the corridor to their communal lounge. With relief, he lowered himself into one of the padded dining chairs and, activating his wrist comm unit, called Banner.

"Can you get Jayza to collect a meal for me and bring it and Shaidan down to our lounge, please? I'm not going to make it to the mess—I've overdone things a bit," he said, ears flicking in an attempt at wry humor.

"That's one of the few sensible things you've said today," Banner replied shortly. "I'll see to it now."

He sighed, easing his leg out in front of him. Banner's anger and indignation that he'd not discussed his ideas for the covert mission with him first were preceding him, and he knew his Second was already on his way to have it out with him. Sighing again, he braced himself for the verbal onslaught.

". . . and you know if you'd told us you were Shaidan's father, we'd have stood with you!" Banner was saying. "If something's so damned sensitive that you don't want me knowing it, Kusac, then, dammit, I'll give you permission to wipe it from my memory once we've discussed it, but at least *ask* me!"

Shocked at his Second's offer, he looked up at Banner.

"I mean it," said Banner, leaning across the table. "I'd rather you messed with my mind after we'd spoken than you acted alone again."

"There's a difference between cooperating and expecting

me to discuss my every thought first," he said, irritated. "It was only a planning meeting."

Banner thumped his palm on the table in exasperation. "I *don't* expect that, but I do expect us to discuss plans before you start allocating personnel!"

"Would you, as Kaid's Second, expect him to discuss everything with you?" he asked with deceptive mildness.

"No, but . . ."

"Then don't expect me to. When we return after our meal, you're as free as anyone around that discussion table to make your objections."

"You've already said you're taking Khadui. It should be *me* watching your back, not him. And why are you so set on leaving before Kaid gets here? You're avoiding him, Kusac."

Jealousy—or protectiveness, he wondered. "I need you working with Kezule," he said. "Kaid doesn't know him as well as you, and the Touibans don't know him at all."

Banner made a sound of disgust. "Knowing him, I don't trust him an inch."

"Can I trust you? Who's your loyalty to? Me, or Kaid?" he asked sharply. "What did you tell him during your debriefing?"

His Second had the grace to look away. "I have never been disloyal to you, Kusac. I told him everything," he said. "Everything I knew. I also told him that though I'll keep watching your back, I can't have divided loyalties between you and him any longer."

"So the pressure's off me, is it? If you're with Kaid, you'll see Jurrel sooner."

"Your safety is more important," he began, then stopped. "Do you know Jurrel is with them?"

"Yes, he's there. I can sense them all."

Banner stared at him. "At that distance?" he asked slowly. "But being there to guard you is more important."

Kusac nodded. "Then would it suffice if I took you with me until we've taken the Orbital and the *Kz'adul*? It isn't sensible for me to risk my Second in the tunnels, Banner. Kaid and the Touibans need an officer with them who's had experience with the Primes and Kezule. You'll probably be needed to persuade Kezule to oversee the whole operation from the Orbital or the *N'zishok* rather than go down with his troops. He and Zsurtul are indispensable."

Banner sighed, ears flicking in irritation just as the door opened to admit Jayza with Kusac's meal on a tray and Shaidan. "Very well, I'll accept that compromise."

The insectoid alien sat on his cushions, bronze colored stick-thin limbs folded up comfortably, looking into the screen of his comm, a comm that was, unknown to anyone else aboard Kij'ik, currently in conference with his handler on the Camarilla world of Ghioass.

"The null zones around Hunter are surrounding him more and more. They disturb us all," Kuvaa the Cabbaran was saying to him, her long furry snout twitching in concern. "Potentialities of future around him are more difficult to read. What have you discovered about them?"

"Nothing as yet," he admitted. "Hunter Kusac beginning his abilities now to question, looking at memories of Kzizysus and his operation more and more. This worries me also."

"Divert him! When his family he meets, then he'll be told what they know. Time running out for him and Sand-dweller female Zayshul to form mental Link. Tonight you must push him into this. From his family must he be more isolated, and from Kzizysus this will divert his thoughts."

Giyarishis spread his small hands wide in a gesture of appeasement. "I believed canceled was this plan as the cooperation between them was achieved."

"Don't think, follow orders," snapped Kuvaa, her vertical crest of hair tilting forward.

"Helpful would be an idea of what potentialities are looming," he began, thinking how uncharacteristic it was for her to be so short-tempered with him. They must indeed be concerned about the Hunter.

"Not for you to know, that's for us. Talk in Council of you losing control of Hunter. Prove Isolationists wrong."

He bowed his head and clasped his hands in front of him in obedience. "Believing I am we never had control of him. Again I will attempt tonight, Phratry Lady," he said.

"See you do," she said sharply.

"A matter of delicacy before you go," he said, hesitating.

"What now? I want to hear nothing about complaints of your colleague Hkairass."

"Hkairass' change to female gender closer than he thought," he said, trying not to glance at the chrysalis standing in the corner of his room, covered with various of his own differently colored spare draperies. "His chrysalis you will need to remove."

Kuvaa stared unblinkingly at him. "I thought he had another year or two left," she said quietly. "Annoying, and disappointing. Pity you TeLaxaudin change gender. Have you a retrieval unit?"

"One is left."

"Fix it to him and activate it. We'll collect him now and send several units in return."

He bowed his head again. "The Hunter cub . . ."

"Forget the cub. See to what you must tonight." She cut the connection abruptly.

Giyarishis sat there regarding the blank screen for a moment before pulling open a drawer and extracting an innocent looking device. Then, rising up in a cloud of pale gray draperies, he stalked in his stiff-legged gait toward the chrysalis and pulled off the camouflage.

Kuvaa had not been her usual self at all, he thought as he carefully fixed the retrieving unit into the thick outer shell. Setting the homing signal, he stepped back and watched it until suddenly it winked out of existence, leaving four units· lying where it had been.

Ghioass

Meanwhile, in the Camarilla Chamber on Ghioass, Azwokkus, the TeLaxaudin Leader of the Reformist movement within the Camarilla, was Speaking from the lectern.

"The cub must we be watching too," he said. "Not impossible the null zones of impenetrability around the Hunter are responsibility of him. He is bridge, naturally has what was created in Hunter artificially." Here he looked at Zaimiss. "Enthusiasm of Isolationists out of control when they decide cub to create without Camarilla permission."

Zaimiss stood, creating a perfumed cloud of injured innocence as his red draperies gently flapped around his body. "Hkairass not here to Speak in defense of himself," he objected.

"Many years it will be before she can," said Htomshu dryly from her corner as Moderate Leader. "Unity tells me Hkairass has changed. Entering her fertile time she is, as is normal with our kind."

There was a sudden hush, and Zaimiss' draperies began to move more violently around him, the scent becoming one of sharp anger. "Not possible!"

"Her chrysalis being taken to the breeding quarters even now. Ask Unity," she said. "Time of celebration for her skepp, this is."

Aizshuss leaned toward his Cabbaran friend Kuvaa. "Some peace we will now have. Isolationists absorbed in choosing new leader will be for some time since no one is clearly to be chosen."

Kuvaa's mobile upper lip pulled back in a smile as her stiff crest dipped forward toward her companion. "It'll be refreshing," she said. "Especially now when they push for a mental Link between the Hunter and Sand-dweller when there is no need."

Aizshuss nodded.

On the dais, Azwokkus continued. "Suggesting I am monitoring of cub as well as Hunter. Null zones might be his making."

"Seconded," said Kuvaa, lifting herself up on her haunches to Speak. "Isolate the cause we must. Nothing our attention should overlook."

"Objections?" asked Htomshu, whose turn it was to head the Council meetings, as she stood.

A low hum and buzz of conversation filled the tree-lined auditorium, but no voices were heard in dissent.

"Passed," she said. "Let Unity record our decision."

Recorded, said Unity, the massive AI that was the core of the Camarilla. *Cub will be monitored to see if there is any connection between him and null-zones around Hunter father.*

"Isolationists wish to push for Sand-dweller female and Hunter mental Link still to be established, despite harmony and pact between their peoples," said Shumass, leaping to his feet in a swirl of green and red strips of floating gauzes.

Azwokkus turned his large swirling eyes on the younger TeLaxaudin male. "Your reason?"

"All agreed it was this should happen . . ."

"Not agreed by all," broke in Kuvaa, raising her snout. "Only one more vote you Isolationists had."

Shumass hummed angrily. "Passed by Camarilla, not yet achieved."

"Time has run out," said Azwokkus. "Tomorrow they leave Kij'ik."

"Tonight remains. Insist will of Camarilla done!"

Shvosi rose onto her hind legs. "What point in this? Potentialities still on chosen path, pact made, no need this action to be forcing."

Zaimiss, still on his feet, his draperies beginning to settle, raised his voice. "I Second Shumass."

"Cannot vote on this issue second time," began Azwokkus.

"Isolationist issues sidelined by Camarilla!" said Shumass, his voice getting higher in pitch as the thrumming sound he was making increased. "Insist it carried out!"

Aizshuss unfolded himself until he was standing. "Out of time are we," he said. "Inappropriate this now is since achieved already goals are."

Shumass rounded on him, mandibles audibly clicking in anger. "Reformist, be silent! Your ideals beneath my feet are dust!"

"Shumass, desist!" said Khassis from her cushions among the Moderates. "Young you are to be on Camarilla, but outbursts of childishness not tolerated."

"Any insulting further of Camarilla members and removed you will be from chamber," said Htomshu, exuding anger scents as harsh as her tones.

"Matter already was debated, decision reached. Not all matters can we accomplish in details discussed here. Goal achieved as said rightly by Shvosi. That important issue," said Aizshuss.

"Demand will of Camarilla be done. Tonight remains," said Zaimiss insistently. "Losing control of Hunter are we, if ever we had him in control. Easier female Sand-dweller is to influence. Through her regain control of him. Unity will confirm my demands within laws of Camarilla."

Htomshu reluctantly asked.

Unity confirms this.

Zaimiss looked around the assembly, spreading his arms triumphantly. "I cannot be denied this."

Azwokkus looked to Htomshu for support, but the position of the TeLaxaudin female's hands showed her inability to help him.

"His demands are lawful," she said, her tone reluctant. "Kuvaa, tell Giyarishis to achieve mental Linking between Sand-dweller female and Hunter tonight."

"We run danger of Hunter reading all that was done to Sand-dweller if this is done," warned Aizshuss. "Unwise this is!"

"Decision made, Aizshuss," said Zaimiss. "I will tell Giyarishis, Htomshu. Let not Shvosi be troubled." He bowed to her and began to move between the cushions toward the exit, his draperies now exuding triumphant scents.

"Then I Speak for making this the last attempt since goals achieved. If Giyarishis fails tonight, no more attempts be made," said Aizshuss.

"Seconded," said Khassis before anyone could speak.

"Passed. Record this, Unity," said Htomshu.

Recorded.

"If failure, Giyarishis him should accompany. I so order," said Khassis.

"At least we've achieved that much," said Kuvaa with a sigh of relief to her companion. *Why is Zaimiss so obliging?* she sent to Shvosi, her fellow Cabbaran, ignoring Aizshuss as he began to give reports on how matters were progressing with the raiders out in the vicinity of the world Vieshen, one of the trading partners of the Prime world, K'oish'ik.

He is getting what he desires, and the Isolationists don't trust us, the older female replied.

He makes me uneasy.

He is hoping to win the position of Isolationist Leader now Hkairass is no longer concerned with such things, replied Shvosi.

And I thought we'd be better off when he changed his gender!

Shvosi gave a mental laugh. *We will be, as they dance around each other trying to outdo themselves to be picked as Leader!*

That I would not rely on, sent Azwokkus, joining their mental conversation through Unity. *A feeling have I this matter decided some time ago and Zaimiss elected is already. Pushing mental Link is not wise. As Aizshuss says, risking Hunter discovering more than what Kzizysus told his family.*

We can do nothing, replied Kuvaa sadly. *Except hope their failure over this is our success.*

Kij'ik, Command Level labs

Kezule found Giyarishis alone in the main lab, sitting on a pile of cushions by a low table, holding a wide-mouthed bowl of some sweet-smelling warm liquid. He felt a reluctance to actually enter the room and remained by the doorframe. He found the insectoid TeLaxaudin intimidating.

"Giyarishis, I need to know if anything happened to the Captain, would my wife be affected in any way?" he asked without preamble.

The TeLaxaudin looked up at him, large eyes swirling as he adjusted them for longer vision. "Why would that be happening? Is only scent marker, nothing more. Anticipating something happening to Captain, are you?"

"Of course not, but we're about to mount a mission to retake the Palace of Light. In war, anything can happen. I just need to know that my wife will be safe."

"Yes," he said shortly and returned his attention to his drink, long tongue uncurling from inside his mouth to daintily suck up the liquid.

"Have you come up with any way to turn off the scent marker yet?"

"No. Computer simulations progress, but nothing have I discovered. Solution may come naturally now you allow them to couple."

Kezule stiffened. It was one thing to turn his back on the Captain and his wife, another to have it discussed openly in front of him. "That is none of your business," he said icily, turning away from the door. "Just keep trying." For some reason, he didn't trust the TeLaxaudin. He intended to take Zayshul with him so he was on hand if anything happened to the Sholan or her.

He made his way to the sick bay where he found Zayshul and Ghidd'ah putting together supplies for them to take onto the *N'zishok*.

"I hope you asked the Sholans for more medicines and dressings for us," she said. "We are very short on the smaller ones and on all analgesics."

"I did," he said, reaching out to take her by the arm. "Carry on, Ghidd'ah. I need to talk to my wife for a few minutes."

"Kezule, I'm almost done; can't it wait another few minutes?" she objected as he drew her toward an empty area.

"No, it can't. I'm due back in the briefing room shortly, and I need to talk to you now. Don't ever sedate one of my people, or the Sholans, like that again," he said, keeping his voice low. "I need Kusac alert right now. He's come up with a workable plan. Thankfully, he was able to burn it out of his system."

"How? And I sedated him for a good reason! He should be resting, not up on his feet. That fight took a lot out of him, emotionally as well as physically."

"That isn't your decision to make. You're not to do it again, do you hear me?"

"I hear you," she said, jaw firming in annoyance. "But if he comes to me and I decide it needs to be done, that's my decision, not yours. Now tell me how he got rid of the sedative from his system."

Kezule now knew when to accept a partial victory so he let the matter drop. "He has Warrior glands like ours. You can talk to him about it later because I want you to come with me, and bring Mayza. I intend to suggest Kusac take Shaidan."

"On a warship, in a war zone? You're mad, Kezule," she hissed. "You said you were taking Ghidd'ah!"

"I'm taking you both. As you said, we are conducting a war, hopefully only a small one. I also intend to teach you how to use the Warrior glands you possess, Zayshul. I've meant to do it these past few months but never gotten around to it. Besides, with that scent marker on you, you need to come too. I'm not risking the Captain's well being as we did when we went to Ch'almuth."

"I can see that makes sense," she agreed slowly. "But the children?"

"They'll be safe, trust me, and on hand to be with us when we've retaken the City and the Palace."

"You sound very sure of yourself."

"I am. This is what I did for a living, remember?" He smiled at her, putting a hand on her shoulder. "Don't worry. If I had any doubts, neither of the children would be going." Over her shoulder he noticed Kusac entering. "Here's your Sholan. I'll see you later. Start packing as soon as you're finished here. You don't have any patients now, do you?"

"None ill enough to be in the sick bay. One of the duty medics can see to them."

Kusac was still hovering by the central reception desk as he passed him on his way out. "We reconvene in ten minutes, Kusac," he reminded him.

Up in the swimming pool level, Giyarishis let himself relax into the Unity net that was spread throughout Kij'ik. He sensed the Hunter on his way to the Sand-dweller to reprimand her for using the sedative. That would be counterproductive. Best he forget about it. He was just thankful that while the Hunter had been imprisoned, when he'd finished his most rapid healing, he'd been able to make him forget his discovery of Unity.

He began to gently nudge the potentialities, making it so that the future in which Kusac forgot why he was talking to her came to pass. His Hunter became distracted by the continuing discomfort in his leg, and seizing the moment, Giyarishis made sure the distractions overwhelmed his purpose.

Zayshul smiled as Kusac approached her.

"What brings you here?" she asked.

He frowned slightly, realizing his feet had automatically brought him here after leaving Shaidan with Jayza. "You know, I can't remember," he said, puzzled.

"Was it to tell me what time you'll be finished tonight?" she asked.

"It must have been that," he said, but there was still a nagging doubt at the back of his mind. Fishing in his pocket, he drew out the card to his rooms. "Here, take that. I've no idea when we'll finish, but Jayza has said Shaidan can sleep in his room until I come for him tonight."

"Your key? But it's your private space," she said, surprised.

"There's nothing private there now," he said absently, still wondering what it was he'd forgotten.

"Kezule wants me to go with him. You should be with Shaidan tonight. We can postpone this till tomorrow."

"There won't be time. We've got the makings of a plan now.

Talking of which, I need to get back down for the meeting. I'll see you later," he said, turning away from her.

As he made his way back to the briefing room, he started to worry about his uncharacteristic forgetfulness. He couldn't afford it this evening, not when they had the finer points of his proposed plan to go over.

Giyarishis began to withdraw from the Hunter's vicinity. He'd done enough for now. Later, when they were together would be a better time.

Officer Level Hall, several hours later

As the military personnel, including the rest of his crew, filed out of the hall to be fitted for their assault suits, Kusac felt the blast of anger from M'kou as the young Lieutenant turned to his father and began talking to him in a low, intense voice. Just out of earshot, he was unable to hear the words, but he knew instinctively what it was about.

"Kezule, I'd like M'kou with me," he said, moving closer.

"This is a private matter," hissed the General, not bothering to even glance in his direction. "I've given my orders. It isn't open to discussion."

"He'll be safe with me, Kezule," he said, putting a restraining hand on the General's arm and refusing to be shaken off. "I know how much M'kou lost when I shot him with that la'quo pellet. Call this a debt I need to repay to him personally."

Kezule turned an angry gaze on him. "He's too vulnerable now!"

"Only your kind have the extra glands that make you faster and stronger in battle and accelerate healing. The rest of us manage without them. So can he."

"You have them!" The anger was dying from Kezule's eyes now. "And he's lost them."

"I know. That's why it's all the more important for him to go on this mission, to prove to himself he is no less a warrior than he was before. You should be able to understand this.

Our covert operation is one of stealth. If it goes as planned, we shouldn't see any fighting."

"Kusac . . ."

He could feel the complex emotions Kezule was trying to keep to himself as if they were his own. "He's my friend," he said simply, letting the General go. "I won't let any harm come to him, Kezule."

"Go," Kezule said to M'kou with an effort. "Get fitted with your suit like the others. You'll accompany the Captain."

"Thank you, General," M'kou said quietly before executing a crisp salute and leaving.

"If you prevented him from going, it would eat at his soul," said Kusac, not taking his eyes off Kezule. "It's what he was bred and trained for, by you."

"I know, but I don't have to like it," Kezule ground out through clenched teeth.

"If it's any consolation, because he does it this time, he'll probably be content to leave it to his brothers in the future."

"I hope you're right, Kusac. I'll see you down in the landing bay at 04:00. Good night."

Kusac watched Kezule stalk out of the hall before leaving for his own quarters, where Zayshul was waiting.

Winter's Realm

Vartra sat on the window seat, staring out at the snow-covered landscape. The branches of the resin trees were still weighed down by the snowfall of a few hours earlier. "Spring's late this year," he murmured. "It's Zhal-Arema already."

The snow white Goddess lying curled on the bed laughed softly and propped herself up on one elbow. "More time for us to be together."

"I should be leaving."

She made a little mewling noise of protest, like a kit deprived of a treat. The sheets rustled as she rose to her feet. "You've been away too much this winter already. You belong to me during this season."

Vartra ignored the implicit complaint, concentrating instead on trying to armor his senses against her. He could smell her faint perfume, spicy and rich, hear her soft tread even on the furred rugs that covered the floor of her bedroom. He resisted the temptation to turn, knowing too well the effect her unclothed body would have on him. Even now the blood was pounding in his ears, and his heart was beating faster as he sensed her stop just behind him.

"Spring will come soon enough," she said, her breath cool on his ear and cheek as she laid a hand on his shoulder. "This is our time."

Like a magnet, her presence drew him to face her. Deep, icy-blue eyes regarded him from within her white face. Around her shoulders, the waves of her hair lay like a cloud seen high up in a winter sky.

"You're cold. Come, let me warm you," she said, reaching to touch his cheek.

Her scent surrounded him and he found himself reaching clumsily to cup her face in his hands. Like a starving beggar, his mouth covered hers, kissing her deeply, burying his hands in her silky hair. He felt her tail flick gently against his legs.

At last he pulled back from her. "You don't warm me, Kuushoi, you never have. Your coolness burns me," he said hoarsely, picking her up in his arms and carrying her back to the bed they shared. "It sears my soul."

"Better that than lie with my oh-so-worthy lukewarm sister," she murmured, wrapping her arms around him as he lowered himself onto her. "Her desire will not warm you at all."

"Don't talk about her like that," he said, his voice thick with passion as he pushed her hair aside and began to kiss and nip at her neck. "She doesn't try to own me as you do."

"Then don't talk of Spring to me," she whispered, arching up to meet his sudden urgency.

Kij'ik

The Hunter had arrived at his rooms now, and convinced Shaidan had something to do with the black, or null, zones that frequently surrounded him, Giyarishis reached out through

Unity and activated the Isolator in the cub's bedroom, putting him instantly into a deep sleep that nothing save morning would wake him from.

That done, he chose the interface in the Hunter's suite and settled back to monitor what they were doing.

"You said you wanted to talk," Zayshul said as he laid himself carefully, facedown, on the towels she'd spread over the top of his bed.

He felt the bed move as she settled herself astride him, then smelled the sudden, pungent aroma of the massage oil as she opened it.

"I do," he said. "The thing is, I don't know how much of what I'm thinking and sensing is imagination."

Her hands, thick with the oil, began to stroke across his shoulders, following the lie of his short but dense pelt. "Your fur is soaking up the oil," she said, her voice rich with amusement as she stopped for a moment to pour more oil into her hands. "You really needed this treatment. I just hope I've got the mix that Banner told me right."

He twisted his head around in an effort to squint up at her. "Banner gave you the recipe? When did he do that?"

"During your meal break. It's a muscle relaxant coupled with a conditioner for your pelt, he said. Something to ease your body and put the oils back into your skin and fur. He said it looked shockingly dry and dull after your rapid healing."

Grunting, he let his head fall back on his folded forearms. Thoughtful of him, but then that was Banner all over—he took his responsibilities seriously. She was working on the other shoulder now, spreading the warmed oil downward toward his shoulder blade, part of the complex joint system that allowed him to switch between upright and all-fours stance. The heating had been turned up because of the chill in the air they'd both been feeling earlier that day, and the scent of the oil was beginning to fill his small bedroom. He found it pleasant, with slightly soporific overtones, probably from the muscle-easing herbs.

"Tell me what's worrying you. Sharing it by talking about it might clarify your thoughts," she said, easing her way slowly, with regular pressure and strokes, down his back to his hips.

"Something and nothing," he said. "I had plenty of time in my cell to think through the events of the past year or so, and it's as if there was a thread running though them, a kind of hidden purpose."

"To what ends?" she asked, beginning to spread the oil over his hips and thighs. "By the way, do I massage your tail?"

The incongruity of the question struck him, and he began to chuckle. "Not unless you want to. The muscles in it are fine." He flicked it up, unerringly wrapping it around her wrist.

She pulled against the coils of it, finding they tightened briefly before releasing her. "Very amusing," she said, swatting his butt lightly. "How am I supposed to know?"

"True," he agreed amiably, allowing himself to sink into the pleasant sensations she was creating. "The ends are here, I think," he added after a moment. "Being on Kij'ik, with you and Shaidan."

"Us? But what about your family? Your mental Link to them is surely stronger than anything."

"It was, but that was destroyed by Chy'qui, remember?" He eased his legs apart so she could work more easily on the inner surfaces of his thighs, wincing slightly at the pressure that put on his wound.

"How can I forget that," she murmured. "But what's your reason for thinking there's a connection? I can't see one." He felt her hands passing around the bandage on his left thigh, leaving that area alone.

"I'm more vulnerable alone. Linked to them, they'll notice anyone, or anything, trying to affect me." As he said it, he realized this was the first time he'd actually put his feelings into words. His sense of unease began to grow, but he folded it deeper inside his mind where she couldn't pick it up.

"What are they like as people?" she asked suddenly.

"My life-mates?" Again he looked around and down at her where she was now working on his lower legs. This time he didn't have to lift his head.

"Yes. And your children. You'll soon see them again."

"They're good people."

"They must be more than that to you."

"They complete me," he said, the words out before he could think of what to say. "We know each other's strengths and weaknesses as no one else could."

"Will you tell them about my DNA in Shaidan?" Her fingers were suddenly less gentle.

"Careful, that's hurting," he said. "I don't know, Zayshul.

Eventually, yes, but not at first. I'm not afraid of how they'll react, it's more than that." He was afraid for them, he realized, for them all, from Kaid and Carrie to Zayshul, Kezule, and their daughter, and Shaidan. Why, he wasn't sure, but suddenly he was deathly afraid for them.

Her hands stilled. "You're afraid," she said softly, her expression changing as her eyes grew wide with apprehension. "I've never known you to be afraid."

He turned over, sitting up to grasp her by the shoulders. "Something's using us, Zayshul," he whispered, flexing his claws so as to avoid hurting her. "Not the Directorate, it was only part of it. Something else, more powerful. I felt it just before I came up to the hydroponics level to confront Kezule that day."

"Are you sure?" There was real fear on her face now.

"I'm positive." He reached out with his mind, feeling for that presence he'd briefly sensed before, at the same time burying his thoughts deep into his subconscious, behind the walls he'd used during the early days of his Link to Carrie, lest something tried to make him forget what he'd discovered. He took the bottle of oil roughly from her hand, putting it on the night table. "We have to protect them, Zayshul—my family and yours—until we find out who it is and how to stop it!"

The lights flared briefly, died, then flared again, growing in brightness.

"What the hell . . ." he began.

Giyarishis collapsed back onto his cushions with relief. He'd had no option but to employ the Isolator. Thankfully, they were in the Hunter's quarters where they'd be undiscovered till they woke in time for the mission. There was not a shred of doubt now in his mind that the Hunter was not under their control. Obviously he had been thinking this through on some level for quite a time or he'd have been unable to discern the connections in his life. And yet, he'd picked up none of this! The null zones—they must have hidden him during those times. He had to contact the Camarilla immediately.

Sitting up again, he reached for the communications device on his belt and sent out the signal. Moments later, a holo image of Kuvaa formed in front of him.

"He is discovering the truth," said Giyarishis. "Invoke the

Isolator I had to, otherwise he and Sand-dweller female both know."

"He must forget," said the Cabbaran female. "In a few hours they leave for mission. Have you pushed him into the Link yet?"

"No, I was listening to them."

"Try forcing the Link once more. If achievable that is not, I will not be concerned. You understand this? But forget he must! Her also."

Giyarishis' eyes whirled with indecision as his hands began to fold around each other. Kuvaa was being most unlike herself, most inconsistent. "I understand," he said.

"Report to me when you're done," she said and signed off.

The TeLaxaudin sighed, putting his communicator away in one of the pouches hidden under his waist draperies. Why would Kuvaa now look on a failure of them to Link mentally as no bad thing when a few hours ago she was pushing for it? Could it be that the Camarilla had changed its mind yet again?

Puzzled still, he obediently began to sink into the requisite trance, calling on Unity to enhance what feeble natural ability he had. Then, with great stealth, he gently tried to insinuate his thoughts into the Hunter's mind. It was difficult, because he'd learned his lessons well from Naacha, and many were the shields he had to penetrate then leave, without trace of his entry being found. Once there, he searched out any thoughts that didn't suit their purpose, making them fade away until only faint echoes were left.

Time was passing too fast, and he had to withdraw and work on the female Sand-dweller. That done, with a light hold still on her mind, he drew the Hunter's to him again, subtly bending them until a faint mingling of them had been accomplished. More, he couldn't do. The mind was fragile in some ways yet strong in others, and forcing it against the natural inclinations of a person was not that easy.

Withdrawing completely, he triggered the release from the Isolator's influence and sat back to watch them.

Kusac blinked then blinked again, seeing the afterimage from the bright flare of the lights.

"What the hell was that?" he asked, pulling her closer.

"Maybe they're still checking out the electrical systems,"

she said, snuggling into him, one oil-rich palm reaching up to caress his neck. "Forget about that, it isn't important."

He hesitated, trying to think back over what he'd been saying before the lights had acted up. Teeth closed over his shoulder muscle, the mock bite sending waves of desire spreading through his body. Her other hand was pushing through his fur, playing with one of his nipples, and suddenly whatever he'd been saying wasn't important anymore.

She'd played with him, pouring the oil onto his chest, massaging it in gently, then moved lower, driving him frantic in his need for her. His conscious mind screamed he didn't want this, not with his family arriving so soon, but the thought was stifled as her mind reached out for his and her sensations flooded through him.

He moaned at the enhancements it brought to his own pleasure, but he knew deep down inside that this was wrong, even as his mind not only accepted what she was sending to him but reached out for hers. Inside, where she couldn't feel it, he was yowling his denial as the merging of their minds began. He was utterly powerless to stop it.

Then, like the force of a winter storm, coldness beyond anything he could imagine froze him, and it stopped. He instantly pulled his mind back, as in a panic he pulled himself forcefully away from her, collapsing on the bed beside her.

His head ached with a fury, and he was bitterly cold, frozen to the bone and beyond, but he hadn't Linked to Zayshul.

Beside him, she cried out in terror, curling up on herself, nursing her own aching head. He leaned forward to comfort her. "It's all right," he said, pulling her up and folding her into his arms. "It's over now."

"My head," she moaned. "I can barely see. What happened?"

The room had begun to warm again, but there was still a lingering chill in the air. "I don't know. We began to Link, but something prevented it. That wasn't us, Zayshul," he whispered. "We were being forced into that Link. I was right—there is something trying to control us."

She was beginning to recover a little, though still massaging her temples. "Then what stopped it?"

"I don't know. But I do know we have to protect our families, as I said before."

Her puzzled expression only made him more sure he'd been right.

"When did you say that?"

"You've forgotten it. Let's get under the covers first and keep warm, then I'll remind you."

Kij'ik, Zhal-Arema, 3rd day (March)

The *Venture 2* stowed safely in the belly of the *Mazzu*, Kezule watched on the Bridge screen as it pulled slowly away from Kij'ik. All they'd planned would now be won or lost with this first strike at the Orbital. He sighed and got to his feet.

"Put out a call to the ready rooms and tell the commandos for the *N'zishok* and *M'zayik* to meet me in the landing bay," he said. "You have the Bridge."

"Yes, General," said the young officer on duty. "Good luck."

He bit back a retort to the effect that luck had nothing to do with it, then thought better of it. Luck, indeed, would need to be on their side.

As he made his way to the *N'zishok's* ramp, he heard a commotion from behind him and turned to see the TeLaxaudin, followed by one of his people who was weighed down with various cases and bags, exiting the elevator.

As Giyarishis stalked over toward him, he heard the low buzzing the alien was emitting increase until it was echoing in the bones of his head.

"I come, needed I might be," the translator said as he was overtaken by the alien.

Kezule reached out to take hold of the civilian following him with the luggage.

"What's this all about?" he demanded.

"I know as much as you, sir. He called me into his office and said he was joining you. Shall I take his stuff in?"

Kezule let him go and nodded. "Carry on." Thoughtfully, he followed.

*   *   *

Giyarishis was not pleased. In fact he was outraged at this peremptory command from the Camarilla, to say nothing of Kuvaa's reprimand for his failure to make them Link the night before.

"It was against his inclination, Phratry Leader," he'd said. *"More forcing his mind would damage. No use to us then he is."*

"Not much use now," she'd muttered darkly, lip curling contemptuously at him. *"We try another way. Harden him. Make him more warrior, less understanding."*

"Isolate him from all this will," he'd objected.

"Not the Sand-dweller General," Kuvaa had countered. *"Is what must be done."*

"But . . ."

"Obey Camarilla will! You accompany Sand-dweller General, influence Hunter from there! Have Unity on ship."

"Yes, Phratry Leader," he'd said resignedly.

It was an immense change of plan to go from wanting closer ties between the Sand-dweller female and the Hunter to alienating the Hunter from everyone but the General.

He thought deeply on this as he stalked behind the officer leading him to his hurriedly arranged quarters. What could he do? Call the Camarilla, demand he speak to someone else—a TeLaxaudin—to verify the orders? His blood chilled at the thought. It was his role to do, not question, and he'd worked for some time now with Kuvaa as his handler. But he was not happy, not happy at all.

Tooshu, same day, 06:00 hours Prime local

"What do you mean he's already left?" asked Kaid, suppressing his anger with an effort after he'd listened to Kezule describe the plan all the way through. "Why didn't your doctors stop him? He's still recovering from a blaster wound in his leg."

"The wound is virtually healed, now," Kezule said smoothly. "He's fit enough for what he's doing. Besides," he added, "stopping him is not the easiest task, as I'm sure you know."

"Following orders was never one of his strengths," he muttered to himself.

"Come now, Kaid—what is your rank, by the way?—neither of us were very good at that when we were younger."

"I have no rank," said Kaid, his tone hardening as his anger increased. "Nor do I need one. We only have ranks when we lead missions. There was no need for this haste, Kezule. Zsurtul bought us six weeks. Call him back."

"No, Kaid. We need to act now, before K'hedduk consolidates his position on K'oish'ik. That's what's important, and Kusac knew this. I admit it took me a while to see I was wrong and he had the right of it."

"This whole undertaking should have been discussed with me first," Kaid said, trying to hold back the snarl that was threatening to escape.

Kezule inclined his head slightly. "Why?" he asked, almost conversationally. "Kusac and I lead this mission, Kaid. His part is for him alone to decide. I called you to arrange a rendezvous point and inform you of our plans. When we meet, I'll be happy to discuss any ideas you have for the HALO drop."

"I'll meet you, but I'm not pleased you've sidelined us like this." This time Kaid did show his teeth.

"And I'm not pleased you lied about Zsurtul," Kezule snapped back. "I know he's with you, and I demand to talk to him now, in private."

Kaid snarled soundlessly. "We're not finished talking yet, Kezule." Reaching forward, he punched in the code to transfer the call to Zsurtul's room.

"Going through the tunnels was your plan, as was using the asteroids," said Carrie from where she sat at the small table nearby.

"I know," hissed Kaid. "He's been reading me—there's no other explanation for it!"

She got up and came over to where he sat at the comm unit. "What bothers you most?" she asked, putting her hands on his shoulders and beginning to massage them. "That he took your plan or that he can read us from all that distance and hasn't yet contacted us?"

"Both," he snarled, reflexively tightening up as she touched him. "I don't know what I expected from him, but I didn't anticipate him being able to read me and ignore us!"

"I'm not happy about it either, but we don't know the circumstances. It may be that he just picked you up and can't actually communicate with us."

"Do you believe that?" he asked, turning his head to look up at her. "We're anxious to see him, but it doesn't mean . . ." He stopped, unwilling to say more.

She sighed, resting her head on top of his, hands stilling. "I hope so," she said quietly. "I don't want to think it could be anything else." She shook herself and smiled, continuing to massage him. "Relax, Tallinu, whatever else, at least we know he's been able to pick our brains and refine what we were talking about, so we have had some input, even if at a distance. How good is his plan?"

"Not bad, actually," Kaid admitted, relaxing under her expert hands. "It's that wound that worries me."

"Banner said he'd used fastheal in their sick bay and his wound was almost gone."

"It would have to have been a shallow, glancing injury for that to happen," said Kaid.

"It worries me too, but maybe it was."

Kaid grunted in disbelief. "Then he was luckier than he deserved to be from what Banner said."

"That's not a nice thing to say!"

"He acted like a fool, even given the circumstances. He should have involved the others. Together they had a better chance of getting safely off Kij'ik. He hasn't yet grasped the most basic concept of a team."

"I can see your lessons were effective, then," she said, putting an edge into her voice.

"I'm not like that."

She said nothing.

"Carrie, I'm not!"

"No? My memory must be troubling me, then."

"Dammit!" The incoming message warning began to sound, and he stopped talking to gesture her away, then leaned forward to take the call.

"I'll meet with you, Kezule, but I want you to tell Kusac to wait at the Orbital for me before going down to the planet. The Touibans are working on remote rovers to dismantle the tunnel traps." He had the satisfaction of seeing Kezule's surprise.

"Kusac intimated the Touibans were with you in large numbers," Kezule said. "We need a minimum of two hundred people in the HALO assault. I have only some thirty-eight warriors available, and I need twenty-five for my fighters."

"I'll see to that." The fact that Kezule was as much in the dark as he was pleased him, dissipating much of his anger.

"I'll pass on the message to Kusac, of course, but he'll have to wait there for our young Emperor to join him. Without Zsurtul, we can't access either the weather controls or the Command Center terminals."

The anger returned. "Out of the question," he snapped.

"I will be there, Kaid," said Zsurtul as the screen split to accommodate him in the conference. "I gave the General my promise to help him in this undertaking to free my people."

Don't try to stop him, Tallinu, sent Carrie. *You can't publicly minimize him in the eyes of others, especially Kezule, otherwise they won't accept him as their ruler. Talk to him later, privately.*

Kaid studied the young Prime's pale face and resolute expression for a moment. "I'm not happy with you risking yourself, Emperor Zsurtul," he said carefully and formally. "You are your planet's last hope; you shouldn't be putting yourself in danger like this."

"What kind of leader would I be if I were not prepared to do what I expect of my followers? I learned that from you, Kaid. I'm the only one who can command the loyalty of the crews of my ships, and a retinal scan from me is needed to radically change the climate controls."

"He's got you there, Kaid," murmured Kezule. "I'll see he is properly protected, have no doubt of that. I'll have my best commando as his personal bodyguard, plus Kusac's team is mostly my people, and they will protect our Emperor with their lives if necessary. Kusac will also be there to protect him, and Banner too, on the Orbital."

Zsurtul winced. "I don't want it to come to that, General."

Kezule inclined his head. "I know, but it's necessary. I'll have my daughter Zhalmo designated as your bodyguard, Majesty, plus two people of her choosing. She's the best I have."

Zsurtul nodded seriously. "Thank you, General. I'll leave you to make the other arrangements, Kaid."

Patience. This was bound to happen soon. He's been brought up to be Emperor and take command of his people. We have to have faith he's learned all we've taught him, Tallinu, sent Carrie. *It seems that he has. After all, he's deferring to you now.*

Kaid grunted.

You need to learn when to let go, Tallinu. You did it with Dzaka, why are you having so many problems with Kusac and Zsurtul?

He had no answer and instead concentrated on Kezule. "Is there anything else, General? Or have we had all the surprises now?"

"I have fighters and no pilots, Kaid. I need sleep tapes to instruct them."

"We don't train using sleep tapes. We might be able to help, though. Send me the specs of your craft, and I'll see what can be done. The Touibans may have that capability."

"Thank you, and please pass on my debt of gratitude to them," said Kezule.

"The debt is mine, General," interrupted Zsurtul smoothly. "Not yours. I will thank them for us."

Kaid watched the stiffness leave Kezule's face.

"As you wish, Majesty," the General said, without, Kaid noticed, a trace of irony.

"I'll call Toueesut and ask him if he can help," Kaid said suddenly.

When the problem had been described to him, Toueesut was enthusiastic.

"This we can do," he nodded, waving his hands. "Needing Sholan pilots we will as we can program our flight simulator to be the Valtegan fighters, but we are of a smaller size than them."

"We'll provide them," said Kaid. *If we can be sure nothing but piloting skills is recorded,* he sent to Carrie.

Nothing else would we let them have, came Toueesut's response, rendering both Kaid and Carrie speechless with shock. Never before had the Touiban spoken mentally to them.

Out here, as Family, there must be no secrets anymore between us, sent the small alien. *Secrets can be fatal in the circumstances we are now in.*

Agreed, sent Carrie.

"We'll get this to you as soon as possible," said Kaid, recovering his composure.

"A few hours, no more," assured Toueesut. "Send data, now I start."

Kezule leaned forward to send the information. "I have one more request of the Touibans," he said. "Kusac actually suggested it. When we've freed K'oish'ik, would you be able to help us move Kij'ik into an orbit around it? It is powered, but only in order to correct its orbit, nothing more."

"Tell us where you are and a shuttle will be going there with technicians to look at it," said Toueesut. "First I must be knowing your purpose for moving it."

"The Orbital above K'oish'ik has only rudimentary defenses because we relied on our fleet for that. It was never anticipated that our Empire could fall. Kij'ik can give us that defense and provide training facilities for the new military we will have to build to defend our world. It will also free my people to become citizens of K'oish'ik."

"We will be needing to assess the possibility, General, and confer with our Family."

Kezule glanced questioningly at Kaid.

"We're his adopted Family," he said.

Kezule raised an eyebrow ridge. "You and Kusac attract the most surprising allies, Kaid," he murmured. "I am impressed."

"What can I say? It must be our winning ways, General," Kaid grinned, amused at last.

"I'll hear from you shortly, then."

When the call was over, Kaid turned his chair around and looked over to where Carrie had resumed her seat. The silence lengthened between them until he spoke.

"You're right, I have to let Kusac go, and Zsurtul—he has his own advisers after all. It's just not so easy to watch a lover take risks, Carrie," he said quietly. "As you know."

"You have to have as much faith in him as he has in you, Kaid, or you'll continue to fall out with each other."

"Do you have faith in him as a leader?"

"Yes, and as a Warrior, you know I do. I trust my life to both of you and always have."

"I suppose you have," he said slowly. "I just never thought of it like that before."

"He's been without us both for nearly half a year, Tallinu. We have to recognize that he's had to rely on himself."

"That's where Banner was supposed to come in."

"He did what he could, but Kusac's like you in that he's been brought up to be a Clan Leader. You were marked to be the Brotherhood Leader—neither of you can easily defer to the other. You're both natural leaders, as Kezule is."

He sighed and held his arms open to her. "Were you always this wise, Dzinae?"

The *N'zishok*

"Zhalmo, I've got a job for you," Kezule said to his daughter as she stood smartly at attention before him.

"You want me to look after our Emperor, don't you?" she nodded. "Makes sense. He'll need a bodyguard. Am I to do it alone, or can I choose my unit?"

Kezule didn't twitch a muscle this time. He was getting used to the females around him being well aware of what he was thinking and about to do. "You'll be working with Kusac, of course, but you can call on another two people to help you."

"No need, sir. The ones I want are already on the Captain's team."

He nodded. "You'll transfer to Kaid's ship when we rendezvous, Zhalmo. Dismissed for now."

"Yes, sir."

He sighed as she left, wondering if there was any point in him wearing the psi damper when he was surrounded by people as good as his daughter. At least Kusac had promised to train them on the courtesies involved in having that ability—though he knew his daughter hadn't been invading his privacy.

Zhal-Arema, 4th day, (March) Winter's Realm

Kuushoi frowned in annoyance as she felt a warm breeze stir the blue-white draperies in her Viewing Hall. The distant sound of leaves soughing in a breeze gently filled the chamber.

"Lady, Vartra comes," said her dzinae Nefae, coming over to join her and bowing low. "It's time."

"Ghyakulla's Realm is close," said Rojae, lounging against a pillar by the doorway.

"I'm aware of that," she said testily, swinging away from the huge ice crystal set in the center of the viewing table where she watched the many mortal worlds to face him. "We have a few days left. Why are you lounging in here, Rojae? You still have work to do!"

Rojae flicked imaginary specks off his spotless white tunic before answering her. "The air is warming, Lady, as you can feel. There's little I can do during daylight. I can only bring frost for you when dark falls." His handsome face, with its soft gray pelt and pale blue eyes, was a study in polite boredom.

"Insolent dzinae!" Kuushoi hissed, clutching her robes as she took a step toward him. "You sprites are getting above yourselves!"

He straightened up, smiling provocatively. "Will you accompany me, tonight, Lady? Spreading frost over the land would help ease your loneliness tonight."

His tone was soft and persuasive, and for a moment Kuushoi considered it, but only for a moment. "Don't try to distract me," she said petulantly, turning away from him to Nefae. She hated this time of year when her reign on Shola was over except for the high mountain ranges, where she ruled perpetually. She hated more that Ghyakulla was calling for Vartra.

"Are we ready, Nefae? Is Winter's growth waiting for the first thaw?"

"It is, Lady," said her dzinae respectfully. "Even in the desert where no snows can reach, only Rojae's frost, all is waiting for your sister."

Her lips thinned and her ears flicked sideways in anger. "There's no need to remind me," she snapped.

Footsteps echoed in the hallway outside, and Vartra, dressed already in the subtle green robes of Spring, entered, followed by Gihaf.

"I've been called," he said awkwardly, stopping just inside the chamber.

"I know you have! Do you think I'm deaf?"

He remained silent, watching her.

"One day, Vartra, you will have to choose between us," she said, her voice brittle. "I know you'll always have to serve your time with her, but you must choose which of us you love!"

"I can't," he said, clasping his hands in front of him. "It's no easy choice to give one who was once a mere mortal, Kuushoi. How can I choose between you? You are both Goddesses."

"Won't, you mean," she said spitefully.

"We have this same conversation every year, Kuushoi. Why can't you be content when I'm with you? You have a husband . . ."

She laughed, her voice echoing off the ice walls. "L'Shoh? He's a creature of reason and logic and rules! He has no fire in him!"

"You chose him, took him when he was promised to Ghyakulla," he said quietly.

"I know what I did, thank you! Go to her, and be damned to you," she said, turning her back on him angrily. "Ghyakulla, take him, but return him by morning!"

"As you wish," he said.

She smelled the sweet scent of nung flowers as Ghyakulla's realm opened up to let him walk through; then, as suddenly as they had come, the nung blossoms, warm breeze, and Vartra were gone.

Gihaf was coming closer, she could smell its scent as it approached, so it was no surprise when it touched her on the arm.

"Lady, you should rest," it said in its soft voice. "Let me take you to your Spring rooms. I've made them ready for you."

Its hand stroked her arm gently, urging her to leave the Viewing Hall, and before she realized it, she was accompanying Gihaf down the corridor.

"I know how tiring this day is for you," it said, its voice gradually losing the softness and becoming deeper. "I have prepared some wine and a light meal for you."

She glanced at it, marveling anew as she watched the soft, feminine features of her favorite dzinae gradually lose their curves and become harder as the masculine planes developed. It grew slightly taller, as if straightening up, but she knew that was only an illusion. When it topped her by half a head, it was fully male, but none of its beauty of face and form had been lost.

"Stay with me, Gihaf," she said as he opened the door into her suite. "I could do with some honest company. Rojae is trying too hard to seduce me out of my mood, and Nefae is being overly subservient, as usual."

"Of a certainty, Lady," he smiled, deep blue eyes lighting

with genuine humor. "Did I not just change for your benefit alone?"

"You did," she acknowledged, letting him lead her to the table set with several interestingly scented dishes. "When we've eaten, weave pleasant, restful dreams for me, my Dzinae," she said, reaching up to touch the soft gray pelt of his face. "I want to forget Vartra tonight."

"As you wish it, Lady," he said, catching her hand and, eyes never leaving her face, licking it languorously before releasing it. "What would you like to talk about as we eat?"

"Anything but the weather," she said with a touch of her previous acerbity as he pulled out a chair and held it for her.

Ghyakulla's Realm

Lazily, feeling refreshed and almost reborn, Ghyakulla sat up and stretched from her toes to the tip of her tail. Trying not to wake the male deeply asleep at her side, she began to slide out of her bed. Now that the Spring Rites had been accomplished, she had matters to see to that couldn't wait. As she rose, Vartra stirred, murmuring nothings as he turned his back to her before settling once more.

Her bower was an open trellis of living trees that formed a roof over the bed below. Sweet-smelling Spring blossoms of several kinds mingled with the omnipresent nung flowers of which she was so fond.

Picking up her discarded tunic, she reached forward to let her hand trail gently down Vartra's spine. She enjoyed his company and was glad she'd had the excuse of Spring to call him to her Realm for the next few months.

Sighing, she turned away, and as she donned the short tunic, she sketched her hand in the air and stepped through the resultant shimmering portal into L'Shoh's Realm.

As usual, he was sitting on his ebon black throne, elbow on the armrest and chin perched on his hand. He looked up at her as she stepped onto the dais beside him.

"Cousin, it's good to see you," he said, getting up to greet her.

Ghyakulla looked down into the Judgment Hall, taking in the somber crimson-edged, black-draped columns surrounding the restless gathering of souls. Her eye ridges creased in concern as she caught sight of his two dzinaes and turned back to look at him.

"I know you find my work distressing," he said, his pleasant voice so low only she could hear him. "But the worthy must be rewarded and the unworthy judged. Let's go somewhere more relaxing. Tallis, you and Vakaad continue without me."

"Yes, Lord," they said, bowing low in respect as L'Shoh held his hand out to Ghyakulla.

When she took it, he drew her behind the throne and into the corridor leading to his private rooms. He ushered her into his own study, a room as different as was possible from the hall they'd left. A warm fire crackled in the grate, and gentle lighting cast a glow on the comfortable furniture and thick carpets. Outside, she could hear the winds that perpetually howled around his castle.

Indicating a chair, he went to get drinks from the sideboard for them.

"This isn't called Winter's Hellmouth for nothing, Cousin," he said wryly, catching her thoughts as he poured them both some mulled wine. "Kuushoi hasn't been near me today, though I gather from the glow you seem to be wrapped in, Spring is now due."

She smiled, taking the glass from him as he returned to her side, sipping daintily from its contents.

Sitting down, he nodded. "She usually comes to me, pouring out her wrath and venom for not remonstrating with you when you send for Vartra." He swirled the contents of his glass before taking a sip. "This time, for some reason, I seem to have been spared."

She sent images of Vartra returning later that day to Kuushoi for a week as Winter still ruled in most of the lowlands, the thaw being late this year.

"So she's sulking for today. Is she continuing to hide our Hunter of Justice from the Camarilla? Ironic that he is a descendant of Vartra."

Nodding, she put her drink on the table by her elbow and leaned forward to regard him seriously.

L'Shoh flicked his ears backward in denial. "Not just my Avatar of Justice, Ghyakulla—ours. You had more to do with creating him than I did. It's taken a long time to get to this point, Cousin; enjoy this small victory. Despite what I do from now on, he could still bring it all to ruin around our ears."

She smiled, letting him see she had no worries about his part in their venture.

"I know you have faith in me," he said, his mouth twisting slightly as it opened in an ironic smile. "I wish your sister had, then we wouldn't have had to resort to your subterfuge to get her to protect our Avatar."

Frowning, she looked briefly away from him.

"I don't like it either," he said, putting his glass down abruptly and reaching out to take her hand in his. "If only it hadn't been for Kuushoi's treachery on our wedding night, you'd be my wife, not her. You know we work well together, Ghyakulla. Kuushoi barely speaks to me."

Pulling her hand away, she looked at him intently. She could feel his genuine regret at the circumstances of his marriage to her sister, but she herself had none. The thought of being confined to the cold of Winter had appalled her, creature of sunlight, warm breezes and forests that she had always been.

Putting her hand up in a warning gesture, she watched his face resume its normal mask of neutrality as he lowered his hand and sat back in his chair.

Obviously following her thoughts, he smiled ruefully. "You're right, you wouldn't have made a good Winter Guardian, nor she a Summer one. I suppose it's as well your sister's devious nature showed itself when it did."

"Events happened as they must," she said slowly, as speech was not how she normally chose to communicate. "You acted nobly, even if she didn't, believing that marriage to you would bring her greater power. You have come to love each other, though she'll not admit it."

Even as he looked at her in disbelief, she sent him images laced with gentle amusement and memories of how he indeed did love his sharp-tongued mate.

I'm no innocent, she reminded him.

Hardly, when you conspire with me to make Kuushoi do our bidding, he replied.

Only she can reach our Avatar at this time. He must counter the darkness that spreads between Ghioass and M'zull and reaches out to taint Shola. It threatens to engulf us all.

· "And when he's on K'oish'ik?" he murmured. "Kuushoi can only reach him because of the cold between the stars."

She smiled gently, letting him know she had other plans already in the making.

"What is it about Vartra that interests both of you so much?" he asked abruptly. "Why are both of you so obsessed with him?"

Ghyakulla shrugged, telling him in mental pictures that it was his mortality that made him so unlike Varza, who had preceded him. He was peaceful, gentler in every way than the Entity of War had been. *He is my natural mate.*

"Yet he refuses to choose between you and your sister."

Her eyes clouded over, becoming distant as she looked to some time and place beyond him. "He will choose when it's time," she said, rising to leave.

CHAPTER 3

The *Tooshu*, same day, Zhal-Arema, 4th day (March)

MUCH to the annoyance of Carrie, Jo, and Kitra, Kaid had left the three females and taken the rest of their team down to one of the lower decks to run them through their battle suit and weapons' drills.

"Absolutely not, it's too dangerous to have you along. You don't have the necessary experience," was all he'd say about the matter before heading off to work with the others.

Knowing how angry she was about this, he was surprised when she interrupted him with a sending.

Valden hasn't turned up for his kitchen duty, and Zsurtul's nowhere to be found.

Sighing, he acknowledged her, knowing he'd have to deal with this himself since she was obviously refusing to do so.

"Run them through the drill one more time, Garras, then dismiss them," he said, turning to leave. "Tell them to take their kit to their quarters so they can modify it where necessary."

The older male nodded as he took over.

"They can't have just disappeared," Kaid was saying in frustration half an hour later, after talking to the cubs in the kitchens and searching their quarters for the missing pair.

"Apparently they have," said Carrie dryly, continuing studiously to read the novel on her comp pad. "You'd better contact Toueesut and warn him."

Ears flicking in annoyance, Kaid turned and stalked off down the corridors. When he was out of sight, he stopped and tapped in the code on his wrist unit for the Touiban's personal comm.

"Toueesut, Zsurtul and Valden are missing again. Can you put out an alert on them?"

"Not needing one. They are in the comms room we set up for him to be reaching the M'zullians. Most amusing it is what they are doing."

"What are they doing this time?" he asked with a now familiar sinking feeling in his stomach. How much more trouble could those two get up to before they met with Kezule? Letting Zsurtul go with Kusac was beginning to look more and more like an attractive proposition if it meant keeping him out of trouble, and Valden's way.

Trouble and Valden are synonymous, observed Carrie.

"Better it be if you are speaking to them for yourself," chuckled the Touiban, signing off.

He called Jurrel up as he headed off at a brisk walk toward the elevator up to the comms room. "I thought I put you in charge of keeping an eye on Valden. How come he's up to more mischief with our young Emperor?"

"You told me to report for battle dress drill and that I was to consider myself back on active duty," Jurrel said reasonably. "I can't do both, Liege. Not unless you put Valden on active duty too."

"Hell will thaw first," he muttered, half to himself, as he hit the call button for the elevator. "Keep him with you during training. May do him some good to see what the future holds for him when he's finally graduated."

"Aye, sir," Jurrel replied.

The small room was filled with a press of fatigue-clad Touiban bodies, all twittering and gesticulating avidly to each other as they watched what Zsurtul and Valden were doing. At the Prince's elbow, one stood out by his very stillness. At least, he assumed it was a male . . . both genders looked the same to him. Valden and Zsurtul were sitting at the room's main console, their actions hidden from him by the press of bodies.

Glancing over the multitude, he could see no sign of Toueesut or any of his swarm.

"What's going on here?" he demanded, lowering his voice and underscoring it with a faint growl of menace.

As one, the group began to break up and re-form into their own swarms—then, with much trilling, they surged toward the doorway with a complete disregard for his presence in the opening.

Hurriedly he stepped back into the corridor, waiting until their hasty exodus was over before stepping into the room again.

Valden and Zsurtul, heads bent together, were focused on the terminal at which the young Sholan sat, typing furiously. He could see a look of unholy glee on the youth's face and a smile of satisfaction on Zsurtul's.

"What the hell are you two doing now?" he demanded, striding over to them to look at the screen.

"A moment," said Zsurtul, holding up a warning hand. "This is delicate."

As Kaid swallowed his retort, Valden hit a final key then sat back in his chair with a sigh. "Done!"

"What have you done this time?" Kaid asked, his voice terrifyingly quiet.

"It's like a tick, Commander," said Valden, looking up at him, ears tilting in deference to his superior.

"A parasite," agreed Zsurtul from beside him.

"It isn't meant to be found, just to hide in various places and feed off the system," explained Valden.

"Drawing energy from it, interfering with genuine messages and corrupting them . . ."

"Sending people and goods to the wrong places . . ."

Palace of Light, K'oish'ik

"What d'you mean you can find no trace of the TeLaxaudin or their equipment?" K'hedduk asked, his voice ominously quiet. "You were allowed to head the Palace Security only because you claimed you could do the job."

"I can, Majesty, but not even I can find them if they're no longer here." Kezain hesitated for a moment and glanced at his other five colleagues around the Council table. "We think they left before you claimed—rightfully of course—your throne. They weren't at the banquet the night of the attack, and usually one of them attends."

K'hedduk noted the faint trace of Kezain's fear scent in the air and the way the other department Directors kept their attention on their comp pads—all save his Head Inquisitor.

"Impossible. I made sure all shuttles were grounded before I acted," he hissed. "They're here somewhere, and so is their technology!"

"Not if they left by other means," said Kezain nervously. "Means we cannot fully imagine."

"Don't make excuses for your own incompetence. They can't have vanished into thin air! Lufsuh, take over questioning the captives. Have the Palace and the City searched again. I want them found."

"I've had the Palace searched three times, Majesty, and the City," blustered Kezain. "Even Inquisitor Lufsuh is finding it impossible to extract information from the Pretender's remaining counselors! There are rewards posted on every street corner here and in the City and villages outside . . ."

"Enough!" K'hedduk snarled, bringing his hand down hard on the table. "Find them! Or Fabukki will replace you!"

TeLaxaudin labs, City of Light, 2 weeks earlier

"Quick! Hurry! We have very little time," said Ayziss, draperies fluttering as he stalked around the research labs, following the three armed U'Churians as they hurriedly placed translocator units on every piece of equipment that the anxious TeLaxaudin pointed out to them.

"Do you want to take everything, Researcher?" asked one, stopping to look at him. "It would make our job faster if we just took the lot."

"Yes, yes do it," hummed the small alien. "Make sure you take all records! Nothing must be falling into their hands, nothing. I go see how my colleagues are doing. Tell me when done."

He ran off unsteadily on his spindly bronze legs, passing quickly along the corridor to the medical labs area. Through Unity, which was working overtime right now, he knew they were well on the way to completing their tasks, but he felt safer with the others in case they were discovered. Pushing open the door, he found another six U'Churians busily marking all the many breeding tanks and ancillary equipment for retrieval.

Shoawomiss looked around as he entered. "Is it complete?" he asked. "Are you finished?"

"Not yet. How long before the Sand-dweller attacks?"

"Unity says they are on their way," said Kouansishus, eyes swirling as they focused on him. "Not needing to disturb us for this, ask yourself you could."

"Is worrying, waiting till last minutes like this," hummed Ayziss. "What if Unity be wrong? What if someone finds us?"

"Camarilla watching, we be brought instantly home," said Shoawomiss in disgust. "You fear too much. Go do your job! Do you not trust Unity when it comes to us?"

"Yes, yes, Unity I trust, just not these perfidious Sand-dwellers!" said Ayziss, wringing his hands together, emitting a scent that he knew was fearful but was unable to stop. "This one is the worst of them, he cares nothing for life . . ."

"Then you know who to support on the Camarilla," said Shoawomiss quietly. "It is Isolationists that get us to this state with their insane schemes."

"Enough!" said Kouansishus sharply. "Have job to do! Unity says they draw very near!"

"Waaaa!" Ayziss' humming rose plaintively into almost a shriek as, wringing his hands even harder, he began to fold down into as small and compact a shape as he could.

Suddenly darkness and a coldness as deep as that of space folded around him. Just as suddenly light and warmth returned, and with it the familiar scents of home.

"Come, Researcher Ayziss," said the gentle voice of his U'Churian homekeeper as she leaned down to help him to his feet. "Warm scented oil baths to soothe your shattered nerves are waiting for you all in the Arrivals room."

"Such a coward you are, Ayziss," said Shoawomiss with disgust as he turned to thread his way past their U'Churian troops and through the piles of equipment now lying in the huge warehouse.

"Not understanding the trauma I suffer," began Ayziss, accepting the U'Churian female's hand to stand up.

"Shh, we will be there soon," she said, ushering him before her to the exit. "They probably felt just as traumatized as you but managed to hide it."

"Such a comfort to me you are," he hummed.

*　　　*　　　*

Lufsuh stirred and reached for the carafe of water in front of him. "Majesty, Kezain may be right," he said quietly as he refilled his drinking bowl. "I've seen how much equipment is missing. For it to be removed in any normal fashion would have disrupted the lab area, the Palace, and transport to the landing pad outside the Palace walls for at least a day. That didn't happen. Our resources are limited. If you want the turret defenses and the force field that surrounds the Palace repaired and working, we'll need everyone we can spare— unless you wish to draft more of the City's population into the Palace?"

K'hedduk's lips parted in a hiss of rage. There were already too many of the peasants about for his peace of mind, but only they had the mechanical and electrical expertise needed to repair the ancient defenses. Without them up and running, until his Generals and their Warriors arrived in six weeks, he was wide open to any counterattack. All the relays for the force field had proved to need rewiring, and the turrets were clogged with a mixture of sand and rust and needed to be dismantled and repaired. At least the Command codes to activate them—long assumed to be obsolete—had been accessible.

"Draft more of them to search the City again, and have my troops replace them where possible in the Palace, Kezain," he ordered. "Question the medical scientists and the lab staff. They worked closely with the aliens."

Overhead, the lights began to flicker, then dimmed, casting the Council chamber into a sepia half-light.

"That'll be them checking the power circuits, Majesty," said Szayil, Director of Power. "The cables for the force field relays are ancient, as you know . . ." he tailed off into silence under K'hedduk's angry gaze.

A nervous tapping at the door drew their attention to it. An aide slipped in, murmuring vague apologies while sketching a bow toward K'hedduk, then hurried over to Szayil.

He watched as Kezain surreptitiously wiped the sweat from his face and Szayil began to visibly pale. From outside, he heard a sudden burst of raucous music playing over the public address system. Thankfully, the walls muted it.

Szayil glanced across the table at his colleagues, then gestured the aide over to them. Face almost white, he then rose to his feet.

"Majesty, I must leave. There's a—situation developing that needs my personal attention."

"I suggest you tell me now what's happening," he said, keeping his temper with an effort. Fear scent assailed him from both sides of the room now as two more counselors got to their feet and the aide tried to back out of the chamber as inconspicuously as possible. The Primes were a spineless breed, and he despised them, but for now, they were all he had.

"There's been power failures in several areas of the Palace, Majesty. Communications are down, and the water-pumping station has gone off-line. My colleagues and I must see to it now."

"We expected some problems, Majesty," said Lazkoh. "We're trying to rebuild an ancient system without replacements . . ."

"We have enough water in storage for three days," Lazkoh hurriedly reassured him. "Parts are being manufactured and delivered by the U'Churians in . . ."

K'hedduk raised his hand abruptly, silencing them all. "Don't drown me in details and justifications, just get it fixed! And someone, get that damned music turned off!" He pushed his chair back from the table and stood up.

"Communications are a priority; get them restored first. I must be able to contact the fleet. Why haven't the backup generators cut in?" he demanded.

Szayil looked confused. "We have no backup generators, Majesty. Never, in living memory, have we had power failures before. It comes from two sources, atomic and solar. For both to be drained is unheard of."

K'hedduk took a deep breath. As his hands clenched on the tabletop, he could feel his nails biting into the wooden surface.

"This Palace was originally a military Command Center, built to defend itself and its Royal family. Right now, even a day-old female hatchling could break in! I want emergency lighting and communications up within two hours, Szayil! Route power from other areas if you have to! Report to me then—I'll be in the Artisan's Quarter. You're all dismissed."

Fuming, he headed down the corridor to the elevator, aware of the sudden increase in temperature as the air-con-

ditioning broke down. There would be changes made here, by
all that was holy! It was time the home world was returned to
its former glory.

Realizing he was outpacing his gene-altered guards, he
slowed his steps as he came level with the first of the Royal
statues. Some of his anger dissipated as he passed it. Already
all the statues in the Palace had had their heads replaced with
his own likeness instead of that of the previous Emperor.
There would be time enough to commission new ones; for
now it was more important that those that existed bore his
image to remind the rabble in the Palace and the City that he
was now the God-King.

The *Tooshu*

"Power failures and brownouts?" echoed Carrie, who had
joined them.

Zsurtul nodded. "I was able to tamper with the local communications too. At present, they can't reach the fleet, nor can
they communicate with the nearby towns that provide the in-
dustries they'll be using to replace cabling and worn-out parts
for the ancient defenses."

"Music, too. Don't forget the music," Valden grinned,
bouncing lightly from one foot to the other, tail swaying
enthusiastically.

"Music?" echoed Kaid.

"Playing over their P.A. at random times. Not that they had
anything decent, but I chose what Zsurtul said was martial
music—nice and loud."

"What you did might seem amusing," said Carrie angrily,
"but if they discover someone's been hacking their system
from a distance, they'll know it was us!"

"No, Carrie," said Zsurtul, reaching out to touch her arm
briefly in reassurance. "They won't find out. We've made it
look like the system is old and degrading on its own. It wasn't
difficult, because it is." He pulled a wry face, a very Human
gesture. "It's one of the things that needs to be replaced
urgently."

"It will be, Zsurtul," Kaid assured him. "We won't be leaving K'oish'ik until you're as impregnable as we can make you. Kezule wants the asteroid, Kij'ik, towed into orbit over the capital. It'll be a major asset to your planetary defenses."

"Indeed," agreed the young Emperor, his expression lightening. "It may even mean the General will stay on K'oish'ik this time."

Carrie tried not to glance meaningfully at Kaid, but Zsurtul noticed just the same.

"You're wrong. General Kezule won't try to rule through me," he said in a tone they were beginning to recognize. "He refused to be my father's chief adviser and head of what we called our military. This time, I hope he will not refuse me, especially in light of what happened when he left."

Was that a note of censure I heard? Carrie sent to Kaid.

Possibly, but he's certainly stopped any further discussion on the subject, Kaid replied, his mental tone wry. *Seems to me we gave him the right military training in leadership skills that his father lacked. However, he's a little too astute to be relying on what he knows about our body language. I think there may be some truth in Toueesut's belief our princeling has some mental abilities.*

"We're finished here," Zsurtul interrupted, moving away from the console. "Shall we adjourn to the rec lounge?"

"By all means," said Kaid smoothly. *He's taken the whole situation very neatly out of our hands.*

"We also messed up their orders for cables and stuff," said Valden with a laugh. "That K'hedduk is going to be so mad when he finds out. It'll look like a comp error, of course."

Kaid stopped suddenly and turned on the youth. "You are not to go off and do anything on your own, do you hear me? Any bright ideas, come to me! I'm not having you risking everything for the joy of pulling a fast one on K'hedduk and his people!"

"Of course I won't," huffed Valden. "I don't know why you'd think I would. I'm working with Prince Zsurtul now."

Carrie opened her mouth to reprimand him, but Kaid stopped her with a mental *Don't. You'll only make it worse.* He moved aside to let Valden out.

"We smile and put up with it—for now," he muttered to her as they followed the two youngsters out.

Ghyakulla's Summer Realm

Kuushoi was angry, and she knew it showed in the way she held herself as she strode imperiously through the bushes, tail lashing angrily, until she found her sister.

"Why did you take him?" she demanded. "You had no right! He was to be with me another two days! Winter is *my* season, he belongs to me!"

Ghyakulla turned a faintly surprised face to her, flicking her ears in a Sholan negative.

"What do you mean you don't know what I'm talking about? I'm talking about Vartra, disappearing in an instant before my eyes, that's what. You chose your moment well, Sister, I'll give you that!" she said bitterly. "He left me, unfulfilled and angry, at the peak of our joining! Much good he'll be to you in an equally frustrated state!"

He is not yours, or mine, she sent, a slight frown creasing her face.

"I refuse to argue about that right now," Kuushoi said petulantly.

The Summer Goddess reached out to lay a hand on her enraged sister's shoulder, a gentle smile now on her lips, the green draperies that exactly matched her eyes billowing lightly around her in the warm air.

"Yes, I'm distracted," Kuushoi admitted, her body beginning to unbend a little as images from her sister filled her mind. "As you asked, I'm maintaining a null zone around Vartra's child, Kusac, and it is exhausting me. If you didn't take Vartra, then who did?"

A look of pure rage crossed her face, fading only slightly when her sister gave her a gentle shake and turned away from her, gesturing her to follow.

"The Camarilla!" she hissed, following. "This is beyond accepting, Ghyakulla! How dare they take *my* lover like this! It's one thing that they meddle with the mortals, but that they, mere ephemerals, should put themselves above us like this! I want this stopped, Sister! You've persuaded me not to intervene until now, but this is beyond endurance!"

Ghyakulla stopped at her fountain, reaching out to pick up a simple pottery cup, made from the clay of her own garden. Filling it, she held it out to her sister, smiling briefly before a more somber look crossed her face as mentally she reassured her.

Kuushoi accepted it gracefully, arranging the pale blue tunic she wore before perching on the edge of the softly tinkling fountain.

"So you're finally going to act," she said with satisfaction. "Very well, I'll leave it to you for now, but if this happens to me again, I warn you, I will take my own actions! Bad enough I am forced to share Vartra with you without him being stolen from my very bed by them!"

She sipped the drink while Ghyakulla bent to pick up one of the jeggets that had crept nervously out from the nearby bushes.

"One of your pets? I don't know why you bother with them," Kuushoi said. "The people consider them vermin, you know."

Her sister said nothing, merely tickled the little creature under the chin.

"Oh, very well," Kuushoi sighed; rinsing the cup and putting it back in its small niche. "I'll go back and wait for him to return and leave matters to you." Her earlier temper was now receding fast. She knew it was her sister's influence, and she didn't really resent it. After all, she had voluntarily accepted the calming water.

Standing up, she looked at the jegget, which was obviously enjoying the attention it was getting. "It's probably for the best that you have Summer, Ghyakulla, even though I am your elder," she said grudgingly. "I certainly wouldn't have had time for those vermin. Good-bye."

Turning, she made a slight gesture, opening a gateway from her sister's realm to her own. Shimmering in the warmth, the gate, fashioned of ice crystals, stood before her. She stepped through it and was gone.

Ghyakulla remained where she was, shivering slightly at the faint hint of chill in the air that her sister's portal had left. She was happy in her realm, and the thought of inhabiting Winter as the wife of L'Shoh, the Lord of Hell, had never appealed. Yes, it had been for the best that her sister had stolen the Entity meant to be her husband.

She sighed, her breath dissipating the chill, her thoughts turning to Vartra. Though it broke her heart, Vartra would have to be sacrificed to the Camarilla. If she and L'Shoh intervened, they would show their hand too soon. The faction that had taken him assumed Vartra was an Entity, but he was not: He occupied a special place in the pantheon, a mortal living on as a demigod. The Entities needed to be ignored so that their final solution would come to fruition. Her peaceful Warrior's very existence now depended on his own ability to withstand what that faction of the Camarilla would do to him.

Walking back to her bower, she turned her thoughts to two of her other charges—Noni and Conner. Now her mouth opened in a gentle smile, the sadness she felt briefly dissipating. Now there was a good match. Both of them had served her well over many years. They deserved the happiness she'd hoped they'd find together. However, there was more for them to do.

With a thought, she called her two assistant dzinaes, Agalimi and Aduan, the spirits of Shola's two moons.

Shola, Stronghold

Lost in his own thoughts, Conner hadn't noticed the commotion at first.

"Look! Look up!" The man running toward him was screaming. "They'll kill us all! Run, run for your life!"

He stopped, confused by the sheer terror in the other's voice, uncertain if he was drunk or mad. Hands grasped him, fingers biting like claws in the sleeve of his robes.

"Listen to me, darnmit!" the man yelled into his face, making him gag at the wave of his sour breath. "They found us! You have to run, get under cover, or they'll kill you!" Wide, staring eyes glared at him from a pale face.

"I'm sure it's not as bad as you think," he began, keeping his voice calm and reasonable.

"You idiot! If you don't believe me, then believe your own eyes," the man snarled, shoving him aside and continuing his mad dash for the houses that ringed the square.

All around him, the people were running for cover, some pointing at the sky overhead, many of them screaming. One or two, like him, simply stood and stared.

He looked up, gasping in shock at what he saw. High above them, it hung in the air, looking like the kind of bauble peasants would hang on the prayer tree for their chosen deity. Moonlight shimmered and glinted off it, making it appear almost ghostly, a thing of less substance than presence. A spindle end projected from its top and hung below it. Between them, a platform hung in nothingness, banded by four slim struts that formed the outline of a globe.

A flash to one side of it drew his attention. It was followed by a streak of light, then another, and finally by a flare so bright that even when he blinked, he still saw it.

Movement from the platform—a cloud of tiny lights, like fireflies, leaving, swarming toward where he'd seen the explosion—caught his eye.

"Our defenses aren't strong enough yet," said a voice at his elbow that he almost recognized. "If only we'd had some warning."

He spun around to face the man, but his face was hidden in the shadows of the clock tower.

"I don't understand," he stammered, glancing back at the beautiful monstrosity in the sky.

"There aren't enough ships berthed at the platform. The attacks came too soon for us." A low snarl underlaid the voice.

A flare of light, like a bolt of lightning, hissed and crackled through the air, impacting on the central building of the Palace behind him. Stone blocks exploded violently, sending red-hot shards high into the night sky to rain down on the courtyard. Over it all, a high-pitched whine and the smell of burning filled the air.

The red glow of flames lit the man's face, and as he watched, it began to alter. The ears shrank, becoming smaller, the bridge of the nose filled out until it formed a smooth line to the forehead, and the mouth widened and narrowed, top lip forming a gentle V shape.

It was the eyes that held him—large, bulbous green eyes, with vertical pupils.

With a choking cry of horror, he stumbled backward, desperate to escape the demon. Quicker than his eye could follow, a hand snaked out to grasp hold of him.

"You must warn us, Merlin Llew," the green-skinned demon said.

"Leave me alone!" he croaked, plucking at the clawed hand. "You caused this!"

"Not me. Look around you. These are my people," the green demon said. "Look!" he commanded.

He looked, seeing for the first time that he was no longer in his village, that this was not the market square but a huge stone courtyard, lined on one side by buildings and massive statues and on the other by a row of open-air stores, many fronted by tables and chairs.

"See the people!" the voice commanded.

Against his will, he let his eyes focus on those fleeing in terror. All were green skinned and bald like the demon that held him captive.

He recoiled again, Llew's mind shrinking from a reality he couldn't accept.

"Look at me, Merlin Llew. Open your eyes and learn what the future holds if you don't remember."

He squeezed his eyes even more tightly shut, terrified beyond comprehension, then another bolt hit a building close by, filling the air again with red-hot stinging embers and his nostrils and ears with the stench of burning flesh and screams of agony.

"You'd condemn them to this because they're different, Merlin?" the voice asked more gently.

This time, the voice was familiar, and against his better judgment, he opened his eyes.

Letting out a low moan, he would have collapsed to the ground had he not been held. His reaction only brought him closer to the being as it changed form yet again.

Gone was the green skin; instead a covering of fur was growing across its face as the ears lengthened into those of a cat, the mouth became smaller, bifurcated, and the nose shrank to more Human proportions then darkened. Hair grew from the bald scalp, cascading down to the being's shoulders and beyond.

"You must remember, Llew, remember when you are the Merlin Conner, and tell us we were not prepared for the attack on K'oish'ik."

Memory struggled to the surface. It was a voice he'd only heard once, but it was unmistakable.

"Kusac?"

The Sholan laughed gently, canines shining red in the reflected light of the fires blazing around them.

"No. We have met before, here, in Stronghold." The voice was altering, becoming high in pitch, more feminine.

Conner blinked, watching as the Sholan's pelt blanched, turning white in a matter of moments, and he stood in his own bedroom before a small, blue-eyed female, dressed in pure white.

"I was sent to unlock Llew's memory," she said, letting him go to run gentle fingertips across his cheek, leaving a trail of coolness behind them. "So you are a Human. It seems I have ignored your kind too long," she murmured, letting her hand fall to his shoulder and, obviously appraising him frankly, walking around behind him. "I should visit your world of Earth again."

He shivered, aware of both the chill that emanated from her body and the heat from her eyes as they seemed to bore through his thin sleeping robe.

"What am I to remember?" he asked, fighting to keep his teeth from chattering.

"Patience," she purred. "I would study you a little longer."

Clasping his arms across his chest in a futile effort to keep warm, he waited. He felt his hair being moved aside, then her cool nose touched his bare neck; she was only taking in his scent, logic told him.

"Ah, your people chose you well, Conner. The fires of life blaze fiercely in you, and your seed is still strong: just as it should be for a Guardian."

Her voice was deeper, languorous. Her hand strayed around to caress his throat while against his neck her breath was cool. "And you're still unmarked on either throat or neck. Perhaps I'll return to spend some . . . quality . . . time with you." Her laugh rippled like the sound of wind through icicle-laden trees.

He shivered again, reinforcing his mental shields in an effort to distance him from her, but a cold heat began to lap slowly across the nape of his neck, scattering his concentration and leeching what warmth remained from him.

Kuushoi laughed again, letting his hair fall back into place and stepping around in front of him. "Your kind is very fragile. Come, let me warm you now, as I warm the new season's growth under my blanket of snow." She spread her arms, mouth widening in a Human smile.

He hesitated, trying to gather his wits. She was altogether too beguiling.

"Your virtue is safe from me—this time, Conner," she purred, her eyes mocking his indecision as she pushed his arms aside and stepped forward to enfold him. "I only entertain the unattached, and you have no mate." Her nose tucked itself under his chin—for she was shorter than him—and gently nudged his jaw upward.

Powerless to move, as his mind screamed "No!" a sudden gust of warm, blossom-laden air swirled around and between them, then was gone.

Kuushoi hissed angrily as she leaped back before turning her ice-blue gaze on him again.

Nung flowers, he thought, it had smelled of nung flowers . . . and it had broken Kuushoi's spell of ice.

"Tell Kusac alone that his salvation, and that of his Clan, will be found only when he becomes his enemy. Some evils can only be fought from within. You are to guide him, Merlin Conner, help him make wise choices when the time comes. My worthy sister," her lips lifted briefly in a soundless snarl, "reminds me you are her creature, and bids me tell you that the sand-dwelling reptiles, the Primes, their land withers from neglect. She looks to you to return them to the old ways. What point is there in surviving invasions only to succumb to neglect?"

He nodded, more from reflex than any ability to control his frozen limbs.

She tossed her head, smiling again. "My message is delivered. Now, Conner, I'll trade you a gift for a gift. Show me your gratitude and grant me a kiss, a foretaste of that Human passion I will one day claim voluntarily from you." Her hand reached out, and she began to draw a lingering finger down the center of his body.

Grasping her hand, he leaned forward, lips barely touching hers, only to be captured in a kiss that sent fire and ice coursing through his body, igniting responses that had lain dormant since he'd said farewell to his Nimue.

Kuushoi broke away, hand to her lips, eyes sparkling with pleasure. "Ah, Conner—if only you served me and not my cold sister, then perhaps Spring and Summer would be bearable," she murmured.

Like quicksilver, her expression changed, becoming somber. "Since you gave the kiss freely, I give you one more piece of knowledge for Kusac. Time is fluid, as you know. When he becomes his enemy, he will set in motion events that can be resolved by his choices alone. Like Llew's High King, he must know which one is true and live the past that has been already written, or all that has been achieved these two years will be undone, and Shola will fall."

"I don't understand. What has this to do with the High King?"

"Remember Llew's life, remember Artos," she said, forming the name with difficulty as she stepped back from him. "Remember your King, the one who sleeps under the hill—remember how Llew couldn't influence his choice. Maybe this time, the Merlin's words will be heeded by the sired as well as by the sire, Guardian. Perhaps this time, Justice's Sword will bind all sides in a lasting peace. Just maybe . . ." Her voice and form faded till nothing remained—except the bitter cold.

Conner woke with a start, still deeply distressed and chilled to the bone but with the echoes of arousal still coursing through him. He remembered everything—with too much clarity.

"She should have let me accompany him to Avalon," he

muttered, pushing himself out of his bed. "Man of my age has no business outliving his King. But She knew better. Now I get to stay behind and be plagued by visions of demons not even Morgause could have dreamed up!"

Reaching for the black robe that lay on the chair by the side of his bed, he shrugged it on, tying the belt loosely around his middle as his feet fumbled, one at a time, under the bed for his sandals.

His mind, meanwhile, reached out through the building, checking to see who was still awake. He found only a few hardy souls—a youth still busy with his books, several praying in the chapel, another kept awake with a toothache. He snorted, heading for the door out into the corridor. Not his problem. If they thought him tamed, they had the wrong man. Let King Rhydderch's surgeon see to it, it was no longer his concern. He was leaving, returning to the deep woods.

Lighting in the corridor was dim as he padded cautiously toward the main staircase. Behind their drapes, he could hear the windows rattling with the force of the wind howling outside.

"I'll build you a place where you can study the stars, Brother," he muttered. "You'll be the first to see your sky ships! Thinks she can buy my silence and peace of mind with empty promises, does she? Liar! She wants me here for that pale husband of hers, the one they call King! He's no King— there's been no true King since the High King fell!"

Tears started in his eyes, and he stopped, leaning against the wall, overcome with grief.

"Goddess . . . Mother . . . you should have let me fade into legend with him, not chained me here, half mad, among the living!"

He dashed the tears away on his sleeve and stumbled on. "Why do I bother appealing to you? You know as much about pity as the witch does—and this is her season!"

The main staircase was ahead of him, and beyond it, the castle door and freedom. For a wonder, the guard was missing from his post. Putting on a spurt of speed, Conner hurried down the stairs. As he drew level with the counter, a figure stepped out in front of him, barring his way.

"Can I help you, Master Conner?"

About to correct him, he bit down on his tongue. The guard didn't recognize him!

"Stand aside, man. I have business outside," he ordered.

"I can't do that, sir. It's a wild night out there. You'd do better waiting till morning."

"My business is the King's. It can't wait," he snapped, trying to thrust him aside.

"I understand, sir," the guard replied, placing a large hand in the center of his chest and effectively holding him still. "If you'd wait a moment, the King himself is coming to speak to you."

Conner snarled, and reaching out mentally, he began gathering energy from the very stones that covered the floor. "You lie!"

"Sir, there's no need to do that," exclaimed the guard, snatching his hand back as if burned and backing off a few paces.

A hand touched his arm, instantly draining him, sending him staggering weakly into the guard.

"Master Conner, you're right, he is lying," said a gentle male voice from behind him as his arm was grasped firmly, steadying him. "There's no need for you to leave Stronghold. You've been time slipping, Master Conner, to Llew's life, not your own."

"Llew?" he asked querulously. "There is no Llew. He's dead. I am the Merlin."

"Indeed you are," said the voice soothingly as he was gently turned to face the youth.

Peering at him, a thought struck him. "Why do you and the guard wear your furs indoors?" he asked, suddenly confused.

"We've just returned from the forest," the youth said promptly. "She sent me to bring you to her. My name is Teusi. Surely you can't have forgotten me?"

"Teusi," he said, rolling the name off his tongue, testing it for familiarity. "Yes, yes. I remember you." Some darkened corner of his mind did, indeed, remember the name. "She sent you to fetch me?"

"That's right. Noni's waiting for you."

Another familiar name. She was the older healer and Guardian here at the Brotherhood. Teusi was her apprentice.

Teusi tugged gently on his arm. "You're cold. There's a hot drink waiting for you upstairs."

He heard the noise of chanting off to his left, but it was an unearthly sound, made by no Human throats or voices. It was strangely comforting despite that. Slowly, his confusion was beginning to recede.

"It's only the acolytes and priests at their prayers," said Teusi. "You're safe at Stronghold, Master Conner."

"Stronghold." He blinked owlishly, looking around him, this time seeing not the castle of Llew's sister and her Royal husband but the Brotherhood fortress on Shola.

His knees buckled suddenly as a gust of wind came shrieking under the front door, and he realized how close he'd come to disaster, but Teusi's steadying arm was still there to support him.

"It's all right, Master Conner, you weren't really in any danger. Chaddo called us as soon as he saw you. He realized you weren't yourself. Let's get back upstairs for that hot drink, shall we?"

"Please," he said gratefully, allowing the young male to help him. "I apologize for waking you like this."

"You didn't wake us, Master Conner. I assure you it was someone quite different who did that."

Conner glanced at Teusi as they climbed the stairs, but the youth obviously intended to say no more.

"You can come through here, Conner," Noni called out as they entered the outer room of her suite. "I'm not dragging myself out of bed for you!"

Teusi led Conner in then took his leave, closing the door quietly behind him.

"Propriety?" said Noni, raising her eye ridge questioningly at him as she read his thoughts. "Propriety is what I decide it is, Conner." She patted the empty side of the bed. "Sit. Have your hot drink and pass me mine. Who's to see you visit the Healer in the dead of night, eh? And if they did, so what?"

Reluctantly, Conner approached the bed where Noni, wrapped in a shawl, sat propped up, lowering himself onto the side of it.

"The drinks," she reminded him. "You should enjoy it, it's a variation of one of your Human nighttime drinks."

She accepted the mug he handed her, waiting until he'd tasted his before taking a sip herself.

"Chocolate," he said, surprised.

"Nice, isn't it? Added some of my herbs to it—gives it a little spice," she said, still watching him carefully. "That will warm you up. Now, why don't you tell me what caused Kuushoi to wake this Llew's memories and have you trying to escape from Stronghold?"

His mouth widened in a slow grin. "Is there anything that happens here you're not aware of?"

Noni hesitated, discarding the flippant answer that had instantly come to mind. "Plenty," she said. "But Ghyakulla, your Earth Goddess Gaia, told me to help you. Kuushoi's not the same as most of the Goddesses—Entities really—she likes to play with people every now and then. Her reaction to you was—unexpected, that's all I know. She's the Goddess of Winter."

Conner shivered, his face taking on a closed look.

"Talk to me about it," said Noni quietly, putting her hand over his, instantly picking up his fear of Her returning to him, but not why. "Tell me what happened to make Llew's memories overwhelm you so. Why was it so important?"

"We teach," said Conner, letting Noni peel one of his hands away from his mug to hold in her furred ones. "And advise, as we always have. It wasn't so much that Llew was important, more what the Goddess wanted him to do for her, who he was to teach." He looked sideways at her. "I can't understand why it was Kuushoi—I serve Gaia, the Earth Goddess, not her."

"It may be past the first day of Spring, Conner, but a glance through the window will remind you, Winter still rules here in the mountains. There's no love lost between the sisters, at least on Kuushoi's side, though in the end, she has to do Ghyakulla's bidding. She's the Earth Goddess here. What makes you— or Llew—so determined to leave Stronghold in the middle of this storm?"

Conner drained his mug before answering. "Toward the end of his life, Llew had a vision of the future—our future—that so terrified him that he lost his mind for many months. He was still mourning the passing of the High King of Britain—the lad he'd been given to raise as his own—and the fact that the Goddess refused to let him go with him to Avalon. That, combined with his vision, was too much for him to cope with."

"He tried to kill himself?"

"No." Conner smiled faintly. "It's not that simple. The High King was mortally wounded in his final battle and was taken by boat to the Goddess' isle while he still lived. He refused to let Llew accompany him. Legend has it that to this day he sleeps under a hill, awaiting his country's hour of greatest need."

"I can understand his anger at being left behind," Noni said. "But the vision, what did he see?"

He shook his head, leaning past her to put the empty mug on her nightstand. "I was told to pass that on only to Kusac."

"Then it concerns those reptilian Valtegans," she said. "You were muttering about sky ships down in the hallway."

"All I can tell you is that Kuushoi took me into Llew's vision, as if I were actually living through it," he said, his eyes taking on a distant look.

The hand resting in hers began to tremble slightly as he remembered. Then he began to shudder violently, withdrawing his hand from hers as she moved to put the mug aside.

"I'm sorry," he began.

"Hush!" she said, with a trace of her normal acerbity. "What you going to do? Sit and worry yourself to death alone in your room? Get that blanket on the chair," she ordered him. "Wrap it to around yourself and come back here beside me. You're chilled to the bone!"

He did as she bade him then stood holding the blanket. "I've disturbed you enough," he said. "I can go back to my own room . . ."

"Don't make me lose patience with you, Conner," she interrupted. "I know well enough you don't want to be alone in case She returns! Now, get back here beside me!"

Conner sat down again, putting the blanket across his lap and legs. "I'm not that cold," he murmured.

"Tell me about this Llew and why you were trying to leave Stronghold."

"The vision that Llew had, the very same one I experienced, terrified him to the point that he almost lost his mind, as I said. He turned his back on all Human company, leaving his sister's castle for the wild woods, where he lived as a hermit. His memories of that time are obviously somewhat sketchy."

"I expect they are," Noni murmured, watching his eyes beginning to droop a little. Her herbs were beginning to work. "So how did he come to be back in the castle?"

"It was his twin sister Ganieda's home," he said. "Though she knew he needed periods of solitude in the wild, she was determined to find him and bring him back to the castle that winter. The countryside was once again a series of small

kingdoms fighting for supremacy, and her husband, King of
Strathclyde, valued her brother's counsel. Their soldiers found
him, disheveled and unkempt, and dragged him back to the
palace . . ."

His voice had become quieter, taking on a strange, almost
lyrical quality, like that of a storyteller. His accent changed,
and he switched to what she assumed was Llew's native Welsh.
She realized she was listening more to his mind than to the
actual words.

"See, your room is as you left it, Brother. No one has entered since you
left," his sister said as a servant scurried around lighting the candles.

"Fire's lit," he said, narrowing his eyes as he noticed the girl wrinkle
her nose in disgust when she passed him.

"I kept the fire going. No one else has been allowed in here till now.
I had to keep the room dry because of your books."

He sniffed, not willing to acknowledge she'd done well. He was still
angry with her for dragging him here, but so far, anger hadn't gotten
him anywhere with her or the guards.

There was a knock at the door. "Where do you want the bath placed,
Mistress?" asked a young male voice—one of the pages, doubtless.

"In front of the fire," Ganieda replied, going over to the chest at
the end of his bed and opening it. "We eat in two hours, Merlin. Time
enough for you to bathe and dress. Look, here is the robe I made for
you last winter." Turning, she held it up for him to inspect.

He ignored her and the pages busily placing the wooden tub by the
fireside.

"Winter's here. You know we had the first snowfall today. You
wouldn't have survived till Spring," she said quietly, laying the robe on
his bed and searching in the chest for linen undergarments. "They said
they found you living in a cave with a wolf pack. I don't know how you
managed to survive."

"Wolves don't betray their own kind. They kept me warm, brought
me food," he muttered. "I'm not wearing that robe. You can put it away.
What do you think I am? Some kind of idiot to be paraded for your
husband and those parasites he calls his nobles? Look at it! Covered in
gibberish symbols! It's only fit for a Court fool!"

"The symbols impress the Court, Brother, you know that. You liked
it well enough when I was embroidering it."

"I hated it from the first. Never wore it, did I? You want me in the
hall," he said, drawing his rags around himself and standing straighter,
"then you can have me as I am. And you can forget the bath!"

"Wear it for me, Merlin," she said, closing the chest and coming over to him as a procession of servants entered warily carrying buckets of steaming water. "And you will bathe. If you refuse, I will bring my ladies to help me bathe you myself."

This time he looked at her, catching the steely glint in her eyes. She was his equal, no doubt of that.

"Leave me one maid to wash me, then," he said, changing his tactics.

"I'll stay, Mistress," said a pert female voice from behind him. "I'm not afraid of Master Merlin."

"Nimue's here," Ganieda said. "Wouldn't you rather she attended you than Briony?"

"That useless slut? Keep her away from me!" he snarled. "Doubtless she's been making free of her virtues with any man in the town while I've been away."

"Don't speak of her like that!" his twin said sharply. "She's not like that, and you know it! She's remained here, cloistered in her rooms with her studies the whole time. She was inconsolable when you left!"

"Begone, girl! I won't have you arguing with me!" he said, beginning to peel off his rags. "If I'm to bathe and make ready for the meal in two hours, I need to start now. A fool decked out to amuse fools—it should be entertaining."

"Merlin . . ."

He could hear the appeal in her voice and that she was close to tears, but it meant nothing to him.

"Go! Get you to the side of that upstart you wed and tell him the fool will appear in the hall as requested."

With a stifled sob, his sister left, slamming the door behind her.

"You shouldn't speak to the mistress like that," said Briony when they were alone. "She's been worried sick about you. And the Lady Nimue too."

He rounded on her. "Lessons in manners from a trollop?" he thundered, staring at the comely serving girl. "Just who do you think you are?"

She stared back at him, arms akimbo on her ample hips. "Not afraid of you, for one, you bad-tempered old bugger! You ain't exactly impressive standing there in next to nothing, stinking like you've been living in the kennels with the hounds, you know."

For almost a minute he stared at her, completely taken aback by her attitude; then he began to chuckle, his humor restored for the first time that day.

"I don't suppose I do, girl."

"It's Briony," she said, advancing toward him. "Now, let's be having the rest of those rags off you."

No place below the salt with the common folk was he allowed. No, his brother-in-law was insisting he sit at the high table for all to see, he discovered, when, grumbling and swearing, he'd been fetched for the evening meal.

"You look nice, Brother. Briony did well with your hair," she said, reaching out to touch a silken white lock that lay on his chest. "Even managed to get the tangles out of your beard. She didn't get you to tie it back, though."

"Aye, and it costs me plenty in pain, Sister, and for what?" he snapped, jerking his head away from her. "She'd have had me braided and tricked out like a nag for sale on market day! I hate being put on show, and that's all this is! The Morrigan herself would laugh to see me in this outfit!"

"We sent my men after you for your health, Merlin . . ." began Rhydderch, making the sign against the evil eye—one echoed by his wife at the mention of the Mistress of Crows.

"You did not!" His voice rose even as he lifted his hand to point at his brother-in-law. "You brought me back to improve your standing among the other petty kings! Think I am a fool, Rhydderch? I may be mad, but I'm not stupid!" he snorted. "You've dragged me from the Goddess' work to be naught but a trophy in your Court. And what a Court!" he sneered, gesturing toward the Great Hall behind Rhydderch. "Look at them! All they care about is eating, drinking, wenching, and fighting! Did you learn nothing at the table of your High King? I need be about Her business, since not one of you cares for the land and the people any longer."

"That's enough, Merlin!" hissed the King, trying to keep his voice low so as not to attract attention from those in the Hall. "You know I control my men as best I can. Winter's here, in case you hadn't noticed, and there's little else for them to do but stay within the confines of the Keep!"

"There's plenty, if you've a mind to do it. Make alliances, patrol borders, keep the brigands in the woods from raiding outlying farms. Ach, you make me sick! There was only one man with the depth of vision to unite all your warring factions, and he's gone." He was tired, too old for politics.

"Yes, he is," said Rhydderch sharply. "I'll thank you to stop harping on about him. I brought you back to help me make changes, but you left, in the dead of night, on the eve before a meeting of the nearest lords! I've not forgotten that, Merlin! Only because Ganieda begged for another chance for you have you gotten this one! Right now I am trying to make alliances with the nearest Angle warlord. His envoys arrived earlier today."

He barely heard what the other said—it was as if his voice were at the bottom of a deep well. Blinking, he frowned and looked at his sister.

"Why am I here? I should be outside, watching the skies, studying the stars for ships that sail in the night." Even he heard his voice taking on a slightly querulous tone. "I must find a way to reach one not yet born who lives across the seas of night. One of fur and scales, both mammal and reptile in one body."

Rhydderch swore. "I thought you said he was better! He's still raving mad, moonstruck! I prefer him when he fights with me. At least then he talks some sense!"

"He's not," she said, leaping instantly to her twin's defense.

"Moonstruck? Nay, never that," said Merlin, rallying his wits again. "She came, the witch came, all glowing white with ice in her veins and her breath the blizzards of Winter. But I'd have none of her, even though she wanted this skinny ancient body of mine. I serve Gaia of the Summer lands, of Avalon, and She bids me study the stars. I can't stay here, I must return to the woods."

"Shut him up," hissed Rhydderch, grasping Ganieda firmly by the arm and shaking her as he saw his resident Druid approaching. "I'll not stand for trouble from the Druids this night—I've enough on my plate dealing with the visiting Angles from across the border." Letting her go, he turned abruptly and left, intercepting the Lawgiver and drawing him toward the high table.

"Merlin, you must stop this wild talk of starships and strangers," she pleaded, blinking back fresh tears. "We need your help. Rhydderch is trying to arrange a meeting with the leader of the largest Angle war band. If he succeeds . . ."

"I know well what it will mean," he interrupted. "But I also know what will happen if I cannot reach this youth from the stars."

"Help us tonight, and I promise you I'll build you a place of your choosing where you can live in comfort and study the stars."

This caught his attention.

"You swear? On Cerridwen's Cauldron and your hopes of another life?"

"I swear."

He smiled, the first genuine one for nearly a year, one that smoothed the lines of fear and worry from his face and made his eyes glitter in the candlelight. "Then let's to dinner," he said, catching her by the hand and dragging her into the Great Hall and up to the high table.

I wouldn't say your body is scrawny, a voice murmured in his mind, drawing him briefly out of Llew's life and back to his own.

Disoriented, he raised his head, looking down to see himself in bed with Noni lying unclothed beside him. He started to sit, but her hands, claws carefully sheathed, grasped him around the waist.

"Where you going, my bonny man?" she asked, using the Human words. "You need me. This Llew has been fighting to dominate your mind since you were Chosen because of his vision. And I need you." Her voice dropped to a low purr on her last words.

He let her pull him back down and felt for the first time the softness of her pelt against his own bare skin as she pressed him close against her.

A shuddering sigh of pleasure was the only response he could make.

"Don't even think to tell me you're not schooled in the arts of love. I know better," she whispered in his ear before sinking her teeth gently into the lobe. "Since you're too much the gentleman—" again a Human term— "I'm going to have to be the one to stake my claim on you and leave my mark for that minx Kuushoi to see."

Her words were punctuated by little nips until she reached the base of his neck; then the bites changed, sending erotic waves of desire and lust racing through his body. Before he knew it, his throat was arched up, vulnerable to her, and her eyes were glittering down at him.

"Old? No older than me," she purred, pushing him onto his back, "and just as virile if what I feel pressed against my belly is what I hope it is."

Beyond words, still half in Llew's memories, he watched through almost closed eyes as her face descended toward his neck, mouth opening wide, affording him a clear view of the long canines and the row of short incisors between them.

"Goddess help me," he whispered, reaching out to cup her head in his hands and draw her closer.

As you are Her male vessel, I am Her female one, Noni sent as her jaws closed over his larynx.

He felt engulfed, had never been so close to death, nor to physical fulfillment as their minds met and began to intertwine. Even with her jaws around his most vulnerable place, he grasped her waist, lifting and positioning her so that as she began to bite down hard, he was entering her.

Equals. I never thought to meet an equal, she sent, her mind spiraling around his.

The pain of her bite was swift, then gone, and her mouth was seeking his with smaller nips. He could taste his blood on her lips—sharp and metallic, an unexpected aphrodisiac.

His hands stilled her head as he caught hold of her lower lip, biting down equally sharply before she could prevent him.

Blood is life—I shared mine with you, now I take yours to seal our union, he sent.

Then he was beyond thinking rationally as she proved her skill a match to his own.

Against his wishes, Nimue, as publicly demure as ever, sat to his left, serving him from the laden platters. Many had been surprised to see him. The promise of a tower from which to study the stars kept him civil, and as the meal wore on, she grew bolder, reaching under the table to place her hand on his thigh.

"Permit me to visit you this night, Master Merlin," she said quietly, leaning against him as she offered him slices of the choicest venison with her other hand. "I've missed you. Your bed will surely be cold without me."

Flaxen braids, bronze jeweled clasps decorating their length, fell almost to the floor. Her complexion was as pale as the alabaster vases that came from their Eastern traders, but her eyes—they were dark, almost violet, and fringed by long lashes that cast kohl-dark shadows on her cheeks.

"How old are you now?" he asked abruptly.

"I reached my sixteenth year this autumn, Master."

"You should marry. The King can find you a worthy husband, as is your due."

Her face crumpled slightly. "Do I displease you so much, Master? You chose me yourself from among many of your students to be your apprentice."

"I was wrong. You deserve a life of happiness, not one beset by tending an old man wracked by visions and prophecies. I'll speak to the King tonight."

Her hand slid farther, finding his lap. Irritated, he removed it.

"Enough, child. I have other work to do. I'm leaving the Court, returning to the forest and the animals. I have no further need of an apprentice until it's my time to return to the College at Old Sarum."

"But your bedfellow, yes, for tonight at least," she murmured, smiling sweetly, persisting despite his attempts to push her hand aside. "You taught me well, Master."

Her efforts, even though he had blocked them, were having her desired effect. Enraged by the weakness of his body, and finally grateful for the ornately embroidered robe, he thrust his chair back and stood up.

"Leaving already, Master Merlin?" leered the Druid, glancing over at him.

"I have higher work to do than waste my time in this hall of corruption," he snapped in the sudden silence that fell. "You prostitute yourself to curry favor with those barbarian warlords, Ganieda. They have no intention of allying with you—they are spies for their Angle lords. You suffer their lewd talk and gestures for nothing!"

He turned on Rhydderch, holding onto his returned sanity with an effort. "Deal with your own concerns in Strathclyde, Lord King, I'm returning to my woods to study the stars and avert disasters worse than any the Angles with their feeble intellect and blighted imagination can encompass!"

With that, he left the table and, stepping down from the dais, began to stride down the center of the great hall.

"Stop him!" the Druid called out, jumping to his feet. "He must not leave! Not even the once great Merlin can insult the King like this!"

Merlin stopped, turning back to look at the high table.

"I speak the truth, as I always have. Would you stop me?" he asked amid the stunned silence.

"You tax even my patience, Merlin," said Rhydderch, his voice taut with anger he couldn't afford to let loose.

"Your mind has gone; you will be returned to the College," said the Druid sharply, leaning forward on the table. "Why else would you insult our honored guests? It's time you were replaced, Merlin!"

He shook his head slowly, trying to read the potentialities of this moment. They were there, just beneath the surface, if only he could catch them . . . "I have several years left to me yet. The College knows this. You know this."

"I know you're trying to disrupt this alliance with your talk of spies and conspiracies," snapped the other.

He felt it strengthening, swirling, then suddenly all the possibilities coalesced. Why was Briac here? What could have brought such a senior Druid as far as Rhydderch's Court when it was known the King had him as a counselor? Why hadn't he seen it before—or was his madness what Briac had counted on?

"So, you'd dabble in politics now, would you, Briac?" he asked, stripping the other of his title. He reached for Nimue's mind, looking for the proof he needed—it was there, the reason why she'd stayed cloistered away from the public Court during his absence.

"You tried to seduce my apprentice," he accused, raising his voice so it echoed throughout the hall. "You plan to replace me as the Merlin, then betray my King for your own gain? Think again, Briac! Look in his room, Rhydderch. You'll find letters he's exchanged with the Angle warlord, letters plotting your downfall!"

Around his shoulders, he felt his hair beginning to stir as if it were alive as he reached down with his mind for the energy of the Earth herself—the energy locked in the very stones of the floor beneath his feet. The power was there, but it was taking too long to gather it. He spread his hands, drawing in the energy of those around him, letting it spread throughout his whole being.

"He lies! Arrest him for treason!" the Druid yelled, his face now flushed with anger. "What are you afraid of?" he demanded when no one moved. "He's a fool, a mad old fool! His power is spent!"

Chairs scraping back made him spin around to face a group of the King's favorites.

"Well, Duncan? Have you the courage needed to lay hands on me?" he demanded contemptuously.

"Don't harm him!" he heard his sister shout. "Check the Druid's room first!"

He sensed Rhydderch reluctantly nod his consent even without turning around, but he didn't let his guard down. Even though the favorites relaxed their stance, he remained taut. Every instinct warned him the danger was not yet past.

"I'll stop you," said a harsh voice from behind him.

Merlin turned his head, catching the other's eye. "You're either a brave man or a fool, Daffyd," he said quietly, lifting his arms out from his sides and letting the energy visibly play along them like a nimbus. He could smell the ozone now; feel the tingling it caused as every hair on his body began to lift.

"Stay where you are," he commanded, letting just enough loose to strike the warrior in the chest and send him reeling against the table. The small crack of thunder that accompanied the bolt of energy echoed ominously around the hall, and those before him scattered, overturning their benches in the process.

He turned to face the high table and Briac. "You forget who I am," he said, gesturing with his other hand and extinguishing the candles in the lower part of the hall. "I'm no spent force, Briac. I serve no man, call no King Master, nor come at the bidding of the College—unlike you."

In the flickering light, he created the illusion of himself growing taller, broader, more threatening. "Take his blade from him," he ordered the guards who stood by the high table.

Briac lurched across the table, grabbing the nearest knife.

"Stay away from me," he said, holding it before him as he backed slowly away from the table. "He's lying! It's all illusions, trickery, can't you see that?" His hand reached out for Nimue's arm.

Lightning struck him first, playing along his limbs, wracking his body with convulsions. Briac screamed, a high-pitched, thin sound that continued for a few seconds after his scorched body fell to the floor. The smell of overcooked meat began to fill the air.

"You have your proof, Rhydderch. See to your Angle guests. I serve only the Goddess, and She bids me return to the woods. Remember that well, and don't seek me out again!"

Turning on his heel, he extinguished all but the candles by the now surrounded Angles and strode out of the hall.

"You were very restrained with them," Noni repeated.

"Unh?" he muttered, blinking up at her.

"I mean Llew was," she corrected herself.

He reached up to rub his hand over his eyes. "I slipped again, didn't I?" He was still groggy with sleep.

"You did, but I reckon that could be the last time," she said, moving out of his line of sight.

Soft fur slid against his naked hip and awareness of where he was returned as he realized sunlight was streaming in through the window.

"At least we know why Llew's memories have been plaguing you these past months," she continued, sliding an arm unself-consciously across his belly. "He was given a vision of the far future, one that affects us now."

"It would seem so," he said, tensing as he tried to remember anything other than Llew's memories from the night before, but they were so entwined with his own, he couldn't tell one from the other. It could be nights with Llew's Nimue, or his own . . . Had anything even happened between them?

A low vibration against his side surprised him moments before Noni began to chuckle. It was a deep, rich sound, echoed in the purr that was now vibrating through them both.

"You can't remember last night, can you? Don't know how to behave!"

He could feel her amusement at his predicament.

"First lover I've had in some thirty-odd years, and he can't remember. Don't ever say the Entities have no sense of humor, Conner!"

He shifted, turning on his side to look at her, being careful not to touch her. Her arm, he noticed, moved with him, keeping its proprietary hold on him.

"Lovers?" he asked, his senses taking in her relaxed body, the slightly openmouthed Sholan grin as well as her widened yet relaxed ears. Obviously his attentions had not been unwelcome.

"It was bound to happen sometime, Conner," she said, more serious now. "We both knew that on some level. No point prancing around each other at our age. Besides," the grin dropped into a full smile. "The attraction was mutual. You play a grand tune, my man, for a male of any age!"

He laughed at her outrageous compliment, finally moving in close to her.

"Shall I remind you?" she asked as he embraced her and began rubbing his cheek against hers.

"Later, maybe," he murmured, breathing in her scent as he buried his face in the short pelt of her neck.

Her purr deepened as she arched against him, tilting her head to one side.

"Ah, you're so like a Sholan," she whispered, opening her mind to let him feel the sensations he was creating for her.

"And you, my dear, are all feline," he murmured before closing his teeth on her exposed throat.

Conner came out of the bathing room to find Noni sitting at her dressing table, brushing her long hair.

"I've got bite marks on my throat," he said, going around behind her and taking the brush from her hand.

"So you have," she agreed, watching him in the mirror as he took over the brushing. "Think I'm going to let some young female in Stronghold try to claim what's mine, to say nothing of Kuushoi?"

He stopped brushing for a moment. "You know about that?"

"I don't play games with your mind, Conner. Something woke me last night, and I knew Kuushoi was here. When Llew's memories possessed you, they took me in too."

"Ah." He resumed brushing for another minute or two then handed it back to her and began braiding the snow-white hair. "Then you know everything?"

"Not everything. Only that you were afraid of Her return-ing and what happened when Llew was returned against his wishes to Rhydderch's castle." She reached for a hair clasp on her table and passed it back to him.

"You have lovely hair," he said, fastening the long braid off. Sadness was building in him, and he tried to close off his thoughts from her.

"So have you, and no, we didn't become lovers because of Kuushoi, so you can stop thinking that right now," she said tartly, rounding on him. "You and I know damned well there's more between us than that!"

"I know," he said, reaching out to touch her face. "I have to leave Shola and travel to where Kusac is."

"But not today, and you'll return to me," she said, grasping his hand. "Won't you?"

"In truth, I don't know, Noni. The Goddess has given me other work to do there." He felt her wince as her claw tips began to extend and prick his hand and realized he was hold-ing her too tightly. He relaxed his grip a little. "It's not wise for us to get so involved . . ."

She made a noise of disgust. "We were already too involved before last night!"

"Noni, I've said one too many good-byes in my life, I can't bear another," he said forcefully.

"Then don't," she said, standing up. "Come back to me."

"Come with me!"

"I don't travel," she replied automatically.

"I know, but I must," he said gently, lifting her palm to his lips.

"They haven't even retaken the Prime world yet," she mut-tered. "We can enjoy the time we have here, then, who knows? Perhaps I'll join you later."

He stared at her. "You'd consider it?"

"I must be going senile," she muttered. "Yes, I'll seriou consider it if you are away for more than six months."

"Two."

"Three months, and no sooner! Take it or leave it!"

He laughed, picking her up and planting a kiss on her cheek, much to her feigned indignant yowl just as Teusi walked in.

"Your pardon, Noni, Conner," he stammered, backing out. "But there's a search on for Master Conner—they think he's missing."

"Go tell them I'm with Noni and we're going to the Senior's room for first meal," said Conner, putting Noni down.

"Umm . . . That'd be for second meal, Master Conner," said Teusi, grinning.

"Second meal! Goddess save us, imaginations will be running riot," Conner murmured.

"Oh, I think not, when they see your neck," said Teusi.

"Out, brat!" shouted Noni, lobbing her brush at him. "Don't you go spreading any rumors!"

"Won't need to, Noni," he laughed, beating a hasty retreat as the brush sailed harmlessly past him.

"Seems like we're already an item, whether we want it or not," said Conner, walking over to retrieve the brush and throw it on a nearby chair as they left.

"You'd think they could find something better to gossip about," grumbled Noni as Conner ushered her into the corridor. "Wait. I need you keyed into my room," she said, stopping him by the security access panel.

He inclined his head slightly as he waited for her to input her number then place her palm on the sensor panel. "I'm honored."

"Now you," she said, stepping back as a couple of students came out of one of the other rooms.

Pretending not to notice, the young females politely sidled past them before heading off at a brisk pace. A muffled giggle drifted back.

"I have to go to Vartra's Retreat this evening. If I'm back late, let yourself in," she said, glaring at the youngsters' retreating backs. "Teusi will look after you. Why is it that when you do something personal, there's always someone about to mind your business?"

"It comes of living in an establishment like this," said Conner calmly, keying in his palm print. "What takes you out there tonight?"

"Business. I'll tell you about it when I can," she said shortly, taking hold of his arm as they started down the corridor.

"Your stick . . ."

"I don't really need it every day," she said with a grin. "Makes me look more intimidating, don't you think?"

"Oh, I think you manage fine on your own," he said with a chuckle.

"Why did you call this meeting of the Guardians, Noni?" asked Lijou that evening as he escorted her into Vartra's Retreat.

"Ghyakulla told me to," she said. "She's preparing for this war in other ways, you know."

"Does this involve Conner?" he asked shrewdly.

Noni shot the Guild Master of the Brotherhood priests a glance. "Aye, it does. You know that the Entities have been curious about our Humans since they first arrived, don't you? Well, they've chosen one who is already a Guardian."

"I knew Conner was more than he seemed. And the fact that he and you are a couple now?"

"A couple?" Her face softened. "I suppose we are, at that. Seems strange after a lifetime alone to find someone now." She shook herself. "That's got little to do with it, Lijou. Shortly he'll be telling you he has to go to the Prime world. He's been carrying in his ancient memories a prophecy for our time that the Entities told him to deliver to Kusac. Ghyakulla also wants him to help them heal their world by returning them to their worship of the land. That's what I'll be telling the other Guardians tonight."

"It seems the Humans have been part of our destiny since the beginning. Will they accept Conner?"

"If I'm not mistaken, they'll have no choice," she said, her voice taking on a harder tone. "I have Teusi shadowing him. Your Brotherhood training's coming in useful for the lad, and I thank you for it."

"It was nothing, compared with what you do for us," he murmured, nodding to the priests as they made their way to the meeting room. "Why is Teusi shadowing him?"

"Because he'll be called here by Ghyakulla herself," she said. "He won't know why, and he might not even be aware of coming here. That's why I want Teusi there to help him when it happens."

Lijou opened the door for her. The scent of nung blossoms began to fill the air as they entered.

"Looks like it may happen sooner than I thought," she muttered.

Aware of her sudden fear for Conner, Lijou took her by the elbow and steered her toward the nearest sofa. "She won't let him come to harm, of that I'm sure," he whispered.

A warm Spring breeze filled the room as in the center of it, the air began to shimmer and shift. Glimpses of another realm, one of trees covered in brightly colored blossoms and flowers could almost be seen as silence fell. Then it was gone, leaving an afterimage of a golden-pelted female—and Conner, very solidly standing there, shocked almost out of his wits.

"See to him," Noni snapped, but Lijou had already left her side and sprinted over to catch the Human as he began to stumble.

As Lijou began to reassure him and lead him over to Noni, she ignored the sudden demands from the others to know what was going on. Instead, she took the time to answer a mental call from an extremely worried Teusi.

"Who is this Human, and why's he been brought here, Noni?" demanded Keaal loudly, amid the sudden babble of voices.

"I am sure Noni will explain," said Rhaid, raising her voice in order to quell the others. "If we give her the chance. And introduce our visitor."

"This is Conner, a Human Guardian from Earth. He's been chosen by Ghyakulla to join us as a Sholan Guardian and to speak for the Humans who have become part of us," she said, reaching out to take Conner's hand. "He's been sent to help us in the coming war."

CHAPTER 4

"EVENTS not going as planned," Aizshuss hummed, pacing up and down in front of the small fountain that graced Kuvaa's inner courtyard. "Why? How has Hunter avoided forming mental Link with the Sand-dweller female when Isolationists pressed for it? How he created these . . ." he searched for a suitable word, "null areas, blackouts—within Unity, where we cannot see him?"

"Emotional attachment between them been achieved . . ." began Kuvaa.

"Is not what we've worked for!" The TeLaxaudin stopped pacing as the thrumming sound that underscored his words became louder.

"Giyarishis could try again to influence him while he sleeps," began Kuvaa.

Aizshuss made a derisive sound. "Unimportant. How our influence he avoids matters now!"

"Perhaps more for this female, he cannot feel," Kuvaa said. "Emotional ties to his own mate there is, and the Third."

"Time on *Kz'adul* Hkairass told Camarilla that should have severed," said Aizshuss. "Said the implant Directorate installed, those ties had broken."

"Obviously not," Shvosi replied. "Manipulating deep emotions and ties to others a complex matter; his go deeper than expected. I never in favor of this, nor were you. What we do now is more important. He must be controlled. If not, future could be bleaker than reunification of Sand-dwellers."

"I think we have underestimated the Hunter all along," said Kuvaa, trying to keep the nervous tremor out of her voice. "Humanity in him not foreseen. Perhaps from there his continuing need for his partners stems, and instincts to keep Sand-dweller female at a distance."

Azwokkus stirred on his cushion, leaning toward the young Cabbaran female. "That unimportant, Kuvaa," he said gently. "Never what we wanted, was plan of Hkairass' faction. Our responsibility is for enhancements Kzizysus performed, for monitoring and controlling him. This not happening."

"Why so important?" she asked, wrinkling her snout. "His will is as ours—oppose reunification of Sand-dwellers."

Aizshuss stopped in front of her, abruptly folding himself up and squatting down. Eyes swirling rapidly as they adapted to the nearer field of vision, he leaned toward her, exuding an even stronger scent of outrage as his mandibles began to move more rapidly.

"Hunter for intelligence, among other qualities, was chosen. Much we wished hidden has he pieced together due to null zones."

Azwokkus let loose a sudden burst of humming that rose rapidly in pitch until it passed out of her audible range. The effect on Aizshuss was instantaneous. Rocking backward on his feet, he almost overbalanced, then, recovering, turned to face him. A brief exchange followed, punctuated by competing scents, brought to an end only by the intervention of Shvosi.

"Enough!" she said, trotting across to them, side-swiping Aizshuss as she passed. Then she butted her head into Azwokkus. "Isolationists we fight, not each other!" she snarled as both the TeLaxaudin, limbs flailing, tried to pick themselves up. "Laugh at us they would if Unity not excluded from here. Kuvaa young, learning Camarilla ways—bad examples not needed from our leaders!"

Aizshuss stiffened, then inclined his head toward both Shvosi and Kuvaa, his draperies flicking slightly as the outraged scent was changed to one of almost neutrality. "Apologies. Age forgets how learning takes time."

"Apologies," Azwokkus hummed gently, accepting Kuvaa's hand to pull him upright on the yielding cushions.

Thank you, she sent, knowing his embedded devices would allow him to pick her up through the physical contact.

Did not I tell you we respect your physical strength? he replied with a trace of humor.

"Our weapon against M'zull, the Hunter is," said Aizshuss, his tone this time more even. "I explain. If Hkairass not convinced us the Hunter's psi abilities and emotions destroyed by torture and implant, Reformists would not agree to return his abilities and enhance them. This, even though best hope that way lay of preventing reunification. Enhancing made him our weapon, gave him abilities greater than any Hunter before. Risk is . . ."

"He discovers what Camarilla have done," finished Shvosi.

"But we did good," said Kuvaa, confused as she looked from one to the other of her three mentors.

"Some," said Azwokkus, mandibles quivering. "Not good trying to force mind Link to Sand-dweller female. Object he might to new abilities, Sand-dweller implants . . ."

"Our monitoring of him," added Shvosi. "That he did notice, once."

"Twice," corrected Kuvaa, beginning to understand. "He seeks us, not stopping Sand-dweller reunification. He needs direction, to forget what he has uncovered."

"Exactly," agreed Azwokkus. "Isolationists' policy exposed us to discovery because we losing control of him."

"If we ever had it," sniffed Shvosi pessimistically.

"If we ever had it," agreed Aizshuss. "Now best chance of diverting him is through his family. Hkairass' party miscalculated. We correct it; ascendancy to main party is ours. We shape future with more concerns for nexuses."

"We fail . . ." Kuvaa stopped, shuddering at the thought of what could result.

"We not fail," Azwokkus hummed. "Through him, we reach his family, control them if not him."

"But potentialities not obvious," she objected. "All in flux now."

"Because he remembers. Stop memories, flux settles, our way is clearer again."

"And Humans? Where they fit into this?"

The other three exchanged glances.

"They don't," said Shvosi quietly. "Until recently, they were nothing to us."

Asteroid Field, same day

"Red Leader to Command. Cargo acquired. Rejoining unit now."

"Acknowledged," said Kezule, watching the *Mazzu* with its trail of small meteorites head slowly toward where the *M'zayik* was herding a now sizable collection of floating debris.

It had been a slow and boring task, not without its dangers. The *M'zayik* had managed to get itself holed, and only the quick actions of its crew had avoided loss of life. Now, floating well outside the influence of any stellar bodies, they were finally ready to mine the largest three.

As he watched, the *M'zayik* activated its beam, pushing a group of rocks into slightly closer proximity to the main group. The large ones hung motionless toward the rear. Even with explosives buried deep inside them, they posed a deadly threat to K'oish'ik. If they got too close before they were detonated, the resulting debris would rain down upon the helpless inhabitants. He intended to make sure that could not happen.

"Ready for stage four, Command," said his Comm officer.

"Initiate," he said, checking the clock. They were still slightly ahead of schedule. "Tell them to take their time. I want no casualties. We have ten hours left before rendezvous."

Huddled on the rock floor near the center of his prison, Vartra sensed their presence outside the confines of the opaque force field within which he was being held. Curled around himself, his tail wrapped across his limbs, he'd tried to keep warm during the long night, but the rock had slowly leached all heat from him. He was unclothed, plucked as he had been from Kuushoi's bed, he knew not how long ago. There was no way for him to reckon time here. He only assumed that it had been night because they'd left him alone for so long.

Well, Hunter priest, willing to cooperate with us now, are you? The sharp thoughts of his main captor stabbed through his mind like a knife, starting up the headache again.

"No finesse," he muttered to himself. "Just savages."

Feed him, give him blankets, sent the other, its thoughts less abrasive. *No use him expiring of cold and hunger. These Sholan Entities are as weak as I said they were.*

Two folded blankets suddenly landed on top of him, and a tray of food slid across the floor toward him from the edge of the "field."

He lay there, too stiff and cold to move.

Cover yourself, and eat, now! Unless you want to suffer reprisals!

He stirred, slowly uncurling, dislodging the blankets. Reaching for one, he pulled himself onto it, breaking his contact with the icy floor. The other he tugged closer, then, clumsy and stiff, he opened it up and managed to wrap it around his shoulders.

You demanded food, said the other. *Eat.*

Staggering to his feet, he clutched his blanket tightly and took the few steps to the tray. Lifting it up in one shaking hand, he backed off back to his place, almost falling down on the other blanket. He picked up the bowl, moving aside the green leafed plants to find the fruit and clusters of grains below. It might be long enough before he was given any more food, better to fill his belly now.

Picking up a cluster, he put it in his mouth, spitting it out as soon as he saw what lay beneath it.

"Bugs! I don't eat bugs," he snarled, throwing the bowl aside.

Is meat, you Hunters eat meat. And grains and fruit.

"That's jegget food! We eat real meat, from animals, not bugs!" he snapped. "You call me a Hunter? Well, that's what we do, hunt meat." He bared his teeth in a feral snarl, looking around his prison so no matter where they were they would see it.

Jeggets?

"Rodents on Shola."

He reached for the bulb-shaped container of liquid on the tray, almost afraid to find out what it contained, but his thirst was worse than his hunger right now, and that in itself was strange. Normally he needed to eat and drink only occasionally.

He took the top off and squirted some of the liquid into his hand, sniffing it.

Fruit juice, sent the gentler mind. *Nothing more.*

Faintly, at the edges of his senses, he almost heard them arguing mentally with each other. He dipped his tongue in the liquid in his palm; it was indeed fruit juice, sharp and refreshing, and he drank thirstily.

A plate suddenly slid across the floor, coming to rest against his foot. So they could see him clearly, and the force field was definitely only one way, designed to keep him in. He glanced at the plate. This time it held a chunk of cold meat and a large piece of bread.

Now eat, Hunter. Then we talk.

He shuddered as he picked up the plate and began devouring the meat and bread, dreading what he knew was to come.

All too soon, his meager meal was finished. As he laid his plate aside, the now familiar pain lanced through his already aching head, felling him to the floor in agony.

Tell us about the Hunter, said the harsh mind as it began peeling away his mental defenses a layer at a time. *Tell us his nature. Many follow him—who does he look to? Who influences him?*

He could barely think, the pain was so intense, but he retained just enough control to start pulling his consciousness deeper into himself.

No! I'll tell you nothing, he sent. But his deeper self was crying, *Goddess, Ghyakulla, where are you when I need you? Help me!*

The *Profit,* same day

"*Venture II* to *Rryuk's Profit.* Requesting permission to approach for docking," said Kusac, slowing the *Venture* until, their velocities matching, he was trailing the *Profit.*

"*Profit* to *Venture,* permission granted. We've rigged up a temporary docking ring on the dorsal surface—can't miss it, it's lit up like a festival tree. Once you're docked, we'll engage the electromagnets and a force field to keep you in place."

"Affirmative," he replied, frowning briefly. The voice, and the accented Sholan with its almost perfect pronunciation, was vaguely familiar. He shrugged it off—a coincidence, nothing more, caused by the fact the ship had once been Tirak's—and concentrated on moving into a tight trail position. "Be advised we have docking clamps on the exterior of our vessel."

"We copy that, *Venture*," said the *Profit*.

"Taking over comm, Captain," said M'kou quietly.

"Acknowledged."

"Two thousand feet and closing," said Banner, beginning to count the distance down for him.

The rear of the *Profit* was starting to fill their forward view. Senses strained to the utmost, he began to gradually increase the speed—too close and they'd end up a fireball.

"Fifteen hundred."

Soon . . . but not yet, his instincts told him.

"One thousand."

Not yet . . .

He felt as if he could reach out and touch the *Profit*—he could certainly feel the life-forces of those inside her.

"Nine hundred."

He could sense the *Venture* all around him, humming as if she were alive. She? Why she, part of his mind wondered.

"Eight hundred and closing," said Banner.

Raising the *Venture's* nose a fraction, he was acutely aware of the instant response as she began to lift, almost straining against his control as he stepped up above the other ship. She felt like an extension of him now, not something separate. A touch more acceleration . . .

"Closing at three hundred feet, with thirty feet clearance."

Slowly they began to overtake the *Profit*.

"One hundred feet, holding at thirty feet clearance," said Banner.

A margin of drift had set in, and carefully he nudged her back on course. Checking the forward view, he saw the ring of beckoning lights ahead. Below him, against all reason, he could "see" the dorsal surface of the *Profit*.

"Approaching zero distance, holding at thirty feet clearance. Docking ring is eighty-five feet in, Captain," said Banner.

"Acknowledged," he said, pulling back on the speed as he sensed Banner's hand hovering near the copilot's controls.

"Counting from eighty-five now. Eighty feet."

Slower, even slower, till they seemed to be barely moving, he nudged the *Venture* forward.

"Activating docking beacon," said J'korrash.

"Sixty feet. Height constant at thirty feet."

He cut the speed again as the collision warning blared out. "Silence it," he snapped just as M'kou did so.

"Thirty feet. Height constant at thirty."

"Prepare to cut engines," he said.

"Aye, sir," said J'korrash.

"Ten feet . . . five . . . zero feet. Line above achieved," said Banner as the docking beacon began to chime gently.

The humming of the motors sank gradually as he slowed for the final time, once again matching speed with the *Profit*.

Briefly, he took one hand, then the other, off the controls to flex them. "Descending now," he said.

"Copy that," said Banner. "Twenty-five, twenty . . ."

He tuned out the sound of his Second's voice, concentrating on the feel of his ship, the high-pitched whine of the engines, and his instrumentation as he eased her lower and lower until, with a slight bump followed by a brief grinding noise, they'd docked.

"Cut all engines," he said. "Engage docking clamps."

"Engines cut," said J'korrash. "Docking clamps engaged."

Mentally disengaging himself from his ship, he closed down his station then leaned back in his chair, feeling drained. He became aware of the sudden lightening of the atmosphere around him.

"Well done, everyone," he said tiredly as a low buzz of conversation broke out among the crew.

"The *Profit* bids us welcome, Captain," said M'kou, turning in his seat to look at him. "They say they'll be ready for us to debark in about ten minutes, once they've secured our docking rings."

He nodded, lifting up his armrest to reach the bottled water and high energy snack packed in there, wondering when he'd learned to fly using his psi senses as well as his normal ones. Ripping open the packaging, he took a large bite out of the fruit and cereal bar.

Around him, his crew were running their own shutdown checks and closing down their stations. He leaned forward, activating the stealth shield around the *Venture*. With that on, as they approached the Orbital, the Venture would be invisible.

Banner got to his feet, stretching from head to tail tip before coming over to stand beside him. "Nice piece of flying, considering how little experience you actually have."

"It had to be," he said, accepting the compliment for what it was worth. "We're riding on top of our fuel tanks, after all. Tends to make one very exacting."

"There is that," Banner agreed with a slow grin.

Kusac snorted gently and opened his water, taking a long drink from it. "I only put the wind up your tail once."

"Sure you did," grinned Banner, turning away.

"I thought I recognized your voice," Kusac said to the black-pelted U'Churian as he emerged in the *Profit*. "When did you change ships?"

"Some time ago," said Tirak, holding his hand out in greeting and grasping Kusac by the forearm when it was returned. "Well met, Captain. Are you well?" he asked, a look of concern crossing his face as he saw how thin Kusac looked.

Kusac nodded, moving aside to allow the sandy-pelted male above him to climb down to the deck. "This is Jayza. Captain Tirak of *Watcher 6*. And my Prime crewmembers, Noolgoi, M'kou . . ."

Tirak held his hand up as he surveyed the others making their way down. "Don't tell me now. I'll never remember them all. Come to the mess, get a hot drink inside you, and we'll talk. You can introduce them all there."

"You know the plan." It was a statement; the knowledge was at the forefront of Tirak's mind. He turned his inward, searching for memories of Kaid's time on the *Profit*.

The U'Churian nodded, ears flicking in assent. "Kezule briefed us himself," he said as they headed over to the mess. "It's a bold plan. I like that. We're to help you take the Orbital, Kusac, guard you and your party."

Pulling himself back to the here and now, he glanced at the black pelted Captain. Their species were so similar yet also very different. "I'll be glad to have you along," he said, feeling the other instantly relax. "I'm not foolish enough to object to help when I need it," he said in an undervoice, making Tirak start slightly.

"You telepaths," the other laughed. "I still find you a little unnerving. It was Kaid who thought you'd refuse us, not Kezule. I'm glad that medical procedure Kizzy did seems to have worked so well for you."

"Oh, it worked," he replied, keeping his tone light as they stood back and let the others crowd into the small room. "Are the rest of your Family here? The Cabbarans? I thought that I'd have a word with Naacha, thank him for his help during that time."

"They're here, checking over all our suits right now, trying to create a joint communications system. We've got another six hours."

"Five hours, fifty-seven minutes," Kusac said automatically. "Have you managed to get that link set up to the *N'zishok*?"

"Completed an hour and a half ago," confirmed Tirak. "No one will be able to pick up our ship-to-ship transmissions. Naacha and Annuur haven't been able to do much about the suits yet, though. Once down on K'oish'ik, we'll have to stay in close proximity to each other to be heard with all the interference from the storms they plan to create." He gestured to Kusac to enter first.

"Captain!" said Sheeowl, getting to her feet as they appeared. "Good to see you again!"

"You're limping," said Manesh. "What happened?"

Surprised that Tirak's security officer had picked up his now slight limp so quickly, Kusac took one of the empty seats. "Got shot in the leg a while back. I'm fine now; it's more or less healed."

"Have it checked before you suit up, please. I need to know how it affects you if I'm to watch your back."

He nodded. "You know about Zsurtul, the Prime Prince ... Emperor," he amended. He had to get used to using Zsurtul's new title—if they didn't, the youth would never have the respect his position demanded.

"I know. Kezule said his daughter Zhalmo would be his personal bodyguard."

"She will. She's with Kezule, en route to meet with Kaid and the young Emperor. She's good. We trained her ourselves. This is one of her brothers, Lieutenant M'kou," he said, indicating the young male and watching as the slightly plump U'Churian ran a practiced eye over him.

"We've two civilian engineers with us," said M'kou. "They're going to take over operation of the weather controls."

"Understood. They'll stay in the *Profit* until we send for them, then ..."

"No, they come with us," interrupted Kusac. "If anything goes wrong—a warning is sent, equipment damaged—they're right on it, no delays."

"You've forgotten about Annuur and Naacha, and they're battle trained. I suggest it would be better for them to handle that side until we control the Orbital."

Reluctantly Kusac nodded. "Very well. Have you contacted the Orbital yet, told them about your engine problems?"

Sheeowl glanced at her wrist. "In ten minutes," she said, getting up from the table and beginning to squeeze her way out. "I'll get down to the Bridge now, Captain Tirak. Oh, Captain Aldatan, this is Thyasha, our new comm operator. She's taking Giyesh's place."

Kusac nodded a greeting to the young female, noting she wore her mane of hair shorter than the other two females on Tirak's crew.

"Tirak, I suggest we retire to your office and go over the plans one more time before briefing our crews," said Kusac.

"Agreed," said Tirak. "It's a little tight for room in here."

They walked down the corridor, and as he opened his office door, Tirak said in a low voice, "Having the young Emperor with us is the only thing that is worrying me about this mission."

"We need him," said Kusac patiently, following him in. The office was small, containing only a desk, two chairs, and a couple of cupboards—the usual cramped standard for any ship of this size, no matter the species. "Without his retinal pattern, we can't reprogram the Orbital weather center or the main Command Room in the Palace."

"I know. It doesn't stop me worrying, though. We came prepared. Antipersonnel gas, weapons, and armor. And before you ask, all my team have seen combat— before Jalna," he added with a grin, going over to the cabinet at the back of his desk.

"Jalna was a lifetime ago," Kusac murmured.

"It was indeed. Let's drink to happier times and a successful mission," the U'Churian said, pulling out a small bottle and a couple of glasses. "Take that chair, and I'll bring mine around to join you." He waved the hand with the glasses in it in the general direction of the more comfortable of the two chairs near the desk before depositing the bottle and glasses on the surface and turning back to pick up his own seat.

"Sounds like a plan," Kusac said, sitting down in the padded wooden chair. "How did you say you came to be on the *Profit* again?"

"I didn't," said Tirak, carrying his chair around to the other side of the desk. He sat down with a sigh and reached for the bottle. "You'll like this. It's a liqueur, triple distilled and very expensive. It's made from berries that grow wild on hillsides around our ancestral home on U'Chur. They lay it down for ten years, then distill it, then it's laid down for another twenty."

As he opened the bottle, Kusac smelled a light and aromatic scent.

"None of that throat- and gut-burning rubbish you get even in the best bars and restaurants. This is only sold by auction to a very select clientele."

"Nice glasses," he observed, watching as the other carefully poured about an inch of the heavy, almost purple liqueur into each.

"Special glasses too," said Tirak, closing the bottle and picking up a glass to hand to Kusac. "Its name translates to Land's Blood in your language, and the glasses depict the scene of the Soil Goddess and the Sky God creating the sun and stars."

He accepted the drink, holding it up for a moment, turning it to see the images engraved within the actual glass itself. "Very beautiful."

"Not as beautiful as what's in it. Here's to a successful mission, and happier times," he said, raising his glass in a salute to Kusac.

"Indeed," said Kusac, doing the same before taking a sip

The taste was as light and aromatic as the scent, warming his mouth and throat gently as it slid like silk down into his stomach. He was impressed. "This is good."

Tirak laughed. "I knew you'd like it. I brought it with me to share with you. It's from my private stock. It's good for all that ails you, helping whet the appetite or digest the meal. I hear your Governor enjoys it."

"Then your clientele isn't too elite," he said with an attempt at humor. It hadn't escaped him that Tirak had again neatly sidestepped his question.

"I'm sure some could be procured for you," chuckled the U'Churian Captain, amused.

"You obviously had some time to prepare for this trip."

"As you say," Tirak agreed, putting his glass down. "We were called home to make this delivery. The Matriarch didn't want genuine merchants going to K'oish'ik at such a sensitive time. And when your request to join your mission came, she gave her consent, said it was good you would have a crew worthy of you." He flicked his ears in self-deprecation.

"And the body armor you have with you?" Kusac persisted, absently putting his hand up to the back of his neck where a nagging headache had begun to develop. Tirak's explanation wasn't entirely convincing, but the pain in his neck and head was distracting him enough to keep him from consciously reading the other's mind.

"Standard for us. We had it with us when we landed on Jalna, just never had the need to use it when we first arrived or the chance to get into it when we did. As for the rest, not knowing what we were flying into and given the pacifist nature of the Primes, we wanted non-lethal options. I like your new look, by the way. The earring suits you, and the beadwork bracelet is very ethnic—don't think I've seen anything like it before."

"It's Prime, made for their first major fertility festival on Kij'ik—they were gifts. As they had no priests, I helped out," he replied. The pain was beginning to migrate up to the back of his head. It could be postural—he had been pushing himself hard in an effort to get fit again, despite the pain his injured thigh still gave him.

"Sounds like you were kept busy. You'll have to tell me about it later. What's this Kezule like? I hear he's one of the ancient Warrior elite, the ones that killed what they couldn't conquer."

"He's slippery, more kinks in his mind than bends in a stream," Kusac replied, taking a larger mouthful of the drink. "But he's also motivated by his sense of honor, and he's on our side. He'll do what he said, put Crown Prince Zsurtul on the throne, see him crowned and surrounded by advisers whose judgment and loyalty he can trust, then walk away."

"Good. Now to business. You've got the layouts of the Orbital and this tunnel system with you?"

"Not only that, but I have several of the late Emperor's

bodyguards with me—ones who set up the modern security devices in there when they revamped the security system," said Kusac, reaching into the largest pouch on his belt.

"I've a couple of extra crew on board, by the way," said Tirak. "Members of the *Profit's* new regular crew, to handle the cargo and shuttle when they go down."

He nodded. "I wondered how you were going to manage that. Your people have made deliveries here before. Will the Primes send out a collection vehicle in the weather that we'll be creating?"

"Not sure, but the warehouses are near enough that they can start unloading some of the lighter goods into them. Don't want them sitting on their tails and drawing attention to themselves, after all."

Tirak's wrist comm sounded, and as he answered it, Kusac spread the plans on the desk.

"Captain, need Sholans and Valtegans in battle suits in deck 2 workshop," Annuur said. "Maybe we have way to communicate while underground."

"I'll go and take M'kou with me," Kusac said. "Banner can cover your briefing, at least for the Orbital portion of the mission."

"They'll send someone down," Tirak said, signing off. "I'd rather you did the briefing. Is there some reason you want to see Annuur, because once this is over . . ." He tailed off into silence, obviously a little puzzled.

"Not particularly," he lied. For all he knew, Tirak was as involved as Annuur and Naacha in what had been done to him on Shola after the operation to return his psychic abilities. "Our suits are Prime made. The others don't know the specs as well as I do."

Tirak nodded. "Makes sense. You'll cover the tunnel mission with me when you're done?"

"Of course. I'll take M'kou with me to describe the various security measures to Annuur," he said, getting up. "I want to get this out of the way fairly quickly. My crew could do with some rest time before we reach the Orbital."

"I'll have Manesh set up some camp beds in the cargo hold next to the one we're using as the ready room."

He'd worn a heavy battle suit only four times, all drills, but the training in how to put it on, and quickly, had been in-

ained into him by Kaid when they'd trained at Stronghold.
'he Prime-made ones were essentially the same, and he'd run
several drills for them all on their way here.

The suits were now mounted on the back wall of individual
stalls, down in the *Venture's* lower deck Ready Room. All he
had to do was back into it, place his feet into the shaped boots,
his tail into the jointed extension, then pull the various limb
and groin pieces into place, sealing them on the inner edges
and at the joints. Last, he reached up to pull down the chest
piece. His arms felt heavy, weighted down as they were by five
hundred pounds of still slightly loose-fitting body armor, but
until he had it in place, he couldn't power-up.

Settling his chin into the formed hollow, he clicked the chest
plate into place, reaching around to either side to activate the
seals. A faint hiss, and it was done. He leaned forward, pulling
against the gentle tug of the suit's cradle. Immediately he felt
the interior shrink as it began to mold itself to the shape of
his body. Moments later, as soon as it had nestled itself firmly
around his neck, the power came on and the five hundred
pounds of armor weighed nothing at all. Had he been wearing
his helmet, he'd have seen the various holo displays on the
lower right come to life, giving him a constant feed on both
his health and the state of his armor. Instead, he lifted his left
forearm and glanced at the secondary readout there. Thankfully, it was ignoring his headache.

Internal suit temperature was rising to compensate for the
coldness in the *Venture*—since it was effectively parked, only
emergency light and heating were on— magnetics on the boots
were off as it had sensed the ship's own gravitational system,
air was off as he wasn't wearing his helmet, and his built-in
weapons were ready to activate.

Switching the latter off, he turned, now totally unaware
of the weight of his suit, and reached into the niche where
his helmet was stowed. Picking it up, he clumped out into the
cargo hold where M'kou had almost finished donning his gray
armored suit.

"Ready?"

Picking up his own helmet from the jury-rigged stall, M'kou
nodded. Kusac gestured for the young Prime to precede him
to the hatch down into the *Profit*. He'd learned from experience the last few days that his suit's padding cinched his injured thigh a little too tightly for comfort as he walked, and

he didn't want M'kou to see him limping as he acclimated
it. It wasn't enough to trigger the suit's automated system, bu
it was enough to cause him a fair degree of discomfort, even
with his heightened tolerance of pain.

While they were waiting at the elevator, he leaned his head
close to M'kou's.

"Don't look directly at Naacha, the one with the blue tattoos on his face," he said very quietly.

Startled, M'kou pulled back to look at him.

He held his gloved hand up to silence M'kou, then beckoned him close again.

"He's their mystic. The tattoos can have hypnotic effects
on some people," he whispered when they were in physical
contact again. "He's also a telepath. Different, as we all are,
but more than capable of reading us. So no communications,
understood?"

"Aye, Captain," he whispered. "Don't you trust them?
Need we be cautious of all of them?"

"Be cautious anyway." Finding Tirak's crew on the *Profit*
was just a shade too convenient. "They're allies, but like everyone, they have their own agenda."

M'kou nodded as he backed off and thumbed the elevator
switch.

Walking in the powered armor was easier on his leg this
time, but he still found the fit around his injured thigh a little
too snug for comfort. Obviously some swelling still remained,
so he'd been careful until now to not to remain suited-up for
too long when they'd been training.

Annuur looked up as they entered. "Good to be seeing you
again, Captain. M'kou, this is?"

"Lieutenant M'kou," he corrected before the young male
could, keeping an oblique eye on Naacha as the Cabbaran
mystic came down from his angled worktable and began to
circle around them, his hooves clicking on the metal floor.
M'kou watched him, fascinated, until Kusac nudged him in
the ribs.

"Prime construction obvious," the mystic said, stopping
in front of them. "Helmets give to Annuur." With that he
abruptly turned and went back to his workbench.

Kusac moved closer to Annuur and put his helmet down on the bench in front of him. M'kou did the same.

"Seats over there, you bring closer. Too tall are you," said Annuur, gesticulating vaguely to the other side of the room.

"This is Annuur, and the other Cabbaran is Naacha," he said to M'kou. "I forgot you haven't met their species before. They're Tirak's Family, and his navigators."

"A pleasure," he murmured.

Annuur looked closely at him, nose wrinkling and lips pulling back in his smile. "One of General Kezule's kin." He held out his paw. "Good meeting, Lieutenant. Hope we can make comm links for all our suits when underground. Only talk each other, of course. Atmospherics will be blocking all else."

M'kou took the proffered hand in his gloved one, trying not to stare at the tiny hooves on the end of each digit before he released them.

Annuur turned his attention back to Kusac. "Comms, are they Sholan or Prime, Captain?"

"Bit of both. Certainly Prime and Sholan compatible."

"Ah. Easier this will be, then," said the Cabbaran with satisfaction, lifting Kusac's helmet and turning it upside down to inspect the interior. "Only two systems then needed to talk to each other—ours with yours."

"We'll be joined by Crown Prince Zsurtul and another Sholan when we've retaken the Orbital."

"No matter—they can talk, we can talk to your Emperor. Will suffice," the Cabbaran muttered, poking at the interior controls. "I concentrate now. Give other helmet to Naacha."

Kusac picked up M'kou's helmet, gesturing for him to fetch the chairs. Here was his chance to have a quiet word with the mystic.

". . . Surprised how little time that took," said M'kou. "You've been very quiet since you spoke to Naacha, Captain. Is anything wrong?"

Just managing to prevent himself from stopping dead in his tracks, he made some noncommittal reply. A hollow feeling was forming in his gut. Mind racing, he glanced around briefly to orient himself—they were heading back along the corridor to the cargo area designated as the Ready Room. His hand tightened automatically on the hard shell of his helmet. The last thing he remembered was . . . Naacha's face and the swirling blue tattoos. Curious, that . . .

A sudden chill ran through him, starting at his left shoulder—a feeling as if all the heat were being sucked from him, despite the fact that his suit had its own internal temperature regulation. Words, almost intelligible, seemed to whisper through his mind, accompanied by a fleeting image of piercing blue eyes in a snow-white Sholan face. He forced himself to concentrate, the effort so intense he stumbled.

Remember, Hunter. Remember why you're angry with them, but don't let it cloud your judgment. He heard them then the memory of what they said was gone, like warm breath evaporating on a winter's day.

M'kou's hand was there to steady him. "Careful, Captain," he murmured. "How bad is the pain in your leg? Are you really up to going on this mission?"

"I'm fine," he said, almost snatching his arm free of M'kou's as he remembered why he'd wanted to talk to Naacha.

Dammit! He'd been duped yet again, and as easily as if he'd been a youngling just starting training at the Telepath Guild! Once again he'd let his anger override his caution.

Every instinct called out to him to immediately turn around, head back to the workshop, and have it out with Naacha from a safe distance where he couldn't be affected by the other's mental abilities, but too much was at stake for that. Memories of Kaid's lectures on anger control and the proper use of Litanies began to run through his mind, doing nothing to improve his mood as he fought to prevent his tail from lashing from side to side. Cursing inwardly, he continued accompanying M'kou back to the Ready Room.

"Captain," M'kou said hesitantly. "Your tail . . . The blades along its armor may not be turned on yet, but it's still dangerous."

He stopped; mentally taking a deep breath, then began to recite the Litany for Clear Thought as he forced his tail into a neutral position, hanging straight down toward the ground. M'kou's very real concern for him—and his own safety in the narrow corridor—were written clearly on his face.

"I'm fine, M'kou," he said, forcing his voice to sound calm. "I wouldn't go if I thought I would endanger the mission. It's only making me limp slightly now and then. The powered armor makes walking easier, but the lining is gripping the wound a little, that's all."

The Prime's face lightened. "In that case, let me see to dressing it properly. It's no sign of weakness to be more comfortable," he said as Kusac hesitated. "In fact, if I dress it in the Ready Room, it will perhaps give the others more confidence in you when they see you aren't ignoring the injury."

"Very well," he said, a portion of his mind automatically checking the slightly weeping wound at the back of his thigh as he forced his main thoughts back to the business at hand. He couldn't let his team's morale be affected right now by having it out with the Cabbarans, but when this was over ...

M'kou left him at the iris, heading off to the sick bay for what he needed. It cycled open just as he was reaching for the key panel.

"I was about to come and find you," said Banner, stepping aside so he could enter. "We've only got ..."

"Four hours and ten minutes left, I know," he said automatically, stepping inside. "They'll be up in approximately two and a half hours to fit their comm modulators."

"Cutting it close."

"Take them that long to make the number we need," he said, making his way over to the briefing table and benches that had been set up at one end of the Ready Room. "If they can't fit them in time, we delay our docking procedure."

Banner nodded, apparently satisfied.

He unsealed his gloves, taking them off and putting them on the table beside him as he began to start unfastening the seals on his body armor, aware of the suit powering down and its interior retreating from contact with his body.

"Need a hand?"

"Thanks."

As he unfastened the right leg sections, he turned away from Banner, hoping to conceal both the slightly stained dressing at the back of his leg, and its matching patch on the inner protective lining of his armor. He needn't have bothered.

"It's not blood," he said quietly, forestalling his Second. "The inside's rubbing on the bandage, making the wound weep a little. M'kou's going to redress it."

Banner nodded, ducking behind him to check for himself.

"Yeah, looks like that's what it is, right enough. I'll get your armor cleaned, then."

Mrowbay, carrying a dressing tray, came padding in with M'kou, gesturing for him to stay on his feet. Both crouched down behind him. He held his short black tunic aside, giving them room to work as M'kou cut the dressing free and the U'Churian ran a scanner over the wound.

"That was deep," Mrowbay murmured. "Right through the muscle, but as you said, it's almost healed. I assume if we pad it back and front, the suit will conform to that shape rather than try to compress it?"

"Yes," said Kusac, submitting to their ministrations impatiently. "M'kou can see to it, Mrowbay. No need to take up your time."

"With respect, Captain, I've got more training than anyone here," began the medic.

"Not me," he snapped. "You forget that it was Kaid who treated my wife here when she was shot on Jalna, and I have his memories and skills."

There was a small silence. "M'kou is still in his armor, Captain, but if you'd prefer to do it yourself . . ." Mrowbay let his sentence hang there.

Dammit! He shouldn't be letting his anger affect the way he handled his team.

"My apologies to you both," he muttered. "Mrowbay, please continue dressing my leg. M'kou, take your suit off and then accompany our people back to the *Venture* to collect their gear. I'd appreciate you getting my weapons. Banner knows where they are. Final briefing is in forty-five minutes."

"Aye, Captain," he said, straightening up.

As Mrowbay began to place a series of padded dressings around the wound area, Kusac kept an eye on the others, ignoring the slightly rough handling he was receiving. For him, it was merely a minor irritation, nothing more. His attention diverted by Banner's return, when the medic pressed on the center of the wound at the back, he stiffened and let out a loud hiss of pain.

"Sorry, Captain, just wanted to be sure you still had sensation there," said Mrowbay blandly, smiling up at him as he fastened off the encircling bandage. "Now would you walk across the room, please? I want to make sure it's not binding anywhere."

Clenching his teeth, he moved off, crossing the fifteen feet there and back with barely a discernible limp.

Mrowbay grasped his wrist, checking his pulse. "A little elevated, but acceptable," he said quietly. "It's obviously still paining you, Captain, but not enough for me to ground you, in the circumstances. I suggest you set your suit's power for a slightly heavier gravity, let it do the work for you. I have some mild analgesics that don't cross the brain-blood barrier I can give you as well. They last about twelve hours, so you should be good for the whole mission."

Kusac nodded. After the pressure Mrowbay had put on it, it was aching pretty badly, albeit at a background low-level range. It was enough to drag him down, though, and impair his reflexes in the long run.

Stripping off his treatment gloves and putting them on the tray, Mrowbay got to his feet. "Captain Tirak asked me to remind you to join him in his office when we were done. I can send the meds there for you."

"Thank you, Lieutenant," he said, his mind suddenly elsewhere. Something aboard the *Profit* felt . . . off . . . not quite right, but he was damned if he could tell what it was.

Reaching out, he probed every corner of the ship, finding nothing. But his headache was now gone. Still vaguely uneasy, he followed his crew out as they left for the *Venture* then headed for Tirak's office.

On the *N'zishok*, Giyarishis sat back on his cushions, exhausted. He'd only just managed to warn Annuur to withdraw from the Unity net and close it down before the Hunter had traced him or it. This was unprecedented. The Camarilla purposely operated on a frequency no known telepathic species, save the Cabbarans, could use, let alone sense. When he recovered from the shock, he must contact Kuvaa.

The *Tooshu*, earlier, en route to the Prime solar system

"You're not coming on the *Soohibo*, and that's final," said Kaid, his face taking on the closed look Carrie had come to know so well. "Before this goes any further, I know all the arguments you're going to use. No, you're not a child; yes, I can give you orders as Leader of this mission; yes, you are different from T'Chebbi because what happens to you, happens to me—I can't be torn between running the mission and your safety during it. Yes, I know you want to see Kusac as soon as possible and that you were the only one to believe in him, but you'll have to wait a few more days until we've retaken the City. And last, and most important, there isn't a battle suit that you can safely wear because none of them fit you."

"Getting to be a regular know-it-all, aren't you?" she said, a growl of anger underscoring her words. "Psi suppressants make you cranky, you know."

"Jo and Kitra aren't going for the same reasons," he said, ignoring her gibe and softening his tone.

"I only want to go to the Orbital. The fighting will be over by then, so I won't be in any danger. You forgot that argument."

He sighed, ears tilting backward. "So I did, but it changes nothing. There still isn't any armor for you."

"You're saying if I had armor . . ." she began.

"I won't let you trap me verbally, Carrie," he warned.

"Do I lack the training or knowledge of anyone else you're taking? Because most of your arguments are personal, not objective."

"You have my and Kusac's knowledge, plus enough training, despite the lack of experience, to use it," he agreed reluctantly. "But you're more vulnerable . . ."

"In what way? The armor's powered, so I'll be as strong as any female Sholan in it."

"There is no armor for you," he repeated, exasperated. "This whole venture could be some kind of trap. We help Kezule and suddenly find ourselves his prisoners."

"Then right there, in a little over five days, you and I are dead—unless I'm with you. Same goes for Rezac and Jo, and Dzaka and Kitra. All of us with a Leska partner are at risk. You take all that into account too, Tallinu?"

It was Kaid's turn to growl in frustration, but he was spared having to answer right then as the door opened and Rezac came in.

"I drew the short straw, so first off, don't bite the messenger," he said, mouth widening slightly in a half grin. "If you two are going to keep arguing until it's time to leave, you better to your quarters because at least they're shielded—you're both broadcasting your annoyance with each other over the whole ship. Technically, neither of you should be going on a mission halfway through your Link day."

"I can cope," Kaid snarled.

"We can't," said Rezac. "You won't want my advice, but here it is anyway. Jo and Carrie are right. Apart from their lack of armor, you have no good, objective reason not to take them."

"You're right, I don't want it!"

"People like us can't live our lives always taking the safe option, Kaid. If we do, we're as good as dead," Rezac said. "That goes for Jo and Carrie too. If we want to protect them, we can't put ourselves in danger."

"Didn't you hear me? There are no suits for them!"

"Yes there are. Toueesut had them made for all three of them—Jo, Carrie, and Kitra."

Carrie watched Kaid's ears vanish into his hair and tried hard to suppress her pleasure at Rezac's news. So Toueesut had managed to finish them in time.

"Tallinu," she said, leaning forward to touch his hands where they lay clenched together on the table. "Kusac told you back on the *Khalossa* that we didn't intend to hide from danger any longer. That was a joint decision. Now we're Leskas, I expect us both to take such decisions together, not you to impose yours on me. You don't have the moral right. If Jo, Kitra, and I shouldn't go, then neither should you and Rezac or Dzaka."

"The Touibans are picking you up too," added Rezac. "They're having some difficulty understanding your double standards, and frankly, so am I."

Kaid stared at him for a moment. "Don't you want Jo kept safe?"

Rezac shrugged and came over to join them at the table. "Yes, and no. She's a warrior, like me. If I stop her being what she is at heart, then it'll kill her just as quickly as a shot from a gun, an aircar accident, or choking on a nut will. Don't forget the problems I had with Zashou," he added, his eyes clouding over briefly. "She was a pacifist and wanted to stay safe, hated everything I was and am. We can't have it both ways, Kaid. We don't need a mate who's our equal whom we protect to the point where we destroy her and our relationship."

"You're right," said Kaid abruptly, his hands relaxing und€
Carrie's. "You and Jo can come," he said to her. "But Kitr₂
stays. She's still only fifteen."

"Then sweeten it by taking her on the *Soohibo* and giving her a real task to perform for the mission," said Rezac.
"She's on hand then if anything happens to Dzaka. To be honest, I think they'll both be relieved she's not in the front line,
so long as neither of them think she's being treated like a
kitling."

"I'll leave you to find something for her to do, in that case,"
said Kaid dryly, "since you're so full of good advice today."

"No problem," grinned Rezac as he got to his feet. "When
we board the *Soohibo*, why don't you and Carrie stay in your
quarters until nearer the rendezvous time? Garras can take
charge till then."

"Good idea," said Carrie, before Kaid could refuse. "It'll
give everyone else some peace at least."

"Depends," growled Kaid, one hand clasping hers tightly
and shaking it. "You, Dzinae, and Jo, not to mention Kitra,
have to go through some battle-suit drill before then!"

"Fair enough, but remember, all three of us have your
knowledge of the drill," she grinned.

"Nothing replaces experience. Where are the suits now,
Rezac?" Kaid asked, turning to look over his shoulder at his
father.

"Along with the rest of ours, in the Battle Dress room we're
using on the *Soohibo*. Everything we need has been loaded
now," he added. "They'll be ready for us to embark in about
ten minutes or so."

Prime Orbital Station

It looks like a child's gyroscope, he thought, plucking the word
from Carrie's embedded memories as he watched the Orbital
through the main viewscreen.

Built around a vertical spindle, the central levels spread out
in disks around it, the widest being the commercial docking
ring. The blue shimmer of a force field shone in four bands

reaching from top to bottom of the Orbital—bands that could become a solid sphere of protection if necessary.

Right now, the only ships berthed there were the giant *Kz'adul* and several smaller cargo shuttles.

"They may have repaired the clamshell doors at the front, but I see they haven't gotten rid of the blast marks we left on the outside," remarked Tirak, turning to him with a grin.

They were mere spectators on the Bridge right now, leaving the two other crewmembers to the task of controlling the ship.

"*Profit* to Orbital, requesting docking permission," said Mrowan, the current Captain.

"Granted, *Profit*," said the Prime controller. "You've been assigned Bay 3, next to the *Kz'adul*. The Orbital is currently operating under military law. A copy of our rules and regulations will be sent to you before you'll be allowed to debark. It is advised you read them carefully. Ignorance of them will not be accepted as a defense for breaking them."

"Copy that, Orbital. Can you update me on what's new since my last trip?" asked Mrowan.

"Your ship must be powered down completely except for prior to takeoff; no hand weapons can be carried, and don't even look at the armed guards on the main concourse," recited the official. "There's more of the same in the rules."

"Don't know that I can power down until we've fixed the fault in engineering," said Mrowan. "A meteor hit us, holed our hull . . ."

"I know," the official interrupted. "You'll have to take your chances with the Commander of the *Kz'adul,* then. I'll pass your message over to him."

"Take my chances?"

"*Kz'adul's* there to ensure no ships behave in a way that could be construed as a threat to the Orbital. You act in a suspicious manner, break any of the new regs, and he'll torch the *Profit's* ass, blow you right out of the sky. Between you and me, you sneeze around here and it's taken as a plot against our new Emperor," said the official, lowering his voice to a conspiratorial level.

"Like I believe that," retorted Mrowan. "He'd put a hole in the Orbital if he did that! I thought you guys were pacifists."

"Won't harm the Orbital unless you're hooked up to our umbilicals, and you can't do that with your engines running," he pointed out. "Least that's what the new Security Chief on *Kz'adul* says."

"So who . . ."

"Copy that, *Profit*," he was interrupted loudly. "I'll pass the information concerning your engine problems to our Security Chief. We'll withhold the umbilicals until such time as you have fixed the problem and can power down. Be advised we have reports of a meteor storm heading this way. Be alert for possible hull breaches until we activate the force fields."

"Someone must have come in," murmured Tirak. "Probably one of those enhanced people J'korrash told us about."

"Thank you, Orbital. Making our approach now," said Mrowan.

"In one way, I'd hoped not to be right beside the *Kz'adul*," said Kusac. "Solves one problem but creates others for us. Good to know Kezule's meteors are arriving on schedule. We better join the others in the cargo area."

Tirak nodded, and as one, they turned to leave.

Of the Cabbarans, only Annuur and Naacha were unarmored.

"Some skills of our own we will use. Put them at their ease at first," said Annuur.

"Surely you're very vulnerable without armor," said Kusac, accepting his assault rifle from Banner. He'd already stowed his handgun in its recessed holster on the outside of his thigh and made sure his vibro sword was firmly attached to his belt.

"They will keep to the rear as soon as any fighting starts, don't worry," said Tirak. "They're used to combat situations. I told you that the Orbital has never seen any Cabbarans before and that Annuur and Naacha would go out first to lead attention away from us."

"I hadn't forgotten," Kusac said, lifting his helmet and putting it on. As it met the locking ring, he gave it a slight turn, then, as it sealed, he heard the suit's air supply start up.

This helmet, unlike the Sholan ones, was larger, giving him more room inside for the necessary TAC and status displays. Immediately, the HUD lit up, showing him the positions of all his armored team on the right, and on the left, a scrolling status display of his suit. Keeping an eye on it, he turned on the comm system.

"You on-line, yet, Red One?" Banner was asking.

"On-line now, Red Two," he confirmed. "Red Team, check in now."

He waited while they all acknowledged their presence on the comm net.

"Accessing layout on HUD now," he said. "Red Two, Blue One, pull up yours." Having the Orbital's layout at hand throughout the mission would be of immense tactical advantage to him, Banner, and Tirak. They'd split their forces into two teams, each of them leading their own people.

On his HUD, the ghostly green outline of the loading bay and the concourse beyond it appeared. He scrolled through it, accessing the other levels with a punch of his chin on the controls inside the helmet. This had all been checked and rechecked during their flight here, but it never hurt to put it through its paces one more time. In his opinion, technology was wonderful—when it performed as expected.

"Take up positions behind the cargo," he said, satisfied, as the hollow thumps and bangs of the docking umbilical corridor being extended and locking onto the Orbital reverberated through the cargo chamber.

The elevator descended with Mrowan and his crewmate Rroshan. External pickups heard every sound, amplified to the level each individual preferred, so Kusac had no problem hearing Mrowan telling them all had been settled, and though the *Kz'adul* was monitoring them carefully, his crew was clear to start unloading the cargo not already on their own shuttle while he worked on the engine problem.

Though unarmored, the two Cabbarans were wearing comm sets, hooking them into the battle channels on the suits.

"Move out when ready, Annuur," Tirak ordered.

"Affirmative, Captain," murmured the small alien as he and Naacha trotted over to Rroshan at the docking lock.

Now they had to wait until Annuur and Naacha planted the small devices that, when activated, would black out the Orbital's internal comm system for a precious ten minutes, while leaving their own protected one as well as the *Profit* intact. In pouches on their leather harnesses, the two also carried the gas masks they'd need when he and his teams began releasing the sleep-gas canisters.

Mentally, he followed them, watching as if from a distance, the surprise of the few station crew they came across as they made their way through the curved concourse to the port of-fice on the other side. There, the three of them engaged the official they'd spoken to when they docked in conversation regarding the purchase of spares for the *Profit*.

Finally, Annuur's voice broke into his concentration. "De-vices planted and activated successfully, Red One. Rroshan released sleep gas in office. Naacha does same in mess. Secu-rity cameras on five-minute delay to avoid suspicion. I go now to bar area."

"Acknowledged. Good work," he said. "Stay outside the Port Office when finished. Have you an estimate of personnel numbers currently on the Orbital?"

"Few. Forty crew, no other ships. *Kz'adul* crew not allowed on Orbital as our scans showed. Three guards, no more. Out-side elevators leading up to weather platform. Are implants, members of old Imperial guard, officer said."

"Wait for us by ship supplies," ordered Kusac, moving out from behind the cargo crates. "Use stun settings if you can. We want to keep casualties among the ordinary Primes to a minimum. Exiting now, Annuur."

Immediately outside was the Orbital's air lock, a small chamber about ten feet wide and as long as their half of the docking bay. When they'd cycled through that, they stepped out into the spacious loading area, empty except for a couple of forklift vehicles.

Beyond that was the concourse, the ring shaped corridor running around the Orbital off which were the various main-tenance areas, stores, offices, and sleeping accommodations for ships' crews staying over. Living quarters for the station staff and the scientists operating the weather facility were on the level below, accessed by an elevator next to the Port Office that Rroshan was in the process of disabling.

Cautiously Kusac emerged into the corridor, checking in both directions. "Appears clear," he said, gesturing his team to follow him out.

A sudden noise from across the corridor made him spin around, lifting his assault rifle just as Banner's spat. The Prime standing in the open doorway of the public restrooms fell bonelessly to the ground.

"Check it out!" he hissed, annoyed with himself.

Banner, rotating his weapon to gas grenades, was already running over.

"Heading out now," said Tirak as they began to move in the opposite direction.

Kusac acknowledged him. "Jayza, J'korrash, M'yikku, take Life Support as planned, then join Tirak and his team working their way antispinward. We're taking the elevator corridor and transient quarters. Remember to isolate the weather platform level from the sleep gas. Red Team, follow me," he ordered as Banner rejoined them.

"I let off a grenade. If anyone's in there, they're asleep now," his Second said.

Kusac nodded. "M'kou, keep me updated on any Port comm activity," he said, moving off. "Noolgoi, Khadui, cover our rear."

"Aye, Captain," the three Primes murmured.

Slowly, keeping close to the inner wall, Kusac led his team toward the corner where the corridor leading to the elevator up to the weather platform headed down to the Orbital's central hub. Off it were the entrances to the rec room and the dorm—and one of the three guards.

Just at the junction, Kusac stopped, beckoning Banner forward. Making a couple of Brotherhood hand signals, he ordered his Second to fire a gas grenade down the corridor to disable the guard.

"Khadui, cover me," ordered Banner before taking a quick look around the corner.

The guard was facing the elevator. A swift hand signal to Q'almo and the young Prime had crossed the opening and was ready to cover him.

Stepping into full view, he fired the grenade then stepped back out of sight.

It landed at the guard's feet. Startled, the male looked briefly at the object, then, as it began to hiss and release its transparent odorless gas, he turned and charged down the corridor toward them, his gun spraying gouts of energy at the opening.

Khadui began to shoot, changing his load to energy pulses when he saw the stuns were having no effect.

Stepping into the opening again, Banner let loose two precise shots to the rampaging Prime's chest, felling him only feet short of the entrance.

"What the hell is that?" he demanded, kicking the prone alien with the heavy toe of his boot to make sure he was dead.

"I have no idea," said M'kou, venturing around the corner in Kusac's wake to look down at the leather-clad body.

Bending down, he flipped the dead alien over onto his back. Bulking about twice the size of the average Prime male, this one was even larger than Kezule. Lurid tattoos depicting a scene of violence covered the green-skinned skull. The clothing was just as atypical, consisting of a scuffed leather jacket, trousers, and heavy boots.

"One of K'hedduk's gene-altered monstrosities, no doubt," said Kusac, moving past him and the body, rifle held ready.

"Excuse me?" asked Banner.

"There was one on that broadcast from the Prime world, Banner, Jayza, take the rec, M'kou, the dorm. If there's anyone in there, they'll certainly know something's going down," he said, watching the elevator. "Khadui, Q'almo, guard the concourse."

He watched as they hit the access panels, then, as soon as the opening was wide enough, fired gas grenades through it.

"Empty," reported Banner.

"Three, huddled in their beds," said M'kou.

As the door on the dorm closed again, reversing his rifle, Banner hit the access plate hard, smashing it. "Should keep them in there for a bit once the sleep gas wears off."

Kusac grunted approval and, hitting the comm button inside his suit with his chin, called Tirak.

"Finishing up here, Red One," said Tirak. "All stores and supply offices are closed. Place is deserted, it being station night and us the only ship with station leave. Should be at your location in five minutes."

"Copy that. Red Seven, report."

"Are done, Captain," said Annuur. "Bar had six people in, all asleep now. Mess had ten, again sleeping soundly." The little Cabbaran chuckled. "Rroshan returned to ship. We wait for you."

"Join us at the elevator. Red Five, report."

"Red Five. We've finished, Captain. The station general store had only the shopkeeper in it, and he's now sleeping the gas off at the rear. We closed it off. Life Support is pumping the gas through the station except for the weather platform level."

Red Five, join us at the elevator. Good work, everyone."

"Captain," interrupted M'kou. "Someone on the *Kz'adul* is ___ng to reach the Port Office. They're going to get suspicious ___en no one answers."

"Then reply. You're the diplomatic one, use your skills and ___ving it," Kusac ordered, tuning into the Orbital's channel. "I'll ___nitor."

"Aye, Captain," M'kou answered, a tinge of apprehension ___ his voice.

The call concerned the approaching meteor storm. The *Kz'adul* wanted to be patched through to the weather staff for ___ update on whether they were triggering the force field and ___ they would need to undock prior to this.

"Negative, *Kz'adul*," said M'kou, his voice now holding all ___he confidence Kusac could want. "We have a problem with ___ne of the force field generators right now. Our engineers are ___ealing with it. It's not anticipated the storm will come close ___nough to cause any damage to the station."

"Thank you, Orbital, but our Security wishes to confirm ___his with the weather staff."

"Not possible, *Kz'adul*. Weather staff has advised us not ___o disturb them at this time. They have their hands full right ___ow."

Kusac could hear angry low-level voices discussing the ___natter at the *Kz'adul's* end, but eventually the comm opera- ___or came back with, "Thank you, Orbital. *Kz'adul* out."

Around him, the Prime members of his team let out a col- ___ective sigh of relief.

"You should have more faith in M'kou," chided Kusac, ___rinning. "Nicely handled, Lieutenant."

"Thank you, Captain," M'kou murmured.

He felt the other's surge of pleasure at his mild praise.

"Your opinion matters to me, Captain," said M'kou quietly, ___rigging a private channel to him.

He started and looked around at the young male, surprised ___he other had read his body language so easily even when he ___vas wearing bulky battle armor.

"Thanks," he murmured.

Leaving Tirak's team to guard the lower level, Kusac and ___is group headed up to the next one where the Orbital's main ___ower, avionics, scanners, and life support were located.

"Stay alert," he warned them as the elevator came to a "Don't take it for granted that everyone is immobilized. guards might well be carrying gas masks and be alerted to (presence."

The elevator opened onto a ten-foot circular corridor. D. rectly opposite it was the door to the command office. Th corridor to the only elevator accessing the actual weathe platform lay just beyond it, as did the last of the guards. Tw air lock irises gave it added security.

"Banner, Khadui, J'korrash, take the office. The rest c you, with me as planned," he ordered as he thumbed the doo open, rifle poised in case anyone waited outside.

The corridor was clear except for a huddled form lyin near the open office doorway.

Banner darted forward, closely followed by J'korrash an Khadui. While he bent to check the prone body, they checke out the inside of the office.

"Empty," they confirmed, moments later.

"This one's out cold," confirmed Banner, standing up.

Kusac and the others emerged, making their way slowly t the air lock at the entrance to the corridor.

"M'kou, stay with me. Banner, take your unit and chec the rest of the level," he ordered, taking up a covered positio to one side of the air lock as M'kou passed him to take th other side.

Their search was rapid and confirmed that all other stai members on duty had been rendered unconscious like the on in the main corridor.

"Ready?" asked Kusac as he prepared to thumb open th iris.

"Ready," confirmed Banner and M'kou.

The iris petals wound back silently into their frame, reveal ing the prone body of another of the gene-altered guards.

"One down, one to go," muttered J'korrash.

"All clear below," Tirak's voice murmured inside Kusac helmet as he made the first of his regular updates.

"Copy," Kusac replied as they silently covered the twelv feet to the next iris.

Taking up the same positions, they repeated the procedur Once again, they met the slumped figure of one of the guard

Bending down, Kusac set his rifle to stun and at close rang zapped the guard where he lay. "Banner, go back, do the sam to the other one. I'm not taking any chances," he said. "The way that one on the lower level withstood the gas had me worried. They might throw off the effects too soon."

"How can they?" J'korrash asked. "With the gas in the life-support system, it's a constant feed into their air supply until we turn it off."

"Kusac's right," said Banner, reluctantly. "One mistake could see us all dead."

"Blue One, elevator area is clear. Send Annuur and Naacha up now, and two people to cover the corridor."

"Acknowledged, Red One."

By the time the two unarmored Cabbarans arrived in the company of Manesh and Sheeowl, they had the elevator door open and waiting for them.

"We'll need to go up in two trips. You sure you can handle the weather controls if need be until Emperor Zsurtul arrives?" asked Kusac.

"Affirmative, Captain," said Annuur, trotting past them into the elevator. "Naacha, you come next. I go this trip. Will take a few minutes to scan the system, discover how it differs, then we can take over. If any damage, can repair, but longer that will take us."

"Let's just make sure there's no damage," said Banner, joining him.

"Agreed," said Kusac as he, followed by J'korrash, Noolgoi, Jayza, and M'kou, got in with them.

As the elevator door opened, they came face-to-face with yet two more of the leather-clad guards.

Jumping to the front of his Primes, Kusac fired instantly, keeping the trigger depressed for several seconds. An arc of energy lanced from his rifle to first one then the other of the two guards, felling them. Beside him, he caught sight of Banner doing the same as his weapon sprayed the room beyond them.

Only one of the guards got off a shot, but crushed together as they were in the elevator, it couldn't miss.

Kusac felt the blast hit him in the chest and staggered slightly backward, but the special coating on his armor deflected it—to Banner.

Cursing himself for growing sloppy and not checking the room out mentally first, he let go of the trigger and scanned the room beyond. No more guards, only one dead and smoking corpse in front of the central control banks and four terrified scientists crouching under their desks. His heart still racing, it took him a couple of deep breaths before it began to beat more normally.

"Vartra's bones," Banner swore quietly as Kusac turned to see that his friend was all right. "Where in L'Shoh's name did they come from? I'm fine," he said, waving Kusac's concern aside. "Thank the Gods the Primes put Sholan coatings on our suits, though!"

A faint wisp of smoke hovered over the control bank, and the section beyond began to spark.

"Annuur, get onto that," snapped Kusac, stepping out into the room. "M'kou, speak to them. Reassure them, tell them why we're here. Noolgoi, get Naacha up here on the double! We have damage to the weather system! J'korrash, see to the comms. Make sure no one can contact K'oish'ik without our permission."

"Aye, sir!"

"You jumped in front of us," said M'kou, following him. "Why, Captain?"

"Our suits have reflective coatings that absorb most of the damage from energy weapons," he said, going over to check on the dead guards. "It wears down, of course, but I knew your armor couldn't take a point-blank shot like that. And we had Annuur with us. See if you can find some kind of fire extinguisher, Jayza. Put him out. Then find some cupboard—they must have some—to stow him and get the air changed in here," he said, standing up. "The smell must be appalling."

"Aye, Captain."

CHAPTER 5

KEZULE was waiting for them in the docking bay when the shuttle from the *Soohibo*, the Touiban's primary drop ship, landed.

"It'll be good to see the General again," said Zsurtul as he and Valden waited at the air lock with Kaid, Dzaka, Garras, and Jurrel.

"I'm sure it will," murmured Kaid.

The air lock opened, and they began to move down the ramp. Kaid's first impression was one of organized chaos. From several directions he could hear the hiss and spit of welding torches; people and machines bustled about, loading the one-person fighters into launching gantries set at either side of the bay. No one cast even so much as a curious glance in their direction.

Standing nearby was a shuttle where a small unit of black-clad guards waited, General Kezule prominent in their center. Unlike them, Kezule and his escort were unarmored and unarmed.

At the General's signal, they marched crisply forward, stopping some ten feet from the end of the ramp. Springing to attention, they saluted Kaid as Kezule, accompanied by two people, one obviously female, stepped forward to greet them.

Kezule inclined his head in a respectful gesture to Zsurtul.

"Enlightened One," he said. "My condolences on the death of your father. He will be avenged, I promise you. Meanwhile, we welcome you and your companions to the *N'zishok*."

Slightly startled, Zsurtul glanced obliquely at Kaid, as if for reassurance. Kaid merely flicked an ear at him.

"Thank you, General Kezule," Zsurtul said, his tone a little uncertain. "It's good to see you again. I don't want any ceremony. Please, have your people stand at ease. This is my friend Valden. I think you know the others."

Kezule gestured, and the honor guard relaxed. "As you wish, Prince Zsurtul. It is good to see you again—and looking so well, if I might say. This is my daughter, Lieutenant Zhalmo, who's been assigned to you as your personal bodyguard. And my son, Head of our Security, Lieutenant M'zynal."

Kaid realized he wasn't alone in picking up the Prince's instant interest in Zhalmo as the young male stepped forward and took hold of her hand in a very courtly way.

"My bodyguard?" Zsurtul said, smiling and bowing. "Hard to think of one so beautiful performing such a lethal function."

"A necessary one, Highness," said Zhalmo, trying to look anywhere but at the Prince as the color of her face darkened in obvious embarrassment.

Kaid watched, shocked to find himself as amused as Kezule.

"Kaid, we meet again," Kezule said, breaking the silence as Zsurtul finally let go of Zhalmo's hand.

He glanced briefly at Carrie, giving her a nod and saying, "I remember you," before turning his attention to Dzaka.

"We met on Shola, in my Liege's house," said Dzaka, his voice chilly.

"My son, Dzaka," said Kaid. "And Jurrel, another of our Brothers."

"The young warrior I took prisoner along with the child," said Kezule. "You have my apologies and my respect, for what it's worth. I took no pleasure in taking either of you hostage. It was a necessary action at the time. I'm sure if the positions had been reversed, you'd have done the same. You remained a worthy adversary, Dzaka, just like that young female of yours."

"Enough of this idle chat," said Kaid, breaking into their conversation.

"Time grows short," agreed Kezule, glancing back at him. "I see you're all armored. Kusac left suits for you and Carrie. They're from the *Venture*. Prince Zsurtul, if you'll accompany

Zhalmo and M'zynal to the armory at the rear of this bay, they have a suit waiting for you."

"Valden, you and Jurrel help Dzaka load the tunnel remotes on our shuttle. I'll go with the Prince," said Carrie as Zsurtul and Valden began to walk off.

"We'll stick to the suits we have," said Kaid.

"They have Prime modifications, including their style of helmet," said Kezule.

"The ones with the faceplate filter that causes nausea when others look at it?" Kaid's attention had been caught, despite himself.

"The same," agreed Kezule, gesturing to the shuttle. "Shall we talk in there while we wait for Prince Zsurtul? I can have the suits brought to the shuttle for you."

Kaid considered it as he followed the General.

"I'm hardly about to sabotage the suits of my allies, Kaid, not when I need their continued help."

"Have them sent over," he said as they began to walk up the ramp. He didn't want Kezule doing him any favors—even if the suits belonged to them anyway.

Kaid waited until they were in the passenger area before giving vent to his anger. "You had no right to have Kusac tortured!" he snarled as Kezule sat down in one of the seats.

"I didn't torture him, and he tried to kill me."

"You kept him and his son hostage!" Kaid loomed over Kezule, ears flattened to his skull in a show of anger that was just short of how he really felt.

"No. I kept Shaidan hostage for a short time. I needed Kusac's help, Kaid, and he wouldn't have given it willingly. None of you would have. Don't forget that I also rescued all your children and released the rest of them to Kusac."

"That doesn't excuse what you did!"

"On the contrary, what I did was totally justified. He tried to kill me, and though he failed, he did succeed in shooting my son with one of those drug pellets. His crew was making illegal and potentially lethal weapons, obviously with his knowledge. I did what any rational commander would have done. I held Kusac responsible for his own actions and those of his crew, and I punished him accordingly."

Kaid's hand closed on the headrest of Kezule's seat, his powered gloves puncturing the cover as he clenched his hand. "He'd just been shot and seriously wounded in the leg with a pulse rifle," he said, lowering his voice. "You could have killed him. Banner told me what that tape held—you could still have caused him incalculable mental damage!"

"He was unconscious within minutes of the tape beginning—I know because he was being constantly monitored."

Kezule hit Kaid's arm aside and stood up, almost nose-to-nose with him. "Do you take me for a fool, Kaid? I needed Kusac alive, but I had to punish him! I couldn't touch his crew, that would have been unjust—they were only following his orders!"

"When you two are done posturing and threatening each other, maybe I can get to the point you've missed, Kaid," said Carrie from behind them.

Both males turned their heads to look at her.

"Where is Kusac's son?" she demanded. "Hand him over to us now!"

"His son is safe with my daughter and wife," said Kezule. "Kusac left him in our care, I can't give him to you."

"I don't believe you," said Kaid automatically.

"You'll see Kusac at the Orbital," said Kezule. "You can ask him yourself then. What would I gain from lying to you? I need your help and your trust to regain our world for Zsurtul. Kusac has given me his. Do you think I would risk all that for spite?"

Kaid reluctantly stepped back, letting his arms fall to his sides. "You're right," he said, forcing back his anger. "You're many things, Kezule, but not foolish. I apologize for doubting your word." The words almost stuck in his throat.

"Understandable, under the circumstances," murmured Kezule, glancing around at Carrie standing behind him. "I trust you're satisfied too? Or will you once again threaten to rip the knowledge from my mind?"

Without warning, Carrie's armored fist flew out, landing Kezule a whack on the side of his jaw.

"Don't you ever," she ground out, a snarl of rage in her voice as she cranked her arm back for a second blow, "touch *any* of my cubs again!"

Kaid barely took in what was happening before Kezule had recovered his balance from the first blow and had grasped hold of her fist in his hand, pinioning it there and effectively holding her still.

"Burn it!" the Valtegan swore, putting his other hand to

his bleeding mouth. "You Sholans have too much emotion at times! Much as I deserved your anger, Madam Aldatan, I didn't deserve that! I never harmed your cub!"

"Carrie! In Vartra's name, stop it!" exclaimed Kaid, grabbing for her as she struggled against Kezule's grip.

The General let her go instantly, leaving her to Kaid as he went to find the restroom at the rear of the shuttle.

"Dammit, what the hell did you do that for?" he demanded as she stopped struggling.

"He kidnapped Kashini, and held Shaidan hostage—that's twice he's had my cubs at his mercy," she snapped. "Never again! He'll do well to learn just whose wrath he faces for that!"

"You could have broken his jaw with that punch," he said. "Dammit! Think of the consequences if you had!"

"Serves him right," she growled, unrepentant.

"Don't touch him again," he warned, "or I'll send you back on the shuttle to the *Tooshu*! I mean it! I'm going to see how he is."

Kezule was washing his mouth out, still spitting some blood. The side of his face was swelling and changing color despite the cold pack he'd taken from the first aid cabinet there.

"I apologize for my mate's behavior," said Kaid awkwardly. "Are you badly injured?"

Kezule straightened up, the cold pack pressed to his jaw. "I'll survive," he said, his voice sounding slightly muffled. There was a faint glint of humor in his eyes. "Lost a tooth, but luckily we regrow them. I wondered what you both saw in that not-so-fragile-looking Human female. Now I know. Looks like your domestic life is as stormy as mine."

Kaid glowered at him. "Don't get me wrong, Kezule. Had it been any time but now, I wouldn't have stopped her, armored or not. But we can't have you going out of here looking like that, no matter how much personal satisfaction I get from seeing it," he said, sending all manner of mental threats and anger in Carrie's direction.

Moments later she came storming into the small washroom herself. "Out of my way," she ordered Kaid, pushing him aside. "Since you're so worried about what people will think, I'll deal with it."

Even Kezule backed away from her.

"Don't worry, I'm not about to hit you again," she said,

grinning evilly at him as she began to take off her gloves. "I can't promise this will work, but I'll try healing it for you. That is, if you've enough courage to let me try."

Kezule's eyes darkened in momentary anger as he came forward, taking the cold pack away from his face. "No one accuses me of lacking courage, Madam."

Tossing her gloves to Kaid, she reached up and grasped Kezule by the other side of his jaw, pulling his face down closer to hers, ignoring his small exclamation of pain.

"Nice knuckle marks," she murmured before placing her right hand over the swollen and cut area and closing her eyes.

Kaid watched with his mind as well as his eyes, sensing what she was trying to do.

I need to draw on you for energy, she sent to him. *This isn't easy for me. I haven't done this successfully since my days on Keiss with Kusac.*

Take what you need. We can't have Kezule going out of the shuttle in this state. I know he deserved it, but . . .

I know, she said. *We're trying to gain an ally here.*

Kezule's face suddenly took on a look of total shock, and he almost jerked away from her. At the same moment, Kaid felt a sudden surge of energy passing from himself to her, and then it was over. Letting go of Kezule, she slumped back against him momentarily then straightened up.

"It'll still hurt," she said tiredly, "but you deserve to suffer some of the pain at least. You had no right to involve our cubs in your fight against us!"

Kezule looked in the mirror, putting a hand up to run it unbelievingly across his now normal cheek and jaw. He winced briefly. "A female of many talents," he murmured, turning back to them. "You may not think it, Carrie Aldatan, but I am a person of honor and scruples. Involving either your daughter or Kusac's son wasn't a decision I took lightly. And at no time did I ever intend harm to either of them. Shaidan was treated the same as my own daughter."

"My trust of you will come very slowly, Kezule, if at all," she said. "If I can't see Shaidan, I want to talk to him."

"Again, I must refuse. I don't know what the Captain has told him about the rest of his family. I can't take the risk that he knows nothing about you."

"You can't . . ."

"He's right, Carrie," said Kaid reluctantly. "We can't interfere. He's Kusac's son."

And quite possibly mine! she retorted.

We don't know that.

With a low growl of anger, she snatched her gloves from Kaid, then turned and walked out of the restroom back to the passenger area.

"The things I do for my people," Kezule muttered, throwing the cold pack into the waste bin and following Kaid out.

"Life gets complicated when you really have to lead, doesn't it?" said Kaid, feeling a fleeting sympathy for the General.

Prince Zsurtul, now wearing one of the gray Prime battle suits, arrived with the others in tow as they rejoined Carrie.

"I trust your talk was pleasant," Zsurtul said, looking from one to the other and frowning slightly.

"Informative," said Kezule blandly. "I had better take my leave, Majesty. Your third bodyguard is with Captain Aldatan—his name is Q'almo. Kaid, I'll have the suits sent over in a few minutes. May all our Gods be with you on this mission."

"And with you, General," said Zsurtul.

Zhalmo accompanied her father, waiting for the others to be out of earshot before stopping. "You know you said we'd know our mate when we met the one," she said softly.

Startled, Kezule turned to look at her. "Excuse me?"

"I think I've just found mine."

"The Prince? You can't be serious, Zhalmo! He's got too much drone blood in his ancestry."

"Has he? Maybe he only looks like he has," she said with a slight smile as she turned to leave.

Giyarishis had been monitoring the meeting carefully, pleased that the emotions of all had been so highly charged that they'd spared little attention to their surroundings. Now he closed down his small section of Unity and pondered what he'd learned.

The Hunter's intrusion through the female Human on behalf of the Sand-dweller would have been applauded not so long ago, but now they wanted him to become more aggressive, less caring of others. Pushing him against his nature would not be easy. Too much and he'd notice, as would those around him. A word too soon would alert him to his unaccustomed behavior, make him change back. Too little pushing and the desired result would not be achieved. He'd need to watch him for moments when he felt anger and build gradually on those until the desired behavior pattern was so established that even censure from others wouldn't alert him to what was happening.

This was not something he particularly wanted to do, but, as always, he would do the Camarilla's will to the best of his ability.

"What prompted you to heal Kezule?" Kaid asked her when he'd gotten them underway to K'oish'ik's moon, behind which they were to conceal themselves.

"Kusac," she said shortly. "He sent to me, told me to try."

"Kusac?" He turned to look at her in surprise. "You mean he ..."

"No, he just sent that to me, nothing more. I couldn't reply." Her voice had the tone she used when she didn't want to talk and Kaid knew it was wiser to leave her alone.

Prime Orbital

Under the watchful eyes of their two civilian engineers as well as six of Kusac's people, the weather platform was operating again. Annuur and Naacha had finished repairing the damaged unit and were now back on the *Profit* with the rest of their sept.

J'korrash had gone back to the lower-level Life Support and, taking the gas feed off-line, had purged the air supply. Now it was safe for them all to breathe.

Kusac, Banner, and M'kou had taken over the Port Office and were sitting there waiting for Zsurtul to contact them. M'kou was busy talking to the *Kz'adul* on their private gossip channel, posing as the Port Officer. Already he'd gained a lot of useful information.

Tirak came in, rifle slung over his shoulder, helmet hanging from one hand. "The Orbital's secure," he said quietly. "The lower accommodation level has been totally isolated. We've rounded up all the personnel on the upper levels, apart from the scientists on duty, and they're in the rec room under guard. Sheeowl's prepping the shuttle next to the *Profit* now."

Kusac flicked an ear in acknowledgment and checked his suit's wrist comm, for effect rather than because he needed to. He could sense them out by K'oish'ik's moon. "We should be hearing from Kaid any time now."

"Alpha One to Beta One. Checking in."

"That's them," said Banner, sitting up and looking over to M'kou, who instantly put the *Kz'adul* on hold.

"Alpha One, acknowledged.," said Kaid. "We have the first message available for your patron now. Contact is Shikku, in the science lab."

"Understood, Beta One. Patch him to us now. We're ready to reply."

"Be ready to take a live feed to the Orbital if need be," Kusac warned in an undervoice as M'kou linked the *Kz'adul's* private channel through to Kaid's shuttle.

"How do you know this'll work?" asked Banner.

"Prince Zsurtul was well known both in the Court and to the staff on the *Kz'adul*, especially those in the sciences because he was into everything, like any cub," said Kusac. "I suppose you could call him a bit of a rebel in his culture—he tried to be one of the people when he could. He was well liked by everyone, I'm told."

"Shikku, you didn't come to see me on your last shore leave," said Zsurtul's slightly reproachful voice. "Are you well? It's been a long time since we last spoke."

"Highness? Is it you?" The voice was hushed, disbelieving. "Where are you?"

"It's me, Shikku, and I'm close by."

"Highness, wherever you are, you must leave, now! Believing you safe is all that's keeping most of us going!"

"I am safe and with allies. We need your help, Shikku."

"I'll do what I can, Highness, but that won't be much. We all learned early on that we couldn't stand against the new Emperor. He's brought back the Inquisitors—and there are collaborators everywhere who report the slightest thing to them."

"The *Kz'adul*, how many people loyal to K'hedduk are on board? How many warriors?" asked the Prince.

"Only a dozen or so are loyal to K'hedduk—everyone knows who they are. We have five of his thugs on board—large and violent genetically altered peasants with not much intelligence that are fiercely loyal to him. There's always one of them and one of the implants on duty on the Bridge, two in Engineering, and two more in the main air lock to the Orbital."

"I need you to organize those you trust, Shikku. We're going to reclaim the *Kz'adul*."

"We can't fight the Emperor's soldiers, Highness!" The voice sounded shocked.

"You won't have to," said Zsurtul calmly. "I told you I have allies with me. You and your people only need to do two things for us, and we'll see to the rest. First, make sure the collaborators are locked in their rooms—it is ship's night there now, isn't it?"

"Yes, Highness, and on K'oish'ik."

"You will need to damage the door-locking mechanisms outside the collaborators' rooms, and post two people there as guards to make sure they don't get out."

"We can do that," confirmed Shikku, his voice firming again. "What else, Highness?"

"We need to dock a shuttle with the *Kz'adul* to get our soldiers on board. You'll have to create a diversion to get the guard off the Bridge. We'll be using the portside emergency docking bay on the fourteenth level."

"That could take over an hour to set up . . . The soldiers, are they Sholans?"

It was Zsurtul's turn to be surprised. "Yes, some are. How did you know that?"

Shikku chuckled. "We know you were on their world, Highness, and prayed you'd remained safely with them."

"I couldn't remain there while my people are suffering, Shikku," murmured Zsurtul. "The Sholans are accompanying some of our own warriors—General Kezule's commandos. Give them all the assistance you can. In fact, please download the deck plans of the *Kz'adul* to them."

"We will, Highness. I'll get back to you as soon as I have word." This time there was real hope and enthusiasm in the Prime's voice.

"Thank you, Shikku. I hope when you next have shore leave, you keep your word to come and visit me."

"I will, Highness."

The channel went quiet as Shikku signed off.

M'kou stirred and looked to Kusac for further orders.

"Ask him to address the Orbital now."

"Greetings, Kusac. I heard your request," said Zsurtul. "What do you need me to say to them?"

"Just that the Orbital is in the hands of forces loyal to yourself, Prince Zsurtul. Let them know those in custody will be released once the City and Palace of Light are in your control," he said, raising his voice.

"You have them imprisoned?"

"We don't know who's loyal to you. Until we can sort them out, I'm not prepared to take chances on any sabotage. They're only confined to the recreation room and the lower living level—they have adequate food and water available."

"I see," said Zsurtul, obviously relieved. "I'll speak to them, of course."

"You handle it, M'kou," said Kusac quietly, getting to his feet. "I've one or two things I need to see to. I'll be back shortly."

"Need any help?" asked Banner, preparing to get up.

"No, you can't help me with this," he said. "I'm going next door to the sick bay for peace and quiet to do a little work, that's all."

He picked up Banner's instant concern and stopped beside him on his way out. "I'm fine. I want you to see everyone gets a chance for a quick meal break now. Zsurtul's end will take an hour at least, as he said. If you like, you can bring me something to eat in about fifteen minutes."

"I'll get right on that," Banner nodded.

Putting his helmet on the medic's desk, he sat down and began taking off his armored gloves. Already he'd begun mentally reciting the Litany for Relaxation. He wanted to see if he could make contact with the Sholan hostages on the Prime world below. Before they began the main mission, it made sense to find out if they were still alive and to glean any information he could from them, especially their location. And avoid talking to Kaid, he admitted to himself. Part of him was dreading that meeting because he knew Carrie would be there too.

An oval paperweight carved to look like a curled beast drew his attention. Closer inspection showed the creature was some form of reptile, sinuous, scaled, with four legs and a tail that, as he turned the object around, looked to be almost as long at the body. The gaping mouth had an impressive array of teeth. Cast in some yellow alloy, it was indeed a work of art. It most closely resembled the small lizards found in old brick or stone work in the summer on his estate. Turning it over in his hand, idly he wondered how large the original was and if it even still existed on the world below. Kezule had said something about the civil war fifteen hundred years ago having caused the extinction of many native animals as the starving population ate anything that moved.

He turned his mind inward, relaxing completely before reaching out for the two captive Brothers. As far as he knew, he'd never met them, but among so many Prime minds, theirs should stand out.

Lowering his mental shields, slowly, he allowed himself to sense the minds below. Despite his care, the sudden burst of noise was deafening, making him clench his hands in real pain. The sound of their thoughts hissed and spat and crackled through his mind like white noise from a radio receiver.

Automatically his barriers went up, cutting off the contacts. He'd allowed his search to be too general. Trying again, he narrowed the mental bandwidth to one he knew Sholan thoughts operated within, then widened it a fraction.

The noise was still intense but less so than before. Old Human sayings about needles in haystacks came to mind, but he pushed his random thoughts aside and concentrated on finding two or three sparks in the morass of sound that were indisputably Sholan.

A flicker there—different from the others. He latched onto it, discarding the rest, narrowing his search to its band alone.

Shamgar stumbled, holding onto the chair in their narrow cell for balance. As he straightened up, he stiffened, ears flattening to his skull.

"What's up?" asked Vayan. "Stubbed your toe?"

"No, I'm . . . being spoken to," he said almost inaudibly.

"Stop clowning around, Shamgar," said Vayan. "I'm not in the mood for a dose of your humor right now."

Shamgar didn't reply. Instead he made his way, slightly stiff legged, toward their tiny window and looked out into the courtyard beyond.

"Gun turrets at positions 1 hour, 14 hours, 17 hours, and 22 hours," he said, his voice sounding flat and expressionless

"Shamgar!" his friend hissed, sitting up on his bed. "This isn't amusing! It's downright weird!"

"Yes," said Shamgar before collapsing in an unconscious heap on the cell floor.

With a shudder, Kusac withdrew from the unconscious Brother and slumped back exhausted in the chair. He hadn't intended to be so rough with Shamgar, but it had taken a great deal of mental energy to reach him, and there hadn't been much left for subtlety. He'd need the food Banner was bringing to boost his energy levels again.

A tap on the door and M'kou entered, carrying three bowls of maush on a tray.

"I thought I'd join you," the Prime youth said coming over to the desk. "Banner is getting us food. J'korrash is on comm duty now." He set the tray down and handed Kusac his drink before grabbing a nearby chair.

Kusac accepted it gratefully, realizing he was still holding the paperweight in his hand. "What kind of beast is this, M'kou?" he asked, passing it over to him.

M'kou examined it for a moment. "I really can't tell, Captain. It's too badly damaged." His voice had a flat quality about it that was unusual for him.

"Very amusing. So what is it?" he asked, taking a sip of the drink.

"I'm not making a joke, Captain," he said, passing it back to him. "See for yourself."

The metal appeared to have been melted, become pliable, malleable to the point where it had been squashed in someone's hand—his. On one side, clear as day, were the imprints of his fingers, complete with claw tips.

Startled, he glanced up at M'kou.

"You did the same to a chair in the briefing room on Kij'ik," said the other carefully. "My guess, from what remains visible of the beast, is that it's a norrta, a burrowing lizard that exists on the surface of our world."

The door began to open and without a second thought,

Kusac stuffed it into a small compartment on his left thigh armor.

"I'll help Banner," said M'kou, jumping up, obviously relieved not to have to discuss it further.

Kz'adul

Two hours later, their shuttle attached to the exterior of the large Prime ship, they were waiting on their side of the air lock.

"Rifles on stun," Kusac ordered, pulling up the deck plans, "except for those enhanced thugs. Shoot to kill them outright. No point in taking chances. Remember there are collaborators on board. Anyone suspicious, stun them. We can sort it out later. M'kou, open the air lock."

Inside, the *Kz'adul* was quiet, the lighting so subdued it was almost on emergency power.

"Looks like our side's plan is on course," said Tirak quietly to him as they emerged. "Hope they've made sure to lock all the doors on our route."

"I'm sure they have," said Kusac.

Keeping close to the walls on either side, they made their way carefully down the deserted corridor to the first access hatch they needed. Shikku had arranged for an altercation to happen in one of the cargo bays at the rear of the main landing bay, a location close to Engineering and the main air lock. Trouble there should bring two of the four guards running. The one on the Bridge would be lured away by the fire alarm from the Officers' Mess on the same level. Their hatch was a service one that would bring them out in the adjacent cargo bay. The signal for them to attack would be the flickering of the main lighting in there.

"Good hunting," Kusac said to Tirak as he and his team halted.

"Good hunting, Captain," said Tirak, sketching a rough salute to his helmet before he led his family deeper into the ship to the hatch they needed. They were headed up to the mess kitchen to deal with the Bridge guard. This time, the Cabbarans had remained on the Orbital.

Noolgoi moved forward to open the hatch, swinging the door wide. Inside, a corridor just wide enough for them in their suits split off from a central well to the left and right. In the well itself, a rotating mechanism brought a small platform into view every thirty seconds, one that then sank below the level of the deck they were on, taking repair crews and their equipment down to the lower decks and access corridors.

"IR filters on," ordered Kusac. "Down four levels, then step off into the side corridor till I join you. We'll form up in Fire units as we exit. Banner, go first," he said, clapping him on the shoulder. "Noolgoi, you're last. Close the hatch behind you. Move out."

While waiting, he ran a quick check on his suit's combat systems, scanning the telltales on his HUD for each member of his team, triggering the autotracking system and the targeting grid before turning them off again. When it was his turn, he stepped onto the platform and grabbed hold of the handgrip, turning around as he sank slowly down to the level they needed.

Crates had been stacked to give them cover when they exited the hatch. Just beyond those they could see that the dividing wall between the cargo bays had been retracted at one section.

His people deployed, Kusac called Q'almo on his comm.

"Red One in position, Base."

"Copy. Informing contact now."

Strident voices were coming from the bay beyond, getting louder by the minute. One voice, deeper and harsher than the others, rang out, the words indistinct but the intention more than clear. Kusac braced himself, opening his mental shields just enough to read the situation while signaling his people to be ready.

As the lights flickered twice, a shot rang out, followed by a second harsh voice demanding silence.

"Move out!" snapped Kusac, gesturing Banner to go first. "Two guards. One dead ahead, other at 2 o'clock from him."

In a rolling advance, darting from cover to cover, both Fire units headed for the opening. Noolgoi was first in, followed by Kusac on the other side. Kusac's shot took the guard immediately ahead of him in the upper chest, sending him flying backward. As the other began to turn, a look of shock on his face, Noolgoi's shot hit him in the legs.

As he fell, the guard's weapon came up and a shot spat out. Without even thinking, Kusac lunged for Banner, ramming him aside while letting off a long pulse of energy that severed the guard's arm and went on to burn its way through his torso, cutting off the ascending shriek of agony midcry. They hit a stack of packing crates that disintegrated under their combined weight, sending them sprawling on the deck.

The civilian Primes scattered as a third guard came charging into the bay. He didn't get far. The blast from four energy rifles hit him, sending him crashing back the way he'd come.

J'korrash ran to help him and Banner up from the remains of the shattered crates while the others kept watch.

Getting to his feet, Kusac punched a private channel to Noolgoi. "Next time, when I say kill, do it," he snarled angrily before closing it.

"Clear these civilians out and stay alert! There's one more guard, and he knows we're here."

The fifteen Primes huddled behind the crates eased themselves cautiously into the open. Banner grabbed one of them and pointed to the injured crewmember lying in the middle of the floor retching.

"Take him with you," he said.

Pale and shaking, the male scurried over to help his fallen workmate.

"Just what we need, a shipwide hunt," Kusac muttered in disgust. His anger was dissipating, leaving in its place a small residue of shock over how easily he'd almost lost his Second.

"Thanks," said Banner. "Didn't see that rifle coming up."

"Neither did I. I sensed it." He clasped Banner's arm to take the sting out of his terse reply. "Let's get after that fourth guard."

"Aye."

Carefully they began to pick their way around the dead bodies. The sound of someone dry-retching stopped them.

"Vartra's Bones!" swore Banner. "Noolgoi! Deep breaths,

dammit! You can't throw up in your suit—you'll choke on it!"

The sounds got worse.

"I'm on it, Lieutenant!" said M'yikku, shouldering his rifle. Swiftly he began unfastening Noolgoi's helmet, pulling it off and holding it while the young male turned and staggered to the nearest crate. Holding onto it, he was violently sick.

"Maybe that meal break was a mistake," muttered Kusac, signaling Khadui and M'kou to go cover the doorway.

"We're lucky he's the only one," said Banner, guarding their rear with Jayza. "Considering how few of them have seen real combat."

"There is that." Unspoken was the thought that at least they didn't need to worry about their own people.

"Got him in time, Captain," said M'yikku, reaching down to grab a piece of stray packing waste and handing it to his brother. "He's cleaning himself up now."

"Get that helmet on, Noolgoi!" he said angrily. "We're losing time, putting innocents at risk!"

"Yes, sir," the youth gulped, grabbing for his helmet.

Banner exchanged a grin with him as cautiously, on Q'almo's relayed instructions, they made their way along the scuffed access corridor to the main air lock. On the way, Kusac had him call Tirak, giving him a terse warning about their firefight and the remaining guard. The U'Churian and his team were still en route to the Officers' Mess area.

Constantly scanning ahead, Kusac held up his arm and abruptly halted them.

"He's just beyond the junction, with a hostage. There're half a dozen other civs with him. Banner, set for wide-angle stun. Take them both, and as the hostage falls, I'll kill the guard. J'korrash, M'yikku, cover us. Single shots, kill anyone who looks threatening. Noolgoi, stun any Prime civs who get in our way. We can't let him get onto the Orbital."

Slowly, carefully, they inched their way to the junction, hearing the curses of the remaining guard and cries of pain from his hostage.

Anger filled him, but he controlled it, lifting his arm to signal to the rest of his team.

Moments later they erupted into the corridor. The large guard towered over the Prime civilian, who, face cut and bloodied, was being dragged toward the air lock. Several other Primes beyond them were attempting to block his way by their sheer presence alone.

"Duck!" yelled Banner as he fired, his beam overlapping his targets and catching a bystander.

A split second later, as the hostage began to fall and the guard stiffened, Kusac shot using a sustained burst.

It caught the guard's upper chest, the splash hitting him on the neck and face, flinging him into the midst of the fleeing Primes and sending them all sprawling.

Following, Kusac stood over the charred remains, making sure the warrior guard was dead before reaching down to easily flip him off the two civilians trapped beneath.

"See to your injured," he ordered. "The hostage is only stunned. There're three bodies back in the cargo bays—bag them all, and get this one down there with the others."

Flipping channels, he called Q'almo. "Red One to Base. Mission accomplished. What's Blue's status?"

"Blue's mission accomplished also. They have the guards restrained and are bringing them in now."

"Negative on that, Base. I ordered termination of all guards. We do not have the facilities to restrain them effectively."

"Guards are unconscious. They're being taken to *Kz'adul's* detention facility."

Kusac snarled softly to himself and grabbed one of the Primes. "Take me to the detention area now!"

"Alive, the collaborators can release them," he said to Banner as they hurriedly followed their guide to the nearest elevator. "I'm taking no risks."

"I said nothing," said Banner.

"Didn't need to, I read you loud and clear."

"Tactically, I agree with you, but killing them in cold blood . . . kinda sticks in the throat."

"How often do you get second chances in this game?" he asked.

"Point taken."

They met up with Tirak outside the detention block. One of the guards, a large leather-clad one, had just come around and was putting up a ferocious struggle against the two U'Churians holding him.

Slinging his rifle over his shoulder, Kusac sidestepped them and pulled out his sidearm, pressing it just below the male's ear.

For a moment he stopped struggling to look at Kusac.

"You mean to frighten me with that toy, little vermin?" the Prime warrior asked, baring his teeth in a manic grin. "I laugh at your threats!"

"No, I intend to kill you," Kusac said, then pulled the trigger.

"Was that necessary?" asked Tirak as the sound of the muffled shot died away and Sayuk and Nayash eased the limp body to the ground.

"Yes. Primes like him you will kill on sight, as you were ordered to do," he said, closing the distance between him and their other captive. "We haven't the strength or resources to take them captive. They aren't worth your compassion. Those they've beaten, tortured, and killed are."

"He's unconscious and not one of them, Captain!" objected Mrowbay, trying to stop him as he again held the gun to the captive's head.

"Do as Captain Aldatan says," said Tirak. "This is his show, not ours."

Kusac held his fire only long enough to answer Tirak's medic. "He's been implanted with that device on his skull—as I was," he said, his voice cold and inflectionless. "He can be controlled remotely by K'hedduk or anyone with a controller. He dies now, as they all do."

He felt no shred of remorse as he shot the Prime. These, the old Imperial Guard, were volunteers, not victims. Until the City and Palace were once again in sane hands, they died. Then the decision wouldn't be his to make.

Holstering his pistol, he turned to one of the civilians cowering near the air lock, trying to help those who'd been injured.

"When the casualties have been seen to, take these bodies down to the rear cargo bays," he ordered. "We're not here to harm you, only to release you from K'hedduk's rule."

"We know, Captain," said the Prime, standing up and meeting his eyes. "We don't fear you or your people. You're the Sholan allies of our Enlightened One, Prince Zsurtul, May His Name be Revered Forever."

Kusac nodded. "Good. Tell all your people they did a fine

job, and we regret that any were injured." He turned away to speak to Tirak.

Zsadhi . . . The whispered word was no louder than a sigh, so quiet he wasn't sure he'd even heard it.

"We need to get to the Bridge now, Tirak," he said, dismissing it from his mind.

"Follow me," said Tirak.

"Why such concern over them, Banner?" M'kou asked quietly. "These altered Primes are worse than the M'zullian half-breeds. Terminating them is the surest way to eliminate their threat."

"I've no problem with that," said Banner.

"You just didn't expect it of your Captain. There comes a point where one realizes compassion is best kept for those who deserve it. Didn't your Brotherhood perform assassinations in your recent past?"

"Yes," he said shortly. Damn, M'kou was just a little too astute and knowledgeable at times.

"Ah, it's because Captain Aldatan was originally a telepath that it worries you."

"I already told you I don't have a problem with his decision," he said, quickening his speed till he caught up with Jayza and Khadui. "Stay alert. There could still be collaborators on the loose."

"Aye, Lieutenant," said Jayza.

On the Bridge, they were greeted by relieved Primes led by Commander Q'ozoi and Shikku, anxious for news. Kusac had them patch through to Kaid's shuttle so Prince Zsurtul could address them himself. When he'd finished, Shikku contacted the other three ships, informing them the Orbital was expecting an in-bound shuttle with readings from the approaching asteroid shower.

"When we sever comms between all the ships and the planet below, it'll be up to you to contact the other craft and try to subvert them the way we did here," said Kusac, preparing to put his helmet back on. "Or to get them to leave orbit to go after the larger asteroids."

"Won't be easy," said Q'ozoi. "The crews of the *Zasho* and *Shazzu* are predominantly military. The majority of the old Imperial Guard is on board, and some of the implanted

M'zullians like these we've taken prisoner. Only the *Zh'adak*, our brother science ship, is civilian."

"The *Zh'adak* is the same size as this, with the same weapons, so it presents the largest danger. Try it first. We want to avoid fighting them if at all possible."

"But we can't do that!" exclaimed Shikku, shocked. "Shoot our own kind?"

"Then they'll shoot us, and we'll die as we try to retake your Palace for you!" Kusac said harshly. "So make your arguments persuasive!"

Back on the Orbital, they found Q'almo updating Kezule. Once he and Kusac had engaged in a spirited exchange, then fine-tuned the remainder of the two missions, the General signed off, and they waited for word from Kaid. Timing was crucial now. They only had a window of twenty minutes left before they had to take off in the *Profit's* shuttle for the surface of K'oish'ik.

Kusac and Tirak had decided to leave the Cabbarans and Thyasha on the Orbital to ensure all went as planned. Tirak and the rest of his crew were to accompany them down to the planet, then rendezvous with the remainder of the main force once they'd dropped to the planet's surface. Banner and Jayza would leave with Kaid for the Touiban drop ship, *Soohibo*.

"Alpha One requesting docking permission from Orbital Port Office." Kaid's voice.

Smiles broke out among those waiting in the office.

"Granted, Alpha One. You've been allocated the shuttle dock in Bay 3."

"Copy that, Port."

Kusac pushed himself up off his seat. There was no point in delaying the meeting. "Jurrel's with Kaid," he said to Banner. "Shall we go? M'kou, you'd better come too."

Banner's smile lit his eyes as he stood up and grabbed his helmet and gloves. "Be good to see him again."

He followed Banner and Jayza out, tightening his mental shields while mentally reciting any Litany that came to mind in an effort to prepare himself for the ordeal he knew was to come. This would be far worse than the row he'd had to engineer with Kaid before leaving Shola, because for Vartra knew how many weeks, he'd have to see both of them every day.

They waited in the cargo area for them to cycle through. Finally the air lock opened.

Six suited figures, three of them obviously Sholan, three humanoid, stood in a tight group in various stages of removing their helmets.

M'kou was the first to move forward.

"Enlightened One," he murmured, bowing to Zsurtul. "We're relieved to have you safely here."

"Did you doubt it?" the Prince asked with a wide grin, reaching out to draw Zhalmo to his side. "These are my friends, M'kou. Your sister you know, of course." He indicated the others. "Kaid, Carrie, Jurrel, and Valden. This is Lieutenant M'kou, son of General Kezule and Zhalmo's brother."

"Welcome to K'oish'ik Orbital," M'kou said. "I wish these were happier times."

Kusac ignored the exchange. He'd glanced at Kaid, unable to prevent his ears from tipping slightly backward when he did, but now he only had eyes for Carrie as she removed her helmet, letting her long blonde hair spill incongruously over the gray metal of her Prime-made battle armor.

It hurt, Gods but it hurt almost more than he could bear to see her standing so close, smell her scent, and be unable to run to her. With an effort, he turned back to Kaid and found it no easier to look at him.

"We must get Prince Zsurtul up to the weather platform immediately," he said. "The asteroids are nearing us now and will soon begin to penetrate the planetary atmosphere."

Kaid nodded. "We can talk on the way up. Jurrel, no need for you to come."

As he turned to leave, Kusac saw Banner bounce over to his sword-brother and embrace him, the gesture instantly returned. He envied them the simplicity of their relationship.

"So the *Kz'adul* is ours," said Kaid, his voice calm and measured, as he fell into step beside Kusac. "Rather ironic, considering our past. Any problems?"

Kusac was relieved that Kaid was prepared to put personal matters on hold for now. "None. As soon as the Prince changes the weather patterns for us and the ships are isolated from K'oish'ik, the crew on *Kz'adul* will try to subvert the other three ships to our cause. The *Zasho* and *Shazzu* are only 1,000 tonners, formidable enough, but the *Zh'adak* is the same size as the *Kz'adul*, with the same firepower."

"Will your team be taking those ships too?"

"No. Thyasha, Tirak's new comms op, will remain with the four Cabbarans. They'll do it, along with the help of the Primes from the *Kz'adul*."

"Let's hope we get them all."

Kusac nodded to Sheeowl, standing guard at the first elevator. "If we don't, the *Kz'adul* takes off, supposedly for the asteroids, in another twenty minutes. In fact, she'll rendezvous with Kezule and the *Tooshu* behind their moon. The Touibans will transfer enough soldiers to man the weapons and then, if the threat of the large asteroids doesn't draw them off, the *Kz'adul* and the *Tooshu* can engage the remaining Prime ships while Kezule leads the drop mission from the *N'zishok*."

Kaid raised a surprised eye ridge as M'kou punched the call button. "You persuaded the General to stay on board? I'm impressed."

Kusac shrugged. "Wasn't that difficult," he murmured. The opposite had in fact been true. They'd had a fierce interchange until Kusac pointed out that he needed the General out of the combat zone to liaise with all the various elements of the mission and guide them through the Palace by means of monitoring their helmet vid cams.

"You're the General, Kezule. Do what you do best—organize us all into one integrated attack force. We can't risk both you and Zsurtul on the ground," he'd said.

The elevator door opened, and suddenly he was crowded in face-to-face with her. She smiled, and he had to look away, but not before he saw the hurt he was causing.

"It's been a long time," said Kaid quietly. "You look thinner."

"A little," he said, readjusting his rifle, searching for something—anything—neutral to say. "You're the same."

"No. None of us are. Are we?" Kaid said it so quietly he barely heard him and looked up in surprise.

The elevator stopped, the door opening, spilling them all out onto the main control level. He backed away from them and turned to lead the way to the next elevator.

"I need to see to the *Profit's* shuttle," he said to Kaid as they reached it. "M'kou can handle this. You don't need me."

Kaid's hand snaked out and grasped him, his powered glove uncomfortably tight around his bared wrist.

"We have remotes for you from Toueesut on our shuttle.

Don't leave without them, Kusac. They can sense any new traps in the tunnel. And we need to talk," he added.

"I'll get Jurrel and Banner to load them," he promised, then looked Kaid calmly in the eyes until the other released him. "We'll talk. I can't leave without the Prince," he said. "Q'almo, accompany Prince Zsurtul. You're now one of his designated bodyguards."

"Aye, Captain."

He waited until the doors closed before leaning against the wall and closing his eyes. Every breath brought their scents to him—hers as sweetly musk as he remembered, his deeper and sharper, male. Memories of nights together rose, refusing to be banished until he forced himself to remember the danger to them.

Blinking furiously, he straightened up and strode away.

What's happened to him? Carrie asked. *He's changed so much, and he's blocking us on every level!*

We'll find out later, Kaid replied. *Let's see Zsurtul start this bad weather, and then we'll go down and get him on his own.*

"Highness! Enlightened One! Gods be praised, it is you!" exclaimed the senior scientist, bowing low as they emerged in the actual weather lab. "We hardly dared hope it was true."

"As you see, here I am, Doctor," said Zsurtul, reluctantly giving up Zhalmo's hand.

"Gratified as we are by your visit, Highness, may I ask why you honor us with your presence?"

"I need to access the weather control, Doctor . . ." Zsurtul hesitated, waiting for him to supply his name.

"Doctor Kochess, Highness. If it's because of the meteorites, they shouldn't come close to us, but . . ."

Zsurtul held up his hand, silencing him. "Not directly. I need to change the weather drastically on the surface so that the City of Light suffers such severe thunderstorms that it loses contact with the ships now orbiting our world."

"The effect doesn't need to be gradual," interrupted Kaid. "In fact, if it is swift enough that they assume the Orbital has been damaged, so much to the good."

"But we have the force fields to protect us . . ." began one of the others.

"Which you can't use with the *Kz'adul* berthed here. I'm assured that worrying about why the Orbital has been damaged will be the last thing on the minds of those in the City during this storm," said Zsurtul, his voice taking on a slightly brittle quality.

Doctor Kochess smiled slightly. "I begin to understand, Highness. To do that, we need you to initiate the manual override. Incidentally, there is a failsafe built into the system that will allow you, if you have the codes, to sever communications between the ground and the ships. There's no need to hope that the storm does it."

"That's good news," said Kaid. "Do you have the codes, Prince Zsurtul?"

"Since K'hedduk hasn't been able to tamper with this system, I assume the code my father gave me should work here."

"If you would come over here, Highness," said Kochess, leading the way to the other side of the central control bank. "There is a DNA and retinal scan procedure you must take to activate the override."

Zsurtul followed him, waiting patiently while Kochess pressed the controls that brought the retinal scanner out of its recess. In front of it, a palm sized panel started to glow.

"Please place your hand on the panel and look into the small lens. You'll feel a short burst of heat under your hand as it takes a sample of your skin."

It was over in a moment.

"Identity confirmed. Crown Prince Zsurtul Shan-Cheu'ko'h, welcome to the Orbital Weather Platform," intoned the artificial voice. "What are your Highness' instructions?"

"Initiate manual override," said Zsurtul, trying to keep the slight tremor out of his voice as he glanced at Zhalmo standing by his side. "Praise to thee, O waters of Life, coming forth from the earth, that your people may be fed," he recited, then fell silent.

· "The God-King has spoken," said the computer. "As you command, so it will be. Manual override initiated. The station is yours, Highness."

Zsurtul looked at Doctor Kochess, then at Kaid. "I had the code," he said.

I think it has really hit him that his father is dead, poor lad, Carrie sent to Kaid.

"That's all that's required, Highness. We can now access the controls, including those that will isolate the ships from the Palace of Light."

Kaid joined them. "Show me the approaching asteroids," he said.

"Over here," said a voice from behind. "I'm sorry—no one has introduced you," the scientist apologized.

After hasty introductions, Kaid studied the approaching asteroids.

"It's only just begun," said Kochess helpfully.

"We should have a good six hours of them," said Kaid. "I need that storm established as soon as possible."

"If you tell me what is planned, I can more easily tailor it to your needs."

"We're dropping soldiers under cover of the storm, specifically at its height. Dawn is only three hours away—I need a storm that keeps the sky as dark as night for as long as possible. Torrential rain and lightning, the works."

"You want a supercell one, then. The problem with those is that the more severe the storm, the more likely it is to become a danger to yourselves and any airborne vehicles you may be using."

"We'll be safe in ablative shells when we're dropped," said Kaid. "I've been in severe storms before; our equipment can handle it. We're insulated."

"The usual time for storms to start is in the late afternoon," murmured Kochess. "You need heat after all, and moisture, to start the process."

"It's day on one side of your world right now," said Kaid.

"There is that, of course, but we are a fairly arid world, with landlocked seas . . . Leave it with me. We'll come up with what you need."

"In our time frame? We need that storm to be at its height within three hours at most. In fact, we need it to be fairly severe within the next hour."

"Yes, yes, now let me work." Already Kochess was deep in his own thoughts as he darted from one to the other of the control units set on the hub of the room, checking the displays on his colleagues' screens.

"What about communications?" Kaid reminded him.

"We'll call down to the Port Office and let you know. I assume that is your base of operations, yes? Now go, leave us to our work and concentrate on your own." Kochess suddenly remembered that Prince Zsurtul was there. "Highness, I meant no insult to your allies . . . but we all work best if left to get on with it."

"I understand, Doctor Kochess," said Zsurtul.

He knew it was Kaid before the hand even fell on his suit shoulder.

"Now," was all he said.

"We can manage the rest," said Banner. "Take what time you need."

Kusac left the *Profit's* cargo hold with Kaid. In the empty loading bay, he stopped and turned to face him, heart already pounding.

"Not here," said Kaid, his face expressionless. "In the bar, where we won't be disturbed."

"There's only one thing I need to know right now," said Kaid, closing the bar door behind them. "Did you leave the cub Shaidan in Kezule's care?"

"Yes. Shaidan's safe with him. He's on the *N'zishok* with Kezule's wife and young daughter," he said, surprised at the question. He walked over to the bar and leaned against it.

"Well and good." Kaid studied him carefully before coming to stand in front of him. "After our last meeting, I swore when next I saw you . . ."

"Don't. You know I was under orders . . ."

"I know. You couldn't have chosen to say anything more calculated to push me aside if you'd tried. But you knew that."

This was the last thing that he'd expected from Kaid. Anger, recriminations, but not this. He could feel his throat constricting, making it difficult to breathe.

"I had to stop you from following me," he whispered, still, by an effort of will, keeping his eyes averted.

"Oh, you did that, all right. If I'd had my wits about me, I'd have seen it for what it was."

He felt Kaid's fingers touch his neck and looked up then in shock.

"You always did get a tight throat when you got stressed," Kaid said, hand curling around his throat and beginning to massage it gently.

He grasped the hand, pulling it away. "Kaid," he began,

then let his head drop forward until their foreheads touched. He drew in a deep, shuddering breath, losing himself in the familiar scent and touch of his Triad partner. "I'm sorry. I meant none of what I said that day."

"I know you didn't. And I'm sorry I didn't trust you, didn't believe Carrie when she insisted there had to be a good reason for what you'd done," said Kaid, turning his hand in Kusac's until he could clasp it. "Banner told me everything that happened on Kij'ik. You've nothing to explain. We're both just glad to have you back."

Like a shower of cold water, Kaid's words reminded him what was at stake. "It's not that simple," he said, gently pushing away from him. "You know about the scent marker. What you don't know is that it acts like a drug, and I can't be without it—without her." He searched Kaid's face, praying he'd understand. "And I've gotten used to it, and her, Kaid. I wouldn't change it if I could."

"She's a Prime, Kezule's wife." A statement, nothing more. Testing him to see what his response was.

"I know." Now the big lie. "That's not important. I love her, Kaid."

Silence and a steady, unflinching gaze from Kaid's eyes—eyes more gray than any other color right now. "I see. That . . . kind of complicates life, doesn't it?"

Relief flooded through him. Kaid had believed the lie. "It was the Directorate, not Zayshul's doing," he said. "Kezule knows this, as do most people now."

"And Kezule has no objection? He has changed, then," murmured Kaid.

"I have to go, Kaid. We'll talk again later, on the surface, when this is all over."

Kaid nodded. "Don't take any chances, Kusac, even though you've got the people who trapped the tunnels with you. K'hedduk's no fool—he'll have put his own traps in. Use those remotes."

"I will. Believe me, they're very welcome. M'kou's already experimenting with one of them on the shuttle." He hesitated, suddenly no longer anxious to leave. "You'll tell . . ."

"Carrie knows," Kaid said. "She has something to tell you—news you should hear from her before you go."

"I really can't delay any longer . . ." he began, moving away from the bar and Kaid as Carrie pushed the door open.

"It will only take a moment, Kusac," she said, coming over to them. "You need to know in case anything should happen to any of us."

He frowned, wondering what it could be.

"You have a son," she said.

His face cleared, and he nodded. "Shaidan. I knew about him from the first. I thought Banner would have told you that."

"Not Shaidan. A cub, a twin to the daughter Kaid and I had."

Shock hit him like a punch to the belly. "What? How is that possible? Unless it was that first night on Haven . . ."

All pretenses at distancing himself from them were gone. He could see from her expression that the feelings he'd hidden from Kaid were now written clearly on his face. He struggled with his emotions, trying to get them back in order.

"He was conceived then. We called him Dhaykin. He's dark like you, Kusac."

Another son—a cub! "Your daughter, what did you call her?" he asked hoarsely. This was all he'd ever wanted—to be with those he loved and share cubs with them.

"Layeesha. Already she looks out for her little brother," Carrie said, coming closer.

Two more reasons to protect them now. "I have to go, and you have to let me," he whispered, fighting to keep the pain he felt at parting from them from showing. "Take care in the coming battle, both of you!" He reached out, grasping her by the shoulder, pulling her close until his lips fastened on hers in a bruising kiss that flooded his senses with the magic of their vanished Link.

Shocked again, he wrenched himself away from her only to be caught up in Kaid's arms.

"Stay safe, sword-brother! We'll see you at the bar or in L'Shoh's Hell!" Then he was released and loping for the door, leaving them behind. On his cheek he could still feel the touch of Kaid's tongue, and on his lips, the echo of a Leska's kiss.

Carrie put her hand to her lips, a strange expression on her face as Kaid put an arm around her armored shoulders.

"What is it?" he asked.

"His kiss . . . It was as if we were Linked, Kaid. Like before."

"It couldn't have been," he said. "Do you sense anything from him now?"

She shook her head. "Nothing. It was as if his shields came down just for a split second when we kissed. I don't believe he's in love with her."

"Hold tight back there," said Tirak over the shuttle's comm. "It's going to be one hell of a ride! Those folk on the Orbital certainly cooked you up a storm!"

The shuttle began to jerk and buck like a riding beast with a burr under its saddle. Kusac gripped the safety rail and looked over his team. Noolgoi had his stomach under control, though he looked somewhat pale. Not that he likely had anything left in it after the way he'd thrown up on the *Kz'adul*.

Zsurtul was sitting beside Zhalmo, his jaws clenched tight, but if he was any judge, the Princeling would rather die than throw up in front of a female he wanted to impress. The rest looked a little shaken but fine. Which left Khadui.

"How you doing?" he asked the older Sholan quietly.

"Better than a drop ship," the older male said through gritted teeth. "I'll last. Least we got our helmets off."

"Can't raise the landing pad, Captain," said Sheeowl to Tirak. "Too much interference."

"Keep trying." Tirak said as they suddenly began to drop like a stone before just as suddenly leveling out again.

Kusac felt his stomach lurch and eyed the bucket someone had thoughtfully fastened to the wall opposite. If anyone was going to be sick, it wasn't going to be him, he decided grimly, clamping his own jaws tightly shut and swallowing hard.

"Got a fix on the landing beacon," said Sheeowl. "Captain looks like they've got that force field up after all."

"I see it," said Tirak. "It looks unstable to me."

The craft went through another series of gut-wrenching dips.

"Got them on audio now, Captain. They're putting the lights on for us. They want us to taxi into one of the warehouses. What do I say?"

"Say yes. I'll stall them, make it look like the wind blew us down on the pad. Mrayan, you can taxi us in." He raised his voice. "You hear that, Kusac? Get your people ready to move out as soon as we touch down. We'll all need to lie low at the edge of the pad till they kill the lights."

"Copy that," Kusac called out. "Helmets on now," he ordered, lifting his own off his lap. "Those with remote sensors, check they're firmly fixed to your suits. Run safety checks again; any errors let me know immediately. Make sure you can't lose your tool packs. We'll need them if we hit any cave-ins."

"Why didn't we just use the regular entrance?" Valden asked.

"It's a concealed exit, not an entrance," said J'korrash. "Only meant to be opened from the inside. It's easier to use a controlled charge in the soil to open a shaft for us than to blast the exit open."

"The hill is predominantly limestone and is riddled with natural tunnels. Captain Tirak has a cover for the hole that will conceal it," said Zsurtul. "Anything that does show will be thought of as a cave-in due to the rain."

"By the time daylight comes and this storm clears, we'll hold the City and the Palace, and no one will care about the hole," said Kusac. "We expect some flooding, possibly even cave-ins, which is why we're carrying tools. Valden, remember to compensate for their weight if you have to use the suit jets at all."

"You have jets on your suits?" asked Zsurtul incredulously, nausea forgotten as he leaned forward to look at Khadui's lower leg pieces.

"Valden, that's enough. You're here on sufferance because we need you to hack the AI," said Kusac absently, his mind moving to other matters.

"I didn't say a thing!" the youth objected indignantly.

"I heard it," he replied as one by one he reached out to touch the minds of the rest of his team. For this mission, he wanted a light Link to each of them. "The Primes copied our armor to make these suits. Doubtless your next generation armor will incorporate a lot of what we use, Prince Zsurtul."

"Captain, I'd prefer if you just called me Zsurtul," the young Prime replied. "I don't want to be different from anyone else on this mission."

He could empathize with that, having run away from the family responsibilities that had been forced on him three years before.

He grunted noncommittally in reply. His own checks completed, he readied himself for the landing.

Good as Tirak was, he didn't have to fake much of the unscheduled landing at the edge of the pad. High winds drove the shuttle down, and it was only the U'Churian's piloting skills that enabled him to align it exactly where he wanted.

"Out now!" Tirak barked, turning the controls over to Mrayan and getting out of his seat.

Kusac was up first, opening the side hatch. As he dived out into the pelting rain and raced the few yards to the edge of the pad, he saw that they were hidden from the warehouses not only by the foul weather but also by the shuttle itself. Beyond the edge of the landing surface was a slight drop into a ditch, then beyond that the scrubland that surrounded the walled city.

Rifle held clear in one hand, he flung himself facedown in the churning muddy ditch. Around him he felt the slight impact as the others landed close by, saw their telltales on his HUD. Automatically his free hand checked that the remote sensor from Toueesut was still safely attached. Barely audible above the noise of the gusting wind and the rain battering on his armor, he heard the shuttle lift into the air again and head out across the pad for the warehouses.

He raised his head slowly, finding it was level with the pad, but he could see only vague flickers of light through his visor and the driving rain.

"Switch to IR," he said. He saw the shuttle then, glowing brightly between the open doors of the warehouse—he could even make out the huddled outlines of the six Primes waiting for it.

As soon as the shuttle was inside, before it had even landed, the doors slid closed. Scant minutes later, the pad was plunged into total darkness as the landing lights went out.

"Wait," he cautioned them, reaching out mentally to see if he could eavesdrop on Mrayan's conversation with the Primes inside.

When he was sure all was proceeding normally, he contacted Tirak.

"Ready," he said. "We'll stay down while you blow an entrance in the tunnel for us. The fewer of us on our feet, the better."

"Aye on that," agreed Tirak. Signaling Sheeowl to follow

him, he carefully raised himself into a crawling position and headed into the darkness.

Kusac felt the small concussion shock vibrate the ground under him and waited for Tirak to let him know all was ready.

"We're through, Kusac," said Tirak.

"Coming," he said, securing his rifle with the suit latches and coming up in a low four-legged crouch. He crawled over to where Tirak and his group were kneeling around a four-foot hole in the ground, grabbing for the flashlight that hung at his side.

He shone it briefly into the hole so he could see the tunnel opening out below. "Neat hole," he murmured. It looked as if it had been cut out with a cookie cutter.

"Right tool for the right job," said Tirak. "Better get down now. With this rain, it'll collapse soon. Sheeowl's rigged a rope for you."

A rattling on his suit announced the start of hail.

"To me, in your ranks," he said over the team channel.

Reaching out, he grasped hold of the rope, then, having second thoughts, sat back on his haunches. "I think I'll send down a 'bot first."

Unclipping it, he fiddled for a moment with the activating switch, then held the small mud-brown oval shape against the rope.

"What's that do?" asked Tirak.

"Touiban device," he said, almost letting it go in shock when six tendrils, three on each side, whipped out and caught hold of the rope. Instantly, a new telltale appeared on his HUD. When he did release it, it began to rapidly scramble down into the hole.

"Kathan's beard!" swore Tirak, who'd leaped back in surprise. He approached Kusac again, his own flashlight picking out the small ovoid shape as it rapidly descended. "How d'you keep track of it? It's almost perfectly camouflaged!"

"It's on the HUD," he said, watching the device let go of the rope, drop to the tunnel floor and begin what he could only think of as sniffing. "Toueesut said it would change color if it found anything. Hell," he said, shifting his weight and leaning closer to the edge. "It *has* found something! J'korrash! Did you have a trip wire or trap around here?"

"At least you know it works. What now? Don't get too close to the edge—that soil is waterlogged," warned Tirak.

"I'll wait till it signals it's disabled it," he said, watching his footing. The 'bot identifier, projected onto the inside of his helmet visor, had begun to blink yellow.

"Not one of ours, Captain," she said.

"Better move back," said Kusac, fitting actions to his words. "It could be explosives."

They waited, tensed in case there was an explosion, but a few minutes later, the telltale returned to blue.

"Clear now," he said, moving back to the edge of the hole and grasping the rope. He held his other hand out to Tirak. "Once again, good hunting, Tirak."

"And you, Captain."

Hand over hand he lowered himself swiftly down the rope. When his feet touched the ground, he chinned his helmet controls, turning on his low light sensor, then looked around for the 'bot.

It sat about a foot away, beside a now deactivated land mine.

"Ancient but effective, especially in such an enclosed area," he muttered to himself as he quickly surveyed what he could see of the tunnel around him.

"Didn't catch that, Captain," said Khadui from above.

"A land mine," he said. "Safe now. Hold on while I take a look around me."

The debris from the hole Tirak had created had fallen to the back of the tunnel, almost filling it, leaving their way ahead clear except for a scattering of soil and stones. The walls were a mix of naturally eroded limestone and rock, fused by intense heat when the Valtegans had artificially enlarged it. About ten feet wide at this point, the roof was only eighteen inches above his helmet.

"All clear," he said, moving away from the rope and into the tunnel proper. As he did, the 'bot scurried some fifteen feet ahead of him then stopped, blending into the darkness at the edges of his visibility. He examined the walls again, moving closer, seeing the water that was seeping through the untreated limestone and running down the walls to pool on the earth-covered floor. A quick survey showed that a drainage hole had been cut at the juncture of wall and floor, and the water was managing to escape through it. The surface underfoot was still slick with mud—and he knew there was a downward slope just ahead.

"Watch your footing everyone," he warned as Khadui landed just behind him. "Floor is muddy, with water running down the walls onto it."

"Probably hasn't seen this much rain in a good many years," said Khadui, clearing the access hole and performing the same checks he'd just done. "No lichens or mosses I can see."

"None in this area," Kusac confirmed. "We'll need to watch our time. I allowed us ninety minutes for the tunnel and getting into the Command Room."

"Let's hope there are no surprises the 'bots can't handle," said Khadui, eyeing the deactivated mine.

"Glad I sent it down first," Kusac muttered as J'korrash landed beside them. "I take it this wasn't one of yours."

"No, Captain."

"Now we know for sure they've trapped this area," said Khadui.

CHAPTER 6

Palace of Light, same night

"THE force field is up now. Why can't it stay up?" demanded K'hedduk, pacing from his desk toward the window to look out at the pale actinic rippling light that arced above the Palace.

"Two generators are faulty, Majesty," said Fabukki, one of his M'zullian followers who had come to the Prime world with him. "We're using them for this test, but if we keep them in the relay, they will fail completely, distorting the shape of the force field."

"Meaning what, exactly?" demanded K'hedduk, returning to his desk to push the map of the Palace and surrounding City toward his Security Chief. "Show me."

"Meaning we will have no force field covering the area beyond the front entrance wall to the Palace or the one on the east side beyond the parking area," said Fabukki, indicating the defective generators and their arcs on the map. "Instead the field will default to a weaker path, roughly along the front of the walls. Weaker because it will have to cover more distance."

"There's still a generator at either corner of those walls. Doesn't that mean each will only have to cover half the length of the wall, less distance than it does on its normal arc?"

Fabukki shifted his feet. "It's not quite that straightforward, Majesty," he murmured. "Before we lost contact with the Orbital, I was told the shipment of replacement parts had arrived. Given the violent nature of our current weather and the asteroid storm, I doubt their shuttle has left there. Indeed, it may even have been destroyed—we have no way of knowing until offworld communications are restored."

"I thought I'd made it clear that communications with our ships are a priority. They're our first line of defense," said K'hedduk, narrowing his eyes as he looked at Fabukki.

"There's nothing we can do right now, Majesty," said Fabukki, deferentially. "Not until the storm ends, or someone on the *Kz'adul* checks on the Orbital to find out if it has been damaged, as we fear."

"There should be failsafes, alternative ways to override the main computer system other than accessing it in the sublevel Command Room! I want a system set up that has redundancies built in, other ways for me to access the main controls and the Orbital! I should be able to see exactly what that meteorite shower is doing. It's unconscionable that I should be out of communication with my fleet at this time!"

A tapping at the door brought their attention to it. A youth entered, bowing low before scurrying over to K'hedduk, holding a piece of paper out in front of him.

"Message from the landing pad, Majesty," he said, handing it over and unobtrusively retreating.

"This whole damned planet is a joke," K'hedduk hissed as he unfolded the note. "We were brought up to believe it was the holiest of worlds—the place of our emergence, where we evolved! How advanced it would be in comparison to our humble planet, we were taught. Advanced? Everything is ancient, worn out, crumbling, not steeped in history—steeped in threadbare decay more like! Nothing works! Even our internal communications are down again tonight! This wouldn't be tolerated on M'zull!"

"Not everyone has had the good fortune to have been born on M'zull like us, Majesty," said Fabukki smoothly. "Once our support arrives, we'll have the personnel and resources to effect the major changes that are needed."

K'hedduk looked up sharply from the note. "We?"

Fabukki bowed low. "Your pardon, Majesty," he murmured. "I meant you, of course. We all exist merely to do your bidding."

K'hedduk grunted and screwed up the note. "The U'Churian shuttle has landed and is being unloaded in the warehouses now. You'll have your parts within two hours."

A peal of thunder rent the air, echoing around the walled courtyard outside his office.

"Assuming that damned storm lets up enough to allow them to transport the parts here!" he hissed, throwing the balled up piece of paper into the waste bin. "What's the state of the gun turrets?"

"Good," said Fabukki. "The rewiring and renovation of those around the exterior of the Palace has been completed. They were able to reroute the controls during the work, so full control has been restored. Obviously, the weather has halted work for now on those in the City precincts."

"What about all the security scanners?"

"Without access to the main controls, Majesty, it has proved impossible to remove the retinal scans of the late Royal family from the memory banks, but yours have been entered successfully. They're ready to switch them back on at your command."

"Then do so now. I'm disappointed that more progress on breaking the codes in the main command computers hasn't been achieved. I'd expected your people would have done that by now. It's damned annoying having to argue with that AI every time I need to make changes. I need a way to override it!"

"I don't have my people here, yet, Majesty. At present I'm forced to work with those who lack the enthusiasm to solve the problem."

"Perhaps they need a bigger spur than you're providing."

"That's Kezain's department, Majesty. Even so, I doubt they need greater encouragement. Head Inquisitor Lufsuh visited them. Three are still in the dungeons, and one is dead. It only served to make the remainder work even more slowly. If they didn't lack a backbone, I'd say it was passive resistance, but . . ." He shrugged and left his sentence hanging.

K'hedduk sighed. "In the circumstances, you've done well," he said grudgingly. "If Kezain continues to be a liability, we'll need to have you officially take over from him." He was annoyed that a dead Emperor could still thwart his plans from beyond the grave because of a set of computer codes only he had known.

"He serves his purpose, Majesty, in letting the commoners relate to him, whereas I'm seen as an outsider. I'll have people waiting at the gates for the relay parts. They can work on the faulty units without us needing to take the force field down completely."

"That's at least reassuring," said K'hedduk. With no communications from the ships orbiting K'oish'ik, he felt more secure knowing that at least the Palace was protected from not only the asteroids that were falling but also any possible incursion.

"One last thing, Majesty. The female, Kezule's daughter. You said to transfer her to the harem section in the morning. Her own room, as I remember."

"What about her?"

"You mentioned I might . . ."

"Yes, yes, you can have her for what is left of tonight, after the force field is repaired," he said, waving his Security chief away. "I have plans for her future. Pity my people weren't able to capture more of those females alive."

Fabukki bowed. "As you say. It's late, Majesty. Perhaps you should also consider retiring for the night."

"Soon," he said. It had been a day or two since he'd visited his Empress; perhaps he'd do so now. She was certainly more amenable since he'd had the Palace doctor start sedating her. Not as heavily as the other harem females, of course. He liked his with some life in her, just not too much aggression.

Kz'adul, same night

"*Zh'adak*, this is Commander Q'ozoi of the *Kz'adul*. Be advised we are tracking the meteorite storm and have found several large objects in the midst of it. We need you to investigate."

"*Kz'adul*, Commander Ch'akkuh here. We hear you. Zoshak in Science has updated us on the asteroid situation. Unfortunately, Security Officer Zsaffer refuses to leave our designated orbit. He wishes to confirm your order with the Palace first."

"Communications with the ground are out, Ch'akkuh. He won't get confirmation. If those larger asteroids keep their current course, they'll enter the atmosphere in approximately

five hours, and pose a serious threat to the City of Light."
Q'ozoi looked at Shikku.

"Suggest they come here and talk to our Security," whispered the Science officer. "Understood, Q'ozoi," the Captain
of the *Zh'adak* said, "but the decision isn't mine to make.
Without orders from the Palace, Zsaffer won't authorize leaving our current orbit."

"As senior ship, we can issue the command, Ch'akkuh, and
I'm doing just that. We'll undock from the Orbital and cover
the City against the meteorites. Tell Zsaffer he's welcome to
come here and discuss it with us."

There was a short silence. "We're breaking orbit, Commander Q'ozoi, and will rendezvous with you in approximately thirty minutes. May I suggest you join us on the
Zh'adak?"

"Very well, Q'ozoi out." The Commander looked at
Shikku.

"Captain Tirak left us some canisters of sleep gas," said
the Science officer. "They would come in very handy if you
could gather all K'hedduk's security personnel in one room,
Commander."

Q'ozoi nodded. "Get a team ready in that case. Have you
got any portable breather units in the labs?"

"Ones small enough that we can conceal in pockets," confirmed Shikku. "I'll go get them organized, Commander. How
large a group do you want to take onto the *Zh'adak*?"

"Four of us," said Q'ozoi after giving the order to undock
from the Orbital. "If Ch'akkuh and Zoshak can get K'hedduk's
five people isolated in the air lock area, we can neutralize them
with that gas and throw them in detention."

N'zishok, 90 minutes to Drop, Zhal-Arema, 6th day (March)

This time, when they approached the *N'zishok*, Kaid was directed to the starboard docking area, passing the *Couana's*
shuttle moored securely to the port side as they went. Once
on board, they were met by M'zynal and taken directly to the
main landing bay.

Carrie's senses were immediately assaulted by the sheer variety of sounds and smells. Fuel was foremost—sharp, and tasting of hot metal and burned insulation. Underlying it was the smell of Valtegan sweat.

Fighter planes were being towed by mechanics to the refueling point, then taken to their launching area. To one side, the racks for the egg-shaped drop capsules were being loaded, while the launching sequences were being tested with what appeared to be spares.

"The General's over there," M'zynal said, indicating the launch control booth as they began weaving their way between the craft. "He's going to coordinate the mission from the Bridge."

"Then he does plan to stay on the *N'zishok*," said Kaid with satisfaction.

"He knows where he's needed most, Captain."

"We've a conference on the Bridge with the *Tooshu* in half an hour," said Kezule, getting up as Carrie, Kaid, T'Chebbi, and Garras entered, leaving the others outside. "The thirteen who'll be on the HALO drop with you are in the commons on the same deck. I assumed you'd want to meet and address them first."

"I'd prefer that."

Kezule signaled to one of the civilians hovering nearby. "Organize some refreshments for us in my office," he ordered. "We've got ninety minutes until drop time. I've just had word from the *Kz'adul* that the *Zh'adak* is now ours."

"Good news," said Kaid as they followed him back out. "We'd rather avoid a third assault front if possible."

"We should be able to. Commander Q'ozoi of the *Kz'adul* has left the Orbital and ordered the *Zasho* and *Shazzu* to rendezvous with it. There are ten of the implanted ex-Palace guards on each of the cruisers. If we can get them all in one room, we can transmit their shutdown codes and knock them out. When they regain consciousness, they'll be in the *Kz'adul's* brig."

"I assume K'hedduk's other agents are there."

Kezule glanced across at Kaid as they stopped by the elevator. "Those from the *Zh'adak* are, but Captain Aldatan took no prisoners from those on the *Kz'adul* or the Orbital."

Kaid nodded, hiding his surprise from the General.

"Met with heavy resistance, did they?" asked Garras casually.

"No more than expected, once he realized how aggressive K'hedduk's gene-altered thugs are. Killing them then saved me doing it later."

The elevator arrived, eliminating the need for anyone to reply.

Kusac wouldn't kill captives, sent Carrie. *Or if he did, he'd have a good reason for doing it.*

Later, he replied.

"You thirteen will be in three Fire Teams led by myself, Banner, and Garras," Kaid said to the group seated in the commons. "The rest of you will be backing us up, taking out the gun turrets once we've knocked out the force field generators. I'm assured only the eight on the perimeter have a full 360-degree field of fire. Those inside the outer Palace wall can't shoot more than a foot above the twenty-foot-high walls or farther than their opposite wall."

A hand went up. "Whom do we take our orders from?"

"That's sir or Captain Kaid to you," growled Banner from where he was perched on the edge of a low cupboard. "And you take your orders from the General."

"Yes, Lieutenant," the youth responded quickly, trying to not glance sideways at his father.

Kezule stirred in his chair at the head of the table beside Kaid. "I thought I made it clear you were to treat our Sholan allies with all due courtesy," he said, a hiss of displeasure in his voice.

An embarrassed silence fell until another hand went up from among the thirteen who were to accompany Kaid.

"Who is in which team, Captain Kaid, sir?"

Kaid picked up a list of names and read them out. "The first group will be in a Fire Team with me and Carrie. The second will be led by Banner and Jurrel; and the third by Garras and my son Dzaka. We'll work as one unit along with one of the Touiban Fire Teams, targeting the force field generator designated as number 1. We already know the force field is up, but it is unstable as two generators are out—numbers 6 and 8. They'll still be targeted because we can't assume they'll stay down. Until we disable the force field, we'll be sitting targets for the laser turrets, and until the field is down, our fighter units can't hit them. We'll all be relying on the support that you give us," he said, glancing briefly over to the fighter pilots. "How many of you have HALO dropped before?"

"Those who remained on K'oish'ik as the Palace Guard," said M'zynal. "The rest of us have done time in the simulator though."

Garras grunted. "Will have to do. Better get them pumped up with antinauseants, though."

Kaid saw with amusement the various uncertain looks the youths exchanged.

"It's been done," Kezule murmured in a quiet aside to him. "Just to be safe."

"You all have cameras installed in your helmets. General Kezule will be monitoring the mission from the Bridge and will issue orders via the Team leaders. Those are the only people you obey. In the event your Team leader is taken out, report to the General for new instructions. Courtesy of the Touibans, on your HUDs you have sensor telltales showing you not only the location of your teammates, but of all friendlies. Enemy troops will show up in red. Remember, though we're not the main attack force, we are vital to the retaking of the City and Palace. If all goes well, the force field will be down by the time we land, and the fighters will have taken out most, if not all, of the turrets. Any questions?" Kaid waited for a moment or two before continuing.

"In that case, Fire Teams, go and get suited up then assemble by your designated drop capsule," said Kaid. "General, I'll hand over to you."

As the ground troops filed out, they stole curious glances at T'Chebbi, never having seen a female Sholan before. At just five and a half feet tall, she was smaller than the males and more lightly built, her long dark hair worn in a single thick braid at the back, but her face framed by several small ones that were currently clipped up out of the way. From it her ears rose high on her head, their width showing off her highland origins. What could be seen of her pelt was multicolored in grays and browns. Aware of their interest, she widened her mouth in a very toothy, feral grin, making Carrie, sitting beside her, chuckle quietly.

"You know your targets," Kezule said to the pilots. "And you know what depends on the success of this mission. I have every confidence in you. Dismissed."

Once they'd gone, Banner got to his feet. "We'll head down and supervise, unless you have anything else for us to do."

Kaid shook his head. "Carry on."

"I go with him," said T'Chebbi, shouldering her rifle. "Want to see this place for myself."

"Don't frighten them too much," said Carrie, sotto voce, patting her on the cheek.

"If any of your people need to use the simulators, we do have enough time," said Kezule.

No way, Carrie sent to Kaid, eyes narrowing as she looked at him. *I'll cope.*

"We're all prepared, thanks," he replied. *You stick close to me unless I say otherwise.*

I have every intention of doing that!

"Let's retire to my office," said Kezule, getting up. "The call from the *Tooshu* can be routed there."

Zh'adak, same time

"Commander Q'ozoi of the *Kz'adul* to the *Shazzu* and *Zasho*. Leave your current orbits and head for the asteroids approaching K'oish'ik. Several large bodies have been located within the cloud that pose a danger not only to our world, but also to the Orbital. Locate and destroy them."

"Negative, *Kz'adul*. We only take orders directly from the Emperor."

"Communications with the Palace are impossible because of conditions on the surface below us and the asteroids."

"My military advisers say our orders are unchanged. We will remain in our designated orbits protecting the Palace of Light."

"There will be no City or Palace if even one of those large asteroids hits the surface," said Q'ozoi tersely.

"We will remain in our designated orbits, Commander," repeated the *Shazzu's* Captain.

"Fikkush, I am ordering you and Ne'zego to rendezvous with me on the *Zh'adak* to discuss this matter. In the event of a break in the chain of command, I have the authority to take charge of the fleet. I am doing so now."

There was a short silence. "We'll meet you in fifteen minutes, Commander."

Tunnels

"Watch your footing," Kusac warned, looking back as Zsurtul made his way gingerly toward them. "The surface is slick with mud."

"This is the escape tunnel?" the Prince asked.

"Yes, Majesty, but it isn't normally waterlogged like this," said J'korrash.

"It's only an emergency exit to the landing pad," M'kou said.

"Quit gossiping," growled Khadui from up front. "There's a camera ahead. They may be monitoring for sound."

Kusac joined him, raising his rifle toward the tiny blinking red light, then stopped. Shooting it would likely draw the attention they were trying to avoid. Expecting nothing, he reached with his mind, surprised when he realized he could sense not only the camera but also the relay controls. It took only a moment to ensure that the water running down the walls managed to penetrate somewhere vital. The red light dimmed, then went out.

"Disabled it," he said, lowering the rifle and moving on.

The tunnel began to narrow slightly as they made their way down the slight incline. From behind came the sounds of slipping and occasional muted curses. Then the tunnel began to level out as the ceiling sloped lower until they had to bend their heads to avoid scraping their helmets on it.

Kusac hung back, waiting for the Prince in the middle of the group to come level with him.

An exclamation from Khadui, followed by a sustained sliding and bumping, ended in a loud splash. There was a moment's silence when even Kusac was concerned; then the older Sholan began to curse. He interrupted his flow briefly to say, "Watch out for the steep slope ahead."

Muffled laughter escaped from everyone.

The sound of Khadui surging to his feet, then beginning to wade through the water, silenced them.

"The suits are watertight, right?" Zsurtul asked.

"Yes, Majesty," murmured Zhalmo, taking hold of his arm and gently urging him onward. "Air and watertight."

"Turn on internal air supplies," ordered Kusac. The suits should automatically close the filters and engage the stored air as soon as they detected water above Sholan ankle height, but he'd rather not leave it to chance. "How deep, Khadui?" Khadui's had at least, since his telltale was still green.

"About chest high—over four feet I'd say. It's a big puddle. Over twenty feet long from what I can gauge."

"Ignore the water," he said, addressing them all. "Just ensure your boots have a firm grip, and keep your weapons up out of it!"

"Aye, sir."

Do I detect a special interest in our Princeling? he sent in an amused tone to Zhalmo as he passed her on his way back up to the front.

We inherited the ability to know our genetic mate from our Father. He's mine, she replied.

Is that all? That piece of information didn't surprise him.

No. I find him—endearing, she replied, with the equivalent of a mental laugh. *He feels the same about me.*

So I see. Just make sure you guard him well.

With my life, Captain! There was no levity in her mental tone this time.

Kusac caught up to Khadui in the middle of the water.

"It's getting shallower now," the older male observed. "Why they made it slope down . . ."

Kusac triggered the tunnel map up on his HUD. "We're passing under the outer wall of the City. Probably dug deeper for safety. We've covered over three hundred feet now. Still another fourteen hundred to do."

"We're about right for time so far," said Khadui. "How is the 'bot doing?"

"It's about ten feet ahead of us. I can see it just emerging from the water ahead."

Khadui grunted. "Handy little gizmo. We should try to keep 'em for the Brotherhood if we can."

"Nothing comes free," said Kusac. "There will be a price for the Touiban help, I'm sure."

Khadui glanced at him but said nothing as they began to wade up the narrow incline out of the water.

The ground had more or less leveled out, and they were able to make better time. Kusac tried to keep them to an even pace. Arriving earlier than planned would be as bad as arriving late. It wasn't easy as the dust on the floor of the tunnel had turned into a sticky slick mud that meant they still had to be careful of their footing.

"Water ahead," said Khadui after about five minutes.

"I see it," he said. "Looks like it's a big pool this time. And the tunnel's narrowing."

"It opens out into a reasonably large cavern," said J'korrash.

"How large?"

"A hundred feet or so, from memory," she replied.

"We'll have to wait for the 'bot to get to the other side," he muttered. "Put yours down too, Khadui. This is more a lake than a pool. We'll need two of them to cover it."

"Aye."

He stopped at the edge of the lake, staring across the sheet of barely moving water to the other side. J'korrash was right, it looked to be a hundred feet across, give or take ten either way.

He heard a deep hiss of indrawn breath from Zsurtul as the others came to a stop behind him.

"Any idea how deep it could be, J'korrash?" he asked.

"Not really, Captain. As deep as the last one, at least."

"It's beautiful," said the Prince in an awed voice. "Look at the pillars! And the spikes hanging down from the roof! And over there—it's like folds of drapery!"

Too focused on the way ahead to take much note of the other features in the cavern, Kusac looked around in time to see Zsurtul reach out to touch a nearby pillar.

"Don't!" he said sharply. "Zhalmo!"

Too late to stop him, Zhalmo reached out and pulled the Prince back as the pillar collapsed in a shower of dust and chunks of limestone.

"The stone becomes fragile as it dries out," Kusac said as the cloud of dust settled, and he scanned the roof for any more movement. "You're damned lucky it was one of the thinner pillars. They formed when there was a constant stream of water running through here. When it stopped, everything became dry and brittle. Don't anyone touch anything. Fragile as they are, we don't need any rocks falling on us."

"The 'bots have reached the other side," said Khadui.

"Let's get moving," said Kusac, stepping into the water.

It was deep. Even Kusac felt a slight twinge of concern as the water began to lap against his neck, the ripples he made causing it to splash up against his visor. As it rose over his head, his visibility shrank to a few inches because of the sediment on the bottom he was stirring up.

"Switch to sonar," he ordered. "And follow me and Khadui exactly; we've had experience in water."

"We have?" Khadui asked on his private channel as Kusac's Second-in-Command.

"Yes," he lied, using the same channel. "We know how to navigate without hitting land masses, don't we?" He was relying totally on inherited memories from Kaid for this as he picked a safe route for them among the small boulders that without the water, they'd have been able to avoid easily.

"True," murmured Khadui, doing the same.

Palace of Light, Emperor's lounge, 02:15 hours local

"I don't care what it takes, keep that damned force field up! You're the one who woke me to tell me it's raining meteorites!"

"Majesty, the City is unprotected, and it hasn't yet been hit," said Fabukki. "They're burning up in the atmosphere before they reach the ground. If not for this storm, we'd have an interesting display of . . ."

"Shut up, Fabukki!" K'hedduk hissed as he paced between his office window and his desk. "Have the parts arrived yet? Can you repair the damaged units without lowering the whole field?"

"Not yet, Majesty. They're being loaded onto the vehicles at the warehouse now. They should be here in half an hour.

The units can be repaired without taking down the field, but it's dangerous for the technicians."

"Unimportant. Do it. What's taking them so long to fetch the parts?"

"They have to unpack them first, Majesty. I've dispatched four covered vehicles—one for each . . ."

"I don't need details," he snapped. "What about the lighting? How much longer do I have to endure this emergency lighting?"

"The rain has caused failures on the rooftop solar generators, which are being repaired now. The force field is helping, of course, by preventing any more water flooding into them, but it is taking time to pump the water out. They anticipate another two hours of work."

"And communication with the weather station?"

Fabukki gestured expressively. "Who knows, Majesty? I am sure they are working on it. The *Kz'adul* is a science ship, after all, and can effect any repairs needed. Until the meteorite shower stops, we're unable to launch a shuttle. Everything we can do is being done, Majesty."

"I don't like being stranded like this, Fabukki," K'hedduk muttered. "I don't like at all."

"There's still the ship we arrived in, Majesty. It's easily accessible by you, and it can withstand even this meteorite shower. You're not stranded on K'oish'ik."

K'hedduk stopped his pacing to look at Fabukki. "You're right," he sighed. "This is an inconvenience I should have expected on such a backwater as this. Stay vigilant, Fabukki. I will see you in the morning."

"I'll monitor the repair of the force field generators personally, Majesty," said Fabukki, bowing low as K'hedduk headed for the door.

N'zishok

The launchers for the pods were ready and loaded when Kaid and Carrie rejoined their small team and Kezule's commandos in the landing bay.

"Time to load up," said Kaid, taking up a position in front of them all. "You have all taken the simulations, you know what to expect. This is no different. Do a last-minute check on weapons and ammo, check the person beside you's suit seals, then mount up. Any problems, no matter how small, let me or Control know immediately. I intend to bring you all safely through this mission. Is that understood?"

"Yes, Captain," came the chorused answer.

"Dismissed—and good hunting."

As the assembled commandos went through their final checks, Kaid turned to Carrie.

"Are you sure this is what you want? There'd be no disgrace in you staying behind, even now."

"I'm going," she said firmly. "I'd be lying if I said I wasn't scared, I am, but I'm still going."

He nodded and reached out to check the readout on the panel on her left forearm. "Well and good," he said. "Stay close to me."

"I will," she replied, watching as he flipped its cover and pressed several buttons. "What're you doing?"

"Making sure you don't get sick on the way down," he said as she let out an exclamation of surprise. "That's the suit's automed. It's just giving you a shot of antinauseant. It's always a bumpy ride down, and this is your first one."

She put her hand inside the neck of her suit, rubbing where the hypo had pierced her. "Thanks for the warning," she muttered.

Kaid smiled briefly and touched her cheek. "Now you know what to expect if it has to treat you." *See you medicate Jo,* he sent to Rezac.

Will do.

"You're being cheerful!"

"Hey, Carrie," T'Chebbi called out to her from her position two pods up as she started checking the people nearby. "See you at the bar . . ."

"Or in L'Shoh's Hell," chorused the other Sholans there amid laughter.

"You're on," Carrie shouted back, trying to keep her voice steady.

"Your suit'll medicate you even if you get too anxious," he said. "It isn't designed to act only if you're injured. Time to get into your pod. Helmet on, please."

She stood looking at him, the helmet dangling in her hands, for all the world like a cub about to go to the dentist.

He picked up the long braid that still hung outside her suit, tucking it in down her back. *Don't look at me like that, Dzinae,* he sent. *We'll both be fine. Everyone will keep an eye out for you.*

They shouldn't have to, she replied. *I know I'll be fine.* She looked away and lifted up her helmet, lowering it over her head and twisting it so that the seal locked.

It took Kaid only a moment to check her out, and then he was helping her into her pod.

It was snug, there was no other way to describe it, Carrie thought as she backed carefully into it, first stepping over the lip.

Go right back, Kaid sent. *Lean against the back wall—there's a small perch you can rest on.*

Leaning back, she found it—it fitted snugly under the seat of her suit, touching the back of her upper thighs.

You'll not be alone, Kaid sent as he moved away to see T'Chebbi into her pod. *Either Dzaka or I will stay in mental touch with you all the way down.*

Understood, she replied, trying to relax a little, but the tightness in the pit of her stomach wouldn't go away.

They'll be closing the pods in a minute or two, sent Dzaka. *Kezule controls them from this flight deck. You'll feel a rumbling beneath you, then a series of jerks as each one advances along the line . . .*

She tried to keep her attention on what he was saying, but as soon as her pod closed and she was alone in the darkness, feeling the pod's interior press against her suit, cushioning her, she began to panic. It was too like the old nightmares she'd had as a child in cryo when leaving Earth—when she'd sensed her mother dying and been unable to wake up and sound the alarm.

Carrie! Kaid's thought was insistent, demanding her attention. *Turn on your helmet light. Sorry, I should have suggested that earlier.*

She tilted her head inside the helmet, knocking the control with her chin. Instantly everything was bathed in a white glow. Not that there was anything but the cushioned interior of the unit pressing against her faceplate to see, she thought wryly.

When the pod opens, sent Kaid as a rumbling under her feet began, *remember the drill. Count to ten and trigger your parachute. It'll break your fall and lower you closer to the ground, where you can fire your suit's jets.*

Carrie—

Kusac? she sent, taken completely by surprise. *What's wrong? Are you all right?*

I'm fine. Just slow your breathing, cub. Take long, slow breaths, Kusac sent. *You'll be fine with Kaid.*

I know, she replied, barely noticing her pod lurching forward. *Where are you? What's happening?*

Nothing. We're still in the tunnel. It's flooded in places and slowing us down a little. Did Kaid tell you to watch the elevation countdown on your HUD and turn off the jets at ten feet?

Just about to, Kusac. Kaid's mental tone was slightly dry. *Good to hear you again.*

Take care, and good hunting to you both, sent Kusac.

Suddenly a great force seemed to grasp the pod, thrusting it out from the *N'zishok* into space.

Tunnels

"Our junction's ahead," said J'korrash. "We turn right at it."

Kusac grunted and glanced again at the time display on his HUD. Nearly half their allotted time was gone. They still had to reach the entrance to the Control Room, break through, and overpower the guards there. The 'bots were doing their job well—two more traps had been found, both quickly disabled. It was the flooding and earth cave-ins that were delaying them.

"Another fall-in ahead," said Khadui. "Not as bad as the last one, from the looks of it."

"On my way," he said, increasing his pace to catch up with the older male. Stopping beside him, he surveyed the pile of rocks and mud partially blocking their access to the junction.

"Need to clear them both," said Khadui, raising his rifle.

Kusac swung his around on its sling and lifted it up to bear on the right-hand side. Holding the trigger down continuously caused the bolts of energy to form an almost continuous stream that on hitting the barrier began disintegrating it in a cloud of mud and dust. The delays were beginning to irritate him. In an effort to dissipate it, he became so focused on what he was doing that he almost missed Khadui's exclamation of shock.

He didn't miss the raucous shriek of rage, or the flash of a long dun-colored body hurtling out from the rubble toward Khadui.

He swung his rifle around, ready to shoot, but by then the beast had toppled Khadui to the ground with its sheer weight. There was no chance for a clean shot. Swinging his gun back, he pulled out the knife fixed to his belt.

"Get Zsurtul to the rear!" he ordered, advancing.

He recognized it when he got closer. It was the same beast as the melted metal carving nestling in one of his pouches. A norrta, M'kou had called it.

The violently lashing tail swept toward his feet, forcing him to jump out of the way as the beast, fastening its jaws on Khadui's arm, began to worry it, snarling and hissing as it tried to drag him back to its lair.

Khadui, struggling to reach for his own knife, let out a sharp yowl of pain.

Anger surged through Kusac, and without thinking, he lashed out with the only weapon that would reach—his mind. As the beast froze, he threw his knife.

Passing within a hair's breadth of Khadui's visor, the Brotherhood blade struck the norrta straight between the eyes, penetrating almost to the quillons. Seconds later it collapsed, blood pouring from its nose and mouth, dead.

Eager hands pulled the large reptile's carcass off Khadui and helped him to his feet. M'kou went to retrieve the knife.

"Once again you're to be complimented on your throwing skills," said the young Prime, handing it back to him. "And your mental ones," he added quietly. "I think it was dead before your knife hit it."

"Quite possibly," Kusac said, taking the knife from him and checking that it was clean before putting it away.

"You don't seem surprised."

Before he had to answer, Zsurtul was pushing forward. "Are you all right?" he demanded of Khadui. "Let me see. Norrtas have corrosive saliva. We have to clean the wound."

"The suit should see to it," said Kusac, leaving M'kou to join them. "Let me see, Khadui."

"I'll do," said his Second, his voice sounding decidedly unsteady. "The suit's already medicated me."

Kusac took hold of his arm and examined the damage to the suit. A large half circle of ragged punctures had penetrated the armor around Khadui's left wrist where the glove attached to the arm. More worrisome, in the center was a fused, burned area through which sealant foam was slowly oozing before coagulating.

"Patch it, M'kou," he said, turning his attention to the control panel on Khadui's other arm. "Suit's lost its integrity. How bad is the wound?" he asked as he checked the telemetry.

"Hurt like hell at the time," said Khadui. "Fine now. What's it say?"

"Four punctures, each with some saliva damage that's been neutralized. Damn thing secretes an acid!"

"I said it did," said Zsurtul. "We need to take the head off so the teeth can be pulled. Lend me your sword, please, Captain."

Kusac frowned at him as he released Khadui. "What the hell for? So it can drool more acid over whoever is carrying it?"

"We must have the teeth," Zsurtul insisted. "It's traditional. My father told me that in the far past, in their rites of passage, young males had to kill a norrta single-handedly. The teeth are made into a necklace. Khadui and you must have your trophy to show you survived the attack and killed the beast."

He looked over at the creature lying only a few feet away. It was large, at least twice his height in length.

"We can come back for it later," he said turning away. "I can't spare anyone to haul that beast's head around."

"It might come in useful, Captain," said M'kou. "After all, wasn't it an omen you found a carving of it on the Orbital?"

"Since when did you become superstitious?" he demanded of the young lieutenant. "Do what you damned well want, so long as it doesn't delay us any longer! I've one person injured already, and we're getting too close to our deadline!"

He turned away from M'kou and began walking toward the right-hand tunnel entrance. "We have forty minutes left not only to reach the Control Room but to break in and take over the Palace and its defenses." The clock in his head was ticking down at an alarming rate now.

"There is only another 350 feet of tunnel, Captain," said M'kou, accepting Khadui's sword. "Ten minutes at most."

"I didn't expect to meet that down here," said Kusac, as he watched the 'bots scuttle ahead. "This is the second rock-fall we've seen; there could be more ahead as we pass farther under the Palace."

He waited for them, his suit picking up the almost inaudible hum as the vibro blade was activated. One slice and the head would be severed.

"Seal it with a blaster," he ordered. "I'm not having it leave a trail and possibly attract more of them, or stink the tunnel out ahead so the Primes smell it as soon as we break in." The germ of a plan was beginning to form in his mind.

They were on their way again, the head of the beast stowed in a backpack, Zsurtul and Valden talking about it in excited low voices, with the occasional dry comment from Zhalmo. Up ahead, he could already make out what looked like another partial blockage.

Calling up the map on his HUD, he checked the area out. "J'korrash, there's a dip in the tunnel ahead and a rock pile that doesn't look natural. Check out the map." He stopped just before the 'bots would reach it.

She was at his elbow a moment later. "You're right," she said. "It's not ours, Captain. Ours were mainly trip wires to alarms, and the 'bots found them all so far. This is K'hedduk's work."

"I'll send the 'bots on ahead," he said, pulling the remote for them off his belt. "We should all back off another five feet or so."

Increasing their range, he watched the faint telltales on his HUD as the 'bots scuttled past the partial barricade and down into the dip.

"They've not stopped, and we can't see what's beyond it until we're actually there." He looked up at J'korrash, seeing only the faint image of her face through the special Prime coating on both their helmets. "I need you and Q'almo to go ahead and scout it out. Be careful, it's likely to be a trap."

"Understood, Captain," she said quietly, turning away to call for Q'almo.

Guns held ready, the two advanced slowly to the barrier, skirting around it then disappearing from sight.

"There's nothing obvious to see, Captain," she said a few moments later. "It's a small cavern, and apart from the barricade, it looks the same as we left it."

"Stop when you get to the center," he said.

"Aye, sir. Approaching there now. Still seems normal. No, wait."

The channel fell silent.

"J'korrash, report," he snapped after a minute's prolonged silence.

"Sorry, sir. Seems to be another blockage, this time filling most of both tunnels where our route splits up ahead. We can't see from here whether it's natural or not."

"The 'bots are just ahead of you. What're they doing?"

"Nothing," said Q'almo. "They can't go any farther. They don't seem to have found anything, though."

"It could be mined," he muttered to himself as he mentally ran through all Kaid's knowledge of dirty tricks, searching for an answer, and coming up blank. If there were explosives, the 'bots would surely sniff them out—unless they were buried deep in the fake fall-in. "Stay where you are," he ordered. "We're coming in. Zhalmo, take Valden and Zsurtul to the rear and keep them there."

They advanced slowly toward the barricade, edging carefully past it until they were inside the small cavern. Even with all his senses straining to find anything unnatural in the area, he could sense nothing that was out of the ordinary.

Ahead, the floor of the cavern was uneven, with several large boulders strewn haphazardly about where the long gone river's flow had left them. Just beyond the center, some twenty feet away, J'korrash and Q'almo waited for them.

"Single file. Stay close to the walls," he said, leading by example. "If anything happens, it should be safer there. J'korrash, Q'almo, head for the other side. Work your way closer to the rockfall."

Time was wasting again, but they couldn't afford to be careless this close to their goal.

He held up his hand, signaling those behind to stop just

before he got to the halfway mark. J'korrash and Q'almo were approaching the second barrier now.

"Blockage seems to be mainly across the right-hand fork, Captain," said J'korrash, her voice a soft whisper. "We'll still have to dismantle some of it to get through, though."

He did some rapid calculations, mostly involving the time they had left—twenty-six minutes and forty-five seconds.

"Back off fifteen feet, then hit the left-hand side with five thirty-second streams from the rifles," he ordered. He had no option but to risk the lives of the two commandos. They had to get into the Control Room in time to turn off the force field and the gun turrets, or the area outside the Palace walls would become a killing ground. Nerves taut, he settled back against the wall, watching them, gun ready for anything that presented itself as a target.

Slowly the two soldiers backed off until they were at the distance Kusac had said. As one, they began to shoot at the rockfall, streams of energy leaping from the barrels of their rifles and splattering over the surface.

Far away, out by the Orbital, Kusac felt Carrie's fear and reached out to her.

Just slow your breathing, cub. Take long, slow breaths, Kusac sent, keeping as much of his attention as he could on what J'korrash and Q'almo were doing.

Inside her helmet, she nodded, forcing herself to hold her breath a little longer before taking another gulp of air.

That's right. Now let it out, Kusac sent, his tone gentle and patient.

With an effort, she began to release the breath as a great weight continued to press her deeper and deeper into the pod's padding.

She heard a mental chuckle, and afterward she swore she felt the touch of Kusac's fingers on her cheek.

Good, cub. You've been launched; that's the worst part over. It's plain sailing from now on. I have to go. I'll see you in K'oish'ik.

Kusac? Kusac! she cried out. "Don't go yet!" The break in their contact hurt so much.

He has to, Dzinae. He has his own people to look after, sent Kaid. *I'm right behind you. Just breathe slowly like he said, and you'll be fine.*

Fighting down the panic, she began to gain control of her breathing and tried not to envisage how she was tumbling toward the planet's surface at a speed that was already beginning to burn the outer ablative shell off the drop pod.

It's designed to burn up a layer at a time, sent Dzaka, his mental tone steadying her and driving away the last of her panic. *I'll be here for you, Carrie. My father will contact you when he can, but he has to oversee the whole mission too.*

I understand, she replied.

A murmur of conversation from behind him caught Kusac's attention, drawing it back from Carrie to the scene in front of him. He turned around, catching sight of Valden stepping away from the wall to stare up at the cavern roof. Zsurtul was already reaching out for him, ready to draw him back.

"Valden!" he shouted.

At that precise moment, the barrier on both tunnels broke open with a roar that deafened them all.

Kusac barely had time to launch himself backward, not for Valden, but for the Prince; then the wall of water engulfed them all.

As the water hit him, it flung him forward into Zsurtul, allowing him to grab hold of the young Emperor and lock him tight against his body. He felt another body hit them both—Zhalmo—and cling onto Zsurtul from behind as the force of the water tossed them. Briefly, he wondered if Valden was safe; then he was slammed against a boulder, bent around it, and was swept away again.

All it needed was a crack in the visor, and any one of them would be dead. He tightened his grip on the Prince as the water surged between them, threatening to drag them apart as it sucked them backward, swirling them about until they were once again slammed into a solid surface.

This time, his head hit the back of his helmet with enough force to stun him. He felt his grip on Zsurtul begin to relax and gave a low moan of pain as nausea swept over him.

Someone was saying something, but the cries of fear and distress from the others were drowning it out.

Just as he was about to lose contact with the youth, he felt himself grasped firmly by the waist, and again by one arm. He heard a dull clunk as something hit his helmet, and he fought to focus beyond the blurry lights of his HUD.

"We've got you safe, Captain." Now he could hear. The voice—Zsurtul's—was reverberating inside his helmet.

He blinked several times until his vision began to clear. Yes, it was Zsurtul, with his helmet pressed up against Kusac's.

Control was coming back to his limbs now, and reaching out, he grasped the youth by the arms, trying to ignore his pounding head. He sucked in a breath at the sting in his neck as the suit decided to medicate him.

"Thanks," he said. "Zhalmo?"

"She has hold of us both," Zsurtul said. "The worst seems to be over now. The water's calm."

Water. That's what had been behind the barricade!

"An effective trap," said Zhalmo as the three of them began to slowly sink to the bottom. "If we hadn't been in armor, we'd be dead."

"I want K'hedduk alive, remember that," said Kusac as he began checking his HUD for the rest of his team. "Where's Valden?"

"I'm here," said the youngster.

All telltales were present and, for a wonder, green, including those of J'korrash and Q'almo. Even the two 'bots were still operational.

"Report in!" he ordered, feeling the cavern floor beneath his feet and trying to get a grip on it with the artificial claws in his boots. "Anyone injured or with a suit breach?"

They reported in, one at a time. Only J'korrash and Q'almo knew they had suit damage as the sealant had activated to repair it.

Now that the immediate danger was over, reaction was setting in for them all. Time to get everyone moving again and focused on their mission. The rifles would be thoroughly soaked and needed stripping down before they could risk using them. The pistols, stowed inside their suit thigh compartments, should still be dry, but he couldn't take the risk.

Twenty-nine minutes left. He began swearing under his breath.

"Very graphic, Captain. I'll try to remember some of them," said Zsurtul, with a forced laugh.

"You do, and Kezule will really try to skin me!" he said.

"My money would have to be on you, Captain," said Zhalmo. "May I suggest you don't let the General hear Sholan cuss words, Majesty?"

Aware that everyone was hearing their small talk, now that his head had cleared, he was able to sense their banter lifting the mood. He responded to her in kind.

"If you do, he'll learn a few more from me, Zsurtul! Head out to our tunnel exit, everyone! We've a job to do—and wet rifles to see to first!"

Their responses were crisp and businesslike, he was glad to hear, even though he knew most of them were still shaken by the experience—hell, *he* was.

"Remember, we're not dead yet, and they've only made us more determined to succeed," said Zsurtul, his voice firm and confident.

Our Princeling continues to amaze me, he sent to Zhalmo.

I know, she replied.

Had he heard pride in her mental voice? Was she that attached to Zsurtul after knowing him for such a short time?

Shaking his head slightly, he began to turn around, using the wall to help propel him. It was like moving in zero-gee but without being able to magnetize his boots to a metal surface.

The suit's system suddenly recognized his difficulty and increased his gravity. Now he was firmly on the cavern floor. Walking was still difficult because of the water, and he couldn't see more than a few inches beyond his faceplate because of the amount of mud and silt that had been churned up, but his HUD scanners were still functional and showing him which direction to take.

A few exclamations of surprise came across their channel as the others suddenly found themselves able to walk vertically too.

Within minutes, they were all clear of the water and standing just inside the left-hand fork of the tunnel.

Inspecting the rifles, Kusac found that two had been badly damaged—one bent beyond repair, the other possibly repairable in a workshop. He was pleased no one had dropped his or her weapon. Searching in mud for it wasn't something he could waste time on.

"Bury them under those rocks so we can retrieve them later," he said. "Meanwhile, get your pistols out. They need to be checked for water. Rest of you, strip the energy cells out of your rifles and dry them and the contacts. You have two minutes. Valden, give your rifle to Q'almo to deal with, then check your pistol, and, starting with mine, check everyone else's. Q'almo, when you're done, check everyone's suit for external damage."

"Aye, sir."

Crouching down on his haunches, he pulled out his pistol, laying it down before opening the sealed belt pouch containing his gun cleaning kit.

Quickly and efficiently, he popped his rifle cell free, mentally thanking Kaid for the hours of cleaning drills he'd put him through. It was good to be able to rely on his own experience this time.

Ninety seconds later, he was done. Slinging his weapon over his shoulder, he packed his kit away, checking to see how the rest were doing.

Khadui, J'korrash, and M'kou were finished and helping those beside them. Valden had completed his handgun inspection—they were all dry and functional, though the youth's own weapon had been jammed in its recess, and Q'almo had had to force it open.

He sat there impatiently, every second ticking down in his mind. By two minutes and five seconds, everyone was finished.

"Good work," he said, getting to his feet.

M'kou's suit was the only one to have taken on any water. A search found one small dent in the left leg piece, which was quickly rectified by slapping a temporary patch over it.

"You'll do," he said, after double-checking it for himself.

"The water's gone into my boot," M'kou complained, shaking his leg.

Khadui laughed. "Shaking it won't help. One of the joys of being an Operative, M'kou! Welcome to the Special Forces!"

"If you're all ready," Kusac began in an ominous tone.

Everyone scrambled to his or her feet.

"Check that your suits have returned to normal gee, and let's get moving."

In midstride, he was stopped dead by yet another shriek from Carrie. Stumbling, he staggered into Khadui, only to be grabbed by M'kou.

"Captain! What's wrong?"

Dragged into Carrie's mind by her terror, he barely heard him.

*   *   *

Carrie screamed long and loud as the shell surrounding her suddenly disintegrated, and she saw herself plunging through the air to the ground far below.

Carrie! The chute! Release your chute! sent Kaid, but Carrie's terror was too great for him to reach her.

"Chute," Kusac muttered. "Open the chute, cub!"

He seized her mind in an iron grip as, in sheer terror, her head searched blindly for the right control.

Here, sent Kusac, containing her fear, calming it as only he could. When she hit the control, he sensed the small ancillary chute opening and beginning to pull the main one free.

Now turn off the light. You want your night vision on, with IR filtering. Concentrate on the controls. You practiced it often enough today. That's right, he sent as she finally got the chute to deploy. *The light, Carrie, turn it off too ...*

The sudden jerk of the fully deployed chute came as another shock, and instinctively she grabbed hold of the cords. Then she was floating, and Kusac had gone again.

"He must have hit his head harder than I realized," said Zhalmo. "Get his helmet off, I need to do a visual check on him!"

He was aware of being pulled about as Khadui began to examine his forearm panel, and Zhalmo and M'kou started working on his helmet seals. He could do nothing to tell them he was all right, that it was just Carrie's fear that had pulled him out of himself.

"What did he say?" demanded M'kou.

"Something about chutes," said Khadui. "His telemetry's fine, the automed treated him when he hit his head."

"Cub? Whose cub?"

"Shut up, M'kou," snapped Zhalmo, finding the emergency latches on Kusac's helm and triggering them.

"But ..."

"It's his wife, dammit! Now do something useful!"

Just as he was beginning to recover, he was jerked back again.

Kusac! The chute's breaking off!

"Jets," he mumbled. *Jets, Carrie. Count to ten then trigger them.*

Too late! Turn them on now, Carrie! Kaid's mind, his mental training pushed aside in his need to save Carrie, was pure raw power as it thundered through both of theirs. *Now!*

Do it, sent Kusac, letting all caution go as he forced her mind to Link completely with his.

He looked through her eyes, seeing the ground so close—too close. Fumbling, he forced her hand over to the jet controls on her right forearm. Moments later, *they* were thrust momentarily upward as the jets broke her descent. The pressure forced her to remain upright, but as the burn lessened, he felt her begin to wobble.

A moment of panic almost overwhelmed even him, but Kaid was there, his strong, steadying presence taking control for the final moments.

I have you—both. There was surprise in his tone, and Kusac knew his sword-brother hadn't expected to find him there, Leska Linked to Carrie—and now to him.

Explanations would be wanted, demanded probably, ones he couldn't yet give them. He began to withdraw, then stopped.

We're not at the Command center yet. There were traps, a large reptile . . . We're all fine. Stay hidden till I send to you. And, Tallinu—get someone to the hostages fast. They plan to take the female to the harem this morning. They're here. He sent the images he'd taken from Shamgar while on the Orbital.

What? Kaid cursed briefly. *I'll see to it. Be quick, our air cover's due in twenty minutes. We'll wait for your signal. Stay safe, sword-brother.*

Take care! sent Carrie as he broke contact.

And you.

Keeping up the pretense that Zayshul mattered more to him than they did would be even more difficult and painful now.

"Captain, drink this," said Zhalmo insistently, pushing a container against his lips.

Still confused, he opened his eyes, blinking as he tried to orient himself. It had been . . . too long since he'd mind Linked with either of his Triad, and the experience had left him not just aching at the loss, but not quite sure he was back in his own body.

As the liquid began to dribble down his chin, he swallowed

convulsively, bringing up his hand to push the container away. It left a bitter taste in his mouth, one he knew well.

"There's nothing wrong with me," he snapped, struggling to sit up. When had they gotten him down onto the ground? "Where's my helmet? What's it doing off? Gods, that damned norrta head stinks, Zsurtul!"

"He's fine," said Khadui, holding out a helping hand and pulling him up to his feet when he took it. "One of those telepathic contacts, that's all."

"Captain?" asked Zhalmo.

"My helmet, please. I'm fine, Zhalmo. I don't need your analgesics. We have to hurry; the drop squad has landed. At least none of the rest of you took your helmets off!"

"Have you . . ." began M'kou, handing him his helmet as Zhalmo began to stash her small medkit away again.

"I've told them to wait for word from me before attacking," he said, lowering his helmet over his head and latching it in place.

As soon as the seal engaged, he felt the flow of oxygen start up.

Khadui tossed him his rifle, and they began to move off.

"Zsurtul, does that norrta stink like that all the time, or just when it's dead?" he asked as they jogged around the bend toward the last junction.

"Oh, it always smells like that," said the youth cheerfully. "Smells worse when it's been dead a couple of days, so my father told me."

"We're out of time now, can't be subtle about breaking into the command room. If we blew a hole in the wall, stuck that head through . . ."

"They'd panic," Zsurtul confirmed. "Anyone with any sense would. An enraged norrta is capable of knocking a wall down."

"Then that's what we'll do. M'kou, you and J'korrash have your gas canisters loaded up. I want them fired into the room as soon as we breach the emergency exit. You have enough explosives, Khadui?"

"Plenty, but I'll take some of those you're carrying too, Captain. Just to be sure."

Ghioass, **Camarilla**

Kuvaa stood in the empty Camarilla chamber watching Unity's projection as the potentialities meandered their way across the interface. For the last few days, unusually, the projection had been slow, almost peaceful. Except at the nexus point. It was there she was watching. There were things happening she didn't understand, was not sure how to interpret.

"The Hunter becomes stronger," said a voice behind her.

Turning, she found Khassis there. "Yes, Skepp Lady, he does."

"What will he become, I wonder?" The TeLaxaudin reached out and touched the center of the flowing, swirling mass of colors with a long, thin, bronzed digit.

Kuvaa tried to suppress her sharp intake of breath as she watched the colors eddy around the Elder's finger.

"A representation only, Kuvaa," said Khassis, amusement in her mental tone. "Look."

She thrust her hand deeper into the projection, letting the swirling ribbons of light cling to her wrist before sharply withdrawing it. Wisps of light shimmered in the air, hung for an instant then winked out of existence.

"It remains here."

Kuvaa's gaze was riveted on Khassis, where the colored ribbons roiled and twisted around her wrist like a living entity.

"How . . ." she began, then stopped as Khassis held that hand out to her.

"You manipulate matter. Take it from me."

"But why?" she asked, even as she reached for it.

Khassis let the strands twist and wriggle from her into the outstretched paws of Kuvaa.

"Time you learned how to directly affect the potentialities if you are to counter the plans of the Isolationists. This is as real as you want it to be."

Stunned, she stood there, colors swirling around in her paws like a miniature whirlpool of light. The colors were changing slowly, losing their brilliance. "Real?" she whispered. "You said it was a projection."

"Until you make it real. If you let them fade, then the moment will pass, and your direct intervention will be impossible. Make it real. Do it now, before it's too late."

"Do what? I don't understand."

"In the center, do you see where hot and cold dance together?"

She looked, unable to see what the elder was talking about. Then, a brief flash of blue-white caught her eye. "Yes!"

"Ah, then it is not just me," Khassis said with satisfaction. "Touch it with your mind and abilities, bend it to your will."

"Why? What is it?"

"Something I've only seen once or twice—an influence beyond us, one that hides itself from our control."

"I thought that was impossible."

"I thought so too until I first saw it. The moment passes, you must act swiftly."

"And do what? What is the desired outcome?" She was confused, unsure. In her hands the colors were fading, turning a dark earth brown.

"What outcome do you want?"

"I can't decide! I'm a Junior, I have no say!"

"Now you have. Do it now, or let it pass. Better you than Zaimiss."

The thought overwhelmed her, left her wondering why Khassis had chosen her. Then her resolve hardened, and she looked at the Elder.

"No," she said. "Everything should not be controlled. What if I choose wrong? I will leave it as it is, let the unknown element remain." She closed her paws on the now motionless brown puddle, watching as it squeezed between her hooves, dribbling down to the floor, dissipating before it landed.

"Your friends wait outside for you," said Khassis. "Tell them I am content. Time to find a replacement for you."

Kuvaa was left alone again, wondering what had just happened. Then the words hit her. "Replace me?"

Always there must be Juniors learning our skills, Kuvaa, sent Shvosi. *Now your turn, as Senior, to teach.*

But . . . she began.

Enough! sent Azwokkus. *Confused is she! Promotion, that was, Kuvaa. Join us, we tell you.*

She gave a last look at the projection as she dropped down onto all four feet and trotted along the path between the cushions and sloping recliners of her people, to the exit. Had the last few minutes really happened?

"Very real," said Azwokkus as he came to meet her, his pastel blue and lilac draperies exuding a pleased aroma. "The power have we to make changes on our own. Discipline and belief that we do make errors, cannot know everything, is vital for position we hold."

"I could have changed—everything—at that moment?" The thought shocked her.

"You did not," reminded Shvosi, joining them. "Celebrations we have now! Not every day one is lifted from Junior to Senior!"

"Too much power," Kuvaa murmured as she let them herd her toward the restaurant. "Could be abused too easily."

"Checks in Unity there are," reassured Azwokkus.

"Nothing is infallible. Hunter hides from us. What if one of the Camarilla did this?"

"Not possible. Hunter is different, a nexus, wild element."

"If he can be, so can one of us." She stopped and looked at them both, crest and ruff of coarser hair rising in a display of determination. "I will make security of Unity my personal field."

K'oish'ik

In the driving rain, none of the guards at the wide main gates into the walled city saw the low black shadows slip past them in the lee of the cargo haulers carrying their load of spares for the Palace force fields.

Keeping flat to the ground, Captain Tirak and his team waited till the gates had been shut again, and the guards had scurried back out of the rain into their posts.

Silently, one at a time, they rose, each running a few yards closer to the edges of the houses before falling flat and signaling the next to move. When they reached within thirty feet of the first of the nonfunctioning generators, Tirak pulled a small pistol free from his belt and, aiming carefully, pulled the trigger.

There was a small *phut* of released air, nothing more.

"Marker confirmed," Sheeowl whispered.

The pistol stowed away again, Tirak led his people toward the next generator in the relay.

"Captain," hissed Sheeowl. "To your left, five hundred yards away—looks like a gun turret!"

Pulling a pair of binoculars free of his belt pouch, he raised them to his eyes, looking for the object. Letting out a low curse, he lowered them. "Intel said nothing about gun turrets inside the City walls! Check out the rest of the grasslands for more of them."

Switching the main channel off, he activated a secure private one. "Ghost One, did you copy that?" he asked quietly.

"Aye. Located two pairs on either side of main highway and neutralized them. Send your people farther afield. Proceeding into City now."

CHAPTER 7

THEY were five minutes behind his schedule by the time they reached the end of the tunnel, but he'd managed to regain the dispassionate calm that had filled him on the *Kz'adul*. The longer they took to breach the Command Room, the greater the risk to those on the ground above them. He could not—would not—let that affect their actions here and now.

Before them, set into the living rock, was the large blast-proof door. He knew by just looking at it they couldn't breach it. He walked past it, trailing his gloved hand just above the rock surface, probing with his mind for the flow of energy from the stone that he knew would have to be there.

Stopping abruptly, he patted the wall and looked over to Khadui. "Here," he said quietly. "The rock's thin here and lined with brick on the inside. Place the charges here. Have that head ready, Noolgoi."

While Khadui was setting the explosives, he took the 'bots from Valden, quickly reprogramming them as he'd been shown.

"Give me the third one, M'kou," he said, placing the second on the tunnel floor by the first one. "Call up the Command Center layout on your HUDs now. We're entering in the guardroom. See where the wall-mounted laser guns and the exits are. No one must get out or set off an alarm. Note the laser turrets and retinal scans— disable them only if there are no living targets and the 'bots aren't dealing with them."

He stopped, taking the last 'bot from M'kou. "Noolgoi, as soon as that charge goes off, stick the norrta head in low through the opening, count to ten then throw it in, then fall back so we can get through. J'korrash, M'yikku, you're with me. I want those gas grenades going off the instant Noolgoi shoves that head into the gap. Next in are Noolgoi and Q'almo. Khadui, M'kou, you'll be in front of the Prince, guarding him once we're inside. Pulse shots only, both of you. Immediately on our left is the door to the elevator area from the Throne Room—you'll deal with that, we'll handle the main guards. To our right, at the other end of the room, are the guard post and the door to the Command Room. It's soundproofed, so they won't hear us. We'll clear the guardroom while you handle the access room. There are three lasers set into the wall. One covers the door to the elevator room, one covers the guard post at the far end, and the remaining one covers the rest. We'll clear that room. Noolgoi, you'll take up position watching the elevator while the rest of us regroup and head for the Command Room. Once it's taken, go to your designated posts and guard Zsurtul and Valden. Any questions?"

He waited for their low chorus of negatives before continuing.

"Gas grenades first, then over to energy slugs. Shoot anything that moves. Zhalmo, keep Zsurtul and Valden to the rear. You two," he said, looking up at the Prince and the young Sholan as he placed the last 'bot on the ground, "have pulse rifles—use them to kill if you have to, forget about wounding. Try to avoid damaging any equipment if you can. That goes for all of you."

"Ready, Captain," Khadui said, stepping back several feet and priming the detonator.

He nodded briefly. "Do it. Good hunting, everyone," he said.

With a muffled crump, the charges blew a ragged gap in the wall.

As Noolgoi shoved the norrta's head into the opening, Kusac activated the three 'bots, and J'korrash and M'yikku fired several rounds of gas canisters into the opening.

The smell of the norrta had the desired effect. The three guards sitting around the table remained frozen in shock long enough for Kusac, J'korrash, and M'yikku to let loose their gas canisters over Noolgoi's and the norrta's heads.

The sound of them hitting the ground instantly brought the guards to life. Two bolted toward the back of the room, the third, obviously one of the altered thugs, rose to his feet and, snatching his rifle from the floor beside him, began to advance toward the opening.

Noolgoi heaved the creature's head through the opening, diving to the left to leave the way clear for Kusac.

His rifle already ratcheted over to pulse fire, with his free hand Kusac swiped at the nearest edge of the hole, sending several more feet of brick wall cascading to the ground. In the same move, he propelled himself inside the room, firing an almost continual burst at the advancing male.

The guard slowed, staggering slightly as he continued to raise his weapon.

Diving to the right, past the range of the laser, Kusac continued shooting, this time at his legs. Roars of pain filled the air. Moments later, a second stream of energy from J'korrash hit the guard square in the chest, cutting short the cries and finally sending him toppling to the ground.

A quick glance at his HUD told him the 'bots were already scurrying toward the lasers, and the two remaining guards had taken refuge in the reinforced guard post at the far end.

A single shot turned the farthest laser, the one presenting the most danger to them, to a smoking ruin as J'korrash came level with him. He heard the sound of scrabbling and a sharp pop as the 'bot above his head dealt with the one there.

M'yikku vaulted through the opening to join them, glancing over at the still twitching body of the thug only feet away.

"They don't even look like our species any more," he muttered. "K'hedduk's a menace to his own kind."

A shot hit the edge of the table, sending splinters flying into the air, focusing their attention back on the reality of the two guards now hiding out in the reinforced security post at the far end of the room.

Kusac signaled J'korrash forward. "Neutralize it," he ordered. "Noolgoi, Q'almo, take the elevator room now."

"Aye, sir," said J'korrash, ratcheting her rifle over to short-range missiles. Moments later, the post exploded with a dull crump in a shower of debris.

The dust had barely begun to settle before Kusac was running over. On his HUD, he could see that the 'bot had dealt with the remaining turret. Scanning the debris, he found a few cooling remains that had been the now dead guards.

"Clear here," he said, shifting his attention to the heavy door leading into the Command Room proper.

The sound of a short firefight came from the access room, then Noolgoi and Q'almo were giving the all clear.

"Bring Zsurtul up now," he ordered. "We need him to open this door."

Once again, Zsurtul gave the password. This time, the AI responded with, "The God-King has spoken. Greetings, Emperor Zsurtul Shan-Cheu'ko'h. May you reign and live forever. What are your instructions, Exalted One?"

Uncertainly, Zsurtul glanced at Kusac and Zhalmo. "I . . . um . . ."

"I hope you've plans to rid the Palace of the usurper, Highness," the AI said. "I have done my best to isolate him from my crucial functions, but even now the technicians are working on . . ."

"Enough!" said Zsurtul hurriedly. "Open the door, ZSADHI, but don't alert those inside I'm here. Also, deactivate the lasers and retinal scans inside the Control Room." He turned to look at Kusac. "Not all in there will be collaborators. Surely they don't all have to die?"

"We won't shoot the unconscious ones," he said, keeping his attention on the door. He was experiencing a vague feeling of déjà vu. The word that Zsurtul had used sounded familiar, but where had he heard it before?

"Gas grenades ready," he warned. "Zhalmo, get Zsurtul and Valden to the back again."

As the door unlocked and began to swing open, Kusac shoved the muzzle of his gun through the aperture, letting off two gas grenades before falling back to ratchet around to pulse fire and let the others unload their grenades into the room.

Exclamations of shock and surprise came from inside, followed by coughing and the sound of running feet.

By now the door was fully open, and they could clearly see the seven technicians, hands over their faces, running for the door, followed by a single implanted Palace Guard who was pulling out his sidearm.

Kusac dropped him with one precise shot.

Before the first of the civilians reached them, they were stopping in midstride and crumpling bonelessly to the ground, unconscious. Only two made it past him, and those were taken out by himself and J'korrash.

"Get the dead out of here," ordered Kusac, stepping into the room to do a visual sweep. "Secure the unconscious ones, then put them in the guardroom. Sling the dead in the tunnel for now. Zsurtul, Valden, it's up to you. We need that force field down and the turrets disabled as soon as possible. Zhalmo, Q'almo, M'kou, don't leave your Emperor's side."

Stepping over the bodies, he made his way over to the central console. Rifle slung to one side, he leaned on the chairback, searching the panels of keys and buttons for those that controlled the environment.

Finding the one he wanted, he turned the air-conditioning up to full to flush out the sleep gas.

Out of the corner of his eye, he saw Valden reach up to remove his helmet. "Don't be foolish! It'll take about ten minutes until the gas has dissipated. You can take off your gloves, but nothing else until I tell you it's safe."

"Sorry, Captain, I forgot," the youth replied, taking the seat beside Zsurtul.

"I cannot give you access to that function, Highness," said the AI for the seventh time. "It has been isolated from my control."

"Dammit!" swore Kusac, hovering behind Zsurtul and Valden. He was beginning to dislike the anonymous pleasant tones that the computer utilized. "What *do* you still have control over?"

"Answer the Captain. He is one of my Generals," said Zsurtul absentmindedly as he continued going through various diagnostic routines, trying to access the areas K'hedduk had managed to isolate.

"I'm in!" said Valden suddenly. "I can access the gun turrets—well, some of them," he amended as Kusac stepped over to him.

"Which ones?"

"Those on the perimeter beside the force fields," he said. "I've turned them off. I can't access those inside the Palace walls, though."

"That's something," Kusac muttered. "Turn off their main power now, and I'll contact Kaid and let them know."

"They're on emergency power anyway," said Valden.

"Looks like the storm took out their rooftop generators before they got the force field up."

"I need you all to have your retinal scans taken," said Zsurtul suddenly. "The Palace has extensive security measures based on ZSADHI recognizing you."

"We haven't the time," said Kusac. "Just turn all security measures off for now. We can't take the risk of anything firing on Kaid and the others."

"Captain," said the AI "You requested a list of the areas over which I still have control. They are as follows: all security gates and doors into the Palace and the Detention center, security scanners and lasers at main staircases and outside the Royal apartments, all levels of alarm systems, communications systems within the Palace itself, though I do seem to have a troublesome erratic memory error . . ."

"Enough!" said Kusac. "Turn off your virus, Valden. Give control back to the AI, and then we can change the codes."

"How'd you know about that?" demanded the youth, turning around so quickly he almost dislodged Kusac's helmet from the console.

"Take it easy, youngling," said Khadui, grabbing it before it could fall.

Kusac let out a growl of annoyance. "Just focus on what you're supposed to be doing! I'm going into the guardroom to contact Kaid and the HALO team."

K'oish'ik surface, 03:15 hours local

"We're on," Kaid said quietly over the Command channel to all eight Fire Packs. "Form up with the rest of your Pack now. Aerial support should be here any time to give us cover."

Can you alert the captives, Kusac? Kaid sent.

Will do, came the terse reply, then his mental presence was gone.

Kaid sighed and turned to Carrie just as a large dark shape came lumbering toward them through the driving rain.

"I with you, Carrie," said a well-remembered voice in their headsets. "Kaid says I watch your back. Better I do than last time. Nothing will I let near you," the young Sumaan said firmly as he settled his large bulk on the ground.

"Ashay!" she exclaimed, reaching out to put her gloved hand on the knee of the large suited figure beside her as the reptilian Sumaan bent his mobile neck down to her level.

Stay with him at all times, Dzinae, sent Kaid. *He's heavily armored and can look out for both you and himself if need be. I'll stay with you whenever possible.*

"Toueesut, Heokee, let me know when you start the main gate assault."

"Aye, Kaid," was all the reply Toueesut made.

Kaid rose to his feet, making sure that his small team was beside him. At least while they'd waited for word from Kusac, he'd been able to orient them on the exact part of the City wall he wanted to penetrate. They'd waited out the delay by making their way to a point only a few hundred yards from the fifteen-foot-high wall.

"Packs Two through Eight, move out on my six," he ordered. "Missiles to the front with me."

You'll be with me if I need Ashay to breach the wall, Carrie. Remember to keep clear of our armored tails, he added.

Aye, she sent.

Carrie held her heavy assault rifle close as she followed behind Kaid. Around her she was aware of the shapes of the others and the comforting bulk of the Sumaan fighter on her right-hand side. Though nervous, she wasn't unduly so. They'd been in less clear-cut combat situations before. This time she knew who the enemy was, and she was well armored.

Kaid called a halt just short of the high wall, ordering them to hunker down once more and wait.

The order to advance came suddenly. "Heavy units to the front. Take down that wall."

"Aye," said Zsafar and Shartoh, running forward with their missile launchers. Another four people joined them. Moments later, a section of the wall erupted in a fountain of debris that was quickly dissipated by the rain.

"I go!" said Ashay, almost before Kaid gave him the order. "Carrie stay here."

She watched the youth bound across the gap between them and the irregular hole in the wall, his heavy hind legs propelling him forward in leaps and bounds. *Like a cross between a dinosaur and a puppy,* she thought.

More like a large and friendly velociraptor, sent Jo.

Grinning, she turned to look at the other woman and almost missed Ashay's shoulder ramming the side of the wall while his tail delivered a mighty blow to the other side, opening the gap up to one they could now easily get through.

"I didn't realize they were so powerful!"

"Oh, yes, and still some growing I have to do," said Ashay cheerfully as he shook the debris off his suit and trotted back to them.

"Good work, Ashay," said Kaid as he passed him. "Let's get in there. Maaz'ih, you're on point with me."

She followed at the rear, stepping through the gap into the City grounds just before Ashay did. Through her visor she could just make out the outline of the domed force field glowing around the Palace and its walls, and the dark shapes of the surrounding city.

"Buildings to the left," murmured Garras.

"Animal shelters," said Maaz'ih. "Beyond them is the farmhouse."

"Check it out," said Kaid. "See if there are any lights showing."

"None, Captain," Maaz'ih said a few minutes later.

"Let's move," Kaid said.

"I'm reading a power source ahead," said Zsafar suddenly. "Looks like a gun turret."

"Maaz'ih?" Kaid demanded.

"I know nothing about them, Captain. They must be new. No lights in the animal shelters."

"Or very ancient," muttered Zsafar, continuing to fiddle with his scanner. "Power source is almost depleted, and I'm picking up an underground elevation system under it. My guess is they've been buried for a long time."

"Is it functional?" Kaid demanded, halting them.

"If it were, the farmhouse would be a ruin," Zsafar said dryly.

Carrie, ask Kusac . . .

On it, she replied, already reaching out for him. *Not under the main AI control, he says. They can't access that network, doesn't even show up.*

"Damn," Kaid muttered. "Zhookah, take it out."

"Wraiths to Jeggets, making first sweep now," said a voice in Carrie's helmet. *"Targets identified by markers. We have two, repeat two targets in red zone and two in the field."*

"Copy," said Kaid. *So that's what Tirak was up to,* he sent to Carrie. *Painting the turrets for our fighters.*

Seems like, she agreed. *Who gave him the orders, though? That, I'll find out later.*

Ahead of them, the dark shape of the gun turret seemed to crumple as the missile hit it.

"First strike on its way," Kaid told them over the Command channel. "Time to head on up and join the party."

They were still a good fifty feet away from the broken generator when the lasers on the fighters hit it. It erupted with a satisfying *crump*, leaving a small pillar of debris hanging momentarily in the air. To their right and left, other missiles were exploding around the edges of the force field or actually against it.

With any luck they'll overload it, and it will shut down, Kaid sent to her.

"They know we're here now," said Maaz'ih, his tone one of satisfaction.

"Packs, disperse to your allotted targets," Kaid ordered as they began to advance on the Palace walls.

A dark shadow darted across the surface of the force field, guns streaming plasma bursts at the generator on the corner to their left. Chunks of soil and rock were propelled into the air from the shots that missed; then suddenly the whole corner of the wall bellied outward before collapsing. The force field flickered, the blue-white glow dimming then brightening again as the field compensated for yet another missing generator.

"Generator 1 is down," said Rezac. "Field is defaulting to a straight line between 2 and 7."

"Alpha One to Jeggets. Generator 6 is also down. New targets are 2 and 7. Repeat, concentrate efforts on 2 and 7, and the force field will collapse."

Kezule, she thought, aware of Kaid changing his plans even as he absorbed the new information.

"Copy. Packs Two and Three, take out relay 2. Packs Four and Five, unit 7. Rest of you with me," said Kaid. "We're going in through that breach. Pull up your TAC maps now. I need those laser turrets taken out ASAP."

Stay with Ashay, Carrie, he sent, heading off into the night at a run.

Palace of Light

"We're under attack?" K'hedduk repeated, sitting up in bed and staring disbelievingly at Fabukki.

"Look out the window, Highness. The force field is absorbing damage—for now. We must leave immediately!"

"Take charge of the troops and set up defenses on the first floor," ordered K'hedduk, flinging back the bedclothes and getting to his feet.

"I'll send up your bodyguard, then see to that, Highness."

"No! See to our defenses," he hissed, heading for his dressing room. "I'll be safe as long as no one gets past you!"

"Yes, Highness," murmured Fabukki, bowing as he left.

Many things were running through K'hedduk's mind as he pushed the racks of clothing aside until he came to where he'd concealed his body armor. Returning to M'zull with the Empress beside him, he could spin the truth any way he wanted. She was his link to the Throne of Light; he needed her. But taking Fabukki along, never mind any of the other four of his original crew, all witnesses to his inability to hold this backwater planet, was not part of his plan. He intended a victorious return, one where he and the Empress had narrowly escaped Fabukki's plot against him.

Struggling into the suit, he thumbed on his communicator, praying it would work. It did. "Zoshur, we're under attack. Take the troops down to the first level and prevent them gaining access to the Palace at all costs."

"Yes, Majesty," came the reply. "Want anyone up there as bodyguards?"

"No. You take control along with Fabukki. Make sure he stays with you. I'll be safe here."

He cut the connection and, thrusting the communicator into a belt pouch, grabbed his helmet. Hurriedly he crossed the bedroom and headed for the communicating door between his room and his Royal harem, where he kept the Empress.

NL

Palace of Light, grounds, about 03:20 local

Red and gold light blossomed from the wall opposite, catching Carrie's gaze as Ashay took her firmly by the arm and pulled her to his side.

"I guard you now, Carrie," he said, lowering his long, suited neck until his head was level with hers. "Stay in safe zones we must, where turrets cannot hit us."

Momentarily overwhelmed by the information that Kaid was mentally processing and the orders he was calling out to the other seven Fire Pack Leaders, she nodded her head, forgetting Ashay probably wouldn't see the gesture.

"I can see them on my TAC screen, Ashay," she said, finding her voice at last as Ashay led her through the breach in the wall and into the outer grounds of the Palace.

The telltales of each team were showing clearly on her HUD as the Packs with them spread out, targeting the laser turrets spaced out on both sides of the outer wall. Realizing she was clutching her rifle too hard, she loosened her grip, readying it, but there seemed to be no opposition to them—no enemy telltales.

Placing her between the wall and himself, Ashay let her arm go to grasp his own firearm more firmly.

"Back here we'll stay," he said, even as Kaid's order to him came over her helmet comm. "We watch for enemy coming through doors ahead. They go to disable turrets and set rear charges behind generator,"

"I know," she said quietly. Her heart was beating faster now, and she could feel herself breathing more rapidly.

Dzaka, hold your Fire Pack back with Carrie and Ashay. Watch these main doors. We're heading for the parking lot and the rear of generator 7.

Aye, his son acknowledged, moving forward till his Pack flanked Carrie and Ashay on both sides.

Red and orange plasma flares blossomed across the surface of the force field where it lay diagonally across the far side of the Palace courtyard.

"Watch the doors," Ashay advised. "Others the laser turrets are targeting."

The actinic glow of the force field was beginning to flicker and darken, not only at ground level, but also across the surface of its dome where the fighters were still targeting it.

At worst, we'll wear it down, Dzinae, Kaid sent. *It can only absorb so much damage before it fails.*

Take care, she sent back, eyes straining to see him among the flares of multicolored lights.

Of course, and don't look for me, focus on those doors!

I need to know where you are.

On the HUD, he replied briefly.

Switching her attention back to the main entrance to the Palace, she glanced at the HUD display, finding the telltale that was Kaid easily among the others. From the look of it, he and his Pack had already made it to the far side, taking out the turrets as they went. Now all that held them back was the force field itself.

Once more, red and orange flares lit up the night as they began bombarding the wall between them and the generator

Light lanced toward her, but Ashay was already lifting her out of its path as he simultaneously sent a fusillade of shots toward the suddenly active security post flanking the main entrance.

Six more streams of energy joined his and seconds later, the turret and guard post exploded in a shower of debris. Already Dzaka's Pack was targeting the other post, and she barely had time to get one shot off before it, too, was destroyed.

The force field ahead was suddenly shot through with red and green, and then they were pitched into profound darkness as generator 7 was finally destroyed.

"7 down," she heard Kaid say in clipped tones over the Command channel.

"Copy. Backup on the way. Proceed to east side entrance," Kezule replied.

"Acknowledged. Dzaka, Ashay, rendezvous with me now."

"On our way," Dzaka replied.

She reached Kaid's side just before the area was suddenly swarming with loping Touibans heading for the main doors.

They'll distract any defense while we break in the side entrance, Kaid sent to her.

A loud explosion from inside the covered parking area momentarily drowned out the terse conversations among the rest of their Fire Pack.

"Turret out, door open," said Jurrel. "Preparing to advance."

Carrie could hear the pleased tone in his voice.

"Go," said Kaid, heading up into the covered area ahead.

As she followed, she tracked Jurrel on the TAC map on her HUD. He and his Pack were edging into the open corridor, keeping to the safe zone where the turret set above the side entrance couldn't reach them.

Dodging among the parked vehicles, Carrie found herself wondering how Ashay, at over seven feet tall, could possibly manage to keep himself under cover.

He stays out of the light, hugs the walls, sent Kaid from just in front of her. *Worry about yourself—stay focused, Carrie!*

I am, she replied tartly, following him as he and the others dashed across the last open space to the back wall.

"Turret down" said Jurrel. "Safe."

"Copy," said Kaid, carefully edging his way around the gaping hole where the door had been and into the small yard beyond.

"Any news on 2, Alpha One?" he asked. "Until it's out, the force field cuts right through the central courtyard."

"2 down!" Rezac's voice filled her helmet. "Field is failing."

"Copy. Proceed to west target entrance. Pack Leader, you hear that? Generator 2 is down. The field should collapse any time now," said Kezule.

"Understood," Kaid replied. "T'Chebbi, take point. Jurrel, follow her."

"Copy," they both replied.

The side entrance led them into a narrow street, empty in the torrential rain, between the tall buildings of the west wing of the Palace. In a rolling advance, they proceeded along it until Kaid called a halt.

"Central courtyard ahead," Kaid said. "Packs Two and Three, report."

"Target area appears clear," said Jayza. "Continuing toward captives."

"Copy." *Rezac?*

Barracks empty as we anticipated. Almost at cells now.

Take them to rendezvous immediately. They are noncoms at this time. On no account are our Brothers to join us.

Understood.

"Packs Seven and Eight, the power plant is at the far end of the main courtyard. Six, you're still with me, making sure they get there. Move out!" he ordered.

"Force field is down, Pack One," Carrie heard Kezule say as the sickly blue-white glow that lit the night ahead of them suddenly went out. "Contact with Control Team established. Internal security is now ours. It is safe to proceed into the Palace."

"Copy," said Kaid, gesturing his Pack forward. *Kusac made it,* he sent to Carrie.

Good.

03:25 hours local

Like shadows, they slipped from doorway to garbage dumpster, working their way silently toward the far end of the courtyard. At the exit to the last building, they stopped while Jurrel and T'Chebbi scouted ahead, one down either side.

"Reception committee," said Jurrel from his vantage at the north end of the alley. "One large gun emplacement dead ahead, ten soldiers, not armored. In front of small fountain."

"Two more this end, and thirty troops," said T'Chebbi. "Guarding corridor into Palace."

"Maaz'ih, Shartoh, Dzaka, take positions," he ordered.

As the heavy gunners loped forward, Carrie could sense Kaid weighing the odds.

"Looks like a pitched battle ahead of us," he said, his tone a slow drawl. "We need a clear path to the covered street that heads north out of the courtyard. Once we've got it, we hold it till Packs Seven and Eight return."

"In position," said Shartoh. Moments later, the other two checked in.

"You know the drill—take 'em out," Kaid ordered, his voice sharpening to a crisp command.

"They're moving civilians in front," said Jurrel.

Do it now! Before.... Carrie began.

"Go!" Kaid repeated, cutting over her thoughts.

The silence was shattered by the dull *crump* of successive explosions, followed by the sound of rapid gunfire. Carrie shut her mind and tried not to think of who was being wounded. There was no choice—what were a few deaths against the whole City and Palace, to say nothing of the worlds beyond that.

"Done, but need backup! Coming out of the woodwork at us!" called Jurrel as the shooting continued.

"Move out and engage," Kaid ordered, gesturing them forward with a wave of his arm. "You know your targets!"

Carrie followed close on his heels, Ashay loping alongside her as they stopped at the entrance to the courtyard.

Focus only on the job! Kaid's sending jerked her gaze away from the bodies lying sprawled in unnatural positions around the smoking ruins of the gun emplacements.

Aye, she sent, fingers tightening on her rifle.

"Carrie, take out the damned trees. I can't see past them," Kaid ordered, ducking into the store doorway.

Ratcheting the grenades into active mode, she raised her rifle and fired. There was only a slight kick against her armored shoulder, then, seconds later, the palms surrounding the central fountain exploded in a spray of shards of wood and pulped greenery.

"Better," he grunted, diving toward the fountain wall for cover.

Carrie had no chance to follow him as gouts of energy from the doorway opposite tracked his path.

The next ten minutes passed in a haze of chaotic activity. It was followed by moments of intense silence, broken only by sporadic shooting as each side tried to maneuver to their advantage.

Sweat began to trickle down her back until the suit's internals sensed it and compensated. She could sense Kaid's hand with its missing finger begin to ache, feel him flexing it to ease the pain—and his instant reassurance that he was fine.

Stay there! Kaid's sudden order was followed by a compulsion to remain that shocked her to the core as he and the rest of his Pack, on fours, dove out into the open and raced for the remnants still blocking access to the covered street.

She watched them rear up suddenly, vibro swords and

knives drawn, the blades edging their tails slashing as fast as their weapons. It was over in the blink of an eye, and then they were back in the lee of the central fountain's low wall.

"Seven and Eight, go!" Kaid ordered, sliding into a controlled stop by the low wall.

"On our way," she heard Dzaka say as his and Jurrel's Packs raced for the entrance.

The air was filled with the whine of energy weapons and the sound of their explosions.

"T'Chebbi, report," said Kaid curtly, glancing over to where she and Ashay still hid in the alleyway.

"Both guns down. Need backup. More of them coming from Palace." Her tone was terse.

"Understood," he said.

As soon as he lifted his arm to gesture her and Ashay forward, she began to run, fear lending her extra speed. Sliding to a stop on the loose gravel that now peppered the courtyard, she flung herself down into a crouch beside Kaid, Ashay hunkering down behind her.

"I need you and Ashay to remain here and cover us," he said. "Use those warrior instincts of yours."

Through his visor, she saw his canines gleam white as he flashed a smile at her. She nodded.

He turned away, his attention now focused fully on his Pack and relieving T'Chebbi. "On our way," he said, rising to his feet.

Command Room, Palace of Light

As Zhalmo left the Control Room to check in on those by the elevator, Zsurtul got to his feet. Tilting his head from side to side to ease the cramp in it, he moved over to where Kusac sat perched on the edge of the console nearest the door.

"Zhalmo. She is a good fighter," the Prince said quietly, lowering his head so it was level with the Sholan's. "A perfect choice for a bodyguard."

"Indeed," said Kusac, looking at him thoughtfully. "Kezule's choice."

Zsurtul met the amber eyes with his own, forcing down his species' natural instinct to look away. "Beautiful too."

"Beautiful and deadly, the best combination," Kusac agreed. "And her loyalty and friendship know no boundaries."

Zsurtul nodded, his mind drifting slightly as he gathered his courage. "They say you knew Carrie was your natural mate as soon as you met her," he said in a rush. "Is this true?"

Kusac blinked then looked away. "Why do you ask?"

"Did you know?" Zsurtul asked again, wondering where his newfound courage came from.

"Yes. I knew, and so did she," he replied. "But why should . . ."

"I think I've found mine . . . In Zhalmo," he said quickly before he changed his mind.

Kusac's amber eyes regarded him again, seeming to look right into the core of his being. Then the Sholan nodded. "I believe you."

Zsurtul felt suddenly weak with the release of tension and clutched at the console to steady himself. "You do?" Somehow he'd expected the Sholan to deny the possibility.

"You don't need my belief, Emperor, only your own."

Zsurtul found himself nodding his head slowly in agreement. "You're right, of course. I intend to make her my Queen." He winced inwardly at the implicit challenge in his voice.

"She's certainly of Royal blood," was all that Kusac said.

Zsurtul opened his mouth to speak when suddenly he was filled with an overwhelming sense of danger threatening his mother.

"I have to go!" Zsurtul said, spinning around and taking off at a run for the emergency elevator up to the Royal Apartments.

"What the . . ?" he heard Kusac say as he left the main room.

Careering through the guardroom, with a sweep of his hand he shoved aside those on duty by the elevator, flung himself into it, and closed the door.

"Stop him, dammit!" Kusac yelled, launching himself off the edge of the console and heading after the young Emperor. "Zhalmo! Stop him!"

By the time Zhalmo and the others had regained their footing and collected their wits, the elevator doors had already closed, and the Prince was gone.

Her reply was slow in coming and when it did, it was accompanied by curses. "He's gone, Captain. Took the elevator up to . . ."

"I know where he went," Kusac snapped, pushing his way through the now crowded guardroom to the smaller one beyond. "Is there any other way up from here? An emergency stairwell?"

"No, Captain. We came in the exit, and . . ."

Kusac waved her to silence, reaching out with his mind, trying to read Zsurtul, discover what had made him run off. He met the natural barrier of all the Primes, this time even stronger than before. All he could glean from the youth was a sense of fierce determination.

"How long before it returns?" he demanded, rounding on J'korrash. Then he caught sight of Valden and M'kou. "Get back to that damned AI!" he roared, ears flattening to the side and baring his canines in a real show of anger. "This doesn't take all of us! Lives depend on your ability to reroute control of *all* security systems to here!"

As they hurriedly disappeared, he turned back to the young female. "Well?"

"Two or three minutes only, Captain," she replied, raising her chin and trading stares with him.

Rapidly he ran through his options. He needed to stay here. Taking control of the Palace from K'hedduk was his first responsibility. Khadui was the obvious choice to send with Zhalmo, but he was injured . . . and he didn't want to deplete the numbers he had here.

"Get that elevator back down," he said, making up his mind. "Zhalmo and J'korrash, you go after him. I can't leave here yet. How many levels can he exit to?"

"Three," said J'korrash. "The Throne Room, Audience Hall, and the Emperor's private chambers."

"Dammit! He's gone after his mother!" he snarled as realization hit him. "Get suited up again. Start at the top and work down, Zhalmo, unless you can track him by scent or your psi abilities. Any trouble, send to me. Don't take risks, but get him back here even if you have to stun and carry him!"

"Understood, Captain," said Zhalmo. "I apologize for not . . ."

"Don't waste time blaming yourself. Just bring him back safely," Kusac interrupted, turning away from her to return to the Control Room.

"Yes, Captain."

His mind focused only on the overwhelming fear he knew came from his mother, Zsurtul hit the button to take him up to the Imperial private apartments—his, now. They were there, her and that . . . animal . . . who had killed his father. Rage filled him, dimming his vision until everything seemed washed with red.

Part of him sat back wondering at the lack of fear he felt as he clenched his teeth together and pulled his pistol free from his belt. All the lessons he'd learned at the Sholan Warriors' Guild came back to him now, and taking up a stance in the corner farthest from the door, as it opened, he was ready for anyone on the other side.

The concealing curtain was pulled back, giving him a clear view of the opposite wall. He listened, straining every nerve for any sound before cautiously stepping out into the bathroom. Remembering those below, he reached back inside to lock the elevator on this floor—he couldn't afford to be stranded here.

Cautiously easing himself along the side of the wall, he risked a quick look around the corner into the rest of the room to make sure it was indeed empty. A few steps took him to the door into the main suite. He stopped and pressed his ear to the door; he waited, listening, but the pounding of his own heart threatened to drown out any noise there might be in the room beyond. Opening the door carefully, he peered through the gap. Yards away, a massive leather-clad Prime, lurid tattoos decorating the top of his head, was bending over a cringing female.

The guard looked up, eyes instantly locking with his. Panic washed through Zsurtul, turning his limbs to lead as the male uttered a hiss of rage and reached for his gun while stepping toward him. At his feet, the female turned to look, uttered a sharp cry of recognition, and flung herself around the legs of the guard, attempting to stop him.

"Run, Majesty! Run!"

Before he could move, the guard shot at him while reaching down for the female; he grasped her by the shoulder, wrenched her off himself, and flung her aside.

The wood exploding just to the right of his ear released him from his fears. Flinging the door wide, he crouched down behind the frame, his finger tightening on the trigger of his gun. Three bolts of energy lanced toward the guard. His roar of pain abruptly cut short, he went flying backward to land on top of one of the fragile low antique tables.

Shouts from his mother's room off to his left had Zsurtul diving out of the doorway for the cover of an armchair as two more guards, normal Primes, not gene-enhanced thugs, came rushing out.

Zsurtul swept a spray of continuous fire across them, sending them crashing, dead, to the ground. Reaction kept his finger clamped tight on the trigger as the beam of energy continued, cutting a swathe of destruction across the room until he realized it was over and there were no more guards. Forcing himself to relax his grip, he released the trigger and got carefully to his feet. Smoke from splintered and burned furnishings drifted in the air, mixing with the stench of burned flesh, and the metallic scent of blood.

"M'ikkule!" he called. "M'ikkule!"

A small moan answered him, and on shaking legs, he rose to his feet and ran toward the sound.

"You're hurt," he said, helping her to sit up. Blood from a cut on the side of her head was running down her face, and more oozed from the four deep puncture wounds in her shoulder.

"Leave me, Majesty," she said, trying weakly to push his hand aside. "Save your mother. He was wearing a ship suit when he came for her."

Zsurtul hesitated only a moment. "Our allies are attacking," he said. "Help will be here soon. Hide until then."

"I will, Majesty. Now go! Save your mother."

Leaving his former mistress, he ran back to the elevator. If K'hedduk was wearing a space suit, then he must have a ship nearby. There was only one other way out of the City—through the tunnel leading to the northern exit. Did the M'zullian really believe he could make his way from there to the landing area to steal the Royal ship from the warehouse?

"Elevator's finally coming down," Zhalmo said into her helmet mic as a small indicator on the wall access plate lit up.

"This system is antiquated beyond reason," snarled Kusac, putting a hand up to his ear to adjust the fit of his external pickup. "It needs to be updated immediately!"

"I'd say it was serving its original function admirably," said M'kou, looking up at him. "We are being delayed in pursuing our Emperor, while he is free to go where he chooses."

Kusac shot a look of pure anger at the young Lieutenant before turning his attention back to the console.

"Have you located the *N'zishok*, yet?" he demanded of the AI.

"Yes, Captain," the bland electronic voice replied. "I am negotiating protocols with it now. Communications should be established shortly."

"Captain," said Zhalmo. "It's stopped again. I believe the Prince has descended to the Throne Room level."

"You'll have to deal with it now, Zhalmo," he said. "I'm about to be patched through to General Kezule."

"Aye, Captain. It's moving again, this time responding to us. We should be in pursuit of him any time now."

Update me when you have news, he sent to her, then cut that mental connection to begin searching not for the young Emperor but for the minds of the Empress and K'hedduk.

Zsurtul's headlong rush down the narrow tunnel concealed in the ancient wall of the Throne Room was brought to an abrupt halt as his mind was suddenly filled with the sound of Zhalmo's voice.

Majesty, stop! We'll go after your mother, but you must *return to the safety of the Command Room!*

With an effort, he began running again. *Follow if you must, but I will not leave her with K'hedduk any longer! He has a ship hidden somewhere!*

Where? she demanded.

"How should I know?" he muttered aloud and mentally. "I'm only following their scents right now!"

"Kezule, we have a situation here," Kusac said. "I need one of the fighters to take out any outbuildings to the north of the Palace that are large enough to conceal a ship the size of a Royal barge."

"The fighters are out of fuel and munitions, Kusac. They're returning to the *N'zishok* now. K'hedduk?"

"With the Empress," Kusac confirmed. "What about the Touibans? Can they do anything?"

"Too far out to reach you in time, as are we all."

Kusac heard a few soft swear words before the Valtegan General continued. "All we have are the ground forces. Kaid's Packs are the nearest. I'll move the *N'zishok* closer to intercept in case he manages to launch."

"What about the *Kz'adul*?"

"We have our own situation here—the *Shazzu* decided to attack the *Zasho* when it changed sides. We've sent the *Kz'adul* to help."

"I'll talk to Kaid," he said, taking off the headset and handing it to Khadui. "Take over here."

The older Sholan nodded, taking it from him and sitting on the edge of the countertop.

Kusac leaned back in his seat, sighing, then rubbed at his tired eyes with one hand.

"Captain, your food and water rations," said Noolgoi, holding out a tray bearing a sealed pack of food and a bowl-shaped cup of water.

Absently Kusac took them from him, nodding his thanks. The sachet of food he set down on the console; the water he began to sip as once again he cast his mind out, this time to contact Kaid.

Carrie heard the message at the same moment Kaid did, then heard him curse softly.

We're pinned down here, Kusac. I'll have to send one of the teams in the power stations. And Zurtul's gone after them?

Yes. Zhalmo and J'korrash are following closely behind. I can't leave yet . . . Dammit, I have to! If anything happens to him . . .

A sudden loud pop drew Kusac's attention back to the world around him. He blinked, trying to orient himself, then looked at the now empty clenched hand where his cup had been. Those around him were still exclaiming and looking up in shock.

Go, sent Kaid. *Leave Khadui in command there. I'm dispatching Jurrel's Fire Pack now. Good hunting, sword-brother.*

And to you, he replied automatically, withdrawing.

"What was that, Captain?" asked Valden, a concerned look on his face.

"Just me popping one of those food packs," he said, sweeping up the one on the countertop. "I'm going after Zhalmo and the Prince, Khadui. Take charge here."

Pushing himself up from his seat, he strode over to where his gloves and helmet sat. "Jurrel's Fire Pack has been dispatched to intercept them."

Once in the elevator, he opened his hand slowly. In the center of his palm nestled a small pile of white powder. He tilted his hand and let the clay drift down to the ground. Shaking himself mentally, he rubbed his hand against his thigh before settling his helmet over his head and sealing it. What had he done to the cup, he wondered as he drew on his gloves. Vaporized it—drawn out all the water? There had been a faint wisp of . . . something . . . around his hand when he'd first looked at it. This was the second time today that he'd physically altered an object with no idea of how it had happened.

Captain, we've met up with Prince Zsurtul and are proceeding along the hidden passageway to the exit, sent Zhalmo.

I told you to bring him back here!

He refuses, Captain, and he is my Emperor-elect. I must obey him.

I'm on my way to join you. Where is the entrance?

You won't find it unaided, Captain. I'll send J'korrash back.

Very well, but do not engage K'hedduk under any circumstance. Do I make myself clear?

Aye, Captain. I'll make sure we wait for you.

Like the faint beating of butterfly wings, Kusac felt the alien touch at the outermost edges of his mental shielding. Instantly he stopped trying to track Zhalmo and Zsurtul, closing down even the tenuous Link he'd left open to Kaid and Carrie. Instead he put the energy into strengthening his shields and reflecting back anything sent to him. Almost, it was enough, but still it came, probing gently at his defenses, trying to insinuate itself into his thoughts, to make him turn back, leave the young Prince to his appointed fate.

"Dammit!" he muttered, almost coming to a stop as he shook his head in an effort to deny the siren song.

"Excuse me, Captain?" asked J'korrash, her voice suddenly loud inside the helmet. It broke the spell.

"Nothing," he replied, speeding up again, hands automatically tightening on his rifle as he followed close behind her.

"Khadui, I want an update on the current state of all Fire Packs now."

"Aye, Captain. Collecting the data."

Anything to keep his mind occupied and the subversive thoughts at bay! For a moment, a sense of déjà vu overwhelmed him; then he remembered where it was he had felt this exact sensation before—on Kij'ik, just before going to confront Kezule! This was the same alien presence, and once again it was trying to control him . . .

"Now, Khadui!" he snapped. "I need it now!"

"Aye, sir! Pack One has retrieved the packages and is now escorting them to the designated safe zone . . ."

"Captain!" Zhalmo's voice cut across Khadui's. "There's a hangar here—the ruin isn't, it's a hangar for a small interplanetary craft! There're ancillary vehicles here, too—towing ones, and fuel . . ."

"Do not enter the hangar, Zhalmo! You must keep the Prince out, even if K'hedduk escapes!"

"I'll do my best, Captain," she said as a single shot rang out. "Majesty, no! Zsurtul, come back!"

As one, he and J'korrash began to race down the last stretch of tunnel. It seemed to extend forever as they both listened helplessly to the sound of weapon fire interspersed with angry voices. There was a muffled exclamation from Zhalmo, then silence.

On his HUD, her telltale, and Zsurtul's, changed to orange and began to blink.

"Zhalmo, come in," said Kusac. "Report in! Dammit, J'korrash, call for a medic evac, top priority! Give them our location."

J'korrash was already doing it as he finished speaking.

A faint glow ahead heralded the end of the tunnel, and as they raced toward it, Kusac felt the faint presence suddenly withdraw. The evac team wouldn't arrive in time, he realized with frightening clarity, and he had a key role to play in the outcome.

"J'korrash, drop!" he ordered, grasping her arm and pulling her to a halt.

"Captain?" she asked, obviously confused.

"Drop to the ground, dammit! I need to get past you!"

As she dropped prone, he slung his rifle over his shoulder,

quickly latching it in place before dropping down himself onto all fours.

It took only a fraction of a second for the suit to recognize his altered stance and accommodate it. Servomotors kicked in to help him spring forward over J'korrash and land some ten feet farther down the passageway.

"Follow!" he ordered, increasing his pace until he was running flat out. He knew the suit could only maintain this speed for a limited time, but right now that wasn't an issue.

Sounds of her helmet being unlatched came loud and clear over Zhalmo's channel as Kusac tried to put on yet another spurt of speed. The exit was so damned close now!

Male laughter rang out briefly. "So, I have one of your daughters, Kezule! You've just given me the best claim I could have to the Throne of Light! A wife of Royal blood—blood undiluted by these damned Primes, and the heir to the throne lies dying—if he isn't already dead. We'll meet again soon, Kezule, but next time, I'll come in force."

Moments later, Kusac slewed to a stop at the hangar entrance. His teeth began to ache as the whine of motors cut through the air, rising in pitch. Already the craft was hovering in midair, turning slowly, positioning itself to align with the gap in the roof above.

The cold rage that he'd controlled until now was flooding through him—K'hedduk was responsible for breeding the hybrid cubs like his son Shaidan, he had put him in the hands of the Prime who'd illegally implanted him with a control device that had destroyed his natural psi abilities—and he was escaping.

"We won't wait for you, K'hedduk! Guard your doors well, because we will bring the war you crave to you!" he snarled.

Dropping to his haunches, he pulled his rifle free, automatically ratcheting it around to the grenades. Raising it, against all logic, he began to bombard the craft until he was out of shells. It was futile, and he knew it, but . . .

The grenades exploded harmlessly against the ship's force field, sending waves of energy spilling down to the ground below to kick up the loose soil and debris lying there.

"Khadui, tell Kezule that . . ."

"I heard, Captain. Relaying the message now."

"Captain!" J'korrash grabbed him by the arm, pulling him

around as K'hedduk's craft rose abruptly into the lightening sky. "He didn't take Prince Zsurtul!"

Flinging his rifle at her, he rose fluidly to his feet and ran over to where the limp body of the Prince lay in the lee of a battle-scarred towing vehicle.

Zsurtul lay sprawled on his back, his usually sandy skin a deathly greenish white. On the right side of his suit, from a single blast hole, white wound sealant foam bubbled and oozed sluggishly across his armor in partly solidifying rivulets.

Ripping his gloves off, Kusac placed his fingers against the main artery in Zsurtul's neck, feeling for a pulse. He could sense the youth's life ebbing away and had almost given up hope when he felt a faint fluttering. Without thinking, he reached for Zsurtul's mind, catching and holding it the same way his son had done for him not so long ago.

"Dammit, Zsurtul, stay with me! We need you!" he muttered. Looking up at J'korrash, he said, "Get him out of that suit!" Sitting back, he reached up to remove his helmet. "I'll do what I can, but it may not be much. When you're done with the suit, I'll need whatever meds you have on you."

He couldn't call on Carrie for help this time—she and Kaid needed all their wits about them in their current situation, still pinned down as they were by enemy fire. He'd also be wide open to any attack from the alien source. How could he be sure it wouldn't try to subvert him, make him kill Zsurtul rather than heal him? On the other hand, if he couldn't make a difference, why try to prevent him from getting there?

Slinging his helmet aside, he leaned forward and began to help J'korrash peel the ruined chest piece away from the injured youth.

The fog that seemed to surround Kusac was slowly beginning to clear. Broken beams crisscrossed the bright blue of the sky above him. A single shaft of sunlight pierced the dim interior of . . . Briefly, he felt his eye ridges meet in a frown. Everything was still hazy, thinking made his mind hurt. A sense of well-being began to fill him—he was warm, relaxed, there was nothing for him to be concerned about. He concentrated on watching the motes of dust dance in the light, feeling his eyelids getting heavier and heavier.

"The Captain's down!"

Again his forehead creased. That wasn't right. He wasn't

down, he was just . . . tired, deathly tired. His eyes flickered
and closed.

04:00 local time

As dawn began to break, Kaid watched the wave of Touiban
reinforcements he'd had to call in undulate across the slightly
sloping rooftops toward them.

"How did they get up there?" Carrie murmured.

"Jets," said Kaid briefly. "They can jump higher than we can
to start with."

"You should be ordering your people to withdraw and be
taking good cover now Captain Kaid," he heard Toueesut's
voice say on the Command channel. "Some debris this explosion will generate, and unavoidable it is that some flies your
way. We will be waiting their withdrawal."

"Understood. Retreat to my position, T'Chebbi. We'll
cover you."

"Aye, Captain."

Kaid watched as T'Chebbi began to order her Fire Pack
to withdraw. One by one they pulled back, taking cover first
behind the huge fragments of the fallen statues, then ducking
down the nearby alleyway to join them from the rear.

T'Chebbi was last to leave. Letting off a fusillade of shots,
she turned and began her dash to the block of masonry. A shot
hit her in the back, making her stagger, but she kept her footing and continued to run.

"Dammit, get a move on, Sister!" Kaid snarled, raking the
enemy positions with a burst of continuous fire. "I'm not coming out there to save your sorry ass!"

She chuckled faintly in reply.

Another series of shots, this time from a window to their
right, spattered the ground around her as she slid down into a
crouch by the stonework.

They all heard her short grunt of pain as she seemed to
slump against the stone. On his HUD, her telltale began to
blink orange.

Swearing, Kaid clicked his gun to grenades, rose to his feet, and swinging his rifle up to bear on the window, let off several volleys.

As he did, something punched him hard in the shoulder, making him gasp for breath and stagger slightly till his suit compensated for it. His left hand suddenly numb, he felt the rifle slip from his grasp and heard it clatter to the ground as hands reached to pull him back into cover.

"I'm fine," he snarled, trying to push them away with his right hand. "See to T'Chebbi. I need to adjust my meds!"

"Let me," said Carrie, leaning forward from behind him as he gasped at the sudden onslaught of pain.

"I be fetching her," Ashay announced, starting to rise.

"Stay, Sumaan warrior," came the sharp command from Toueesut. "Captain, you are down I see. We will effect the rescue of your Sister. She should be clear of our blast zone, but we will accommodate her presence so fear not for her safety."

"Aye," Kaid grunted, struggling to sit up as Carrie flicked back the control panel cover on his injured arm. He felt the sting on his neck of the suit's meds, and the pain began to fade rapidly.

Beside him, Ashay sank to the ground again, trying to make himself as small a target as possible.

I need...

I know what you want, she sent. *I disagree, but I will do it.* In his mind's eye he could see her face clearly, her eyes worried but understanding.

He leaned back against her, resting briefly, waiting for the stimulants he needed. Again the sting, then his senses, dulled by the pain and analgesics, sharpened once more.

Do not *try to use that arm,* she warned as he sat up, watching the Touibans. *T'Chebbi is still alive.*

I know.

Under supporting fire, one of the Touiban soldiers leaped off the rooftop, jets flaring, and began a sharp descent toward T'Chebbi's position. The faint actinic glow of a personal force field surrounded him. As he reached halfway, the explosive rounds were shot down into the enemy positions.

"Didn't know anyone had managed to perfect personal shields yet," Carrie murmured.

"Experimental it is, Carrie," came Toueesut's reply. "Etishu will protect her and see her safe, have no fears."

How do you feel now? Carrie asked.

Good.

Liar. You're still in a lot of pain. I can sense it.

It's distant, like it isn't mine.

Be careful, she warned. *If you have no sense of pain, you could do worse injury to yourself.*

He glanced obliquely at her. *I can handle myself, Dzinae. You forget how long I've been doing this.*

They watched as, bare seconds before the whole frontage exploded, Etishu landed beside T'Chebbi, picked her up in his strong arms, then enveloped them both in his shield.

Maaz'ih swore loudly. "If that was a small explosion, I don't want to see their large one!"

"Aye," Kaid said soberly, trying to peer through the dust for signs of the Touiban and T'Chebbi. He could sense her presence, but she was unconscious.

"Returning to landing area base, Hive Leader," they heard Etishu say as the white-suited Touiban, still holding his Sholan burden, shot back up into the air on an intercept course with the lowest part of the roof. "This one needs urgent attentions of our medics."

"Captain! What's that?" Zsafar's call drew Kaid's attention instantly.

Looking up in the direction the commando was pointing, he watched as a streak of light that was obviously an interstellar craft headed upward. Suddenly it accelerated, almost vanishing from sight, leaving behind the faint echo of rolling thunder.

"K'hedduk! That tree-climbing runt has gotten away!" Kaid snarled.

"The General is aware of this and is on an intercept course . . . Wait." Toueesut fell silent.

"What?" Kaid demanded after two or three minutes' silence.

"The weather platform reports a massive disturbance causing it some damage as a small craft entered hyperspace inside the gravity well. K'hedduk has indeed escaped us."

The regret in the Touiban's tone was evident. Kaid began a litany of low curses.

Dust caused by the explosions was settling now, and they could see that the first and second floor facade of the buildings forming one side of the central courtyard had been destroyed. They could see inside the partially demolished interiors of offices and what looked like part of a function suite. In front of it, the remains of the two statues and the fountain were now a small crater. Debris blocked the passageway into the main Palace. Of the enemy soldiers, there was no sign.

"Remain where you are, Captain Kaid," said Kezule. "We are now in the Palace itself and clearing it floor by floor. I need a Fire Pack there to take care of any who try to escape by that route. You, yourself, will be picked up by an evac team to be treated."

"I'm fine, Kezule . . ."

"You will report to the evac team." Cold fury underscored Kezule's voice this time, but Kaid knew it was not directed at him. "Take your Pack with you, and leave the others there as guards. Our Emperor has been seriously wounded, and I am told Kusac is also injured. The Empress has been found dead. I will lose none of you this day, do I make myself clear?"

"The Prince and Kusac?" Kaid said. "How?"

"I have no details as yet. I am on my way. Likely you will see them at the evac center before me. Another reason I want you there, as protection for Emperor Zsurtul."

"Aye, I'll go then," he said.

I have Jurrel on his Team channel for you, sent Carrie. *Kusac healed the worst of the Prince's injuries, but he still needs medical attention.*

Kusac?

Unconscious. No visible suit damage. I think he's probably passed·out from lack of energy after healing Zsurtul.

He could hear the unease and surprise in her voice.

He's never done this before, Kaid. I hope he's all right.

We'll find out soon enough, he sent then turned on Jurrel's Team channel. "Report, Jurrel. Where's Zhalmo?"

"You don't know? K'hedduk took her—as his claim to the throne."

This new shock hit him hard. They may have won this battle, but their losses so far had been unacceptably heavy. "Does Kezule know?"

"Yes, he was told immediately J'korrash and Kusac knew."

That, and the Prince's injuries, explain his rage, sent Carrie.

"Status on both the injured."

"The Prince is stable. His injuries are fairly bad but not life threatening now, from what J'korrash says. Kusac—I can't see anything wrong on his suit monitor. The only meds it's administered are glucose and a rehydration fluid, which it's still dispensing. Evac is on its way to us."

"Tell J'korrash to accompany them. You rejoin T'Chebbi's Team and take control of it when you've seen them on the craft. She's already at evac HQ and I'm on my way there shortly."

"Aye, sir."

He relayed Kezule's orders to the Fire Packs; then, sighing, he shifted his position, making himself comfortable so he could lean back against the wall of the fountain.

Can you sense him? he asked after a short silence.

Yes—and no. Even unconscious he's using shielding I have never before sensed—almost as if he expected someone to mentally attack him. There's no way I can reach him, Tallinu.

What he was going to say next was lost as the sound of a Touiban evac craft filled the air.

04:20 local time

A field hospital had been set up inside the warehouses at the landing pad by the simple expedient of landing a small hospital ship. Around it, food and rec tents had been hastily set up for those not needing beds but unable to return to their units.

Kaid and his Team had barely arrived when a stir of excitement drew anyone who could walk to the outer doors.

"Find out what the fuss is about," Kaid said irritably to Maaz'ih as they headed for the ramp into the hospital. He hadn't the patience for this—he was too concerned over the state of T'Chebbi, Kusac, and the Emperor-elect.

He was still at the reception area, fending off efforts from the Touibans to admit him while trying to find out T'Chebbi's condition when a sudden silence fell.

Every instinct made him spin around, pistol already drawn, to face the new arrivals. In front of him, protected by four guards wearing blue draperies and carrying large staff weapons, stood a party of six bronze spindly-limbed TeLaxaudin.

A low vibrating hum came from the lead one. "Injured you have. We return to treat them now the imposter has left," the electronic translator it wore intoned. "The Sand-dweller Emperor and the Hunter healer—tend them we must. To them lead us now."

"I don't think so," said Kaid, ears flicking out to the side and down. "Just where in L'Shoh's Hell did you come from?"

The guards instantly moved to the front of the party and pointed their staff weapons at him.

The lead TeLaxaudin lifted one thin hand and waved them back. "Your weapon you will not need. Come from nowhere, Captain. Already here we are. We hide from the imposter. Physician Kouansishus am I."

Slowly Kaid reached up to activate the headset. "Shartoh, what's the name of the head TeLaxaudin physician in the Palace?" he asked, keeping his eyes on the speaker. "Why didn't you warn me they were here?"

"Um . . . Ayziss, or maybe Shoawomiss, if I remember right. And we're so used to them, Captain. They've always lived in the Palace."

"What about Kouansishus?"

"Kouansishus was the head one," interrupted Zsafar. "Ayziss was head of Research, not Medicine, and Shoawomiss was in charge of medical research."

"So confirmation you now have," said Kouansishus, bobbing his head slightly. "Our patients wait our arrival."

Kaid holstered his gun. "They haven't arrived yet," he said. "You will not be treating the Sholan, though. We'll see to him ourselves."

The TeLaxaudin's draperies began to move slightly. "The choice yours is to make, but advanced medicines we have to restore him more quickly."

"Prince Zsurtul and Kusac's evac has arrived, Captain Kaid," Maaz'ih's voice sounded in his headset. "We'll be escorting them in."

"So, they arrive now. Show us a treatment room. Our equipment will follow."

"You won't need your soldiers. We've been asked to guard the Emperor-elect," said Kaid as a hum of conversation broke out toward the entrance.

"Remain will one. Us you will not use the way you dealt with Kzizysus," came the sharp reply.

"Uh . . . One, then." He had to admit, they had a point.

"Prepare yourself and you we will treat also."

"There's no need. I will see to him, thank you," said Carrie stepping in front of him and taking hold of his good arm.

From outside came the sound of raised voices—the lilting tones of the Touibans' speech underscored by a deeper Sholan voice they knew well. They only had time to exchange a glance before the door into the reception area swung back with a crash. Kusac, still wearing his battle armor, preceded the stretcher bearing Prince Zsurtul. He looked around, taking in the situation at a glance, acknowledging their presence only with the barest of nods.

"I want a Touiban surgeon to be present at all times," he said to the Touiban at the desk, ignoring the TeLaxaudin. "They must understand and check any TeLaxaudin procedures before they are carried out—and I will remain at the Prince's side. This is the will of myself and General Kezule."

"As you wish, Captain," said a physician, stepping out from the crowd. "If you will be following me, I will lead you to the treatment room we have made ready for His Highness."

Kaid caught sight of J'korrash at the rear of the crowd.

"Report, Lieutenant," he murmured into his headset.

"He came around suddenly," said J'korrash. "Just before we were told about the arrival of the TeLaxaudin." She hesitated. "He's still weak, Captain. He should be having treatment too, but he refuses to listen to anyone."

"I hear you, J'korrash. Leave it with us now and join my Fire Pack on guard duty."

"Aye, sir."

As she signed off, he realized a Touiban was standing beside him, trying to get his attention.

"Your turn now it is for treatment, Captain Kaid. If you will be accompanying me I will take you to your physician."

"You'll go now," said Carrie, reaching up to remove his headset. "I'll deal with this."

Kaid saw the look in her eyes and sighed. He wouldn't win this fight, no matter what he did. "Then come with me," was all he said. "I want news on T'Chebbi as soon as there is any."

CHAPTER 8

BITTER cold enveloped him, sending uncontrollable shivers through his body. Consciousness returned abruptly, and he came to to find himself, helmetless, on his back, surrounded by concerned Touiban faces. Every sense screamed danger to him. With a wordless cry, he flung himself off the stretcher, landing in a combat-ready crouch, pistol already in his gloved hand. Then the weakness and fatigue hit him, and he began to sway, feeling dizzy and sick to his stomach.

As people rushed to support and reassure him, he steadied himself, straightening up as he felt the sting of the suit medicating him again. At the same instant, the temperature inside it began to rise to a normal level.

Realization of what had happened to him came at last, the sense of danger now dimming. A quick glance told him he was on the landing pad outside the warehouses. As he holstered his pistol, a gnarled Touiban hand held out his helmet. Nodding, he accepted it. Pulling the comm free from inside, he put it on. Looking over their heads, he saw J'korrash and flung his helmet to her.

He activated the comm link. "Kezule . . ." he began.

"You're conscious? Good," came the reply. "What happened to you, and how badly injured is the Prince?"

"Exhaustion," he replied, cutting him short. "I did what I could in the way of healing. Zsurtul won't die now, but he's still badly hurt."

"Stay with him. There are TeLaxaudin there—I don't completely trust them . . . Can he wait till Zayshul and I arrive?"

"No. I'll stay with him and see that only the Touiban medics treat him, unless he needs something urgently that they can't provide."

"Are you well enough . . . ?"

"I'm fine," he interrupted, nodding to the Touibans who were gesturing that they must take the Prince inside. "I need a brief battle update."

"The City is ours, as are the Palace grounds. The battle continues inside."

"Good. Keep me posted," he said, closing the connection as another, lesser, wave of fatigue made him stagger despite the suit's ability to support him.

08:00 local time, Palace of Light

"He will be crowned within the hour," Kezule hissed into the transmitter in the headset he wore, as, flanked by heavily armed and armored guards, he took the stairs up to the Throne Room three at a time. Behind him, at his gesture, his escort of commandos peeled off to either side, taking up positions at regular intervals.

"You told me Zsurtul was out of recovery and awake, that thanks to Kusac's prompt actions, his life was no longer endangered. Release him and the Captain to my commandos so they can be brought to the Throne Room now, Zayshul!"

Switching the transmitter off, he turned his attention to the Palace AI.

"ZSADHI, you have the codes for all friendly troops. Initiate a level 2 Palace lockdown," he snapped. "Allow free access only to those on your current list."

"Lockdown initiated," replied the artificial voice. "Arming security lasers now."

"On stun," Kezule reminded, glancing briefly at the glowing red eye of the one on the left-hand side of the double doors ahead of him.

"Of course, Lord General Kezule," replied the AI in what sounded like a tone of justified outrage. "I expect you want me to inform you of anyone who . . ."

"You have your orders," Kezule interrupted, passing between the doors and into the Throne Room itself. "Damned impudent machine!" he muttered under his breath. "I don't remember it being this presumptuous before!" It was taking a supreme effort of will to suppress the rage that was threatening to break loose right now.

"You were a minor Royal on your last visit, Lord General. It was not in my remit to engage you in . . ."

"Be silent!" he commanded, coming to a halt and surveying the almost empty room. "Get the public broadcasting equipment online and ready to use when I give the order. D'haalmu, reinitialize the manual security checkpoint. Designate a team to police it." He looked across to where his daughter, Shartoh, was approaching him.

"Shartoh, have you removed the skins of the two dead Sholans? And where has the Empress' body been taken?"

"They're all with the embalmers, General," she said, coming to a halt and saluting him. "The Sholans are to be placed in small caskets to be returned to their Ambassador. As for the Empress, from the position of her wounds, it looks as if she was struggling with K'hedduk, perhaps to protect her son. Anyway, we cleared the area as you requested, then searched it for any traps or explosive devices. There were none. Guards have been posted both in here and in the Royal Chapel next door. Our Sholan contingent is checking out the other floors, room by room. Any prisoners have been taken downstairs to the old dungeons."

Kezule nodded. "Good work, Lieutenant. Were any . . . remains . . . of the late Emperor located?"

Shartoh looked away from him. The desecration of a dead body did not happen often, and it had affected all of them badly.

"We removed all the trophy heads from the stakes on the Palace walls, as requested. One, thought by its location to be the late Emperor, was also sent to the embalmers."

"And the remains on the throne?"

Shartoh glanced back at him, eyes widening in shock. "I forgot . . . I'm sorry, General, I'll see to it immediately."

"I'll see to it myself," he said, reaching out to stop her. This was not a task he'd have her do. "Have the surviving members of the Court been located?"

"Only a few, General. We're gathering them in the Court Chapel, in the priest's quarters where they can clean up and get ready for the ceremony."

Kezule sensed her hesitation. "What?" he demanded.

"Don't you need a priest for the coronation?"

"No," he said brusquely, walking past her toward the back of the hall and the actual Throne of Light itself. "It can be performed legally by a member of the Royal Family, a throwback to the days when the King was the accepted head of the ruling family." Even as he said it, he wondered where the knowledge had come from. He brushed the thought aside as inconsequential. All that mattered right now was finding the damned Imperial Crown. Without it there could be no coronation. With any luck, K'hedduk had no idea the crown worn by Emperor Cheu'ko'h was a fake, made because the real one was too heavy for everyday wear.

Footsteps echoing on the gold-flecked blue-tiled floor, Kezule made his way quickly over to the pillars leading to the shrine of the throne. Between one step and the next, he faltered as memories began to clamor for attention.

He was kneeling on the red carpet before the throne, waiting to accept his next commission from the Emperor—his Emperor, Q'emgo'h—the commission that would take him to Shola to guard the Royal Hatchery there—and lead him inevitably to this moment in the then far future.

Hard on its heels came others, of him kneeling not before an Emperor but before a Queen. Head down, he knelt in the obligatory position of submission, daring to cast a quick glance up at her. She was tall, of middle years, but still a striking beauty. His mind recoiled from the memory in shock. This was impossible! There had been no free females in his lifetime—until now.

With a jolt that rattled his thoughts, his foot hit the ground again. Slightly off-balance, he staggered, a feeling of confusion passing through him. Coming to a stop, he looked around the room as if trying to remember why he was there.

The crown: He'd come for the crown. Starting forward again, he took the three steps up to the throne in one stride, cut sharply to the right of the golden seat, and, passing behind its sunburst backing, headed for the colossus of the God-King Q'emgo'h.

Fully fifteen feet high, the intricately carved marble statue was decorated in a mixture of gold, inlaid precious stones, and vibrantly colored enamels. Wearing only the Warrior's pleated kilt, held at the front by an elaborately carved knot from which a single engraved fold fell below its short hem to his knees, the statue's pose was one of majesty. Royal staff in its right hand, right foot resting on a footstool, Q'emgo'h stared regally ahead. Around his forehead was a simple silver band bearing the protective head of the same predatory bird that adorned the throne.

The raised foot rested on a footstool decorated with the likenesses of their enemies. Without needing to look, Kezule knew he'd find all the subject races of his time depicted there—the Mryans, Delmoi, Hrana and the Vieshen, but not the Sholans. They'd not yet been added in his time. Briefly, he wondered if K'hedduk had had the time to add them. He doubted it from the number of statues he'd passed all now bearing the head of the usurper.

There was just enough superstition left in him that he hesitated before grasping hold of the statue's calf and pulling himself up onto the footstool.

"General . . ." Shartoh said from behind him, a tone of shock and censure in her voice.

He ignored her; he knew what he was doing. It was the head of the staff he needed. Where better to hide the most valuable treasure in the Palace than in plain sight? Reaching up for the massive thigh, he groped along the carved folds, claws searching for a firm grip, then hauled himself up, swinging his legs up until he was crouched on the Emperor's thigh.

Slowly he raised himself upright, keeping his attention focused on the carved staff before him. The head of it was yet another representation of the Royal raptor, but on its head sat the real Royal crown. Resting one hand against the Emperor's gold encased chest, Kezule reached out for it. It was heavy, as befitted the crown of the Emperor of not only all the Valtegans but of all their subject races. It was no light thing to rule such a vast Empire, and the weight of the crown was meant as a constant reminder of this.

The gemstones on it were artificial, and the crown itself, hollow—just like the Empire, came the unbidden thought. He shivered reflexively, almost losing his footing. Immediately he squatted down again, sinking his claws into the ridged folds of the Emperor's carved kilt.

"Shartoh, take this," he said, leaning down toward her and holding out the crown. "Be careful, it's heavy."

"What is it?"

"The Imperial Crown," he said. His arm was beginning to ache with the effort of holding it out for her. "Quickly!"

Slinging her rifle over her shoulder, she reached up for it with both hands, taking the weight from him.

"I have it," she said.

He released it, the relief to his tensed muscles instantaneous.

"Burn it! You didn't say it was *this* heavy!" she exclaimed, staggering slightly.

Kezule cast her a reproachful glance as he straightened up and leaped to the ground beside her.

"Wearing a crown is not a light matter," he said, taking it from her.

Zsurtul, pale and unsteady on his feet, was helped from the litter to the Throne of Light. As he grasped hold of the carved armrests and lowered himself onto the cushion-strewn stone Throne, he looked questioningly at Kezule.

"Your father's remains are being tended to by the Palace embalmers," Kezule murmured. "I saw to it personally, Majesty."

Zsurtul inclined his head briefly, then leaned back in the Throne and closed his eyes as Zayshul fussed around him.

"Tiredness, nothing more," said Kusac, aware of Kezule's and Zayshul's concern as he let his suit take over the task of keeping him upright. The Touiban doctors, then Zayshul, had tried to check him over thoroughly, but the most he'd let them do was check his suit diagnostics and give him high-energy drinks. His leg, though almost completely healed, was hurting like hell, and he could barely keep his eyes open, but he dared not take anything yet.

Shartoh returned, and Kezule stepped aside to talk to her.

"I haven't yet thanked you for saving my life, Kusac," said Zsurtul, opening his eyes and with an effort turning to look at him.

"You're a fool, but a brave one," he replied. "Don't let anyone ever tell you that Warrior blood doesn't run in your veins, because it does."

A faint smile quirked the young Emperor's lips. "You certainly saw enough of it when you rescued me. They said that you healed me, that there should have been more damage than I had . . ."

"They say too much," he growled. "You concentrate on recovering. You have a world to govern and a war to fight."

"You're right," Zsurtul said after a moment's silence. "There's much to be done."

Zayshul handed Zsurtul a bowl. "Drink this. It'll help you get through the next couple of hours. You really shouldn't be doing this, Majesty."

Zsurtul sat up and took the drink from her, draining it in one gulp. "I'm well enough to perform my duties to my people," he said, handing it back to her and waving her away.

Kezule came back, this time sketching a small bow before he ascended the steps to the Throne.

"We're ready to begin, Majesty."

Zsurtul nodded, looking around the hall, lined now by Touiban, Sholan, and Prime guards. It hadn't escaped damage caused by the fierce fighting in the open square outside. The large windows at the far end were shattered, and the three smaller stained glass decorative ones were missing a few of their panes.

"We'll need to get those windows repaired," he murmured.

"In good time, Majesty. Let the Court in now, Shartoh," Kezule ordered. "ZSAHDI, start the broadcast."

Kusac started to move away from the Throne, but Zsurtul's hand closed on his armored arm, preventing him. "You stay, Kusac."

Out in the courtyard, Dzaka and the others watched as a hologram of the Throne of Light with Crown Prince Zsurtul sitting in it suddenly appeared in the air in front and above them.

"Kusac's all right then," said Garras, as, like the hundreds of Primes and the armored Touibans in the courtyard around them, they watched Kezule step forward carrying an ornate crown.

"I told you he was," said Dzaka absently.

Garras glanced at him, seeing his slightly vacant look. "You relaying this to Kitra?"

"Yeah, she's still mad at being left behind," he replied, focusing on the hologram as Zsurtul reached out to lay his hand on the Imperial Crown and repeat the oath after Kezule. "Zsurtul's out of danger, but still badly injured, Kaid says. Kusac healed him, repairing a badly damaged organ . . ."

"Repairing?" asked Rezac. "How repairing?"

"Kaid doesn't know. All he can tell us is that from the hole in the Prince's side, the organ should have taken fatal damage. There are signs it was regrown . . . no, re-formed. Zsurtul should be dead."

"But that's . . ." began Garras.

"Impossible? No. Zashou and I could do that once," said Rezac. "Not healing, but destroying tissue using our mental abilities."

Garras turned to look at Rezac.

"It's rumored only the First Telepaths could do that," he said slowly, switching to a private channel on their suits, one only Rezac could hear. "Who are you, Rezac? Where did you come from, because I've never believed you were Kaid's brother?"

"There's no mystery. Kaid told you what happened, Garras."

"You came back from Jalna with them. We were all too wrapped up with Kusac at the time to give you much thought, but I've been looking into it, and he had no family. So who are you?"

"Ask Vanna, she'll confirm we're related," Rezac said, making a gesture to silence the other. "I need to concentrate on what Kaid's sending me."

Garras growled his displeasure. "Vanna will tell me nothing, and I already know you're related—you are too alike not to be." He stopped and looked more closely at him. "Are you his son?"

Rezac snorted his amusement and turned to watch Zsurtul being crowned. "Hardly!"

"Then that only leaves . . . his father. But that's impossible . . ."

"Now you know," said Jo quietly on the same channel. "He and Zashou were trapped in a stasis cube that the Valtegans dropped on Jalna. They all come from the past, from Vartra's time. He and Zashou were two of the first enhanced telepaths."

Garras' jaw fell open, and he stared at Jo until Rezac's elbow thumped him in his armored side.

"Look," he said.

Kezule had stepped back and bowed before moving to the other side of Emperor Zsurtul's throne from Kusac. For the first time, Kusac caught a glimpse of the crown.

Made of a metal lighter in color than gold, the front of the crown had the serpentine head and neck of one of the beasts he'd seen decorating various areas of the Palace. Leathery wings swept back from a bulge at the back of its neck, sweeping around to cup Zsurtul's head. They arched over the top, the wing struts meeting in the center.

A memory tickled at the back of his mind—not his, Carrie's.

A prehistoric bird—or a Dragon. It looks like a Dragon! he thought, then his attention was pulled away from it to what Zsurtul was saying.

"I rule today because of the help of our allies, the Sholans and the Touibans. For that, I thank them, and I make good my promise of formal alliances with them. I rule today not only by inheritance but by Right of Conquest—I fought alongside our allies to free us from K'hedduk's yoke. By those rights, I retroactively give Ch'almuth its independence and do now dissolve the Empire and relinquish the title of Emperor. One world is enough responsibility for one person. As from now, I will be known as King Zsurtul. There has been no Empire for 1500 years; it's time we all faced that reality."

Shocked exclamations and the buzz of conversation greeted his announcement, and as Zsurtul waited for the noise to abate, Kusac saw a sheen of sweat begin to gather on his face. He glanced at Zayshul as she began to move toward the youth and shook his head in a negative gesture.

"General Kezule I appoint head of what military forces we have. Have the prisoners brought now. I'll pass judgment on them myself. We'll all rest easier knowing they've been sentenced."

Kezule leaned forward as the young King" s voice began to falter. "Majesty, there is no need to . . ."

"I will see to it myself," said Zsurtul, more firmly.

Kezule inclined his head then signaled to M'kou. "As you wish, Majesty, but this is no time for clemency."

Zsurtul's hands clenched the arms of the throne till his knuckles showed white. "They'll get none from me."

"Execute all the altered ones with tattoos except the leader. We need him for questioning," said Kusac abruptly.

"We don't know who the leader is, despite our initial questioning," said Kezule, glancing up at him.

"I know who he is," said Kusac, scanning the faces of the assembled nobility and soldiers. He was picking up small areas of fear accompanied by anger. "As for the implanted guards, let them be kept under house arrest until the TeLaxaudin have deactivated them. If they could remove my unit, they can disable theirs. The Palace guard had no choice but to follow their implants' programming."

"And if they can't?" asked Kezule.

"Then we will offer them a painless and honorable death," said Zsurtul. "There will be no more implants."

"There are M'zullian agents here," said Kusac. "Counselors of K'hedduk's. I can smell and feel the fear of those around them."

"Your nose is better than mine," said Kezule. "I thought the M'zullians were darker than the Primes."

"Not all," said Kusac, flicking his ear briefly in Carrie and Kaid's direction when he saw them at the back of the Throne Room. "K'hedduk wasn't dark skinned—or he has a means to appear lighter."

Their conversation stopped as they sensed, by smell as well as the reaction of the crowd, the arrival of the prisoners. The people parted, opening a wide path for them to approach the foot of the throne. Kezule immediately stepped in front of the King.

All Kusac's senses were now focused on finding those who were loyal to K'hedduk among the Royal Court.

First came the four altered Primes who had survived the battle. Each was manacled and held by two of Kezule's armored commandos. Kusac tuned out M'kou's voice as he listed their crimes, keeping his eyes flicking over the gathering until he heard Kezule demand the name of the leader, then his attention returned to them.

"Do you think we'll cooperate with you inferior cattle?"

demanded one, struggling with his guards. "K'hedduk will return, and when he does . . ."

Kusac pushed past the General, drawing his pistol as he did. Without breaking his stride, the single pulse of energy from his gun hit the thug between the eyes, dropping him like a stone, leaving his guards struggling to support his dead weight.

At the last one, Kusac stopped. "Zoshur," he said, grasping him by the arm and pulling him free of the guards. "Here's their leader," he said, hauling him forward then flinging him down on his belly before the throne steps. "You don't need the others."

"Execute them," said Zsurtul, tiredly. "Have this one returned to the cells to await questioning."

"K'hedduk's counselors are next," said Kezule quietly as Zoshur was hauled off and the remaining two were dragged out to the balcony to be publicly executed.

"Bring Prime Counselor Shyadd to me first."

"He's being treated for injuries right now, Majesty," began Zayshul as a small commotion at the rear of the hall drew all their attention.

"Shyadd," said Kusac, without even glancing in that direction as he continued to keep his senses and eyes roaming over the gathered crowd.

Kezule signaled to the guards at the rear of the hall to let the Council member approach.

"Majesty." Shyadd bowed his head in respect when he reached the foot of the throne. "Your counselors were forced to work under K'hedduk. Please don't judge them too harshly. They did what they could to protect your people—except for one or two who were more . . . enthusiastic in helping K'hedduk."

Sparing a glance at him, Kusac took in the bandaged hands and the signs of bruises and cuts on the Prime's face.

"They could have refused, as you did," he said.

"Not as easy to do as say," Shyadd murmured. "We Primes are not known for our bravery."

"Time some of you were," Kusac said, going back to scanning the assembly as the counselors were brought before their King. He could sense something in a small group toward the back of the hall, near the exit to the balcony, but he couldn't quite pinpoint those concerned.

Ignoring the excuses and pleas from the counselors as they

were called forward, he concentrated instead on them. Jumping down into the crowd, he pushed his way through as he strode toward them. As he did, one began to back away, then suddenly turned and fled toward the large broken window behind him. As the Prime leaped into the air, Kusac's shot caught him full in the back, propelling him out and down to the courtyard below.

"Garras, see he's dead," he subvocalized into this throat mic, increasing his pace till he reached the others.

They tried to scatter, but those around them prevented it.

"He's Fabukki," said one, pointing at one of the small group. "He was Head of Security in the Palace!"

"They're lying," said the Prime, a look of outraged innocence on his face as he stood his ground. "Using your presence to settle old jealousies."

Kusac grasped him by the arm and thrust him toward the two Touiban guards who had rushed to his side.

"We need him alive. He's a M'zullian," he said, surveying the three who had been with him. Mentally, he reached for them, forcing through their shielding to scan them, leaving them holding aching heads.

"Collaborators," he said, losing interest in them to check the rest of the assembly. "They sold out their own to K'hedduk."

"Take them into custody," ordered Zsurtul from his throne. "They will be judged later. Bring Fabukki here."

"Dead," Garras confirmed through his headset.

Kusac paced through the crowd, his senses intent now on finding the other two M'zullians. He was aware of Carrie and Kaid at the edges of his mind, demanding an explanation, but he shut them out, needing all his concentration for the job at hand. The Primes around him moved aside, giving him a wide berth, some even flinching if they thought his gaze fell on them. He stopped; the fear-scent was getting thick now, masking those he wanted. A slight movement from the extreme left caught his attention, and his head swiveled around to track it. He had them now!

He pounced, grasping each by an arm and dragging them up to the dais to give to Kezule's guards. "Two more M'zullians," he said, stepping back to the General's side. "Members of K'hedduk's crew. The one I shot was also one. We have them all now. They've got mind-blocks—I can't read them yet."

"Good work," murmured Kezule. "Majesty, keep them alive for questioning."

Zsurtul nodded and waited for Kezule to issue the orders before turning to his late father's counselors.

Meanwhile, he sensed Kaid's acceptance of what he'd been doing and withdrawal from the edges of his mind.

"Your rank is forfeit," Zsurtul said. "Your sentence is to serve our people in the restoration of our world. You will be part of the workforce to repair the city and give aid to our people all over K'oish'ik. Till then, you will live in the barracks under the watchful eye of our loyal military. Take them away."

Slowly Zsurtul turned his head to regard Shyadd. "Counselor Shyadd, you retain the rank my father gave you as Prime Counselor. You have until midday tomorrow to choose those who will serve under you as heads of the various departments. Present your list to me at that time in the Council chamber. Meanwhile, retake possession of your office and anything else you need."

Thanking him, Shyadd bowed as low as he could and slowly backed away.

"What's next?" asked the young King, leaning briefly against the back of his throne.

This time, Kusac sent to Zayshul, asking her to give him a mild stimulant and some liquid nourishment.

Reaction had begun to set in, along with pain from his leg. While she was busy with Zsurtul, he surreptitiously triggered a stimulant and analgesic from his suit's automed. As they hit his system, a wave of light-headedness coursed through him, and he leaned back against the side of the Throne.

"Six of the twenty M'zullian/Primes who were on Shola survived, Majesty," said Kezule, glancing at Kusac and frowning. "In fact, they surrendered to the Sholans at the first opportunity, but I intend to have them executed."

"Wait," said Kusac, pulling his scattered thoughts together with an effort. "They surrendered?"

"It surprised me, too. They asked to be spared and wished to speak to Kaid."

"Take them to the barracks cells and let Kaid speak to them," he said, looking up and sending to his sword-brother to join them. "He knows them better than any of us."

"Do as he asks," said Zsurtul tiredly; sipping at the drink the Doctor had given him.

Kaid, accompanied by Carrie, stopped at the foot of the throne and saluted the young King. Kusac could see he was favoring his injured right arm even though he was back in his armor.

"Majesty," Kaid said.

"You will speak with the six surviving M'zullians you trained on Shola and assess their loyalty to us and their ability to follow their appointed officers. They surrendered to your people and asked for you."

"I was told of their surrender, Majesty, but haven't yet had the opportunity to speak to them."

"They can await your leisure now, Captain," said Kezule, gesturing to Kaid and Carrie to move to one side. "The Inquisitors are next." He indicated the bound red-robed Primes at the back of the hall.

Zsurtul's expression changed to one of barely suppressed fury. "Execute them all. I will not have them in my presence a moment longer. There will never again be Inquisitors."

"Keep the leader," said Kusac. "I want to talk to him, find out what he knows about K'hedduk and his crew."

"Do it," said Zsurtul. "Have him under constant guard. Are we done with the prisoners?"

He looked exhausted despite the stimulant.

"Yes, Majesty," said Kezule.

"I want all trace of the harems destroyed," he said, rousing himself. "If they haven't been yet, all the ladies in them must be treated and returned to their families. I need a list of their names so restitution can be made from the property belonging to the disgraced Counselors."

"It will be done," assured Kezule.

"General," Zsurtul said, raising his voice. "Your first task after securing our world and organizing what aid you can for the Ch'almuthians is to rescue your daughter Zhalmo Shan Q'emgo'h, my future Queen, from K'hedduk."

Kusac watched as Kezule's crest lifted and his nostrils flared. His softly spoken "Majesty . . ." was lost in the renewed buzz of conversation from the assembled courtiers.

"You will rescue her, General," said Zsurtul, and though his voice was low, his tone brooked no argument. "And she will be my Queen."

"It can be done," Kusac heard himself say. "There is a way, with the help of the Ch'almuthians."

Kusac could feel Kezule's and Zsurtul's eyes boring into him and, at the edges of his shielding, consternation from Carrie and Kaid.

"Then see to it, Captain Aldatan. You rank second only to General Kezule as my military adviser," said Zsurtul, the drink slipping from his hand as he fainted.

"Stop the broadcast, ZSAHDI," Kezule ordered. "M'kou, empty the hall. This audience is over."

"Affirmative, Lord General," said the AI, causing Kaid and Carrie to look up and around in surprise.

"I'm taking him to the hospital now, Kezule," said Zayshul, gesturing for the floater to be brought up.

"No, take him to my suite, Zayshul," he said. "And before you start arguing, it is opposite the hospital. I can ensure his safety there, I can't in the hospital."

Reluctantly, she nodded.

M'kou, having issued the necessary orders, turned to him. "Captain, you look like you're going to pass out too."

"I'm fine," he said, grasping the arm of the Throne as he felt himself about to stagger.

"Kusac, a mission to M'zull would be suicide," said Kaid, coming swiftly to his side. "You haven't recovered from your own injuries yet."

"We never leave one of our own, do we, Kaid? Zhalmo is one of my people now."

"You're not fit," insisted Kaid.

"I will be by the time three weeks in jump space are over."

"Going to M'zull is a suicide mission, you know that," said Carrie. "You can't do that to us, Kusac, not after . . ."

He turned his head to look at her. "I'll go. She's one of my people, Carrie. No one, least of all her, deserves what K'hedduk will do to her."

"You have a plan?" asked Kezule, joining them. "What happened, how did he manage to take her?"

The pain on his face was clear for them all to see.

"As I understand it, Zhalmo was just behind Zsurtul and was unable to stop him from opening fire on K'hedduk. He was trying to save his mother," said Kusac, turning to the General. "Zhalmo hadn't gotten a clear line of sight when K'hedduk shot Zsurtul. She ran to help him, while K'hedduk, recognizing her, used the Empress to capture her. He then killed the Empress and took off just as we got there."

"Your plan?"

"I'm working on it," he said. "It involves the Ch'almuthians."

Understanding dawned on Kezule's face. "If we can bring this off . . ."

"It's madness, Kusac," said Kaid. "We get our people back if we can, but this is beyond us!"

"If it was your daughter, Kaid, you'd grasp at any straw," said Kezule. "I won't let you risk your life, though, Kusac."

"Kaid knows exactly what it's like to try to rescue a child of his own, General," said Kusac, as wave after wave of exhaustion passed over him and he began to feel physically sick. "He's just done that. I told them to take the cubs to our estate, Kaid. I had no idea Rhyaz would try to keep them. I'm sorry, and I'm glad you have them safe now."

Now he was swaying, and his vision was fading in and out.

"M'kou, get the Captain to the suite next to the King's now!" snapped Kezule, reaching out to steady him before Kaid or Carrie could. "Tell Zayshul she's to see to him as soon as she's done with Zsurtul."

"We'll see to him," said Kaid, stepping in front of M'kou, who neatly sidestepped him and went to Kusac's side.

"No, Captain, my people will," said Kezule. "When he's fit to see anyone, then he can contact you himself. ZSAHDI, allocate rooms for Captain Kaid and his partner and for the chief Touiban and Sumaan in the Guest quarters on the fourth floor. Place all others on the third floor. Send the list to M'kou."

"As you order, Lord General Kezule," intoned the AI.

"Dammit, don't argue over me," Kusac snapped, leaning on M'kou. "I'm safe with them."

"Kaid, I need you to see that any of your fallen are set aside for your own funeral rites," said Kezule. "Shartoh, have them collect the bodies of our enemies outside the City walls and put those of our own dead in the central courtyard. We'll hold the funerals tonight for those who are to be cremated."

Caught neatly by the need to deal with the matter, Kaid had to turn his attention to Kezule. Before he did, he glanced over at Banner, who, with a minute flick of an ear, joined Kusac.

"The only casualties we have are the two Brothers and several Touibans."

"Your Brothers are with the Royal embalmers. They've been placed in small caskets for your ceremony."

"Thank you."

"Kusac needs food, General," said Carrie. "He may not want to eat, but he must, to replace the energy that healing Zsurtul took."

"Tell M'kou, ZSAHDI, and have the kitchens send something to his suite."

Kezule began to leave the throne area, walking down the few stairs back into the main hall. "I assume you wish to contact your people and tell them we have gained control of the City of Light."

"That would be appreciated," Kaid murmured.

"Noolgoi will take you to your Embassy office so you can make the call in private. He'll wait outside to take to you up to your suite afterward."

As they neared the door, Carrie grasped hold of Kaid, pointing to a small dark furred shape in the center of a group of commandos that was heading upstairs. "Look! It's Shaidan! I have to see him!"

"No," said Kaid before Kezule could. "It's up to Kusac, not us."

"Shaidan is with my daughter and their nurse," said Kezule. "He'll be being taken to his father now."

"What's he like?" Kaid asked before he could stop himself.

"His father," said Kezule dryly. "He took it upon himself to be a companion for my daughter."

"Don't send Kusac on a suicide mission, General," said Carrie. "I'm sorry K'hedduk took your daughter, but . . ."

"I have no intention of letting anyone go on a suicide mission. I want my daughter back, not dead. I'll listen to his plan before making any decisions. Noolgoi will remain with you. I have matters I must attend to now." With a brief inclination off his head, he left them.

Jayza, already out of his armor, was waiting in his suite when Kusac arrived.

"Lieutenant Banner detailed me to stay with you, Captain. Make sure you had any help that you needed."

"If you would help the Captain with his armor," said M'kou, staying in the doorway, "it would free me to attend to other pressing matters."

"We'll manage," said Kusac tiredly, reaching to turn off the power to his armor as Jayza came over. He felt the faint sucking sensation as the interior of the suit pulled away from his body. Taking off his headset, he handed it to Jayza.

"ZSAHDI tells me food is on its way here," said M'kou

"I'm too tired to eat."

"Make sure he eats," said M'kou to Jayza, still listening to his headset. "I'm told you need to because you healed King Zsurtul."

"Aye, sir," grinned the youth as he started unfastening Kusac's chest armor.

"I'll see you later, Captain. A guard will be outside your room for security reasons, but you're free to leave when you wish. Oh, I've been told Shaidan is on his way up. Do you want him brought here, or should he stay with the nurse and Mayza in the General's suite?"

"Here, please. Jayza, would you mind . . . ?"

"Glad to, Captain," said Jayza as M'kou shut the door. "There's bound to be board games we can play."

"If he wants to sleep, he can join me," said Kusac, bending to help unfasten the leg pieces.

"You're leg is bleeding again, Captain. It needs a fresh dressing. The hospital is right opposite us. It won't take me more than a few minutes to dress your wound."

"Getting flung about in that water trap didn't help it any," Kusac murmured, straightening up slowly and pulling his tail free.

"A wonder no one was killed," said Jayza. "If you would step out of the armor, please, Captain?

Weighing over 500 pounds, the main body armor was a deadweight capable of standing upright on its own.

"The Touibans will ferry the *Venture* down when it's considered safe and make sure our armor's picked up and stowed back inside it."

Kusac nodded as, holding onto Jayza for support, he pulled one leg, then the other out of the boots. Staggering slightly, he found himself caught before he fell.

"Easy, Captain. It's been a long night," said Jayza, helping him over to the dining table and chairs and pulling one out for him. "I'll be back in a couple of minutes."

Perching on the edge of the chair to avoid pressure on his

thigh, Kusac leaned back and closed his eyes. It had indeed been a long night. He felt stiff and sore, every joint ached. All he wanted to do was sleep.

"Captain, wake up. I need to dress that wound."

Tiredly, he blinked at her, then, leaning on the table, pushed himself to his feet. Once again Jayza was there to help.

"I thought you were with the King."

"I was," said Zayshul. "He only needed to be bedded down and the drips reattached. Don't know how you did it, but the wound in his side is almost healed. He'll only have a faint scar. I saw what remained of his armor."

He grunted, bracing himself against the table while she cut the soiled dressing off and began to clean the wound.

"We got hit by several tons of water," said Jayza, "And flung again rocks and the tunnel wall."

"And killed a norrta, yes, I heard," said Zayshul. "I don't suppose it will do any good to tell you to take it easy for the next few weeks, will it, Kusac?"

"I'll do my best," he said.

"It's not too bad, actually," she said, probing the wound and making him hiss with the sudden pain. "I'm only putting a light dressing on it; I want it to be able to breathe."

"The U'Churian medic put a more secure one on to prevent my armor rubbing."

"You won't be wearing armor for a long time, I hope! Jayza, hand me that larger dressing, please."

He heard the pack being ripped open and then the dressing held in place firmly but gently over the wound at the back of his leg.

"Now the other one. You hold it for me," she said to Jayza. She was just fastening it off when the door chime went.

"Shaidan," he said, raising his head.

"I'm done now. Sit down, and I'll let him in when I leave," she said.

He sat, stretching out his injured leg only to have Jayza grab another chair and lift his leg onto it.

Come back when you can, he sent to her.

But Shaidan . . .

He can stay in here with Jayza. We need to talk as soon as possible.

With barely a glance at anyone else, Shaidan ran into the room past her, flinging his arms around his father.

"I was scared for you."

Catching him around the waist, Kusac lifted him onto his lap, noticing how his son automatically settled himself on his good leg.

"It's my job, what we all do in our Clan, as I told you," he said.

"Long postings like this don't usually happen, though, Shaidan," said Jayza, busying himself closing the armor and stowing the headset in its external niche ready for transportation.

The door chimed again, this time for one of the kitchen staff bearing a tray of food.

Shaidan rested his head against his father's chest. Kusac heard the guard telling Jayza he'd checked the food and it was safe. He sighed inwardly. Yet another task for him when he'd rested. K'hedduk had concealed himself among the kitchen staff, and he'd need to see there were no more traitors there.

The servant brought the tray in and, putting it on the table, lifted off the two large covered dishes.

"Stew, Captain, with fresh bread and a vinegar and oil dressing to dip it in." Four bowls and spoons were placed on the table, then a jug and four cups. "And hot maush to refresh you and your companions."

"Thank you," he said tiredly.

"Are there any board games we can use?" Jayza asked as, eyes as large as saucers, the servant tried not to stare at Shaidan as he bowed and began to back away from the table.

"You'll find games, books, and other entertainments in the library. It's straight ahead from here, the second room on your right past the garden."

"Garden?"

"There is a garden on this level, and if you take the elevator up one more level, you'll be on the larger, rooftop garden. I hear there is even a fountain."

"A fountain?" Shaidan's brow creased.

"Water spraying out from a pool," said Kusac, nose twitching as Jayza removed the covers from the dishes and the aroma from the food filled the lounge.

"Shaidan, let your father eat," said Jayza, pulling out the chair beside Kusac for the cub. "Sit here beside him. I bet you had a rushed first meal and are hungry now."

"You eat too, Jayza," said Kusac, sitting forward as Shaidan scrambled down. "Or I won't."

Jayza laughed and grabbed the chair. "I'm not going to argue. That smells too good."

It was nearing dusk when Carrie and Kaid, having slept, eaten, and checked that T'Chebbi was recovering from the burns on her back, knocked on Kusac's door.

Banner answered the door and came out into the corridor, closing it behind him.

"Doctor Zayshul is with him right now."

"What haven't you told us about him?" demanded Carrie, looking up at him.

"I've told you all that I know. Mostly, it's exhaustion. From what I can gather, King Zsurtul had rather a sizable hole blown in his side and lost part of an organ that can't regenerate. Kusac healed that and closed the wound. Zsurtul's still got a way to go before he's healed, but without Kusac's help, he'd have died before we could have evacuated him to the field hospital."

Kaid stared at him. "Are you sure? That's something only the First Telepaths could do. What about his own wound?"

"I'm sure. Healing himself obviously drained him a lot, but he was regaining weight until now. They got caught by a water trap in the tunnels. K'hedduk had blocked their route just beyond a small cavern. When they broke down the barrier, it caught them. Kusac was thrown into some rocks while trying to protect King Zsurtul. That opened up the exit wound again on the back of his thigh. If they hadn't been in their suits, they'd be dead."

"What about Shaidan? Is the cub here?" asked Carrie.

"Yes, he's inside with his father," said Banner, gesturing at the door behind him.

"He should be with the others, not here," said Kaid, frowning.

I'm not leaving my father! The sending was so loud and clear that even Banner heard it.

The door opened suddenly, and Kusac stood there, clad in a colorful Prime wraparound robe that reached his knees.

"We'll talk tomorrow, at the evening banquet," he said. "You'll meet Shaidan then."

Kaid stared at him, shocked by how thin he was and how he leaned against the doorframe for support.

A wry smile briefly lifted the corners of Kusac's mouth, and he flicked an ear in acknowledgment of Kaid's observations. "Healing takes a lot of energy, you both know that."

Even as Kaid watched, the pallor around his sword-brother's eyes and nose began to fade, and he seemed to stand straighter.

Kusac glanced back into the room. "Shaidan, no. Keep your energy for yourself. You're too young to be trying to help me," he said sternly.

Without thinking, Kaid reached out to put his hand on Kusac's shoulder.

"No, Kaid." Kusac batted his arm away. "You've none to spare either. You got shot in the arm." He hesitated a moment. "I'm glad T'Chebbi isn't badly wounded. I'll go see her too as soon as I can."

Kaid nodded. "Burn wounds on her back, but not severe since the suit treated them fast. She's more uncomfortable than anything else."

A slightly distant look crossed Kusac's face. "Send a unit to the sewage plant, Kaid—there's a group of collaborators there now with a couple of the missing Inquisitors."

Kaid cursed softly and turned to leave, but Kusac reached out to stop him. "ZSAHDI, relay orders now and in future from Captain Tallinu to his troops."

"As you command, Captain Aldatan," said the AI.

"The AI has receptors throughout the Palace. If you want privacy, just tell it," Kusac said.

"How can we trust it—or Kezule?" asked Carrie.

"The Lord General Kezule is honorable," said ZSAHDI, its tone as full of rebuke as was possible. "It is beneath his dignity to stoop to using me to spy. Unless you request my services, I do not monitor private quarters or conversations."

"I'm tired of answering that question," said Kusac, frowning. "What would we do in the same situation, Carrie? My presence here with my son should be proof enough of his good will. You don't need to verbalize to communicate anyway! You're here because of Kaid's rank and as a courtesy to me. If you prefer to berth outside the Palace, in the City, you're free to do so."

Kaid had kept one ear on their conversation while relaying orders to the nearest patrol. Finished, he turned his attention back to them.

"Here is fine," he said, putting a hand at the small of Carrie's back to urge her not to inflame the situation further. "We don't know Kezule as well as you do. Our last dealings with him personally were when he kidnapped Kashini and Dzaka. Carrie's just anxious, as any mother would be, to make sure that Shaidan is fine."

Kusac's ears tilted back and his tail, which had been flicking slightly in irritation, stilled. "I haven't said who my son's mother is. Now is not the time to discuss it," he said, turning back into the room. There was finality in his tone neither of them missed. "I need to sleep. We'll talk tomorrow, as I said."

As the door closed firmly behind him, they were left looking at Banner, whose face and the set of his ears was a study in blankness.

"He's changed," said Kaid.

"He's very protective of Shaidan," agreed Banner, examining a hangnail. "They're very close."

Carrie swung around, pushing Kaid aside to stride down the corridor toward their suite.

"You . . . men!" she snarled in English. "You're all alike!"

"What did I do?" asked Kaid, throwing a puzzled look at Banner before following her.

"You trained him to be like you!"

Shaidan was bursting with questions. As he limped past where his son sat at the table, the board game for now abandoned, Kusac stopped to ruffle his hair. "We'll talk tomorrow, Shaidan, I promise. Right now, I'm too exhausted to even think straight, let alone answer your questions."

Shaidan tried to keep his ears upright as he slowly nodded his head.

"Patience, cub," Kusac smiled, bending down to rub his cheek against his son's before continuing into the bedroom where Zayshul waited.

Finally he could let go of the self-control that was all that had kept him on his feet. As he sagged against the closed door, she was there to help him over to the bed.

"You should have let Banner deal with it," she scolded, lifting his legs up and placing the injured one back on the supporting cushions.

"I did what I had to," he said, settling against the wedge of pillows. He shivered, looking across to the open window, and pulled the covers over himself. He shivered again, putting his hand up to brush his face as an eddy of cold air touched it.

"Nights, even in late spring, can be cold," she said, moving over to close the window. "I brought the complete meal drinks you asked for. The Touiban was most helpful."

"They're good people. We're lucky to have them as allies," he said as she returned to the bedside and took a canister out of the night table's cupboard to hand to him.

"You need to eat solid food as well," she warned, sitting down beside him. "That isn't enough on its own."

"I will, I just need to boost my reserves right now." He popped the can open and took a long drink.

"The crisis is over. It's time for you to recover properly. I'm taking you off duty for the foreseeable future, and I shall tell Kezule that."

"There are some things I have to do, like speak to the prisoners."

"No patrols and no leading missions," she said firmly.

He chuckled. "Yes, Doctor. Going back to what we were talking about . . ."

"Yes, I had noticed that though the scent marker is slightly fainter, it's still there, but the compulsion isn't."

"I removed that, but we can't admit it if we're going to find out what's happening to us."

"You removed it . . . Just like that?" she said slowly.

"I can't explain it," he said awkwardly. "I just sensed where and what it was and changed it. No one else will notice, though, so we still need to be seen to be taking time alone together."

"Do you know anything about the threat?"

"Not yet, but whatever it is didn't want me to help King Zsurtul. Something is trying to control my mind, and I think it's succeeding occasionally."

"But why would anything—anyone—want to control you?"

"I've no idea. It isn't as if I'm that important here."

"Oh, but you are," she said. "You've been placed second only to Kezule in charge of the military and security on K'oish'ik. You've volunteered to head a mission to rescue

Zhalmo, Kezule's favorite daughter and, if King Zsurtul is serious, his future Queen."

Kusac chewed at his lip thoughtfully. He hadn't looked at it from that perspective. "Oh, he's serious, but I have no idea what prompted me to say we could rescue her . . ."

"Kusac. . ."

He looked up at her. "I *do* have a plan, Zayshul. I owe her. Like M'kou, she was always honest with me, even when I tried to use her."

She gave him an old-fashioned look. "I don't even want to ask about that."

There was a gentle scratching at the door.

"Shaidan," said Kusac. "We've been alone in here long enough to keep the rumors going. It should be reasonable enough for you to leave now."

"I don't smell of you, though," she said, rising to her feet.

He beckoned her to lean down toward him and when she did, rubbed his face and jawline across her cheeks and neck. "That should do it," he said, letting her go.

"You have scent glands there?" she asked, surprised, as she stood up.

He smiled briefly. "Oh, I meant to ask, does the Palace have a pool?"

"The Emperor—King Zsurtul I mean, has one in his private gymnasium, and there's a public one over on the other side of the Palace, in the living quarters."

"Might be an idea to go there too," he said. "Explain the lack of our scents on each other."

"I still have my old apartment here."

"Could be useful," he nodded. "Thank you for the drinks, Zayshul. Can you let Shaidan in and ask Banner to come in too?"

She nodded, going to the door and letting Shaidan in as she left.

The cub stood at the entrance uncertainly. "Lieutenant Banner says it is time I got ready for bed, Pappa. Where am I to sleep?"

"With me, of course," said Kusac, holding a hand out toward him.

Face lighting up with a grin, Shaidan scampered over to his father, scrambling up onto the bed beside him.

"Pappa, is it now?" he asked, amused, wrapping his arm around him as Shaidan leaned against him.

"Mm," the cub nodded. "It's what the others call their fathers."

"I suppose you can pick them up again now."

"Only Dhyshac. He says he's a Brother now. Will I be one too?"

"Yes, but you'll also help your sister Kashini rule our Clan."

"You wanted me, Kusac?" said Banner from the doorway.

"Yes. I wanted to be sure they've given you and Jayza quarters of your own."

"Kezule put us in the suite next door. I got Jurrel posted there too, as you said."

Kusac nodded. "We're going to sleep now. Take the night off, go mingle, find out what they do for entertainment. You know the drill, get a feel for them and the mood of the people."

"What about Shaidan?"

"He's old enough to get himself ready for bed. Zayshul put his things in the drawers over there. You go, we'll be fine. There's a guard outside the door, and if I need you, I'll call you on my wrist comm. Go," he said as Banner hesitated, a dubious look on his face. "Report to me tomorrow morning. I'd be doing it myself if I weren't so damned exhausted."

"I'll see you tomorrow, then," said Banner.

Zhal-Arema, 8th day (March)

Dusk was approaching as Kusac, dressed in his Brotherhood black robes, accompanied Shaidan up to the rooftop gardens.

"We're not to be disturbed by anyone," Kusac told the guard on duty at the elevator.

As the doors opened, Shaidan let out a long drawn-out "Oohh" of wonderment and clutched his father's hand tightly.

"That's a fountain," said Kusac as he drew the cub with him out of the elevator toward it.

Shaidan had never seen anything like it before. Ahead of them, from a rectangular pool, sprays of water from half a dozen jets arched upward into the air for about six feet before curving earthward again and falling in a misty spray of water.

"It's beautiful," he whispered, almost afraid to break the silence. "I can smell the dampness in the air! Can I touch it?"

"Not today. You're dressed up for the banquet."

A gentle breeze ruffled Shaidan's pelt, tugging at his tunic hem, sending the shorter hairs at the sides of his head that had escaped from the braids, across his face. He brushed them aside, turning to look up at his father. "That's the wind?"

Kusac nodded and led him toward the western edge of the garden where trees hid the fencing. "It's gentle now, but it can get very strong."

Shaidan closed his eyes as they walked into the breeze, feeling it pass over his face and limbs like a gentle caress. Traces of foreign smells came to him, and opening his eyes, he widened his nostrils, sniffing deeply of the scents carried on the evening air.

"There's so much to smell," he said. "Scents I've never smelled before. It's so different from looking at it in picture books or on your comp pad. It's nothing like Kij'ik!"

"This is a world, Shaidan, not an enclosed station in space." Stopping beside a shrub, Kusac pointed to the flowers. "Smell them. Flowers are often scented."

Shaidan reached for the flower, holding it carefully in his hand as he sniffed deeply—then promptly sneezed.

"You aren't meant to stick your nose into the pollen," his father laughed, taking a handkerchief out of his pocket and handing it to his son. "Your nose is all yellow with it now."

Shaidan wiped his nose vigorously and shoved the hanky into his tunic pocket. "Look, that bush has red flowers . . . They're a different color and shape! Can I go look?"

"Yes, but look up at the sky first."

Shaidan looked up. As far as his eyes could see, there stretched the sky and the land.

"Look, something's on fire!" he said, pointing toward where the dull red orb of the sinking sun disappeared behind the garden's trees.

"That's the sun. It's a star far up in space that heats this world. I know you learned about them on my comp."

Shaidan followed as his father pushed the greenery aside to

make a path for them to the railing. "I remember, but I never thought it would look like this!"

Now they had a clear view of the sunset.

"All those colors, and the . . . clouds?"

His father nodded as Shaidan grasped the bars and peered through the railings. "There are different dangers on a world, Shaidan. In its own way, it's as dangerous as living in space."

The breeze was stronger now, blowing his hair back from his face, even the heavy braids. "It could blow me off here if not for the railings. How can something you can't see be so strong?"

"Many invisible things are strong, like my love for you," said Kusac, putting a hand on his shoulder. "Think about our Talents. We can't see or touch them, but they're very real. Look how the clouds change color as the sun sinks lower."

Shaidan followed the pointing finger, looking at the streaks of purple and red clouds against the deepening turquoise sky. He sighed deeply. "I didn't know colors like those existed in life."

Before his father could answer, the Palace AI chimed gently, then spoke.

"Captain, you will be late for the banquet."

"Time to go," said Kusac. "We can come up again another day."

"I'd like that," said Shaidan as they turned to push their way back through the bushes.

Do we have to do this? Shaidan sent as they passed the Security post into the anteroom for the banquet hall.

Yes. It's time for everyone to know who you are and that you are my son. Have just a little more courage, cub. You've shown so much already in your short life. I promised you'd meet your mother tonight, and you will. It's time for you to take your rightful place in our En'Shalla Clan, Shaidan.

The ushers were running too and fro busily as they stopped just by the doors. Kusac looked his son over for the last time. Their pelts had been brushed till they gleamed with all the blue-black fire of the Aldatans, and Shishu had made matching braids, decorated with beads, on either side of their faces. Against the black of Shaidan's ears, and one of Kusac's, blue gemstone earrings glittered brightly in their silver settings. They looked Sholan, yet not.

The chief usher bustled up to them. "Captain Aldatan? Are you and your son ready? You're seated next to King Zsurtul."

They glanced at each other, both afraid, both dreading the next few minutes, but knowing there was no other way to do this. In his hand, Shaidan's fluttered nervously. Kusac gave it a gentle squeeze and then began walking into the banquet hall, the usher pacing beside them.

As they passed between the tables, Kusac noticed that the Royal Throne had been moved from its position on the dais to the other side of the hall. A second seat, for a Queen, had also been added to it, though for now it was empty. Where the Throne had been was closed off with heavy drapes.

The sound of chattering faded as they made their way to where Zsurtul sat with Kezule on his left then Carrie and Kaid next to the empty spaces left for them on his right. Most of the Court had never seen a young Sholan, and the sight of one now made them stop their conversations and stare openly at them.

It was now so quiet that the click of their claws on the blue lapis tiled floor sounded loud to their ears.

"I am so proud of you," murmured Kusac. "This is the only way to get the truth of who you are across to them all."

Shaidan looked up at Kusac, a small smile touching his lips. "I understand, Pappa."

They came to a stop in front of the High Table.

"May I present Captain Aldatan to you, Majesty?" said the usher with a low bow.

"King Zsurtul," said Kusac, bowing to him. "This is my son, Shaidan. He was one of the hybrid Sholan/Humans created by the Directorate. K'hedduk used genetic material from myself and my mate, Carrie, Shaidan's mother, to create him."

A susurration of shocked conversation broke out, and Kusac held up his hand for silence. When it fell, he continued, aware of Kezule tensing in his seat.

Trust me, he sent to the General, much to the shock of the other.

"Shaidan is not just a mix of Sholan and Human genes. It seems K'hedduk wasn't content with the other seven experimental cubs. Shaidan is unique in that he also has Prime genes, genes stolen, as ours were, from Doctor Zayshul. K'hedduk's plan was to keep them all as slaves, to use them against us in a war to reunify the old Empire. This will not happen now, thanks to General Kezule and yourselves and our other allies. I bring my son Shaidan before you as a free citizen of all three races—Sholan, Human, and Prime—a bridge between all of us, to bring us closer together."

As he spoke the last sentence, the world around him seemed to lurch. Suddenly he was no longer in the banqueting hall but in a place of trees and fountains. He shook his head, forcefully banishing the images, pulling Shaidan in front of him, holding him close as he came back to reality.

"Most importantly, I bring him here tonight to meet his mother and his Triad father and take his place in his Clan," he said.

"My home will always be a second home to you, Shaidan," said Zsurtul, smiling. "Join us at the table."

Carrie had risen to her feet by this time, and now he dared to look at her. He saw only her need to be at his side and to hold their son; she cared nothing for the fact he also had Prime genes.

He opened his mind to her and Kaid, wincing slightly at the intensity of their feelings for him and Shaidan. *I apologize, but I had to do it this way so there would never be questions for him to answer, so Rhyaz couldn't bury him and the others ever again.*

I want to meet my son, sent Carrie.

You did right, sent Kaid with a mental chuckle. *There's no way now these cubs can be hidden from the Alliance!*

He led Shaidan around to the back of the table and stopped in front of Carrie.

"Is she really my mother?" asked Shaidan nervously, looking from his father to the furless Human female.

Kusac nodded.

"Are you too big to be hugged?" Carrie asked, bending to his level, her voice breaking slightly.

"I don't think so," said Shaidan.

Carrie swept him up into her arms, hugging him for all she was worth, looking at Kusac over the top of his head as she did. "He's so like you," she whispered. "So very like you."

Kusac watched as Shaidan's arms crept tentatively around her neck to return the hug. "I don't think I am too big at all," he said as tears began to well up in his eyes and spill down his cheeks.

"Don't cry, oh, please don't cry, cub," said Carrie, trying to wipe the tears away. "You have a family now, you belong to us. You'll never be alone again, I promise you!"

Shaidan pulled back a little, dashing his tears away with his forearm. "I'm not crying, I am not," he said, his voice trembling with the effort of stilling his sobs.

"Of course you aren't," said Kaid, reaching out to ruffle between his ears. "Hello, Shaidan, I'm Kaid. I stand in for your father when he can't be there."

"More than that," murmured Kusac. "But that will do for now."

From behind him, he heard a gentle trilling. "Clan Leader! How good it is to be seeing you again and meeting soon with your son for the first time."

"Toueesut! Well met indeed," said Kusac, turning around to greet the small Touiban. "I've heard much of your people's great exploits in the battle. We must talk of them after we've eaten."

"Indeed," said Toueesut, his mustache bristling with obvious pride. "Indeed we shall and at great length so I can hear the news of your own exploits in the tunnels."

Shaidan was looking thoroughly bewildered by this time, so Kusac, with a gentle murmur of explanation, took him from Carrie and led him to his seat at the table.

As he took his own next to the empty Throne seat, Zsurtul leaned over to talk to him.

"Thank you again for saving my life, Kusac, especially at a time when you needed the energy to heal yourself."

"You'd have done the same for me," he said. "You look better today."

"I feel better too. Our good Doctor Zayshul tried to bully me into not holding this traditional victory feast, but a leader has to be seen to be strong for his people, even when he is not."

"Unfortunately true," nodded Kusac, sitting back in his seat.

"I'm really honored to meet you at last, Shaidan," said Zsurtul. "Your bravery is an example to us all."

"I didn't do anything, Majesty," Shaidan said.

"But you did. I have heard how you looked after your brothers and sisters and, lately, General Kezule's daughter, Mayza."

"She's only a cub; of course I look out for her."

Zsurtul laughed and sat up again, wincing slightly in pain. "I can see you're an Aldatan." He gestured to the usher and raised his voice to fill the hall. "Let the feast begin with the list of the fallen whose memories we honor this evening."

Kusac sensed Carrie watching him and turned to look at her where she sat on the other side of Shaidan.

Was all the protectiveness and mystery because he has some Prime genes? she asked. *You should know us better than that, Kusac.*

He had no ready answer to give her and was glad to be diverted by Shaidan snuggling up closer to him.

It's taken a long time to unravel what K'hedduk did. He didn't exactly leave many records of his meddling. In fact, he made it seem that Zayshul had done it.

Where does Zayshul's scent marker fit in?

Startled, he glanced away, closing down the Link between them. "Later," was all he said as he began to stroke Shaidan's head and try to remember the details of the strange mental leap that he'd had.

CHAPTER 9

"THAT was some entrance he made last night," said Kaid, going over to the breakfast table to sit next to Banner.

"One worthy of you," said Banner, pouring out more maush for himself. "Want some?" he asked Kaid, hesitating over a clean cup.

Kaid chuckled. "No, thanks, we breakfasted a couple of hours ago. I dropped in to see if Kusac was up yet after visiting T'Chebbi."

"He went for a swim first. He should be here anytime." He put the jug back on its hotplate.

"A swim?" Kaid raised an eyebrow.

"Yes, the King has a pool in his private gym. Water has a religious importance for the Primes and Valtegans. There's a huge pool on Kij'ik."

"Ah. I wonder if we can get access to it. Swimming is good exercise. And Shaidan?"

"Shaidan's with Mayza, the General's daughter, and the other youngsters in the nursery here. Kusac said he wants him back in his regular routine. They're well guarded."

"That doesn't concern me. I'm more worried that he's separated from his own brothers and sisters."

Banner gave a slight laugh. "I wouldn't worry. He's been talking to Dhyshac since the *Tooshu* arrived in orbit here."

"He has?"

Banner nodded, picking up a length of thin, crisply fried meat to crunch on. "Don't worry too much about them, Kaid.

They may be ten years old physically, but they've not even been awake and conscious for a year of our time. This," he gestured in a wide circle with his arm, "will fade in their memories once they're back on the estate with the other kits. They'll always seem slightly strange and otherworldly to us, though, because of the way they were matured."

"You seem to have a fine understanding of·them," said Kaid dryly, reaching out to snag the other piece of crispy meat on his plate.

Banner grinned across at him. "Only of Shaidan. He's bombarded us with questions about families and Shola for some time now. He wants to belong so much it's painful to see at times. And before you ask, he most of all wants, and needs, to be with his father. You should bring the others down here, not keep them up on the *Tooshu*."

"Maybe we will. I have a feeling the center of the war just moved away from Shola to here. If that's so, we could be here for a long time."

"Aye, that's been our thoughts too," said Banner.

"Has Kusac said any more about this plan to rescue Kezule's daughter?"

"Not to me."

"See if you can dissuade him from it," he said, getting up. "Whatever he owes her, it isn't worth his and a team's lives."

"If you think he's hell-bent on a suicide mission, you're wrong, Kaid. He might have been once, but not now. Not since he died."

Kaid froze and looked at Banner. "Tell me," he said quietly.

"I didn't know about this until a day or so ago. When Kezule put him in the punishment booth, he did it when he knew that Kusac would black out almost instantly and avoid experiencing the punishment."

"I remember." A puzzle was suddenly becoming crystal clear to him now.

"They were monitoring his telemetry from a room nearby when all his life functions flatlined. By the time they reached him, he'd pulled out of it himself and gone into the start of that healing coma he was in for the best part of a week."

"How long was he gone?"

Banner had to strain his ears to hear the quietly spoken words. "It can't have been longer than three minutes."

"Shaidan helped him; he didn't do it alone. It was he who pulled him back to life," said Kaid, sitting down again as the strength left his limbs. "We felt him. He reached out through the gestalt and pulled us in for the energy to do it."

"He did? Damn, he's got some range has that kit."

"To be able to follow his father down into death and pull him back from the brink, no wonder they're close!"

He sensed Carrie's concern, wondering what it was he'd discovered that had distressed him so. He sent a reassurance her way then came back to the reality of the breakfast table as Kusac, with hardly a limp, walked in.

"You're up late," he said, walking over to the serving tables at the side of the room. "How's the arm?"

"A glancing shot. I've had worse," said Kaid, pulling his scattered thoughts together with an effort." I've been up for a couple of hours. Did you enjoy the swim?"

"Yes," said Kusac, lifting the lids on the various heated dishes to see what was inside. "Gods, real food again! Meat that had four legs and wasn't grown in a vat!"

"They certainly believe in eating heartily," agreed Banner, grabbing his last slice of crunchy meat before Kaid was tempted to.

"I'll ask Kezule if those of us on this floor can all use the pool," said Kusac, finally deciding on eggs and slabs of tenderly fried meat. "I presume Banner told you about the significance of pools to the Primes and Valtegans?"

"He did," Kaid replied.

"Sorry we had to leave the banquet early, but both Shaidan and I were exhausted," said Kusac, coming over to sit down beside them. "I'll answer what questions you have now."

"I'll leave you to it as I'm on duty shortly," said Banner, rising.

Kaid nodded good-bye and reached for the maush jug. "I think I'll have some of this after all," he said, pouring himself a cup. "Want some?"

"Please."

Silence fell and lengthened until they both began to speak at once.

"We found out how you were tricked into coming to Kezule," said Kaid.

"How are the twins and Kashini?"

They stopped and looked across the table at each other, faint grins on both their faces.

"You first," said Kusac, pointing his fork at him.

Kaid shrugged. "The twins are doing well. Being younger than his sister Layeesha, Dhaykin was not as strong when he was born, but that lasted only a few weeks. Last time we checked, a couple of days ago, both were thriving. Kashini, that little jegget, is into everything without us there to stop her!"

Kusac's smile grew wider. "I can imagine."

"My turn. You aren't seriously thinking of going to M'zull to rescue Kezule's daughter, are you? The way they react to even the scent of us, it'd be suicide."

Kusac scooped up another forkful of eggs before replying. "I assume Banner told you about our visit to Ch'almuth and how the M'zull are culling them every few years."

"Yes. We sent a Touiban unit to investigate their satellite and see what they can do to fix it. Haven't had an update from them yet."

"Good, they need to be able to defend themselves. Kezule met the M'zullian ship this time, killed the crew and sent it back, making it look as though there had been an accident in space and it never got to Ch'almuth. They'll be back, though, and we'll need to help the Ch'almuthians. They and we will get only three days warning, though."

"Three days? That's not much considering the distances involved."

"Banner didn't mention the ancient corridor device that had been set up between Ch'almuth and M'zull? There are two more—from Kij'ik to Ch'almuth and maybe a nonworking one here somewhere. The tech can't be reverse engineered; we tried. Ch'almuth was the granary of their old Empire, staffed with a few military people and a lot of the worker caste."

"He mentioned it in passing. So they developed a fast transit system to reach there. Nice, if you can do it. Pity we can't work out how. Maybe the Touibans can?"

"Maybe," he said doubtfully around a mouthful of meat.

"So the gist of your plan hinges on this cull that the M'zullians will do shortly."

"Yes. If I can get the info I need about their Palace setup, we could perhaps hijack this ship and return with not the

Ch'almuthians they are expecting, but a bunch of commandos from here as well as maybe some of us. In full battle armor, we shouldn't stand out so much."

"Tails," said Kaid succinctly. "And our leg shapes."

"I did say I had an idea, not a full plan," said Kusac, glancing over at him as he picked up his drink. "I'm hoping we have someone among the prisoners capable of drawing a plan of their Palace for us, because I don't think for a minute a race as warlike as the M'zullians, left to their own devices for fifteen hundred years, didn't either relocate the Palace or improve vastly on its design."

"It might be doable," said Kaid thoughtfully, turning the idea around in his head. "Let's see what intel we can come up with first."

"We don't have long now. The M'zullian ship will be coming for its Ch'almuthian cargo soon."

"We should have some turn-around time, though, at least a day. L'Seuli's ship is due tomorrow."

"Is it? Well, that's not my concern, Ambassador Kaid," he said with a big grin. "I'm still contractually obligated to Kezule."

"We left Shola illegally to find you, you ingrate," said Kaid with a hint of a growl.

"I haven't time for the diplomatic niceties, Kaid. I've been given a job to do, and I have to do it. You, on the other hand . . ."

The sound of approaching footsteps stopped their banter, and moments later, Kezule walked in.

"Kusac, I need your help questioning the prisoners," he said, stopping at the end of the long dining table. His Valtegan accent was more pronounced than Kusac had ever heard it. "I nearly killed one of them. I don't trust myself with them."

"I think perhaps this is my area," said Kaid. "Kusac has scores to settle, same as you. I can be more impartial."

"That's not your decision to make, Kaid," said Kusac, aware from Kezule's posture just how much anger and rage the other was holding in.

When will you all stop treating me as if I am retarded in some way? Kusac sent. *Don't contradict me in front of Kezule! He's on a knife-edge right now because of his daughter.*

"Kezule, apparently K'hedduk was hiding out in the Palace kitchens," Kusac said. "I suggest we order a sweep through there and make sure of everyone's identity."

"M'kou has seen to that, but if you feel we need another one . . . ?"

"I would be happier. Things have quieted down a bit now, so anyone trying to hide as a member of the staff would feel safe. As for the prisoners, I want Kaid to question the thug Zoshur, Banner to be pulled off his detail to take Lufsuh, the Inquisitor, and our two Brothers, Shamgar and Vayan, should question the two M'zullians."

"ZSADHI, send my orders to them."

"As the Lord General commands."

"We need a medic and a couple of guards with each unit, Kezule," said Kaid, finishing up his drink.

"I've got them there already," said the General grimly. "I learned a thing or two when I was your prisoner. Let's go."

On the way down to the lower dungeons, Kusac told Kezule the basis of his idea to rescue Zhalmo.

"It could work at that," said Kezule, some of the tense lines around his brow smoothing out. "If you could bring this off, Kusac . . ."

"I make no promises," he warned. "It all depends on whether we can get information on the layout of their Palace, or where Zhalmo is likely to be held, from the prisoners. And the right timing. It will take K'hedduk three weeks to reach M'zull. If they come for their cull before then, we'll have to wait for their next visit. That means sacrificing more Ch'almuthian children, which neither of us wants to do."

"Agreed. Hopefully K'hedduk will have told them of his setback and they'll wait for him to arrive before doing anything else. They're leaderless right now, until he returns."

"Leaderless? How so?" asked Kaid as they got out of the final elevator and began walking along the corridor past the guards and the ancient cells that lined one wall. "I thought they had their own Emperor."

"K'hedduk would not have been so bold as to usurp the throne here unless he was sure that his elder brother back on M'zull had been deposed," said Kezule, stopping to open the door into an office. "We'll wait here for the others. There are screens to let us monitor the prisoners at all times."

The two guards on duty leaped to attention on seeing him, and Kezule gave them curt orders to find more chairs.

"No, K'hedduk will return to M'zull as its Emperor with some tale about the jealousy of his underlings leading to his forced retreat," the General continued.

"You mean bolting like a chiddoe!" said Kaid.

"Chiddoe?" asked Kezule.

"Long back legs, small white tail, long ears," said Kusac, snagging a chair when Kaid gestured him to do so.

"Ah, those, my staple food on Shola. They feared my scent so much it soured their flesh." He frowned as if in memory of the unpleasant taste.

"Was anything we assumed we knew about you correct, Kezule?" asked Kaid. "Because there's little resemblance between you now and then."

"The times I now live in forced many changes on me, but that was always the strength of my kind—our adaptability," the General said, taking a seat in front of the banks of monitors.

"Did we do you such a disservice, bringing you forward to our time?"

Kezule turned around to look Kaid full in the eyes. "At the time, I thought so, but not since I realized I had a purpose here and now, that of saving my species from what it has become. We should be like you, all one caste, not three. A Queen artificially created that many centuries ago, when our Empire was founded. But Kusac can tell you of this," he said, turning back to the screens and dismissing the matter.

There were four main prisoners and a group of four other individuals who had been collaborators. The latter were huddled two to a cell while the former were lying or squatting against the wall in individual cells.

Kusac sat quietly, watching them, his mind wandering briefly to his cell on the *Kz'adul*. It had at least been cleaner than the ones here, and he'd had a bed.

"Where are the medics?" asked Kaid, leaning on the back of Kusac's chair.

"In the guardroom, taking a break. Their stomachs are not as strong as they thought," said Kezule wryly.

"Interrogation is a specialized technique," said Kaid.

"I know," said Kezule. "And better done by those with no issues with the prisoner."

A knock on the door, and there stood Banner with Shamgar and Vayan.

"Reporting for duty as requested, General Kezule," said Banner, making a sketchy salute.

Watching, Kusac's mouth quirked in a ghost of a smile. So Banner was taking that tack with the General, was he? Then he'd let Kezule deal with it unless it got out of hand. Shamgar and Vayan's salutes were exact to the gesture by comparison.

"See the guards in the guardroom for your prisoners. They'll give you any current transcripts. The medics are in there too. Take what time you need to familiarize yourself with what we know about them first," said Kezule.

"Aye, sir," said Banner.

"I'd better join them," said Kaid, leaving.

"You were worked on by Inquisitor J'koshuk," said Kezule when they were alone.

Kusac stirred. "Yes."

"And I by your Commander Rhyaz."

"J'koshuk was on a personal crusade," said Kusac. "I didn't know it all at the time. He'd tortured my wife's twin sister to death and recognized Carrie. K'hedduk was only interested in what pain to me would do to my Triad mates."

"Ah. I've seen them work. In my opinion, they hold all that is bad of our people within them. They don't just hurt you physically, they take your mind and twist and bend it out of shape. I nearly killed the Inquisitor."

"Why?"

"He tried to manipulate me," Kezule hissed. "He wanted to die quickly, but he won't. I'll have every scrap of information he holds wrung out of him before he's allowed to die!"

"I believe we'll get more of the info we need from the two M'zullians," said Kusac quietly, sitting back in his chair. "If we do mount a mission to M'zull to rescue Zhalmo, we need to know where the Palace is and, ideally, its layout."

"You're right," said Kezule after a moment's thought. "You're planning that our people will be on the ship taking the Ch'almuthians to M'zull, aren't you?"

"That's the idea, but we need to know our way around, where to land, where to take them, so we have time to find Zhalmo and extract her safely. I'm hoping we get most of the info from the two M'zullians and the rest from the crew of their ship at Ch'almuth. Incidentally, what would happen if we tried to disable the corridor device? How would they react? It would ensure we had the time we need to prepare for this mission."

Kezule looked away from the screens to him. "I have no idea how they would react or what would happen," he said slowly. "I don't even know if ours on Kij'ik to Ch'almuth will still work when we have the station in orbit here."

"We'll have the chance to test it when it arrives tomorrow."

"Indeed," said Kezule. "My best guess would be that they will still be in some confusion after the coup, if not publicly, then certainly the top military and the Court, and even more when K'hedduk informs them of his defeat. They may not have time to worry about why the corridor to Ch'almuth has closed down."

"If they do?"

"They're busy taking all they can from the now dead world of J'kirtikk, so their resources are stretched," said Kezule thoughtfully. "They won't have been expecting an attack, and we know that K'hedduk told them how passive the Primes are. Now, however, he'll have told them to pull back because we have the Sholan Alliance and their allies on our side. Difficult to say what he'll do about Ch'almuth. He'll be wanting to concentrate on home defenses and will expect us to follow up with a punitive action."

"They still have the weapon that wiped out two of our colonies," said Kusac. "An all-out war isn't what we want."

"That pellet gun, and the spray—yes, I found that as well," said Kezule dryly. "Could they be adapted to be used on a whole world?"

"Not in that form, and the dangers to any of your people carrying it would be the same as to those you're fighting. They'd lose the speed and the reflexes as well as the Warriors' ability to heal themselves."

"The M'zullians are an aberration. They deserve to be wiped out," said Kezule.

"Agreed, but don't you need their genes?"

"They present too much of a danger to our species. I would eradicate them all if it were in my power to do so." Kezule's crest had risen slightly, and his hands were clenching the chair arm tightly.

"I'm inclined to agree with you," sad Kusac, "but the Alliance won't."

"Giyarishis is working on your formula now. I need to know if it is possible before I make a decision. Cutting Ch'almuth off from M'zull would also mean cutting it off from us. They'd have less warning of an imminent arrival, and we'd arrive too late. As it stands, if the corridor on Kij'ik still works, we can reach them in time to help. Any decision on cutting them off from M'zull would have to be theirs."

"It was just a thought. I'm toying with ideas right now. One thing we'd need, unless this mission is to be Primes only, is suits that conceal our different body shape, which is not so easy."

"The chameleon shielding might be adapted. I'll get someone on that now," he said, reaching for his communicator.

"They're beginning," said Kusac, nodding at one of the screens where Shamgar and Vayan could be seen entering a cell.

Governor's Palace, Shola, same day

Sorli, Master of the Telepath Guild had sat up all night reading the slim volume, and what sleep he'd been able to snatch before leaving for the Palace in the capital, Shanagi, to see Lijou, had been fraught with nightmares.

"Master Sorli," said Lijou, getting to his feet as he was ushered into the inner office. "A pleasure indeed to see you. What brings the Telepath Guild Master to my office at such an early hour?"

Lijou gestured to the informal seats, and Sorli gratefully sank into a soft easy chair.

"Bring refreshments for us both, if you please," said Lijou to the attendant before he left.

"It's this book," said Sorli, pulling it out of a deep pocket in his robes. "I found it in our library. It's a book of ancient prophecies and must have come from one of the precataclysm ruins that my predecessor, Esken, ordered "blessed" with explosives when he tried to hide our past from us."

"But what in this has gotten you so worked up?" asked Lijou, accepting the battered book from him and beginning to flick through the pages.

"One was found before, by the same author, warning us of the la'quo stones. He called them Green Seeds of New Regret. This one speaks of more weighty matters, if that is possible, and touches on our own deities and our destiny."

"Granted that one was correct, but it doesn't mean . . ."

"This one talks about a time when we face our largest threat, which has to be now, hasn't it? We will be judged by L'Shoh's arbiter. His Sword of Justice will be released among us. Do you know what that means, Lijou?"

He could see that Sorli was getting quite agitated and was glad when they were disturbed by a knock at the door that proved to be the arrival of c'shar and sweet cookies.

The ritual of pouring the c'shar and offering the cookies did calm the Telepath Guild Master down somewhat.

"Now tell me again what you think this passage is saying and why it relates to us now. It's almost in the job description of prophecies to be nonspecific so they can be used to keep countless generations in line, you know."

"I know, but there are passages that refer to the plight that lately Kusac Aldatan found himself in. Believe me, Lijou, I don't want it to be true. Justice on that scale would be unthinkable. We all say we want justice, but what we really want is fairness, and true justice isn't necessarily fair: It must be modified by compassion—you know that, you've been a Guild Master far longer than I have."

"Show me some of these passages, Sorli," said Lijou, putting down his mug to hand the book back to him.

Sorli took it and turned the pages till he came to the passage he wanted. "Read this," he said, handing it back.

"And the Avatar will be forged through the countless fires of hell. All he holds dear will be stripped from him, even to his life and his name, until he stands, alone, before the deities to be told their bidding. L'Shoh will say, *"Go forth and be our Sword of Justice among all the peoples of the worlds. Smite down those who have done evil, chastise with the blade those who have done wrong. Let none come before me but those whose souls are tainted with the dark."* Then the Avatar, as dark as the night skies, will bow and take the Sword of Light from L'Shoh and say, *"It shall be as you wish, Lord of*

Justice. None shall escape my Blade of Truth, be they living in the hells of our oppressors or the Halls of Light itself." Stirring prose indeed, Sorli, but how you can tie Kusac into it, I can't see."

"Kusac has lost everything, Lijou, even his good name."

"And had it restored, Sorli, don't forget that," murmured Lijou, continuing to read.

"What do they call the Palace on the Prime world?" asked Sorli quietly as he took a sip from his mug.

"The Palace of Light," he replied absently.

"Not a long stretch to Halls of Light, is it?"

"I suppose not, but it's all symbolic, not literal, Sorli. Kusac is very much alive and in no position to do something this sweeping anyway."

"When he returned from his last mission, the Jalna one, he was changed. He had lost his Talent, his Leska, and his way. Then comes this mission to the one Valtegan who was his bitterest enemy, the one who kidnaped Kashini, who . . ."

Lijou held up his hand, stopping Sorli in midflow. "I do know all this," he said gently. "Believe me when I say, yes, it could be Kusac, but it could also have been other people in our past. We don't lack heroes, do we? I will read the book and make Rhyaz aware of it. But honestly, there is nothing about Kusac's situation right now that would lead me to believe this refers to him or, if it does, that he is in a position to do anything about it."

"Did you read the next part, where Ghyakulla tells him to become one with his enemy so he will know their weaknesses? Isn't that just what he's been doing this past half year or more?"

Lijou pulled himself out of the book with an effort. It was just too easy to read into it what Sorli had.

"Yes, I did." He closed the book and put it down on the table. "The Primes are not our enemies, Sorli, and I doubt if Kusac harbors any ill-feelings toward us for sending him on that mission." He wasn't really certain about that. Rhyaz, at least, he had promised a reckoning. "I will take your concerns seriously and pass them on to Rhyaz, you have my word." That this should have rattled their usually unflappable Telepath Guild Master was in itself a reason to take it seriously, and he wasn't about to add to his worries by saying that he did have some good reasons for thinking this applied to Kusac. He'd show this to Noni and Conner and discuss it with them, then report to Rhyaz.

"Now tell me how your family's doing. It seems ages since we visited and chatted about our wives and cubs."

Zhal-Arema 10th day (March)

"Have you any idea how difficult it is to get hold of you, Kusac?" asked Carrie, walking over to where he sat at breakfast in the dining room.

"I've been busy, Carrie, nothing more." It was true; he had been busy.

"There are things we need to discuss, and they can't wait," she said sitting down opposite him.

"Like what?" Her scent came drifting across the table, smelling of the special oils Vanna's cousin made for her, taking him back to happier times.

"Shaidan for one. He's my son too, and I feel he should be with his brothers and sisters on the *Tooshu*, not down here."

"He stays here with me. I'll not break my promise to him," he said. "Bring the others down here—it's wrong to keep them cooped up in space. Shaidan had never seen a sunset or felt the wind on his pelt till I took him to the rooftop the other night."

"The others will stay on the *Tooshu*," she said as firmly.

"Why? Let them walk on grass, feel the wind, smell the fresh air, and play in mud till it squishes between their toes— even chase butterflies! They need to taste freedom. They'll be safe here. Unless you think Kezule let them go in the hopes of one day getting his hands on them again?"

"Of course I don't think that!" she said, her skin flushing.

"Hmm," was all he said as he went back to eating, trying not to let himself be too distracted by her presence.

"I don't! It's kidnapers and assassins I'm afraid of."

"The other cubs would be under the same stringent security as Shaidan and Mayza, Kezule's daughter, are. He's not about to let harm come to her."

"Cubs need boundaries . . ." she began.

"They also need freedom to play and to be cubs, Carrie," ? countered. "Give them a little time now, and they won't ?uddenly take off on their own with a burning need to explore. They've been controlled all their short lives. Give them that time, Carrie."

"I don't see you letting Shaidan loose on the world!"

"Since the battle was over, he's been swimming with Mayza in the King's pool, and Shishu took them to the cattle pens to pet the newborn calves yesterday. They came back reeking of cattle dung, but happy and excited. What have you let the other seven do?"

"All right, I get your point. I'll discuss it with Kaid and their parents later today. In return, I want to know about this scent marker."

Startled, he looked up at her. "I told Kaid."

"I'm not Kaid. I want to hear it from you myself."

"It's too public here, and I'm almost late for a meeting with Kezule and the King," he said before shoveling the last mouthful in and standing up.

Then send it to me, she said. *I know you can because you helped me during the HALO drop.*

Trapped, he straightened up and retreated behind the Warrior within him. All along, he'd known he'd have to lie to her to protect her. Now was the time.

"The night before I was returned to you, K'hedduk sent one of his females to rape me and steal genetic material to make Shaidan. She smelled of Doctor Zayshul, so I thought it was she. She drugged me and bound Zayshul's scent with mine, hoping I'd tell everyone what had happened, Zayshul would be blamed, and the alliance between the Primes and us would never happen. Only . . . I didn't tell anyone."

Carrie's face had grown paler as he spoke. "Why not?" she whispered.

His eyes took on a bleak look for a brief moment. *Because I enjoyed it after enduring so much pain from J'koshuk.*

When she said nothing more, he continued. *I still love you, Carrie, but I'm linked physically by this scent marker to Zayshul, and we can't dissolve it.* He wanted to say—I'm lying to protect you, I love you more than life itself, can't you tell?— but he couldn't.

I see.

He could feel her thoughts even though his were hidden

from her. *I fought so hard to prove your innocence and travel so far—for what? To find you in the arms of a Prime female?*

"I have to go," he said quietly.

"Go, then. There's not much left to talk about, is there?"

He hesitated a moment longer, then left before his courage failed him.

Nlè

The shuttle, flanked by a wing of fighters, flew low over the town, giving Zsurtul a clear view of just how bad the urban decay and poverty was.

"I don't understand," said the young King, looking away from the portholes to where Kusac and Kezule sat at the table. "My father was a good person. I know he implemented many schemes to help rebuild and revitalize our cities. What happened to them?"

"Your father relied too heavily on his advisers, King Zsurtul, and most of them were not honest men," said Kezule. "Take us back now, Khayikule, if you please."

"It appears not. This visit has taught me much, but how do we go about repairing it?"

"We need to visit each township and city and set up officers who will report directly back to you on conditions in their area. The people need to be united into helping themselves when given the tools to do so. Most importantly, they need to see you as the ultimate ruler again, Majesty. Doubtless petty lordlings will have taken over the more prosperous areas. They will need to be investigated and dealt with."

"There must be some honest Primes on this world," said Zsurtul.

"There are many, Majesty; we just need to find them and reward them for treating their people decently. It's time to bring back the old system where each area sent a representative to your Court to sit on your Council. That will be one reward for being honest."

"You could start with repairing that old irrigation system we've seen," said Kusac. "With a proper water supply, you'll have more crops and less hunger. It'll also employ many of the people now idle. I also advise that as soon as you can, you take all heavy industry offworld and onto your moon again."

Zsurtul nodded. "Those dark clouds from the foundry looked most unpleasant for those living nearby. Would the Ch'almuthians help? They have the worker genes; some of them injected into my people would perhaps stop them contemplating goodness knows what while their world falls around their ears!"

"They agreed to help me on Kij'ik, Majesty; I'm sure they'll be willing to help you," said Kezule.

"General, I know you wanted to have nothing to do with the Court and ruling K'oish'ik, but I really do need your expertise. What we are talking of doing on a large scale, you had started on Kij'ik. I'm asking you to accept the title of First Prime and remain here to help me accomplish what looks like a task for several lifetimes, not one."

Kezule was silent for several minutes. The only sound to break it was the faint tapping of his claws on the table.

"I'll stay, Majesty," he said finally. He looked across at Kusac. "You told me to dare to be different and leave a positive legacy behind. You were right. Rebuilding our people into one caste again is a worthwhile task for any Prime or Valtegan."

"Congratulations, Kezule," said Kusac. "You're the right person for the post. You bring to it the knowledge of where your people went wrong in the past so those mistakes won't be made again."

"Thank you from the bottom of my heart, General," said Zsurtul, reaching out to take Kezule by the hand and shake it.

"I may have the memories, but half the time, I'm damned if I know where they come from," Kezule muttered, returning the handshake.

Kusac's ears pricked at that, but he held his peace for now. Later, when he and the General could be alone, was time enough to ask him about that.

"Your Brotherhood arrives later today," Kezule was saying to him. "With them here, and if that corridor is working, we can make short shrift of moving those Ch'almuthians who want to emigrate here."

"I'm sure L'Seuli will have no objection to helping," said Kusac, grinning.

"What we will need is prefabricated buildings and facilities for them to live in until either those in the towns and cities repaired or a new settlement is built," said Kezule.

"There's plenty of room on the plains below," said Kusac, looking out of the porthole as they neared the Palace again. "There's even a river. Perfect place for a temporary camp where people can be processed to their final new homes."

"With the Ch'almuthians we'll have the two main castes," said Zsurtul. "What about the Warriors and M'zull?"

"We don't need them. We'll recruit and train our own people. If Inquisitor genes could survive, then out there must be some rogue Warrior genes. The Ch'almuthians themselves bred the few Warriors that were on their world back into their gene pool, so we'll get them from there."

"And there're your commandos," said Kusac.

Kezule's face darkened. "We lost nearly half of them in the defense of the Emperor, damn K'hedduk!"

"His coup has decided one factor," said Kusac. "We no longer need to guess where he'll hit next. He has to come here, to K'oish'ik, and retake it, or unless I am very wrong, his Generals will depose him. You will have your revenge match at some point, Kezule."

"You're right. That runt of a half-breed will lose his throne on M'zull unless he makes us his priority."

Zsurtul winced visibly at that.

"What?" asked Kezule, puzzled.

"I'm not exactly of pure blood myself," Zsurtul murmured.

"Nonsense!" said Kezule, reaching out to grasp his young ruler by the shoulder. "It's my bet that if we looked, we'd find you are a mix of the genes of all three castes, Zsurtul. You conducted yourself as a Warrior any father would be proud of."

"But I didn't save my mother or your daughter, and I nearly got myself killed."

"You tried, and you fought against K'hedduk," said Kusac. "How many in the Palace have done even a fraction of that?"

"As First Prime, I can award you the Medal of Valor, if you want," said Kezule with a slight smile. "In fact, that's a damned fine idea! You'll be the first ruler in many centuries to have actually earned it."

His color heightened, Zsurtul obviously was casting about for something neutral to say. "Oh!" he said, suddenly digging in his pocket. "I keep forgetting to give you this."

Kusac took the rectangular red leather box and turned it over in his hand, seeing the ornate clasp on the front. "What is it?" he asked.

"Your necklace of norrta teeth," grinned the youth. "The Palace jewelers made a lovely job of it, even made the case out of its hide for you. Have a look."

He hesitated, but the wave of pleasure in giving him this gift was so strong from Zsurtul that he hadn't the heart not to flip the catch and open the case.

Nestling on a bed of deep blue velvet, the five inch-long serrated teeth glowing ivory in their sliver settings, lay the necklace. It was almost barbaric, but the finely wrought links of chain between the teeth and at either end gave it a beauty beyond that. He lifted it out of the case to examine the chain more closely.

"It's made of links," he said, "and each one is riveted."

"Yes," nodded Zsurtul. "It's the traditional design for it. It is a Warrior's necklace, so the chain is a very fine one made of rings of mail interlinked. Wear it for good luck, Captain, not that I think you will need it. You get five teeth because you killed it, and Khadui got the other four."

"Impressive," said Kezule, bending to look at it. "I thought they were exaggerating about its size, but apparently not. Even in my time, killing one as large as that alone was a feat of bravery."

"Put it on, Kusac," said Zsurtul. "You should wear it with pride. Kij'ik arrives today, doesn't it General? What do you plan to do with it?"

"Turn it into an offensive station. I'm hoping we can call on Touiban help to get the cannon working again, amongst other things. If we are going to be K'hedduk's main target, we need to be able to defend ourselves properly."

"There's nothing the Touibans enjoy more than clambering over old technology and trying to make it work again," said Kusac, dropping the chain over his head as their shuttle began to circle around to land in the front courtyard of the Palace. "I'm sure they'd be willing to help." He closed the case and put it into his belt pouch.

Ghioass, the Camarilla Council chamber, same day

Khassis stood on the podium at the lectern as behind her the representation of the current potentialities of the future dimmed and faded.

"All can see, war no longer encompasses the realms of our children or their allies. Accomplished that we have. Next, unified are the Sand-dwellers and Hunters. Side by side they fought. Before no aliens they tolerated, now many they call friend. This done without forcing Hunter male to Sand-dweller female. Little left now to do, except watch their final solution to Warrior Sand-dwellers."

A rustle as Zaimiss got to his feet. "All are threatened by warlike Sand-dwellers. Final solution must ours be, not theirs. We have the experience, the vision of futures, not they. I Speak for obliterating them. While one survives, a danger to all they are."

Shoawomiss rose. "Even do we Moderates doubt Warrior Sand-dwellers of M'zull have any use. But genocide not light decision."

"Use drug Hunters produce," said Shvosi sitting up on her cushions. "Alter into sterilizing one. Easy Shoawomiss to do, he there. Genocide not committed but threat gone after this generation."

"That option more acceptable," said Shoawomiss, the lenses in his eyes spinning as he looked around the hall. "We would Speak for that. Only females need be targeted."

"No. They steal females from grow-world. All on M'zull must be sterilized for safety," said Shvosi.

"Threat remains. Even sterilized will they plunder grow-world," said Zaimiss. "Only death stops other potentialities from occurring."

"We have not the right to decide this," said Kuvaa, rising onto on her haunches. "Gods we are not! Means we have to give memories to Sand-dwellers, overwrite those they have. This should we do to them. Turn them aside from war is best solution!"

"Well said, Kuvaa," said Khassis, looking around the murmuring hall. "Three proposals have you to think on. Destruction of all Sand-dwellers on M'zull, or sterilization, or, finally, memory adjustment in hopes it buries their nature forever."

"Isolationists preach noninvolvement. Now they ask to

meddle openly in destruction of whole caste of Sand-dwellers. How justify this?" demanded Aizshuss.

"We rectify errors made by you when you concentrated on saving Primes, not curbing M'zulls," snapped Zaimiss.

Arguments went back and forth for some time with the majority of those in the Council favoring a more permanent solution. Finally Azwokkus rose from his cushions, his draperies dispersing a calming scent.

"There has been much talk. Vote now we must. I Speak for memory wiping. We are not Gods and must remember this."

"I Second that," said Kuvaa.

With a glance at each other, they sat down.

We will not win, sent Shvosi through Unity to Kuvaa. *Too much fear of them there is.*

They make me afraid, but some things are not right for us to do!

"I Speak for termination of all Sand-dwellers on M'zull," said Zaimiss.

One of his Isolationist friends Seconded him, as expected.

"Shoawomiss?" asked Khassis. "You Spoke for sterilization. Do you still Speak for that?"

"I do," said Shoawomiss, bowing to the female TeLaxaudin.

Again he was Seconded.

"Now the vote."

It was a tied vote, equal numbers supporting genocide and sterilization, and as Shvosi had predicted, their proposition lost.

"Azwokkus, your votes will decide which path we take. Use them wisely."

We support sterilization, he sent to Shvosi and Kuvaa. *But this not the end of our proposal.*

We meddle too much, grumbled Kuvaa.

Hush, young one. Compromises divert attention, sent Aizshuss.

Having spoken to all his voters through Unity, Azwokkus gave their decision to Khassis. "We vote for sterilization, only as lesser of two evils," he said.

Khassis frowned at him. "Your strong comment is noted. Unity, tell us the decision now.

"Majority vote is for sterilization of M'zull Sand-dwellers," said Unity.

Shoawomiss got to his feet again, his drapery swirling like a cloud around him. "This task to Giyarishis must be given. My work is increasing with need to let Primes breed naturally. No more can I be taking on. Preliminary work he doing already on this."

"Noted. Kuvaa, you will instruct Giyarishis on what he is to do," said Khassis. "We will send him when he is ready the compound he is to use."

Kuvaa rose up onto her haunches, her mobile nose wrinkling as if she smelled something bad.

"I do the Camarilla's will," she said.

"Attention I wish to draw to Hunter," said Zaimiss. "Nexus he still is. Why do black moments surround him from time to time? Has answer to this puzzle been found?"

Khassis looked over to Kuvaa again.

"None yet. It is not the cub, as was thought. Neither Hunter nor Sand-dweller aware it happens."

"Irrelevant this is," said Khassis. "Matters there progress well. No deviation from his path is there to be seen. This session is now closed."

As they filed out, Aizshuss suggested they eat at a quiet U'Churian restaurant he'd discovered not far away.

"I have Giyarishis to contact first," said Kuvaa.

"No, no, eat first you must, young one," said Aizshuss, one fragile-looking hand grasping her harness and pulling her toward him. "Weak with hunger you are, from studying late last night. Not so, Shvosi?"

"Is so. Saw her light on I did myself."

Too surprised to object any further, Kuvaa let the two Te-Laxaudin and her fellow Cabbaran hustle her along the walkway to the small restaurant.

Despite the fact the U'Churians, at six feet tall, towered over both species, there was a room set aside with furnishings obviously made for them. Once settled comfortably and their orders given, Aizshuss turned to her.

"Occasionally, very occasionally, does this happen. The compound for wiping memories we will give you to send to Giyarishis before the one for sterilization is ready."

"What do I do with the one that is the will of the Camarilla? Surely my substitution will be discovered?"

"No, for you will assume the one you are given is right," said Shvosi.

"When the other arrives, put in place you forget, for it is an error, no? Already you have been given it."

"Some things are just wrong, you said, Kuvaa, did you not?" asked Shvosi.

Unhappily, Kuvaa nodded. It seemed that being a full member of the Camarilla was far more complex than she had imagined. "I do it."

Prime world

It was late afternoon as Kusac and Shaidan crossed the Palace's western courtyard. They'd been taking a break in the formal gardens there for Kusac to give his leg some gentle exercise as ordered and to enjoy some time outdoors with his son.

Shaidan! The call was loud and clear, and they both swung around to see who it was.

"Dhyshac!" said Shaidan, waving back to his brother, who had left Tanjo's side to run at full pelt toward them.

Shaidan turned a hopeful face up to his father. "May I?"

"Go on," said Kusac, letting his hand go. "Just stay clear of the builders!" All around them the debris caused by the battle was being loaded onto hoppers and taken to be dumped. Reconstruction had already begun on weight-bearing walls and other high priority areas.

As if it had been a signal, the other six children left Tanjo's side too and made straight for where the two younglings now stood looking at each other, unsure what to do or say next.

Gaylla had no such problems. She flung herself at her brother, winding her arms around his neck. "I missed you!" she cried, almost knocking him off his feet.

"Hello back," he said, hugging her. Then he was at the center of them all, being hugged by each in turn, even Dhyshac.

Kusac watched for a moment or two, nodding to Tanjo as he hurried in their wake, then began to stroll over to them, pleased and surprised that Carrie had taken his advice and brought them down to the planet.

"You must be Captain Aldatan," said Tanjo, holding out

his hand in the brief Telepath's greeting. "I'm Tanjo, Liege. I do apologize for the way they rushed over, but we only just landed, and they're very excitable."

"It's good to see them behaving like cubs, especially Shaidan." Kusac gave a brief nod to the two guards accompanying Tanjo.

The cubs were casting surreptitious glances in their direction now. Kusac could see apprehension in the lie of their ears and tails. Shaidan, however, had his set at a jaunty angle.

"I wonder what he's telling them."

"Probably of your Warrior prowess," said Tanjo with a small laugh. "They're as thirsty for knowledge of their parents as plants in a drought."

Startled, he looked back to Tanjo. "Only Shaidan is mine, isn't he? I couldn't detect any of the others having my blood."

"Only Shaidan," agreed the Brother as the cubs came over to join them. "I'm glad Liegena Carrie brought them down to K'oish'ik. They need to be able to scamper around fields and streams and be young for the first time in their lives."

"That's what I told her. For now, though, perhaps you'd better head into the Palace with us and see M'kou about where he's billeting you all."

"That would be most helpful."

"The Lieutenant is in the office next to the King's," offered one of the guards as Kusac led the way to the Supplies entrance.

No sooner than they had entered the Palace than Kusac was hailed by ZSADHI on his wrist comm.

"The *Va'Khoi* has taken up a parking orbit at the Weather Orbital, Captain. Commander L'Seuli sends his regards to you and says he will leave presently to rendezvous on the surface."

"Pass the news to M'kou and Captain Kaid, please."

"As you command, Captain, it will be done."

Seeing Tanjo's surprised look, he said, "Palace AI. It has a quirky way about it. It's got nodes all over the Palace; so if you need anything, just call out for it. That's right, isn't it, ZSADHI?"

"As the Captain says, Brother Tanjo. Well come to the Palace of Light. You and your charges are now in my data banks, though I will need you to stop for a quick retinal scan at the first checkpoint. It is my duty to see that you are comfortable and secure and that your needs are met. You will be staying in the nursery on the King's private floor, the fourth level. If you would proceed there now, I will guide you through anything else you need to know."

"Thank you, ZSADHI," said Tanjo.

"I'm on my way up there anyway, so I'll take you. Now you're in the data banks, you should have no problems at the various checkpoints. Security's high right now," he said, leading them all to the first checkpoint.

"Captain Aldatan." The guards on duty saluted crisply, then relaxed a little.

"I see you met up with the party from the *Tooshu*," said the officer in charge. "If your companions would mind just stepping on this marked tile one at a time, so ZSADHI can scan them, I'd appreciate it."

"Certainly," Kusac said, gesturing to Tanjo.

The process took only a few minutes, and then they were all crowding into the small elevator up to the fourth floor.

As they spilled out, Kusac gestured his son over. "Shaidan can show you the nursery from here. I have to go down to the Admin level now."

"Thank you, Captain. No doubt we'll see each other again soon."

"I'm sure we will," said Kusac, stepping back into the elevator.

The *Va'Khoi*

L'Sculi got to his feet as the U'Churian and the Cabbaran were ushered into his lounge.

"Captain Tirak, and Annuur, a pleasure to see you again," he said, offering his hand, palm uppermost, to them.

Tirak barely touched his fingers in greeting, but Annuur sat up on his haunches and put his hoof-tipped hand squarely into the Sholan's and shook it before letting go.

"A telepath now, are you?" the Cabbaran asked, dropping back down onto all fours.

"I am, but how did you know?" he asked, a faint smile on his face as he gestured them to take a seat.

Annuur trotted over to the large pile of floor cushions placed specially for him, and after a moment's pummeling them into a comfortable shape, dropped down with a sigh of contentment.

"You use Telepath greeting to Tirak, and you carry the scent of your partner. A Leska maybe?"

Tirak laughed, nudging the Cabbaran with his booted foot before sitting down. "Always so diplomatic, Annuur. Word travels, Commander. You have our congratulations on being gifted with a Leska."

"Thank you. I'm blessed indeed," L'Seuli murmured as he took his own seat again. "Can I offer you refreshments?"

"No, thank you, this is a quick visit. You'll be expected down on the planet shortly."

"What news have you, then?"

"We haven't yet resumed trade with the Mryans and Vieshen in this sector because since we lifted our embargo on their goods, they've decided to put their prices up. Their regular traders have been behaving more moderately at our station, though, which is why we've allowed them back."

"Some new undercurrent there is," said Annuur. "They look at us and whisper now, or fall silent when either of our species comes near."

Tirak nodded. "It's like watching young ones at lessons— they know some secret we don't, something that concerns us. Damned if we can find out what it is, though. Meanwhile, the raiding goes on as before, except that Chemerian ships are still least often hit by them."

"Let me just recap on this," said L'Seuli. "The Mryans and Vieshen were once slave races owned by the Valtegans."

"Is so," said Annuur, bobbing his long head, whiskers twitching at the end of his long, mobile snout. "They are least pleasant of the four races. Vieshen are feathered species not to be trusted. Young males secrete stones inside and are coated with secretions that made them most valuable to ancient Valtegans."

L'Seuli look at the Cabbaran in horror. "You mean . . . they actually killed their own young to sell these stones to the Valtegans?"

"Regretful am I to say they did. But only for minerals do we deal with them."

"I hate to ask what the Mryans did."

"They were slavés, used to mine and do heavy work, nothing more. Argumentative they are and prone to fights. Like beings of nightmares they look and are behaving."

"They sound like species to avoid, not trade with! Is it possible that the Chemerians are deep in with them? How do they behave around them?"

"Same as ever—rarely is a Chemerian seen in the station public bars and stores," said Tirak. "We've been watching them closely, and agents of both species have visited the Chemerian Ambassador in his quarters there, but they have legitimate trade agreements with them. Unless we can prove some collusion over the attacked ships, we can't move against them, even to putting recording devices in their quarters. There has to be trust there, the Matriarch says, or no one will come to trade with us." Tirak pulled a face at that. "Sometimes diplomacy holds us back from proving what we know is happening."

"Do you think it involves more than just raiding merchant ships?"

"No way of knowing yet. The raiders are sticking to the same space lines and patterns of behavior. Believe me, if we see a deviation from the norm, we'll let you know and flag it as high priority."

"Maybe we should send a few trader ships to your station, Tirak, ones with hidden armaments and crewed by Brothers. If we're attacked, maybe we can get some useful prisoners."

Tirak shrugged. "You're welcome to try. We have, but they're too fast, even for the *Profit*."

"Raiders with expensive ships, not likely. They have backers, funding, so we think," said Annuur. "Best we be watching them carefully and find out who—their own worlds or Chemerians."

"Agreed. What of the M'zullians?"

"Watchers all see them continue plundering dead world," said Annuur. "This interesting."

"We've seen no reaction to K'hedduk's departure from here as yet, but it would take some little time for them to respond. Plus, we don't know exactly what the situation is on M'zull. Was there a coup? If so, then one assumes the Generals are in charge, but how loyal will they remain to an Emperor who failed to keep K'oish'ik?"

L'Seuli's wrist comm buzzed discretely. "Time for me to head down to the surface," he said, getting to his feet. "I have a meeting with King Zsurtul and his advisers to attend. Thank you both for updating me in person on the *Watchers*. We'll meet again before I leave."

Tirak and Annuur rose. "We have to get going too. I think there's a banquet planned for this evening in your honor."

"In that case, my Leska Jiosha's coming. I'll not suffer alone."

Tirak laughed. "They're not so bad. Zsurtul's revamped everything to get most of the pomp and ceremony out of it, but he would be dishonoring you and the Brotherhood if there weren't a formal dinner. I hear it will be a small one, though, in deference to the fact he's still recovering from injuries he sustained trying to stop K'hedduk from leaving."

"Really? The youth has spirit then. Till we meet again, Tirak, Annuur."

K'oish'ik, Council chamber

Kezule turned off the holo images that they'd taken the day before when he'd shown Zsurtul the state of his world outside the City of Light. The drapes over the windows at the far end of the room slid back, letting in the sunlight again.

He sat down, the chair under him audibly tilting slightly to one side as he did. "You can see quite clearly for yourself that the Prime culture, left alone, is dying out, and we need to regenerate. Now we do have some resources of our own—Kij'ik is being towed here and should arrive sometime this evening to be placed in a geostationary orbit around K'oish'ik. On it is my fledgling colony. It will be ferried down here as soon as we have built at least a temporary township for them just outside the city here. As you came in to land, you may have seen it, L'Seuli."

"I did. It progresses well. We have brought with us the prefabricated materials you requested, Kezule."

"We thank you indeed," said Zsurtul.

"Our other resource is the people of Ch'almuth. They were once an agricultural world with a small military and scientific presence. They have managed over the last fifteen hundred years to return to what the Valtegan people once were, not three castes but one. They are reaching a population level where they are happy to let those who wish to emigrate come here. All we lack is the means to ferry them to K'oish'ik in large enough numbers."

"There's an added problem that M'zull has for many years been raiding Ch'almuth not only for supplies but for their young people, mainly the females, as breeding stock," said Kusac. "We anticipate another such incursion any time now. The details on our current situation were sent to your ship as soon as you docked. I don't know if you've had time to read them."

"My aide did and brought me up to speed on your situation. I'll study them myself tonight. As I understand it, your main needs are the building materials we brought for you from Shola, a way to bring the Ch'almuthians who want to emigrate here, and a way to defend the Ch'almuthians from any M'zullian attack."

"Not so much the latter," said Kusac. "The Touibans have managed to repair the Ch'almuthian weather platform, which, as it turns out, is also armed. They have that now as well as a couple of fair-sized ships, so they can defend themselves against the craft that will be sent to do the cull. However, this visit will be the last for five to ten years, if all goes as the M'zullians expect. If we let it go ahead as planned, it would give the Primes some time to get up and running here. Five years is half a generation to them. We should have three weeks grace at least until K'hedduk lands on M'zull. "

"We need fighter planes, their pilots, and warriors, Commander L'Seuli," said Zsurtul. "We need to train more of our military, and for that we are looking to you for help. I know how good the Brotherhood training is."

"You were trained by Kusac and Kaid at the Warrior Guild, weren't you?" said L'Seuli with a faint smile. "I remember that now. We'll need to thrash out the details, but I can leave about two hundred Brothers and some ten extra fighters, but that's all for now. We have to be prepared for the war to start nearer to home than here. We can also go to Ch'almuth and bring at least a thousand people here for you, if that would help."

"Enormously," said Zsurtul, the relief evident on his face. "The task of rebuilding my people back into one species again is enough of a burden without the prospect that the M'zullians will launch an all-out war on us."

"As to that," began L'Seuli.

"The war will happen out here at some point, L'Seuli," said Kusac impatiently. Why couldn't others see the reality as clearly as he did? "They need this world to recreate their Empire, and since we sent K'hedduk fleeing, his tail between his legs, he will be focused on K'oish'ik. Remember the Valtegan mind-set." He cast a sideways glace at Kezule as he said that. "The balance has changed. Now we can decide whether to take the war to him from here, or wait for him to come to us."

"He's been defeated, very publicly," said Kezule, his voice clipped with self-control. "However, he can prove that it was due to failed communications between M'zull and K'oish'ik, that the expected reinforcements did not arrive. That, and the presence of my daughter as a captive, will buy him some time on M'zull. We do know now that while he was here, his Generals staged a coup on his behalf and deposed his brother, the Emperor, so he does have all the resources of M'zull at his fingertips. But his Generals will turn on him at the first sign of weakness. At some point, he has to regain K'oish'ik to regain his honor and remain their Emperor. I believe he will try to take Ch'almuth first as the easier target."

"He sees us as a barbaric backwater, Commander," said Shyadd, speaking for the first time. "He'll come, but he'll come in force to wipe us out for daring to stand against him, and for succeeding, thanks to the bravery of our King, yourselves, and our other allies."

"The reason we can't take the war to him remains the same," said L'Seuli. "Now we do have superior numbers, thanks to the demise of J'kirtikk, but they still have the weapon that destroyed all life on two of our worlds. And if we survive that long, inevitably it will come down to fighting on the planet's surface. On the ground, we know from experience, none of the Alliance can beat the M'zullians on sheer brute strength, speed, and ferocity. The outcome is still not predictable."

"Pity we didn't have a couple of planet-buster bombs," murmured Kaid, pulling a stim twig out of the pack in front of him.

L'Seuli looked askance at him. "If they existed, there's no way even the Brotherhood could defend itself for using them."

"Nice thought, though, you gotta admit that," Kaid drawled, sitting back in his chair. "We don't want to leave anything of them to rise up again in another fifteen hundred years, do we?"

"Thankfully, that's not for us to decide," said L'Seuli. "Is there anything else you need, King Zsurtul?"

Kusac and Kaid exchanged glances that said it all.

"There is. Since everyone here at this table is fully occupied, can you possibly spare a priest to help me replace the old Emperor cult with one belonging to one of our older Gods or Goddesses? Something more peaceful, perhaps a fertility deity."

Kusac turned back to see L'Seuli blink in surprise.

"Yes, I can do that," he said. "There's no one I can spare on the *Va'Khoi,* but I will ask Father Lijou tonight when I return to the ship if he can send someone."

Ghyakulla sat back on her heels, and wiping a smudge of wet earth from her nose, smiled.

On Shola, Conner looked up from the book he was reading to Noni.

"I have to leave tomorrow," he said quietly, reaching a hand across the table to her.

She took it and squeezed his till her claws pricked his flesh. "So it begins, does it?"

"It does, the Gods help us all."

CHAPTER 10

Zhal-Arema 11th day (March)

IT had been another bad night, one of disturbing visions of faceless beings and unaccomplished tasks that woke him every few hours. Luckily, Shaidan had asked to sleep with his brothers and sisters for the last two nights, so the only one disturbed by it had been him.

He was already late for his meeting down in the cells with Kezule, so breakfast had been what he could pile on a slice of bread and eat on the way down. Now it lay in an indigestible lump in his gut, which didn't improve his temper.

He joined Kezule in the office, sitting down to watch the bank of monitors.

"Kij'ik arrived last night," said Kezule. "They're preparing to test the corridor."

He grunted noncommittally. "When are you bringing down the civilians?"

"When we have somewhere for them to live. They're safe on Kij'ik for now. We have to worry about those who come from Ch'almuth first as they'll have nowhere to stay."

"They can always be berthed in Kij'ik for the time being. Less work than trying to build a shantytown around them."

"No, I don't want to open up any more of the station until it is fully operational. We had too many botched systems running there. We'll give them the materials," said Kezule, "and provide some help. They'll do the rest and will be on hand to help other newcomers when they arrive."

"I suppose."

"Where's Kaid today? I expected him here but Banner is standing in for him."

"It's their Leska Link day. They need to spend the next twenty-eight hours alone, sharing their minds. You won't see them until tomorrow." Was that what was bothering him? He pushed the thought aside and sat up, trying to take an interest in what was happening. "I take it there's nothing new since yesterday?"

"Nothing. I don't believe that gene-altered monstrosity has anything to tell us. He certainly wasn't chosen for his intellectual ability. Are you sure you can't mind read the others?"

"I've told you, someone has enhanced their natural barriers that prevent me making a deep enough contact to get what I need from them. If I do force a contact, they'll have a stroke and die." Anticipating the next question, he looked at Kezule and said, "You were a different case. You only had the natural protection, which Carrie could force through."

"Do your worst to the thug," said Kezule. "He's of no further use to us."

"I'm certainly done with him. I'm more interested in the M'zullians and why they aren't as afraid of us as the ones on Keiss were."

"Those, from what you've told me, were Warriors. These two aren't, they're a more intellectual strain. The same memories aren't passed on to every caste, you know."

"I'd assumed they were, without really thinking about it." It felt as though the more he learned about all the different castes of Valtegans, the less he seemed to know.

He reached out to turn up the volume on the monitor for the cell of Lufsuh, Head Enforcer of the Inquisitors.

Banner was sitting astride a wooden chair, arms leaning on the back, facing Lufsuh, who was tied another. To the right of the prisoner stood Kho'ikk, whom he recognized as one of the few commandos that K'hedduk had taken prisoner.

"You're the last of the Inquisitors, Lufsuh," Banner was saying. "You meant nothing to K'hedduk; you were merely a stepping stone to power. He considered you disposable. Not a nice thought, is it, that your ruler thinks you're worthless?"

"He's a betrayer," said Kho'ikk, spitting on the ground. "He betrayed his brother to take the Throne of Light for himself, then betrayed you when he left you stranded here during the battle. He's a coward, not fit to rule, and you're a bigger fool for protecting him now!"

"Why should I tell you anything? You'll kill me no matter what I do or say. Perhaps I despise you more than K'hedduk," said Lufsuh, trying to turn his head away from the brightness of the light shining in his face. "The hatchling you set on the Throne may not be the equal of K'hedduk, but he is a Prime. He trained on Shola as a Warrior, and I hear he fought in the battle." The V shaped mouth split in a toothy grin. "The blood of Warriors obviously flows in his veins. Be wary of him. One day he will tire of bowing to lesser beings like you, and . . ."

Kho'ikk's hand lashed out, delivering a blow to the side of Lufsuh's head.

"Silence!" he hissed. "Our King, unlike yours, would never betray his people or his allies!"

Lufsuh shook his head and turning to face Kho'ikk, spat blood at him. "Whatever you think you know about us as a race, forget it. You know nothing about us! You are the dust beneath our feet!"

"They're fanatics, every last one of them," said Kezule. "There is no talking to them."

"I can see why you nearly killed him. He's taking control of the situation," said Kusac, his own hackles beginning to rise. "Have you one of those punishment collars handy?"

"There're several in the guardroom, with a couple of control bracelets. K'hedduk used them on the Council members."

"Good," he said. Pushing his chair back, he got to his feet and headed out to the guardroom for them.

Stopping only long enough to put the control bracelet on, he knocked on the cell door. Kho'ikk opened it, standing back to let him in.

Reaching inside himself, he fanned the anger he knew was still there and triggered his fight response. Where his hair wasn't braided, it rose up like a cloud around his face. His hackles, visible because of his sleeveless summer tunic, stood up along his shoulders, and his tail bushed out to nearly twice its width as it began to sway more quickly.

"You have a prisoner here for me," he drawled, stalking into the room, the very epitome of a Sholan about to go into the kzu-shu red rage. "He's lacking a collar. Why hasn't he been collared?" he demanded of Banner.

"We don't use the collars, Captain," Banner said, getting slowly off the chair.

"All my prisoners wear them," purred Kusac, moving around behind Lufsuh.

One hand snaked out to grasp the Prime around the jaw and jerk his head up while the other snapped the collar in place. He released him as abruptly, making a few hand signals to Banner, telling him to play along with him.

He came around in front of the Prime, kicking Banner's now vacant chair aside.

"Why is he still dressed in his robes?" he demanded. "He's a prisoner. Have him stripped and given something more suitable to wear." When neither Kho'ikk nor Banner moved, he raised his voice to a roar. "I mean now!"

"You think to intimidate me . . ." began Lufsuh.

Kusac depressed the pain button on the control bracelet, holding it down for a count of ten. He watched dispassionately as the Prime's cry of pain filled the air and his limbs jerked convulsively, sending the chair tumbling over on its back.

"I'm waiting," said Kusac mildly, looking at Banner and Kho'ikk.

Banner left the room at a run as the commando rushed to where Lufsuh lay gasping and began to untie him.

"I expect you're very familiar with this kind of collar," said Kusac, picking Banner's chair up and setting it back in place. "You're mine, Lufsuh, mine to torment or reward as I see fit. You thought you had nothing to gain by cooperating? Think again. You cooperate, and you'll suffer less pain." He sat down, legs sprawled at ease in front of him as he allowed his hair and pelt to return to normal.

"I'll . . ."

He hit the pain button again, this time for a count of fifteen. Kho'ikk had to move back quickly to avoid being hit by the thrashing limbs.

"Did I ask you to speak?" asked Kusac. "I know this game well, Lufsuh. I've played it with one of your kind. You cannot win. You will tell me everything I need to know, and then you'll die, but not until then. Do you hear me?"

Lufsuh lay there making small noises of pain, which grew louder when Kusac gestured Kho'ikk to continue stripping him.

The room seemed to fade around him, taking him back to

his time on the *Kz'adul* when he was J'koshuk's prisoner. The collar sent signals through the body's central nervous system, creating wave after wave of agonizing, fiery pain. He knew exactly what Lufsuh was experiencing.

He blinked, pulling himself out of the memory to look at the now naked Prime lying at his feet.

"Rules, every encounter has rules; doesn't it, Lufsuh? Mine are that you answer truthfully every question I ask. If you do, you will be rewarded with less pain and something halfway decent to eat and drink. If you give me the information I need sooner, I'll even see that you are decently buried, not left for the wild beasts or burned as a traitor. Is that understood?"

"I have rights . . ."

Kusac just touched the button again, sending a brief jolt of pain through him.

"Rights? What rights?"

"Alliance . . ." Lufsuh gasped.

"You forfeited those when you and K'hedduk withdrew from that treaty. A new one hasn't yet been signed. I told you, you're mine, Lufsuh. You betrayed your legal ruler, helped to murder him and his offspring and imprison his wife, and you performed her illegal marriage to the usurper! Your crimes are many, Lufsuh."

"Captain," said a voice quietly from behind him. He turned his head just enough to see the medic without taking his eyes off Lufsuh.

"What?" he demanded.

"I must protest . . ."

"Tell it to the General. I'm busy here," he snapped, turning back to his prisoner. "Do you understand my rules, Lufsuh?"

"Yes."

"Good, then we've made some progress. Tell me what K'hedduk promised you to betray your predecessor."

"He didn't," said Lufsuh so quietly Kusac had to prick his ears forward to hear him.

He triggered the collar again, aware that any feelings of sympathy or compassion he might have for the male before him had fled deep within him.

"I'm not lying!" screeched Lufsuh. "He offered me this post or death!"

"So, our first truthful answer. Good. What else did K'hedduk promise you for leading the Inquisitors?"

"I'd be First Inquisitor when he united the two worlds," Lufsuh gasped, the nails on his fingers leaving deep furrows in the dirt floor of the cell as he clenched and unclenched them.

He sensed Banner returning with a pair of pull-on shorts for their captive. Seeing them, he raised an eye ridge questioningly, getting back the reply in hand signals that this was to reward him.

"We make progress at last," he drawled, taking the shorts from Banner and throwing them down in front of Lufsuh. "Here's clothing as a reward for cooperating."

Trembling, Lufsuh pushed himself up into a sitting position, grabbing for the shorts.

"The General asked that you use this, Captain," Banner said quietly, handing him a headset.

He took it from him and put it on.

"Yes, General?" he asked, subvocalizing.

"Find out how K'hedduk got onto K'oish'ik in the first place. There's a security breach somewhere that we know nothing about."

"Aye," he said then turned to Kho'ikk. "Give him a small amount of water before we continue," he ordered.

Kho'ikk filled a pottery bowl from the tin jug of water that stood on the cell's small table and handed it to Lufsuh.

Greedily, he drank it down.

"So you were in K'hedduk's confidence then?" Kusac asked

"As much as anyone was," said Lufsuh, handing the bowl back.

"How was he able to land here without detection?"

Lufsuh squatted on the floor, pulling his legs close to his body to present as small a target as possible.

"Some of the Emperor's Council contacted M'zull several years ago. They offered help in exchange for a coup against the Emperor. Their offer was accepted, K'hedduk said, and he chose to come here and build his own empire."

"Which councillors?"

"Ghoddoh, Zsiyuk, Schoudu, and Noshikk."

"You're lying," he said, activating the collar for ten seconds.

"No! Stop, please!" shrieked Lufsuh, thrashing uncontrollably on the ground. "No more!"

"Pick him up and put him back in the chair," Kusac ordered, knowing that the slightest touch would compound the agony for the Prime. He sat up in his own chair, all traces of relaxation gone.

"You will not lie to me again, Lufsuh. Never forget I am a telepath and can tell when you fail to speak the truth. Now name the Directors who were in league with K'hedduk."

"Ghoddoh, Zsiyuk, Schoudu, and Zhayan," wept Lufsuh, cringing away from Kho'ikk's touch as he was roughly hauled upright and shoved into the chair.

"The first two are dead," said Kezule's voice in his ear. "The other two are in the barrack cells."

The questioning went on for another hour, by the end of which, Kusac was exhausted. He left the cell only to walk into Kaid waiting outside for him.

"What're you doing here on your Link day?" he asked, pushing past him to get to the guardroom.

"Banner sent for me when you ignored his request that you stop torturing the prisoner."

He stopped dead and turned back to face him. "Of course I'm torturing him! You were doing it yesterday because we need information they refuse to give us any other way!"

"He believes you were carrying it too far."

"How far is far enough?" he asked, continuing down the corridor to the guardroom, where M'zynal was waiting for him.

He pulled off the control bracelet and threw it to the young Prime, then did the same with the headset. "The session was recorded, wasn't it?" When M'zynal nodded, he continued, "Then have the other prisoners questioned the same way. It will get us results in the fastest possible time, as you saw."

"Aye, Captain."

"Kusac, torture leaves scars, both on those tortured and those doing it," said Kaid. "Leave it to the others now. If you don't, it'll leave a mark on your soul that you can't get rid of, and one day, you'll never forgive yourself for what you did."

"Do you agonize over everyone you've had to question or kill?" he demanded.

"That's not what I meant."

"Just because I was a telepath first, don't assume I don't have what it takes to be a Brother, Kaid. You have no idea what I had to do on Kij'ik!"

"You're wrong about the Captain," said M'zynal. "He

taught us how to be hard yet have compassion when it was needed."

"I've seen too much of the hard recently," said Kaid. "If you keep it up, you run the risk of desensitizing yourself to normal emotions. I know, it happened to me," he added quietly.

"It's not happening to me, Kaid," he said, keeping an eye on the corridor he'd just come up as the guards led the thug, Zoshur, out to be executed.

Heavily bound, he was still managing to struggle against his captors, but when he caught sight of Kusac, he renewed his efforts, managing to send one guard caroming off the wall.

"I see you, you piece of shit! If I die, you going with me!" Zoshur yelled, dragging the other guard with him as he headed toward them.

"Down!" Kusac yelled, pulling his pistol and aiming.

As one, the commandos hit the ground, the guard rolling clear of his captive as Kusac's pistol gave a cough. Zoshur's momentum carried him forward another couple of steps before he crashed to the ground. Kezule came running out of the office, his own pistol drawn and ready.

The General slowed to a walk, nodding to Kaid as he passed him to check the supine thug.

"Nice shot. Got him right between the eyes. Get this piece of trash out of here," he ordered the guards as they got to their feet. "If we get any more of them, execute them in their cell."

As he holstered his gun, Kusac saw the look on Kaid's face. "Now what? I was only doing what you trained me to do—execution duty. Remember?"

Kaid had the grace to wince as he said that.

"Kaid, go back to Carrie," Kusac said quietly, his anger suddenly evaporating. He took his sword-brother by the arm. "You're broadcasting too much. I'm not turning into some monster. I knew how to get the information from Lufsuh because I'd had that done to me. Though," his face took on a thoughtful look, "I did last a lot longer than he did, but, then, you trained me well."

Go, please, he sent. *I don't need to feel what you're projecting.*

Kaid hesitated, then nodded. "We'll talk tomorrow sometime," he said then left.

Kusac sighed inwardly. Though Kaid was wearing a damper, and he'd been able to block out most of the raw sensuality he was projecting, what he was picking up was like rubbing salt in the wound that had existed since he'd lost his Link to Carrie.

"I'm going to see Giyarishis, Kezule," he said as the General came over to him. "I want to find out if he has, or can make, some kind of drug we can use on the prisoners to make them tell the truth."

"I'll send someone over to the Summer Palace to find the blueprints of the M'zullian Palace." said Kezule. "It makes sense that the Emperor would want those on hand in case of any rebellion."

"Lufsuh said he couldn't find them when K'hedduk sent him to destroy them."

"He didn't know where to look. I spent several days there looking for the location of Kij'ik. I know where it's likely to be. Give me a minute to send someone there, and I'll accompany you to the labs."

Giyarishis had been given a lab on the second floor, in the main research area. They found him in his office, talking to Zayshul. It was a small room, made even smaller because the desk chair had been pushed to one side to make room for Giyarishis' pile of cushions behind the desk.

His leg was beginning to ache by now, so Kusac limped over to the easy chair.

"We need a drug to make the prisoners talk," he said to the TeLaxaudin. "You've got the one taken from me, the la'quo. Can you adapt it?"

The spindly alien began to hum, then the translator cut in. "Cannot. Memories it will affect as well as damage organs for strength and ability to heal."

"That's irrelevant," said Kusac. "We need them to talk; nothing else matters."

"Could it be mass-produced and delivered on a planetary scale?" demanded Kezule.

The lenses of his eyes whirled as he adjusted his vision to look from Kusac to Kezule. "Raw materials we have not. Much needed. There be deaths from workers as well as injury. Affect all castes, Primes, Ch'almuthians, and M'zullians. Delivery system needed, have you one?"

"Not yet," Kezule admitted. "But we can devise one, I'm sure."

"Insects infected with it," said Kusac. "They pass it on when they bite. And there are plenty of the la'quo pellets on Jalna."

"Idea interesting," said Giyarishis. "You got six months?"

"What you're suggesting is wrong," said Zayshul.

"Why?" asked Kezule. "They came here, not openly as soldiers to fight us, but covertly. They killed your Emperor and his family, apart from Zsurtul. Killed several loyal advisers and half of my sons and daughters. They have no rights."

"We can't win a head to head fight with them, Zayshul, so we have to use every means we can. And if saving lives means doing it with drugs and poisons, then so be it," said Kusac.

"Find me something, anything, I can use against them!" said Kezule.

"A compound I work on to strip memories from them," Giyarishis said. "They forget all—dreams of conquering, hate of Sholans, all gone."

"Does it work?"

"On computer, yes. Blood samples I need to test."

"We can get plenty of those from the M'zullians in the cells. If you can combine that research with the one to strip them of their extra abilities, then do it," said Kezule. "I want you to work on it too, Zayshul. We need every advantage we can get if we're to survive."

"What you're trying to do is tantamount to genocide! I won't be a party to this."

"They're not a species, Zayshul, they're only a caste," Kezule said.

"They've survived for fifteen hundred years without the other two castes," she said. "We're the ones dying out, not them!"

"To go back to what I was asking," said Kusac, "are there any drugs we can use to make them tell us the truth? Maybe one of your anesthetics?"

"No, nothing," said Zayshul. "All our anesthetics sedate us completely."

"Then we'll have to stick to doing it the old fashioned way," he sighed, pushing himself out of the chair. "I'll leave you two to it then. I'm going to get second meal and then head back down to the cells and start working on the other two prisoners."

Zayshul waited till Kusac had left, then turned on Kezule. "What have you been doing or saying to him, Kezule? He's become harder these last few days. I don't like it."

"I've done nothing to him. He's a Warrior, Zayshul. That means he does have a darker side. Some people never find it, others only when they need it, and right now, we need to use that darker side of ourselves."

"I don't like it," she said stubbornly.

"K'hedduk's harem you like less, or being dead," said Giyarishis. "Your daughter he will slaughter if he gets in power again here. Get blood samples, more la'quo stones, I do research, find you drug to use."

Shola, Stronghold, same day

It was their regular weekly meeting day, and this time, they'd gathered in Lijou's office.

"The first item on the agenda is one that troubles me somewhat," said Lijou. "Once again, two seemingly unrelated events are coming together. L'Seuli has requested that we send one of our priests to K'oish'ik to help King Zsurtul replace the former cult of Emperor worship with a more suitable one, namely an Earth or Fertility Goddess."

"I take it the other item is this book Sorli found," said Noni, picking up one of the sheets of paper in front of her.

"Yes. The salient points are on the first page of the notes you all have for this meeting," said Lijou.

"It says here that the justice of L'Shoh is meted out by a sword," said Conner quietly. "Is this true?" A familiar feeling was slowly stealing over him as memories began to stir and shift. It was as if his mind were searching for the right one, and while it did, time seemed suspended, waiting for the revelation.

"Yes, L'Shoh's symbol of Justice is indeed a sword, one that cuts away the lies to get to the heart of the truth," said Rhyaz absently as he read the notes.

Merlin ... It was only a whisper from within, but it served to bring back his memories of that time, of another sword bearer and the visions that had plagued him not so long ago.

"I must go," Conner said, his mind still on the visions that had sent his ancient Welsh predecessor mad. "I helped one sword bearer in the distant past; now I must do so again."

"Why must it be you?" asked Noni.

"If I don't go, the warning that tormented my predecessor fifteen hundred years ago will not be delivered in time to save them from attack," he said gently, reaching out to pat her hand.

"Fifteen hundred years ago, you said?" asked Rhyaz, ears pricking toward him.

"Merlin lived about fifteen hundred years ago . . . when on Shola, you were fighting the Valtegans," he added as suddenly even more became clear to him. "There can be no doubt now. I must go to K'oish'ik and Kusac."

"Agreed the timing of the visions and our past history is uncanny," said Rhyaz, "but what makes you so sure that the prophecy in the book Sorli found refers to him, Lijou?"

"Mention of the Entities creating winter in summer, the fact that L'Shoh's Avatar has been tempered on the Gods' anvil by losing everything dear to him . . . and is black-pelted. Just odd things like that," said Lijou with a touch of sarcasm in his voice.

"It also says the Avatar died, and to my knowledge, Kusac is alive and well!"

"Then L'Seuli didn't tell you the rumors. Kusac did actually die—for all of three minutes, during Kezule's punishment."

Rhyaz said nothing, just continued reading. He put the notes down and looked across at Conner. "Tell me again about this vision."

"Merlin found himself transported to another world," said Conner. "One with buildings surrounding a central courtyard and overhead, a space station that looked like a spindle. Points of light winked far out in space, and he knew that each one was a ship come to rain fire and destruction on the city below. His guide there became at turns a Sholan like Kusac and a Prime—I know that now because I have seen the Primes, but then he thought they were demons." He'd half expected to see the vision as he spoke and was relieved when that didn't happen.

"And the gist of the vision?" asked Rhyaz, clasping his hands and resting his elbows on the table.

"The last person his guide became was Kuushoi. She said they were unprepared for the attack, and many died. They lost what advantage they had over their enemy to the point where defeat was inevitable."

"The war has changed its focus," said Lijou. "Even without this vision, we can tell that K'hedduk will concentrate on regaining K'oish'ik. If he does, it will be from there that he attacks us."

"Raiban is going to love this," muttered Rhyaz. "She's already on route to K'oish'ik, ready to insist on taking charge. This will give her even more reason to try to do so."

"We have to depend on Kezule to be equally determined," said Lijou. "I'll have to accept your offer to go there, Conner, I'm afraid. Noni, I am sorry, but . . ."

"There is no other option," she said, her eyes bright with gathering tears. "Too much of the prophecies overlap for it to be a coincidence."

Conner felt her distress as sharply as his own and sighed inwardly. This time with her had been an answer to an unspoken prayer, and he wanted it to continue, but again he was called to do the Goddess' bidding.

"This other sword bearer, Conner—in what way did you help him?" Rhyaz asked, bringing him out of his reverie.

"Merlin was there to teach him that with great power comes great responsibility, that justice without compassion is as bad as no justice, and to try to teach him about Human nature. That was unfortunately the downfall of them both, betrayal by women they trusted."

"In what way?" asked Lijou.

"Arthur's nemesis was his half sister, Morgause. She seduced him without telling him of their relationship and bore a son who ultimately destroyed him."

"Let's hope that story doesn't play itself out again," muttered Lijou. "We do know that the missing cub is Kusac's son with Carrie but that when he was created, K'hedduk included genetic material from Doctor Zayshul."

"These are Earth legends, Lijou. There's no reason to suppose they'll become ours," said Rhyaz. "This," he indicated the notes in front of him, "could all be the ravings of a lunatic. However," he said, holding up his hand to still the objections, "I will tell L'Seuli to stay at K'oish'ik and warn him of what we've discussed here, and we'll send Conner there. We still have the use of one stealth craft. I've been hiding it from Raiban," he admitted with a slight grin.

"I'm truly sorry, Noni, but I must send him. Conner, be ready to leave from here within two hours." He looked around the small gathering. "Is there anything else we need to discuss? You all have a copy of L'Seuli's update from the *Watchers*."

"I'm already packed, Master Rhyaz. I had a warning last night that I would be leaving today," said Conner.

Rhyaz blinked at him in surprise but said nothing.

"Something still troubles you, Lijou," said Noni as Rhyaz prepared to get up. "Out with it, if you please! We need to know anything that might help us at this time."

"It's perhaps something, or nothing. There's an old tale about the end of times in the library here," said Lijou. "It's about L'Shoh's Avatar, called both the Deliverer and the Destroyer. He uses the sword of L'Shoh to cut to the truth of a person and has the ability to travel through the night skies to find them. He appears as all things to all people so none find him strange at first. I find it disturbing to think this may refer to the Avatar judging other species than our own, that he could bring total destruction down on our heads, or be our savior."

"You worry too much, Lijou," said Rhyaz, getting to his feet. "We sound as though we're acting as I'm told the ancient Sholans did, deciding everything on the outcome of the entrails of a chiddoe! You're reading too much into all this."

"I hope so," said Lijou as Conner and Noni got to their feet.

That's why I'm here—to keep Kusac from losing his way and becoming a destroyer, Conner sent to Noni as he put a comforting arm around her shoulders.

Council chamber, Prime world, Zhal-Arema 15th day (March)

"The corridor tested out as working last night," said Kezule. "It formed as was expected, and we shot a message capsule with a transmitter on it through. The Ch'almuthians will let us know when it arrives."

"That is indeed some excellent news to be having, and if all goes as planned, within five more days the new emigrants will be arriving," trilled Toueesut. "Enjoying exploring your Kij'ik we are General, and our engineers are telling us that we can be getting your cannon working very swiftly. The fighter bay is also being cleared, with the scrap metals being brought here for transportation to your foundries. A fighter of yours will we be needing there, Commander L'Seuli, so the launching gantry can be adapted for them. Same we do for our own fighters being berthed there."

"Thank you, Toueesut," said Zsurtul. "That's good news indeed."

"We're still unloading what supplies we were able to get at such short notice," said L'Seuli. "But building of a reception town has begun, thanks to those people who volunteered to help from the City and from Kij'ik, General. I also have this transcript from the *Watchers* who witnessed the destruction of J'kirtikk," he added passing a message crystal over to Kezule. "It shows the weapon they used on our two colony worlds in action and being destroyed."

"Thank you, L'Seuli. Things are beginning to come together," said Kezule, leaning back in his chair. As he did, it tilted to one side, unbalancing Kezule, who gave an exclamation of annoyance and got hurriedly to his feet.

"I thought I asked you to get this chair fixed, M'kou," he said, irritated, as he lifted it out of the way and grabbed the one next to it.

"I did, General," said his son. "Perhaps the floor is slightly uneven there?"

With a hiss of annoyance, Kezule sat down carefully, making sure that this chair was stable. He glowered across the table at his wife.

Kusac hid a slight smile behind his hand as he reached up to scratch an eye ridge and tried not to look across the table to Banner.

"Weren't you married to a daughter of the Emperor, Kezule?" asked Kaid, idly playing with the stylus in front of him.

"Yes. Why?"

"Did it give you a claim to the throne?"

"Not directly. There were many in the family with a greater blood tie to the Emperor's family, but had they all been killed, then yes, it would."

Kaid nodded. "Rather ironic the way we are now preparing to rescue your daughter. Kind of a reversal of what Kusac went through with Shaidan."

Kezule's crest began to rise slightly but he suppressed it. "There is a difference. I meant no harm to Shaidan, whereas K'hedduk will use my daughter, turn her into one of his harem . . ." Catching sight of Zsurtul's look of distress, Kezule left the rest unsaid.

"If we leave as soon as we can," said Zsurtul, "as soon as the Ch'almuthians tell us the ship is on the way from M'zull, she should be all right. He needs her alive, doesn't he? I accept he will force her to marry him, but . . ."

"I'm sure she'll be fine," said Kusac. "He'll be making her his Queen after all, and Zhalmo isn't stupid, she'll do what she has to to survive."

"You're right," the young King said with obvious relief. "She'll know I won't abandon her because we did get the chance to talk a little." His color heightened in obvious embarrassment. "My interest in her is returned, General, I assure you. I'm no K'hedduk to want to . . ."

"I understand, Majesty," said Kezule, taking pity on him as his own anger faded. "No one for a moment thought your interest in my daughter was anything but mutual."

"Let's see the plans of the M'zullian Palace, Kezule," said Kusac. "See if we can form a rescue plan from my idea."

The M'zullian Palace was similar in design to the Prime one, but it had no defensive wall around it, and the surrounding town was closer.

"Of course, we have no idea if it is still the same," said Kezule as the others left their seats to come and stand behind him. "After the Fall they may have had to relocate for a number of reasons, but Lufsuh, the Head Inquisitor, said they do still use the old Palace."

"He also said their defenses are far better than here," added Kusac. "Are there copies of these plans yet, Kezule?"

"I have a copy for you, Captain," said M'kou, handing him a slim folder.

"Thanks. I'd like to go over this with Lufsuh later today."

"Looks like their main landing area for local traffic is just outside the Palace," said Kaid, pointing to an area of the map. "It's large enough for something the size you say the cull ship is to land there, but would it?"

"Given the nearest landing area is a good distance outside the town, I'd say yes," said Banner. "They won't want to risk their new prisoners trying to escape."

"Nowhere for them to go," said Kusac. "That's a military town."

"Even so . . ."

"Point taken," said Kusac. "Looks bad to the natives and all that. Where's the harem?"

"That's the question," said Kezule. "On these plans, it's on the fourth floor as it was here, but we need accurate information."

"Looks like I'll be spending time with our M'zullians then," said Kusac. "I have a feeling they're not your run of the mill ones either. They blended in with the Court here, so they must be used to it at home . . . which means they likely know their way around the Palace."

"Wouldn't you be better off talking to Lufsuh and leaving them to me?" asked Kaid.

"You can take one, certainly," said Kusac, engrossed in the plans. "But I'll take the other. The cull took how many young people?" he asked, picking up his comp pad and activating it.

"Between ten and twenty, mostly young females," said Kezule. "They also took a tribute in goods from them, medicinal herbs and grain, some cloth too. The military crew consisted of eight armored warriors who actually left the ship to supervise the loading."

"That's the part I needed to know," said Kusac. "If they're in armor, they won't know that we've substituted our own people. What color and style of armor?"

"Not quite the same as ours," said Kezule. "The helmet is smaller, and their armor is a sand color where ours is gray."

"The chances of getting enough undamaged suits to use theirs is small," said Kaid. "Would they notice the difference if they were painted the same color?"

"If no one else is wearing their armor inside the Palace, it should pass," said Kezule. "So we need twenty warriors that include a crew of ten, plus ten or so prisoners, mainly females."

"Those playing the captives would be most vulnerable without armor," said M'kou.

"Have you any lighter battle armor they can wear under clothes?" asked Kusac. "Some protection is better than none."

"If they have not, let us be having the materials we require and we can make them lightweight protection on the *Tooshu*," said Toueesut.

"We may not have long enough for that, Toueesut," said Kusac.

"Ten suits for Primes not take long. Not be comfortable as proper ones, but will reflect some damage back from them and have hidden comms in them. Better than going into this battle in their skins, yes?"

"Yes, indeed," said Kusac. "I don't want any of my people injured if it can be avoided."

Your people? sent Kaid.

I trained them; they're my responsibility, Kusac sent back.

You did a good job, by the way. I watched a training session yesterday. Very professional.

Surprised, Kusac smiled at him. *Thank you, that means a lot coming from you.*

I'm still not convinced this rescue is a good idea, though.

"There should be at least ten female captives," said Kezule. "Those I have among my surviving commandos are better used as soldiers, not captives. All the captives need to do is look cowed and frightened and do as we tell them."

"Trust me, Kezule, you want as few civilians as possible on this mission," said Kusac. "They can freeze at the wrong moment, run the wrong way, any number of things that will put not only them at risk, but the whole mission. If we haven't enough females, we'll get some cosmetics and turn the males into them."

"What?" Kezule sounded both shocked and outraged.

"We don't intend to let the enemy get close to them," said Kaid. "All they'll see is the bright face colors and will assume they see females, not males."

"Their scent . . ."

"Get Zayshul to make up something that we can spray on them to at least hide their male scent. Remember, most of their bodies will be inside armor."

"Ah, I forgot that. Then there's a good chance it will work as few of our scent glands are on the face and neck. But will they be that easily deceived?" Kezule looked perplexed.

"People see what they expect to see, Kezule," said Kusac. "That's one of the things you learn in the Brotherhood. Give them some of the major clues that these are female, like the bright face coloring, and their own minds will fill in the other details. They don't need to be perfect."

"Start picking your team, Captain," said Zsurtul. "You

know which ones are better designated as warriors than prisoners. We need to be ready to leave immediately we get warning from Ch'almuth."

"Aye, King Zsurtul," said Kusac, then turned to Kaid. "Can you ask Carrie if she'd help devise cosmetics for the males? The Prime females do use them."

"She says that's not a problem. She'll talk to Shishu about it later today."

"Thanks."

Why don't you send to her yourself? Kaid sent.

Things have been awkward between us since I told her about Zayshul.

"We'll also need to secure Ch'almuth from future M'zullian incursions because once they know we used their ship and corridor to reach them, they'll take reprisal action," said Kaid.

"I'm told their weather platform is now working properly and that our people are renovating the weapons system but that control of it is now back in the hands of the Ch'almuthians," said Toueesut. "Some extra weapons has General Heokee that he is having installed there too as the ones they have are not sufficient for the ships of today."

"They'll need more than that," said Kusac. "The best we can do with three days warning is arrive shortly before any M'zullians do. They can wreak a lot of damage in that time. We need a destroyer permanently in orbit there."

"Sorry, but new orders came through today for me to remain here," said L'Seuli.

"Send the *Zh'adak*," said Kusac. "Load it with fighters—the landing bay should be able to take about forty at least. You have the *Tooshu* and the *Va'Khoi* here, it's a 100,000 tonner, the *Kz'adul*, which is 200,000 tons, the *N'zishok* and the *M'zayik* and two more at 1,000 tons, and Raiban arrives in another nine days, before K'hedduk can reach M'zull. If I know her, she'll come with something the size of the *Khalossa* plus a small fleet. We should be more than amply protected by what we have here."

"We can probably spare at least one of the 1,000-ton vessels too. We'd need to have some of your people as gunnery crews," said Kezule thoughtfully.

"That we could be doing, General," said Toueesut. "We have the spare personnel to be aiding you in this way, and we can spare some fighters as we discussed."

"Then get the *Zh'adak* kitted out with the extra craft and personnel now and send her to Ch'almuth as soon as you can," said Kusac.

"Agreed," said Kezule, looking over to M'kou, who'd been trying to catch his attention.

"Giyarishis says not much progress yet. Says he remembers he was growing some la'quo on Kij'ik, and if we get those plants, that will do for now."

"Arrange it, and pass on appropriate orders to the *Zh'adak* to prepare for the Touibans' arrival."

"Send a message to Ch'almuth, M'kou," said Zsurtul. "Tell them we are making provision for their defense now and to ready anyone else willing to emigrate."

"Yes, Majesty," said M'kou.

"We cannot be a party to delivering any chemical weapons, Kezule, you realize that, don't you? It's against Alliance policy to use them," said L'Seuli.

"We have the treaty ready to sign, Commander," said Zsurtul. "Are you saying that if we continue to pursue this field of study, we cannot join you?"

L'Seuli was silent as he obviously looked around for an answer.

Kusac gave a small laugh and reached for a glass of water. "He can't say that because he knows damned well that the drug you got from me was illegally produced! He means stop talking about it in front of him, King Zsurtul, but he can't even officially say that, can you?"

"Something along those lines," L'Seuli murmured with a frown. "Kaid, you taught him too well—he's become a cynic like us!"

"He did that all by himself," said Kaid, glancing at him as he chewed on his stim twig.

"Have you checked up on the M'zull half-breeds from Shola yet?" Kusac asked him.

"Yes, I did. I think if we split them up so they're not together, or at most only two of them in the same posting, they'll be fine. They did tell me that it was only after the Emperor's death that K'hedduk approached them. Until then, they were taken into custody, drugged by the same ale as everyone else."

"Mind if I check them out before they're released?"

"Be my guest," said Kaid, "but you'll not pick up more from them than I did. They were telling the truth. Seems our methods of teaching them made all the difference, subverted their aggression into a team spirit rather than into individual advancement."

"A lesson I will remember," said Kezule.

"Kusac," said L'Seuli, "I brought the mech you asked for down with me today. It's crated up, of course, and sitting in the courtyard by the barracks under guard. I keyed it into your bio signature. I have no idea why you wanted it—it's only a huge toy."

Kusac smiled. "Toueesut, want to play with me and my new toy?"

The Touiban, mustache bristling with curiosity, looked over at him. "A toy you say? What manner of toy is this?"

"I'll show you after this meeting."

"We found another couple of those gene-enhanced monstrosities in one of the towns a hundred miles from here," said Kezule. "We'll have to check for them in every town and city in a two hundred mile radius at least. We're also working on getting the old public comm system repaired so we can start up regular broadcasts to the whole of K'oish'ik again. That way we can get the people to report any of these thugs so we can go pick them up."

"Is there anything further to discuss?" asked Zsurtul, looking around the table. "Then I suggest we adjourn for today. Thank you all for attending."

"Clan Leader," said Toueesut, dancing around the table to his side. "This toy you mention . . .?"

"Ah, yes, come with me," said Kusac. "Have you seen the MUTAC, Kaid?"

"No, I can't say I have. I've heard of it, though."

Kusac sensed the other's interest was piqued. "Care to come and look at it with us?"

"Sure. It's on the way to the cells anyway."

"Mind if I come?" asked Banner.

"Be my guest."

It seemed to tower above them because of its bulk, yet it was only about twice their height. As the last side of the packing crate fell away and it was fully visible, Kusac stepped back in awe.

"What the hell is it?" asked Kaid, looking up at the white mechanical shape of a Sholan crouched on all fours.

"Insurance," said Kusac as Toueesut began trilling and dancing in delight. "This is the Multi Terrain Attack Carrier prototype, MUTAC for short."

"Insurance, how?" asked Banner as they all moved closer to it.

"Imagine this coming out of nowhere at you," said Kusac, reaching out to put his hand on one of the two jump jets on the leg nearest him. "It can jump or be HALO dropped, has explosive and guided missiles on board and an energy beam weapon mounted on the top. Comes complete with full sensor and electronic countermeasures equipment."

"And it was abandoned by the Brotherhood as unusable," Kaid added. "I remember it now. Why on earth did you want it?"

"How it not work?" demanded Toueesut, coming to a halt beside Kusac. "This is being a marvelous device! A giant mechanical Sholan! It stands up too? Pulls at walls with its claws?"

"Yes, it does all that," said Kusac. "When we can get it to work. It uses a form of levers and pulleys which makes it very slow moving and unwieldy to control."

"What this?" asked a new voice.

Kusac turned around to see Annuur and his sept looking at the MUTAC.

"Heard there was big mechanical monster in courtyard so came to see."

Toueesut turned to the Cabbaran and began rapidly explaining what it was.

"Ah! What like inside? Maybe it can be fixed."

"Exactly what I was thinking, Annuur, so shall we ask the good Captain to be opening it up so we can look inside?"

"It only holds one Sholan," said Kusac. "Very cramped in there, but it has a rear compartment for one injured person. It's designed to be a terror weapon."

"Then it must undoubtedly become one so that on your mission you can take it, and if anything goes wrong it is at hand to come raging in after you!"

"My thoughts exactly," purred Kusac, with an amused glance at Kaid.

There was a discreet cough from behind, and Kusac turned to see two Sholan Brothers standing there with slight grins on their faces. They executed smart salutes, then the darker one spoke.

"The Commander said we'd to report to you, Captain Aldatan. Brothers Jerenn and M'Nar at your command. I see you've got our MUTAC."

"Yours?" Kusac raised an eye ridge.

"Yes, we designed it."

"I know, I was there at the time," said Kusac.

"Doesn't work as well as we hoped it would as we only had a few weeks to make it. It was a punishment for playing an Earth game with giant mechanized fighting units like this on the cryptology computers," said the other morosely.

"Perfect!" trilled Toueesut. "We can have them working with us on this!"

"You're seconded to Toueesut," said Kusac as he ducked under the leg and approached the entry hatch. He saw the locking plate and laid his hand over it.

"I'd stand to the side, Captain," said M'Nar. "The hatch might hit you otherwise."

He backed off as the hatchway began to swing down, forming a ramp that allowed him access to the small pilot's cabin.

"Would you care for a demonstration, Captain?" asked M'Nar.

"In a minute," he said, walking up the ramp so he could look inside. The pilot had to climb up a short ladder to reach the cockpit that was mounted inside the head, but once there, he'd have a good view of his surroundings.

He came back down. "Is there room for either Annuur or Toueesut inside with you?"

"Be a tight squeeze," said Jerenn doubtfully. "There's only one seat."

"Try."

"I think I should be the one . . ." began Jerenn as M'Nar raced up the ramp and began to disappear from sight up the small ladder.

"I think it's too late," said Kusac, amused. "Toueesut? Want to see if there's room for you?"

"Indeed yes!" said the Touiban, bustling forward to follow M'Nar. Sounds of scuffling and a muted "Ouch! Watch my tail, dammit!" then the ramp closed up.

"I'd back off a good way," said Jerenn. "Its movements aren't the smoothest. As M'nar said, though, we didn't have long to work on it."

They backed away, watching as the mech's engines came to

life and it began to shudder slightly. It purred, like a Sholan, Kusac thought as he listened to it.

More and more people were coming into the courtyard now; to the point that Kusac began to worry someone would get hurt. He beckoned over a small group of commandos.

"Dheku, clear this area of all but those who should be here," he said.

"Aye, Captain."

Slowly the mech's legs straightened out of the crouch it had been in, and the jointed tail swayed into a position that counterbalanced it. One front leg lifted up and began to move forward, followed by the opposite rear one. The ground shuddered slightly as the feet landed on the concrete surface, then it began to pick up its pace to a slow lope.

"This, I like!" said Annuur. "Why you not make more of these?"

"The controls aren't responsive enough for use in a battle," said Kusac as they watched it lope around the exercise yard.

"I'll tell you what, though," said Kaid. "It is bloody intimidating. I wouldn't want to get too close to it."

"If the Touibans can get it working properly, I was hoping to take it with us on the M'zullian ship as backup, in case we need to get out of there in a hurry."

Kaid gave him a long, searching look, then put his hand on his shoulder. "It's good to have you back, sword-brother."

Zhal-Arema 19th day (March)

Conner walked down the ramp into the parking area at the front of the Palace. He stopped to look at the building, its white exterior bathed almost golden in the late afternoon sun. Carved figures painted jewel-bright colors marched across the front above a pillared balcony. Each bore tribute which was placed at the feet of an enthroned monarch. To either side of him stood the figures of protective deities sharing in the bountiful offerings. The scene was marred here and there by small chunks of missing masonry and scorch marks, obviously caused by the recent battle.

"Beautiful, isn't it?" said a voice at his elbow. "Easy to see why they called it the Palace of Light. I'm M'kou, General Kezule's aide and one of his sons. Welcome to K'oish'ik."

He turned around, hand already held out in greeting. The young Warrior shook it warmly then reached for his case.

"I'll carry that for you."

"I'm Conner," he said, finding his voice and handing the case to him. "The Palace is magnificent."

"It needs some repairs since the battle, obviously," said M'kou, leading the way toward the covered parking. "But with all that's happening now, only the necessary structural ones are being done."

"Understandable," he murmured as he passed out of the heat of the sun and into the welcoming shade. "Could we go through the main courtyard, do you think? I'd like to see it if it's no trouble."

"Certainly. It did take the worst damage in the fighting. Repair work is still ongoing," said M'kou, opening the door for him and standing back to let him enter first.

The corridor was narrow, but tall, the walls again decorated by scenes of visiting nobles. There was a barbaric splendor about them that didn't belong to the current era.

M'kou opened another door and gestured him through, following close behind him.

"Are all the corridors so beautifully decorated?" he asked.

"Not all, only those used by visiting nobility and the Royal family. Most of this side of the Palace is given over to offices, administration, and housing for the staff here."

They stepped out into an alley at the side of a small building.

"The Grand Courtyard has restaurants and a few stores in it," explained M'kou as he led him along the narrow alley and into the courtyard proper.

Sunshine again dazzled his eyes, making him blink. When his sight cleared, he saw the courtyard of his vision. There was the central pool, now with the broken stumps of trees around it, the huge stone statues to his left and at the far end flanking an ornate doorway. People bustled about, stopping briefly to look at him and nod to his companion before rushing off. Sounds of hammering and sawing filled the air, and everywhere there was a sense of purpose.

"The public temple is over there," said M'kou, pointing to

the distant statues. "The rest of the buildings on this level are offices and Security."

Conner turned around, finding he'd walked farther into the square than he thought. As he looked at the young Prime, the vision became complete. Here indeed was the world Merlin had visited in his vision, and these were indeed the people that long-dead druid had seen. No wonder he'd thought he was going insane.

"Is everything all right, Conner?" asked M'kou, coming closer, his face creased in obvious concern.

"I'm fine," he said, smiling. "I had a vision that I thought was of this world, and I just wanted to be sure it was."

"And was it?"

"Yes, it was. It was this very courtyard that I saw," he said, looking around at the balconies, the carvings and finally the damaged south wall to his left, where the bulk of the building repairs were ongoing.

"Shall we continue into the Palace? The sun is strong even though it's still spring here. It takes a little time to become accustomed to it," he added, watching the Human squinting up at the sky.

"Yes, please lead the way. I do apologize, I was lost in my own thoughts," said Conner, tearing his gaze back to earth and M'kou.

Conner was shown to one of the Guest suites on the fourth floor, where, he was told, the King and his other guests from Shola and Alliance worlds were also staying. There was time for him to unpack and freshen up, then he was taken to meet King Zsurtul.

He stopped to stare through the transparent walls at the garden as they passed it.

"If you like gardens, there's the King's private one on the rooftop," said M'kou. "It's open to all who are staying on this floor. There's also a gymnasium and a pool."

"There is?" sad Conner, carrying on down the corridor. "This Palace is indeed marvelous."

"It's also very old," said M'kou, stopping at the first doorway and opening it for him. "We reckon somewhere in the region of three thousand years. Not all of it is that old, but the central building certainly is. Successive rulers added to it over time."

"Impressive indeed," said Conner as he entered the lounge.

"Welcome to my home, Conner," said the young Prime getting up stiffly from one of the easy chairs. "Your arrival has been eagerly awaited by many people, including me."

Conner went forward to shake hands, then take the seat that was offered to him. "King Zsurtul, I assume," he said as he sat down.

"Yes, and you're the priest Father Lijou of the Brotherhood sent to help us."

"That I am," said Conner, sizing up the youth in front of him. He was young by his people's standards, that he knew from the brief Lijou had given him, but there was more about him than that. There was a drawn look about his face, alien though it was, that showed he'd suffered loss and sadness. Again, he knew this to be true from the briefing.

"I offer you my condolences on the loss of your parents, King Zsurtul. However, I know they have left a worthy successor in yourself."

A faint smile. "Thank you, Conner. Would you like a drink? You must taste our maush—it's most refreshing and has medicinal properties too."

"Thank you, I will."

Zsurtul poured him a generous measure in one of the bowl-shaped cups that sat on the small table between the two easy chairs.

"Perhaps we should start with you telling me exactly what you want me to do," said Conner, accepting the cup and taking a cautious sip of the drink. He was pleasantly surprised. The taste was light and refreshing, reminding him of chamomile tea back on Earth.

Zsurtul relaxed visibly. "The previous state religion was worship of the Emperor as a living God. I dissolved the ancient Empire, what there was left of it at least, when I was crowned. Now I want to replace the religion with something more suitable. There are other deities that we worshiped, of course, but only once a year, or when it was thought that deity could help one."

Conner nodded. "Do you have an organized priesthood of any kind?"

Zsurtul frowned, obviously in anger. "The main priesthood was the Inquisitors who conducted services for the Emperor and found sedition against him. They were all executed except for the head of the order, who is being questioned in the cells. They were the ones who betrayed and killed my family."

"What of the other religions, though?"

"There are a few priests, and were even some priestesses, for La'shol, our fertility Goddess."

"Would it be possible to meet with them?"

"ZSADHI, please ask them to meet us in the public temple in half an hour," said Zsurtul. "And ask General Kezule and Captain Aldatan to join us as well."

"It shall be done, Majesty."

Conner looked around for the speaker.

"It's the Palace computer," smiled Zsurtul. "If you need anything, from information to a nighttime snack, just ask ZSADHI. He has nodes everywhere, but unless you say his name, he doesn't listen in."

"Very useful," murmured Conner, thinking of the nights in Old Sarum when he could have done with an artificial intelligence to get him hot drinks and snacks. "Does La'shol have a temple anywhere?"

"In the City, the people have shrines here and there for Her, but no, there is no place where only she is worshiped. Well, maybe you could say the pool is hers. My idea was to turn the two temples over to her. They both share the hollow pillars full of water and creatures from our holy pool."

"Tell me about Her," said Conner, relaxing back in his chair.

Zsurtul looked dubiously at him. "I don't really know that much," he said. "My mother was more interested in her than I ever was. Water is sacred to us, because we have so little. You'll have seen how small our seas are compared to Shola's as you approached the planet, I imagine."

"Yes, it seemed very arid from space. Would that explain the water-filled glass bricks with complete miniature ecologies in them that I've seen at the entrance to various rooms here?"

"Yes, indeed. We believe all life began from a natural hot spring pool near the Summer Palace. La'shol is the deity of life and crops, the herd beasts, and She is the Goddess present at our weddings. And that's about all I know of her. The priests will know more," he offered.

Conner smiled gently, taking another sip of the maush. "I'm

sure they will, King Zsurtul, but you've given me a good idea
what She is the Goddess of. It sounds like She's the same as
Ghyakulla on Shola, and Gaia on Earth."

"It does?" Zsurtul managed to look baffled and hopeful at
the same time.

Conner began to tell him about Ghyakulla, but before long,
ZSADHI reminded them it was time to leave for the temple.

The public temple was a large room with the glass-paneled
container of water from the hot springs reaching up through
the ceiling to the smaller private King's chapel above. Strange-
looking fish and crustaceans could be seen flitting about in it,
some of them using the bubbles of air from the oxygenator to
hitch a ride.

"Fascinating, isn't it?" said Conner from behind him.

Kusac turned to greet him. "I hope your trip wasn't too
tiring."

"I have to admit to sleeping through most of it," Conner
laughed. "However, I did watch as we left Shola's orbit and as
we came in to K'oish'ik."

"You saw the best parts of the trip, then. Let me introduce
you to General Kezule."

"You have the thanks of our people for coming all this distance to help us," said Kezule, taking the proffered hand and
shaking it.

"I enjoy seeing new places and meeting new people," said
Conner, looking around the main room of the temple.

Four pairs of pillars supported the ceiling, each of them
carved and painted with scenes of people bringing tribute to
the temple. The final scene was the one behind the altar table
of the Emperor enthroned with the same two deity figures
behind him. In front of that was a colossus of the Emperor
carved in dark, polished stone

Rows of wooden seats for the worshipers filled most of the
floor, with aisles between them leading up to the altar. Someone had obviously been tending to the temple because a vase
of fresh cut flowers stood in the middle.

Some twenty feet from them, a small group of six Primes
stood waiting. Zsurtul beckoned them forward. "These are
our priests of La'shol, Conner. Please, introduce yourselves."

The first, a small female with green tints surrounding her
eyes, came forward and bowed from the waist.

"Majesty, Brother Conner, I am Loshu, and senior among us." She indicated the others in turn, starting with the only other female. "This is Shadduk, Nioshik, M'zukosh, and Chykuh."

"An honor indeed," said Conner, bowing back to them. "On Shola, the priests are also telepaths, or Gifted in some way. I can see that we will be able to follow the same course here."

"Excuse me?" said Zsurtul.

"These young people are all what we call sensitives, meaning they have senses beyond the normal ones. Two of you, in fact, Loshu and Nioshik, can be trained as basic telepaths, as can you, King Zsurtul."

"What?" said Zsurtul.

"A telepath?" said Kusac.

"Why am I not surprised," murmured Kezule. "I knew some of our females have an ability," he said, "but I didn't think it was inherited by the males."

"It may not be as strong or as common, but, yes, it's there, General," said Conner. "I can teach the most able ones, and they in turn can teach the others. We'll need to set up a college, of course, a place where we can teach."

"ZSADHI?" said Zsurtul.

"May I suggest that the premises lately occupied by the Inquisitors would provide adequate space for a college?"

Zsurtul smiled. "Excellent idea! There's a whole block that they used, offices, sleeping quarters, they are all yours, Loshu. Let ZSADHI know if you need anything."

Still looking stunned, the young female bowed again. "You have our thanks, King Zsurtul."

"Would you mind if we moved that statue of the Emperor out of here, King Zsurtul?" asked Conner.

"Not in the least," he replied. "It's not my father's portrait, or even my grandfather's. You have complete freedom to do with the chapels what you will—redecorate them if you wish. And if you care to go to the Palace stonemasons' quarters, they may even have a suitable statue of La'shol there. The place is full of interesting odds and ends. I used to love looking round there when I was young."

Conner chuckled. "Then I shall be sure to go visit there. Loshu, would you and your colleagues care to show me around?"

As they made their way out of the temple, Kezule turned

to Kusac. "My daughter Zhalmo, is she one of those with a Talent?"

"She is," said Kusac. "Looks like Zsurtul does know his life-mate after all."

"It does. The irony is that what K'hedduk tried to create artificially was evolving naturally right under his nose."

"K'hedduk was trying to create Valtegan telepaths?"

"When he had me taken to his underground laboratory, he wanted to show off his experiments on the Primes he had imprisoned there. I refused to look," said Kezule, frowning at the memory.

"Was that when you saw the cubs?"

"Yes. Talking of them, how's that little gray one doing? Gaylla?"

"She's doing well," said Kusac, surprised he'd remembered her. "Both her parents are on Shola, though, but she's growing more confident by the day now she feels secure. She'll always be a little slower than normal, but we'll look after her, see she gets a good mate and is happy. She's Clan, after all."

"That's good to hear. Zayshul would like to see her again, I know."

"There's no reason I know of that she can't," said Kusac as they began walking out of the temple.

CHAPTER 11

Zhal-Arema 24th day (March)

CRIES of pain echoed around inside his head as the cell around him faded until it was the white tiled room on the *Kz'adul* and he was the one crying out in agony. It faded again, colors washing in front of his eyes until a darker room formed, with a circle of Valtegan faces staring down at him. The scent of blood was thick in the air. He heard hysterical laughter; then the room spun about him, and now he was one of those staring down at . . .

Angrily, Kusac forced back the shadowy visions/memories—he couldn't tell which they were any more—of being both the victim and the torturer.

Perhaps there had been some truth in what Kaid had said, he thought, shaking his head, grasping the edge of the table till his claws extended into the wood, till he was sure he could actually feel it and believe he was really in the cell in the Palace of Light.

"The harem is here," said the unsteady voice of his prisoner, Zhakk. "On the second floor."

"Mark in any guards and security checkpoints," he said automatically, pushing away from the table. He had to leave. There were too many forces at work in and around him right now.

"Take over, Banner," he said, heading for the door. "See he finishes the sketches."

He didn't stop until he was outside, in the sunlight and fresh air. There, the dark scenes he'd been part of seemed far away, not connected to him any more: He could dismiss them as waking nightmares, caused by too little sleep or by the cheese after dinner last night. Truth was, his nights were always disturbed now and had been since Conner had told him of his vision of an attack on the City.

His wrist comm buzzed insistently. It was Kezule. "Your General Raiban has arrived and is making unreasonable demands. I need you up here in my office now."

"Get Kaid too," he said, turning and heading back into the Palace.

"She's insisting she dock at the Orbital," said Kezule, the irritation obvious in his tone. "Why is it that the females of all our species are less logical, and more prone to irrational demands?"

"Where's the *Kz'adul*?" asked Kusac. "Can she dock there before Raiban could?"

"Yes."

"Tell her the berth is for the *Kz'adul*, which needs urgent repairs," said Kaid, instantly on the same wavelength.

Kezule relayed the message to the Orbital, then ordered the *Kz'adul* to berth for "urgent repairs."

"General, Commander Raiban has agreed to dock at the lunar mining station, but she wishes to speak to you now," said the harried comm operator on the Orbital.

Kezule waved Kusac and Kaid back before saying, "Patch her through to me, sound and vision."

"We meet again, General," said Raiban as soon as her image appeared on the screen.

"Welcome to K'oish'ik, General Raiban. We appreciate your understanding of our current emergency at the Orbital. King Zsurtul has asked me to extend his hospitality to you and invite you down for a banquet in your honor tonight."

"Convey my thanks to King Zsurtul, but before I come down to the surface, I need to speak with Kusac Aldatan, here, on the *Khalossa*." False regret oozed from her every syllable.

Kezule ignored it. "An unusual request, but I'll pass it along to the Captain."

"Please do. I'd hate to disappoint your King by being unable to make the banquet." With that, she cut the connection.

"She's up to something," said Kaid before Kusac could. "She swore to hang your hide out to dry for the stunt you pulled when you left Shola. Whose idea was that, by the way? Pretty slick piece of work."

"Mine," said Kusac. "You sure that I was publicly pardoned?"

"Went out on all the newscasts," confirmed Kaid. "We saw a couple on Haven. Besides, I gave you the papers myself, and I checked them before we left Haven."

"Don't go," said Kezule. "If she wants to remain on her ship, she can."

"She's holding the aid from Shola hostage, Kezule. She won't release it unless I go to her," said Kusac.

"How can she do that?" said Kezule. "Your government sent it, not her."

"She won't admit to withholding it," said Kaid. "She'll just make sure to keep delaying it until Kusac does go. All perfectly reasonable, she'll claim."

Kusac drummed his claw tips on the table for a minute or two, running through various scenarios in his mind, finding the most workable one.

"Is the *Couana's* shuttle planetside?" he asked.

"Yes," said Kaid, the beginnings of a smile on his face.

"We'll use it and take Toueesut," he said, standing. "Kaid, tell Dzaka to meet us at the shuttle in his grays. I'll call Banner and Toueesut as I'm getting changed."

"Dzaka's upstairs. He can pick up gray tunics for us both to save time," said Kaid, getting up.

"Do it," he said. "Kezule, I need paper and an envelope, a plain white one, please."

Kezule reached into his desk drawer and pulled out one of each. "What are you planning to do?"

"Bluff," said Kusac, a feral grin on his face as he took the paper and swiftly folded it to fit into the envelope.

The *Khalossa*

The familiar smell of oil and fuel greeted him as he stepped out of the *Couana's* shuttle onto the deck of the *Khalossa*.

"Almost like coming home, eh?" said Kaid.

"I enjoyed my time on the *Khalossa*," he said. "Mostly."

"Strange how one encounter can change your life," murmured Dzaka.

An aide came over to them, saluting crisply. "Commander Raguul welcomes you to the *Khalossa*, sirs, and asks that you please discharge your business here with General Raiban as quietly as possible."

Kusac and Kaid both broke into chuckles. "We'll try," said Kusac.

"Is your Touiban companion going too?" the aide asked dubiously. "I have no orders concerning him."

"Indeed I be coming with my good friends," said Toueesut firmly in his trilling voice.

"I'll take you to the General, then, sirs."

Stares followed them, but they were used to it. It wasn't every day they saw four Brotherhood in their active grays accompanied by only one Touiban.

Their guide finally stopped outside one of the Admin offices. "Please wait here," he said and, knocking on the door, opened it.

Kusac immediately moved forward and prevented him from closing it. "Thank you," he said, with a widemouthed Human smile that made the aide wince. "No need to announce us."

Raiban, mug of c'shar to her lips, almost choked as they entered.

"Welcome to Prime space, Raiban," drawled Kusac. "I hope your trip wasn't too boring."

Trying not to cough, she waved the aide away. "You surprise me, Kusac," she said, putting the mug down and leaning back in her chair. "I didn't think you'd have the courage to come."

"I'm hurt, General," he said, putting a hand over his heart and a pained expression on his face. "Your words cut me to the quick."

"Hmm. Your stance says otherwise," she said, leaning forward to pick up one of the sheets of paper from her desk and move it closer to her while surreptitiously pressing her buzzer.

"I'm taking you into custody," she said as the door opened again to let in four of the heavy troopers. "I have a warrant for your arrest."

"And I have a full pardon, signed by Governor Nesul. I

think that makes your warrant redundant," he said, pulling the envelope out of his pocket.

"Let me see that," she said, reaching for it.

Kusac twitched it just out of her reach, then hesitating for a few seconds, handed it to her. His hand then went to rest on the hilt of his Brotherhood knife.

She took it in both hands and looked at him. "This is only a piece of paper, Captain Aldatan. It could have an unfortunate accident."

"It could," he agreed as she slowly twisted the envelope in opposite directions, stopping short of actually tearing it. "It is only a copy, and we have Ambassador Toueesut here as a witness."

"Then he can witness your legal arrest for crimes against the people of Shola and for stealing an alien ship from the spaceport," she said, letting the letter drop to the desk and reaching for the warrant.

Kusac's knife thudded into her desk, almost grazing her fingers as it pinned the warrant in place.

He had to give her credit —she didn't flinch. Behind him, he sensed Kaid's mental laugh as he and the other two turned to face the troopers.

"Look at my knife, Raiban," he said quietly, moving forward to lean on her desk. "You see that bronze mark in the grip? You know what that means, right? And notice that it's on the inside of the grip, the side not commonly seen when I wear it. That means I led a covert mission. Your warrant is null and void, Raiban, and you know it. The incident has been closed by our government as I was on a sensitive and secret mission among one of our Alien allies."

He reached out and pulled his knife free, then stood back. "I suggest you send the troopers away and accept that I acted under orders when I left Shola. Besides, do you really think four troopers would be enough?" He let amusement tinge his voice

Cursing under her breath, Raiban ordered the troopers to leave. "You deserve to pay for what you did," she snarled, throwing the envelope back at him. "You disrupted shipping for over three hours at Shanagi! You stole the *Couana* . . ."

"There was no theft because I had told my Clan Leader that what was mine was his, and if he be needing to borrow my ship, then it is his to use," said Toueesut, emitting a scent of reproach in her direction. "No charge of stealing a ship there is against him!"

"I had to make it look good, Raiban," said Kusac mildly. "You have to admit I did that."

She snarled wordlessly, her ears going sideways and down as she looked over to Kaid. "I'll deal with you here on K'oish'ik, Kaid, not that impudent cub! You can leave, Kusac Aldatan, and take your entourage with you! My business with you is finished."

"I'm sorry, General Raiban," said Kaid regretfully, hand resting on the pommel of his own knife. "King Zsurtul has chosen his advisers and I'm not one of them. Kusac is. You'll have to deal with him."

"Go!" she said with barely suppressed fury. "All of you go!"

"I take it you'll start ferrying down the supplies you've brought from Shola for the Primes," said Kusac.

"Indeed, General, the *Tooshu* awaits your orders as it is having lots of cargo shuttles to ship the goods down, and we are anxious to be unloading the Ch'almuthian immigrants we currently have on board."

"Tell your people to contact the cargo officer," she snapped.

"Thank you, General," said Kusac, turning to leave.

"King Zsurtul will want to thank you himself tonight at the banquet," said Kaid, sketching a bow in her direction as they left.

Once on the shuttle, Kusac pulled a sheet of paper out of his pocket and started to read it. Then he began to chuckle.

"That isn't the warrant, is it?" asked Kaid, raising an eye ridge. "You took it out from under her nose."

"Yes," he said, passing it over to him. "It's as real as the pardon papers I showed her. Bluff and counterbluff."

"Ah, the ways of diplomats are strange indeed," sighed Toueesut.

"She's no diplomat," said Kaid, grinning as he read the duty list for the day before. "She did all that just to give him grief, make him come all the way out to her." He handed it back to Kusac, who pocketed it.

"She'll have a diplomat on board, though," said Kusac. "And you can take bets on Raiban trying to stick her nose into our rescue plans."

"That's a given," agreed Kaid.

*   *   *

They debarked at the landing pad outside the City. On the right side of the main road up to K'oish'ik, all was activity as the prefabricated town gradually began to take shape. In what would eventually be the center, they could see a well had been dug. Even now, masons were setting a ring of stones and mortar around it.

"Who'd have thought we'd ever see this day," said Kusac, indicating where a mixed group of Primes, Touibans, and a few Sholans were working together to raise one of the prefab buildings.

"Cooperation is much more rewarding," said Toueesut as the rest of his swarm came dancing up to greet him.

One of the Sholans waved and called out to them. "Hey, Banner! We're getting a catch-ball game going later this afternoon. Want to join us?"

"Sure," said Banner, looking at Kusac who waved him away.

"Kitra's found something she likes in the town market that she wants me to see," said Dzaka. "Are we done here?"

"Yes. Go have fun," said Kusac as he and Kaid began walking up through the bustling throng on the roadway to the Palace.

They wove their way through the crowd until a Sholan bumped into him.

"Watch your manners," Kusac began. The next moment, he was fighting for his life as he dodged a flurry of knife strikes, looking for an opening.

It came quickly, and grabbing his assailant's knife arm, he twisted it aside and then dived in close to palm-punch him in the face.

Kaid danced behind to deliver a couple of blows to the attacker's kidneys. There was a loud snap as the male's arm broke, and with a high-pitched yowl of agony, he fell to the ground.

"What the hell . . . began Kaid, as he and Kusac reached down to haul the now disarmed Sholan to his feet.

"He's dead," said Kusac, looking at Kaid. "He shouldn't be."

Banner skidded to a stop beside them. "What happened? I saw the fight."

"I was attacked," said Kusac.

Kaid knelt down to examine him as Kusac looked around for any more trouble, but everyone was giving them a wide berth. He saw the discarded knife a few yards away and went to fetch it.

"He took poison," said Kaid when Kusac returned. "He's dressed as Forces, but he's no papers on him."

"The knife looks like one of ours, but it isn't," said Kusac, kneeling down beside him. "He was trying to kill me," he said, his voice sounding a tad shaky even to him.

"Definitely," said Kaid. "He has to have come on the *Khalossa*, but how did he get down here so fast? Dammit, I thought we'd gotten all the dissidents long ago!"

"I don't think this was a dissident," said Kusac slowly. "I felt his mind—this was a paid job for him, an assassination."

"It can't be the Brotherhood," said Kaid. "I know they made contracts against us illegal because it risked more than one life because of our Leskas."

"I don't know," said Kusac, activating his wrist comm to call a squad of commandos to get the body. "I'll certainly be talking to L'Seuli."

"Let me handle it," said Kaid. "I've had more experience at this than you. Ghezu used to send an assassin after me every other year."

Next day, Zhal-Arema 25th day (March)

"She'll be here in a couple of minutes," said M'kou as ZSA-DHI updated him through his headset.

"Why she couldn't have remained here overnight," muttered Kezule, getting to his feet with the others.

"She did it to keep us off -balance," said Kusac. "Are you sure you're up to this meeting, Zsurtul? You're looking pale."

"I'm fine," said the young King from where he remained in his seat. "Just tired."

Raiban swept in, followed by someone Kusac knew well, Falma from AlRel.

"Good morning," she said, frowning a little when she saw Kusac and Kaid.

"Good morning, General," said Zsurtul, inclining his head. "Please be seated, and we can introduce our advisers."

"I didn't expect to see you two," she said. "The Brotherhood has no right to be involved in this meeting."

She was surprised to see them, but Kusac could sense none of the reaction that he'd expect from someone who expected him to be dead, or at least seriously wounded.

"They're here as my advisers, General," said Zsurtul as the others resumed their seats. "General Kezule you know, and this is Prime Counselor Shyadd."

"I have to protest at their presence," began Raiban.

"They are my advisers, and they will remain," repeated Zsurtul firmly, staring unblinkingly at her. "Introduce your aide, please."

"Falma, from Alien Relations. He's brought the Treaties from the Alliance and Shola for you to sign."

"Hand it to Shyadd, please. He'll read it through and give me a report on it."

"They're an exact copy of the ones your father signed," said Raiban as Falma withdrew the documents from the case he carried and passed them across the table to Shyadd. "All you have to do is sign them."

"I am not my father, General Raiban," said Zsurtul quietly. "I will study this first, then listen to what my advisers say before I sign anything."

"Signing comes later, Raiban," said Kusac. "First it has to be studied, then negotiated, and finally signed when both sides agree on it. Falma knows this as a member of the Diplomatic Guild."

"Indeed, Captain Aldatan," said Falma with a slight smile of relief. "We members of Alien Relations understand the niceties of such things. By the way, I have a message to pass on to you from your father when the meeting is over. All is well at home," he added hurriedly seeing a worried look flit across Kusac's face.

"The treaty negotiations are none of your concern, Raiban. Since when did you become a Diplomatic representative for either Shola or the Alliance?" asked Kaid.

"I'm here from a military standpoint, to advise on the situation here, especially considering the youth of the new King," said Raiban blithely.

Zsurtul froze in the act of reaching for a glass of water from the decanter in front of him. "I don't remember asking for such aid. Did you, General Kezule?"

"No, Majesty. You have me and your Sholan advisers."

"The situation here is quite volatile, as I see it," said Raiban, obviously settling into her seat for the duration. "You have refugees pouring in from Ch'almuth and a potential war brewing there if you don't give this M'zullian ship the tribute it expects. Level-headed experienced military leadership is needed."

"General Raiban," Falma interrupted quietly. "This is neither the time nor the place for such discussions."

"It is exactly the right time and place," said Raiban.

"They aren't refugees, General Raiban, they are immigrants," said Shyadd looking up from the treaties he was reading.

"Immigrants, refugees," said Raiban airily, waving an expansive hand. "They are still fleeing from the M'zullians. It would be best if you let that shipment go ahead as normal so as not to arouse them, and give us more time to prepare to meet them on a more equal footing."

"Are you suggesting that I have less experience than yourself, General Raiban?" Kezule asked, his tone silky. "You may have noticed that we're sitting inside the Palace of Light that was so recently occupied by K'hedduk. We took it back without your help and with very little damage to either the Palace or the surrounding town. Had we followed your advice, we would still be battling it out today, and the collateral damage would have been considerable. We achieved what you personally said was impossible."

"I wasn't aware the Touibans had sent you one of their warships," she snapped.

"You should have known," drawled Kaid, lounging back in his seat. "It was no secret the Touibans helped get us off Shola. You've become complacent, Raiban, seeing only what you expect to see."

"Impudent! I demand these two be removed from the room or these talks will cease!" she snarled, ears flattening to her head in anger.

"If I may break in here," said Kusac. "Shyadd, I suggest you take Falma and the necessary papers down to your office, where the two of you can get on with your business undisturbed."

Shyadd smiled broadly as he looked at his opposite number. Seeing he was in agreement, he looked at his King for permission.

"Go," said Zsurtul, with a slight smile. "We'll stay here and discuss important matters, like who is the scarier General."

Amid the chuckles, they beat a hasty retreat while Raiban glowered at everyone.

"You don't seem to realize that I cannot command the Ch'almuthians, General Raiban," said Zsurtul, this time getting his glass of water. "They are an independent world, I do not rule them. Also, this shipment, as you call it, is a cull of the young females of egg-bearing age. They are being stolen from their families as breeding stock for the M'zullians. I will *not* let that happen. And finally, we need their ship to mount a rescue for one of General Kezule's daughters."

"I heard she'd been taken captive," said Raiban. "A regrettable casualty of war, but it would be foolish to try to rescue her and put both Ch'almuth and K'oish'ik at risk."

"The war will come here whatever we do," said Kezule. "K'hedduk's honor demands he retake the Palace or his generals will turn on him."

"I disagree. He's far more likely to annex Ch'almuth first as a staging post and for its produce—an army needs to be fed. And I don't see why you're so anxious to bring this war about so soon! No one is prepared to face them when they have the weapon that wiped out all life on our two colonies!"

"He can't use it against us," said Kezule. "His Generals won't let him, even if he was foolish enough to want to do so. That is, if they still have the weapon after their main battleship was destroyed at J'kirtikk."

"What do you mean?"

"It was destroyed at J'kirtikk. K'hedduk can't rule a dead world," said Kusac, smiling slightly. "We've got him where we want him, in a neat trap of his own making."

"Exactly," said Kezule. "He'll be forced into a conventional war with the same constraints we had when we retook the City—he cannot destroy the Palace of Light."

"We don't know for sure their weapon was destroyed at J'kirtikk," objected Raiban.

"We saw, like you, I'm sure, footage of their largest warship being destroyed. Agreed the other ships also dropped that cloud of whatever it was, but most came from the main ship. I'd say their ability to destroy on a large scale is compromised."

"Do we have any idea yet what it was they used on J'kirtikk?" asked Kusac.

"There's speculation," said Raiban reluctantly, "but nothing concrete is known. It was too dangerous for the *Watchers* present to even think of collecting samples at the time. Besides, would you go near something that eats its way though the hulls of ships?"

"Maybe there are two weapons, one they used against ships, the other against living matter," said Kaid.

"Possibly, but the vids show it falling down onto the planet below," said Kusac. "The fact that they are hauling salvage off J'kirtikk suggests that it isn't doing the same damage to metal structures on the planet as in space. As on our two colonies, it probably killed only living tissue, plant or animal."

"Decisions on how to deal with M'zull will be made at Alliance Council meetings, not here," said Raiban firmly. "Everyone will be affected by what you do here, Kezule. We cannot allow you to act independently."

"M'zull is our world, General, our people. You cannot predict how they will react in any given circumstances; I can," said Kezule. "That knowledge is vital when planning any campaign against them."

"*You* will not allow us to make our own military decisions?" said Zsurtul. "And just how do you plan to stop us, General Raiban?"

"Let's stop right there," said Kusac. "King Zsurtul, despite how it seems, General Raiban is only one member of the High Command of the Alliance, and her words don't necessarily reflect what they think. I very much doubt she's here in any official capacity, or she'd have shown us her orders at the start. Besides, you haven't yet signed the Treaties, so the Alliance has no jurisdiction over you."

"Yes, where are your orders, General?" asked Kaid. "Remember, I still have the rank of an Ambassador of Shola, and we still have our own Ambassador here."

"This is a military situation which needs . . ."

"Your orders, if you please, General Raiban," said Zsurtul, sitting up straighter. "The Captains are correct. I would never send any delegate to a foreign ruler without giving him or her orders to hand to them."

Reluctantly Raiban reached inside her uniform jacket and drew out a slim envelope, which she slid across the table to King Zsurtul.

The young King took his time opening the package and reading the contents. As he did, Kusac could sense the youth's mood lightening.

When he put them down, he smiled slightly. "It seems, General Raiban, your visit is a short one, meant to convey the good will of Shola and a promise to aid us if possible. Commander Raguul and the *Khalossa* will remain to aid us in any way we need it. In which case, I thank you for meeting with us." He got to his feet, forcing everyone else to do the same, then extended his hand to Raiban.

"Good day, General. I hope your visit to our world was a pleasant one," said Zsurtul, shaking her hand.

A quiet scratch at the door, then M'kou entered to escort the General back to her shuttle.

"Majesty," said Raiban through clenched teeth. "Do consider well what I've said."

"I will keep it in mind, General," said Zsurtul, resting his hands behind his back.

When she'd left, everyone relaxed again.

"Since I'm among friends," said Zsurtul, sitting down and pressing the buzzer again, this time to ask for refreshments for them all, "how do we manage this situation? Delay signing the Treaties?"

"There should be no need to delay," said Kusac. "Shyadd knows your mind on the important issues; let him negotiate them into the contract."

"It will take several days anyway, Your Majesty," said Kaid, nodding his agreement. "There are always loopholes. If a golden opportunity presents itself, you'll often find you have no time to discuss a plan with the Alliance. Then you have no option but to act instantly."

"Most of the Alliance Treaty is concerned with not acting against Alliance members without due recourse to arbitration and promising aid and troops to common causes. There's nothing really that should prevent you mounting this mission to save Zhalmo," said Kusac. "I know, I studied it in my training for Alien Relations."

"And chemical weapons?"

"Yes, there is an undertaking not to use them," Kusac admitted. "It's defined, roughly speaking for now, as not using any substance that will temporarily or irrevocably alter the perceptions or body chemistry of any person to their detriment."

"Then how do you justify your drug in the pellets and the spray?" asked Kezule, frowning.

"I have no idea," he said honestly. "I only know, on reflection, that they were left rather conveniently for me to find in Stronghold. I assume it's a Brotherhood development."

"What compound is this? It's the first time I've heard it mentioned," said Kaid.

"A la'quo-based one. It's delivered in either a pellet that dissolves when shot into a Prime or Valtegan or in a small spray. It knocks them out for several hours while it destroys the glands they have that give the Warrior caste their extra speed and the ability to heal themselves faster," said Kusac.

"They've kept this very quiet," Kaid murmured. "I picked up nothing of this, but, then, when we saw Rhyaz and Lijou last, I was not in the best of moods." He grinned slightly. "I socked Rhyaz on the jaw for the way he'd treated you, actually."

That surprised him. "Thanks, I think. I have my own score to settle with him when I see him next." There was the beginning of a low growl under his words. "The Brotherhood acts outside the laws of Shola, Kezule, which is why we so often get the jobs that skirt close to breaking laws or treaties," he explained. "Plausible deniability."

"I see. Doesn't that end with the perpetrators thrown to the wild carrion eaters?"

"Occasionally," said Kusac, glancing at Kaid. "But not often."

"When that happens, we do take unofficial appropriate action to mitigate the circumstances," said Kaid. "It often results in a complete new identity as their previous life is lost to them."

"So wc just lie about any chemical weapon we decide to use?" asked Zsurtul.

"No, Majesty. You give your orders to go ahead with the research then leave it to Kezule to handle. He in turn passes responsibility down the line so that if asked, you can both claim no knowledge of it," said Kaid.

"It sounds dishonest to me," said Zsurtul, frowning.

"It's sometimes the only way hard decisions can be made for the good of many."

"It's good advice for you to follow from now on, Kezule," said Kusac.

"This is all so much more complicated than I thought," said Zsurtul, looking at them each in turn. "I want to be a good and an honest ruler—it seems as if you are saying that no ruler can be that honest."

"You can and will be, King Zsurtul," said Kaid reassuringly. "We're talking about extreme circumstances here."

"How can I be sure I know all the facts about any given situation if my counselors don't tell me the full truth, as you're advocating Kezule should do? How can I trust them? This is what caused K'oish'ik to fall into such disarray in the first place."

"I will keep you fully informed on all matters except those on which we agree you don't need to have full details," Kezule reassured him.

"So we can in all honesty sign the Alliance Treaty, and the one with Shola?"

"Yes, King Zsurtul," said Kusac.

Zsurtul nodded, obviously less anxious about the whole matter.

Kusac exchanged a glance with Kaid as both forbore to mention that in signing the private agreement with the Brotherhood, some, like Raiban, would say he was already well on the way to running downwind of the hunt.

Ghioass, Camarilla chamber, same day

"Allies they are now, as potentialities confirm," said Zaimiss from the Speaker's lectern. "No need now to interfere; let them deal with Warrior Sand-dwellers alone. Enough resources on them have we wasted."

Shvosi rose on her haunches. "Second part of matter transformer still on their world. Still capable of being programmed to make nanites. All they need is delivery system, which is easy if placed in capsules. It must be destroyed."

"For generations trouble has been over this unit. Now is time to leave be. Unlikely are they to understand such advanced device," said Zaimiss.

"Learned how to operate it and use it for destructior didn't they?" countered Azwokkus, rising up from his nest of cushions. "While doubt exists, we must destroy it. In hands of any race but us is dangerous, even Hunters."

Aizshuss also rose. "Who lost the device? Whose error is causing all this trouble? Your Isolationist party responsible, Zaimiss! When last in majority, you lost it, you pushed through belief it vanished in hyperspace!"

"This is untrue! You shift blame to us unfairly to blacken our party," countered Zaimiss angrily.

On her cushions at the front of the chamber, Khassis stirred. "Unity, confirm who responsible for missing matter transformer."

"I protest," said Zaimiss. "Facts do not reflect actual happenings at time!"

"Isolationist party in power when matter transformer went missing on the ship carrying it," Unity intoned. *"Their majority in the Camarilla was then 70%, and they used it to push through a decision not to pursue and recover the unit despite protests from the Moderates, the only other party then. They justified it by claiming such activity would draw attention to the Camarilla."*

"Perhaps wrong decisions made that day," muttered Zaimiss. "If retrieving unit so important to you, suggest we use it to program nanites to destroy itself and the Warrior Sand-dweller world. Two problems solved at one stroke. Use Hunter to do this when he visits their world. That be his mission, not retrieving a useless female captive!"

"How can they go there to destroy matter transmitter when they know nothing of its existence? Do you propose now we tell them?" asked Azwokkus sarcastically. "Retrieving female is reason for going! As for using unit to create means to destroy it, not possible."

"Female needed for breeding program," said Khassis. "Is vital to mix their genes and produce strong leadership for final species Sand-dwellers will become."

"Then give Hunter poisoned nanites when he goes there and means to destroy the unit! Be rid of both once and for all," said Zaimiss, his humming voice rising in pitch.

There was a moment of shocked silence from the whole chamber then suddenly the buzz of conversation broke out, almost rising to a fever pitch until Khassis rose to her feet and

...lked forward to replace Zaimiss at the lectern. Reluctantly,
... stepped down, but he remained beside it.

"He twists the Council for his own use!" said Kuvaa,
shocked, to Azwokkus.

The TeLaxaudin made hushing noises to her.

"There will be silence!" Khassis' voice thrummed in a beat
that, amplified by Unity, resonated in everyone's mind.

The noise died down abruptly.

"We create, we do not destroy," said Khassis. "No more
will there be talk of poisons or destruction of the Sand-
dweller Warriors. Such a decision those who live there must
take, not us. Potentialities predict danger to us if we take
such action."

"I challenge your right to say that," said Zaimiss. "That is
decision of Camarilla, not yours, even as Chief Speaker. Unity,
confirm!"

*"The Chief Speaker, as one of oldest among you, may close
a debate if she feels it is in violation of Camarilla rules. There is
no precedent for stopping this discussion."*

Emitting scents of victory, Zaimiss continued. "I Speak for
sending poisoned nanites with Hunter on his mission, and the
means to destroy the unit after he's programmed it to replicate enough poisoned units to end this nest of Warrior Sand-
dwellers."

"I Second that," said Shumass from the floor.

"I protest not all are gathered today. No prior knowledge
had we of seriousness of topic," said Azwokkus. "Full meeting
should decide this, not just those here."

"You have members missing, is your misfortune. More attention need they pay to Unity's lists," said Zaimiss. "Legal
number here gathered. Vote can go ahead. As for potentialities, we retreat from intervention after this, we be safe from
repercussions."

"Then vote," said Khassis, mandibles clicking in anger. "Remember, Camarilla exists not for our convenience but to help
all. Unity, record the vote. Those for Zaimiss' proposal."

Slowly, the For votes came in.

"Those Against," said Khassis.

The votes were faster, but fewer.

*"Thirty votes For Zaimiss, twenty-six Against, and nineteen
Abstentions. Zaimiss wins the vote,"* said Unity.

Zaimiss took the lectern from Khassis as she returned
her seat, a wave of scents of disappointment following her.

"Kouansishus is here. He should return to the Prime Sand
dweller world with poison nanites for Giyarishis to ensure
the Hunter unknowingly takes with him on his mission. He
should be given knowledge of how to program unit to create
more and means to make it destruct after a given time. I leave
details to our science departments and field operatives with
instructions they must obey."

After the session was over, as Azwokkus, Shvosi, Kuvaa,
and Aizshuss stood in a small knot in the foyer of the meeting
hall, Azwokkus' personal messenger chimed softly.

He read it, then looked up at them. "We are to meet with
Khassis at our U'Churian safe house. Did not know she knew
of this place," he said, obviously worried.

"More and more she seems dissatisfied with the Isolationists," said Shvosi. "Perhaps now she ready to join us in reform-
ing Camarilla."

"We not find out waiting here," said Azwokkus. "We must
split up to go there."

"I know delicacy shop with exotic treats even you like," said
Shvosi in a slightly louder tone to Aizshuss. "Come, I take you.
Is in the U'Churian town just outside our city. Is not far."

"My homekeeper is ill," said Azwokkus to Kuvaa. "Your
presence choosing gift for speedy recovery be appreciated.
He is one of our Children. You know more of their kind than
me."

"Have not been to U'Churian sector," said Kuvaa, playing
along in what she hoped was a convincing way. "Only those
here I know. Be interesting to see their own town."

Questions were burning the tip of her tongue, demanding
to be asked right there and then, but she knew they had to
wait until they had left Unity's realm behind for the privacy of
the U'Churian town.

The town of Tharash was connected to the capital, Zuwassoo, by regular shuttle flights. Compared to there, Tharash
was noisy, bright, and brash. Street vendors shouting out their
wares lined the road that wound among the Cabbaran-made
adobe houses from the shuttle station to the center. There it
suddenly opened up into a large plaza lined with many stores

afes. In the center, a water fountain filled the air with
ng moisture and the pleasant sound of running water.

So different," breathed Kuvaa, finding something new in
ery direction she looked.

"The bustle I find sometimes tiring, others energizing," Az-
vokkus admitted, trotting beside her on his spindly legs.

Though an unlikely pair, no one spared them a second
glance other than to make sure not to crowd them. They were
not the only ones there; a group of Cabbarans sat outside a
cafe in its small fenced courtyard, enjoying drinks in the cool
shade of a tree.

"We must get my gift first," said the TeLaxaudin, heading
across the plaza to one of the stores.

"Why do we need a safe house?" asked Kuvaa, suddenly
remembering all her questions.

"A place to speak without the presence of Unity," said Az-
vokkus. "There we can switch on a privacy device we have
that makes us invisible to Unity, even though the net doesn't
extend into this town by agreement with the Children."

Kuvaa digested this as they entered the small shop. En-
ranced, she gazed around at the many flickering rainbows of
light that reflected on the white walls.

"Crystals," she said, looking up at the many different shapes
and sizes hanging from the ceiling.

"Yes. My homekeeper collects them and turned me into
collector too," he said, lenses swirling as he adjusted his near
vision to see them better. "I find the colors soothing as they
play upon the walls."

"You honor my shop once again, Skepp Lord," murmured
a soft U'Churian voice.

Kuvaa turned to see the brightly dressed female U'Churian
bob her head deferentially to Azwokkus.

"Your crystals delight my senses as always," hummed the
TeLaxaudin. "I will have that one there," he said, pointing to a
teardrop-shaped one the size of his palm that sent a multitude
of smaller rainbows chasing across the walls as it spun gently
in the faint breeze from the air coolers.

"Your taste is excellent as always," she purred, reaching
up to take it down from the ceiling. "This one was new in
yesterday."

Their purchase wrapped up securely and tucked into a
pouch on Azwokkuss' belt, they made their way into one of

the nearby streets. Within minutes, Kuvaa had lost her
ings in the maze of alleys.

"You will soon know the way," Azwokkus assured
"Time for you to learn the abilities possessed by Camar.
members. Has Shvosi started your training yet?"

"Not that I know of," she said dubiously, wondering hov
many of the meetings with the tattooed fellow Cabbaran sh
actually remembered.

Azwokkus gave his dry little laugh. "Perhaps she has the
Time to earn your own tattoos, Kuvaa."

Shvosi and Aizshuss had arrived before them and wer
comfortably ensconced in a back parlor. When Khassis a
rived, their U'Churian hosts brought refreshing drinks to su
each palate. While Shvosi spread the delicacies she and Aiz
shuss had bought on the low table, Azwokkus presented hi
homekeeper with the gift of the crystal.

Once their hosts had retreated, Khassis started thei
meeting.

"Getting all Reformists and Moderates together not pos
sible without drawing attention, so we leaders of the partie
meet in privacy. Kuvaa, you here as concerns you deeply. Yo
are handler of Giyarishis."

"Zaimiss set the topic deviously so Reformists not all b
there," hummed Azwokkus. "This decision must not stand."

"Agreed, but legal number present, I could not stop th
vote."

"So what we do now?" asked Shvosi, picking up a piece o
fruit to nibble on.

"We have Kuvaa tell Giyarishis why he must not follo
orders of Camarilla, that it not representative decision." sai
Khassis.

Kuvaa stirred at this and looked at the TeLaxaudin fe
male. "I am unsure what is right here, Skepp Lady," she sai
dipping her head deferentially. "I swore to uphold decision
of Camarilla, and this was one. Like you, I not like it, thin
wrong, but . . ."

"Reticence does you credit," said Khassis. "Potentialitie
do not favor our intervention in so terminal a manner. If w
do, disaster for us it predicts. Zaimiss blind to this in desire t
cut ties to younger worlds and isolate us."

"Is precedent," said Azwokkus. "When Camarilla voted o

nging your species into it, was such a set up vote. Voted No
ey did under Isolationists."

"This is so. I was young then, but remember well. I
nelped bring first Cabbarans to Ghioass and into Camarilla
chamber. Was almost rioting, most amusing," Khassis said
reminiscently.

Kuvaa's mouth dropped open in surprise. "It was . . . You
did?"

"We did. Forced Camarilla's hand that day, had to decide
Yes."

"This depends on you, Kuvaa. You hold key to what happens," said Azwokkus. "Report us you can, or join us."

Her head was spinning with facts and decisions that she
felt she had not the experience to make. "The potentialities
showed disaster," she murmured, thinking it through slowly.
"Impossible to recall all field Agents, and what of rest of our
species? Will look suspicious if those in key areas disappear.
Ones left will take the wrath of Child races. Only way Zaimiss'
plan could succeed is if all of both our species vanish. Even
then, still danger as draws more attention to us both. Search
for us, they will, never stopping till they find us." She looked
up at the expectant faces around her.

"Present course must be continued," she said. "Foolish and
dangerous to all is any other decision."

"How you answer why should we involve ourselves with
their war?" asked Shvosi.

"War been going on long time. Was born involved," she said
dryly. "Ambition of Warrior Sand-dwellers knows no bounds.
Destroy or enslave all species they will. Vote was not majority
will of Camarilla."

"Then it is decided," said Khassis. "Plant imperative to find
and destroy matter transmitter in Hunter we must."

"Hunter I wish to discuss," said Shvosi. "Sadly, Camarilla not place to talk. Annuur concerned Hunter is more
hardened to fate of prisoners. Violence he uses, and his
abilities he uses to rip knowledge from them. This not predicted. Disturbs his triad and the female Sand-dweller. Why
happen?"

"Naacha can check when subliminals he plants," said Azwokkus. "Annuur also talk to Giyarishis."

Khassis rose to her feet. "Time for leaving. This meeting
must not be suspected."

"Kuvaa and I must leave soon. Her tattoo she must get p.
claiming her of Camarilla now," said Shvosi.

"Be proud," said Khassis, preparing to leave. "You unde.
stand spirit of Camarilla as well as laws."

Kuvaa bobbed her head to the elderly female. She'c
thought Azwokkuss was making gentle fun of her when he
mentioned tattoos, but apparently not. Receiving tattoos was
a momentous happening in a Cabbaran's life because it was a
permanent record of achievements or social rank.

"Most welcome you are to come," she said shyly to Azwokkus and Aizshuss.

"I must return to home now," said Azwokkus regretfully
"Much to do with homekeeper ill."

"I come," said Aizshuss. "New experience this will be."

In a private building on the outskirts of the TeLaxaudin towr
of Zuwassoo, a small group of the Isolationists were meeting.

"How you progressing?" demanded Zaimiss as he stalkec
into the meeting room, his green draperies exuding the scen'
of purpose and determination.

"It goes slowly," admitted Kouansishus. "His reality we try
to warp with drugs, and we administer pain, but his mind i:
strong."

"I want his mind broken," hummed Zaimiss angrily. "No:
assume we have long to do this. Hidden from Unity are we for
now, but risk is high."

The Cabbaran Elder Tinzaa stirred. "Why the need for
this?" she asked, wrinkling her nose. "Agreed to help I did, bu
this is not what I expected. Preventing him from contacting
the Hunter we are. Why is more needed?"

"He meddles! No business has he coming to where the
Hunter is, or the Sand-dweller world. Message we send the
Hunter Entities that they not interfere with our mission."

"Others may not be the same," Tinzaa murmured, wrinkling
her long snout. "You tread on dangerous ground. Distancing
myself from this venture of yours, I am thinking of."

Shumass hummed in displeasure. "You have no stomach
for this! I not thought you Cabbarans were so weak. He wil
break soon, Leader Zaimiss, I know this. Weak these Entitie:
are. Food they need, and water. None as mortal as they car
withstand the forces we can bring to bear on him."

"Then do it quickly," hummed Zaimiss, turning to leave.

Zhal-Arema 25th day (March)

Angrily, Kusac slammed the cell door behind him, leaving Banner to get the information their prisoner was spilling and see he got attention from the medic afterward. These long drawn-out questioning sessions were getting him down. Normally, he felt detached from his victim and remembered little or nothing about the sessions save for what he read later in the transcripts. He wasn't the one causing the pain; it was the other's lack of cooperation that was to blame. That had all changed a few minutes ago, when suddenly, like a sleeper pulled from the depths of a hellish nightmare, he woke to find it was only too real.

This was the last M'zullian to break, and it had taken a lot to break this officer. Even now, his prisoner sat, face bruised and bleeding, cradling the broken fingers on his right hand, telling Banner all they wanted to know about the Palace guards and security installations. How had he become that which he hated so much? How had it happened? What dark mood had possessed him so that he forgot who and what he really was in this cold determination to break another sentient's will?

But you needed to be this hard to force them to speak, said a little voice deep inside. *No one else would do what you had to, except Kezule, and he'd have killed them too soon. And time is running out.*

"Dammit," he snarled, pounding his fist into the ancient stone wall, then wincing when it hurt. Distracted, he flexed his knuckles, seeing the blood welling up on the grazes as they began to swell. It hurt like hell, but it did still that hideous inner voice that egged him on to further callousness, the voice he was sure was the same as the one that had tried to stop him healing Zsurtul.

He wished he could go to Kaid, tell him everything, ask for his help—lay his head in Carrie's lap and . . . He could do none of it if he was to protect them from this insidious presence that seemed able to control him without him even realizing it. How could it follow him around like this? Had the TeLaxaudin Kziz-

ysus planted some control device in his brain when he was c
the Cabbaran shuttle? They'd promised no implants, but ha•
he honored that promise? Tirak had been there. Perhaps he
knew something, but would he tell him the truth, or was he
part of some conspiracy to use him? To what ends, though?
None of it made any sense right now, and it wouldn't until he
knew the right questions to ask himself and others.

He began walking, heading aimlessly back to the surface,
making his mind as blank as possible. There was no running away from this; he knew that. The only escape was to
discover what was causing it. A chill breeze fanned against
his face, bringing with it the aromas of food and hot herbal
drinks. Blinking, he realized that he stood at the edge of the
Great Courtyard and that night had fallen. The bright lights
of the cafes, tables set in the courtyard itself now the rubble
was gone, beckoned with promises of food, drink, including
alcohol, and companionship. From where he stood, he could
see several tables occupied by Sholans. A flash of a golden
pelt drew his eyes, and he identified his sister with her mate,
Dzaka.

His stomach growled, informing him he was hungry. Right
now, though, family was not what he needed. Turning his back
on the courtyard, he headed into the main Palace, deciding
he'd call the kitchens and get something sent to his room. On
the third floor, as he was heading down the corridor to the
elevator, he saw Naacha approaching him. Memories stirred:
there was something he'd wanted to ask the Cabbaran, but he
was damned, now the opportunity presented itself, if he could
remember what it was.

He veered to one side to avoid him as he trotted down the
center of the corridor. However, just before they drew level,
Naacha stopped and, rearing up onto his haunches, spoke to
him.

"Wait, Hunter."

Baffled, he stopped beside the alien. "Hunter?" he asked,
letting the other make eye contact with him.

Look away! Something inside yammered at him. *Don't
look at the tattoos!* Of course, he did . . .

It took only a moment for Naacha to take control of Kusac's
mind, but it took a lot more effort to keep it, he discovered,
as, without words, he led the way to the growth labs and the

TeLaxaudin quarters. At the security post guarding the way into the labs, the guards merely nodded at them and stepped aside.

Naacha stopped at Giyarishis' office, empty right now he knew, and urged Kusac inside. Now that they were no longer moving and there was no danger of being disturbed, he was able to strengthen his hold on the other's mind. Mentally ordering him to sit on the sofa and relax, Naacha reached into one of his belt pouches to draw out the small portable sleep tape unit, which, with the aid of its adhesive backing, he managed to fix to Kusac's forehead.

The process of planting the information on where to find the other half of the matter transformer and how to ensure it produced the nanites they wanted and then destroyed itself would take only half an hour. Meanwhile, with the Hunter's mind occupied with the learning tape, he could easily look for the information that Shvosi had asked for.

Dragging one of Giyarishis' cushions nearer the sofa, he sat down to begin searching through the slowly moving electrical signals that formed the Hunter's thoughts. He had just finished and was waiting for the tape to end when Giyarishis arrived.

Folding himself down beside the Cabbaran, Giyarishis showed the other a small ampoule filled with a clear liquid.

"Kouansishus finished carriers for us," he said. "When we use?"

"Timing critical," said Naacha. "Too late, and no chance to insert. No schedule given?"

"None."

Naacha sniffed his annoyance. "Give," he said, holding out his hand.

When Giyarishis had given it to him, he closed his spatulate hoof-tipped fingers around it and began to feel his way into the electronic commands of the tiny self-replicating nanites suspended in the saline solution. Already tired from the work he'd done, this would drain him, he knew. At least with the nanites, there was no need to be subtle. He checked their programming, adding a few more commands to the string, then handed the vial back to the TeLaxaudin.

"Give now. Under the skin they will lodge till needed, then will be released."

Giyarishis got up and went to fetch a hypo spray. "Worried

I am," he said, coming back over as the Cabbaran removed the sleep tape unit from Kusac's forehead. "Kuvaa tell me this will of her party, not Camarilla. We must ignore their orders and do what she commands."

"So?" asked Naacha, putting the device away.

"Conflicting commands already I had from Kuvaa. She push for Link between Sand-dweller and Hunter, then next message she say not do when I ask. Several times this happen."

Naacha shifted on the cushions. "Ask her then."

"She get angry," said Giyarishis, lenses whirling in distress as he pressed the hypo to Kusac's right wrist. "Not sure . . . not sure I talk to Kuvaa sometimes, she so different."

The mystic looked down his long snout at the slender Te-Laxaudin. "Hunter behaving in way that angers those around. You controlled him."

"Kuvaa order it. Even last night she said do."

Naacha sucked in a breath, his whiskers bristling as he did. "No," was all he said.

"Looked like Kuvaa," said Giyarishis, putting the hypo on his desk. "If not, who?"

"Had she new tattoos?"

"No."

"I tell Annuur. Tell him any new orders first. Something very wrong here. Kuvaa got Camarilla tattoos two nights ago."

A movement from the sofa drew his attention as Kusac began to stir.

"Leave," said Naacha, reaching out mentally to keep him unconscious a little longer. "He wakes, you must not be seen."

He felt a light icy pressure against his lips, followed by a gut-wrenching sensation of falling that made him stagger and reach out hastily to steady himself against the wall. The hazy shape of a white-pelted Sholan stood in front of him, her hand moving back as if she'd just touched him. *Remember.* Smiling, she turned and walked away, leaving him shaking with the cold.

He blinked, and the vision was gone, only Naacha and the corridor remained. Unconsciously he rubbed an itchy spot on the inside of his wrist and looked at the Cabbaran. With a grunt that could mean anything, Naacha trotted past him, leaving him standing there bewildered and alone.

Evening, Zhal-Arema 26th day (March)

Kaid's investigation into the assassin had turned up nothing concrete. The Sholan was ex-Forces, discharged dishonorably after serving a prison term for drug-related crimes. His last known residence had been in the Accommodation Guild-house in Shanagi, the Sholan capital. This information L'Seuli had gotten for them. Somehow, someone had managed to secure a position for him on the *Khalossa*. They were still trying to find out who.

Kusac put the report aside on his desk and sighed. The only person who could pull off a stunt like that was Raiban, but it was too transparent for her, in one way. As a covert attempt on his life, it had been done far too publicly, and the dead Sholan had traces of illegal drugs in his system. Raiban, head of Military Intelligence and the titular head of the Sholan Security Council, wouldn't be so stupid as to employ a real drug addict. More questions and no answers.

He ran his free hand across his face then let it drop to the desktop. He was tired; he hadn't slept well again the last couple of nights because of formless, confused dreams about the assassination attempt, Vartra, and Kuushoi. He knew what had triggered them—his hallucination of the other night—but knowing why didn't help. On top of that, it was Carrie's Link day with Kaid, and no matter what he did, he couldn't shut out the echoes of their state.

A sudden burst of heat from his hand drew a yowl of pain from him as he dropped what he'd been holding back onto the desk. Like a child's lump of clay, the chunk of bronze-colored metal that had once, on the Orbital, been an ornament of a norrta, was now formed into a perfect imprint of his curled fingers.

"What the hell . . ." He poked it tentatively, but it was now cool to the touch. Picking it up, he saw that the desk hadn't been burned, only his hand. When he looked at it, he saw angry red welts on his palm and fingers.

He stared at them for a long moment before his common sense cut in and told him to go stick his hand under cold running water. It helped, but not much. Patting it dry on a small towel, he returned to the lounge. Torn between the need to go to the hospital across the hallway and the need to understand what he'd done, he tentatively picked up the lump again. This time, he didn't look at it but rather tried to see past the outer shape, as he'd done with Zsurtul. He nearly dropped it again as suddenly he *saw* the crystalline structure of the metal, where the weak points and fault lines were.

Mentally he reassured himself that there was nothing strange in this, it was merely a skill the First Telepaths had possessed, like Jaisa from their trip to the past. In its present shape, it was a dead giveaway to the fact he'd been able to do something no one in their time could do.

Warmth filled his palm again as the outlines of the metal began to blur. He almost dropped it then and there, but he held on and tried to force the heat to radiate upward, away from his flesh. It was like watching something alive, one of the shapeless blobby creatures that lived in the holy tanks dotted all over the Palace. The metal seemed to become plastic, flowing downward to form a flatter, squatter shape. Gradually features emerged, ones that matched his memory of not the ornamental norrta, but the real one.

The enormity of what he was doing suddenly hit him. Cursing, he flung the metal away and sprang back, overturning his chair and almost tangling it around his legs. He stood in a defensive crouch for a full minute, breathing rapidly, feeling his palms go slick with the cold sweat of fear as he tried to make sense of what he'd done. Gradually, the tension left his body, and he straightened up, his still healing thigh muscles complaining bitterly at the unaccustomed stress on them. Picking the chair up and putting it back in its place, he went over to the low table by the sofa where a bowl of flowers, kept filled with fresh ones from the Palace gardens, lay. Taking one at random, a pink daisy-shaped one, he looked at it the same way, again suddenly seeing in his mind's eye its cell structure. A touch *here*, and *there*, and the pink faded, changing to a sickly yellow.

Shaken, he put it back in the bowl. His burned hand reminded him it needed treatment. A moment's thought in that direction and the pain faded. When he looked at it, only a slight reddening of the skin marked where the burns had been.

For the next half an hour, he went through his belongings

feverishly, taking any likely item and looking at it, seeing how it was constructed and whether he was able to affect its structure. He wasn't sure if he wanted to succeed or fail, but the need to know drove him on till, exhausted and ravenously hungry, he collapsed on the sofa.

When had the changes in him happened? What—or, more important, who—had caused them? Was it the procedure done by Annuur? That had given him his Talent back after Annuur had made new pathways in his damaged neural system and brain. He remembered now that when he'd come back from the dead, Kezule had told him about the Valtegan healing trance and that he, too, had these Warrior organs, and he'd told him again at the planning meeting when Zayshul had sedated him. It hadn't made the impact then that sitting here thinking about it now in cold blood did. Then, there had been too much happening around him—the needs of his command, his son, the need to retake the Palace and City of Light before K'hedduk was too entrenched and M'zull sent him the promised aid—it was only now that he had the actual leisure to think it all through.

Most of the changes in his abilities had not happened on Shola, they'd happened on Kij'ik, and after he and Zayshul had started their pheromone-induced affair. What part did Naacha play in it all? He remembered . . . that he always forgot what actually occurred while he was in Naacha's company, but that afterward there were changes in his abilities. Was this sudden escalation of his ability to change the form of objects due to something Naacha had said or done in their brief meeting in the corridor? How brief had it been?

He frowned, trying to remember. There was some connection between Giyarishis and Naacha, he was sure, as wisps of memories tried to surface. How could that be? They hadn't met till now on K'oish'ik, had they? The feeling that they did know each other was strong, against all reason. Kzizysus and Annuur were another unlikely pair, yet they had collaborated on healing his mind. And Naacha had been there, too. It couldn't be a coincidence.

A feeling of déjà vu began to steal over him, along with a deep lassitude. He'd come to some of these conclusions before, he realized, yet somehow he'd forgotten about them. Forcing himself to his feet despite his overwhelming exhaustion was an effort, but one he knew he had to make. Was this kin to that little inner voice, he wondered? Pushing himself, he left his suite, heading for the hospital area, where he knew Zayshul would be at this time of day.

Abruptly, he changed course, making instead for the outside garden on this level, telling ZSADHI to ask the Doctor to meet him there. The hospital had no outside windows and depended totally on artificial light, and some instinct warned him he must avoid lights right now.

A chill breeze was blowing through the large open windows. Perched as it was on one side of the Palace, the garden was encased in clear windows that could be drawn back to let the air in. Protective screens kept dust and insects at bay. There, the cool air cleared his head as if by magic. The conservatory did have lighting, but right now it was still off to allow any visitors to see the beauty of the sunset.

Feeling much more alert, he found a seat on a stone bench and waited for her to arrive. When she did, he began to tell her everything that was on his mind.

"I don't think it is coincidence that there was a TeLaxaudin present each time," he finished.

She'd listened in silence, watching his face as he spoke. Now she looked down at her hands.

"I know you don't want to hear it, but I was always convinced that Kzizysus was involved in the scent marker and it had nothing to do with me, unless somehow I was controlled without being aware of it. Giyarishis always insisted it was me."

"What if you're right?" he asked. "If it was that dead female all along? The TeLaxaudin helped your people breed after the Fall. Putting a false scent marker on you should be easy for them, and they are old allies of the Cabbarans."

"They did more," she said, looking up again. "They altered me so I could carry my egg safely. The Royal family must carry their own eggs to ensure that only a legal heir is produced. The rest of the people here," she gave a wave of her hand, "use the growth tanks. The egg is removed and the shell taken off, and the child grows in the tank till ready for birth. This sounds odd until you know that we are too small to bear the eggs any more, that the only way the mother can be sure of survival is to use the growth tanks the TeLaxaudin developed for us."

"You carried your own egg? But if there was a risk . . .?"

"That was how the Directorate tried to blackmail Kezule,"

she said. "They offered to secretly remove my egg and let it hatch in a growth tank while I pretended I was still carrying it. As one of the Royal family, in line to the Throne, that would be a treasonable act. Had we been caught, Kezule and I would have been executed and my child destroyed."

"So he refused."

"He had to; the price was to head the revolt and put him on the Throne as a puppet Emperor for M'zull."

"I can see now why he left K'oish'ik so hurriedly," Kusac murmured. He had a whole new perspective on Kezule to absorb. "But you said the TeLaxaudin altered you. How?"

"I have no idea. Even asking them to help was treasonable, but Kezule did that for me. Afterward, they threw him some kind of device they said they had used so he could do the same for the females on Kij'ik when we were there."

"What did it do, exactly?"

"I said I have no idea, and I don't." She shrugged. "Maybe it changed me, maybe it changed the egg so it was smaller. When I checked myself, I could find no obvious changes, but Shoawomiss, the head of the TeLaxaudin here, said it would be a genetic change, not just for me but for my daughters as well."

"So they have the technology to alter living tissue," said Kusac, seeing the fear in her eyes, feeling it echoed in his. "Do I really have those extra organs, Zayshul?"

"Yes, you have them, against all reason, and they work as well as ours do."

"And Shaidan?" he asked, his voice almost a whisper. His son, bred by the Directorate, bearing Valtegan genes and grown in a tube easily accessible by anyone wanting to alter him.

"He has them too. I found them when I had him scanned in the operating room after he'd been shot and his lung punctured."

"You never told me." It wasn't an accusation.

"How could I? Your relationship was so very fragile to start with, I couldn't harm it."

"Thank you. It was probably the right decision at the time."

"I remember more now. Like Kezule having memories of the far past of his ancestors that he didn't possess before."

"What did Kezule say about this? Did he notice?"

"No, and I haven't mentioned it to him really. When I did once, he just shrugged it off. He's different now, not as . . ." She searched for the word. "He doesn't deal in absolutes any more; matters have shades of meaning now for him."

"Shades of gray. Life is shades of gray, never black or white," Kusac murmured.

Silence fell between them as the sky darkened into night and the air grew chiller.

"Do you find you have a habit of forgetting matters like this?" he asked at length.

"I don't really know," she said. "You told me once I had."

"We have to record this somewhere where we can't lose it," he said decisively, standing up. "If we forget, we can look it up and remember."

"How do we remember that we forgot?" she asked.

He gave a wry smile as she got to her feet. "That's the flaw, isn't it? I think it involves lights, but I'm not sure how. The memory is very hazy. I have to go. I'm having dinner with Shaidan tonight."

He was conscious of her eyes watching him as he left, of her wanting—needing—some words of comfort that he was incapable of giving her because he could find no comfort for himself. As soon as he was in the corridor, he stopped and began recording a brief outline of what they thought on his wrist comm, praying he'd remember it was there.

Between one step and the next, time stretched infinitely, and when it stopped, his foot fell awkwardly, making him stagger slightly, leaving him with a distinct sense of unease and the feeling of a job only half completed.

After dinner, he tucked Shaidan up in his bed, leaving on a low-level light for him. His son spent every other night with him now. The need for them both to cling to each other was lessening with time and the return of Shaidan's brothers and sisters. At last the cubs were learning to behave like children, with no worries for the future but when the next food treat or excursion to play in the river was coming. Mixing with the other Prime children had helped a lot.

With Jayza just across the hallway, Kusac felt confident it was safe to leave him alone in the suite for an hour or two while he went to talk to Conner.

*   *   *

The temple had been transformed, Kusac realized as soon as he set foot into it. Gone was the huge overpowering statue of the Emperor. In its place was a much smaller one, more life-sized, of a Prime female in a pale blue robe, standing with one hand on the neck of a young herd beast, and carrying a basket full of stalks of grain and vegetables.

Where the Royal statue's pose had been rigid, this one was full of life. Her expression a gentle smile, She and the herd beast appeared as if caught in motion. There was a natural style to it that was totally different from any other statues or carvings he'd yet seen.

"Beautiful, isn't She?" said Conner, coming out from behind the altar table placed in front of Her. "My new priests and priestesses found this one hidden in the sculpture studios over in the east wing. Apparently it's some six hundred years old. She needed a new coat of paint, of course, but that was all."

"It is beautiful," he admitted. "Is it La'shol, their Fertility Goddess?"

"Indeed She is, but She has more in common with the Green Goddess for this world," smiled Conner, holding his hand out in the Telepath greeting to Kusac.

Kusac returned the gesture. "I can see a resemblance to Ghyakulla," he said, Kaid's memory of the statue he'd seen in the cavern under Vartra's Retreat coming to the forefront of his thoughts.

"She entrusted me with the task of returning Her worship to this poor, neglected planet and Her people. With Her help, they can rebuild and become again what She intended them to be."

"Hmm," said Kusac, dubiously. Then hurriedly, lest he be misunderstood, "I don't doubt your mission, Conner . . ."

Conner laughed and put his hand briefly on Kusac's shoulder. "You doubt that the Ghyakulla here had a good purpose for the Valtegans," he said gently. "Come and see the rest of the temple. Have you noticed the wonderful hanging behind Her statue? Isn't it beautiful?"

"Another recovered treasure?" asked Kusac, genuinely admiring the pastoral scene that depicted a lusher and more bountiful K'oish'ik than now existed.

"Actually, no. It's new," said Conner. "The ladies of the Court and the priestesses have worked this miracle in the few weeks since I came here, in thanks for their deliverance from K'hedduk."

That did surprise him.

"Their souls were calling out in their need for something gentle and replenishing to worship, Kusac," he said, a serious expression on his face. "Not that Zsurtul's father was anything but a benign monarch, you understand, but especially after K'hedduk's harsh rule, they needed something other than a ruler to worship and believe in."

He nodded his understanding. "I see you've refreshed the water tank and made it more of a noticeable feature," he said looking over to the ceiling-high tank that took up almost half the main wall of the temple.

"Yes. It's endlessly fascinating, don't you think?" he asked, drawing Kusac closer to it. "Look at the variety of creatures and plants that live there. Who'd have thought that such a rich variety of life could exist in a hot spring?"

Kusac watched the tiny silver fish darting about, then miniscule, almost transparent shrimplike creatures caught his attention. He moved closer, fascinated, looking to the bottom of the tank to see what else lived there.

"A microcosm of its own, isn't it?" said Conner, placing a hand on the clear front. "Feel the heat of the water. The wonder of how they can exist at this temperature never fails to amaze me. Ghyakulla fills many niches with Her ever-more-wondrous creations."

He placed his hand on the front, feeling the warmth for himself. "It's almost blood temperature," he said, surprised.

"Look at where the bubbles come from the oxygenator," said Conner, pointing. "See how those little reptiles use them to hitch a ride up to the surface?"

"I see it," he said. "Shaidan and the other cubs would love this."

"Then you must bring them when you have time."

"I will," he said, turning reluctantly away from the tank. He'd found it soothing to watch the creatures, but he'd come here to talk to Conner, not to see the temple.

Conner gestured toward the nearby chairs, then sat, waiting patiently.

"I have fragmented memories, Conner," Kusac said quietly. "Memories of needing to stay away from lights for some

...son, of knowing I forget what I've found out about some
...reat to me . . . and others."

"Are you sure it's real? From what Kaid and Carrie say
to me, it would seem that you are acting out of character, especially with the prisoners," said Conner. "I realize that the
basis of this is that you'll not ask anyone to do what you aren't
prepared to do yourself, but . . ."

"I'm doing it too well, forgetting who I am," he said. "I
know how to make them talk because of what I went through
with one of their Inquisitors."

He got to his feet and began to pace in front of Conner,
hands resting on the butt of his pistol and the pommel of his
knife. "What you don't know is that I feel driven to behave
that way. I feel as if I'm not in command of myself at those
times."

"In what way?" asked Conner, clasping his hands on his
lap. "Who are you if not yourself?"

"I'm still me, I don't mean I'm someone else." He stopped
for a moment in front of Conner. "It's as though my will is
being sapped. I don't notice it at the time, only afterward,
maybe as much as several hours later."

Conner nodded but said nothing.

"There's more," Kusac said, pulling the bronze ornament
from a belt pocket and holding it out to the priest.

"It's beautifully made," said Conner. "A norrta, I think they
call it. You and one of your team killed one, didn't you?"

"Yes, but I made that, Conner."

"You made it?" Conner raised his eyebrows in surprise.

He took it back, holding it in his hand and thinking another
shape into the metal before handing it to him again.

"Good gracious," said Conner after a long moment's silence. "It's me, and it's still warm."

"Only the first altered telepaths were able to do anything
like this," he said, retrieving it and putting it away. "I lost my
Talent completely. Then Annuur and Kzizysus performed that
operation on me, giving it back. I can do things no one else
can, Conner, and I don't know how or why. It scares me."

"Sit down," said Conner. "Let's look at this rationally, shall
we?"

"I've tried, but all I get are questions and no answers." He
sat down again, on the edge of the seat this time.

"You say you keep forgetting what you've discovered abo[ut] this threat to you—it is only to you, isn't it?"

"Not just me. It affects Zayshul too." He racked his min[d] for more details. "She said something about Kezule having odd racial memories that no one else has. She forgets things too," he added.

"When did all this start?"

"On Kij'ik."

Overhead, the lights flickered briefly. As Kusac looked up, a gust of cold wind from outside swept through the temple, making the candles on the altar flicker.

"Like that," he said slowly, memories stirring. "The lights flicker like that, and we forget what we were saying—except when it suddenly gets cold." He started thinking of the times he and Zayshul had talked about this and felt a sudden chill in the air. "Only then don't we forget."

He locked eyes with Conner, seeing his own unease echoed on the other's face. There was one name in both their thoughts that for different reasons they didn't want to speak out loud.

Conner broke the silence. "This feeling you're being controlled, because that's what it amounts to, have you felt it at any other time?"

"Yes, when I was running to try to save King Zsurtul's life. It was a compulsion to stay away, almost like a voice in my head."

"Hmm."

"I'm not going insane," he snapped out in exasperation.

"Of course you aren't," said Conner with a smile. "No insane person would come to me and ask for my help."

"You'll say nothing of this to anyone else?"

"Nothing," Conner agreed readily. "This is between you and me. However, I would like to talk to Zayshul and get her perspective on this."

He nodded. "Best take a recording device with you," he said dryly, "lest you also get hit by the amnesia we seem to be suffering."

"That's actually a good idea. Looking at the other issue, your enhanced abilities, what you're able to do is not unknown to me. On Earth, there were even those who could change their form, like the legends of the Selkies. In the sea they resembled seals, but on dry land, they cast off their sealskins, hiding them from prying eyes, and became Human. They could live in their

.uman shape for many years, until the call of the sea became
too strong and they had to return to it."

"Folktales," said Kusac as Carrie's memory of it surfaced.

"Indeed, but hidden in folktales is often a grain of truth.
With great ability comes the need for great control, Kusac,"
said Conner. "We're in a time of troubles and conflict. Who
knows how your abilities will be able to help us, but I'm sure
you've gained them for a purpose."

"Have I? Or are they some aberration caused by the way
my Talent was restored?"

"You can obviously do this changing at will," said Conner.
"And you not only stopped King Zsurtul from dying but actually repaired damaged organs, I was told."

"I don't have much memory of what I did, to be honest. I
just did what was needed."

"Precisely. Imagine the abilities you have in the hands of
a less scrupulous person. Think of the harm such a one could
wreak. Having such a gift can be dangerous because the
temptation to use it inappropriately will always be there. Set
boundaries for yourself; never use it in anger or to destroy.
Use it only in extreme circumstances, or you'll find that using
it becomes like a drug you cannot do without. Remember,
there is always a cost to be paid for using mental abilities."

"I learned that as a cub," he said. "Healing Zsurtul drained
me for several days. Changing inanimate objects has made me
ravenously hungry."

"Sometimes the cost is not so obvious," said Conner gently.
"You have a position of responsibility here and back on Shola.
You must never forget that you owe them your best. Their
honor is your honor. Never act hastily or lash out in anger,
despite the temptation."

Kusac laughed mirthlessly. "Ask Banner to tell you about
Dzaou sometime. I gave him so much rope he almost killed
me with it because I wouldn't act hastily. I had to be seen to be
fair, even though he was an undermining influence every day
we were on Kij'ik."

"That is what someone in a position of power should do.
Not put himself and his own wishes first, but look instead to
the members of the community."

"That's easily said, Conner. But I left it almost too late to
deal with Dzaou. I was just out of my sickbed after my leg
wound, and he almost killed me."

"And if you had acted earlier?"

He sighed. "I was afraid Kezule would see it as my failure. But strong leadership isn't knocking down those who disagree with you."

"No, it isn't. It's teamwork. It's delegating and, if not following the advice of those people when they give it, at least considering it seriously."

"You're talking about that vision of yours again," said Kusac, trying to keep the exasperation out of his voice. "Do you know what we have right now in orbit around here? We've three massive warships, Kij'ik with its cannon, plus numerous other destroyer class ships! I swear not even a fly could sneak past us!"

"That's reassuring, but how vigilant are those watching scanners for incoming traffic? Do they know we might be victims of a sudden strike?"

"I don't know. That's Kezule's area not mine."

"Then talk to him, tell him to listen," said Conner.

"We know how active the Entities are in our lives, Conner, Kezule doesn't. How do I convince him that the visions of an ancient Earth man are true predictions of what will happen?" This time, his exasperation was loud and clear.

Conner leaned forward and rested his index finger on Kusac's forehead. "I will show you," he said.

He looked up, gasping in shock at what he·saw. High above them, it hung in the air, looking like the kind of bauble peasants would hang on the prayer tree for their chosen deity. Moonlight shimmered and glinted off it, making it appear almost ghostly, a thing of less substance than presence. A spindle end projected from its top and hung below it. Between them, a platform hung in nothingness, banded by four slim struts that formed the outline of a globe.

A flash to one side of it drew his attention. It was followed by a streak of light, then another, and finally by a flare so bright that even when he blinked, he still saw it.

Movement from the platform—a cloud of tiny lights, like fireflies, leaving, swarming toward where he'd seen the explosion, caught his eye.

"Our defenses aren't strong enough yet," said a voice at his elbow that he almost recognized. "If only we'd had some warning."

He spun around to face the man, but his face was hidden in the shadows of the clock tower.

"I don't understand," he stammered, glancing back at the beautiful monstrosity in the sky.

"There aren't enough ships berthed at the platform. The attacks came too soon for us." A low snarl underlaid the voice.

A flare of light, like a bolt of lightning, hissed and crackled through the air, impacting on the central building of the Palace behind him. Stone blocks exploded violently, sending red-hot shards high into the night sky to rain down on the courtyard. Over it all, a high-pitched whine and the smell of burning filled the air.

Transfixed, he experienced the vision right to the end, when Conner finally sat back. "Now do you understand?"

"Yes," said Kusac, hoarsely, shocked not only by what he'd experienced but that Conner could send to him like that.

"Show Kezule this. You have the ability. Do not be afraid to use it. As I've told you tonight, knowing when to use your gifts is the sign of a good leader. There's more you need to know."

"What now?" he asked. "Isn't this enough?"

"It's only the beginning, I fear," said Conner regretfully. "I've been told by Ghyakulla that you're a kind of fulcrum in this war. Much of what you do will affect the outcome."

Kusac began to protest, but Conner raised his hand to cut him short. "Listen to me!" he said, using the voice command that Kusac knew well and instantly obeyed. "Saving Prince Zsurtul's life was one incident. Think what would have happened had he died. There will be more, Kusac, and you will have to meet them all with your entire senses alert. Not everything will be as it seems; you'll need to search beneath the obvious for the clues. I have a feeling this threat you feel is a part of it."

"How?"

"If I could answer that, I would be wise indeed," said Conner. "Call it intuition. Everything is part of a web drawing the key elements and people to the center for the resolution. Look at where you sit now. Would you have guessed that you would be the right hand of King Zsurtul and Kezule a year ago?"

"Of course not!"

"A story for you, one from Llew's past, since his vision is so much a part of our future here."

"A story? How can a story help me? I came to you for help and advice, not a lecture on leadership and stories."

"You will see where it all fits in one day. And perhaps I shouldn't have called it a story, because it was a true happening. It happened when I—Llew—was not at the Court of the High King. They'd quarreled, over a woman, the one Arthur chose to wed. Llew foresaw problems, but his student was in love, so he wed her. Gwenhwyfer was her name, and she had a sister as like her as a twin, called Gwenhwfach. Where Gwenhwyfer was gentle and kind, her sister was made of sterner stuff and was jealous of her position as Queen. She felt someone as devoid of ambition as Gwenhwyfer didn't deserve to be the wife of the High King. If she were Queen, ah, it would all be so different! She'd urge Arthur on to greater and nobler deeds. Enough of this round table with each lord equal to the next! She'd convince the High King it was his destiny to own those lands for himself by conquest, not depend on the good will of his nobles. She, unlike her sister, was like us, with abilities beyond those of the ordinary folk. She'd studied what books she could find, delving deep into the darker arts for her solution."

Conner's voice had a singsong quality to it, drawing Kusac deep into the tale despite himself.

"She found a spell that would switch their personalities so she would inhabit Gwenhwyfer's body, and Gwenhwyfer hers. The spell was successful, and being a canny lass, Gwenhwfach was careful to act as docile as her sister, at least at the start. Of course, Gwenhwyfer, on waking up in her sister's body, ran at once to the Court to tell the King. He, knowing of Gwenhwfach's jealousy, refused to listen to her. Day after day, for a month or more, poor Gwenhwyfer in her sister's body tried to tell her husband what had happened. Eventually he was forced to have her taken out to the gates of Camelot and banished."

"Couldn't he tell his own wife?" asked Kusac.

"Apparently not, and Gwenhwfach was careful not to show her true colors for many months. Meanwhile, Gwenhwyfer had found shelter in the home of a certain knight of Arthur's Court, Lancelot by name. He was the only one who believed her story."

"How long did the deception last? Did she get her husband back—and her own body, in the end?"

"It took a year, but eventually Arthur realized that his sweet gentle wife had become a nagging harpy, always trying to create conflict between him and his knights."

Conner stopped and stared off into space, as if remembering the actual events.

"So what happened?"

"Lancelot found Llew and told him what had happened, begging him to return to the Court and settle the matter. He did and was met by a relieved King who asked him to find out where Gwenhwfach was because his true wife was trapped inside her body. Llew told Arthur to call all the Court together, and he would settle the matter. When they were all gathered, Lancelot brought Gwenhwyfer in. Of course, the false wife began demanded her evil sister be thrown out, that banishment was obviously too good for her, and she should be executed for treason."

"She showed her true nature then," said Kusac.

"Yes. She showed she was selfish, had no love for her sister, and would stop at nothing, even her sister's death, to get her own way. Llew reversed the spell, and Gwenhwyfer, restored at last to her own body, fell weeping to her knees. Arthur, full of apologies, raised her to her feet and banished her sister from the lands of Greater Britain. Orders were sent to every town and village that no one was to give her aid or succor. She was escorted to the Channel and put on a ship, and that was the last that was seen of her."

"A harsh judgment."

"She would have seen her sister killed to keep up her pretense."

"I can't understand how the King couldn't tell she wasn't his wife, knowing she had a sister . . ."

"Who would believe such a plot? Was the sister lying when she claimed to be the true wife, or was the wife lying? Who would you believe?"

"I could tell by touching their minds."

"You could, but Arthur couldn't," said Conner. "Sometimes things are not as simple as they appear to be."

"They never are," he sighed.

"Why do you distance yourself from your wife and Kaid?" asked Conner. "Don't tell me it's because you love Zayshul, because we both know you don't."

"There's a scent marker . . ." he began then trailed off into silence under Conner's gaze.

"Is this feeling of being controlled against your nature part of it?"

Kusac got to his feet. This priest was too damned observant, but then again, Conner wasn't just one person. He carried the memories of hundreds of others in his head.

"I can't involve them in this, Conner," he said with finality. "I know how they will react because I know them, the way you know your predecessors like Llew. Their memories are mine. I need to know why Kuushoi is involved. That's your field."

"I can ask Ghyakulla, but She rarely talks. She communicates in images and symbols."

"Ghyakulla is here?" he asked, surprised.

"Well, yes. That's why I came to help these people open this temple to Her again," he smiled gently. "I don't just sit here and give lessons to them, you know. With the help of the Sholans, we've been going around the area clearing what waterways we can find and taking seeds of native grasses and plants to plant at the margins, trying to bring fresh growth to the land. The Orbital has helped us a lot by scheduling regular rainfalls at night."

"Then please ask her."

"Have you ever been pathwalking? Perhaps it's time for you to meet Her yourself."

He shied away from that idea. "I don't think so. I've seen what happens to Kaid when he's touched too often by Vartra."

"I'll see what I can find out for you, of course. For now, though, I think if you take what Vartra said at face value and consider yourself free of any intervention when outside at night, while it's still chilly, you should be safe."

"Even safe is a relative term," Kusac said, turning to leave. "Thank you, Conner. And thanks for the story."

"A pleasure."

CHAPTER 12

K'HEDDUK'S craft finally settled on the Imperial landing pad in the old Palace courtyard. He'd barely begun the power-down sequence when the platform started its slow descent into the heart of the mountain where the more modern and secure levels were. With a rumble audible even over the decelerating whine of his engines, the overhead blast doors began to close above him, and the shaft was flooded with harsh actinic lights.

The sudden quiet was almost deafening as he leaned back in his pilot's couch and briefly closed his eyes. He was exhausted. Technically the ship could be flown by one person, but it was designed for a crew of at least three. Then there was his captive, Zhalmo. She'd turned out to be as intractable as he'd expected and more inventive than he'd ever thought possible. Her constant attempts to escape her imprisonment or to try to force him to kill her had prevented him from relaxing during the whole three-week flight. When he'd run out of the sedatives in the first aid station, he'd had to beat her then resort to tying her up. Finally, when she'd realized the inevitability of her situation, she'd retreated into her own mind, becoming almost catatonic at times, letting him do as he wished with her—which had annoyed him even more.

On approaching his home solar system, the secure conversation he'd had with the head of his personal bodyguard, Zerdish, and the Generals loyal to him had reassured him that by the time he landed, there would be no opposition left on

M'zull to his claim to the Throne. By now, the last of the a rests and executions should be over.

The platform stilled just as the sound of the engines ceased.

"Majesty, you're clear to debark." Zerdish's voice filled the small Bridge. "The Palace and your people wait to receive you."

"Acknowledged," he said, pushing himself tiredly to his feet.

He headed for her cabin, drawing his stunner before opening the door.

She was still lying on the bed where he'd left her after giving her the sedative that he'd saved for their arrival. There was no way she was making a fool of him by her intransigent behavior. Checking that her wrists were still bound securely behind her back, he grasped her by the arm and pulled her to her feet. She staggered slightly as he led her out of the cabin to the air lock. The outer door irised back to reveal a unit of his personal black-clad guards. They snapped to attention, saluting him as he emerged. He could see them lining both sides of the corridor that stretched toward the underground courtyard. His four best guards detached themselves from their comrades and marched ahead of him. As he passed between the rest, each pair of heavily armed warriors fell in behind him as his escort.

"They overthrew your brother for you, K'hedduk. How long before they turn on you?" Zhalmo whispered, her voice hoarse from misuse as she stumbled along beside him.

"Already dealt with," he said, jerking her onward. "Those alive now have only ever been faithful to me. Have no fear, you're safety is assured on M'zull."

The end of the corridor and a brighter light loomed ahead. Nostrils flaring as she caught the first scent of what lay ahead, Zhalmo tried to wrench herself free from him.

K'hedduk tightened his grip, pulling her closer. "Come now, Zhalmo, no female hysterics. You claim to be a soldier— surely you're used to the smell of a little blood after a battle." His mouth split into a wide smile totally devoid of humor as he dragged her into the courtyard.

"This wasn't a battle, it was a slaughter!" she said in horror, looking at the forest of ceremonial poles, each topped by

vered head, which fronted the Palace's huge metal doors.
ou even had them skinned," she whispered, unable to take
r eyes off those poles with limp green banners hanging
gainst them.

Kezule slowed to a stop, his glance sliding past the waiting
dignitaries to the grisly trophies. He looked them over with
pleasure as his bodyguard fanned out protectively around
him.

"Indeed, my orders were carried out to the letter."

They were all there—those who had slighted and mocked
him over too many years. Those who'd manipulated his weak-
ling older brother into sending him on what they saw as a
fool's mission. He could hear his brother's voice in his head
even now . . .

*"You're ambitious, not bad in itself, so long as you keep your
ambitions to those that glorify me. You want to lead, so lead me
to the City of Light, and ultimately the Throne. I give you this
opportunity to prove yourself."*

So he'd gone, not in force, but in stealth, armed with an
extensive library of sleep skills and a handful of handpicked
followers.

None of you are laughing now, he thought, looking at each
individual head.

"Highness, welcome home!" exclaimed Keshti, the chief
drone of the Royal seraglio, rushing forward and bowing low
before him.

"Magnificence! The Palace rejoices at your triumphant return!" said Garrik, his Chamberlain, trying to outdo the other
with his own groveling obeisances.

Two khaki-clad Generals, accompanied by an officer
dressed in black, were also bearing down on him.

"K'hedduk," said one, giving him a brief nod.

Pointedly, he ignored him and turned his attention to the
one in black. "Zerdish. Report."

Zerdish saluted him crisply. "Your orders were carried out,
Emperor K'hedduk, as you can see. The Palace and the armed
forces are yours to command. The last few possible rebels are
being flushed out of hiding in the city now."

He nodded, tightening his grip on Zhalmo as she shifted
slightly. "And my dear brother?"

Zerdish broke eye contact with him briefly. "He had a
tragic accident, Majesty. When his rooms were checked for

insurgents, he was found dead . . . drowned in his bath. tragic. I had his servant and the guard assigned to protect I executed on the spot."

"A tragedy indeed," said K'hedduk. "Once we've cele brated my wedding, then we can give him a fitting funeral."

"Wedding, Majesty?" repeated Chamberlain Garrik, trying not to look at Zhalmo.

"Which female will you choose, Majesty?" asked Keshti. "If I may make a few suggestions . . ."

"No. I'll have none of my brother's castoffs," he snapped. "Have them reassigned to the Court harem. Keep only those he never touched until I decide otherwise!"

"I'll never marry you!" hissed Zhalmo, struggling in his grip.

"You're my wife already, only the ceremony remains," he said, thrusting her at Zerdish. "Have her taken to the sera-glio, Keshti. Prepare her as befits an Empress for our wedding tomorrow."

"Tomorrow?" Keshti echoed, dismay writ large on his face. He stared at Zhalmo, dressed in torn and bloodstained mili-tary fatigues, as Zerdish gestured two of his soldiers to take charge of her.

"With . . . that?" He looked in distaste at the bedraggled female before him.

"Do you question my judgment?" K'hedduk hissed, grasp-ing a handful of the terrified drone's robe and jerking him for-ward till they were almost nose to nose. He was tired, and the drone's objections were annoying him.

"She's the daughter of Kezule, the only one left with a claim to the Throne of Light, and she *will* be my Empress! See that you make her presentable for the ceremony!"

"Of course, Majesty," stammered Keshti as he was abruptly thrust aside. "But the cuts, the bruises . . ."

"Deal with them! And see she is more docile than she is now. I will not have her spoil the ceremony!"

"As you command, Majesty," said Keshti, bowing and rap-idly backing away from him. Turning, he almost fled after the guards and Zhalmo.

"Majesty, might it not be better to wait a day or two?" mur-mured Garrik. "The last few days have seen . . . many changes, and the people are unsettled. This last purge . . ."

"Was entirely necessary," said General Geddash impatiently, elbowing him aside. "What happened on K'oish'ik? Why did you delay our attack?"

K'hedduk stared at him until the other dropped his gaze and mumbled a low apology.

"I was going to ask you the same question, Geddash. I want to know why you insisted that it would take you several weeks to ready a fleet."

A perplexed look crossed the older male's face. "Majesty, I did not. You told us you wanted to delay our plans, that the situation on K'oish'ik was stable."

"We have recordings of your transmissions," added his colleague. "Granted the connection was bad, but you said there was some problem with the transmitters at your end."

"I'll hear the recordings later," he said, his anger building. "It seems that someone, probably Kezule, has been intercepting our communications. Thanks to him, I was left without your backup, and betrayed by the people I took with me. I barely escaped Kezule's forces."

"The God-Kings be praised that you did, Majesty," said Garrik.

"Indeed," said K'hedduk dryly, clasping his hands behind his back and beginning to move toward the Palace entrance. "Have the heads and hides moved to the Palace walls," he added. "And burn the bodies. No funeral rites for them."

"As you command, Majesty," murmured Garrik.

"Zerdish, send someone to my ship to retrieve the Imperial Crown. It's in the closet in my cabin."

"You have the crown? The Crown of Light?" asked Geddash sharply.

"I have. I was crowned Emperor on K'oish'ik, but apparently that news didn't reach you either. Generals, I want a complete update from you in the morning regarding the situation here and on J'kirtikk and transcripts of the communications that were intercepted. I want to mount a punitive strike on K'oish'ik as soon as possible."

"What about Ch'almuth?" asked General M'zoesh, who'd remained silent till now. "The tithe ship returned damaged and empty except for our own dead. Looks as if there was some accident in transit that killed the crew. The security program took over and returned it to us."

K'hedduk frowned again. "I need real food," he said abruptly. "Ship's rations are barely edible. Join me in the red dining room, and I'll hear your reports now," he said as they passed through the heavy blast doors guarding the underground entry to the Palace. "I need to be sure the Ch'almuthians aren't rising against us too."

"They have no ships or weapons, Majesty," said Geddash confidently. "They're an agrarian world, no threat to us, but we should secure it before attacking K'oish'ik."

K'hedduk stopped abruptly. "Hear me well—our first priority is to destroy the Palace of Light. I killed the old Emperor and his wife, I was crowned Emperor on the Throne of Light, and as I escaped, I killed Prince Zsurtul. I have the Imperial Crown and a bride of Royal descent. I want the City of Light, the Palace, and the Throne razed to the ground so no one can rise against me. We no longer need that ancient pile of rubble. Once it falls, K'oish'ik will be ours, and no pretender like Kezule can claim the throne." He began walking again. "Send the tithe ship if you must. I know your loins are itching for your reward of a young and sentient wife. Use a corvette this time, at least it will test the compliance of Ch'almuth. Once K'oish'ik is destroyed, then we'll take Ch'almuth."

Despite her fear and the drugs, Zhalmo remembered Kusac's training: Observe all you can, it may prove useful.

The fused-rock corridors had given way to more conventional ones, covered in painted battle scenes, leading to an L junction with an elevator ahead of them. They stopped there, Keshti reaching out to call a car. When it arrived, Zerdish pushed her roughly inside. The door closed, and they began to move downward.

"What's so special about this one, apart from her bloodline?" Zerdish asked, giving her a shake.

"Only that," snapped the seraglio head. "Look at her! How I am supposed to turn her into a Queen for tomorrow, I have no idea!"

Zerdish pulled her close, lifting her chin to look at her face. "Might look half decent when the bruises and cuts are healed, but don't worry too much, Keshti—our Emperor hasn't been looking at her face!" He laughed coarsely, running a clawed thumb across her jawline until the drone hit his hand away.

"Uncouth peasant," Keshti muttered.

"That I am," he laughed. "I like my females with no brains and a bit of fight in them, not like this creature."

The elevator came to a halt, and the door slid open. Guards, guns trained on them, were waiting. When they saw who it was, they saluted then stepped back and stood at attention, letting them pass.

The corridor on this level was far more elaborate, the walls incised with beautifully painted figures, again with a martial theme but this time depicting the Emperor in his glory in various poses of dominance over his enemies. Among them, Zhalmo's befuddled senses thought she saw aliens unlike any she'd met before. At the back of her drugged mind, some memory of the slave races of the old Empire stirred, but she couldn't concentrate her thoughts long enough to make sense of them.

She was led into the small room with a desk and more guards, who quickly passed them through into a larger room, empty this time. It was carpeted and lined with chairs. Tables ran down the center, and guards stood along its length and at the exit. When they left there, the vastness of the next room made her head swim. The ceiling seemed to disappear above her in the distance, and she could hear their footsteps echoing off the walls. Past the central fountain they went and into yet another corridor.

At the next doorway, they stopped. Keshti pulled a long chain with a key on it from around his neck and inserted it into the door, opening it. Immediately a large M'zullian, larger than any she'd seen so far and almost naked, stepped out.

"All yours, now, Keshti," said Zerdish, pushing her at him. "Be careful not to lose her!" With another laugh, he gestured to the other two guards, and they left as she was firmly drawn into the room by the giant and the door closed and locked by Keshti on the inside.

"Luzash, take her to Resho and tell her to start trying to undo the damage our Emperor has done. She is to be married to him tomorrow, as his Queen. I need to go sit down and have a sweet drink of hot maush. This is all too much for my nerves, you know," he said, leaning against the wall with one hand. "Oh, and have all those whom the last Emperor slept with removed from the seraglio."

"Removed to where, Master Keshti?" asked Luzash, his voice as deep as he was large.

"To the common Palace harem, of course! Our new Emperor, may his name be praised, won't have them in his seraglio."

"As you command, Master," said the giant, drawing Zhalmo firmly, but surprisingly gently, across the room and out yet another door.

So exhausted she could barely walk by this time, she stumbled against him, and he stopped to swing her up into his arms as if she weighed nothing at all.

"You will be better soon," he said. "Resho will look after you."

Despite herself, she rested her head against his broad chest, letting her eyes fall shut. Moments later it seemed, she was being shaken awake.

"Set her down, Luzash. I'll see to her now," said a female voice.

She staggered as her feet were set onto the floor and clutched at his arm for support. He held her steady for a moment, then withdrew his arm and left the room.

The female in front of her was simply but elegantly dressed in a long flowing robe of pure white. She stared intently at Zhalmo for a moment then began to walk around her. When she stopped in front of her again, she reached out and gently touched a half-healed cut on Zhalmo's cheekbone.

"I heard you were taken in battle," Resho said, "but till now, I didn't believe it."

"Word travels fast," Zhalmo mumbled.

"Indeed it does. We have little to do here but gossip," said Resho dryly.

"I'm a soldier," Zhalmo began, but the other held up a slim hand to stop her.

"No, tell me nothing of yourself yet. Save it for when we can all hear it, all of us who remain, that is." She took her by the arm and, turning her around, unfastened her bonds and threw them aside.

"Come, sit down," she said, leading her over to the sofa against the far wall. "There are two ways you can go from this moment," she said gently, helping Zhalmo sit. "I know you're exhausted, physically and emotionally, and probably heavily drugged from the look of your eyes. Soldier or not, you must be terrified. The easy way is to cooperate with us, because, like it or not, none of us has any option but to obey our new Emperor. If you do, we drones can make your life much easier. Or," she said, sitting down and locking eyes with her, "you can

t us all the way, a battle you cannot win, and earn our anger
well as the Emperor's. So which way will you choose?"

"I want this nightmare to be over!" Zhalmo said, covering
er face with her hands and beginning to weep. "I want to go
home!"

"That cannot happen. All you can do is learn to survive
here. Our new Emperor is . . . exacting in his demands. He may
have been the younger son, but we knew him well before he
left for your world. I can help you meet those demands, if you
let me. First," she said, her voice changing to a more brisk tone,
"let's get you bathed, your cuts and bruises dressed, and some
hot food into you."

"I couldn't eat."

"You will, because you must," said Resho firmly, pulling
Zhalmo's hands away from her face.

K'oish'ik, same day

"It's like trying to find a specific jegget in an infested barn,
Tirak," said the quiet voice of Ghost, the male on the other
end of the U'Churian's comm link. "Granted I can move
about more easily now there are so many Sholans on the
surface . . ."

"That failed attempt was too close for comfort," Tirak
growled, settling himself at his desk.

"Agreed. There was another attempt last night. The assassin
got so close I had to take him out myself. I can't risk discovery
like this. We need to find out who is behind these attacks."

"Agreed. Any ID?"

"Only faked."

"Where's the body?"

"I hid it among the Valtegan dead left for the predators
outside the city walls."

"Should be safe there. Stay alert. You know what you have
to do when you get the opportunity."

"Aye."

There was a quiet tap on his door as Tirak closed the

.connection. He swung away from his desk and the conso
"Enter!"

"Mind if I have a few words with you, Captain?" aske
Kusac, coming in and closing the door behind him.

"By all means," said Tirak, suppressing a flicker of concern
that the Sholan might have become aware of his carefully laid
plans. Thankfully, he still had the mental barrier that the young
Human Kate had put there when they were all on Jalna.

"I've no commitments for another hour or so yet," the
U'Churian added.

"Since you're a member of the Brotherhood, I felt it was
better to come to you with my questions," Kusac said, sitting
on the nearby sofa.

"Questions?" said the U'Churian, puzzled. "I'll help you
any way I can, of course."

"I'm curious about the Cabbarans as a species. How long
have you known Annuur and his sept?"

"More years than I care to remember," said Tirak, wondering where this was leading. "Why?"

"Just curious. I've been rather isolated during the past few
months. Time I got up to speed again on Alliance members
and events. What's their specialty?"

"They're planet-shapers. They heal damaged worlds, work
mentally with the soil if it has been contaminated, and can
turn barren worlds into fertile ones. That's how we met them,
many generations ago. A freak solar flare caused genetic damage to us as a species, as well as to our planet; they came to our
aid. Since then, our peoples have always gotten along well."

"What's the nature of their special navigational skills?"

"They experience jump space differently from us. I can't
exactly explain it, you'll have to ask Annuur, but they can manipulate space and matter as jump points are formed."

"They work closely with the TeLaxaudin, don't they?"

"I believe some do, but not all by any means. The TeLaxaudin have never been to our world, but we've met them through
the Cabbarans on some of our trade stops. Why all the questions about them, Kusac?"

"Curiosity. I'm with Alien Relations on Shola and would,
in normal circumstances, have been fully briefed about them,
but little has been normal in my life lately," he said with a wry
twist of his lips. "Where are Annuur and his sept now?"

"Down in the city, or outside it, rather, with a group of Te-

udin, helping set up some more permanent adobe build-
s for the Ch'almuthians."

Kusac rose to his feet. "I think I'll go watch them for a bit.
Thanks for the information."

"Wait, I'll come with you," said Tirak, finding a sudden
need to accompany him.

"I'll see you down there," said Kusac. "Something I need to
do on the way." With that, he was gone.

Muttering under his breath, Tirak hurried to the door and
yanked it open, but there was no sign of the Sholan in the
corridor. Slamming the door behind him, he took off for the
nearest elevator, just missing it, and Kusac.

As Kusac rode the elevator down to the ground, he felt
sure he'd finally found a clue to his newfound abilities. So the
Cabbarans could manipulate matter, and one of them, a very
important one, Annuur, had been involved in his cure. Were
these changes an accident . . . or by design? Since he'd left
Shola, he'd ceased to believe in coincidences, but if these abilities were by design, what was their purpose? Where was he
being led, and why? He had to see the Cabbarans working and
find out more.

As usual, the central courtyard was busy with an eclectic
mix of workmen still shifting rubble, stone carvers on scaffolds
repairing the damaged facades, and government workers taking their midday meal break at one of the open restaurants
and bars opposite the Palace.

Ducking through the crowds, Kusac loped for the main exit
then headed for the southern sally port that led out to where
the new prefabricated village was being erected. He checked
his wrist unit—still half an hour before he was due to meet up
with Kaid at the shuttle garage.

The scene was one of organized chaos. Dust from the flocks
of shaggy horned animals hung in the air as, lowing loudly,
they were driven down toward the grazing by the nearby river.
The clanging of their bells formed a low descant to the high,
shrill voices of the Ch'almuthian children that were running
everywhere, getting under everyone's feet.

The center of the village was an oasis of relative calm by
comparison, despite the constant coming and going of people
and belongings. It didn't take him long to find Annuur and his

sept, or the TeLaxaudin. They were on the outskirts of the lage, surrounded by a group of almost silent, awed observr Excusing himself, he eased his way to the front of the crowc

In front of a large puddle of claylike mud sat Naacha an Annuur, with Lweeu and Sokarr just behind them. On either side stood two of the bronze-limbed spindly TeLaxaudin. As he watched, the surface of the puddle began to shiver, causing slow ripples to spread outward from the center. As they reached the outer edges, they grew deeper, forming waves that rose higher and then began to coalesce into the beginnings of walls. Each successive ripple added to the height of the outer walls, which gradually rose higher and higher until at a height of about six inches, they stopped.

"More water," said Annuur, rubbing his hoofed hand across his long, mobile snout. "Four buckets' worth."

Adults stepped forward to empty their leather buckets into the drying mud.

One of the TeLaxaudin, dressed in flowing draperies of deep purples and blues, looked around at Kusac and immediately turned to Annuur and began humming.

Annuur made a short, chopping gesture with his hand, and the TeLaxaudin fell silent.

So there was a hierarchy among them, and as on his estate on Shola, the Cabbarans seemed to be the senior partners.

More ripples in the refreshed puddle drew his attention, and he watched as the circle began to divide into sections that would form four interior walls.

It was obvious to him that the four Cabbarans were controlling the mud with the power of their minds, but did they operate on the same wavelengths as telepaths? He thought only Naacha was a telepath. Were the others just less Talented? Was their ability the same as his? He had to know.

Lowering his mental shields, he began filtering out the other minds around him, trying to passively absorb what Annuur, Naacha, Sokarr, and Lweeu were doing. He could sense them working, but not the details, and he needed those. Cautiously, he began to probe, searching for their wavelength. Suddenly contact flared in his mind. Naacha snarled and mentally flung him out of their Link, but not before he'd sensed something more. The Cabbarans' Link to the TeLaxaudin wasn't fully mental; it was enhanced somehow, perhaps by an artificial network, because he sensed many more minds than those physically present. A cold shiver ran down his spine. He'd felt that same network before, on Kij'ik, on his way to confront Kezule.

Light and pain exploded in his mind, the force of it making him stagger and fall to his knees. Panic filled his mind—no, not his, theirs—then another wave of mental pain hit him, and he felt himself toppling as the ground rose up to hit him.

The nomadic market in the town wasn't exactly nomadic because many of the traders lived and worked there permanently from their tented enclosures. The true nomads arrived in the spring and stayed through the summer before returning to winter in the mountains.

Like many wandering people, they had several fortifying beverages, one of which served thick and hot, was similar to Terran coffee. It was to indulge in this that Kaid had brought Carrie to the tent of the most popular seller.

He waited until the surprisingly dainty drinking bowls had been set before them, then the shokka pot on a tray with a dish of honey and a small, steaming jug.

"Boiled water, as requested," the cafe owner said, making a sweeping gesture and bowing as he backed away from the ornate low table at which they sat. "Should the exalted ones wish anything more, just call me."

Kaid nodded and pulled a coin out of a pocket, which he flicked into the air. The nomad's hand shot out and caught it in midspin.

"Good reflexes," Kaid murmured, picking up the shokka pot and pouring for them both. "I would bet they probably retain something of the Warrior genes."

"Could be," she agreed, reaching for the hot water and pouring some into the syrupy liquid. "Those who live in extreme conditions are usually pretty warlike. They need to be tough to survive."

Kaid lounged back among the large cushions, sipping his drink as he watched Carrie absentmindedly continue stirring in her spoonful of honey.

"You weren't this reluctant to read me the riot act when I was at Stronghold," he said at last.

"Excuse me?" Carrie stopped stirring to glance across at him.

"After you rescued me from Ghezu."

"That was different," she said.

"Was it?"

She looked away, laying the spoon down carefully as she pretended to watch the passersby outside the shade of the Bedouin-style tent. "You stayed away from us because you feared your visions and were afraid they'd lead you to harm one of us."

"So you honestly believe he loves Zayshul?" he asked abruptly.

Startled, she looked back at him. "I don't know. He said there was a scent marker ..."

"He's lying. There may have been once, but not now. Neither of us has seen him with her. If he's not questioning the prisoners, he's with Kezule."

"That means nothing. They could be spending the nights together."

He leaned forward, keeping his voice low, despite the fact they were alone. "I've seen the way he looks at you, Carrie, when he thinks neither of us is watching him. He's no more in love with her than I am, nor she with him."

"Why would he lie about it?" Her attention was fully on him now.

"Why, indeed."

"You think he's protecting us—as you thought you were by staying at Stronghold?"

"I believe he thinks he is."

"Why would he think that? There's no threat to us here, is there? That attempt on his life was a one-off incident, you told me."

"As far as I know, it was. More importantly, are you just going to keep accepting what he says and do nothing? You were the only one who believed in his innocence, and you pushed until you got us out here. So, what do you intend to do about it now?"

"He's gotten as good as you were at avoiding me, Kaid, even when we're in the same room."

Kaid had the grace to wince slightly at her words. "You've been doing the same," he countered.

"That's unfair. I made the first overtures to him, and he pushed me away. He took the crystal of the twins and Kashini, but I know he hasn't looked at it."

"You can't keep count of who did what first in a relationship, Carrie."

"What relationship?" she demanded, picking up her bowl and taking a drink from it. "We no longer have one—he made that abundantly clear!"

"None of it makes any sense, though. Kezule's too complacent about the whole matter. The person we brought forward in time would have been consumed by rage had he thought Kusac was even looking at his female, never mind his wife."

"We've all changed a lot since those days," she said tiredly, taking another sip of her drink.

They both felt it at the same moment. Kusac's mind, closed to them both for so long, was suddenly wide open to them. There was a sense of overpowering exaltation, that just as suddenly turned into a snarl of anger and denial before, just as abruptly, it was cut off.

Kaid was on his feet before Carrie had dropped her cup.

The new town, outside the city wall, Kaid sent as they left the tent and began running toward the street leading to the southern exit. *Who's closest?*

Rezac. He's on his way.

There was no sense of physical injury, he sent reassuringly as they pushed their way through the market crowds.

I know, but he's unconscious. Did you . . .

Sense someone . . . something else? Not Sholan?

Alien, she sent, changing their mental frequency to a tighter, private one as they ran toward the southern city exit.

They'd reached the gate by the time Rezac reached Kusac.

He's unhurt, but unconscious, he confirmed.

Keep contact tight. There could be eavesdroppers, sent Carrie.

Aye, he replied. *He was watching Annuur and the TeLaxaudin build adobe houses. Annuur says he touched them while they were working and got hit by a backlash.*

And pigs can fly, retorted Carrie angrily. *He'd hardly forget one of his first lessons as a Telepath!*

He touched Unity! sent Ayziss. *How could he do that?*

Annuur was furious with the TeLaxaudin. *No need to attack him like that! You draw attention to us we do not need! Next time I say too dangerous to come here, you listen! Leave now, before his mates arrive. Unity I shut down now till later tonight!*

No danger, we erase his memory of this, replied Ayziss complacently.

Cannot! His mind is closed to us, Annuur snapped back. *You forget who is in charge here! Leave now! Too many questions his mates be asking! I close Unity now!*

Emitting scents of annoyance, the two TeLaxaudin and their Prime guard stalked back to their flitter.

The red glow in front of Kusac's eyes grew more intense, and he could feel the heat washing over him. The air was acrid with the mingled smells of the fire, red-hot metal, and heated oil. Bellows wheezed, and a fresh wave of heat lapped over him.

"Kaid has been here many times," a deep voice said from beside him.

"Vartra," he mumbled.

"This is Vartra's forge, but I'm not he. Unfortunately, the Smith has been . . ." There was the smallest of hesitations, ". . . detained against his will."

Then who? Kusac opened his eyes and spun around. Before him stood a Sholan as dark-pelted as himself, dressed in unrelieved black.

"It's time for us to finish the job he began."

Kusac's gaze followed him as the male reached for the sword lying on the anvil.

"Many years have been spent forging this, but now it's nearly complete."

Light caught the blade, gleaming off it despite its unfinished state.

"It'll be a fine weapon," Kusac said, unable to tear his eyes from it as it was thrust into the heart of the forge. He watched the crystalline structure of the metal alter as it slowly began to glow.

Not all weapons are made of steel or wood, a gentle female voice said in his mind. *The best ones are made of flesh.*

"Flesh that has been tempered, like steel, in the fires," agreed the male.

Look into the forge.

"I don't want to see," he whispered, unable to look away or close his eyes as icy fingers seemed to creep up his spine.

Images began to form within the heart of the fire as the heat danced on the blade, making it glow brighter and brighter. Helpless, he watched as he struggled, injured, across snowy plains to Carrie's village. Then he felt himself reach mentally for her to stop her following her twin into death. The images of defining moments in his, Carrie's, and Kaid's lives, moments that had changed him forever, flashed by as fast as the flickering of the forge's flames.

The Sword of Justice has always been the wielder, not the blade, Ghyakulla sent as, overwhelmed, he sank to his knees.

"You're stronger than we are now," said L'Shoh, grasping the blade and pulling it from the forge. "Faster, with abilities which give you great power. Justice must be tempered with compassion. It must not be blind lest it become that which it was created to fight."

The Entity picked up a hammer. "This sword has been forged only a handful of times. You face the M'zullians and must decide their fate. The destiny of many worlds rests in your hands."

Kusac cried out in pain, falling to the ground again as the hammer hit the blade, sending a shower of sparks to briefly light the darkest recesses of the foundry.

Again and again the hammer fell, each blow feeling as if it was pounding his flesh, not the steel of the sword. Finally it stopped, and L'Shoh stepped back from the anvil. Through tears of pain, Kusac watched the golden-furred female step into his line of sight to pick up the blade.

Green tunic swirling, she thrust the still-glowing metal into the oil bath. Acrid fumes filled the air as it hissed and sizzled. For him, there was only the sense of blessed coolness sweeping through his body.

Returning the blade to the anvil, she turned to look at him, holding out her hand.

Eyes as green as the grass on Shola considered him carefully as he accepted her help to get to his feet.

Talk to Conner, he can finish the Making. He has the memories of the last Cleadh Mor, the Great Sword of Justice. He can teach you of the dangers ahead.

As she sent to him, her eyes grew larger, filling his vision, their green taking on the shape and form of endless forests of trees.

With a cry, he jerked up into a sitting position, staring frantically around. "The forests," he muttered, reaching up to rub his pounding head.

"Take this." Annuur thrust a mug into his field of view.

He reached for it but Rezac's arm blocked him.

"Is safe, only analgesic he had on Shola," said Annuur hurriedly. "He touched us when working. Got backlash."

Kusac reached past Rezac for the mug, taking it and, on an almost subconscious level, analyzing the liquid as he drank it. There was another compound there—one designed to make him suggestible. No sooner did he notice it than he realized he was automatically neutralizing it.

"Are you all right?" demanded Carrie, crouching down beside him.

"I'm sorry, there was nothing I could do," said Tirak.

"Forgets lessons," said Naacha disdainfully before taking the empty mug from him in his mouth and trotting off to return it to their work area. "Never touch workers!"

Wisps of the vision he had had were teasing his memory, mingling with Naacha's mental suggestions to relax, that nothing unusual had happened. He thrust them aside to his subconscious to deal with later. Now was not the time or place to face down Annuur.

"I'm fine," he said to Carrie, accepting Kaid's outstretched hand to help him rise. "It wasn't a backlash, just an overload. There was nothing you could have done, Tirak," he said to the U'Churian Captain still hovering beside them. "I'm fine, really."

He staggered slightly before regaining his balance. Already the pain in his head was receding. Whatever else, Annuur's potions were good analgesics.

"We can cancel the trip out to the oasis if you're not up to it," said Carrie.

"I'm fine," he repeated. "I'd like to see what Conner and his acolytes have been up to."

"You're in good hands, obviously," said Tirak. "I'd best be getting back to the Palace."

Kusac waved vaguely in the U'Churian's direction as he left.

"There's also their holy hot spring," said Kaid, "though we'll catch it on the way back."

Kusac nodded, following Kaid and Carrie as they led the way west toward the landing area outside the main gates.

"We could all do with the break," said Kaid once they'd left the protovillage behind. "Plus we can do a census of the larger critters that are out there. Good practice using our telepathic skills."

"It wasn't a backlash," said Kusac. "At least, not the usual kind."

"What was it then?" asked Carrie. "Are you sure you're all right?"

"Yes, Annuur's potion got rid of my headache. Actually, it felt as if one of them mentally lashed out at me."

"Annuur?" asked Kaid.

"Not the Cabbarans. I'll need to check it out later."

"I'll get to Rezac to keep an ear open."

"No," said Kusac, stopping to look at them. "Leave it to me. It's only to do with their building, and I have the most experience of the Cabbarans and the TeLaxaudin."

Kaid shrugged. "As you wish."

They reached the landing pad a few minutes later. A shuttle, one of the smaller ones, was powered up and waiting for them. One of Kezule's commandos met them at the entrance, giving Kusac a crisp salute before turning to Kaid.

"All is ready, sir," he said, descending from the craft.

Kaid nodded and climbed up the short ramp into the shuttle. Kusac followed Carrie, glancing to the rear as he took his seat.

"Lot of gear," he observed, buckling in.

"We're setting up a cache inland along the river for future use," Kaid replied, starting up the engines.

Now that he had the chance, he retreated into his own mind, trying to remember his vision, but the details were blurred. He remembered Vartra's forge, a dark, somber male, and a female with forests—endless forests—in her eyes.

He probed the memory, looking for more, finding mention of Conner and a sword.

"We're dropping supplies off for Conner," said Kaid, breaking in on his reverie almost as if he'd been following his thoughts. "Annuur and his sept have promised to come out and encourage the growth of dune grasses and shrubs to anchor the sand and to help build up the moisture content at the edges of this river."

Looking out the porthole, he saw they were flying above a wide, winding river that led deep into the interior. Its dun-colored waters moved swiftly in the opposite direction from the one they were taking, forming small islets here and there. Along the edges was scrubby groundcover of all types.

"Doesn't look that clean."

"It's the inundation," said Carrie. "Runoff from the distant mountains. It'll settle down in a week or two."

Kusac grunted.

"What's Banner up to today?" asked Carrie after several minutes of silence.

"Probably messing with chair legs in the Council chamber or Kezule's office or catching river leapers to let loose in his bedroom," said Kusac.

Carrie stifled a giggle. "That was him? The cubs got blamed for it. Kezule will go berserk when he finds out."

"It's his way of getting revenge—and making Kezule look foolish if he pulls him up for it," said Kaid. "You should stop him before Kezule retaliates, though, Kusac."

"On the contrary, I find it quite amusing. I'm curious to see how far the two of them will let it go."

"There's Conner's group!" said Carrie, pointing ahead of them to a small, lush green area flanking the river. "From the looks of it, they aren't going to need Annuur's skills."

"It looks like Ghyakulla is indeed with them," said Kaid soberly as he began to descend.

"Her eyes are forests," Kusac murmured quietly.

"What?" asked Kaid.

"Nothing."

Back at the Palace, Banner was hanging around the medical staff mess, waiting for one of the Prime technicians he had befriended.

"Sheezar, I've been waiting for you," he said, walking up to her and linking an arm through hers. "Lunch break?"

"No, shift end," she said, mouth widening in a welcoming smile. "I'm on night shift at the moment."

"Then let me treat you to a decent meal in the Grand Courtyard," he said, leading her to the exit.

"Thank you. I'd enjoy that."

"How's the research going?"

"Progressing slowly. We can now ensure the Warrior characteristics can be passed on to any zygote, but that doesn't mean they have the Warrior spirit."

"It's a start, at least," he said as they made their way to

the elevator down to the ground level. "What about your own project, enhancing the adult Primes so they are stronger and faster?"

"That's not as important as ensuring the next generation, Banner."

"If K'hedduk attacks, you'll need every able-bodied person to defend yourselves."

"You're preaching to the converted," she said as they stopped to call the elevator. "I believe as you do, and I have been continuing my own research when I can. My last computer model was the closest yet. I plan to refine it tonight."

"When will it be ready for trials?"

"A good few weeks yet," she said. "I need to test it on animals first."

"If I can help in any way . . . I don't have the medical knowledge, but I can be an extra pair of hands, and I can keep you fed," he said with a grin, waving her into the elevator ahead of him.

She chuckled. "I'll certainly let you know when I reach that stage."

They dropped off the box of seedlings and fertilizer as well as a few cages for Conner, complimenting him and his crew on their work so far.

"Armed guards?" asked Kusac, eyeing the three soldiers keeping watch.

"There're large carnivores other than your norrta," said the Human mildly. "And though we do Her work, the Goddess helps those who help themselves."

"We found some more furred animals," said one of his young female acolytes. "We caught several samples and put them in the cages."

"Indeed, this world is recovering very nicely from its disaster," said Conner. "In the past, the killing of many of the larger lizards and amphibians for food left room for mammals to develop. Nothing bigger than a small dog as yet though, apart from the modified herd beasts that existed then. And we've seen a few of what I am sure are feathered birds."

"Interesting to see how it all evolves," said Kaid, examining an ugly ratlike creature with a bald tail in one of the cages. "Well, we'll have to be off," he said, straightening up. "We have a ways to go to set up this new cache."

"Thank you again for bringing the extra supplies," said Conner, accompanying them back to their craft. "We'll be staying here till tomorrow. The tent and heaters will be most useful."

"Our pleasure," said Carrie, following Kaid into the shuttle.

Kusac hung back a little, waiting till the other two had gone inside.

"Conner, what do you remember about a magic weapon, a sword that was a man?" he asked quietly.

Startled, Conner stared at him, then blinked in confusion. "There have been several. Why do you ask?"

"Ghyakulla told me to."

"I . . . There were two, but only one concerns us, the Cleadh Mor, the Great Sword. I told you about Arthur and the sword called Caliburn, meaning Hard Lightning. His teacher was Llew, the Merlin of those times."

"How can a person be a sword?"

"What are you and your Brothers and Sisters but trained weapons?"

"That I understand," he said with a touch of impatience. "But a sword?"

"The sword is a symbol of might and power and also of eternity. Is it is not the shape of a cross, with the pommel creating the loop of eternal life?" asked Conner, sketching the shape in the air.

"Yes, but . . ."

"How does it become a person? Arthur's sword came from the Goddess, and though it had a physical presence, its power was far more spiritual. Like all men, Llew and myself included, Arthur was all too Human. He forgot that justice cannot be blind and must not be cruel."

"What did he do wrong?"

"His weakness was his strength, sadly. He could not see the evil in men, and particularly in women. He saw only goodness and frailty. This is a lesson you should be aware of too."

Kusac grunted and turned away. "I can't see its relevance to me."

Conner caught him by the arm. "We'll talk more about it tomorrow, Kusac. If She sent you a message, then it's important. Have you managed to get Kezule to heed my warning of an attack yet?"

"I've spoken to him, but we have several thousand people to house and feed, and Ch'almuth to protect. We're spread too thin, Conner."

"Then the city and the Palace will be destroyed."

"The force field is being strengthened and expanded. We're doing what we can."

The shuttle's engines began to power up, and Kusac turned to the ramp.

Again Conner reached out to stop him. "Kusac, come to me when you get back. If Ghyakulla has a purpose for you, there are things I need to teach you, and time is running out."

He opened his mouth to give an excuse, but then he remembered L'Shoh's last words.

You are the Sword of Justice. You alone will decide the fate of the M'zullians and sweep corruption from the highest courts in this galaxy.

"I'll come," he said.

They continued to follow the river inland, flying deeper into the interior, stopping at the entrance to a gorge where the river churned and surged against outcrops of jagged rocks that stretched across its width.

Setting down not far from the cliffs, Kaid cut the engines.

"There's a cave about a hundred yards away," he said. "We're using it to store the cache."

Carrie released her harness and went to the rear of the craft. "What's in the crates? Seeds and such?"

"No, more basic kit. Food supplies, several tents, tools. This will be a base camp. There are a couple of our antigravity cradles to snap around the crates so we can unload them easily," said Kaid.

"Dusk isn't far off," said Kusac, rising. "Let's get on with it so we can get back to the city."

"Agreed," said Kaid, making his own way to the rear and picking up a smaller crate. "I'll get the lighting and security field fixed up inside the cave. You two can unload."

They worked solidly for two hours while Kaid, the lighting rig hung on the walls just inside the entrance, began setting up the force field to seal the entrance once they left.

When Carrie collapsed on one of the crates stacked at the back of the cave, taking a long drink from her water canteen,

Kusac fetched the last crate. As he maneuvered it through the entrance, they both heard the shuttle's engines start up.

"What the hell?" muttered Kusac, leaving the crate bobbing in midair and sprinting into the open, closely followed by Carrie. He could now sense Kaid's determination to leave them there while he returned to the City.

The last rays of the setting sun glinted off the shuttle as it began to rise into the air and head downriver.

Kusac's wrist comm began to beep, and angrily he answered it.

"What the hell are you doing, Kaid?" he demanded.

"Forcing you to reclaim what's yours," said Kaid. "You might fool each other, but not me. You're both going to extreme lengths to avoid each other, now you have no choice. You're at least two to three day's walk from the city, and tomorrow's our Link day."

"You have no right to do this," said Kusac, cold fury in his voice. "I'll call the Palace ..."

"I have every right," interrupted Kaid, "and you can only reach me. I reset the comms remotely with Valden's help."

"Kaid ..."

"You need your life back, Kusac, and so do I. T'chebbi needs me more than you two right now. I'm pretty sure you can reforge your Leska Link to Carrie. Everything you'll need is in the crates—water purifier, backpacks, ammo, food."

"You bastard," growled Kusac with feeling.

Kaid laughed briefly. "I'll see you in two days." The comm unit went dead.

Carrie turned and walked back into the cave. After a few minutes of silent anger, Kusac followed.

They'd unloaded some two-dozen crates, and Carrie had the lids off half a dozen already. Beside her lay a traveling stove, a couple of gallon jugs of fresh drinking water, and several smaller boxes of food.

"I'll start a meal," she said, keeping her eyes on what she was doing. "See if you can find any bedding." She gave a convulsive shiver and looked up at him finally. "And activate the screen, please. It's freezing in here now the sun's gone down."

Too wrapped up in his own thoughts, and locked behind his mental shields, till now he'd missed the warning signs that Carrie's Link day was beginning. Now that his attention had been drawn to it, he could no longer ignore it.

He squatted down to look through the box of military ...als.

"Jegget food," he mustered in disgust, turning the self-eating meals over to check them all out. "I'll go catch us something worth eating."

"Kusac . . ."

"I need to vent my anger," he said harshly, getting to his feet. "I can't stay here right now." He stalked toward the cave mouth, tail flicking angrily, stopping only long enough to turn on the field and key himself into it.

"I'll be back, you have my word." Then he was gone.

"Men!" snarled Carrie, mentally and verbally, picking up the nearest object and lobbing it after his retreating figure. "It's all about *you—your* honor, *your* sensibilities!"

The screen flared blue, sending the lightweight metal cup bouncing back into the cave. "I'm not a bloody pet or a toy to be passed from one to the other of you, dammit!" If either of them heard her, they both prudently remained silent.

The food may have been regular military rations, but Kaid had packed a few luxuries—like coffee, lightweight but warm sleeping bags, protein drinks, clean clothing, antibacterial washing gel, and a safety tent complete with field electronics.

Actually, she was glad Kusac had left her alone as it gave her time to try to sort out her own feelings as she dug a fire pit near the entrance and began stacking armfuls of dried vegetation and shrubs that had been blown or washed into the rear of the cave by abnormally high inundations.

She went outside briefly to gather several large flat stones from the edge of the river, loading them in an empty crate fitted with a lifting cradle so she needed only one trip to get them back to the cave to line the fire pit. Putting a fuel block in the center, she began adding the kindling and lit it with her lighter.

That done, she set a jug of coffee to brew then arranged the sleeping bags on opposite sides of the fire. When the coffee was ready, she poured herself a generous mug. The necessities seen to, she could no longer avoid thinking about him—and them.

Kusac was her first love. He'd held his hand out across a campfire, not very different from this one, and offered her a life among the stars. The life of the Warrior, she had to admit,

but it was the one she had wanted. True, it had been one
danger and hardship, but it was a life as an equal. They h.
shared so much history together in such a short time—was
only three years? He had brought her to an alien world anc
a new family; they'd had children together and made more
friends than she could count. And then there was Kaid, their
Third. She loved Kaid too, but despite the heartbreak and
anger Kusac had caused her, he was her soul mate, and they
shared something that was still unique.

A faint sound from outside made her start, but with her
already heightened senses, she knew it was Kusac.

The force field shimmered as he stepped through, carrying
three bundles the size of small dogs, wrapped in damp moss.

"Coffee?" he asked, sniffing, as he put the parcels down by
the fire. Picking up the stick she'd left there, he began to rake
aside the burning ashes until the stones were visible.

"Some in the pot for you," she said, eyeing the bundles as
he placed them in the pit and covered them with the glowing
embers. She reached out to put more fuel on.

Kusac picked up the dented mug, raising an eye ridge at her
as he filled it from the jug and added sweetener and artificial
creamer. "Someone had a temper tantrum."

"Yes, you did. Some of us can't run and hunt off our anger,"
she retorted, taking another mouthful from her mug.

He sat down on the other side of the fire from her and took
a long drink of the coffee. "Strong," he remarked.

"Those critters are gonna take three to four hours to cook,"
she observed. "I want to eat now. The military meals aren't
that bad."

"Get a couple then, and I'll join you."

"You get them. I fixed the cave and the fire."

As he passed her, she reached for the coffeepot, tilting dangerously close to the glowing fire pit.

"Easy," he said, grabbing her. "I think you've had enough
coffee. You're drunk."

"Nope. I'm pissed at you, Kusac," she said, shaking free
of his grasp and shuddering as his contact wakened her fully.
"You walk out of my life for nearly a year, and when we do
meet, you avoid me and tell me nothing of what happened.
You've not even asked about your new son, Dyshac. You owe
me one hell of an apology!"

e squatted down beside her. "Carrie, I had to go. You
e no idea what it cost me to leave you."

"I know what it cost me fighting to prove you innocent of
e treason charges!" Swaying, she reached out for the coffee-
ot again, but Kusac grabbed it and filled up her mug.

"Had I remained on Shola another hour, we could have
Linked again," he said quietly. "I waited as long as I could, suppressing the pull of our possible Link, until the cub was born.
I needed to know you were both safe, then I had to leave." He
reached out with his thumb to gently wipe away the tears on
her cheeks that she didn't know she was shedding.

"I'm more sorry than you can imagine. My place was with
you, but Shola needed me to leave."

"What about the last three weeks?" she demanded as he
took the mug from her unresisting hand and took a drink
himself.

"There is something here, something sinister, that every
now and then tries to control me. It was on Kij'ik too. Somehow they managed to keep making me forget about it. I was
afraid for you. I had to keep my distance and to pretend that
Zayshul and I were lovers."

"Pretend be damned. You were!" She snatched her mug
back, taking another swig.

"Not by choice. I'm not sure who engineered that scent
marker, but it wasn't Zayshul. She was as much a victim as I
was."

"Well, don't think I'm here for your taking, Kusac! No Link
will force me to pair with you! When I've had enough of this
coffee, I'll pass out and you'll be on your own, just as you like
it!"

"It won't work like that," he said, reaching out again to
wipe the tears off her cheeks. Her could sense her so strongly
now, it was as if time had rolled back for them to the days
when they had been Leska mind-mates. "You know it won't.
Can't you feel your body quickening as it calls out for me?"

"Not for you. For Kaid," she said harshly, pulling away and
draining the mug. "You're there, but only as a Third, not as my
Leska."

"Are you sure? You're right, you aren't a pet to be passed
between Kaid and me, but you never were. You always came
freely to us both."

"I'm not drawn to you any more!"

"My shields are up. If I lower them, I can reforge our Le. Link. Do you want that, Carrie?" he asked softly, leani. closer to her. Gently, he had to go very gently with her becaus she was understandably as angry as hell with him.

She blinked owlishly up at him, finding she couldn't look away from his amber eyes. They seemed to fill her field of vision until she could see nothing but him, and it felt as though he was looking deep into her soul.

"Oh, Gods, don't do that to me, Kusac!" she whispered. "You know how impossible that is for me to resist."

"Carrie, you have to decide. Do you want to choose me now while you still can, or wait until you lose control and pair with me anyway?"

"I want to knock some sense into you! You know damned well pairing would change nothing! I will still be Kaid's Leska."

"No," he said, moving back a little and reaching out to catch a lock of her hair and twine it around his fingers. "I can change that. You would be my Leska again."

"I don't believe you." But there was doubt in her voice now. "What about this threat that you mentioned? I thought you wanted to keep us out of it."

"I do, but perhaps the more of us that are involved, the more difficult it will be to influence us because we'll all notice. I believe they've been manipulating me into staying away from you." He raised the handful of hair to his nose and inhaled her scent. "I missed you so much that I had to lock my memories and thoughts of you all deep in my subconscious," he said settling down beside her. "It was the only way I could survive on Kij'ik."

"I fought to prove you innocent, to find the message I knew you had put on that crystal you left me. No one believed me! It was only luck Jurrel saw it. And you hurt Kaid very deeply. I know why, but you have no idea of the pain you caused him."

"I had to make sure he wouldn't try to follow me," he said, allowing his shields to drop farther. Immediately, where his fingers touched her shoulder, he felt the almost forgotten surge of electricity pass between them. It was faint as yet, not as strong as when she'd still been his Leska.

"I thought I'd never feel this again," he said, the longing for her stark in his voice and on his face.

"I don't know who you are anymore, Kusac," she said, sluring her words slightly as she pushed him away. "You tried to kill yourself rather than live without your Talent." All her pent-up anger was coming tumbling out, and she hadn't intended it to. "You didn't care how Kashini and I felt, or Kaid, or your family! Then when Kizzy and Annuur cured you, you lied about that, and rather than take your full place with us again, you lied and ran away to Stronghold! You don't face up to the trials in your life, you hide from them like a spoiled child!"

"I admit I acted badly in the past, but it wasn't as simple as you make out. I only ever tried to do what I thought was right for you. I stood up to my worst enemy to rescue not only our son Shaidan but the other cubs as well. I have changed, Carrie."

"I'll believe it when I see it! Right now, you're angry at being forced into a Link with me—if you can reestablish it! What I do or don't want hasn't occurred to you. I might not want you back!"

"I didn't want it to be like this."

"Then how? Life doesn't wait for the right moment, you know. It's untidy and inconvenient. I don't want to wait for a youngling to decide it's the right time, I want an adult male who knows his own mind." She stopped, running out of steam, but it felt good to finally get that off her chest.

Her vision was getting blurred, and she blinked a few times in an effort to clear it. Exhaustion was wrapping her in a warm, fuzzy blanket.

"I need to sleep," she mumbled, lying down. "Wake me when the food's ready."

Kusac watched her suddenly go limp as sleep claimed her. He sighed and got up to go back around to where she'd put his sleeping bag. Picking it up, he dragged it beside hers and went searching for some of the Prime herbal tea.

The trouble was, she was right—not completely, but enough to make facing the truth damned uncomfortable. If he wanted his wife back, he was going to have to win her back within the next few hours.

When the water had boiled, he rinsed his mug out then spooned some of the instant maush into it. The scent was instantly refreshing, and while he waited for it to cool, he reached into an inner pocket for the message crystal Carrie had given him on the weather station three weeks before.

He turned it over in his hand. He'd never dared to look at it for fear that it would weaken his resolve to keep his distance from his family, that it would break down the painfully constructed barrier of indifference that he'd built between them.

Was it weakness to cut himself off from all he loved lest it hurt him more than he could bear, or was it strength? There was no easy answer; he knew because he'd searched for one during many a long, lonely night.

He had his life back now, with that pardon, and he'd not even considered what he'd do when this war was over, assuming they all survived it.

The crystal was warm in his hands now as he reached for his mug and sipped the herbal brew. Before Carrie, he'd been alone. When she came into his life, so had many painful consequences—and many more good ones, including new friends he now trusted with his life. Alone, he'd been vulnerable. With his Leska had come strength, the strength to travel to the past for the right to start his own Clan, to become the sword-brother of Kaid, their Third. Yet he'd turned his back on all this, tried to retreat into death and turned away friends and allies because he believed he was weakened by them, that he was stronger alone.

Kaid had been alone for ten years, by necessity, not choice. His sword-brother knew the value of bonds of friendship, the Brotherhood, and family, especially once he accepted he'd found his.

Finally, he realized he was playing into the hands of those trying to manipulate him by isolating himself as he had. His family strengthened, not weakened him, and they could protect each other more easily than he could protect them all alone.

He opened a small recess in the strap of his wrist comm and inserted the crystal, turning it to watch the images on the small screen. Kashini had grown so much and was so like Carrie now. And the twins—Layeesha was Kaid writ small—so like the child he'd been in the far past when they'd walked the Fire Margins. As for Dhaykin, he was smaller, looked fragile, yet his strength of mind reached out from the small screen, as he seemed to stare directly at his father.

As he watched, he heard Carrie stir behind him. Her hand stroked his ears briefly, making them lie down against his skull as a shiver of pleasure ran through him.

"Dhaykin isn't as fragile as he looks," she said quietly. "At first he was, being born a few weeks premature, but his will to live and thrive is great."

"You were right. I thought I was being strong when all I was doing was making myself more vulnerable and hurting those I love," he whispered.

"I can see you did what you thought was right at the time," she said, leaning against his back and resting her chin on his shoulder. "There is no clear-cut right or wrong in life, Kusac, no black or white."

"Only shades of gray." The cube finished playing, and he removed it from its niche and stowed it safely in his pocket again.

"At least you know where you went wrong. I love you, Kusac, whether or not you have your Talent. You, the man," she said, using the English word, "I love with all my heart. You're half my soul."

He could feel the warmth of her body pressing against his through their tunics. Her fingers pushed the braided hair on his neck aside, reaching for the skin beneath. But it was the hot touch of her lips and the flick of her tongue there that undid him.

Turning, he pulled her into his arms, his mouth covering hers in a deep kiss. Her tongue met his with equal intensity. Electricity leaped between them, setting their senses on fire, but it lacked the full contact of their Leska Link.

Kusac pushed her back, breathing hard, his eyes pools of black surrounded by a narrow amber ring. A full restoration of their Link was there, his for the taking because of his enhanced abilities.

"Carrie, you know I want you, but I want you as my Leska. If we make love, I'll not be able to stop myself."

She reached out for his ear, pulling his face closer, her lips feather-soft on his until her teeth closed briefly on his lower lip. "Sometimes, you talk too much," she said, releasing him, then pushing him over onto his back and sitting astride him to attack his weapons' belt.

"Trousers," he muttered, trying to reach past her hands to undo them. "You should wear Sholan tunics with nothing under them, like our females."

"And have all you horny males after me? I think not," she said, running her hand down the seal of his **tunic**.

Pushing himself up, he flipped her over onto her back and began to remove the offending garments.

"With Kaid and me as your husbands?" he mock-growled. "No one would be that brave—or foolish!"

Kneeling between her legs, he leaned forward to touch her face, lowering his mental shields completely as he did. Her mind touched his, and as he drew his fingers down her cheek to her jaw, he felt the magic begin to flow from her to him.

He sucked in a breath of pleasure as she touched his thigh, her fingers tracing patterns of fire there until she touched the still tender scar tissue and he flinched slightly.

Gods, Kusac, that was a horrific wound, she sent as she gently traced its outline on both sides of his thigh.

"I survived it," he said gruffly, pulling her hand away from there to lie against his hip.

Light-headed at the emotions and sensations running through him, he put his weight on his forearms and caught hold of her face, licking and nipping at her cheeks and ears, feeling the heat begin in her belly and spread outward to ignite him.

I never thought to feel this again, he sent, kissing her frantically, tasting her by pressing her tongue to the roof of his mouth.

I love Kaid, but Gods, Kusac, my heart has ached to share this with you again!

Her hands played over his body, sending thrills of the electricity through him.

It will be different this time, he sent, remembering their last time together. *I've been altered. There's no danger I could hurt you now.*

She pulled him down on top of her, grasping his bare flesh with her hand. *Do it. If need be, Kaid can help.*

He sensed Kaid then, at the edges of their minds, Leska Linked to Carrie, yet physically with T'Chebbi.

"Do you trust me?" he asked her, voice roughened by his need.

"With my life."

He thrust forward, letting her guide him as he took her throat in his jaws. As her warmth closed tightly about him, and she began to moan with pleasure, he visualized the Link joining her to Kaid and took hold of it.

There was a flash of pain for them both and an echo of

from Kaid. Time slowed for him as the nature of their
˞k began to unfold in his mind's eye. Hesitating for only a
˞oment, he chose not to sever it but to alter it, creating new
˞onnections, one back to Kaid, the other to T'Chebbi as he
˞eleased Carrie's throat.

He felt Kaid's shock as they began to Leska Link; then he
was pulled abruptly back to the here and now as Carrie began
to move beneath him and rub her palms against her nipples.

Groaning, he reached for her mind as his body surged forward again into hers. The contact was instant and almost overwhelming as images of their time apart flickered through their
conjoined minds, but neither was in a state to make sense of
it right now.

Their lovemaking was fierce as their bodies and minds in-
tertwined into a completeness they had never quite experienced before, and always, not far from them, they felt Kaid
and T'Chebbi undergo their first Link.

Sensations resonated between him and Carrie, taking them
higher and higher until, as one, they climaxed, and Kusac let
out a roar full of overtones of possession.

Exhausted, they collapsed beside each other, bodies still
joined. When he caught his breath, Kusac reached out to open
the seal of her tunic and pushing it aside, slowly cupped one
breast and began to lick and suckle on it.

I never stopped loving you, cub, he sent.

You nearly. died on Kij'ik! she sent, horrified at the
knowledge.

*I did die, through no wish of my own. Never again, cub. I
love you, our children, and life too much to leave it before my
time comes.*

Don't leave me again, Kusac. I couldn't bear it!

I won't. I can reach you no matter where you are now.

Kaid broke into their thoughts. *What the hell did you do?*
he demanded.

*I gave you and T'Chebbi a gift, one that doesn't need every
fifth day together. We can Link any time overnight, with any of
the four of us now.*

We'll need to talk about this! sent Kaid.

*Go make love to your Leska, Kaid, and leave us to do the
same,* sent Kusac, his tone laughing but firm as he cut the connection to them and began to nibble on Carrie's breast, elicit-
ing little Sholan noises of delight from her.

Annuur, Naacha, and Giyarishis made their way to the TeLaxaudin quarters in the Palace.

"Announce us," said Annuur as they reached the door, and
he rose up on his haunches to open it.

Naacha sent a brief message to the TeLaxaudin inside.

"Intruding like this is unacceptable," said Shoawomiss as
they entered without waiting for permission.

"You will transport the three of us," said Annuur, "to your
home world. I need to talk to Unity."

"Can be done from here now Unity been reconnected," objected Ayziss. "What so urgent?"

"Send us now," Annuur commanded as he and Naacha rose
to their full height. "Matter concerns you not."

"Wasteful of translocator and energy," hummed Shoawomiss, signaling Ayziss to get a unit.

"Follow orders!" snarled Naacha. "You are nothing! You
address a Phratry Lord of the Camarilla!"

Ayziss scuttled back with a small handheld unit for them.

"You will do nothing until I return and give you fresh orders in person," said Annuur as Naacha grasped the reluctant
Giyarishis and drew him close between them.

"As the Phratry Lord commands," said Shoawomiss, bowing.

Annuur selected a landing site in the gardens outside the
Council chamber then activated the device.

Their surroundings shimmered slightly, there was a wrenching sensation then they were on Ghioass.

Immediately, Unity welcomed them and asked them their
pleasure.

Conceal us, sent Annuur, *and send a private message to
Khassis that I must meet secretly with her on a matter of great
importance.*

Meet me at Kuvaa's home, came the almost instant reply.

Kuvaa was already there and expecting them as they got
out of the aircar and scuttled under cover from the rain. "Privacy net is active here," she said, gesturing them into the cool
plant-lined interior. "Suitable food and drink is on the table
for you."

nnuur stopped her as she trotted past. "So you have
ned your first tattoos. Well done, child. We need more bold
ung people like you on the Council and fewer ancient bun-
les of bones and sticks who forever mumble, *Isolate us!*"

Kuvaa's nose and ears twitched in amusement and modest
acceptance of the compliment.

They settled themselves around the low table, sampling the
delicacies Kuvaa had laid out for them and listening to the
heavy rain shower. It wasn't long before Khassis and Azwokkus arrived, both swathed in waterproof wraps.

"We are private in here?" asked Azwokkus as Kuvaa
leaped up to help them out of their wet ponchos.

"Completely," said Khassis, joining them at the table. "I had
Kuvaa's home upgraded as soon as she joined us as a Senior."

"Good. There is treason in Unity."

"Impossible," said Khassis.

"Giyarishis is the proof," said Annuur. "I brought him because he was given instructions, by Kuvaa, contrary to those
of the Camarilla." He held up his hoofed hand to forestall the
young female. "It wasn't her because that Kuvaa had no tattoos, and our Kuvaa had been given them that night."

"Is this true?" demanded Khassis, eyes whirling as the
lenses focused on Giyarishis.

"Yes, Skepp Lady," he said, clasping his hands and bowing
low. "Phratry Leader Kuvaa would have had her tattoos by
the time I was contacted."

Shvosi tap-tapped the hooves of one hand on the table,
wrinkling her nose.

"What were you ordered to do?"

"To force the Hunter into a mental Link with the Sand-
dweller female, and to make the Hunter allow the new Prime
Emperor to die when he was wounded."

"You swear this is true?" asked Khassis.

"I would not lie to my superiors," said Giyarishis stiffly,
"and least of all to an Elder, Skepp Lady. I didn't try hard to
prevent him healing King Zsurtul," he admitted, head bowed.

Khassis' mandibles twitched in acceptance, and she waved
a hand at Kuvaa.

"Thank you for having the courage to speak out, Giyarishis.
It shall not be forgotten. We will give you fresh orders shortly.
Send him back to his quarters on the Sand-dweller world."

*   *   *

"This is unprecedented," said Shvosi when they were alor

"Not exactly," said Annuur. "Are we not guiding the Hunt
our way rather than that of the Camarilla?"

"That's different," she said, her humming growing deeper.
"The Isolationists set up the last vote; it was not a fair one.
Their policy of destroying the M'zullians is not why we were
formed. Another solution must be found."

"There has been other interference with the Hunter," said
Shvosi. "We all know of times he is invisible and unreachable
to us, even using Unity. Right now he is beyond us, somewhere
on the Sand-dweller world, outside the City of Light."

"I have another matter of treason to bring before you,"
said Kuvaa. "You know I made security of Unity my study. I
have discovered that the Hunter Entity has been taken again
by the Isolationists—without Camarilla approval."

"Their perfidy knows no bounds," hummed Khassis, mandibles twitching angrily. "Why do they do this? Only trouble
it will cause!"

"This is bad, very bad," said Annuur, head sinking down to
his paws. "Sense of family among Hunters is as strong as ours.
They will stop at nothing to find him."

"He was taken early this month. Nothing has been done
yet that I can sense in the potentialities to find him. In fact, he
does not show in them at all."

"Only matter of time," said Shvosi. "Many followers he has
on Sand-dweller world now."

"Hunter also remembers much," said Kuvaa. "Frequently
we have to erase his and the Sand-dweller female's memories.
Now with Entity here . . ."

"Hunter was left alone in the interior with his mate on their
Linking Day," said Annuur.

"Are Leskas again," said Naacha. "Re-formed his Link.
Made them four now, not three."

"One day, he will come here," said Shvosi, "and demand answers, and it may be the end of us all. Their Entity and Hunter
will both demand reparation."

"We need to purge the Camarilla before that happens,"
said Khassis, clasping her hands in determination. "We will
have to be prepare our defense."

"There is no defense against this Hunter," said Naacha.
"Truth, and providing them the guilty, is all we can do."

Annuur lifted his head. "We must have our suspects watched by Unity's security program, then take steps to isolate them from decision-making so they remain unaware they are exposed. Then we can hand them to the Hunter for justice."

Khassis shuddered at the thought. "I fear you're right. Their behavior cannot be justified. What of the Entity in captivity? Do we do release him?"

"No," said Shvosi.

"Yes," said Naacha, drawing all eyes to him. "I sense another, far more powerful Entity on the Sand-dweller world. She belongs on the Hunter world *and* the Sand-dwellers'— they are Universal. Land flourishes for the first time in a millennium and a half through her influence. The stronger she becomes, the sooner she will challenge us for his return. Best we free him now—with certain memories erased. Our Hunter needs all the aid he can get to defeat the warrior Sand-dwellers. Already I feel his strength growing now his Link is re-formed."

Annuur looked at Naacha in surprise. It was unusual for his telepath to talk at such length. "Hunter is less unstable," he agreed. "Isolationists assume much when they assume this Entity is representative. No powers like the Earth one does he show, yet he has his place in aiding his people."

"So be it," said Khassis, reaching for a device on her belt. "Unity, your central core is summoned to a secret conclave dealing with treason."

They all felt the presence that was Unity change subtly before binding their minds together and creating a zone of utter privacy around them.

What is the security code for this communication, Elder Speaker?

Khassis hummed a sequence of words.

Accepted. I am at your service, Elder Speaker.

Khassis outlined the problem. "Track every Camarilla member and log any suspicious behavior. For suspects, the rule of privacy is negated—monitor them at all times. Update us daily and immediately if someone other than the real Kuvaa should contact Giyarishis or any of those on the Sand-dwellers' world. And cut that connection immediately," she added.

Your will shall be done, sent Unity.

"Arrange for the captive Entity to have his memories of us erased, then find a plausible way for him to escape us as soon as possible. I suspect the guilty ones are the leading cadre of Isolationists, but there may be others. Do you know where he is being held, Kuvaa, since Unity does not?"

Kuvaa reached into a pouch on her harness, pulled out a pad with the data on it, and read it out to Unity.

"Have any others asked you for a private conference and to conceal it from the rest of Unity?" asked Shvosi.

No, Skepp Lady.

"Unity, increase your own security, with guards if necessary. These rogue elements put us all at risk," said Khassis.

"Include Azwokkus in our group," said Shvosi, "and a private Unity channel among only us would also be useful."

This can be done, said Unity. *There is a precedent for it. One was created when there was conflict over inviting the Cabbarans to join the Camarilla.*

"Then reinstate it for us," said Khassis. "How did they not only conceal this captive but appear as Kuvaa to Giyarishis?"

"Speculation only," said Kuvaa, "but I believe they have found a way to make Unity overlook their presence in that location."

"Then we must shut it down," said Khassis. "And prevent this ever happening again!"

This I can do, Elder Speaker, now I know the location, said Unity.

"Very well, do it. But release the Entity and return him to his own realm first, minus memories of this. That will be all, thank you, Unity."

"This will end with the Hunters joining us," said Naacha, "or destroying us."

"As I predicted from the start," said Annuur.

CHAPTER 13

M'zull, Zhal-Arema, 29th day (March)

CARRIE reached for another piece of their still warm baked reptile from the night before's supper as Kusac filled up their mugs with more coffee. The day's heat was already reaching into the cave, although it was only midmorning.

"You're very thoughtful," he said, handing her her mug and leaning back against the crate behind him to finish eating.

"I've been thinking through the memories we exchanged last night," she said, rearranging her overtunic and resuming her position against his side.

Kusac's ears flattened as he put an arm around her shoulders. "There's a lot I'm not proud of," he muttered.

She gave a negative shake of her head. "You were in an intolerable situation. You acted more honorably than I think I would've done. That wasn't that I was thinking about; it was how much Kezule has changed. I think of the two of you, he's been manipulated more by drugs, or mentally."

"That was my thought too."

"The old Kezule refused to tolerate any females near him. Marrying one of the independent Primes would have been unthinkable."

"I know. I believe the Primes did that, though. Without those changes, he wouldn't have been able to live among them."

"Not just the Primes. Those who worked on your brain and mind, after the implant, were the TeLaxaudin and then the

Cabbarans. What made you actually pass out yesterday down at the new settlement?"

"I told you at the time, someone lashed out at me mentally."

"Who?"

"I'm not sure. Not one of the Cabbarans. But the TeLaxaudin . . ."

"Aren't telepaths."

"The TeLaxaudin seemed to use technology to build the way the Cabbarans do mentally. I went down there because I needed to see for myself what they were doing. They had some kind of artificial Link set up between them. I had just sensed it when I was knocked out."

"They can produce a form of communal telepathy using technology," she said. "There were no Cabbarans on Kij'ik, were there?"

"None. Could the changes in Shaidan and me be due to the TeLaxaudin?"

"They're certainly involved, especially as Kezule continued to alter quite considerably while you were on Kij'ik."

"Some of it was due to Zayshul's influence, and his sons and daughters, I'm sure."

"Mmm . . ." she agreed with a smile. "We females always have a good effect on our mates."

"Sure you do," Kusac grinned at her, leaning forward to lick the tip of her ear.

"Then there's the whole Vartra business. He was very active on Kij'ik, and then suddenly he was gone."

"That's very like the Entities," said Kusac.

"Is it? Again, it happened on Kij'ik."

"Only Giyarishis was there, Carrie. He's not one of their top people."

"He doesn't need to be if he can communicate, privately or secretly, with other TeLaxaudin. How did the birthing tanks arrive there, and the supplies? And why weren't you curious about that?"

Kusac went still. "Because my conscious mind was made to forget about it," he said slowly. "And that has only happened on Prime ships, Kij'ik, or in the City. The TeLaxaudin have been with them for fifteen hundred years, genetically modifying them, controlling them, and they did the same to Shaidan and me! The jigsaw is finally beginning to take shape."

He reached out to kiss her. *I didn't realize how much I needed you and your tactical mind until now.*

Only that? she teased.

Gods, no! I need you on a level so deep, I'm incomplete without you.

The kiss swiftly became more than passionate. It would have been so easy to have given in and claimed their twenty-eight hours together, but time was too short for that. Already K'hedduk could have sent another tithe ship to Ch'almuth, and that ship was the core of any plan to rescue Zhalmo. Reluctantly, he pulled away from her.

"We have to call Kaid to pick us up soon. But first, I need you to understand what I'm going to do to us all."

She tilted her head to one side and regarded him quizzically.

"I know how to manipulate Leska Links."

"Well, obviously. You did what we thought impossible, reformed ours and joined Kaid with T'chebbi, who isn't even a telepath!"

"She is now," he said soberly. "I should talk to Rezac. I seem to be able to do many things now that only the First could do."

"Like what?"

"Later. I need to change our five-day dependence, cub, and to make it last less than twenty-eight hours."

Already he'd brought Kaid and T'Chebbi into a Link with them.

I'm changing our five-day compulsion to mate and the need for twenty-eight hours together, he sent to them all. *Among the four of us, our Link will be interchangeable because we'll be like one Leska pair. If we are all apart, we can dampen our need for several weeks. The transfer time for memories can be shortened by being able to do a little at a time, nightly, or every other night, the choice will be ours—every fifth day if we wish, or more often. Nothing else will change—the magic, the mental and physical joining until each pair becomes one entity—that will remain the same. Our Links will just be more flexible, less life threatening if we're separated. The downside is we will be subliminally aware of the other pair all the time.*

How subliminally? asked Kaid.

You'd need to consciously look for it, he sent. *Are you all agreeable?*

If it's reversible, we are. There's so much to do right now, we can't afford one day in five off, sent Kaid.

It's reversible. Carrie?

Only if I can have my fifth day back when this is over, she replied.

Kusac sent her a private mental chuckle and a memory from the night before. *But of course, cub.*

This must be kept from everyone else, he said to them all. *Once we're comfortable with it, I can change the others if they wish. And, Kaid? You'll have to teach T'Chebbi about being a Telepath, as we taught you.*

Aye. That he might need help was unsaid, but both Kusac and Carrie sent them the reassurance that help was always there.

Let your minds be passive once we Link. Think of it as one of the meditation circles we did at Stronghold and the Guild.

He reached mentally for the other two, bringing first Kaid, then a very bemused T'Chebbi deeper into his and Carrie's Link. Once they were all relaxed, he strengthened the bonds among them, enfolding them inside his own consciousness. A momentary panic here, an irritating itch there, were gently quieted until their minds were fully opened to him. He watched their thought patterns as they all began to meld into one, and then he triggered the gestalt. Brain activity flared, sending pulses of energy flowing through their joined minds and bodies. He grasped it firmly, harnessing it before loosening control on their melded minds, letting each of them regain his or her own identity while still Linked.

Carrie's fear built, and he suppressed it with hardly any effort. The gestalt felt like holding a huge squirming eel, one that kept trying to double back on itself and attack him, and he knew he had to act swiftly. Mentally, he fought to program it, to command it to seek out that area in their brains that controlled the Leska Links, and to alter it just enough to allow them to control it, rather than be controlled.

Carrie, follow what I do to Kaid and T'chebbi, he sent. *I need you to help me change myself.*

Aye.

With no more thought, he aimed the now quiescent gestalt at Kaid and T'Chebbi, following it as it flowed first into Kaid's, then T'Chebbi's consciousness like a living thing. Moments later, it was done, and it turned to Carrie.

Ready? He was weakening quickly now with the strain of the work.

Yes. Go for it, she sent.

He felt her gasp of shock; then it was his turn as she grasped what remained of the gestalt and turned it on him. It lasted only a moment, but it seemed far longer as what felt like a nest of snakes squirmed almost painfully around inside his mind. Then it was over, and he and Carrie began to dissipate what remained of the power.

They threw it at the force field, and though he heard the spitting and popping as it tried to absorb the extra energy, he saw nothing. Exhausted, he toppled over onto the sleeping bags, the Link among them all breaking apart.

"Kusac!" Carrie bent over him, checking his pulse and his breathing.

"Fine," he whispered as she eased him into a more comfortable position. "Took more strength than I anticipated. You?"

"Tired but fine; so are the others," she replied, pulling the second sleeping bag over him. "You need food. I'll get some protein drinks for you."

Tell Kaid I won't be fit to travel till late afternoon, he sent.

"Done," she said a moment later as she activated one of the self-heating drinks for Kusac, then one for herself. "You didn't . . ."

Force T'Chebbi on Kaid? No, they both wanted a Link with each other but thought there was no point in even thinking about it.

She helped him sit up and propped the pillow from her sleeping bag behind him before handing him the drink. "And the gestalt?"

A tool more useful than we dreamed — when we have the strength to control it. Many of the First could, but we were weaker.

She hid a huge yawn behind her hand and, emptying her can, waited for Kusac to finish his.

"Do you want another?" she asked, taking the empty containers and stashing them in their garbage sack.

"No, I need to sleep now." His voice was barely above a whisper, and his eyes were already closing as he slipped down between the sleeping bags again. "You need some too. We spent much of the night awake." A pleased smile played around his lips.

With a chuckle, she slid in beside him, happy to be pulled within his arms and close against his side. She could feel the silky softness of his belly fur against her skin and with it, the warmth of his body.

"Yes, there is a rightness about this," he agreed, touching his lips to her forehead then her throat. "I finally feel I've come home to my family." The hard knot of pain in his belly that he had lived with for so long was finally beginning to dissolve.

The City, same day

T'Chebbi hadn't come with Kaid to pick them up, but she was waiting on the landing pad for them with a small aircar when they arrived back at the City.

"Now I can welcome you properly into our Clan," said Kusac, giving her a warm hug and nuzzling her ear.

"Huh, you males too good at making decisions for us! Might have asked me!" She took a mock swipe at his ears as he released her.

"Would you have refused?" He raised an eye ridge at her.

"Is principle," she said haughtily, allowing an amused Kaid to link his arm through hers and draw her into the single cabin.

"It's been over three weeks since Zhalmo was taken," said Kaid. "We need a rescue plan, Kusac, and one to deal with K'hedduk sending another tithe ship to Ch'almuth."

"I've been working on a few," he said. "I'll get Kezule to call a meeting later today, and we can discuss them properly. Meanwhile, consider this. You're K'hedduk. You believe the legitimate heir, Zsurtul, is dead. You married his mother to legitimize your claim to the throne, but you get the chance to take Zhalmo, one of the descendants of the last true Emperor before the Fall. What's your military priority?"

"An Emperor can only be legitimately crowned here, on the Throne of Light, can't he?" asked Carrie.

"Yes."

"To destroy the Throne, the Palace, and everyone in it,"

said T'Chebbi as she started up the aircar and took off, heading over the City walls toward the Palace.

"That's what I was afraid of. Plan for both contingencies and we'll discuss it at the meeting."

"Rhyaz is here. He arrived late last night," said Kaid.

"Is he? I have a bone to pick with him."

"Not in public, Kusac," warned Carrie. "Believe me, Kaid and I had a good set-to with him. If I remember right, Kaid threw him over a chair!"

"You did?" Kusac looked at their Third in surprise.

"Yeah," said Kaid, flicking his ears. "Made me mad to realize what a fool I'd been to believe you meant the things you said."

"Water under the bridge now," said Kusac quietly, grasping his friend by the shoulder.

"Looks like we've got some packing and moving to do, T'Chebbi," said Carrie. "My stuff in with Kusac and yours in with Kaid."

"I need to speak to Zayshul—and Kezule—about that," Kusac muttered, sure it was not going to be a pleasant experience for him despite the good news.

T'Chebbi landed in the lower courtyard and they got out, leaving the aircar in the charge of one of the guards.

"The scent marker is gone now, I take it?" asked Carrie, cocking her head to one side and raising an eyebrow at him as they walked toward the Palace entrance.

"Completely. I turned it off some time ago. I only left the scent there to keep whoever caused it from knowing what I was capable of doing." He hesitated. *I'm sorry I had to lie to you about it, Carrie. I honestly thought it would protect you if I kept my distance.*

"Good," was all she said.

"You do know you'll have to share the bed with me and Shaidan a couple of nights a week?" he said, a slight grin on his face.

"Only for a short time, until he gets used to us living together," she replied. "Then, when he feels secure, we help him set up his own room in the suite."

Kusac nodded his agreement. "I'll leave you and T'Chebbi to your moving for now. Conner's back in the Temple, and I need to see him. Zayshul is busy at the market with her daughter, so I'll catch her later."

Carrie stopped and reached up to pull his face down to kiss him. "I'll see you later, then."

He caressed her face, reluctant to let her out of his sight now that they were one again. "I'll pick Shaidan up this evening and order dinner in our suite," he said. "See you later, cub." For some reason, it gave him an enormous amount of pleasure to say *our* suite, and he felt her agreement.

Conner was in the Temple teaching his group of young male and female acolytes how to cleanse the altar and the small statue of their Goddess. He dismissed them as he saw Kusac walking down the main aisle toward him. As they passed him, each one bowed and murmured a greeting.

"You came," said Conner, smiling and walking toward him. "And there is a difference in you today. You feel more whole."

"I have my Leska back," Kusac said, unable to keep the smile off his face. "I'm no longer lacking the other half of me."

"This is great news! Come, we'll talk in my office." Conner led him back toward the altar and the door off to one side. "You were taken to the Realms, weren't you? Met one or more of the Entities? That's why you asked me about people as swords."

Kusac waited as Conner opened the door, then followed him inside.

The room was medium sized, square in shape, and lit by a series of small windows high up near the ceiling. He frowned, trying to remember the geography of the Palace—he didn't think there was enough room between the rear of the Temple and the next building for bright sunlight to reach them.

"Mirrors," said Conner, gesturing him to a chair as he took another himself. "This is one of the oldest parts of the Palace. Originally they were polished sheets of metal, of course."

"Clever."

The walls looked, and smelled, freshly painted. The King and a procession of various craftspeople followed a trio of priestesses around the room to where their Goddess of Fertility, La'shol, sat enthroned.

"A vast improvement, isn't it?" smiled Conner. "The choice was theirs, of course. But tell me about your vision, or visit, to the Realms."

Kusac told him what he'd experienced, ending with, "As L'Shoh beat the blade, I felt every blow, not as a great physical pain, but as if he were forging me."

"He was," said Conner thoughtfully. "Not your body, but your soul. What did he say again?"

"The forging was done, and you would finish the making of the sword."

"I thought there was more I had to do here," he nodded.

"You've already acquired great power, Kusac, more than any mortal Sholan has ever had. You need to learn to temper that power. Use it seldom and wisely."

"What's the point of it if I use it seldom?"

"It's for those times when nothing else will suffice. You do realize how rare it is to see L'Shoh, don't you? He's chosen you to be His instrument of Justice in the coming war."

"Hmm." He wasn't sure he considered it an honor.

"What would you do? Go from world to world and destroy what didn't meet your criteria of just, fair, and civilized?" asked Conner.

"Gods, no!" he exclaimed. "I hope to return to my home and Clan as soon as the M'zullian issue is cleared up."

"It's going to take longer than you think."

He growled gently. "If it were up to me, once Zhalmo has been rescued, I'd destroy M'zull!"

"What about the innocent M'zullians—the children, drones, and females?"

"There are no innocents," he said flatly.

"You don't know that," said Conner gently, leaning forward. "On my world they say you can't know a person until you've walked a mile in his shoes or been inside her head. You need to understand what it is to be a Prime, a M'zullian, a Touiban."

"I can find out what I need in a moment!" This was beginning to irritate him.

"No, you can't," said Conner. "Do you remember using skill transfers? You learned the skill, but you still had to practice it to know how to use it."

"I remember," he admitted. "But what has this . . ."

"To do with being the epitome of Justice? You have to learn to look at both sides, to make decisions without prejudice, to be ruthless or compassionate as the moment demands, and to understand the natures of the people with whom you deal. There are many species here. Go out and learn to walk in their shoes, be a passive Traveler, then take over for an hour or so and *be* them. You've only ever done this as a lesson in your Guild or to get information, not to understand them as people."

There was some sense in what he said. "Very well, I'll do that. But Conner, I don't want to be an arbiter of Justice!"

"You have no choice, I'm afraid, Kusac. All you've become since you met Carrie has led you to this point in time. Incidents will happen, and people will look to you to make decisions—as you did when you violently weeded out K'hedduk's agents."

"There needed to be a swift punishment," he said.

Conner held up his hand. "No need to be defensive, Kusac. Distasteful as it was, you were right."

"Have you ever sensed something here trying to affect your mind?" he asked, abruptly switching the topic. He didn't want to remember that unexpected coldness with which he he'd treated the prisoners.

"Indeed I have. It had no effect on me and eventually stopped. Why? Have you felt it too?"

"Many times, here and on Kij'ik. Why didn't you tell me? What, or who, is causing it?" He was annoyed with Conner for keeping silent about this.

"You didn't ask me," said Conner, reasonably. "I was unaware anyone else felt it. I think you'll find it has ceased since you became aware of it."

"I want to know who's behind it. They tried to make me let Zsurtul die, they forced me apart from my Triad!"

"That isn't your task right now, Kusac. You have Zhalmo to rescue. She and Zsurtul will found a dynasty that will bring peace to all the Valtegans by blending them into one people again. You are pivotal in making this happen. I will monitor this seditious presence, set traps for it should it return, and keep you informed when the time is right."

"What can you do against it that I couldn't? It kept making me forget what I've learned about it!" He was getting really annoyed now. The safety of his own family was as important to him as rescuing Zhalmo.

Conner smiled gently. "You forget who I am," he said, raising his hand and plunging the room, briefly, into utter darkness.

Kusac felt power flowing from the stones of the floor to Conner, and he shivered as the darkness faded.

"It's a perfectly natural use of the Earth's energy," said Conner. "Come to think of it, I need to teach you that too. However, go Traveling for now and come back in a few days to let me know what you've learned; then I'll teach you how to garner more energy from natural sources."

"We're going to be extremely busy, Conner," said Kusac, standing up. "I'll do what I can when I can. I am taking your advice and telling Kezule to arm the weather station and to not only get the Palace force field up, but also see what we can do to protect the whole City and the village outside."

"That's excellent news," said Conner with a smile. "Perhaps Llew will let me rest easy now."

"I welcome the day when we all can," said Kusac dryly.

"Leave the other matter to me, as I said. I will keep a watch on your family with you. There's no point in rushing in, swords and guns flying, until you have all the facts. Besides, it might just be of some use to us."

"Very well, we'll do it your way, but if it threatens my family . . ."

"That goes without saying," said Conner, rising. "I believe we have a banquet tonight for Rhyaz and his Leska, Alex."

"Quite likely. I've called a Council meeting for this afternoon, I'll find out then." Kusac stopped, listening to ZSADHI'S voice in his small ear-receiver.

"General Kezule requests your presence in the Council chamber, Captain."

"On my way, ZSADHI. Conner, thank you again," he said, turning and leaving.

Heading left outside the Temple, he took the covered walkway between several office blocks, turning left again in front of the Utilities building. As soon as he turned into that section, he saw that several of the lights were out and sensed someone hiding in the shadows. His hackles began to rise, and as his hand reached for the knife at his left side, he stepped into a pool of darkness against the far wall. The junction ahead, by his turn for the elevator, was in total darkness.

He hooded his eyes, trying to prevent the light ahead from causing them to shine. Common sense would have been to back off and send to Kaid for reinforcements, but someone had gone to a lot of trouble to set up this trap, which made it very personal.

Like a shadow, he inched slowly forward, ears pricked for the slightest sound. His enhanced senses could smell the sharp scent of anticipation from the Sholan out of sight around the corner, and his ears picked up the tiniest movements as his would-be attacker shifted his weight impatiently.

Reaching for his assailant's mind, Kusac found it a turmoil of emotions—lust for the kill, and revenge soon to be accomplished: killing this one would make Kaid suffer more—then the thoughts stopped, the mind becoming still as he sensed Kusac's presence.

Suddenly Kusac's foot touched a pebble, making it rattle against the cobblestone pathway. He felt the air move and knew a knife was spinning toward him. Just in time, he dove low for the other side of the narrow passageway, using the wall to bounce off and to propel himself in a forward roll that sent him crashing into the legs of the assassin.

They both leaped to their feet at the same time, facing off with knives drawn.

"Come on, then, mind reader," sneered the other. "Kaid taught you, did he? We were always better than him. You're dead meat!"

Each sentence was punctuated by a slash of the knife as his attacker lunged forward.

Kusac backed away, keeping his guard up, and reached for the other's mind again, this time in an effort to control it; but it was filled with roiling hate and anger—there was nothing sane there to control.

So hard was he concentrating that he didn't sense the cut that came too close, slicing his forearm. The sting of pain banished any desire but to stay alive. The lack of sanity made his attacker doubly dangerous, and despite the army uniform he wore, Kusac knew he was fighting a seasoned Brotherhood Warrior.

Again, he backed off hurriedly, into one of the better-lit areas, letting his attacker think he had the advantage. He faked a stumble, drawing him nearer so he could reach out and grasp his opponent's knife hand, using his strength to pull him in close before slamming his own knife up under his chin. They stood locked like that for a moment, then Kusac wrenched his knife free and allowed the other to fall, dead, to the ground.

Wincing in pain as he bent down to wipe his blade on the assassin's tunic, he realized he'd taken another cut along his right side, one that had sliced through his jacket.

He quickly searched the body, finding nothing except a few coins in the pockets. He retrieved the knife, but it wasn't a Brotherhood one. No way to trace the owner of that blade.

"ZSADHI, is Raiban in the Council chamber?" he demanded. The slice to his side was beginning to burn and hurt almost as much as his forearm did.

"Yes, Captain."

"Good," he muttered, cursing at the pain again as he picked up the corpse and slung it clumsily over his good shoulder.

He exited the elevator, ignoring the flustered security guards who trailed after him as he limped painfully to the Council chamber. Flinging the door open, he headed straight for Raiban and dumped the still bleeding corpse in front of her as they all leaped to their feet with exclamations of shock.

"Call your assassins off now, Raiban, or I swear I'll kill you myself," he snarled, ears turning sideways to his skull, and tail jerking in an obvious show of anger.

"Assassins?" said Raiban, nostrils flaring and ears flattening as she took a step back from the body. "This is nothing to do with me, Kusac!"

"They were wearing forces uniforms, and they came on your ship," he said, catching the glance Zsurtul and Kezule exchanged. "And you swore you'd make me pay for leaving Shola as I did! Who else would do this?"

"Hold on Kusac," said Kaid, walking around the table to look down at the dead Sholan as half a dozen commandos, weapons drawn, rushed in and ranged themselves between Kusac and Raiban. "I recognize him. It's Jebousa. He's Brotherhood, one of the two who kidnapped Dzaka and conspired with Ghezu against me."

"Was this your idea then, Rhyaz?" he demanded, wincing as he swung around to face the Brotherhood Master.

"Not mine, Kusac. Why would I make sure you got a full pardon and then set an assassin on you?"

Kusac growled, a low, menacing sound.

"This matter will be investigated immediately," said King Zsurtul. "Meanwhile, M'kou, have this body removed to the morgue. Captain, you need immediate medical attention. We'll retire to the lounge, meanwhile, and meet you there."

Kusac glanced at his forearm. It was dripping blood onto the polished wooden floor. He gave a low hiss of pain as the cut across his side hurt when he turned to watch Rhyaz as he came forward to check the body.

"That is indeed Jebousa. He's no longer Brotherhood," the Guild Master said. "He became too unstable, so we retired him. There's another force behind this, Kusac. I believe he's actually the third assassin."

"And just when did you intend to inform me about this, Rhyaz?" he asked, his voice suddenly gentle.

"When I had something to actually tell you," the other said, meeting his eyes steadily.

"You take too much on yourself," growled Kusac.

"I have every right," began Rhyaz.

"No. I answer only to Lijou, not you. Which reminds me," he said, suddenly lurching forward to grasp Rhyaz by the front of his jacket and lift him effortlessly up into the air. "I promised you retribution for what you made me say and do to Kaid and Carrie!"

Rhyaz was making choking noises and grasping at Kusac's hand. Just as he reached for his knife, Kusac dropped him and swung his arm back in an arc to land a hard cuff on the Guild Master's ear that sent him flying across the room to land in a heap against the far wall.

"You can thank Alex that's all I'm going to do!"

The rest of them stood rigid, waiting to see what would happen next.

"You're too like Kaid," growled Rhyaz, getting up, straightening his clothes and shaking his head to clear it. "I didn't tell you what to say to Kaid. You made that decision, not me."

"You knew damned well that was the only thing he could say that would make me turn my back on him," said Kaid, walking past Rhyaz and out of the door.

"It's over now," said Kusac, more mildly as he watched a Prime Medic enter.

She hesitated in midstride as she saw the body and glanced at M'kou for instructions.

"He's dead. See to the Captain," said M'kou, gesturing toward Kusac.

Nodding, she approached him, reaching out for his injured arm. "If you please, Captain?"

"It's only a flesh wound," he said, holding it out while she examined it carefully, swabbing the still bleeding wound with the pad she was carrying.

"You need stitches," she said, reaching into one of her fatigues' pockets for a pressure bandage.

"He's got a wounded side too," said Banner, joining them.

He'd stopped bleeding, so she ushered him out of the Council chamber. "You need to come to the hospital for treatment," she said.

"This is a fuss over nothing," he muttered.

"You will go, Captain Aldatan," said Zsurtul. "We'll wait for you to join us before we discuss anything."

Still muttering, Kusac, followed by M'kou, left with the medic.

As Raiban stepped over the body and headed for the door, two commandos fell in on either side to escort her.

"This is an insufferable insult," she said angrily. "I said I had nothing to do with this!"

"You've lied to me before, General," said Kezule, as he and the King followed her out. "Why should we now trust you?"

"Because, like you, I'm a soldier! When I thought he was a loose cannon acting on his own, stealing a Touiban vessel, creating an interplanetary incident, and closing down the spaceport for two hours, that was one thing. I now accept he was on a mission. Besides, if I wanted him dead, I'd Challenge him, I'd never stoop to assassination," she said frankly, looking at him over her shoulder. "You understand that, I'm sure.

Kezule smiled widely, displaying his teeth. "Pray you never find out just how good he is. He gave me a run for my money when we fought."

"ZSADHI, ask Carrie to join us in the lounge," said Kusac, sotto voce as he followed the medic into the King's hospital.

Zayshul was working at the reception desk, checking her few patients' files on the computer. She looked up as they entered.

"Another fight?" she asked dryly.

"Another assassination attempt," he corrected as the medi led him into an examination room.

He winced as she helped him out of his uniform jacket.

We need to talk, he sent to Zayshul as she stood at the doorway watching.

"I'll see to Captain Aldatan, thank you," she said to the medic. "And ZSADHI, ask Lieutenant Banner to bring a fresh uniform here, please."

"How do three assassins get onto your ship and remain undetected?" demanded Rhyaz as they waited while guards pushed the tables and chairs closer to each other in the lounge. "And if there are three, how many more are there, Raiban?"

"I'd like to know that myself," growled Raiban, sitting down. "No stone will be left unturned until I find that out, and who is responsible! This one was one of your people, Rhyaz!"

"We haven't been hired for an assassination in a good few years, Raiban. Besides, you know contracts against Leskas are illegal. Kaid can tell you more about Jebousa than I can."

Kaid settled himself in an easy chair beside one of the small round tables. "He was one of Ghezu's tools," he said. "If he had a personal grudge, it would have been with me. Someone hired him to do this job. There has to be a handler. Find him, and we have our answers."

"I'll have a word with the Telepath Mentor on the *Khalossa* to get right on it," said Raiban. "Can you handle the ground people?" she asked Rhyaz, with a glance at Kaid as well.

Rhyaz nodded. "Alex and I will do what we can. And I've alerted the Mentor for you."

"You'll have to rely on Carrie and Kusac more than me," said Kaid. "Their skills are greater."

"Any ambassadors on the *Khalossa*, Raiban?" asked Rhyaz. "I brought none, though we do have alien Brothers with us."

"None," said Raiban. "The Touibans were already here, but I know there are a couple of the *Watcher* ships berthed at the weather platform because I've seen them and their U'Churian and Cabbaran crews."

"Plus the TeLaxaudin here in the Palace," added Kaid.

"They are above reproach," said Zsurtul.

"All species, even allies, have their own agendas," murmured Kezule.

*   *   *

"What did you want to talk about?" asked Zayshul as she began cleaning the wounds.

"I've turned off the scent marker completely," he said quietly.

"I noticed when you came in. You know, I'm getting quite expert at treating your wounds."

He chuckled. "I'm trying to stop making a habit of getting wounded," he said. "I think whatever has been attempting to control us was also forcing us away from our mates."

"You and your wife are together again," she said, beginning to clip the fur around the deeper knife wound on his forearm. "I can smell her scent on you."

"We do have our Link back," he said. "I wanted to tell you myself. You can say that the scent marker just vanished when she and I Linked again."

He fell silent as she sprayed on a topical anesthetic.

"I apologize for many of my actions, what I did to you, but I have some good memories too. Those I won't forget." He touched her cheek briefly with his free hand.

"Will you tell her what happened between us?"

"She already knows," he said quietly, watching as she expertly began stitching his wound. "When we Link, our minds become one. We exchange all memories since the last time we Linked."

Zayshul paled and looked up at him.

"You've no need to worry. She knows everything—how we were both used and controlled by those who placed your scent marker on me," he reassured her. "We're both free now to return to our own lives."

"I don't know what mine is anymore," she said, wrapping a dressing around his forearm. "Kezule has changed so much from the person I woke on the *Kz'adul*."

"Change is inevitable. We learn to adapt to it, make compromises."

"True. Thank you for telling me in person before I get bombarded by questions from the others."

"I owe you that for what we've shared."

She prodded the cut over his ribs, making him hiss in pain. "That one is more shallow. Luckily your jacket took most of the damage. Just keep both wounds clean, and change the dressings every day," she said, spraying a sealant over it. Turn-

ing, she put the canister back on the counter and reached fc
a lightweight bandage as there was a knock in the door an
Banner entered.

He held out the fresh jacket to Kusac. "Nothing serious, I
hope?"

"Just flesh wounds, though the forearm one was a close
call," he replied as Zayshul wrapped the bandage around his
ribs and fastened it off.

When she was done, he took the jacket from Banner and
accepted his help to put it on.

"They're waiting down the corridor in the lounge for you,"
said Banner.

"I'm almost done, here," said Kusac, accepting the offered
weapons belt and buckling it on. "I'll meet you outside in a
moment, Banner."

"Aye, Captain."

When the door shut, he took Zayshul's face gently between
his hands and kissed her on the forehead before releasing her.
"Thank you again for putting up with me," he said. "I'd like
to think we can remain friends and allies in whatever lies
ahead."

"I would hope so too. There were times when all I wanted
to do was shake some compassion and common sense into
you," she said frankly. "And others when I admired you because you gave so much of yourself to our people. Do you
intend to tell Kezule of your suspicions?"

"Not publicly, but I will talk to him privately about them.
The forgetfulness and the sense of being manipulated has actually been absent the last two days, and I'm not sure why."
He had his suspicions, and they had a lot to do with Ghyakulla
and L'Shoh, as well as reLinking with Carrie.

*I have to go now. I expect we'll meet at dinner tonight. Be
safe and happy, Zayshul.*

"You attract trouble like a dead jegget attracts flies," Banner grumbled as they made their way along the corridor to the
King's lounge.

"I'm attracting assassins," he said grimly. "Ones recruited
on Shola and smuggled onto Raiban's ship. The Gods know
how many more there are, or who's behind it. I thought it was
Raiban, but it's not her style. I need the next one alive enough
to mind read."

"You need your back covered at all times," growled Ban-er, ears sideways in anger.

"Set it up, please," he said. "And for Carrie and Shaidan now that we're back together."

"At last you're gaining some sense! So the rumors are true, then?"

Kusac grinned briefly at him as he opened the lounge door. "Yes."

"I need to get offworld tonight," said the quiet voice in Tirak's ear. "Everyone's so twitchy now, I'll be discovered before I can complete our mission. Kij'ik will do."

"And how am I supposed to get you there?" demanded Tirak.

"That's your job, not mine. Your *Watcher* craft is at the weather station. Schedule a training run or something. I'll be on the shuttle at the landing pad before you arrive. Just divert the pilot's attention long enough for me to slip off onto the station then onto the *Watcher*. You can drop me as surreptitiously on Kij'ik."

"Tonight? There's a Royal banquet for the Brotherhood Guild Master!"

"Even better, they'll be too busy to notice us leaving."

"I'm expected to attend. My absence will draw attention to us!"

"Then you better start working on a good reason to be on the *Watcher*!" Ghost snapped back at him. With that, he cut the connection.

Cursing, Tirak asked ZSADHI where Annuur was then headed out to join him at the new village.

"Just a couple of scratches," said Kusac in answer to the looks as he entered and took his place to the left of the King.

"I'll get to the bottom of this, Kusac, you can trust me. I ordered a census of my people, and the Telepath Mentors are already checking those aboard the *Khalossa*," said Raiban.

Kusac nodded. "Keep me apprised of the situation."

"I want the City off-limits to all but trusted Sholans," said Kezule.

"And who are those?" demanded Raiban, eye ridges meeting in a frown as she glared at the General.

"Kusac's people," said King Zsurtul shortly. "General Rai-

ban, you'll have to excuse us, but you're not part of our pla.
ning meeting. We will see you tonight at the banquet."

Raiban looked around at the gathering and realized she'o
get no support from anyone. Clenching her jaw, she got to her
feet, inclined her head briefly at the King, and left.

"Commander Rhyaz, you and Commander L'Seuli can
bring your own guards to the City gates, where my commandos will meet you. They will guard you inside the City and
Palace," said Kezule. "Your guards will return to your shuttle.
I'll have you and your wife escorted there at the end of the
evening."

"That's acceptable," agreed Rhyaz.

"ZSADHI has security cams everywhere. Anyone not recognized will be stunned on sight and guards called," Kezule
continued.

"Toueesut is included with my people," said Kusac, gratefully accepting the dish of hot maush handed to him by an
attendant. If truth be told, both cuts had been deep enough to
still pain him a little despite the analgesic Zayshul had insisted
he take.

A knock on the door and Carrie entered. As she was
greeted by King Zsurtul and as the Sholans made room for
her beside Kusac, they held a brief mental exchange.

Are you really all right? she asked.

I hurt, he admitted, fingers curling around the hand she
placed on his. *But they aren't serious cuts.*

Carrie flashed a smile and a mental greeting to Kaid, getting one in return as she settled into her seat.

"Kezule, King Zsurtul," said Kusac, "before a tithe ship is
sent to Ch'almuth, I believe K'hedduk will attempt to destroy
the City, and with it the Palace and Throne of Light. Without
it, he knows no one can be crowned Emperor. Remember, he
believes you're dead, King Zsurtul, and that Kezule will take
your place."

Kezule nodded. "Tactically, that would be his priority. However, he could do both."

"He'll want K'oish'ik cowed before dealing with
Ch'almuth," said Kaid. "After all, the tithe only adds to the
Court harem, nothing more."

Zsurtul's face froze into a still mask. "What about Zhalmo?"
he asked in an expressionless voice.

"I'm sorry, Majesty, but until the tithe ship arrives at

Ch'almuth, there's nothing we can do to rescue Zhalmo."
Kusac was aware of Kezule sitting just as still as the King.

"What if he doesn't send one?"

"He will," reassured Kaid. "He's not the kind of person to
let go of anything he considers his. He'll want to make sure
that Ch'almuth isn't ripe for rebellion after the return of the
last ship."

"Zhalmo isn't his!" On the table, Zsurtul's hands clenched
into fists.

"No, she's not," said Carrie gently. "Whatever else, he won't
harm her. He needs her to legitimize his claim as Emperor."

"What is your plan?" asked Kezule, filling the silence.

"We need to use the weather platform and Kij'ik," said
Kusac. "While the rest of you see to the planetary defense, I'll
train my rescue team. My plan is basically what we discussed
before, Kezule. Fill the tithe ship with your commandos wearing K'hedduk's uniforms and battle armor, with a token few
dressed as Ch'almuthians. We'll follow their flight plan, land at
their city then enter the Palace as normal. Then we'll head for
the harem and Zhalmo. She shouldn't be difficult to find since
I'll be able to contact her mentally by then."

"She'll be drugged," said Zsurtul. "There's no way she'd
give in to him."

"I'll find her," Kusac reassured him.

"If you can get in, it would be an opportunity to capture or
kill K'hedduk," said Rhyaz, thoughtfully rubbing his chin.

"Killing K'hedduk won't stop the coming war," said Kaid.
"Another will rise in his place and ensure they hit here first."

"I'll want a team of twelve as soldiers and eight to be the
tithe. We may not need them all, but I want to be sure we
have enough fighters. Is there any way the 'Ch'almuthian
prisoners' can be armored under their clothing?" asked
Kusac.

"Ch'almuthian clothing is worn in layers and can be
bulky," said M'kou. "It's possible it could conceal lighter body
armor."

"If they can carry baggage, they can have helmets in them,"
suggested Carrie.

"Any rescue will make both here and Ch'almuth instant
targets," warned L'Seuli.

"That goes without saying," said Kezule. "You Sholans,
however, are a difficult problem to solve. Even concealing you

as prisoners wouldn't ensure your heads or legs would remain covered."

"I'll be the only one leaving the ship," said Kusac. "I want Kaid to remain on board with Carrie, Banner, and Jurrel, and the MUTAC, assuming Jurrel can pilot it, as backup."

"MUTAC will be ready for you to train within two, maybe three, days," said Toueesut. "Much improved it is with extra firepower and strength. So impressed are we by it, we wish to make some of our own."

"We'll discuss that later," said Rhyaz.

"Discuss it with Garras, Toueesut. He's our Clan's business manager," said Kusac, with a feral grin at Rhyaz. "I think you'll find our people were instrumental in developing it, Rhyaz. You called it a failed experiment."

"Is that so?" beamed Toueesut. "Then I can negotiate for us with the Touiban military, as we are being part of your Clan!"

"This rescue," said Rhyaz. "There must be something we can do to deal them a blow, at least, when you leave M'zull. It goes against the grain not to do them some damage."

"Unlike this Palace, which was never designed as a stronghold, they dug down," said Kezule. "Only public buildings exist in the aboveground levels now, from what our prisoners told us, and the plans confirm. Besides, snatching Zhalmo from his harem, at the center of his world, will make him lose an enormous amount of credibility, and embarrass him publicly."

"Actually," said Kusac, taking another sip of his drink. "I'm looking at the possibility of some of our commandos remaining on M'zull as a small guerrilla force. There's a lot they could accomplish."

"But that's suicidal!" said Kezule. "What can you possibly accomplish on a planetary scale with even twenty warriors, and some of them females, on M'zull? You can't subvert them, most will be genetically loyal to K'hedduk's family!"

"What family? He killed his brother to take the throne," said Kaid. "But you're right. We can't get to their fleet to destroy it. We've read the reports—it's berthed at several orbiting ports in their solar system, not all in one place."

"This is what I want to discuss," Kusac said. "We'll never get another chance to place our people on the surface of M'zull. The alternative is war. So let's look at the guerrilla options now, while we have the opportunity. If the worst comes to worst, they have a chance to steal a ship and get offworld, where we can pick them up."

"I'd still prefer you to take a series of linked charges and set them all over the Palace; then when you take off, blow them," muttered Rhyaz. "Cut the head off the beast, and the command structure falls apart, leaving them ripe for the taking."

"It's unlikely that most of the military leaders will be there. They're more likely to be with the fleet, not on the ground," said Kaid. "One of them will assume command and target both here and Ch'almuth in retaliation, which brings us back to an all-out war."

"Destroy their Palace and Emperor, and they won't rest until both planets are leveled," said Kezule grimly. "Then they'll turn on all of you. It will unite them as nothing else will."

"Much as I would like to destroy the Palace and K'hedduk, it isn't the way," said Kusac, one hand unconsciously going to rub the inside of his wrist. "We have several options. There is the drug that destroys the extra speed and healing abilities for one. If Rhyaz can get us enough of it in time, it can be put in the water supplies all over the planet."

"I have a small amount with me, but not nearly enough of it," said Rhyaz.

Kezule frowned, and Kusac could sense his rising anger. "Out of the question. It's of limited use, anyway. It doesn't prevent their aggressiveness."

"Perhaps the TeLaxaudin have something that could strip them of their racial memories," said Kusac. "Maybe even their current ones." Even as he said it, he had a feeling of déjà vu, as if he—or someone—had said this before.

"How would that help?" asked Carrie.

"They forget about the Empire, and us, and have no reason to fight," said Kusac.

"What makes you think the TeLaxaudin have some such magic solution?" asked Rhyaz sarcastically.

"Because they helped the Primes breed in growth tanks and transfer their memories chemically," said Kezule, thoughtfully. "If they could adapt that for our purposes, then it would be a viable solution. But how would we deliver it?"

"I assume it was put into the tanks as a liquid, so water borne would work. I'll need to talk to Giyarishis first. Meanwhile, I suggest Kaid and I start working on our rescue plans, and you, Rhyaz, and Kezule plan the defense of K'oish'ik. My skills are more toward covert ops than space battles, but we'll fit in where needed in the defense plans."

You're thinking of repeating what the First did—putting telepaths on the main fleet ships so they can cause them to destroy each other! sent Carrie angrily as the meeting broke up.

I'm trying to think of a way to get some of our female commandos, or Ch'almuthians, on their fleet ships, yes, he replied.

Who's going to lead this guerrilla team? she demanded, following them out into the corridor. *You are* not *going to remain on M'zull, Kusac! It would be suicide!*

I don't know who will lead them, or even if there will be a team yet, Carrie. I can oversee it mentally from a distance, though.

"Kusac, a word in my office," said Kezule quietly at his elbow.

Surprised, Kusac turned to look at him, then nodded acquiescence. "Carrie, you, Kaid, and Banner gather the rest of our people and the commandos who lived on Kij'ik, and start forming teams of warriors and captives. ZSADHI can give you lists of those available. Use the large empty room we were allocated next to the Temple on the ground level. I'll join you shortly."

The door closed silently behind them, and Kezule gestured him toward the less formal chairs.

"The scent marker is gone, Kezule," said Kusac, sitting down. "Kaid tricked Carrie and me into a situation where our mental Link could re-form if we wanted it to, and when it did, the scent marker vanished. I haven't yet had a chance to tell you."

"I had noticed," said Kezule, picking up and lighting one of his small cigars from a box on the table. "But it wasn't about that I wanted to talk. You mentioned controlling Valtegan memories."

"I said it was worth looking into," said Kusac. "After all, haven't TeLaxaudin been doing that for centuries in order to help the Primes breed?"

The General hesitated, drawing on his cigar, then letting out the smoke in a series of gentle puffs.

"There are times when I've wondered where some of

my memories have come from," he said finally. "They feel—incomplete—as if only the main facts are there, not the details. Then something tells me I've always had those memories."

"I've read many minds, Kezule. Believe me, deep, old memories can be like that, or they can be overwhelming with the amount of sharp detail," said Kusac, the half-truth coming easily to him. This was his Hunt, and though also a victim, he knew that Kezule had no part in it. "If your memories have been altered, I see no sign it was done to diminish you."

"If you did see signs of that . . ."

"I'd have the hide of whoever did it, literally," he interrupted. "Then give it to you to make a rug or a wall hanging."

Kezule laughed, his first genuine one since Zhalmo had been taken. "And I'd do the same for you."

"Did I ever tell you how our telepaths defeated your Empire?"

"No, you didn't, and for some reason, it never occurred to me to ask you," said Kezule, regarding him carefully.

"Our people placed telepaths as pets with all the major figures in the Court and the military, and gradually they subverted them by making them paranoid about each other. On a given signal, the attack was launched. They made the fleet leaders fire on their own ships, the military on the ground attack each other, and they sterilized the females here on K'oish'ik, as well as turning the guards on each other."

Kezule stared at him. "You used our weaknesses against us. Are you thinking this could be repeated, with Valtegan females?"

"It had crossed my mind."

"It depends how they treat their females. They'll certainly be in harems, and the breeders are given to a very few. They'd have military harems with breeders to reward the military as well as to see that more soldiers were bred from good stock, and public ones with drones for the common soldiers to let off steam. That was the pattern in my day. It's hardly likely high-ranking Admirals or Generals would take their wives out of their homes, even if they aren't drugged and semiferal."

"They might if they thought K'hedduk was casting avaricious looks at them. And that we *can* arrange."

"That would take talented individuals, ones willing to be enslaved by K'hedduk to get close enough to the upper military echelon and the wives to influence them. Do we have any that knowledgeable and gifted?"

"Yes, but I value their Warrior skills more. There may be some among the Ch'almuthians. I intend to recruit from them as well since stopping the M'zullians is in their interests too."

"Indeed."

"As for training them, we can access their own teachers, and Conner."

"They're pacifists, and Conner is a priest," Kezule objected.

"A priest with the lives of many warriors in his mind," corrected Kusac. "If anyone can teach them how to use their abilities deviously, he can."

"Then," said Kezule, leaning forward to stub the remains of his cigar in the ashtray, "let's go talk to him and the Ch'almuthian leader now."

Giyarishis had no sooner learned that Kusac was beginning to piece together their manipulation of Kezule, and their network for Unity on Kij'ik and in the Palace than he sent a private call to Annuur, humming and chirping in utter terror.

"What do I say to him?" he wailed. "They raised violent hands to Kzizysus on their world, the same will be done to me!"

"You lose yourself," said Annuur. "I send you home for rest. Join your Skepp and have long baths, good food, until I call for you. I shall deal with the Hunter."

"Yes, Phratry Lord," said Giyarishis, his instant relief evident in the mellowing tone of his humming.

"Send others home too," Annuur ordered. "I will have them disassemble the Unity network on Kij'ik so nothing is found if they look. Now go."

He'd just finished when Tirak stood framed in the entrance to the aircar.

"Annuur, we need to take the *Watcher* out tonight. Orders."

"Out of question," snapped Annuur.

"Orders, Annuur."

"Mine take precedence." Annuur shouldered his way past him out into the open air.

"What are you talking about?" demanded Tirak, following him. "You can't have orders that don't concern me!"

Annuur stopped dead, turning and rearing up on his haunches. "You forget I leader on my own world. For them, I act too, follow orders. You want to take to your Ghost to Kij'ik, put him on shuttle, go take him there, let him sneak off in landing bay."

Tirak's jaw fell open as he looked at the Cabbaran in shock.

"What? Think we not notice extra weight on trip here? Not sense an extra mind?" Annuur wrinkled his nose at Tirak, amused, briefly, at the other's shock. "Do what you must this time. Not involve us in future. Do not do this again, Tirak. Violates our Family contracts."

He dropped back onto all fours and headed for the city's sally port at an easy lope.

"Dammit, you'd make Kathan himself pull out his beard!" Tirak called after the other's departing figure.

"What kind of trouble?" M'kou demanded of the messenger after excusing himself from the King and Rhyaz. "There aren't any civilians on Kij'ik now."

"People have seen a shadowy figure walking the corridors," said the youth. "They say it's as if he's lost."

"A shadowy figure?"

"That's what they told me."

"How shadowy?"

"Um . . . they say he was almost transparent when he was first seen last night, but now he looks more . . . solid."

"It's their imagination," M'kou said, beginning to catch up to the King again. "They still brewing that homemade Ch'almuthian rotgut up there?"

"I have no idea, sir. There's something else you should know."

M'kou stopped again. "What?" he asked impatiently.

"It's a Sholan."

M'kou stared at him. "A Sholan?"

"Yes. We all know that there are none up on Kij'ik, but . . ."

"Thank you. Tell them I will deal with it, and meanwhile they are to ignore him."

"Yes, sir, but . . ."

"That will be all!" M'kou spun around and headed back the way he'd come.

He remembered a shadowy figure that he and Zayshul had almost seen when watching Shaidan. It had picked the child up and shaken him, moments before Kusac had briefly died on Kij'ik. What had the child called it? Vartra.

"ZSADHI, where's Captain Aldatan?"

"In the Temple with General Kezule, talking to the Human Brotherhood priest, Conner."

"Did you show him the vision?" Conner asked Kusac.

"I didn't need to. Attacking us in an attempt to destroy the Throne of Light is exactly what K'hedduk would do."

"What vision?" asked Kezule, frowning.

"The one of the City and Palace being destroyed," said Conner.

"I don't believe in . . ." the General began, but Kusac cut him short, briefly outlining his idea of replicating some of the actions of the First enhanced Sholan telepaths to the Brother.

"Do we have any telepaths capable of doing this on K'oish'ik, either Primes or Ch'almuthians?" he asked when he'd finished. "The First were not Warriors. Even being near violence made them experience the victim's pain and crippled them with intense nausea."

Conner sat down on one of the seats that had been reclaimed from storage and scratched at his beard thoughtfully. "I'm sure there are," he said. "Are you asking me to locate some? Whether or not they'd be willing to help us is another matter."

Kusac looked at Kezule, who nodded.

"Yes, I'm asking you to locate them for us," said the General.

"Could you give them extra training?" asked Kusac.

"I don't know what your Firsts did," said Conner. "I'll help in any way I can, of course."

"We have one of the Firsts with us."

"You have?" Conner and Kezule said simultaneously.

"Two of them were trapped in a stasis device here," said Kusac. "It's a long story, but we ended up rescuing them on another world."

"Who?" asked Kezule.

"Rezac," said Kusac, sending to Carrie and asking her to bring him to the Temple. "Kezule, Conner, his identity *must* remain secret."

Moments later, Rezac, accompanied by Carrie and Kaid, entered.

"So you're one of those who brought about the Fall," said Kezule, looking Rezac up and down. "I remember your kind well. I had one, if you remember, Kusac. We held you in contempt because you were so weak. Apparently you were stronger than any of us."

Rezac froze, then he shrugged, mouth widening in a smile as his hands moved nonchalantly to rest on his knife and gun. "It was different back then."

You better have a damned good reason for telling them, sent Rezac, his thoughts dark with anger.

How could you tell Kezule who is he? demanded Carrie.

"Peace, Carrie," said Kusac, reaching out to draw her to his side. "Trust me, Rezac, there's no need for violence. We need help that only you, as one of the First, can give. And Kezule, don't taunt him, please."

"Play nicely, children," murmured Conner. "We fight a common enemy today."

Was this wise? asked Kaid.

Vital, Kusac replied shortly.

"Please, sit," said Kezule, moving to take a pew seat himself. "Conner's right: We're not enemies."

Rezac sat, but warily, Kaid beside him.

"What you want to know?" he asked.

"How did you manage to infiltrate the fleet and military commands?" Kezule asked.

"That was the easy part. Your Emperor ordered that we be captured on Shola and brought to his Court. He thought we made good pets and gave us as rewards to his favored Admirals and Generals, as well as to the Planetary Governors. The fact that we were telepathic made us valuable. We could be used to spy on their enemies and rivals, but you know that because you had a pet telepath spy yourself." There was barely suppressed venom in his tone as he said that.

"I'm not the person I was then, Rezac," said Kezule, his tone cool. "I had no choice in the matter: He was appointed to me by the Emperor. You didn't refuse anything given to you by him and live. I only know you were considered dangerous, despite your inability to fight. Incidentally, how did that change?"

"The Talent didn't breed as strongly to future generations," said Kaid. "Plus, there was a virus that infected us all, allowing us to fight."

"Carry on," gestured Kezule.

"We influenced the Emperor to see us as desirable status symbols," said Rezac. "After that, they stopped killing us and just rounded us up instead, shipping us out here. We let ourselves be caught."

Kezule raised an eye ridge. "You impress me. Unable to defend yourselves, you voluntarily became slaves?"

Rezac nodded. "It was a suicide mission, we knew that. I think Zashou and I were the only survivors, and that was an accident. We did leave children and the more frail of our numbers on Shola to ensure the next generation, of course."

"I thought nothing else I could learn about the Sholans could surprise me," Kezule said. "You, however, have just done so."

Rezac and Kaid exchanged glances.

"Could we repeat your plan on M'zull?" Kusac asked Rezac. "Using Primes or Ch'almuthians instead of ourselves?"

"I've no idea," said Rezac. "We became a visible status symbol, as I said, because we looked so different and because of our Talent. As I understand it, only your females are telepaths, General, and M'zull keeps the females incarcerated in harems, as your people did."

"You'll not be able to work on K'hedduk's mind as you did on Q'emgo'h's," said Kezule, frowning. "When I was taken to his research facility, I saw what he'd done to his Sholan captives, and they were telepaths. It was beneath contempt. If you're caught, you won't meet a pretty end. You'll be lucky if you can commit suicide. Those I saw weren't able to."

"You want telepaths placed in the Fleet, with Generals in their homes, and in the Palace?" asked Kaid.

"If we can," said Kusac.

"Then you need to recruit the wives, assuming they are sentient."

"I had thought it might be easier if we made their husbands jealous, made them see K'hedduk as wanting their wives for himself," said Kusac. "Likely all their wives are from Ch'almuth anyway."

"That could work," agreed Rezac. "If they are telepaths. You need to infiltrate the homes and harems first, though. That would take time, and we don't have a lot of that."

"If we could place a small group of guerrillas on M'zull," said Kusac, "one that included drone look-alikes who could find places in the homes and harems as servants, then they could start influencing the minds of the husbands and could recruit those telepathic wives we could find to help us."

"There are only a few people with the experience to do that," said Carrie, "and they're all Sholan."

"There may be a solution to that," said Kusac hesitantly.

"No, no, no!" said Carrie, pulling free of his hold and turning to face him angrily. "I'm not losing you again so quickly! Don't you *dare* plan to remain on M'zull!"

"That would indeed be suicidal," said Kezule. "There'd be nowhere safe for you, nowhere you could hide. I couldn't allow that, nor would King Zsurtul."

"It isn't going to happen," said Kaid firmly. "This idea hinges on the availability of drones who are telepaths. They just don't exist."

"I know, but if I can show our people how to create the illusion of being a drone, we could succeed."

"It took both of us to do that on Keiss, Kusac! And the disguises slipped if we had to defend ourselves. This is far too dangerous to even attempt!"

"You know my abilities are enhanced now. If a small group of us remained hidden and powered the others' illusions, it could be done," he argued. "I'm not trying to minimize the danger," he said hurriedly holding up a hand in negation, "but it is possible."

"Not even I would attempt that, Kusac," said Conner, "and I have access to more power than you can imagine."

"What's this talk of illusions anyway?" asked Kezule. "How can you create an illusion of being something other than you are? Surely that would take some advanced technology."

"Yes!" said Carrie, enthusiastically, turning to Kezule and leaning down to grasp him by the arm. "Maybe the Touibans can construct some kind of chameleon suit your commandos and some Ch'almuthians could wear! That would be far more sensible than you, Kusac, taking a group of Sholans and others and trying to hold an illusion."

"When we were on Keiss, we had to infiltrate the main Valtegan base and send out a rescue message to the *Khalossa*," Kusac explained to Kezule. "Carrie and I discovered we could create the illusion of me appearing Valtegan and so get into the base."

"Was Carrie also Valtegan?" asked Kezule, obviously intrigued.

"No, my twin sister worked in their recreation Center," said Carrie shortly. "I pretended I was her. And Kusac, as a Valtegan soldier, was escorting me to one of the officer's quarters."

"You two are just full of ingenious ideas, aren't you?" said Kezule with a slight smile. "I'd like to see this illusion you're talking about."

"No, Kusac," said Carrie, firmly. "Kezule, no matter what you see, it isn't an option. It took both of us just to disguise Kusac, and we are a Leska pair, at least four times stronger than two single telepaths. It takes far too much energy, makes us weak very quickly, and can't be sustained for long. And the minute we were attacked, Kusac was exposed for what he really is, a Sholan. We don't know if anybody but Kusac and I can even do it!"

"It might be worth finding out, just for the sake of it. One never knows if it could come in useful one day," said Kezule.

"I'll show you," said Kusac, moving a few paces back from everyone. "Don't any of you help me by giving me any extra energy. I need to try to do it alone."

"I don't think the cubs should see this," murmured Kaid, turning to look at the door as he sensed the youngsters approaching with Kitra. "It might frighten them or, worse, give them ideas." He signaled to her to leave.

As he began to slow his breathing, Kusac could sense that even Kaid was intrigued. Remembering what Conner had said about drawing energy from the very earth itself, mentally, he reached down through the soles of his feet, searching for it in the flagged stones of the temple floor. He found it and felt it suddenly surge through him, making his pelt and hair rise about him where his clothing did not hold it down.

Closing his eyes and concentrating, he built a picture of himself as a Valtegan in his mind's eye then began to project it slowly outward. He wasn't prepared for the energy he'd taken in to suddenly take over. The pain hit his legs first; so intense that it took his breath away. He staggered, felt them give under him, and fell to his knees. Then it hit his hips and shoulders, and this time he did cry out in agony as he collapsed forward onto the stone floor.

His limbs felt as though they were being stretched to breaking point, then beyond, as wave after wave of fiery pain wrapped itself around him, searing every part of his body. Just as he thought he could bear no more, the pain intensified as his hip joints were wrenched into unnatural positions.

He could do nothing, only lie there and suffer, unable even to make a sound as he felt himself changing. Forcing his eyes open, terrified, he watched his arms as his pelt disappeared, leaving behind the textured green skin of a Valtegan. Fresh agony poured through him as his fingers lengthened, straightened, and his claws extended to become nonretractable.

In his mind, Carrie's scream echoed endlessly, and he heard Shaidan shriek "Pappa!"

His son's fear mobilized him as nothing else could have done. Slowly he pulled his arms toward him, every muscle and joint sending spikes of sharp pain through him. He managed to push himself up to his hands and knees but collapsed backward, ending up sitting on his haunches. Blinking through tears of agony, he raised his head just in time to see Kaid rush to intercept Shaidan and sweep him up into his arms.

"No, Shaidan!" said Kaid. "You mustn't try to change!"

Conner was already on his feet and reaching for the cub. "Give him to me," he ordered. "I can stop him."

Already Shaidan's body was beginning to arch backward and shimmer slightly in Kaid's grasp.

"No!" Kusac managed to croak as Conner grabbed his son from Kaid. "Shaidan, don't follow me!"

"The time of Testing is here," said L'Shoh, appearing suddenly at Ghyakulla's side in her Realm. He held out his hand peremptorily. "Come. He tried to change too soon. He is not ready."

He must succeed, she sent, taking his hand and with a gesture transporting them back to L'Shoh's Realm. *Everything we are depends on him. We must take him now!*

They materialized to one side of the Entity's dark throne, beside a wide brazier of fire.

L'Shoh passed his hand over it, making the flames leap

higher. In their midst, an image began to form, that of a Sholan transformed into a Valtegan.

Bring him now, Ghyakulla sent as she joined her power to L'Shoh's.

·A blast of heat swirled around him, forming a shimmering cone of fire through which he could barely see the others. It pulled at him, seeming to suck him into the vortex it was creating. He felt himself falling, falling into darkness and cold.

CHAPTER 14

CARRIE flung herself to the empty spot on the floor where, moments before, a very different Kusac had sat.

"He's gone," she said disbelievingly, feeling around the flagstones, oblivious to the heat still in them. "He's gone! Who took him?" she demanded, her voice rising an octave as she looked wildly around her. "Who took him back to the Margins?"

With a glance at Conner and Shaidan, Kaid ran over to crouch down beside her. "You don't know it was the Margins."

"I can smell the fire, Tallinu! Can't you?"

"That doesn't mean the Margins."

Kezule came toward them, stooping to pick something up. "What's this?" he asked, holding it out to them.

Kaid looked, his ears flattening back to his head as he saw what was in the General's hand.

"Carrie," he said, his voice flat and emotionless.

Turning, she saw what he held. Reaching out slowly, she took the two halves of a white flower from Kezule's hand, then a lump of misshapen bronze. As she did, the fresh scent of nung blossom banished the last of the smell of seared stone and fur.

Kaid rose, helping Carrie to her feet and wrapping his arms comfortingly around her. "Not the Margins," he said.

Conner, cradling an unconscious Shaidan, joined them. "I believe he's with Ghyakulla and, despite the display of fire, L'Shoh," he said quietly. "Look, the flower has been severed exactly in half."

"But why? What would She want with him?" asked Carrie. "And what's the importance of the metal lump?"

"Examine it, Carrie. You'll find that there are still remains of its original form. Kusac showed it to me," said Conner as Rezac offered to take Shaidan from him.

She turned it over in her palm, seeing the faint outline of a reptile still on one side of the surface, and on the other, the vague shape of a Human face.

"He was able to reshape it," explained Conner. "He found it on a desk at the weather station."

"I remember that," said Kaid suddenly, letting her go to take it from her hand. "It was a norrta. How in the Gods' names did he manage to re-form it?"

"New abilities have been emerging," said Conner. "Like this one."

"He can change matter, as Zayshul and I could?" said Rezac. "But that took both of us, and we had to be pairing at the time to generate the energy needed to affect people!"

"What's he become?" whispered Carrie, her hand closing on the severed flower and crushing it. She flung it from her. "What have They done to him?"

Turning to Rezac, she grasped hold of Shaidan. "Give him to me," she ordered, pulling her son from his unresisting grasp. "What did They do to my son?"

"Shaidan's sleeping, Carrie," said Conner gently. "I put him to sleep to prevent him trying to follow Kusac."

"You caused this," she said accusingly, spinning around and looking at them each in turn. "All of you! You wanted so much of him for *your* purposes, he had nothing left to be my husband and the father of our children! That's all *he* ever wanted!"

"That's not true," began Conner.

"Shut up and just leave us alone! You've all of you done more than enough!" she snarled. Adjusting her hold on Shaidan, she pushed through them to the exit.

A small crowd of Primes stood there, M'kou among them. As he hastily cleared a way for her, they bowed, chanting something that sounded like a Litany in voices so low she was only just aware of them.

"Tell me if he returns," she ordered M'kou as she passed him.

* * *

Consciousness returned slowly to Kusac, but wherever he was, it was pitch dark. He sent out questing thoughts, trying to check his body, but he could sense nothing—no pain, no movement. He could be in a sensory deprivation tank for all he knew. Pushing back his rising panic, he automatically began reciting the Litanies. He'd learn nothing unless his wits were about him, and even they seemed to want to desert him right now.

Everything had a rational explanation; he just had to find the one that fit. What had happened to him in the last few seconds before he'd passed out? He remembered losing control of the illusion and it turning into a horrifying reality, as he actually became a Valtegan. There had been heat as intense as that at Vartra's forge when L'Shoh had taken him there, a spinning cone of heat with himself at the center—had he somehow triggered the damned la'quo still in his system and been dragged back to the far past of the Fire Margins again? Was he stuck here now, forever separated from all that he held dear, that he'd only just regained? It didn't bear thinking about.

A sudden loud knocking broke the silence, and suddenly his world was flooded once again with light and senses.

"General Chokkuh, you said to wake you when the female arrived. She's here," said a voice from outside the door.

A bed creaked, and his body got to its feet. "Have her wait in the lounge." The voice sounded uncannily close, almost as if . . .

Legs came into view, khaki-clad uniformed legs, ending in heavy boots. Then the owner lurched to his feet.

Oh, Gods, oh, Gods, this is impossible! I'm inside his head!

Terrified, he pulled his mental presence back into itself as far as possible. What would happen if his host found out he was there? Where the hell *was* here, what was he doing here, and how the hell could he escape this?

His thoughts tumbled one after another as he watched through the male's eyes. They passed a mirror, and he caught a fleeting glimpse of his host in it—Valtegan, as if he'd had any doubt.

The General opened the door and stepped into the softer lighting of the lounge. Standing by a stack of shelves was a small figure wrapped in a hooded cloak, her back to them.

"Still looking at my readers," said the General, gesturing the soldier to leave. "They're not for you."

"Oh, I know," a familiar voice said lightly as she reached up to lower the hood, exposing a short bob of golden hair. "I can't read your language anyway, but the shapes on their covers are interesting."

Chokkuh reached out to pull her cloak away and throw it on a nearby chair. She turned around and smiled at him, once more sending Kusac's mental self into a state of shock. It was Carrie!

"A drink first?" Chokkuh asked.

"You are most kind," she replied in a soft, seductive tone, glancing up from under her long eyelashes at him, but there was a note of surprise in her voice.

The General turned away from her to go to the small dining table at the other side of the room where a wine bottle and two glasses were already waiting. As he poured, he watched her approach him.

"Thank you for the dress," she said. "Do you like it?" She turned around slowly, the better for him to see it.

"It is adequate," he replied, handing her a glass as he—and Kusac—appraised her.

Of a semitransparent material, the purple fabric did little to conceal her nakedness under it. Two folds of the diaphanous material swept from behind her neck across her breasts, barely covering them while leaving her back totally exposed. Gathered by a sash at the waist, the rest fell in soft folds to her feet, which were encased in small slippers of the same color.

Where were they, and when? Was this a future yet to come? Carrie hated the M'zullian Valtegans; nothing would make her put herself in such a situation—unless she thought him dead and there was a way she could kill his killers. Hard on its heels came the thought—was he in fact dead? He recoiled further into himself, unwilling to even think about that.

She sipped her wine, coming closer and pressing herself against Chokkuh's side, placing her other hand against his shirt.

"Straight from work?" she asked, wrinkling her nose delicately. "What were you doing this time?"

He took a small drink. "In the field again," he said shortly. "Chasing your rebels."

She took another sip of the wine, her fingers slowly beginning to unbutton his shirt. "Mmm, this is good."

"It should be, it's locally made."

"We do make good wine. Did you catch anyone this time?" his shirt open, she slipped her hand inside and began stroking his chest.

Not like this, Carrie! he almost cried out. *You're being too obvious! Use your mind, not your body, dammit!*

The Valtegan finished his wine in one mouthful and put the glass back on the table; then he reached for her, wrapping one hand around the back of her neck.

"No. We're looking for a hideout in the forests to the east. Do you know anything of it?" His voice was harsher now.

She smiled up at him. "Me? I rarely leave here. What would I know of rebels? They hate women like me."

At last Kusac was beginning to pick up some of his host's thoughts. This was his favorite female, and he was angry with her for asking so many questions.

Oh, Gods, he had to help her, let her know he was here, inside the mind of this M'zullian. She must know how dangerous a game this was! Even on Keiss they'd had a saying, *never be noticed by a Valtegan*, and here she was, throwing herself at this one to get information!

Chokkuh reached out with his other hand, pushing aside the flimsy material covering her nearest breast, grasping it firmly, and letting his claws dig into the surrounding flesh.

She winced, but she kept the smile on her face.

"It would be a pity," he said, flexing the hand still around her neck, "if you should ever betray me, Lise." He released her breast and grasped the dress at the waist, ripping it off her, leaving her standing there rigid and naked. Keeping his eyes on her face, he drew a claw tip down the center of her body, leaving a thin red line. "You have no idea what the Inquisitors could do to a soft-skinned being like you."

"Do you doubt me?" she asked, voice strained by his grip on her neck and throat. "You never have before."

' Call it a warning. You're good at what you do. It would be a shame to lose so—talented a slave."

He released her, taking the glass from her hand and throwing it aside. "Enough talk! You know why you're here."

He didn't want to witness this, but he had only two options: huddle deep inside and shut off his own mind to what was happening, or stay aware and gradually take control while his host was distracted. He couldn't do it suddenly; if he did, he'd be fighting his host constantly when he needed to keep his attention on other matters, like keeping the. both alive.

The M'zullian was rough with her, but as Kusac mentally crept closer and closer to the surface of Chokkuh's mind, he began to sense her, and he realized that she was enjoying this treatment. It made no sense at all as the M'zullian left bite and scratch marks over her body, delighting in her ability to take what he dealt out. A change this basic in her nature could only be caused by a traumatic experience—he knew, it had happened to him, but he'd been tortured. Was she in fact a prisoner and not doing this voluntarily?

His instincts warred with each other, screaming out for him to take control now and stop this abuse, and at the same time telling him that something was not quite right.

At last, spent, Chokkuh fell back among the wreck of his bedding.

"Can I get you more wine?" she asked, slipping lithely off the bed.

"Yes, a little."

Sure-footed, she padded off into the lounge.

Little things were beginning to add up now—she should have been stiff and wincing in pain given the scratches down her back, but it was as if she weren't aware of them. There were other things, too, that made him think that no matter how like Carrie she looked, she was not the same person. Wait, Chokkuh had called her Lise. This wasn't Carrie; this was Elise, her twin. She had no sense of pain because Carrie suffered it all for her! Somehow, he'd ended up on Keiss, back before Elise's death. This shock, among the many he'd suffered so far, left him feeling only numb.

As she came back, carrying the glass, he sensed the tenseness in her body that hadn't been there before.

Chokkuh must have been aware of it too as despite his physical languor, he was instantly alert.

He was setting a trap for her! This had to be the night she was taken prisoner. His immediate instinct was to do something—help her escape, distract Chokkuh. Then, like a shower of cold water, he realized if he did anything, then the present he knew would never happen. Unless Elise died, there would be no Kusac and Carrie. A wave of light-headedness swept through his mind as he realized a younger

.sion of him was already here, struggling through the snow
.th a badly wounded and infected leg. If he did anything to
.elp Elise, he would die or be taken prisoner himself; his crew
would risk capture as there would be no rescue message sent
out, and the Keissians would suffer even longer under the
yoke of the M'zullians. Everything he knew would cease to
be if he interfered.

As if from a distance, he saw Elise give Chokkuh the glass.

He was jolted back to reality when his mind was flooded
with the other's emotions as Chokkuh leaped to his feet and
grasped hold of Elise and the glass of wine. Calling for his ad-
jutant, he stalked into the lounge, dragging her with him. The
door was flung open, and three armed soldiers rushed in.

"Yes, General?"

He thrust the glass at one of the others. "Drink that," he
commanded.

"General, what are you doing? Don't you trust me? Why
give him the wine?" asked Elise, trying to keep her voice
even.

"We'll see," hissed Chokkuh. "I remember sleeping too
deeply after your last visit. This time, someone else can taste
the wine."

The soldier accepted the glass and reluctantly took a small
sip.

"Drink it all," Chokkuh ordered.

Within minutes of doing so, the soldier's eyes began to
droop, then he began to sway on his feet before collapsing
heavily to the floor.

Chokkuh turned on her. "I warned you!" he said, lashing
her across the face with the back of his hand twice before flinging her aside. "Take her to J'koshuk! Tell him he was right, she
is a spy for the rebels!"

Once they had left, still enraged, Chokkuh went to one of
the cabinets and pulled out a bottle of hard liquor. He downed
several shots in one, and then he headed back to his bedroom,
collapsed on the bed, and turned the light out.

While his host slept, Kusac slowly extended his control and
tried to think dispassionately about his and Elise's predica-
ments. It wasn't easy. Apart from the short hair, she was almost identical to Carrie; only he, who knew her so well, could
spot the differences. He tried not to think of what was happening to her right now, but memories of what he'd suffered at

J'koshuk's hands came too readily to his mind. He was grateful Chokkuh hadn't gone with them.

Elise had selfishly pursued her career as a spy in the
M'zullian pleasure city despite knowing the pain and suffering it caused her twin. Dammit, Carrie—a virgin!—had been
the vulnerable one, suffering all the pain of Elise's encounters
as a qwene! It was no wonder she'd been terrified of consummating their Leska Link, and it was even more of a miracle
that she had been able adapt to the Sholan telepaths' way of
life, including taking Kaid as their Third.

He could feel his anger building, and he used it to keep
all thoughts of sympathy at bay. Elise didn't deserve his
sympathy—she had taken a ridiculous risk tonight, and worse,
she knew it. Now she was paying the price, mentally at least.
She wouldn't suffer physically, Carrie would. He'd seen her
wounds himself in the days after she rescued him, and they
were horrific.

Eventually his thoughts turned to why he was here, in this
time and place. Obviously there was a reason, and his bet
was that Ghyakulla and L'Shoh were heavily involved in this.
Which meant it had to do with them wanting him to be an
arbiter of their Justice. But what did they expect him to do?
Save Elise? He couldn't, he knew that now. There was also
the temptation to kill J'koshuk—if he did, then he wouldn't
end up as the Inquisitor's prisoner, and Carrie would never be
raped by him, but what would that change? What the hell was
he doing here if there was nothing he could do that wouldn't
alter the future and destroy all the good that had been accomplished, not to mention wipe out the existence of their
children as well as Kaid and Carrie's daughter.

If he could have moaned, he would. A male could go mad
trying to work through the ramifications of every thought and
action . . . Finally, sleep claimed even his mind.

K'oish'ik

"Explain to me what just happened," said Kezule, looking at
Kaid and Conner.

"In my office," said Brother Conner. "M'kou, please order refreshments for us—strong ones."

M'kou nodded and gave the order to ZSADHI as he followed them to the office.

Once they were settled, Conner began. "Kusac has talked to me over the last few days about his changing abilities. He found out by accident that he could alter the appearance, permanently, of things like that lump of bronze and of living things as well. He experimented on some flowers in his suite, changing their colors."

"That's a long way from shape-changing and disappearing!" snapped Kezule.

"Patience, General," said Conner. "The other day when he collapsed down in the new village, he was taken by the Mother to Vartra's Realm, where he met with her and L'Shoh."

Kezule looked utterly baffled.

"He means our Earth Goddess, Ghyakulla, who is the same as your La'shol," said Kaid. "They aren't exactly deities, but they are Entities, the spirits or aspects of our worlds. Perhaps because we're telepaths, we're more aware of them, and they of us. They certainly interfere in our lives!"

"So you're saying he had a vision of some kind?" Kezule asked, still confused.

"Not exactly," said Conner. "He was mentally taken to one of their Realms, a place outside our perceptions, where they spoke to him about being their Avatar to bring Justice to the Alliance Worlds and deal with the M'zullians."

Kaid had begun to curse under his breath, his hands clenching into angry fists where they rested on his lap. "Where is Vartra in all this?" he demanded.

"Vartra has been absent for some time," said Conner, "and it has annoyed Ghyakulla."

"Vartra?" echoed M'kou. "I've news of him."

"What do you know about Vartra?" demanded Kaid, turning on him. "Tell me now! He's up to his neck in this!"

"He's been on Kij'ik. He was there when Kusac died—I saw him, or his shadow. He shook Shaidan and put him into some kind of trance."

"So he was responsible for sending Shaidan after Kusac!"

"But that's not my news," M'kou added hastily. "They're saying since yesterday, he's been seen on Kij'ik, wandering around the corridors, lost. His appearance, since you can apparently see through him, is disturbing our troops."

"Enough of this Vartra! Where is Kusac?" interrupted Kezule, banging his fist on the table. "I want him brought back now!"

"We can't reach him. He will return when They're finished with him," said Conner. "I believe They may be testing him."

"He was only supposed to be forming an illusion," said Rezac. "How did he manage to change himself?"

"I was asked to teach him what my predecessor taught the last Avatar," said Conner. "One of the things I was going to show him was how to draw energy from the earth. As he was creating the illusion, he tried to do it for himself, and I believe, because he didn't know how to wield the power properly, it took over and triggered the actual physical change."

"How permanent is it?" asked Kezule as a servant slipped in with a tray of glasses and a bottle of spirits, which M'kou took and began to dispense. "Assuming he returns," he added dryly.

Kaid tossed the lump of bronze onto the table, where it fell with a dull thud. "As permanent as he wants, apparently," he said. "We may not be able to reach Kusac, but we can talk to Vartra."

"Take Shaidan," said Conner, accepting a glass from M'kou.

"I don't need Shaidan," Kaid growled. "He's going through enough right now. Vartra has been plaguing me for years with visitations and visions! He'll talk to me."

Conner caught his eye and held it. "They are of one blood," he said gently. "He may not talk to anyone not of his line."

Kaid stiffened, then sighed his defeat. "I'll take Shaidan tomorrow. It'll keep his mind occupied if his father isn't back by then."

Ghioass

"This is intolerable," hummed Zaimiss from the floor of the Camarilla Council chamber. "I demand explanation why

Giyarishis and others sent home, Unity disabled for hours in Sand-dweller Palace and dismantled on Kij'ik! This allowed control over Hunter Entity to fail and him to escape us!"

"Because we. Do. Not. Control Hunter," replied Shvosi from her position on the Speaker's podium. "Annuur in the field, he sees more immediately than us what happens. Had he not done as he did, we would now be discovered."

"Not know this for sure," countered the Isolationist Leader. "Now this Vartra can tell them all that they only guess!"

Aizshuss rose to his feet, eyes swirling as he focused on Zaimiss. "Why you so concerned?" he asked lazily. "Surely this what you want— our withdrawal from the *lesser species*?"

"Not when we need to monitor and control the Hunter!"

"I told you, we do *not* control the Hunter! Study the actions against him *you* have sanctioned, and you'll see most were to prevent him from discovering us."

"Where is he now? He has done yet another disappearance on us!" said Shumass, rising. "A shambles, this is!"

"That's not our doing," snapped Shvosi. "Power failures at our weather controls allowed the Entity to escape."

"Six inches rain before it fixed," said Kuvaa mournfully, wrinkling her snout. "Lightning striking, my garden destroyed."

"I care nothing for that," hummed Zaimiss, glowering at her. "What's your few weeds to me when our plans crumble! Unity, show us potentialities!"

When nothing happened, Zaimiss began to hum angrily, his draperies shifting around his spindly legs as he emitted an angry scent. "Unity, obey!"

"You are not Speaker," said Shvosi with studied gentleness. "Do you forget Unity will not respond to you?"

"Insolence!" Zaimiss' voice thrummed with anger, and he began to stalk toward the podium.

A sudden movement from the side of the room and two guards, one Cabbaran, one TeLaxaudin, moved to block his way.

Khassis got to her feet. "Return to your place, Zaimiss. This behavior not acceptable."

"Since when we needed guards to interfere in our meetings?" demanded Shumass.

"Since your party abandoned all rules of protocol in Chamber," hummed Khassis angrily. "Shvosi, if you please?"

"Unity, display current predictions," Shvosi said, acknowl-edging Khassis' request as Zaimiss sulked his way back to his cushions.

The wall behind her came to life, showing a screen of dark, angry colors with a roiling nexus in the center. Even the near-est ribbons of movement were leeched of their color.

"Look at it!" screeched one of the younger Cabbaran mem-bers. "Utter chaos! We will be destroyed!"

"Be quiet, Rekkur," snapped Shvosi. "This not chaos. This is merely potentialities of now while the Hunter is not in the calculations."

"We should be doing more than sitting here debating," hummed Zaimiss.

"And what do you Isolationists suggest?" asked Shvosi, sar-castically. "Intervention is against what you believe, is it not? There is nothing we can do but wait for his return."

"We can get the Hunter Entity back before he tells all," said Shumass.

"To what purpose?" asked Aizshuss. "He was only once contained because he was actively interfering. Now he cannot. I Speak strongly against that idea."

"I Second that," snapped Shvosi. "Maybe, Shumass, we should rename your party the Meddlers since you leave noth-ing alone! Our purpose is to aid lesser species to survive, pro-mote understanding, and prevent wars, not kidnap and torture them! Yes, we know you tortured the Hunter Entity both times you had him in your control! That was *not* sanctioned!"

"Shvosi, no insults," warned Khassis, coming forward to take the podium from her. "There is nothing to be done till the Hunter returns, so I will close today's session. Until then, representatives from each party may study the potentialities if they wish. The Reformists will be first," she said, acknowledg-ing Shvosi's gestured request.

"That went better than I expected," Khassis murmured as the chamber slowly emptied. "So good of Zaimiss to play into our hands with his anger. Not so good you lose your temper," she added, waving an admonitory finger at Shvosi.

"He is such a meddler, though," said Shvosi, dropping back onto all fours. "But what does this really represent?" she asked, pointing to the screen as Kuvaa trotted up to join them.

"It is showing the potentiality for great chaos," said Khassis, moving closer to the screen.

"And it involves several species," said Kuvaa. "They are all interlinked as usual—the Hunters, the Humans, and the four Sand-dweller worlds, even the dead one. Now why might that be involved?"

"I have no idea," admitted Khassis.

K'oish'ik, late afternoon

Carrie was fixing herself some coffee later that afternoon when Shaidan, asleep on the sofa, suddenly woke and began to scream. Dropping everything, she ran to the sofa, throwing herself onto it and pulling Shaidan onto her lap. Wrapping her arms around him, she held him close and murmured soothing words.

His body stiffened, back arching till he almost fell off her lap as he let shriek after shriek peal out.

She tightened her grip, pressing the small unyielding body against hers and began to rock him gently, still keeping up the litany of soothing words.

The door burst open, and one of the guards rushed in.

"Get out!" she hissed. "It's a nightmare, nothing more. And let in no one until I say!"

As he backed out, she called out to the AI, "ZSADHI, reassure those who need it that we're fine."

"Yes, Sister."

Suddenly, his body went limp, and he began to sob uncontrollably.

"Hush, Shaidan. It's all right," she said, relaxing her hold and reaching up with one hand to stroke his head. "I'm here, you're not alone anymore."

His hands grasped her, holding onto her as tightly as she'd held him moments before. He turned his head, burying it against her chest, and continued sobbing.

With an awful clarity, she realized Kusac hadn't been exaggerating when he said he was the only stable thing in Shaidan's world. And now, after turning into a Valtegan, he'd vanished before the cub's eyes.

"Oh, Shaidan," she said, rubbing her cheek across the top of his head. "It's all right. He'll come back, but you have me, too. Mamma will always be here." She realized that the distance there'd been between her and Kusac had also been there between her and Shaidan. She'd made no effort to bond with her son until now, and the guilt tore at her as she clutched him every bit as frantically.

Gradually, as his sobs began to lessen, she was able to push aside her guilt.

"That's better, cub," she said gently. "I promise you, you'll never be alone again. We're your family, and we'll be with you always now."

He began to hiccup, gradually relaxing and sitting back from her to rub at his eyes. "I'm sorry I'm being such a baby," he said quietly.

"You're not a baby! Seeing what happened to your father would be enough to make anyone cry," she said, reaching out to wipe the tears from his cheeks and hold him closer. "I'm your mama, and you have every right to come and cry on my lap at any time. We all forget how little time you've been awake in our world, but you're not a baby, you're almost a kitling in reality."

"I don't really know you," he said with a hiccup.

"I know, and that's my fault. I promise you, we're going to get to know each other now."

"You've brought your belongings into the suite," he said. "And I can smell my father's scent on you."

"Your father and I are Leskas again. Do you know what that means?"

He nodded slowly. "It means you share a very close mental Link."

"It's more than that. We love each other very deeply, and all our children, and that includes you, Shaidan."

"But you hardly know me, you said so."

"I know I love you, and we've plenty of time to get to know each other—our lifetimes," she said, gently touching her nose to his.

The door suddenly burst open, and Kaid came rushing in. "What happened? What's up with Shaidan?" he asked, running over to them.

"Nothing. Shaidan just had a bad nightmare, that's all,"

said Carrie, signaling him to let the matter drop. "You know Kaid, don't you, Shaidan? He's your Triad father. Leskas often form special marriages, and Kaid is the one we chose. Kaid is your other father, that's why he came here so quickly when he sensed you were upset."

Kaid knelt down beside them and reached up to ruffle Shaidan's hair, then gently tweak one ear. "She's right, cub. Kusac is your biological father, but I'm your father by marriage, and I care about you as much as he and Carrie do."

"Is the nightmare all gone now?" asked Carrie.

Shaidan nodded, looking dubiously from Kaid to her.

"How about I get you a hot chocolate drink. Would you like that?" asked Kaid.

"Yes, please," said Shaidan quietly, still holding tightly to Carrie.

Kaid ruffled his hair one more time, then got to his feet and went over to the drink-dispensing unit to fetch a hot chocolate.

"I need your help tomorrow, Shaidan. How would you like to go on a trip to Kij'ik with me? It seems an old friend of yours has reappeared. His name is Vartra."

Shaidan sat up abruptly. "Go up to Kij'ik? But it's far away."

"Not anymore. General Kezule had it brought here to help defend this world. Would you like to come with me?"

The cub looked at him suspiciously. "How do I know we won't stay there?"

Kaid laughed as he brought the drink back over to him. "You're obviously Kusac's son," he said. "And Carrie's! You're as suspicious as both of them put together. We're coming back because I prefer living on the planet to living on a space station, and we're waiting for your father to return."

"Why do you need me to come with you?"

"Because Vartra can be persnickety and may not want to talk to me. However, He does know you, and you're related to each other."

Shaidan took the proffered mug and sipped carefully at the hot drink. "Related how?"

Carrie began to laugh gently. "I'm going to enjoy this explanation."

"Err, well . . . Vartra isn't quite the same as us," began Kaid.

Shaidan gave him an old-fashioned look. "Of course he isn't. He's an Entity."

"You know?" Kaid asked in surprise.

"How else could he remain hidden from everyone else?"

"Very true," murmured Kaid. "Well, a long time ago, he married a female from your family, the Aldatans. Their children were your ancestors."

"I'll go with you," he said, mouth opening wide in a yawn. "If I can sleep here tonight," he added, his eyes blinking slowly as they grew heavy. He handed Kaid the now empty mug. "Thank you."

"Where else would you sleep?" asked Carrie, hugging him. "It's early yet, but if you want to curl up in your pappa's bed now, you can. Kaid, would you make my excuses to the King and to Rhyaz and Alex, please?"

I'm not leaving Shaidan, she sent to Kaid as she sensed his hesitation.

"Of course. They'll understand your place is with your son at this time," he said, leaning forward to stroke her hair and plant a kiss on her forehead.

Keiss, next day, 3 years ago

Morning came, and the nightmare was still with him. Once again, Kusac tried to retreat from the forefront of his host's mind. After a breakfast in the Officers' Mess of mostly cooked food, the Valtegan went to his office and sent one of his underlings for the Inquisitor.

Minutes later, J'koshuk, carmine robes swirling around his booted feet, strode into the General's small office.

"What do you want, Chokkuh?" he demanded, stopping before the desk. "Some of us have real work to do."

Chokkuh frowned. He despised the Inquisitor. "Watch your tongue," he snapped. "This is a military establishment. You will observe the protocols when addressing senior officers."

"I'm Chief Inquisitor, and you're interrupting my work. Interrogation is an art form where timing is vital . . ."

"I want answers! Locations of the rebel camps!" roared

Chokkuh, thumping a fist on his desk for emphasis. "I didn't give her to you to play with! What have you found out so far?"

"Nothing! I had her softened up last night, ready to start today—only you demanded my presence."

"Go, get out of here," said Chokkuh, not bothering to hide his repulsion for the other. War was clean, honorable: kill or be killed. The Inquisitors' world of torture, spying, and rooting out supposed treachery among their ranks was not.

"Get the information I need as quickly as possible, J'koshuk. If you take too long, the rebels will realize she's been captured."

"As you order," hissed the priest as he left the room.

It was late afternoon before Chokkuh went to the interrogation room. Kusac tried to separate his senses from his host's, but he couldn't. The metallic scent of blood hit him as soon as the door was opened. This was no sterile, white tiled room as it had been on the *Kz'adul*. The walls here had been coated with a plastic-like surface, and the floor was made of the pressed metal usually found in ship corridors. Here and there, drain holes had been inserted so the floor could be sluiced down.

"Well? Chokkuh demanded.

J'koshuk turned away from the group of people clustered around the figure strapped to the examination table and stepped forward to meet the General.

"She's given us nothing but old information," he said. "She's strong, stronger than the Human males I've interrogated. Her pain tolerance is remarkably high."

"I don't want to hear that," Chokkuh hissed, pushing him aside and striding into the room. "What are you doing to her now?" he demanded, looking down at the obviously unconscious female.

"Keeping her alive," said J'koshuk dryly.

"I don't intend her to live," Chokkuh said, grasping hold of Elise by the jaw and turning her face from side to side.

He didn't want to look, he couldn't, but he did. Her face was livid with bruises, as was her body. Her arms and thighs bled sluggishly from several knife cuts as well as many scratch and puncture wounds left by the clawed hands of her captors.

It's not Carrie, he thought, trying to force himself to remain detached, but it was impossible when he knew Elise's injuries were mirrored on *his* Carrie's body.

"I need to keep her alive long enough to get your information," said the Inquisitor. "If she goes into shock, she could die."

Releasing her, Chokkuh reached for the neural prod hanging at the belt of one of the guards. Flicking it on, he pressed it hard against Elise's ribs.

She let out a piercing scream as her body jerked upward, back arching in agony.

J'koshuk grabbed for the prod and wrenched it from the General's grasp. "I told you she needs a break!"

Chokkuh raised his hand to hit the priest, but the guards were instantly between them, weapons drawn in readiness.

Kusac's mind reeled in shock. Had Elise actually felt that? Was she so weak that she was actually feeling pain now?

"She's my captive now, General," said J'koshuk coldly. "I suggest you go and play with your soldiers. Have a drill, or an inspection, and let me do my job."

"I'll have you on report to the Commander!"

"Do that. He's just as anxious for the information as you are. I wouldn't draw any more attention to yourself than you already have, if I were you," said J'koshuk. "It was your incompetence that allowed her to spy on you in the first place."

With a loud hiss of displeasure, Chokkuh left.

Still fuming, Chokkuh headed for the Command Center where the military governor, General M'ezozakk, was conducting the search for the aliens who'd escaped from the scout ship they'd shot down a few days earlier.

Heavy blizzards had hampered their efforts, forcing them to remain on their base and covering the aliens' tracks. The bitter temperatures outside had necessitated them turning up the heating as cold weather made them sluggish. The snow had stopped for now, but the leaden gray skies promised more to come.

As he entered the room with its wall-mounted tactical screens and a dozen workstations, the lights dimmed, then flickered, almost fading before they steadied at half the level they'd been before. The TAC screens abruptly shut down. M'ezozakk hissed in anger.

"Divert the power to the main screen," he snapped. "Chokkuh, get down to the generator building and see what caused this brownout! I want full power restored here immediately. Shut down whatever you need to achieve it!"

For a split second, Chokkuh contemplated refusing the menial job; then, saluting smartly, he turned on his heel and left. A trip across the bitterly cold compound to listen to more of the Humans' excuses was preferable to remaining in close proximity to the thwarted Governor General.

He headed along the corridor to the relief guardroom for an escort of four soldiers. They'd learned the hard way that only a show off force kept the enslaved Human population under control. Apart from the rebels who'd left the settlement, the Humans weren't foolish enough to stage an outright rebellion. They used other, less overt, methods to make daily life on Keiss a constant battle of wills between their species.

The heated light-combat armor was stored here. Once they were suited up, he had the Duty Sergeant punch the day's codes into the weapons locker and dispense energy rifles. Though all troops stationed permanently on Keiss went armed, armor and rifles were only issued when leaving the Command Center.

Intrigued despite himself, Kusac began to mentally uncurl from the corner of Chokkuh's mind where he'd taken refuge. He was getting an unprecedented picture of the M'zullian warriors' lifestyle, albeit on Keiss, but it might expose some weaknesses that would be exploitable. By now, he had realized that as long as he didn't draw attention to himself, the Valtegan was totally unaware of his presence.

He listened as Chokkuh repeated the orders to the Sergeant before they left the Command Center.

The outside video feed, on backup power, had shown the area around the exit to be clear. Chokkuh ordered the outer blast door opened.

Helmet faceplate open, the freezing air almost burned his nostrils, but it was crisp and clean and a welcome change even to the Valtegan after several days cooped indoors by the severe weather. Kusac could sense his host's dislike of the cold, and as he carefully probed for more, memories of cold-weather training surfaced. Temperatures like this, below freezing, made them slow and sluggish, and they were trained to find or make a safe shelter, eat at least half their rations, then go into hibernation sleep until found. Kusac filed the information away for later—this was an important aspect of their training that his Prime commandos lacked, and it needed to be addressed as soon as possible.

Power was generated by burning a local fossil fuel mined in the mountains. The storms had prevented the cargo shuttles from collecting fresh supplies. Naturally, the Humans hadn't bothered to let their overlords know that stocks were dangerously low until now. However, the break in the weather meant six cargo shuttles had gone to collect the coal and were due back anytime. Until then, it was a matter of rerouting power to essential areas.

Chokkuh and his escort headed out into the cold and trudged along the paths cut through the deep snow to the routing station. There he gave orders to close down the recreation dome and route all remaining power to the Command Center, medical facilities, and the sleeping quarters until the temporary fuel shortage was over.

That done, he called the comm center and ordered them to inform everyone to return to their quarters and remain there until they were given fresh orders.

Chokkuh's memories told Kusac this happened two or three times each winter. The Valtegan hadn't punished the labor force since the shortage wasn't technically their fault. Besides, the Humans had a nasty habit of going on strike and refusing to work if any of them were singled out for punishment. Kusac mentally chuckled at the reality of the overlords being at the mercy of a workforce that downed tools at the slightest opportunity. There was indeed much to admire about the Human colonists on Keiss who had helped form the character of the woman he loved more than life itself.

As Head of Security, with much of the base closed down, Chokkuh ordered an extra two units of guards to patrol the dome and the troop quarters. Sabotage was rare, but a situation like this provided an ideal opportunity.

He spent the rest of the day in the Command Center helping to oversee the scouting parties searching the plateau and nearby woods for any signs of the crew of the wrecked scout ship. All they knew for certain was that they were bilateral and ferocious warriors. The firefight there had cost both sides dear, and all they had to show for it, apart from half a dozen of their own dead and wounded, was the burned-out shell of the shuttle and a few charred bone fragments they couldn't identify.

Heavy snow had covered their tracks, but Chokkuh had known they'd make for the forest and the cover it afforded, so he'd ordered his troops to search there.

By late afternoon, the expected delivery of fuel from the mine had arrived. The first large flakes of snow began to fall as they were unloading, and he had to order the scouters to pick up the search teams before it became the expected all-out blizzard.

All day, Kusac had remained a passive observer. He knew on one level that the other him was aware of Carrie and was struggling through the snow on his injured leg, trying desperately to reach the village in which she lived. Her memories of the terror and agony she'd gone through as J'koshuk tortured Elise were also there.

Chokkuh returned to the interrogation room after his evening meal, standing at the back, listening rather than watching. Unlike J'koshuk and his ilk, who bred among their own to strengthen their sadistic tendencies, he had no interest in overseeing the actual torture. All he wanted were the results.

Kusac tried to ignore the low-pitched whimpers Elise was making by telling himself she was suffering no real pain. It was Carrie who felt every blow, whose body was suffering many of the same wounds. Suddenly she let out a shriek that startled them all.

Without thinking, he reached mentally for Carrie, but her mind was incoherent with pain and terror. He tried to strengthen her, lend her energy, only to realize that in this body, he couldn't. Instead, he began to send to her before he realized what he was doing.

For a moment, his mind was seized and held, but it was pure instinct, as if she were grasping his hand. Chokkuh moved closer, and as he did, Kusac saw the extent of Elise's injuries. He wanted to stop them, to save Carrie more pain. He'd finally placed Chokkuh as the Valtegan who had kidnapped Kate and Taynar and killed a brave scouter pilot. Kill him and none of that would happen either.

He could do nothing to help, but perhaps he could at least delay the hunt for his crewmates. So much hinged on this moment of time, yet he couldn't even risk raging at fate inside his own mind lest he be discovered and all that the future was in his time be unraveled.

His vision blurred, and as his mind was released, he watched clawed green hands moving rapidly—far too rapidly—across the girl's body, leaving behind a trail of flowing blood and new wounds. Around him, the people flickered and moved, changing positions, coming and going through the door into the room, as time seemed to speed up.

Help me, said a voice in his mind as Elise looked up at him.

With a gut-wrenching lurch, time slowed down again.

"Well, General?" asked J'koshuk. "Shall I cut her or not?"

"Start with her fingers," he heard Chokkuh say.

Help me! Save Carrie! she screamed in his mind.

I will, he replied as a strange calmness crept over him. This was why he was here. This was the one thing he could and had to do.

She turned her head slowly to look at J'koshuk as he placed the knife over the fingers of her right hand.

"You'll learn nothing from me," she said, and she began to laugh as Kusac reached out to touch her heart and still it.

Her body jerked once, her laughter dying as she did. Her face relaxed, then her body went limp.

"She's dead, you fool!" hissed Chokkuh, but his voice sounded distant as Kusac felt his consciousness begin to fade.

Why did you have to laugh, Elise? was his last thought.

Kij'ik, next day, Zhal-Arema, 31st day (March)

Kaid taxied the shuttle into the main landing bay of the asteroid, following the signal lights set into the floor to his designated bay. He had to admit to being glad of the opportunity to see the place where his sword-brother had been living for so many months.

"We nearly got found," said Shaidan.

"Oh?"

"Mmm. It was the *Zan'droshi,* the other Prime ship, and one of the *Watcher* ships. The General still had the ancient ship attached to the side of Kij'ik, and he shut us down and rotated the Outpost to hide it. They cut the gravity."

What the hell had a *Watcher* ship been doing around the Prime ship?

"Oh, it landed inside," said Shaidan. "I wasn't listening to your mind," he added hastily, seeing Kaid's look. "I just heard you thinking."

He grunted. "You should be shielding more strongly, kitling," he said. "You'll find yourself unpopular if people know you can hear them all the time."

"But I can't. I can only hear my family and . . . you're family?" he said, his voice faltering.

Kaid raised an eye ridge at the child. "Yes, I'm family."

"Are you angry with me? Did I do something wrong?"

"No, Shaidan," he said, reaching out to ruffle the cub's hair between his ears. "Always be as honest as you are now with family, but don't let yourself be aware of all our thoughts. Everyone is entitled to privacy. I don't suppose you know which *Watcher* ship it was, do you?"

"Not exactly. I do know that the sept of Cabbarans on it are on K'oish'ik now, though."

"Are they indeed?" he murmured as he shut down the engines and began to release his harness. Annuur and Tirak's ship. So they had personal dealings with the Primes, had they?

"You sure you don't have a problem coming back here?" he asked Shaidan as he helped the youngster out of his seat.

"No. I met my father here. There are no bad memories for me, Pappa Kaid."

"Good."

"What do you want me to do? Vartra always found me, I didn't ask him to come to me," said Shaidan as they made their way down the short corridor to the air lock and opened it.

"We're going to one of the briefing rooms first to meet with the Captain here. He'll update us on where Vartra's been seen, and we'll go there for starters," said Kaid as they emerged onto the ramp.

A black-clad escort was waiting for them. One of the commandos stepped forward and saluted them smartly.

"Commander Kaid, welcome to Kij'ik. Shaidan, welcome back. Captain Zaykkuh is waiting for you in the Officer Level Briefing room."

"Hello, Shartoh," said Shaidan, looking up at the female Prime.

"Hello," she smiled, falling into step beside him. "How are you liking life on the planet?"

"Very much. I have my parents now, and my brothers and sisters. Did you know there's wind down there? And sunsets and sunrises?"

She laughed. "Yes, I do. I lived there before coming to Kij'ik, you know. I'm glad we're closer to home now, though. We get planet leave every other two weeks now."

Kaid listened to them chatting as they made their way to the Briefing room, glad to hear the youngling behaving like a normal cub at last, and surprised at the obvious affection that the female commando had for him. It gave him food for thought.

Captain Zaykkuh stood up as they were ushered into the room. "Commander Kaid, Shaidan. Welcome to Kij'ik. I'm Captain Zaykkuh. Please, come sit down. Refreshments will be arriving shortly."

Kaid, his hand on Shaidan's shoulder, approached the far end of the long table where Zaykkuh stood. Accepting the other's extended hand, he shook it, noticing that the Captain used only the right amount of pressure, no more, and filed that fact away. Obviously he was used to Sholans.

"Would you prefer our maush or c'shar or coffee?" he asked as Kaid pulled out a chair for Shaidan then pushed it in toward the table. "We have all three drinks here. Fruit juice for you, Shaidan?"

"Yes, please."

"Maush will be fine," said Kaid, sitting down.

Zaykkuh nodded to Shartoh who saluted and left.

"I'm very glad to see you here," said Zaykkuh as he sat down. "Having a restless spirit walking around the Outpost is unsettling my crew. Not that any of us believe that the dead aren't . . . dead."

"Vartra isn't exactly dead," said Kaid. "He's one of our Gods."

Zaykkuh blinked at him in surprise. "I was told he was a dead relative of yours and Shaidan's."

"Not of mine. He's Kusac and Shaidan's relative."

"Then how does he come to be a restless spirit?"

"It's complicated," said Kaid. "He lived during a very troubled time on Shola. It happened at the same time as your Fall. We call it the Cataclysm because a chunk of our moon hit our world, causing planetwide devastation. Vartra emerged as the leader who pulled all the survivors together and kept our civilization going. He was the founder of what Shola is today, in fact. When he died, his soul was taken by our Earth Goddess, and he joined them as one of our deities."

"Your deities are that real?" There was disbelief on Zaykkuh's face.

"So are yours, you just don't know it yet," said Kaid with a half smile. "In fact, though they will appear as Primes or Valtegans to you, they are the same as ours."

"An interesting concept," said Zaykkuh. "However, you will understand, I'm sure, that I would really appreciate it if you could take this Vartra with you when you leave. We children of Kezule haven't had any religion in our upbringing, beyond giving the Emperor, King Zsurtul's father, his due as a supposed God. This is all very alien to us."

Kaid laughed. "This is new to us, too! It isn't often a deity gets lost off our world."

A gentle knock, then the door opened and a steward entered bearing a tray of drinks and pastries, which he set before them.

Zaykkuh passed them their drinks, taking one himself, and then gestured them to help themselves to the pastries. Shaidan looked to Kaid for a nod of assent then quickly grabbed one.

"Good to see the young one more relaxed," said Zaykkuh. "I'm surprised Captain Aldatan didn't come, though. He was always very protective of his son."

"He's otherwise occupied," said Kaid, sending a silencing thought to Shaidan as he was about to explain why his father wasn't there. "Besides, he is my son too, through marriage."

Zaykkuh nodded. "Ah, I had forgotten that. How is the Captain?"

"Fine," said Kaid shortly, sipping his drink. "Tell me where Vartra has been seen."

"Mainly around where the Sholan temple was. I mean, still is, because we've had no need to dismantle it. I'm told that at first he was very transparent, but when I saw him late yesterday, he was certainly looking more . . . solid. He doesn't seem to see us, or he ignores our attempts to communicate with him. Do you know why he should be here in the first place?"

"He came to speak to me," said Shaidan around the pastry. "He couldn't reach my father, so he came to me."

"Why did he come to you?" asked the Captain.

Shaidan fell silent and concentrated on eating.

"Shaidan?" said Kaid.

"I can't say. I promised," the cub muttered, sitting back in his seat and trying to make himself seem small.

Kaid reached out and flicked an ear gently. "It's all right, cub. No one will make you break your oath." He looked back to the Captain. "Has Vartra been seen today?"

Zaykkuh shook his head. "Not yet. I'll take you to where he was seen yesterday. He looked lost and confused."

"I've no idea why he should be," said Kaid, finishing his drink. "From all accounts, he seems to have been wandering about here for several months before this. Have you finished, Shaidan?"

"Yes, thank you, Pappa Kaid," the cub said in a small voice.

"Shall we go?" asked Kaid. He wanted to get this over and done with. Too many awkward questions were being asked, and they had given him a lot to think about.

"Certainly," said Zaykkuh, getting up.

The Captain took them down to the next level and along to the gym that had been set up as the Sholan temple, then, at Kaid's request, left them there.

Kusac's team had done a pretty good job, considering the lack of amenities and the fact that they'd not had any religious artifacts with them. He was pleased to see the gas flame there—it proved what Kusac had said about Kezule going out of his way to accommodate him and his people. And the small sculpture of Vartra—sure it was crude when compared to the polished ones turned out by the crafters on Shola, but it was damned good for a Brother with no real resources or tools. Without thinking, he made obeisance to the altar, sending out questing thoughts to see if he could sense the Entity, but he sensed nothing.

Shaidan found a spot on one of the prayer mats at the front and sat down. Kaid joined him and stilled his mind, absorbing the feel of the Outpost and its inhabitants. After a while, he

called his attention back to the here and now to find Shaidan
leaning against him.

Reaching out, he put an arm around the cub's shoulders.
Do you know the Litanies yet, Shaidan?

Yes, Pappa taught me, he replied. *I've been practicing
them.*

Shall we see if we can find Vartra?

How?

*Just send out our thoughts and look for Him among the
many minds here. Can you do that?*

Shaidan frowned in concentration. *I can try. I know how to
find Pappa's mind.*

*Just think of Vartra, how He felt, what He looked like, and
then reach out to find Him. I'll show you.*

All right.

Kaid sensed the image of Vartra forming in Shaidan's mind;
then the cub began to add on his impressions of the Entity.
His concentration wavered a little, but Kaid mentally reached
out to strengthen the image of Vartra, leaving Shaidan free to
build up the sense of the Entity.

*You're doing fine. I couldn't have done as well as you at your
age,* sent Kaid encouragingly. *Can you sense Him?*

No. He's not here, Shaidan replied.

*Then let's see if we can call Him, shall we? All we do is proj-
ect that image and call His name mentally.*

He didn't know how long they'd been sitting sending out
their call when he was suddenly aware of another presence in
the room.

"Oh! He's here!" whispered Shaidan.

He opened his eyes and turned his head to look over his
shoulder. There, by the door, stood an almost transparent
Vartra.

"Who called me?" the Entity asked in a slightly querulous
voice as He moved slowly into the center of the room.

You talk to Him, Shaidan, sent Kaid, releasing the cub.
Don't be afraid. He won't harm you.

Scrambling to his feet, Shaidan turned around to face
Vartra. "I did," he said, as Kaid rose to his feet beside him.

Vartra stopped several feet away from them, His eye ridges
meeting in a frown. "Do I know you? And by what right do
you disturb me and call me to this place?"

"I'm Shaidan. You came to talk to me here, on Kij'ik."

There was only a slight wobble in his voice, Kaid noted with pride.

Tell Him you're blood-kin and have the right to call Him, he sent. *Say we're on an orbiting space station, and we need Him to come with us to the planet below.*

"I'm blood-kin," began Shaidan, but stopped when Vartra held up His hand, commanding silence.

"I can hear him," He snapped, moving closer still until He was within a couple of feet of them. "I'm not mind-deaf!!" He sniffed audibly in their direction, turning His head to take in each of their scents. "Yes, you're blood-kin, he isn't. Talk to me yourself!"

"Talk to Pappa Kaid," said Shaidan, moving closer to Kaid and clutching at his arm. "He knows what to say, I don't! You're frightening the people here."

"Am I?" Vartra grinned, showing his teeth. "Well, now. I wonder why that would be?"

"We can see through You. They think You're a ghost!"

Obviously startled, Vartra lifted his hand up and stared at it. "What happened to me?" He whispered, a look of fear coming across His face as He lowered it again. "I can't remember anything! Not even how I got here."

"You came to speak to the cub and his father," said Kaid, a wave of sympathy for Vartra sweeping over him. He knew what it was like to suddenly lose one's past. Years of being used as the Entity's messenger, given tasks that he had feared were beyond him at the time, were suddenly wiped out in the face of the other's obvious mental torment.

"You gave me messages for Pappa and for the Doctor here," said Shaidan, looking around from behind the comforting bulk of Kaid's body. "Don't You remember me?"

Distracted, Vartra looked down at the cub. "What?"

"You've forgotten me. You helped me think for myself, undo what that doctor did to me." A look of pain briefly contorted the cub's features, and Kaid could feel his hurt and the deep anger at what had been done to him and his siblings.

Obviously so did Vartra, for He knelt down beside Shaidan, holding His hand out to him. "Then for that, I'm glad, even if I don't remember it," he said gently.

Hesitantly, Shaidan reached out his other hand toward the Entity. As their fingers, then their hands touched, Kaid watched in amazement, as solidity seemed to flow from the cub into the Entity, giving Him form and mass.

Vartra's eyes shut, and He inhaled sharply, gripping Shaidan's hand more tightly as the child left the safety of Kaid to go to Him.

"You're home now," said Shaidan, spontaneously wrapping his other arm around the Entity's neck in a hug. "My pappa, Kusac, my mamma, and Pappa Kaid will keep You safe. They're Your family too!" he said fiercely.

Vartra laughed softly, but it was a laughter that spoke of pride in His own. "I know they will," he said, returning the hug as he looked up at Kaid. The beginning of recognition came into his eyes. "Kaid? Is that you?"

"Yes, Lord," said Kaid, bowing to Him. "You came here where Kusac and his son were, to help them, then You disappeared. Two days ago You suddenly reappeared, but You were . . . less than yourself. We don't know what happened to You."

"It seems," He said, gathering Shaidan into His arms and standing up, "that my memories of my time here have been erased."

"It certainly does seem that way," said Kaid. "Ghyakulla is with us on K'oish'ik. The Primes have reinstated the worship of their own Earth Goddess. Here She's known as La'shol, but they're the same."

"Then we'd best join them," said Vartra grimly. With his right hand, he sketched a symbol in the air; afterward, Kaid swore that between one blink and the next, he saw it glow.

A warm summer breeze, laden with the scents of blossom—including nung flowers—wafted across them, and then a portal opened, showing the flickering image of the temple on K'oish'ik.

"Come," said the Entity, stepping through it.

Thoughts of shuttles left behind, and Captains left bewildered, raced through Kaid's mind; then, as he saw the portal begin to shrink, he leaped through it.

They have been told, came Vartra's thought as he landed hard on the flagged stone floor of the temple beside Shaidan, in front of a still surprised Conner.

"Vartra's back, I take it," the priest said after a moment.

Kaid looked around. There was no sign of Vartra.

"He called for Ghyakulla, and she returned us all home,"

said Shaidan. There was a definite shake to his voice now as Kaid picked him up and settled him in against his hip as if he had been five years younger.

"Don't worry, Shaidan," said Kaid. "In our family, you'll likely get more than used to the ways of the Entities."

Ghyakulla's Realm

He emerged in the clearing he knew so well. The rock fountain trickled merrily down over the layers of stone into the catch basin at its foot. Behind tall banks of bell-shaped light purple flowers was the bower he shared with her during spring and summer, and to his right was the table where they ate. He knew she was coming when a pair of snow-white jeggets scampered into the clearing. They stopped at his feet, rearing up on their hind legs to chitter at him.

"Lady," he said bowing his head as she entered the clearing, long skirts all the colors of summer flowers swirling around her bare ankles as she ran to him.

She cupped a hand around his cheek, smiling up at him and sending him images of pleasure at his return and concern that he'd been lost.

"My memories of what happened have been stolen," he said, briefly touching her hand before pulling away from her. He walked to the fountain, leaning on the edge of it, his back to her. "I must know who did this to me!"

A blast of icy air filled the clearing; then Kuushoi, closely followed by her dzinae Gihaf, stepped out of her Winter Realm. Moments later, a wave of heat presaged the arrival of L'Shoh.

"At last, they've returned you," Kuushoi said. "How *dare* they interfere with Us and imprison him!"

"Welcome home, Vartra," said L'Shoh, inclining his dark head toward him as Vartra turned away from the fountain to greet the new arrivals.

"You know who it was?" Vartra demanded of the white-pelted Entity.

"Silence," said Ghyakulla slowly, frowning at her sister. "The matter is in hand."

"You expect the ephemeral, Kusac, to deal with them?" Kuushoi asked scathingly. "He has enough to contend with dealing with the M'zullians!"

"He is the Avatar, you know that," said L'Shoh. "He alone will deal with them on behalf of all of us. It has been decided."

"He's a mortal! He hasn't the strength or the abilities to . . ."

"Enough!" said Ghyakulla, showing a rare spark of anger. "You will not inflame Vartra to rashness, Sister. We have decided what will happen, how the matter will be dealt with. We cannot fight ourselves—we depend on arming others to do this for *their* mortal realm. Our Avatar has been tested and not found wanting."

"You might not be able to fight, but I . . ."

"Will do nothing," said L'Shoh, striding to her side and taking her by the arm. "It's time you visited *my* Realm, wife," he said firmly.

"Don't be ridiculous," she said, attempting to pull free. "We long ago gave up the pretense of being married."

"Then it's time we renewed it," L'Shoh purred, pulling her close against his side. "I find I have need of some feminine company, and it will keep you from being tempted to meddle."

It's summer here, my time, sent Ghyakulla. *She cannot meddle even if she would.*

"Wait till they go to M'zull," hissed Kuushoi, giving up what she knew was a losing battle. "There they will be in the mountains, among the snow, my Realm, Sister!"

Ghyakulla projected the image of summer on M'zull, even if there were Sholans and Primes among the snowy mountains. "My season," she said, adding the words for emphasis.

"You'll still be with me," said L'Shoh. "Don't forget I have the right to call upon you during Summer."

Kuushoi hissed her displeasure at him.

Go now, you disturb my peace, sent Ghyakulla, gesturing a portal for L'Shoh into existence.

"Lady Kuushoi, if you please?" said Gihaf, making a courtly bow. "Winter is where I belong, not here."

"Go, faithless one!" snapped Kuushoi, gesturing. Gihaf winked out of existence.

Vartra watched them leave then turned back to Ghyakulla. "It's been a long time since he demanded her company during summer," he murmured. "But I do have the right to face them, whoever they are."

Taking him by the hand, she drew him back to the fountain. "They are not your geas, the Valtegans are," she said softly, reaching for the pottery cup that sat on the lip of one of the small pools of water. Leaning forward, she filled it and handed it to him. *If your memories can be recovered, this will return them,* she sent. *If not, then they are lost to you.*

Lifting the cup to his lips, his eyes never leaving her face, he drank.

Images of him rousing his people after the Cataclysm played in his mind, sent by her, then those of him unable to stand up to the unnamed enemy. The meaning was clear—he was a leader, not a fighter.

Aid him by filling him with hope when all seems lost, she sent. *That is your strength. Did the cub not say you helped him break free of K'hedduk's programming? This is your task. Let those born to fight do what is appointed to them.*

He nodded slowly as his anger began to dissipate and peace began to fill him. Handing the empty cup back to her, images of a time of rest and healing began to steal over him, followed by knowledge of a fight well fought, beyond what could have been expected of him.

Food is ready for us, she sent, taking him by the hand and gently urging him toward where the table stood. *Glad I am you are home with me.*

He stopped her, reaching out to cradle her face in his hands and gently kiss her, letting the last of his worries about the mortal realm fade. He knew how much talking, even forming thoughts into words cost her, never mind the confrontation with her sister.

And I'm glad to be home with you,.

Thank you, she sent to L'Shoh. *He needs this time. There is work enough ahead of him.*

My pleasure. It's time my lady wife forgot other males during the Summer season and remembered she has a Lord.

CHAPTER 15

K'oish'ik, Zhal-Ch'Ioka, Month of the Hearth, 2nd day (April)

"WELCOME back," said Conner's voice as strong arms helped him to sit up.

His sight was blurred, but he could see the glass held in front of him.

"Drink this," Conner said, putting it to his lips.

Gratefully, he reached for the glass and took a gulp, only to start coughing as the fiery liquid burned its way down his throat. Then it hit his stomach with warmth that spread throughout his body.

"What the hell is that?" he gasped, trying to ignore the fact that the hand he raised to rub his streaming eyes was still Valtegan.

"Brandy. A strong medicinal Earth drink."

He grunted and moved to get up, but Conner tried to press him back.

"Rest a minute, Kusac. They've all been told you're back," the priest said, wrapping a blanket around him.

Then he remembered. "How do I tell her I killed her sister?" he whispered.

"Did you?" asked Conner gently. "Or did you save Carric's life?"

"I could have prevented so much suffering," he said, letting himself be gently pushed back down on the flagstones as he clutched the blanket around him. "But it would have changed what is now."

"It would indeed. You did what was right, Kusac." Conner's hand clasped his shoulder, squeezing it reassuringly. "You realized you were with Elise, not Carrie, and when it mattered, you were able to do what was needed. You saved Carrie's life, prevented her from being terribly mutilated, and released Elise from the horror of her captivity and torture."

"You know too much about this," said Kusac, closing his eyes in an effort to stop his tears. "How? Was this a test, or real?"

"Did your experiences and actions have a lasting effect on you and others? Yes, it was real, and it was a test. Had you chosen to do so, you could have altered the future out of all recognition."

"How do you know what happened?"

"Ghyakulla showed me," he said. "You passed Their test and are in fact the Avatar of Justice for this time."

"Zsadhi, the Sword of the Gods," whispered another voice. "The legend is true!"

As Kusac lifted his head, he caught Conner's abrupt silencing gesture to M'kou.

"I'm not a legend," he snapped, sitting up and shivering with cold and exhaustion despite the blanket. "I'm me, nothing more! Conner, she's coming. I'll not have her see me like this. I have to change back. Tell me how to draw energy properly from the earth."

"Still your mind, then sink your consciousness down into the stone floor and the earth beneath it," said the priest. "Feel the soil, the rocks that are the bones of the earth, then tap their life force. You didn't go deep enough last time."

"Thank you," he said, pulling the blanket closer. "Some Avatar I am," he muttered. "My sword is on Shola!"

"Is it?" asked Conner, smiling enigmatically as he tucked his hands into his sleeves. "I think you'll find Carrie and Kaid brought it with them."

Kusac huffed, then turned his mind inward. His years of mental discipline made it easy to raise his body temperature as soon as he sensed the free energy of the earth. As he let his light trance carry him deeper, he felt that energy begin to swirl and flow through and around him.

Murmuring a few words of thanks to Ghyakulla, he grasped hold of it, drawing it in as if he were breathing. He could feel his strength returning, and he began to visualize himself as Sholan again.

This time, the change wasn't quite as painful, but feeling every hair on his body forcing its way through his skin to the surface was not pleasant. As his legs began to change, he fell back to the ground and cursed himself for not realizing that a sitting position wasn't wise given his complex hip and shoulder joints.

Finally, it was over, and the hands in front of him were once again his own. Shaking with fatigue, he pushed himself back into a sitting position, pulling the blanket that had fallen away from him, back around his shoulders again.

"Next time, I think I'll let the blanket go," he murmured. "It might have fused to me."

"I believe you'd just have absorbed it as another energy source," said Conner, accepting M'kou's help to stand up. "Your clothes vanished that way. M'kou, would you hand him the flask on the seat over there? It's a protein-rich drink. He's had no food or drink for three days."

"Gladly," said M'kou, fetching and opening it.

"So time there and here was the same," he said, gratefully accepting the hot drink. "How did you know I'd return today?"

"Tonight," the priest corrected him with a gentle smile. "I didn't. It's been made fresh each day, ready for your return. We've all been waiting for you."

"Well, Old One, I know intimately what it's like to live as a M'zullian. M'kou," he said, looking over to the young male. "We need cold-weather gear and training for you all. Temperatures below freezing and deep snow."

M'kou pulled a face. "I'll speak to the General about it, Captain."

The sound of bare feet hitting the stone steps behind them drew their attention, and Kusac began to struggle to his feet. M'kou's hands were instantly there to help, to take the flask from him.

He knew she'd been aware of his return, but like him, she hadn't tried to contact him mentally yet. By an unthought agreement, they didn't dare trust their own senses right now.

The curtain at the foot of the stairs was thrust aside, and she stood there, her hair a wild mane about her face and shoulders, dressed in a short blue sleeping tunic, feet and legs bare. She looked unbearably fragile.

"Carrie," he said then he was almost knocked off his feet as she flung herself into his waiting arms.

"You're back," she said, pulling his face down to hers and covering it in kisses until their lips met.

You scared me, she sent as she pulled her close, feeling her living warmth seep into his body, her love surrounding him.

I scared myself, he admitted. *You're the other half of me. Without you, nothing matters.* She smelled of sleep and of his son Shaidan. The blanket, forgotten, fell to the floor.

What happened? Where were you?

Not here, not now, he replied, aware of Kezule and Kaid arriving. Reluctantly, he drew back, still holding her. *When we're alone.*

"Are they always like this . . ." began Kezule

"Passionate?" asked Kaid with a smile. "Not really. They're being remarkably restrained since they're in public."

"You'll need to excuse us," said Kusac, turning to look at them. "I'm in dire need of food and sleep. We'll talk tomorrow."

"Is everything all right?" asked Kaid, suddenly concerned.

"Everything is as it should be," Kusac reassured him as he reached down for the blanket, but Kaid was there first. *Thank you, Brother,* he sent.

"Tomorrow at 4th hour, after first meal, in the Council chamber. I'll update you."

"You need a medical check immediately," said Kezule. "You changed shape twice—there could be damage you can't sense."

"There's none. Tell him, Conner."

"He's fine," the priest nodded in agreement. "I monitored him as soon as he returned. His body and mind are as sound as they were before."

"I need you fit for the rescue," said Kezule.

"Tomorrow," said Kusac firmly, his arm around Carrie's shoulders as he led her to the stairs.

Banner got up as they entered their suite.

"Shaidan's still asleep," he said. "Glad to see you back, Captain."

"Thank you, Banner," Carrie said as Kusac murmured his thanks. "We'll talk tomorrow."

Nodding, Banner left.

"I have to tell Shaidan I'm back," Kusac said as the door closed. "He has nightmares if I'm not there."

"I noticed. You need to cut that Link with him, Kusac," she replied, heading for the cupboard where the cans of protein drinks were stored. "It isn't healthy for him."

"I will," he replied, throwing the blanket over a chair back. "But gradually, so he doesn't feel rejected. I know it's not healthy for him to be on the edges of our Leska Link, but I have blocked him out when appropriate."

He was back within a few minutes and joined her on the sofa, reaching for both her and the open can on the low table. He drank it all down before beginning.

"I don't know how or why I changed like that, Carrie," he said quietly, burying his face against her neck and breathing in her scent. "It scared the spit out of me—and still does if I'm being truthful."

"Where did you go?" she asked, taking hold of his free hand and lacing her fingers between his. "There was heat, like when we went to the Margins. I was sure you'd been called back there."

"No, not there, or then." He hesitated. "I'm tired, cub. Everything that happened is still fresh for me. I haven't made sense of it all yet, but I need you tonight. I need to know at the core of my being that we're alive and together. If I don't tell you now, you'll find out anyway when we pair, and I don't want that." His hand tightened on hers till he felt his claws extend, then reluctantly he slackened his grasp.

"You really are afraid," she said quietly. "Just tell me, love. It can't be any worse than what we've already been through."

"Do you remember when Kate and Taynar were kidnapped by a Valtegan on Keiss? His name was Chokkuh."

"I remember."

"He was Head of Security on Keiss."

"Oh," she said in a small voice.

"I woke inside his mind, on the night Elise was arrested."

The silence lengthened. "How did he find out about her?"

"I don't know, but she was his favorite, and he warned her not to betray him. She did."

Carrie took a ragged breath and leaned against him. "Tell me it all."

He did, leaving out only her death. "I couldn't help her, or you, cub. If I had, our lives and many others would have been changed, the whole future from then on altered forever."

She was crying now, tears rolling slowly down her cheeks until she wiped her hand across her face. "It happened, Kusac, because it had already happened. We could go mad even thinking about what you could have done differently. You couldn't change anything. How did she die? No, don't tell me. I don't really want to know."

Turning, she buried her face against his chest, sobbing openly now.

"I have to tell you," he said, reaching up to stroke her head as he held her close with his other arm. "J'koshuk . . . he was going to . . . mutilate her on Chokkuh's orders because she wouldn't talk."

"Worse than he already had?" she wept.

"Worse. You lost your fingernails when Elise did. I couldn't risk you suffering more, cub, I couldn't! The Gods help me, I killed her, Carrie, not J'koshuk or Chokkuh . . . it was me. I had to choose between you and her, and I chose you." There, he'd told her. Now he wanted for her response.

She stiffened in his arms. "How?" He could barely hear her.

"Gently, I promise. I stopped her heart," he whispered, holding her closer, afraid she'd push him aside, be done with him for ever. "I'm sorry, Carrie. I had to do it to save you. Both of me felt your suffering, and she asked me to save you. Somehow she sensed me inside that M'zullian."

A moan of horror escaped her, and then she began sobbing. This time in anger.

"If you hadn't been there . . . If you hadn't saved me . . . How could she have been so *stupid*? She never thought twice about risking *my* life, damn her!"

"Not till the end," he said, beginning to rock her gently as he had Shaidan many times. "I had sensed you earlier, reached out mentally for you. I think that's how she knew I was there but didn't realize it until that moment. I was her only hope to escape them and save you." Relief overwhelmed him as he realized this hadn't put the wedge he'd feared between them.

"She must have suffered dreadfully," she wept, "and so must you, trapped in that Valtegan's mind, watching what they were doing . . ." Abruptly she pushed herself away from him and sat up.

"If you were there, then you were always there, we just didn't know till now."

"I know. I was sent back by Ghyakulla and L'Shoh."

When she continued to look at him expectantly, he sighed and reached to pull her close again.

"They want me to be Their Avatar of Justice, decide what we should do about M'zull."

"I hope you said no," she said sharply, swiping her forearm across her face again.

"I tried," he said, nuzzling her neck. "But as Kaid has frequently said, They have a habit of not listening and giving you no other choice."

"Tell me exactly what happened," she said, wriggling in his grasp as he began to lick at her neck and nearest ear.

"I've a better idea," he murmured, catching hold of her ear lobe with his teeth. "You can have it all now, directly from my mind."

"What about Shaidan? He's part of our Link because of . . ."

"Dealt with for now," he said. "And he'll sleep through the night."

You're incorrigible! she sent, putting up only a token protest as his mouth closed on hers.

"Mmm," he replied.

K'oish'ik, Zhal-Ch'Ioka, 3rd day (April)

Kaid and T'Chebbi joined them for breakfast, but it wasn't until Kusac had taken Shaidan to the nursery to join the other children and returned that he reluctantly brought them up to date on what had happened to him. He did keep one or two details about Elise to himself and Carrie, though.

"Let's hope you aren't dragged back in time again," said Kaid, a growl underscoring his words.

"I don't think I will be," he said slowly. "This time was . . . different."

"How we explain it to Kezule?" asked T'Chebbi.

"More or less as I explained it to you, leaving out the Avatar part."

"I don't think you can," said Kaid, pushing his drinking vessel toward Carrie as she lifted the jug of coffee and offered it around.

"Coffee? That's not like you." she said, pouring for him.

"I think I'll be needing it," Kaid grunted. "The Primes see Kusac's shape-changing and disappearance as part of a legend of theirs—one tied, coincidentally, to a savior hero who'll bring justice to all."

It was Kusac who growled now, with annoyance. "Seems every world has one."

"Your return as Valtegan solidified it. They call him Zsadhi. Same as the Palace AI," said T'Chebbi.

"Like Conner's ancient Terran Avatar, he was wounded to death, as were you, but will return to them in their hour of need," added Kaid.

"Coincidence," muttered Kusac, snagging the last piece of crispy fried meat from the communal plate.

"Does it matter?" asked Carrie, sipping her coffee. "These legends aren't going to affect our plans, are they?"

"Only in that among the Primes and Ch'almuthians it calls upon ancient memories and loyalties, which is certainly to our advantage," said Kaid. He smirked at Kusac. "Having our very own God with us would certainly be a rallying point. Just don't get any delusions about . . ."

"Dammit, Kaid, if you don't know better than that by now . . ." Kusac began angrily

Kaid began laughing, and he rolled his napkin into a ball and threw it at Kusac. "Calm down, Kusac. We know who you are; we know you won't get carried away by all this nonsense."

Catching the napkin, Kusac threw it back at him. "It's not that funny," he said. "The last thing we need is a bunch of religious maniacs following us around."

"But them committing acts of civil disobedience in this Zsadhi's name would certainly help destabilize their society," said Carrie.

"Excuse me, Captain," interrupted the gentle tones of the AI "General Kezule asks that you all join him now in the Council chamber."

"On our way, ZSADHI," said Kusac, grimacing as he said the name. He found all this talk of avatars and heroes unsettling. "I don't suppose either of you brought my sword with you?" he asked.

"I did," said Carrie, getting up from the table. "It's in its case in my large bag in the closet. I'd forgotten about it till now. Shall I get it for you before we leave?"

"I'll get it later, thanks," he said, feeling an inevitability of fate settling around him like a mantle.

"I have things to do," said T'Chebbi, taking her leave of Kaid before heading off on her own.

Only Kezule, M'kou, and Zsurtul were in the chamber.

As he expected, Kezule wanted to know about his miraculous shape-changing ability. Regarding his disappearance, however, he was content to accept that Kusac had been pulled back to an incident in his past on Keiss and hadn't pressed for more details.

"Can you sustain the Valtegan form for long?" Kezule asked, sitting back at ease in his chair.

"I believe so," said Kusac. "I was still one when I returned."

"What about your other abilities—changing the colors of the flowers, for instance. Could you change a person's color, make a Prime seem a M'zullian?"

"Possibly. I'd have to practice on more plants, then living animals, before I'd be comfortable even thinking about affecting a person."

"What about gender?" asked M'kou suddenly. "Could you make a female appear male?"

Kusac glanced over at him. "I have no idea. I'd need volunteers at some point, and I'm not at all comfortable at the though of experimenting with lives. If you're thinking I could mask the Prime females as males, they'd possibly lose their telepathic abilities."

"Why? Their minds would be the same even if their bodies altered," argued M'kou.

"I'm not comfortable working on people yet," he repeated.

"If your experiments with animals were successful, we've the condemned traitors we could use," said Kezule. "This could pave the way for a group of commandos to be left safely on M'zull."

"They'd be unable to change back on their own, *if* it was possible," warned Kaid.

"I'd have to be there too," said Kusac, tapping his claw tips thoughtfully on the table. "This could make a couple of ideas I had possible."

"Not unless I'm there as well," said Carrie firmly.

"I don't think I can do this without your help," he admitted, reaching for her hand where it lay beside his on the table. He saw the look on Kaid's face and grinned. "They're only ideas, Kaid. It would all hinge on being able to change other people."

"So share the ideas," growled Kaid.

Kusac shrugged. "Rezac was able to affect matter. I want to see if I can awaken his ability again. His knowledge and experience would be invaluable, and he's actually worked on people. As for ideas, what do we need to actually achieve to neutralize the M'zullians?"

"We need to do more than destroy their fleets and their military HQs on the surface," said M'kou. "If that's all we do, they will rebuild and come after us again. Maybe not for a hundred or more years, but they will come."

Kusac nodded. "We need to destroy the very way they live. Their lives are dominated by the military. All the males belong to it, even their merchants. The nearest things to civilians are the drones and the females, right, Kezule?"

The General nodded. "Drones will make up a fairly large group. They fill many niches that the Prime females fill here. They run the nurseries, the homes of the upper echelons of the military and the Court, perform menial jobs, and are the only sexual partners available to the ordinary soldier. In short, they are present everywhere, even in the Royal harem."

"And unlike the females, they have freedom of movement. I assume they have very few rights."

"If it's the same as it was in my time, they are property, not citizens," said Kezule.

"What about their personalities?"

Kezule shrugged. "I never had anything to do with them," he said. "They were sterile, and most were sexless, though there were those who had basic functionality as males or females. They provided sex partners for the soldiers in my fleet. Having none of the hormones needed to breed, they lacked the aggression of both. The males had none of the organs that enhance our speed and healing. Apart from that, they were unaltered in any other way."

"A slave population," said Carrie. "They can't have much

love for the rest of the M'zullians. They could be ripe for rebellion, and they're present in every location we need to hit—the fleets, the military bases on the planet, and the Palace."

"They aren't warriors," objected Kezule. "Their time is regulated, so their absence would be noticed. Though they may have desires for position and power, they're like the Primes in their inability to be aggressive."

"We need a solution that can be implemented quickly, not one that will take months, maybe years to bring to fruition," said Kusac. "We have very little time before they mount an all-out attack on Ch'almuth and here and then the rest of our worlds. We need to know their weaknesses, Kezule, traits we can exploit to turn them against each other."

Kezule pushed his chair abruptly back from the table and for a moment stood looking impassively down at them. Turning on his heel, he walked away from them, stopping at the large TAC screens. Hands clasped behind him, he stared at the screen, which currently showed a view of the courtyard outside. His anger was a palpable force in the room.

"General," said Zsurtul quietly. "You will tell us what we need to know."

He sat back in his chair, waiting, aware that Kaid and Carrie saw this as a test of Zsurtul's authority as well as proof of Kezule's change of heart.

The silence stretched, then as abruptly, Kezule turned around. "We were controlled, all of us, by being fed a diet of raw meat," he said harshly. "It fed our aggression. Only the Officer Class were given the spice laalquoi, which you call la'quo, to moderate it. In my captivity on Shola, I was given some, but not enough. If you want to take the fight out of the Officers, saturate their food and drink with that!"

"They're not your people, Kezule," Kusac said. "You're not betraying your own kind. The M'zullians are not true warriors as you were. There is no honor in them, or their leader. We both know that."

Kezule's eyes narrowed; then, taking a deep breath, he nodded slowly, mouth twisting into a parody of a smile. "No, they are not."

He returned to the table, bowing to Zsurtul before taking his seat again.

"The Ch'almuthians have a drug they use as an anesthetic,

based on a natural mutation of the la'quo plant," said M'kou. "They farm it in fairly large quantities."

"Find out its exact effects and the doses," said Kaid. "It could be of use to us."

"When those of us related to the Royal family were called to the Court," said Kezule, clasping his hands on the table, "our staff prepared special meals for us, gradually adjusting us to eating cooked food. However, the food was still heavily laced with laalquoi."

"What of the lower ranks?" asked Kusac.

"They were almost a different breed from us. They advanced by fighting their superiors for their positions if they felt they could perform their jobs better. They formed alliances among their ranks and fought it out. Failure to perform satisfactorily wasn't an option—if they didn't, they were torn apart by the opposing faction. We Officers exuded a scent that prevented them from attacking us; it created fear in them, a visceral fear they couldn't conquer."

"How did you advance to your position?" asked Carrie.

"Politics and merit," he said. "Oh, we were as violent as the lower classes in our own way, but with a veneer of civilization covering it. We didn't fight to the death, though the weak were weeded out early on. No, our early years were more brutal in a way, because deaths were rare. Once military training was over, the physical violence was left behind. From then on, we were the leaders, and our power struggles were more— bloodless and political."

"What makes you assume the M'zullians are still like that?" asked Kaid.

"The ones on Keiss were," said Carrie, a shadow crossing her face. "I have Elise's memories of them."

"I can second that," said Kusac quietly. "So the weaknesses we need to target are the reaction to the fear scents of the lower ranks, and the potential for the uncontrolled violence, and the drugging of the Officer ranks?"

"You can control both with laalquoi and fear scents, though the Officers will react differently to the scent," said Kezule.

"All of them are afraid of releasing fear scents," said Carrie, tapping her fingernails on the table in an unconscious imitation of Kusac's habit. "Basically, they are paranoid about how they react to any stressful situation. We can target that. The more paranoid they are, the more suspicious of each other they'll become, which is what we want, isn't it?"

"Feed their paranoia," nodded Kaid. "Turn them against each other. If we can keep them focused on that, we may be able to reach their wives and recruit their help."

"Assuming they are all Ch'almuthian females," said Kezule. "If they're the nonsentient ones I knew, you won't have much luck."

"They're drugged out of their minds, Kezule," said Carrie, looking over to him. "If we can take them off the drugs, then their innate sentience will surface."

"How useful will females be who have lived all their lives drugged senseless in a harem?" asked Zsurtul.

"We won't know till we try, will we?" asked Carrie. "Don't underestimate their desire for revenge, though, nor those of any Ch'almuthians."

"They take Ch'almuthian males as part of the tithe," said Kusac. "What would they do with them?"

"They'll likely use them as breeding stock," said Kezule. "They'd be kept imprisoned, then mated to selected females to strengthen certain characteristics in either the general soldier population, or in the Officer cadre."

"A thought," said Carrie. "What if we also work on the sentient females—make them afraid of K'hedduk, especially those in the harem? It would unsettle the Court and all the Officer cadre."

"There's so much we can't know till we get there," sighed Kusac.

"Then let's plan for what we can do," said Kaid. "We can't train locals to be guerillas and mount a rebellion, but we can make K'hedduk think that one is happening. Covert ops aimed at key targets, both military and civilian, perhaps leaving behind a message of some kind, to make them think a rebellion is in progress and building. We can then use our telepaths to direct their paranoia in the directions we want. Kezule, do they have the Zsadhi legend too?"

"It existed in my time, yes," he replied. "I assume they still have it since it still exists here and among the Ch'almuthians."

"M'kou," began Kusac, then stopped as the youth, with a faint smile, slid a folder across the table to him.

"I thought you'd want to read up on the legend," he said quietly, passing out the other copies.

"Thanks," said Kusac.

"In that case, all we need do is scrawl the word Zsadhi at the scene of our demonstration of the power of dissent," said Kaid, opening his folder and beginning to scan the pages within.

"We'll need explosives of the kind that they use on M'zull," said Carrie.

"Maybe," said Kaid. "If we use ones from here, it may make them even more paranoid. They'll start wondering if the rebels are in touch with us, which would mean that the fleet will become suspect. We want that, since we can't get to the ships ourselves."

"True," said Kusac, looking over to Kaid. "Looks like we're at the point where we need you and T'Chebbi putting together a Wants list. Essentials only, since we'll be doing a HALO drop on our way out after rescuing Zhalmo. Kezule, can you get a holo projection of the countryside around the Palace on M'zull? It would be invaluable. Maps too."

"It's already being worked on," said M'kou. "Should be ready in a couple of days."

Kusac pushed his chair back. "Then I'd better get to work with Rezac. Carrie, can you see to the telepaths with Conner, please?"

She nodded as she rose.

"I'll get on with arranging the cold-weather training over on the *Tooshu's* virtual hall, and organizing supplies with T'Chebbi," said Kaid.

"Kezule, do you know if the Cabbarans have ever been seen on K'oish'ik before now?" Kaid asked when the others had left.

"Not to my knowledge," he said, looking questioningly at King Zsurtul.

"Not in my time," said the youth. "ZSADHI?"

"I have no records of them visiting us, Majesty."

"That's odd. I know where you're coming from, Kaid," said Zsurtul thoughtfully.

"What's odd?" asked Kezule.

"The Cabbarans and the TeLaxaudin are working closely together on Shola, like old allies," said Kaid. "Yet they have

never been here, a virtual outpost of TeLaxaudin activity."
He hesitated a moment. "Shaidan told me that Annuur and
Tirak's *Watcher* ship docked with the *Zan'droshi* when it un-
expectedly approached Kij'ik, Kezule. Why would it do that if
they're strangers to your people?"

"*Watcher* orders, maybe?" suggested Zsurtul.

"Perhaps," acceded Kaid. "L'Seuli is still in the area. I'll ask
him. Meanwhile, if you have no objections, I thought I would
go talk to the TeLaxaudin."

"To see if they will admit to an alliance with the Cabbarans? Good idea," said Kezule, gathering together the papers
in front of him.

"For all they have apparently done nothing but good for
your people, you don't seem to trust them, Kezule. In fact, you
trusted Kusac, a known and deadly enemy in your time, with
the life of your King rather than them when Zsurtul was injured. Why?"

Zsurtul looked at the General in surprise. "You ordered
that?"

"I did, Majesty," Kezule said. "Who better to guard you
than the one who risked his life to save yours? As for the Te-
Laxaudin, call it an old soldier's gut instinct, Kaid. We had one
on Kij'ik with us. In fact, he was waiting for us when we arrived. I hadn't told anyone where we were going, yet there he
was with the hydroponics section up and running, ready for us.
It was just too convenient. And no, I didn't ask him. Somehow,
every time I intended to, it conveniently slipped my mind," he
hissed, his crest beginning to lift in obvious annoyance.

"I take it you don't want to come with me, then," said Kaid,
unable to resist the jibe.

Kezule rose and glared at him. "No, I'll leave that pleasure
to you!" he snapped.

"Excuse me, Lord General, but there are no TeLaxaudin
on K'oish'ik. They all left three days ago," said the AI.

"Left?" echoed Zsurtul, obviously stunned by the news.
"But they've always been here! What will we do if we need
them?"

"We're better off without them," said Kezule. "What can
they do that we, or our new allies, can't do?"

"But the breeding tanks . . . the children."

"King Zsurtul, look around you, at some of the younger
members of your Court," saidKezule. "In the city the number

of pregnant females grows almost daily, and they are all able to bear their own young! The main reason you needed them is gone."

Kaid nodded. "He's right, King Zsurtul. So they left three days ago, when Kusac had his accident down in the new town. Convenient."

"It's as if they're always two or three steps ahead of us," said Kusac from the doorway. "How can that be? Are they spying on us all the time?"

"Either that or someone else here is," said Kaid grimly, walking toward him. "Let's go see what Annuur has to say."

"ZSADHI, alert the Royal guard to escort the King to his quarters and remain with him until I return," ordered Kezule, getting up. "Majesty, the safest place for you is in your quarters."

"Then I'll go to the nursery where the cubs are," the youth said, rising. "I won't have them at risk either. They are your vulnerability, Captain," he said, looking directly at Kusac. "And yours, General."

"Thank you, Zsurtul," Kusac said, turning to leave.

"What about Tirak?" asked Kaid.

"They're all down at the new town," said Kusac. "ZSADHI, put a guard around their ship and their shuttle at the new town. They're not to be allowed to leave the area."

"Yes Captain," said the AI.

Although at first he kept up, eventually their four-legged loping run left the General behind.

We need to keep Naacha away from both us and Annuur, sent Kusac.

Why?

He's their telepath, and he can hypnotize you with those tattoos on his face. Watch out for Tirak and his folk too—they're the muscle for them.

Understood. Do you plan on talking to them there? asked Kaid

If we can. They may try to escape if we ask them to come to the Palace.

What about taking them into the shuttle? At least we'd have them contained.

And hand them ourselves as hostages? snorted Kusac. *No, outside. They may try to run, but we can catch them.*

They left the city behind and circled around to approach the new township from the rear, near the road to the cattle pastures where the new buildings were going up.

I can't believe that either species would act against us, muttered Kusac. *Look at all the help they've given the Alliance, and the good they have done for the Primes.*

Because it also suited them, reminded Kaid. *You told us your memories have been edited when it suited them.*

There is that, he agreed as he began to slow to a walk, then, in the cover of a patch of bushes, reared upright to walk the last hundred or so yards so as to arouse less attention.

A small herd of cattle was coming toward them, the bells around the necks of the lead herd beasts clanging rhythmically as the three young Ch'almuthians, using switches and various whistled commands, drove them toward their pastures farther upriver.

Kusac and Kaid swerved to avoid them.

"Bit late to be taking them out," Kaid observed, glancing at the sun as Kusac pointed toward the small group around the house that Annuur and his sept were erecting.

A sudden commotion was breaking out there, and the air was split by the sound of high-pitched shrieks and snorts that could only come from the Cabbarans. The herd beasts began grunting and lowing, bunching together before they suddenly bolted, moving toward them in an ever-widening wave of solid horned bodies.

Trapped in front of them, Kusac and Kaid dropped again to all fours and began sprinting for safety.

Kusac's sight began to narrow as he tried to outrace the beasts, his mind searching for and finding Annuur as part of his mind was still monitoring the fast-approaching herds. Kaid, slightly closer to the river than he had been, would make it to safety, but he wouldn't.

Kusac! sent Kaid as he began to turn back toward him.

Go! he sent, using Command on his sword brother. *Make for the water!*

He turned, racing for the lead beast and leaped, narrowly missing the widespread horns, landing on its back, his claws sinking deep into its flesh. Screaming, it tried to halt but was driven on by those behind it. Twisting around, he let himself drop astride it; then he leaned forward and sank his front claws into its neck.

It stiffened its legs, arched its back, and, leaping forward, tried to buck him off, still shrieking and lowing its terror. Those around it began to veer away, and Kusac found himself with the open space he needed. He snarled loudly in its ear then sank his teeth into it, at the same time exerting pressure on its neck with his right hand as he dug his claws in even deeper.

Terrified, the beast turned and began to run back into the town, its continuing shrieks opening a clear path for it. People scattered in all directions as it, now trying to outrun the predator on its back, lengthened its stride and ran for dear life.

He spared a thought in Kaid's direction, finding him safe in the river, watching his progress in horror.

They were coming up to the shuttle now, and he could see that the guards there had been taken out and were lying unconscious on the ground. The shuttle was under power, the air lock closing. Annuur, however, was still ahead of him, heading through the town, scattering the market stalls and people in all directions, running for all he was worth.

The beast's hide was covered in coarse fur, but it didn't afford him much purchase. Crouching low, he sank his rear claws simultaneously into its hide, keeping the beast on a straight course, following Annuur's path of destruction. Once they reached the open countryside, he began to gain on him. When they were level, he released his hold on the animal, and using his powerful hind legs, he kicked off and leaped to the ground, landing on all fours at a full run just behind the fleeing Cabbaran.

Lengthening his stride, he let himself go into full Hunter mode, seeing and scenting only his prey. He waited until he was almost past him before leaping, his jaws closing over the Cabbaran's neck as he braced his hind feet in the dirt and pulled him to the ground.

Annuur squealed and tipped over on his side. Over and over they rolled in the dust, finally coming to a halt with the Cabbaran on his back and Kusac straddling him, jaws still fastened tightly around the other's throat.

Breathing heavily, he held his stance, waiting until his vision began to return to normal and he'd caught his wind. Beneath him, Annuur, eyes closed, also lay panting.

I want answers, he sent, lifting Annuur by the neck and shaking him. *No more getting Naacha to make me forget!*

He heard the shuttle taking off, heading straight for the landing pad outside the City's main gates.

They've left you behind, Annuur.

Release me, sent the Cabbaran, opening his eyes. There was no fear in them. *You will have what you need.*

How can I trust you after this? he demanded. *You tried to kill Kaid and me!*

No. Call it our test. You passed, by the way.

Between his jaws, Kusac felt the hint of a chuckle trying to escape from the Cabbaran's throat and growled menacingly.

No more lies or tricks, he warned, tightening his jaws fractionally, cutting off Annuur's air. Then he released him, but he put his hand on the Cabbaran's chest, pinning him to the ground.

"We're not your enemy, nor are we working for them," said Annuur, still struggling for breath. "Didn't we give you back your Talents, enhance them for you?"

"So *you* turned me into a freak!" he snarled.

"No. We gave you more than the skills of your Ancients, and Naacha trained you to use them to deal with the M'zullians."

"You didn't do this for me or for Shola, so don't lie to me, Annuur! You manipulated Zayshul and me! Stole our memories . . ."

"Time short, Kusac," the Cabbaran interrupted. "Do you want the solution to wiping out the racial memories of the M'zullians? Again, M'zullians your enemy, not us."

Taken aback, Kusac could only stare at him. He couldn't believe this small being's arrogance and lack of fear, never mind his absurd claims.

"The pouch on my right side," said Annuur. "Take it. What you need inside. Do not show to anyone else. You will know what to do with it when the time comes, Hunter."

He blinked, suddenly realizing that Annuur was gone. He sat back heavily in the sand, utterly bemused, then realized he held a pouch in his right hand.

"They've done it to me again," he snarled, hand tightening on the soft leather. Something small and hard at its center stopped him. He opened it, tipping the contents out into his right hand. It was a small, clear cube, and inside it, something seemed to move. He lifted his hand closer to see better, and as he did, the cube seemed to dissolve, leaving a slightly shiny substance pooling in the middle of his palm.

He watched in shock as the liquid began to sink into his skin and disappear. "What the hell?" He shook his hand, then rubbed it as he felt a crawling sensation under his skin. Letting out a roar of anger, he raised his head as overhead the *Watcher* became a silver streak heading out into space. "Annuur, you bastard! What have you done to me now?"

He sat there, unmoving, until Kaid came racing up to him. "Are you all right?" his sword-brother demanded, slewing to a stop beside him in a spray of sand.

"Yeah, I think. I lost him, Kaid. He just . . . disappeared from under me."

"They're gone, Tirak and his crew too. They fooled us all."

"You don't believe me," he said, turning to look at Kaid. "I had him, right here. Look. I got this from him." He held out the now empty pouch.

Kaid took it from him and turned it over in his hand. "It was certainly his," he said, smelling the Cabbaran's scent on it. "Was there anything in it? And how could he suddenly disappear?"

"It was empty," he said automatically, rubbing his palm against his thigh. "You don't know what it was like on Kij'ik," he said, getting tiredly to his feet. Every muscle ached, and he knew he was bruised in many places. "Supplies that had to have come from them would suddenly appear on the Outpost with no explanation of where they'd come from. Once another TeLaxaudin arrived, then left as suddenly and mysteriously."

"Didn't anyone question Giyarishis about that?"

"No. Not one of us thought to do it," he said, his voice full of suppressed anger.

Time and time again, he'd been used for their own purposes. They'd taken advantage of his disability to alter him into the Gods knew what! They might even have aided K'hedduk in placing the control device on him in the first place. Even as he thought it, his mind balked. No, they hadn't done that, but they had made use of his lack of Talent to turn him into something more than he'd been.

"There'll be a reckoning, Kaid, I swear there will!"

"Indeed there will," Kaid agreed, reaching out to take him by the shoulder. "But we've more pressing business now. We have Zhalmo to rescue and a planet of M'zullians to deal with. Afterward, we'll track down both the Cabbarans and the Te-

Laxaudin for treason. We'll need to make a report to L'Seuli so he can deal with them on the Council."

"You don't understand, Kaid. They aren't the enemy," he said, knowing he spoke no less than the truth. "But the ones that used me, they were. It's personal, not political."

"Then we'll talk about it later."

"There's nothing to discuss," he said with finality. "Don't tell L'Seuli. They were a group apart from those on the Alliance Council. The Ambassadors will deny any involvement. Once this is over, I will find them and get the answers I need."

"We'll find them," Kaid corrected him.

"When we do, it's my Hunt, Kaid, not yours. I need to know my family will be safe."

"I hear you," said Kaid as they began walking back to the City.

Watcher 6

Annuur materialized in the cargo area of the ship where the rest of his sept was waiting. Quickly righting himself, he began to moan.

"My throat! My throat! It is bruised and punctured! Sharp teeth has the Hunter!"

Lweeu, making sympathetic noises, rushed forward wielding a jar of antiseptic cream which she began to apply liberally to the afflicted area.

Naacha grunted in amusement. "You exaggerate. His mouth gentle. No punctures."

"No punctures but bruised from teeth! Many bruises. You were not sat upon by him!" exclaimed Annuur.

Another snort of amusement from Naacha; then, assured his leader was relatively unhurt, he headed back down to the navigation couch.

"You gave him the nanites?" asked Sokarr.

"Yes, they are within him. They will migrate to join those designed to destroy the matter transformer and reprogram them to do that only when it has created enough of memory-destroying ones."

"And you remembered the trigger word?" asked Lweeu, putting the salve away into one of her pouches.

"Yes, yes!" he said testily, pushing them aside. "He forgot he saw them and how I vanish. We go down now. Need to send signal to Camarilla for gateway."

As he settled himself into his couch, he asked, "Our family, do they sleep upstairs?"

"Soundly," said Sokarr. "Will be good to go home. Real beds again. No more mud."

"Fresh food," said Lweeu wistfully. "Baths."

"Room to be alone," muttered Naacha.

"Send signal, Lweeu," ordered Annuur.

"Signal sent," she replied. "Where will our family be while we on Ghioass?"

"Same as us. They go to village in mountains, wait out time there," said Annuur as they watched the jump point forming in front of their ship. Annuur began to steer toward it as Sokarr called out that the Prime ships were now following them.

"*Watcher 6*, you are not cleared to leave Prime Space. I repeat, you are not cleared to leave. Please return . . ."

"Kill sound," snapped Annuur as they picked up speed and entered the gateway.

Predictably, Kezule was furious at Annuur and Tirak's escape and the realization that they had been manipulating him and Kusac all along.

"Whatever was happening, no longer is," said Kusac when they met with him and Zsurtul again in the library. "It's over. I don't think they were acting against us. Think of all the good they did, for you personally as well as for the Primes. Had they wished to destroy the Primes, they would have done it long ago, after the Fall, when they were at their most vulnerable. They didn't." He kept to himself how they had tried to prevent him saving King Zsurtul. He needed to think this through fully before saying anything to anyone about this, even Carrie.

"Then why flee as they did?" the General demanded, pacing the room.

"I have no idea. But they're all gone from here and Kij'ik, both the TeLaxaudin and the Cabbarans. Whatever their agenda was, it's finished."

"Mysterious as this is, Kusac, and I agree it isn't our main concern right now," said Kaid. "We need to focus on rescuing Zhalmo and dealing with the M'zullians."

"You're right," said Kezule, halting beside the King. "However, I will have their quarters searched and find out what I can." He looked over at Kusac, seeing the tiredness in every line of his body. "I'm told the way you chased down the Cabbaran on one of the herd beasts was spectacular," he said. "Go soak in the pool, both of you. It'll ease those sore muscles. I'll send a masseur to see to you."

"Much as I would love to, we're really pushed for time," said Kusac.

"Go, that's an order," said Zsurtul, adding his voice to Kezule's. "We need you both fit and well."

Kusac nodded gratefully.

"As for the *Watcher* docking with the *Zan'droshi*, we've spoken to the Captain, and it seems that Captain Tirak called them, requesting a pickup as they were running low on fuel. It was a routine meeting, nothing more," Zsurtul continued.

"Was there a TeLaxaudin on the *Zan'droshi*?" asked Kusac.

"No. We only had one on the *Kz'adul* because he asked to come with us. It isn't normal for them to be on our ships."

"Just a coincidence then," murmured Kusac, turning to leave.

"It would seem so," said Zsurtul. "The TeLaxaudin have always been a law unto themselves, coming and going as they saw fit, but always they have aided us. I can find no fault with any of their actions on K'oish'ik at least. I can't speak for the *Kz'adul*, but as soon as your captivity was discovered, Giyarishis was anxious to help you, Kusac."

"I wasn't in much of a state to notice anything at the time," Kusac said.

"I did inform Carrie you were both safe," Zsurtul added. "Likely she'll join you at the pool. Until later, then."

"We'll meet back here at 18:00 hours," said Kezule. "You can update us on your talk with Rezac."

Dismissed, they left the library and headed for the entrance to the pool.

"He's taken to this kingship thing well, don't you think?" said Kaid.

"He was born to it," said Kusac. "He's making a good king,

though. And he's a Warrior." The last held a note of fierceness in it as he looked at Kaid, almost daring him to disagree. "It was always there; it just needed our culture to bring it out."

"Indeed," said Kaid. "You won't find me disagreeing with that. I believe more Primes could be fighters if they weren't brought up to believe the opposite." He let a small silence fall as they passed through the guard point into the corridor leading to the King's private gym and pool.

"That was some wild ride you took."

"I had no choice. I knew I wasn't going to make it to safety. My claws hurt," he said, flexing those on his hands unconsciously. "I had a hard time holding onto that damned beast."

"Let me check them," said Kaid stopping abruptly and holding out a hand.

"They're fine, just tender."

"Let me judge. You know how easily they can be permanently damaged if you let an injury go."

Sighing, Kusac allowed Kaid to examine them, pressing them out of their sheaths to examine the claw bed.

"You're lucky," he said, letting his hands go. "You've a couple of bruised ones on your right hand and a slight tear at the nail bed on your left index finger. I'll dress the finger after our swim, and you can use the bruise ointment on the others. You do have some left in your first aid kit, don't you?"

"I ran out of it on Kij'ik," he admitted as they went through the door into the pool area.

"No problem, we've plenty of our own stores on the *Tooshu*. That's one thing we'll need to see issued to all our team. Better take that dressing off your forearm too, it's filthy now."

Kusac glanced at the dressing. "Yeah, it is a mess," he agreed. "It's almost healed now. Just like old times, eh?" he added, breathing in the familiar smell of the heated mineral water as he led the way to the changing area and showers. "Getting ready for a mission."

"You're thinking of Jalna," said Kaid." You seem to know your way around."

"The pool rooms are all built on the same design—either this one or the one at their Summer Palace," Kusac replied, unbuckling his belt and hauling off his tunic, wincing as he did so. "Dammit, I hurt everywhere," he muttered, throwing his tunic down on the bench.

"You took a hefty fall when you leaped off the beast."

"You saw it?" he asked in surprise.

"Couldn't miss it. Your ride through the market square cleared everyone out of the way," he chuckled. "Granted I was running after you as soon as the way cleared, but I had a good view of you."

"Did you see Annuur disappear?"

Kaid hesitated. "I thought I saw Annuur running off with you in pursuit, but I couldn't be sure. I only saw you jumping off the beast. I believe he was there, though."

"Why? Because of the pouch?"

"That and because on the *Kz'adul*, the TeLaxaudin and the Primes would suddenly appear and disappear. Until now, I'd forgotten about that. And that matches what you said happened to you on Kij'ik."

"I *will* remember what they made me forget," Kusac said. "And when I do . . ." He left the sentence hanging and sighed. "You're right, I must focus on the job ahead of us. Time enough for that when we return."

"Aye," said Kaid, slapping him on the shoulder. "Leave it till then. There's nothing we can do right now with them all vanishing like that. Maybe they'll get careless while we're away, leave a clue or two as to where to find them. Now let's wash this dirt off ourselves and then go soak in that warm water."

The pool room was smaller than the one in Kij'ik, but then it was constrained by the size and age of the Palace.

"Mineral waters?" asked Kaid as they walked along the lounging area.

"The primordial pool of their religion," said Kusac absently, heading for the ramped entrance to the water. "They believe life on their world started in such a pool. Although they're warm-blooded reptiles, they do share some characteristics of their ancestors. They can absorb the water and minerals, to an extent, through their skin."

"It's hot!"

Kusac grinned at him as he waded into the water. "It's a volcanic mineral pool, Kaid, of course it's hot."

"You mean the original was," said Kaid, following him in.

"So I'm told. It's out by their Summer Palace, up in the mountains, where it's cooler," he said, submerging his body and treading water, letting the heat begin to ease away his aches.

"This is a cross between a bath and a swimming pool," said Kaid, starting to swim. "I hadn't realized how much I'd missed either. What's on the island?"

Kusac looked over to it. Like the one on the Outpost, it was planted with bushes and shrubs.

"Not sure," he said, pushing off from the bottom and beginning to swim over to it. "Kij'ik had small clearings among the bushes and a jet pool. This may be the same."

"Jet pool?"

"A small, hotter pool fed by jets of water that massage you," said Kusac.

They'd reached the shallows at the edge of the island and left the water. As soon as they stood up, they could see the jet pool, and Kusac headed straight for it.

Climbing down the steps, he moved around till he found a ledge that suited him and sat down, letting the jets play over his aching shoulders and sides.

"You should try it," he murmured, closing his eyes and resting his neck on the padded rim of the pool.

"I will in a minute," said Kaid. "I want to see the rest of the island first."

Kusac grunted a reply and relaxed, letting himself drift in the hot water. He was almost asleep when a loud splash, followed by his son's mental voice, made him sit up, suddenly alert.

Pappa!

Shaidan, what are you doing here? he asked, watching as his son swam over to join him.

I have something to show you.

You should be at your lessons. Couldn't it wait till evening?

It's second mealtime, and no. You're here now, the cub sent, scrambling out of the water and running over to him.

"You shouldn't be wandering around the Palace on your own, cub," said Kaid, emerging from the bushes.

"I don't, but I knew Pappa was here," Shaidan said, sitting on the edge of the jet pool. "This is important."

Kusac moved around beside him. "What's so important you had to sneak away from Brother Tanjo to tell me?"

"Gaylla will have told him I'm with you so he doesn't worry," Shaidan reassured him. "I found something that shouldn't be here."

Kusac glanced at Kaid who squatted down beside them. "What did you find?"

"I don't know what it is," he said, "but I know you will."

"Then how do you know it doesn't belong here?" asked Kaid.

"It's not part of ZSADHI, and it's the same as the one on Kij'ik."

Kusac stiffened. "In what way?"

"It links places and information together. I remember thinking it was odd on Kij'ik, because it didn't go to anywhere, like to a processing unit. It just . . . was."

"Where was it on Kij'ik?"

Shaidan shrugged. "Everywhere, Pappa. It ran behind the walls."

A memory surfaced, of sensing such a network when he was on his way up to Challenge Kezule and demand his son and freedom for him and his crew. He'd sensed it near the elevator he'd used. Then events had rushed upon him. He'd been injured, shot by a civilian Prime for no reason anyone had determined at the time or after. The shot had been intended to kill him—it was sheer luck it hadn't. Had Giyarishis, the TeLaxaudin on Kij'ik, controlled that male through this network? Yet Giyarishis had helped him heal.

"What're you thinking?" Kaid asked quietly.

He shook his head, signaling *Not yet,* to him. Grasping the edge of the pool, he hauled himself out of the water.

"Show me," he said to Shaidan.

"It was in the back wall here," said Shaidan, leading him away from the pool and among the bushes.

They'd felt their way along the whole back wall, both physically, and mentally, but had found nothing.

"It was here a week ago," said Shaidan, close to tears. "It was!"

"I believe you," said Kusac, ruffling his son's ears. "But it's not here now."

Shaidan pulled away and ran to the far edge of the small island, where it joined another wall, and began passing his hands across it.

"Shaidan, it's time you went back to Brother Tanjo and had your meal."

"No, wait! There's something here," the cub said, looking over his shoulder at them.

Reaching out with his mind, Kusac felt it immediately. It was like a small section of a net, crisscrossing in all directions, made of filaments thinner than a hair. It felt almost alive, and there was something familiar about it beyond the fact that it was what he'd sensed on Kij'ik. Suddenly, it was gone.

"What the hell!" exclaimed Kaid, running over to where Shaidan stood, closely followed by Kusac. "I *felt* that, and I felt it disappear!"

"I haven't told anyone but Carrie this," said Kusac grimly as he ran his hand over the wall, making sure the small piece of web was indeed gone. "That day when I got knocked out near Annuur and his sept in the new town, I sensed this then. It wasn't physically there, but it connected their minds—the Cabbarans and the TeLaxaudin. It was part technology and part organic. I don't think it's a coincidence that now Annuur has left, so has the last of their network. In fact, I think I was knocked out because I sensed it."

"So do I," said Kaid, equally grim.

"Have they been spying on us?" asked Shaidan.

Suddenly remembering his son was there, Kusac cut their conversation dead. "Well done for noticing that and telling me about it, Shaidan, but now you have to get back to Brother Tanjo and your classes."

"But why was that network there? Were they spying on us?" Shaidan persisted.

"I don't know, Shaidan," Kusac replied. "But it's gone now, and that's what really matters. Come along, I'll walk you back through the showers and get a guard to escort you to Brother Tanjo," he said, putting his hand on his son's shoulder.

Wait here, I'll be back shortly, he sent to Kaid.

When he returned, Kaid was relaxing in the jet pool.

"They're not just spying on us," he said as he climbed in beside him, "they're actively affecting what we do, manipulating us!"

"How do you figure that? Not that I'm disagreeing."

"We know Kezule's been altered quite considerably, and not all of it has been the Primes. He's been given ancient memories to fuel his desire to recombine his people into one race again."

"Agreed, but it's a benign change."

"How about the changes in me? They are due to Annuur and Kizzy, and both of them were on the *Kz'adul* as well. How do I know that the whole implant business wasn't a way to ensure they could 'cure' me?" he demanded.

"I think you're being a little paranoid," said Kaid carefully. "If they had, they'd have monitored you on the way home, made sure you didn't . . . harm yourself. I'll agree they took advantage of your loss of Talent, but not that they caused it."

Kusac grunted, angling himself so that the jets hit the source of pain in his right shoulder. "You're probably right," he said reluctantly. "But what else are they responsible for?"

"That scent marker of Zayshul's?"

He considered it briefly. "No, that was K'hedduk's doing, however it may have suited them for Zayshul to start believing it was her. To be fair, it may also have been my insistence that she was lying that made her eventually believe it was her." He sighed.

"You thought she was," Kaid reminded him. "How would that be of use to the Cabbarans and the TeLaxaudin? What's their agenda anyway? If we can work that out, we'll have an idea of how they've interfered."

"I don't know!" he said testily. "But I do know I felt that I was being pushed at Zayshul!"

Kaid sat up abruptly. "That might be the key," he said. "Pushing you at her could be assumed to alienate us. It certainly annoyed Raiban when Kezule trusted you more than any other Sholan."

"Kezule's reaction was also far from typical," said Kusac thoughtfully.

"Speaking of atypical, so was your treatment of the prisoners."

"There were times," said Kusac slowly, "when I felt I was two very different people."

"You were. We thought you were on the edge of a breakdown, but we couldn't get near you to help," said Kaid seriously.

"Another way to alienate me from you," said Kusac, suddenly realizing the depths to which he'd been manipulated. "How did they do it? And why? When he was on Shola, Annuur made no attempt to turn me against you."

"I don't think it was Annuur or even Kizzy," said Kaid.

"I think it was the other TeLaxaudin, or at least a faction of them."

Slowly Kusac lifted his right hand, staring at his palm. "You're right. Annuur gave me something, something to help me against the M'zullians." He remembered catching Annuur by the neck and shaking him, and he remembered the pouch.

"What is it, Kusac?"

"The pouch, it wasn't empty," he said, looking at Kaid.

"What was in it?"

"I don't remember. Dammit! He and Naacha are always messing with my mind!"

"Yet you still don't consider them enemies. Curious."

"I know it sounds ridiculous, but no, I don't. I remember him saying. *We aren't the enemy, the M'zullians are.*"

A silence stretched between them for several minutes as each was preoccupied by his own thoughts.

"Try this out, Kusac," said Kaid. "The Cabbarans and U'Churians are closely linked. They work as a single family unit, with the U'Churians like Tirak providing the muscle. Correct?"

Kusac nodded.

"We also know that the Cabbarans and TeLaxaudin work together. Perhaps they use the Cabbarans as their muscle. I know that the TeLaxaudin are terrified by their own shadows. When Carrie and I questioned Kizzy on Shola, he almost collapsed, and he shrieked for Annuur."

"Yes, that fits what we know about them, and it makes sense," said Kusac.

"Add in that the Cabbarans saved the U'Churians when a solar flare hit their world and almost destroyed it . . ."

"And that the TeLaxaudin did the same for the Primes . . ."

"Both are old species, older than all of our races, and both excel at manipulating matter and people, one with mental powers, the other with advanced technology," said Kaid.

"See what you can find out about them from L'Seuli," said Kusac after a short silence. "When we're done with M'zull, I will be visiting Annuur and his people. They will pay for what they've done to me and my family and to Kezule's. No matter what good they've done, they have committed crimes against us, and they *will* pay for it."

"There may be two factions," said Kaid. "We need to be sure of our facts before we act."

"We won't know until we confront them. If they can set up networks here and on Kij'ik and on the *Kz'adul*, then using the same methods of rendering us unconscious, they could do it anywhere!"

He was furious to think how he'd been used, how they'd tried to drive a wedge between him and his family. If he was being honest with himself, he had to admit that there was a fair amount of fear there too—that his every move had been watched and monitored, and he hadn't noticed it.

"I believe you did notice it," said Kaid, making him start because he hadn't realized he'd spoken aloud. "I know you did, repeatedly, and they had to go to greater lengths each time to make you forget what you'd learned."

"What makes you say that?"

"Because at times, certainly after we retook K'oish'ik, your behavior bordered on extreme. I told you, we thought you were heading for a breakdown."

"That bad?"

"Yeah. We couldn't stop you because of Kezule, who condoned it."

"They're gone now, Kaid. How can we tell if they return? Should we warn L'Seuli and Shola?" he asked, a troubled look crossing his face. "They'll think us mad."

"L'Seuli won't, because we can show him. He's staying at Ch'almuth, isn't he? We can speak to him when we get there. As for knowing if they return, I think we will. It may take a little while, but we'll notice discrepancies, gaps in time, as we did on the *Kz'adul*."

"I'll talk to Conner about it. He noticed something early on but countered it. He may know a way to keep them out of our heads."

"Good idea. I think that's your masseur," Kaid said pointing to a figure at the other end of the pool room. "Let's leave all this for now."

CHAPTER 16

Ghioass, an hour later

UNITY'S alarm system sent out a call to all members asking them to gather in the Council chamber.

Zaimiss accosted Annuur in the doorway.

"Why you back?" the TeLaxaudin demanded, his humming a shrill, discordant sound reflected in the purple and green hues his draperies were taking on. "Your place in field, not here! On what authority you send back all Agents and return? You overstep yourself again, Annuur, and you shall suffer for it!"

"Threaten me, do you?" snarled Annuur, rising up on his haunches and glaring down his long, mobile nose at the spindly being. "You are not Head Speaker of Council, nor will ever be! Remove yourself from my path! Now!"

"You dare address me like that? You are no one, and soon be less than that! A major crisis you have caused in time streams."

Annuur snarled again, letting it build to a bark of sheer rage. "Move, or I move you!" he said, nose wrinkling and whiskers twitching as he displayed his sharp shovel-like teeth and began to step forward, hoofed hand reaching for Zaimiss.

The other blanched, his bronze skin going a dull ocher color as he swirled away inside the Council chamber.

"Be careful," hummed Aizshuss from behind him. "We are capable of violence if pushed, and he has a reasonable tech arsenal at his disposal. Even for the sake of losing him, I don't want you harmed."

"He ambushed me," objected Annuur, dropping down onto all fours again to enter the chamber.

"Even so, our path is dangerous enough. Do not risk yourself. We need you," said Aizshuss, following him.

"Glad you do," he muttered. "This meeting not enjoyable. Censure for me again is top of their agenda."

"Better they do that than take action."

They filed in, sitting among the cushions of their own party. Greetings were passed across to each other, and Annuur was pleased to find that the majority of the Reformists, and even some of the Moderates supported his return. As the last few hurried to their positions, a general quiet began to descend on the auditorium, and Khassis, the Head Speaker, rose from among a small group of Elders of both species and walked up to the lectern.

"I called this meeting because of unprecedented decision of Chief Agent Annuur to dismantle Unity network on Kij'ik, and the Palace of the Sand-dwellers. He also sent home all field Agents in both locations. Though just returned, Phratry Leader Annuur agreed to Speak to us of this controversial decision."

"What Chief Agent?" demanded Zaimiss angrily from his cushion. "When he designated such?"

Unseen by him, a gray-pelted Cabbaran rose to his haunches.

"Speaker recognizes Elder Needaar," said Khassis, clasping her hands to her chest and dipping her head in his direction.

"The young today are lacking in manners," he said in a voice that though low with age was strong nonetheless. "You, I forget your name, are merely member of the Council. You think we Elders, who raise and lower Council members and appoint Agents, commune with such as you?" He shook his head. "Good you have long life ahead, lot to learn have you! We appointed Annuur many years ago."

Annuur rocked back on his haunches, surprised at the support from that quarter. He'd not expected his cover to be exposed so quickly.

"What?" demanded Zaimiss, eyes swirling in anger. "You . . ."

"Be silent, Zaimiss, or ask to Speak," said Khassis, using the voice amplification in the lectern so her words thundered out around the chamber. "Another incidence of this and I call guards to expel you!"

Hissing in rage, his drapery swirling from cool blues into hues of yellow and red, Zaimiss rose to his feet. "I wish to Speak," he said, voice humming stridently.

Beside Annuur, Aizshuss leaned his head toward him and whispered, "See the danger of adopting latest mood fashions." He let out a low rattling hum of laughter, swiftly stifled behind a small hand.

Annuur glanced at Shvosi who sat beside the Reformist Leader. She rolled her eyes, nose wrinkling in a grin. "Not all tech is to advantage of wearer," she murmured softly.

He settled back in his cushions, deciding he'd been too long away from the Council if there were such rifts as these developing, not just between the factions but also between the Elders and the Isolationists. Always restrained in their views and participation, it seemed some of them at least were stepping outside their usual roles, if this support of him and censure of the Isolationist Leader was becoming a trend.

"Speaker recognizes Isolationist Leader Zaimiss," said Khassis with scant courtesy.

Zaimiss took a deep breath, glanced at the Elders, and bowed to Khassis. "I will await Annuur's speech with interest," he murmured then sat down abruptly.

Khassis' head bobbed once. "Then I call upon Chief Agent Annuur to take the floor and Speak of his mission decision."

Moving back from the lectern, she waited for him.

Annuur rose to his feet and began to thread his way out to the aisle, feeling the hands of his Reformist comrades briefly touch his shoulder in a show of support as he passed them.

Up the path edged with tiny sparkling lights he trotted, stopping briefly at the fountain to dip his muzzle in the spray in a gesture of reverence for the liquid that was Life to them all. Then he approached the lectern, and Khassis was bowing to him. His nose wrinkled in worry. What were they planning? This was not at all what he had expected.

Wish you'd given me a clue what this is about, he sent to her as he reared up to touch hands with her before she retreated to the Speaker's cushion a few feet away.

Night had fallen as they'd entered the chamber, and now the only lighting was that of the lamps among the oases of trees and bushes around the edges of the chamber. In front of him was a sea of faces, but they were indistinct in the gentle half-light.

Through Unity, he could feel a mixture of emotions washing from them to him—expectation, support, and of course censure, but for now, the latter was in the minority.

He rose up and placed his hoofed hands on the edge of the lectern, balancing himself, taking the strain off his hindquarters and back.

"I return today with news not welcome to you," he began, looking around the gathering. "Many field Agents have we. All but those in Hunter Alliance are returned to here. Even now in mountain village awake the children of my family, placed there to wait out this crisis. Same true of other Agents with families of U'Churian children. Why do I take this step so drastic? To protect them all."

He stopped, gratefully accepting the small bowl of water brought to him by one of the U'Churian Council servants. Lapping till his throat was no longer dry, he placed it in the holder to one side of the lectern.

"Apologies. Just landed have we after arduous mission I undertook to protect the one assigned it by you. The nanites have been delivered to the Hunter, at great risk to my own hide. It had to be done in such a way he thought he had gained the aid from me. Unity, replay the moment from my memories," he said, leaning forward and opening his mind to Unity.

"As you wish, Phratry Leader," murmured the soft voice.

Behind him, the massive wall screen began to lighten, and images formed, of him running through the township, dashing into piles of baskets and sacks of produce, pulling them over to create a barrier behind him. As he obviously glanced over his shoulder, the screen showed a herd beast with widespread horns not far behind. Crouched on its brown pelt was a hunched black form.

The view pulled out as Unity extrapolated, showing Annuur as well as the beast that was chasing him. As the Cabbaran left the town and headed out into the scrubby land beyond, the beast was getting closer and closer. Foam coated its mouth, spraying out to either side. It let out a pained lowing as the figure atop it leaned to one side, making it change its direction.

It overtook Annuur and the black shape resolved itself into a Sholan, who suddenly launched himself from the beast's back onto the Cabbaran, mouth and teeth gripping him around the throat. Over and over they rolled, finally coming to a halt with Annuur lying on his back, belly and throat exposed to the Hunter who straddled him.

When it was over and the images faded, Annuur tiredly lifted his head. "The Camarilla's will has been done," he said. "What cannot be seen is how much he remembers. He *knows* Naacha hypnotizing him to forget, as you heard. He and Sand-dweller Warrior know what was done on Kij'ik, how we altered the Warrior's memories, gave him ancient ones, how we prepared the Outpost for him, made him choose to leave their world and go there with a party of his people—there is little they do not know! And how do they know this? Because of two things! We ignored requests to watch the Hunter cub, and we were never more than marginally in control of Hunter."

He stopped to drink again, and as he did, a low hum of conversation broke out.

"Speaker! I wish to Speak!" called out Shumass, standing up, his hands waving in agitation.

Annuur waved a hand absently as he continued to drink. All the dust he'd tumbled in was still in his throat. For him, it had been a scant hour since the Hunter had jumped on him.

"How we know they have this knowledge? We expected to take Annuur's word?"

"Phratry Leader, Chief Agent Annuur to you, you impudent grasshopper," growled the Cabbaran Elder Nkuno.

Shumass glared at the Elder then added sarcastically, "Phratry Leader, Chief Agent Annuur."

Putting the bowl down again, Annuur looked over at the TeLaxaudin. "Unity, confirm the Hunter and Sand-dweller Warrior know these things."

"Unity confirms this."

"No," he said, showing his teeth, "my word is not all you have! More they know. I left small portion of Unity behind at Palace, and confirmed it is they know even more. They know nearly everything we have done to Hunter and Sand-dweller!"

Gasps of shock and mutters of rage underscored his words.

"You withdrew all Agents before this event," countered Shumass. "How you explain that?"

"Hunter's memories returning. He confronted us, and Naacha was just able to hide knowledge from him again—then his mind gone, taken by those Entities like the Hunter priest you Isolationists entrapped!" He pointed at Zaimiss for emphasis. "Now priest back among these Entities, and we have them against us too! Think we not know you torture him? Lucky for us all he escaped when he did! Longer in captivity would enrage them more!"

"What do we care about those Entities?" scoffed Zaimiss, rising and getting permission to Speak. "Entrapped one already we did, can do again!"

"That one not a real Entity!" snarled Annuur. "You not know the full rage of even a Hunter, never mind a Hunter Entity! Be afraid. They have empowered the Hunter, made him their Avatar, his geas to bring Justice to the Hunter Alliance. Think you we will escape?" he demanded. "Think again! You want proof? Unity, reveal the potentialities in time!"

The screen darkened, showing ribbons of light crisscrossing each other, flashing briefly then dying, and at the heart of them was a light, a brightness tinged with red, that was slowly expanding.

"That is the Hunter. He will bring destruction on a scale never seen, or bring light of Justice to those needing it. His decision, tempered by our treatment of him. Unity, replay scene before Sand-dweller King crowned when Hunter dispensed Justice to traitors! I remind you how swift and lethal his Justice is!"

The screen blanked, then re-formed with the image of Kusac at King Zsurtul's coronation.

"Execute all the altered ones with tattoos except the leader. We need him for questioning," said Kusac abruptly.

"We don't know who the leader is, despite questioning them," said Kezule, glancing up at him.

"I know who he is," said Kusac, scanning the faces of the assembled nobility and soldiers. He was picking up small areas of fear accompanied by anger.

The scene changed.

Kusac pushed past the General, drawing his pistol as he did. Without breaking his stride, the single pulse of energy from his gun hit the thug between the eyes, dropping him like a stone, leaving his guards struggling to support his dead weight.

At the last one, Kusac stopped. "Zoshur," he said, grasping him by the arm and pulling him free of the guards. "Here's their leader," he said, hauling him forward, then flinging him down on his belly before the throne steps. "You don't need the others."

"Execute them," said Zsurtul, tiredly. "Have this one returned to the cells to await questioning."

"K'hedduk's counselors are next," said Kezule quietly as Zoshur was hauled off and the remaining two were taken out to the balcony to be publicly executed.

"Bring Prime Counselor Shyadd to me first."

"He's being treated for injuries right now, Majesty," began Zayshul as a small commotion at the rear of the hall drew all their attention.

"Shyadd," said Kusac, without even glancing in that direction as he continued to keep his senses and eyes roaming over the gathered crowd.

Kezule signaled to the guards at the rear of the hall.

"Majesty." Shyadd bowed his head in respect when he reached the foot of the throne. "Your counselors were forced to work under K'hedduk. Please, don't judge them too harshly. They did what they could to protect your people—except for one or two who were more . . . enthusiastic in helping K'hedduk."

Sparing a glance at him, Kusac took in the bandaged hands and the signs of bruises and cuts on the Prime's face.

"They could have refused, as you did," he said.

"Not as easy to do as say," Shyadd murmured. "We Primes are not known for our bravery."

"Time some of you were," Kusac said, going back to scanning the assembly as the counselors were brought before their King. He could sense something in a small group toward the back of the hall, near the exit to the balcony, but he couldn't quite pinpoint those concerned.

Ignoring the excuses and pleas from the counselors, he concentrated instead on them. Jumping down into the crowd, he pushed his way through as he strode toward them. As he did, one began to back away, then suddenly turned and fled toward the large broken window behind him. As the Prime leaped into the air, Kusac's shot caught him full in the back, propelling him out and down to the courtyard below.

"Garras, see he's dead," he subvocalized into this throat mic, increasing his pace till he reached the others.

They tried to scatter, but those around them prevented it. "He's Fabukki," said one, pointing at one of the small group. "He was Head of Security in the Palace!"

"*They're lying,*" said the Prime, a look of outraged innocence on his face as he stood his ground. "*Using your presence to settle old jealousies.*"

Kusac grasped him by the arm and thrust him toward the two Touiban guards who had rushed to his side.

"*We need him alive. He's a M'zullian,*" he said, surveying the three who had been with him. Mentally, he reached for them, forcing through their shielding to scan them, leaving them holding aching heads.

"*Collaborators,*" he said, losing interest in them to check the rest of the assembly. "*They sold out their own to K'hedduk.*"

"*Take them into custody,*" ordered Zsurtul. "*They will be judged later. Bring Fabukki here.*"

"*Dead,*" Garras confirmed through his headset.

He paced through the crowd, his senses intent now on finding the other two M'zullians. He was aware of Carrie and Kaid at the edges of his mind, demanding an explanation, but he shut them out, needing all his concentration for the job at hand. The Primes around him moved aside, giving him a wide berth, some even flinching if they thought his gaze fell on them. He stopped; the fear-scent was getting thick now, masking those he wanted. A slight movement from the extreme left caught his attention, and his head swiveled around to track it. He had them now!

He pounced, grasping each by an arm and dragging them up to the dais to give to Kezule's guards. "*Two more M'zullians,*" he said, stepping back to the General's side. "*Members of K'hedduk's crew. The one I shot was also one. We have them all now. They've got mind-blocks; I can't read them yet.*"

The screen blanked.

"That is the Hunter's Justice," said Annuur. "Swift and merciless. The cub found the fragment of Unity I left behind and showed his father. Who was it said, "Ignore the cub, he is worthless"? So worthless he found what we concealed from Hunter."

"Speaker?" said a voice from the Elders' corner. Annuur looked over to see another TeLaxaudin standing.

"Speaker recognizes Elder Zoasiss," said Khassis from where she sat.

"Had you not recalled Agents, would Hunter have discovered and questioned them?"

"Absolutely. He hungers for information."

"Ghioass—would he have knowledge of our location?"

"Yes." said Annuur shortly. "For now we are safe. Rescuing kidnapped Sand-dweller female and setting up base in mountains on M'zull important now."

Zoasiss nodded, gesturing at Annuur as his eyes swirled. "Thanks of Elders you have for prompt action. Well founded was our trust in you."

Annuur bowed to him as the Elder sat down.

Shumass raised his hand again.

"What now?" growled Annuur.

"I say your actions precipitated return of Hunter's memories," said Shumass. "Choice of giving nanites to him caused mental trauma. Hypnotizing him, then planting nanites not have this result! Yours is error of judgment."

"Perhaps, had I not recalled Agents earlier because of return of memories. Reunited with family he is, no chance to approach him with any methods we can use now! Forget that he is enhanced? Not just by us, but by his Entities too! Untouchable he now is."

"Why you think we Spoke for pushing him away from family?" demanded Shumass.

"It was done far outside City, where we cannot reach with Unity!" snapped Annuur. "You blind yourself to truths in effort to throw blame onto me."

Khassis got to her feet and joined him at the lectern. "Exhausted you are," she said with compassion in her voice. "We thank you for coming here so swiftly. Are any more questions?" she asked, looking around the chamber.

"Yes, Speaker," said Shvosi, getting up. When the older Te-Laxaudin nodded at her, she continued. "I Speak for ending this session. Much evidence put forward by Unity and Chief Agent Annuur. Time to digest it needed, and time for Chief Agent Annuur to rest and recover."

"Sound suggestion," said Khassis, nodding. "I Second that. Additionally, I want summaries of actions from all Speakers in this whole Hunter matter. Will be reviewed by Council of Elders, then results dispersed to you by Unity. Then to Chamber for open discussion we will come after reviewing all evidence."

"I Speak for laying charge of incompetence, of acting too hastily, on Chief Agent Annuur," said Zaimiss with heavy sarcasm on Annuur's title.

"I Second that," said Shumass.

"Out of order," said Elder Nkuno. "Investigation into whole matter now ongoing. Apportioning blame now out of order. Wait for reports we will."

"Unity, record that decision," said Khassis sharply.

"It is done, Speaker."

"I adjourn this meeting," said Khassis. "Annuur, our thanks again."

Annuur nodded and dropped down onto all fours. Staggering slightly, he left the Speaker's area and headed back to where his friends waited for him.

"That was totally unexpected," he murmured, allowing Shvosi to take some of his weight against her shoulder when he stopped beside them. "Elders rarely step in."

"Not by us," said Kuvaa very quietly. "Time to find the guilty and punish them. More happening in Council than you know. You come with us to my home now. Warm bath, plenty good food, and privacy to talk there. Your sept can join us if you wish."

"Thank you, I will accept," he said tiredly.

K'oish'ik, later same day

It was afternoon before he had a chance to see Rezac in his suite. He'd needed an update from each section leader to know how they were progressing. Carrie was still busy with Conner and their telepaths, testing their abilities and teaching them more. The next day, they would join the others on the *Tooshu* with the Touibans for cold-weather training. With all the resources of a major battle cruiser, they had the facilities to quickly make the new gear that they would all need for the mission to M'Zull.

The final selection of telepaths would depend on their ability to use their Talents under combat and extreme weather conditions.

Raiban had left the day before for Shola, and L'Seuli for Ch'almuth, where he would conceal the ship behind the moon, out of sight of any approaching craft.

The MUTAC was back down on the surface of K'oish'ik and being tested by M'Nar and Jerenn. Now it was controlled from a form-fitting couch, and the pilot was attached to it by electrodes as well as hand and foot controls. When they moved, it moved; if they wanted it to stand, a control swung the couch into an upright stance and the MUTAC stood. It took a little getting used to, but they were quickly becoming proficient. Once they were, they would be teaching Jurrel as he and Banner were on the team.

What had been minor aches before the swim and soak in the pool had fast become major ones afterward, and Kaid had threatened him with Doctor Zayshul if he didn't rest in his suite till at least the evening, taking some anti-inflammatory meds and applying copious amounts of bruise ointment. His injured finger had been treated with wound sealant and a light bandage to protect it, but it made for some clumsiness. All in all, he was glad to spend the afternoon resting.

Surprisingly, Carrie had not fretted over him, as she would have in the past, once she had seen for herself that he was safe. They were all getting more used to their life as members of the Brotherhood and all that it entailed.

Rezac announced his presence before he reached the door, and Kusac invited him to come straight in.

"Help yourself to coffee or c'shar," said Kusac from where he was resting on the sofa, gesturing to a small drink dispenser on a side table as he entered.

"Thanks," said the other, fetching a mug of coffee then joining him. He took the easy chair opposite. "What can I do for you, Kusac?" he asked.

Kusac chuckled. "Still not keen on titles, are you, Rezac? Here and now, that's all right, but you'll need to use them in front of the Primes, you know, and on the mission. We need to keep the line of command clear to them."

"You want me to go with you?" he asked, ears pricking up as he sipped his drink.

"Yes. You're one of the original enhanced telepaths, and I need your expertise. I saw for myself what some of your companions could do—Jayza for instance."

"I can't do it now, not since Zashou and I contracted the fever that changed us into what you are," shrugged Rezac.

"Watch," he said, holding his hand out. In it was the lump

of bronze that Carrie had returned to him. As he concentrated on it, slowly it began to soften and flow into a new shape. He was surprised to find it was much easier to change the metal than it had been before. Controlling the heat the change generated was almost automatic.

Rezac let out an involuntary sound of surprise and leaned forward. "What the hell?"

Kusac closed his hand around it then held it out to him. "Take it," he said.

Putting his cup down and reaching out, Rezac took it from him, turning it over in his own hands. "It's me," he said softly, looking up at Kusac.

He nodded. "I can change matter," he said. "Not just tricks like this, but flesh as well."

Rezac handed it back to him. "I saw you change into a Valtegan, then disappear. The Primes are full of it, calling it a sign from their Gods."

Kusac made a gesture of dismissal. "Superstition," he said. "I can't say for sure how the ability came about, but that's not important. I need your help to develop this talent into something we can use on the mission."

Sitting back, Rezac rubbed his forehead. "Kusac, it took me and Zashou both to affect matter, you know this. All we did was make the embryos in their eggs sterile—drones, if you prefer—and that was more a matter of temperature control than anything else. We didn't have time to explore our gift before we had to allow ourselves to be captured and brought here."

"I'm sorry if returning to K'oish'ik has been painful for you," said Kusac.

Rezac sighed, leaning forward again. "Not really. The Palace and City today are very different, and the people are nothing like the Valtegans of our time. Being with Jo has put nearly all those demons to sleep," he added with a slight smile.

"I think I can reawaken your old abilities," said Kusac. "Will you let me try?"

"What? Why would you want to do that?" he asked, shocked.

"So you can teach me, and we can work together."

"Ah, perhaps you didn't understand me when I said Zayshul and I had to pair to be able to do anything," he said, reaching for his drink to cover his embarrassment.

Kusac laughed. "I'm not suggesting we do that! Apart from anything else, Carrie and Jo will be there too."

"Thank goodness for that! As for getting that ability back, I'm not sure about that. If it depends on us having to pair with our mates before we can do anything, you'll find it of as limited use as we did."

"Oh, I intend to make sure that we don't have to do that," said Kusac. "I think the key to it is the gestalt. Yes, we'll likely be vulnerable while working, but we'll have the others to protect us, unlike in your time."

"I'm sure you've considered how the Valtegans reacted to us in your time," said Rezac. "One whiff of our scent will send them into a killing frenzy. We aren't going to be able to get very close to them."

"We are, if we are M'zullians," he said quietly, putting the piece of bronze on the low table between them.

"You're joking! No, you're serious, aren't you?"

"Deadly serious," he said. "It's the only way we can remain on M'zull and live. We also need to change the females with us so they at least appear male, or they'll end up attracting every male from miles around."

Rezac took a deep breath. "I don't know that I want to go trying to change people, Kusac."

"We'll need to practice before it comes to that, first on inanimate objects, then on plants, and finally on animals. When we're ready to try it with people, there are condemned prisoners in the cells."

"If we get it wrong . . ." he began.

"One will monitor, the other change," said Kusac. "If it goes badly wrong, the monitor can give a quick death to the subject."

"Dammit, you're taking a lot on yourself, Kusac. We aren't Gods, you know!" he said with a flash of anger.

"I don't think we are. It might be impossible for us to do this, but we have to try, and as soon as we can. Believe me, I will not spend one life, even a traitor's, lightly."

Rezac nodded slowly. "You need to know that I hate the Warrior class, the M'zullians," he said, looking into his mug. "I don't care how many of them die to achieve our means. I can just tolerate the Primes and Ch'almuthians, but only just. If this is what it takes to end their threat forever, I'll do it."

"I understand. I need to do one more thing," he said. "I need to alter your Link to Jo, as I've altered mine to Carrie and Kaid's to T'Chebbi."

"How?" asked Rezac, narrowing his eyes and tilting his ears back in the beginnings of anger.

"I need to eliminate the five-day dependency of all Leska pairs coming with us. Instead, you'll be able to exchange memories every night. I don't need to tell you the benefits of that."

Rezac's ears righted and his brow smoothed. "No, you don't. I'd be happy with that, though our mates might complain," he said. "However, one thing you have overlooked—if we are all males . . ."

"That's why I need more than just me able to change people," he said. "The base camp will have to be safe enough for us to change back to our own shapes if need be. Other than that, no sex and absolutely no shape changing off the base will be the rule."

"That should work," Rezac agreed.

"I need you Linked to Jo for the first change. It can be undone, of course, but the less that makes us vulnerable to the enemy on this mission, the better."

"Kusac, there are matters in my past . . . things I did as a youth . . ."

"I'm not interested in your memories, Rezac," Kusac said with finality. "Unless you think about something so strongly while I'm working that I can't miss it, I won't even be aware of what you're thinking about. Recite the Litanies if you wish; they'll effectively block any other thoughts."

Rezac gave a faint smile. "Yeah, they'll do that," he said. "You have to understand that I don't trust easily. I always felt the odd one out. Some made me feel that way, pushing their privileged backgrounds in my face, calling me trash."

Kusac leaned forward to put a hand on Rezac's knee. "You led the rebellion against the Valtegans, Rezac. Not just that, you survived till our time, to bring us your knowledge and skills. You know that among us, you are an equal, and for those who know your past, you are a living legend of what determination and hope can achieve."

"I'm not looking for praise," said Rezac, ducking his head in embarrassment.

"But you're getting it," said Kusac, slapping his knee lightly then sitting back. "I need you and Jo to Link mentally before I can affect your Link."

A slightly distant look came over Rezac's face. "Ready," he said.

Having done it twice before, it was the work of moments to make the changes with Rezac and Jo.

"Done," he said. "Now comes the difficult part. You and Jo can unLink now," he added.

"Our Link doesn't feel any different," said Rezac.

"It will tonight," said Kusac. "Now I need to explore the connections in your mind. I need to find the altered pathways. Are you ready?"

"Yes."

Reaching out again, he entered Rezac's mind, this time charting the various telepathic pathways. This was a familiar exercise as like all student telepaths, he'd done his time at the Telepath Medical Guild to see if he had a talent for healing. He was looking for damage, an area once used but now lying wasted.

Rezac's mind was as tense as an overstretched drum, making the task harder for Kusac. It was as if he were looking within a clenched fist, trying to see the open palm. Gradually, as time passed, Rezac finally began to relax and a few minutes later Kusac found what he was searching for.

The lesion was small, but it was at a junction for several bunches of nerves. He followed the main pathway in both directions, making sure he was right before he even attempted to do anything more. How to fix it was the question—he didn't want to risk re-creating the missing tissue because that would require taking some from elsewhere.

You're getting too complicated, sent Carrie. *Just tell it to heal itself. That's more or less what you did to change our Link.*

It was a lot more complicated than that.

There's nothing to lose by trying, she replied as her presence faded.

Mentally shrugging, he decided to try a variant of that and touched his consciousness to either end of the lesion, creating a bridge between them. There was a sudden flare of light and energy, and he was flung violently from Rezac's mind to find himself lying on the sofa, blinking and with a violent headache.

"Gods almighty, Kusac!" Rezac snarled. "What the hell did you do? Try to blow the top off my head?"

"Are you all right?" he asked, pushing himself upright again and trying to focus through the stabbing pain at Rezac, who was slumped in the chair.

"No thanks to you," he grumbled, rubbing his eyes. "I have a pounding headache now! Wait. You've done it. Oh, my Gods, you've done it, Kusac!"

"Really?"

"Yes! Look!" Rezac lunged forward to pick up the lump of bronze. Moments later he handed it to Kusac in a new shape, that of a perfectly formed egg. "I can do more with it than I could before!"

Kusac turned it over in his hands. "I think you just know more about controlling your abilities," he said.

They looked at each other. "Time to see Conner," said Kusac, putting the bronze egg down and absently scratching behind his ear.

Conner was busy with his group of acolytes making wreaths out of greenery and summer flowers. He looked up as their shadows fell over him.

"Take over, please, child," he said to the young female with him before turning to them. "I've been expecting you," he said. "Let's talk in my office."

"You have?" said Kusac as they followed him to the rear of the temple.

"I felt the surge in energy as you healed Rezac," he said, ushering them into his office. "You need to know how to use this ability properly, don't you? Well, I can help. Sit down."

"Then there is an easier way to change matter?" asked Kusac, scratching thoughtfully at his neck as he sat.

"Easier? No, but a different way," said Conner, taking a flower out of the vase that sat on his desk and putting it in front of them. "To change the nature of something, you need to know it from the inside out. Same with a person, as you found out, Kusac, when you were inside the mind of the Valtegan. You need to know what it is like to be a Valtegan to become one."

"Does that mean we can only change ourselves?" asked Rezac.

"No. It has been done before, but seldom. It's more like an illusion, one that is skin deep, but no more. At least, if you are making someone look like another of the same species," he amended. "To change a Sholan to a M'zullian is much more complex. I don't know if you'll be able to achieve that with anyone other than yourselves. My advice is to stick with what is easy. Alter the skin color of the commandos to match those of the M'zullians if need be, and make the females appear male and exude a male scent. Don't forget that!"

"We—Zashou and I—were able to affect the gender of embryos in eggs," said Rezac.

Conner nodded. "Yes, that's less complex than changing the sex of an adult person. Like some reptile eggs on Earth, their gender is temperature dependent."

"I now believe we didn't change the temperature, Conner," said Rezac. "For a start, we didn't know that. We actually changed the gender and made them all sterile."

"You did?" Conner's eyebrows raised in surprise. "Then perhaps your abilities will be greater than those of my predecessors. Whatever you do, you will need an enormous amount of energy. The lessons I gave Kusac will help you. Draw energy from the living earth, or you will find you are depleting your own body's resources beyond your capacity to replenish them quickly."

"How do I do that?" asked Rezac.

Kusac quickly Linked to him and passed on the information.

"Oh! It's obvious, isn't it, once you know," said Rezac.

"Indeed," smiled Conner, picking up the white flower and passing it to Rezac. "Try to change the color of this flower."

"I changed Kusac's lump of bronze into an egg shape," said Rezac, flicking his ears back briefly. "Why do I need to do something as simple as that?"

"You think it simple?" asked Conner. "What it will teach you is delicacy. You don't need to pour as much effort into changing a flower as you did in changing the bronze. Try it and see. Make it red."

Grumbling, Rezac began to concentrate on it. Moments later it began to shrivel and wilt.

"What the hell?" Rezac exclaimed, dropping it and leaping to his feet, overturning his chair in the process.

"Now imagine this was one of the commandos and you were attempting to change his skin color," said Conner gently.

"Point taken," Rezac growled, picking up his chair. "Pass me another one."

At 18:00 Prime time, they met again in the Council chamber, this time with Rezac, Toueesut, Carrie, and Banner there as well.

"I had the TeLaxaudin quarters searched," said Kezule, "but they were empty of anything belonging to them. The labs were searched too, but there was nothing to give us a clue as to where they came from."

"What about on Kij'ik?" asked Kaid.

"Same there."

"So that's a dead end," said Carrie, doodling on the pad in front of her.

"Regrettably," said Kezule. "How did your experiments go, Kusac?"

Kusac glanced over at Rezac. "Show them," he said.

Rezac leaned forward to take one of the flowers out of the vase on the table. Carrie watched as gradually the pale lilac of the bloom deepened and became a vivid purple. Rezac held it out to Kezule who took it, a puzzled look on his face.

"It may not look much," Rezac said, "but I killed the first one. We can change the color of flowers without damaging them."

"We needed to learn how deep a change is needed," said Kusac, rubbing his forearm. "This means we should be able to safely change the skin tones of our commandos to match those of the M'zullians."

"Well done," said Kezule.

"That's not all," said Rezac. "We did some work on altering the eggs of one of the river reptiles. The first few exploded very messily," he grimaced.

"We were finally able to change the sex of the young inside them," said Kusac. "You can tell what sex they are by their color. Obviously the embryos were dead after we finished with them because we had to break the shells to see the results of our experiments."

"Impressive," said Kaid, rubbing the side of his jaw. "But how does this help us?"

"We want to be able to affect the M'zullian's eggs if need

be," said Rezac. "Refine what Zashou and I did before. Also we're working up to seeing if it is possible to change the gender of an adult creature. If we can ... then perhaps we can turn some of the female Primes into males for this mission."

"To be honest, Conner has reservations about that," said Kusac, reaching up to scratch behind his ear.

Carrie looked up at him and frowned. It wasn't like him to scratch himself like this. She could feel the irritation he was experiencing there, and instinct made her glance sharply over at Kaid.

"He thinks the best we can achieve is a skin-deep illusion for them to appear male, with the scents to match the gender."

Kezule nodded. "Anything is better than putting them at risk. Can they wear scent-concealing lightweight suits under clothing to mask their scents?"

"Possible. We'd have to ask Toueesut," said Kaid, looking over at him as he ran his claws across his neck.

"Suits for under combat armor can be adapted for this purpose," said Toueesut. "Is small adaptation we can be doing."

"I'd rather have them as the main protection and disguise. We've still a long way to go with our experiments before we're ready to try working on people," said Kusac.

"Carry on with your experiments," said Kezule, making notes on his pad. "And keep us informed. How's the winter training going, Toueesut?"

"It goes very well. Your commandos do not like the cold and move slowly in it, but with the heated clothing they are doing much better. This will work, indeed it will. Another two, maybe three, days and they will be coping well."

"Thank you," said Kezule. "Banner, the fighters from the Sholan and Touiban ships—how is their training, and that of our new Ch'almuthian pilots doing?"

"Going well," said Banner. "Launch time is getting much faster, and the new pilots are doing well with the basic maneuvers and formation flying."

"Kezule," Carrie interrupted. "The cattle, do they have skin parasites?"

"I have no idea," said the General looking surprised. "Why? Is it important?"

"Yes," she said as Kusac picked up on her thoughts and began to groan. "If I'm right, then all the Sholans will need delousing, especially Kusac and Kaid. The cattle will need to be treated too."

Kaid opened his mouth to protest, then began to scratch vigorously at his neck again. "Dammit! She's right. I hate the delousing stuff," he muttered.

"We can zap them ourselves," protested Kusac. "There's no need for delousing. Besides, we don't have anything we can use here."

"You delouse or you aren't sharing a bed with me!" said Carrie. "I'm not catching them from you!"

"Skin parasites?" asked Kezule, puzzled, looking from one to the other.

"Biting insects that live on the host," said Carrie. "I bet there are some on the Prime cattle now."

"None that affect us," said Kezule. "Why would they attack you?"

"Fresh blood," said Kaid. "Also, we're furred, so they can cling onto us."

"M'kou, get the labs onto making something up for the Sholans," said Kezule.

"Weekly wash with it from now on," said Carrie firmly, edging her chair away from Kusac's.

"ZSADHI says they're indigenous to Ch'almuth," said M'kou. "We have nothing like that here. We'll need to fumigate the new town and the herds to kill them all. Apparently they can only live on that world—or on Sholans," he added.

"We must have picked them up today," said Kusac, getting up. "Our quarters will need doing too, Kezule," he said.

"Can't take you two anywhere, can I?" said Carrie, grinning despite herself.

"I suggest you head back to your quarters for now," said Kezule. "We'll see to getting the necessary treatment for this. Apart from that, good work all of you."

"Sonics," said Toueesut. "We use sonic units on our ships and in homes. Portable ones we can bring for people and herds. Like doorway animals pass through and zap, no more unwanted little itchy passengers!"

"That sounds much better than a delousing," said Kaid, his ears perking up again.

"I send for several units and one for herd. Also those to be treating rooms we have. Suggest all Palace be done just to be sure."

"Good idea." Kezule nodded.

Guess we'll be eating in our suite tonight, Kusac sent to her as they began to leave the chamber. *Chance for a romantic evening.*

Not unless I'm convinced you don't have even one insect in that pelt! she replied.

Carrie!

Don't Carrie *me! Do you want to inflict what you're suffering on me? You better hope Toueesut's sonic devices work!*

You're mean, he sent, trying to reach the middle of his back to scratch and to ignore Carrie's laughter.

Not convinced the sonic device was good enough, despite the Touibans pointing out that they were also prey to such parasites, Carrie found that the Sholans staying in the barracks had a generous supply of the parasite wash. She begged some for their use and handed it out to all those living in the Palace with dire threats of what would happen if they didn't use it immediately.

"You can't make them use it, Carrie," said Kusac as, his pelt thoroughly wet, he took the pungent bottle from her and began to lather it all over himself.

"Can't I? Tell me who their Clan Matriarch is?"

"You, of course, but . . ." He sighed, admitting defeat.

"Exactly. They have to obey me," she grinned, folding her arms across her chest as she watched him.

"I don't see why if the sonics was good enough for the furnishings, it wasn't good enough for us," he grumbled, rubbing it over his legs. "You might at least offer to do my back for me—you know I can't reach it properly."

"No way. That stuff smells," she said, wrinkling her nose.

"You know, you could be infested too," he said, keeping his head down so she couldn't see the glint in his eyes.

"Don't be ridiculous. I've been nowhere near the cattle, and I'm not itching."

"You said it, prevention is better than a cure," he said, lunging out of the shower stall and grabbing her.

She let out a shriek as he pressed her close against his chest. "You're getting me all wet, Kusac! Let me go right now!"

"The more I think about it, the more I'm sure you should share my shower," he said, ignoring her shrieks as he pulled her under the stream of hot water with him. "After all, I don't want you to reinfest me, do I?" he grinned, holding her tightly as she tried to squirm free.

"You evil-minded, flea-ridden fur rug!" she spluttered, trying to push her soaking wet hair out of her face as the water continued to cascade over her.

"That's no way to talk to your Clan Leader," he purred in her ear, nipping the lobe gently with his teeth. "If you can order us to douse ourselves in this evil-smelling stuff, then I can order you to do it too."

"You jegget, Kusac! You absolute jegget!" she said, thumping him on the chest with her balled up fists while trying not to laugh at the same time.

Zhal-Ch'Ioka, 7th day (April)

"Why're we walking to the swimming hole rather than going in the aircar with Master Tanjo and the others?" asked Shaidan as he and Carrie walked along the edge of the river. The swimming hole had been constructed at Conner's request, not just for the cubs but for anyone. The mornings, however, were set aside for the cubs.

Carrie settled her backpack more comfortably on her right shoulder and looked down at her Sholan son. "I wanted us to spend some time together, Shaidan. We need to get to know each other better. I promised you we would."

He nodded and kicked at a small stone in his path. "If I'm your son, why don't I look at all like you?" he asked after a few minutes' silence.

"If, Shaidan? You *are* my son! When your father and I first Linked, changes began to happen to us," she said, deciding that only the truth would satisfy him. "I became more Sholan, and Kusac, your father, became partly Human, like me. Even though you and your brothers and sisters look Sholan, inside there is much that is Human like me, especially with your Talents. Your sister Kashini does have a look of me about her."

"She does?" That had caught his attention.

"Mmm. Everyone who knows her says her face and mine are alike, and like me, her pelt and hair are blonde."

"Do you see yourself in me at all?"

Carrie stopped dead and caught Shaidan by the arm, halting him. Crouching down to his level, she looked him straight in the eyes. "Yes," she said, reaching out to tuck a lock of his hair back from his face. "In you I see much of my personality, as well as your father's, the Gods help us! You're as determined to do your own thing as both of us put together! Physically, yes, you resemble him, but to me you look like Shaidan, no one else, and I love that person."

"Oh," he said quietly, looking down at his feet.

"No one could doubt that you are Kusac's and my son," she said, stroking his cheek. "It's there for all who know us to see, Shaidan, in the way you carry yourself, and speak. We Sholans always see beneath the surface of how a person looks."

He looked back up at her, mouth widening in a slow smile. "You're Sholan too?"

Carrie grinned and flicking his ear, stood up. "Indeed I am, kitling. I ceased being Human when your father and I Linked, as I said."

"What about that part of me that's from Aunt Zayshul?" he asked as they began walking again.

"Be proud of it," she said without hesitation, smiling down at him. "I'm your mother, and Kusac is your father. Your DNA was manipulated after you were conceived, and some of Aunt Zayshul's was added to alter you, give you the speed and power of the Prime people. When you are old enough to share cubs with a female you love, those traits, we've been told, will not be passed on. They are unique to you."

"Oh," he said again.

What's really worrying you, Shaidan? she sent. *Do you doubt I love you?*

No, I can feel it, he replied. His mental tone belied his uncertainty where his voice had not. *I 'spose I'm worried that you can love me when I'm so different from you.*

You're looking with only your eyes, she sent, allowing her shields to fall a little so he could Link more fully to her. *Look beneath the surface, read me. You've only ever Linked with your father. I love him, and Kaid, and you're no different from them.*

His mental touch was gentle and deft, much like Kusac's. It took only a moment or two then he startled her as his small hand suddenly took hers and he sighed.

"Pappa was right. You are special," he said, falling in step with her.

She laughed. "He said that, did he? Well, so are you! Now come on, let's get to the swimming hole before Tanjo and your brothers and sisters wonder where we are!"

The rest of the morning was spent playing water volleyball and tag, and by the time Tanjo called a halt for second meal, Carrie was ready for the break.

"How do you manage to keep up with them?" she asked the older Brother as she toweled herself down before eating.

"I always enjoyed working with the young ones," said Tanjo, giving himself a final shake before wrapping a tunic around himself. "I'm glad Kaid gave me the chance to do so again."

"Well it certainly seems to agree with you," she said, sitting down on one of the rugs they'd spread on the ground. "You're looking far more relaxed and rested than I've ever seen you."

"These kitlings are very special," he said, regarding his chattering charges as they finished drying off, then fetched their backpacks and came over to join them. "See how Shaidan looks after Gaylla, and how the others look to him? He's a natural leader."

"I worry that he takes on responsibilities beyond his age," she sighed.

"Oh, don't worry about him," said Tanjo with a chuckle, reaching for his own pack. "He's learning how to rely on the adults around him to look after them all, just as a kitling should."

"Good, it's about time," she said, turning to greet the cubs as they descended on them.

Gaylla made a beeline for her, sitting down beside her, then insinuating herself onto her lap.

"Shaidan said since I have no mommy here that I could borrow you when I needed to," she said. "He said you have lots of extra love to go around."

"Did he, now?" she said, amused, automatically accommodating her body to the cub's and putting an arm around her.

"Mm, yes, he did," nodded Gaylla, sticking a thumb into her mouth. "Can I call you Mamma Carrie?"

A shamefaced Shaidan, carrying Gaylla's pack as well as his own, came to sit on her other side.

"I think it might be better to call me Aunty Carrie," she

said. "I am your Aunty after all, and you do have a mommy of your own."

"You are?" asked Gaylla, her eyes widening to saucer size.

"Yes, I really am your Aunty." She smiled down at her. "Now, how about you take that thumb out of your mouth and have something to eat? I'm sure it'll taste nicer."

The Palace kitchens had done themselves proud by providing each of them with a covered bowl full of strips of cooked fowl and smaller containers of vegetables. There was even a sweet fruit dessert. Bottles of fruit juice accompanied the meal.

Once they'd eaten, the cubs began to stretch out in the hot sun and gradually fell asleep, full of good food and worn out from the morning's exercise.

Even Carrie lay down on the rug for a nap, feeling Shaidan curl around behind her as Gaylla automatically inched backward into the curve of her body.

She woke about an hour later, and not having the Sholan's natural instinct to doze in the heat of the day, she slid out from between the sleeping cubs and headed back to the river to cool off.

Diving into the water, she began to swim leisurely over to the other side when, without warning, hands grasped her and pulled her under the water. Turning on her attacker, she kicked furiously at him, struggling to break free, but he was too strong. A hand snaked out and grasped her by the throat, squeezing tightly as he began to drag her upriver out of sight of the others.

Kusac! Help! she cried mentally as she grasped her attacker's wrist and hand and tried to break his grip, but she was dragged inexorably with him. They surfaced just as her aching lungs began to scream for air. Gasping, she struggled as she was dragged out of the water onto the bank and among a small group of shrubby trees.

"Don't bother fighting or sending to your Leska," snarled the Sholan, tightening his grip on her throat as she began to kick out at him. "I got a psychic damper turned all the way up—he can't hear you."

"What do you want?" she gasped.

"You, for now," he said, reaching for a piece of rope he had concealed there. "You cry out, you'll bring the tutor and the cubs down on us, and you don't want that, do you?"

She shook her head and stopped struggling as he pulled her hands behind her back and tied them there.

"Why are you doing this? You know they'll find me, and your life won't be worth anything."

"I want him to find you," he said, pulling her to her feet. "I can't get near him, but he's going to have to come out here alone to get you back! Now get moving!"

He was armed now and rammed the muzzle of his gun into her side as he began to drag her inland.

It was another hour before Tanjo and the cubs began to stir. The Brother noticed her absence immediately and sent the kitlings to check if she was in the river swimming. When they returned and said she was nowhere to be seen, he began to mentally search for her.

"She's not here," said Shaidan, looking very worried. "I can't feel her anywhere."

Tanjo sent immediately to Kaid, reporting her disappearance and asking that a flitter to be sent to pick them up.

Within fifteen minutes, it arrived with Kusac and Kaid and four commandos. They loaded Tanjo and the cubs onto it, and then it took off to drop them at the Palace then return.

"Kaid, you and two of the commandos take this side of the river," said Kusac, heading down to the water's edge. "I'll take the other."

"Aye," said Kaid, gesturing to two of them and wading into the water.

Dropping down to all fours, he searched the river's edge until he found her scent and traces of the struggle as she was dragged out of the water. The trail was easy to follow, almost as if it were intended that he find it.

Kaid, found her scent. Her kidnaper was Sholan and he's taken her inland. I'm following it.

Wait for us, sent Kaid. *If her trail is that noticeable, then it's a trap.*

I don't care! Catch up.

"He's coming," said the Sholan with satisfaction, peering out of the entrance to the shallow cave in the hillside. "Now you can call him and tell him to come alone or I'll kill you."

"I won't," she said angrily, struggling to get to her feet.

Grabbing a handful of her hair, he pulled her to her knees.

"You'll do it or I will shoot you," he snarled, putting the gun her side. "I don't care if you live or die, it's him I want."

"Who are you? What have you got against my husband?"

"Send to him!" he said angrily, jabbing her viciously in the side with the gun.

"No."

Cursing, he released her hair and backhanded her across the face hard enough to topple her onto her side.

"You will do it," he spat at her as he hauled her up again.

"If you kill me, I can't call him," she said, spitting blood. Her face ached from the blow, and her bottom lip was beginning to swell.

"I can still shoot off your foot or your hand," he growled, pointing the gun at her legs. "Now do it! And I warn you, I can tell what you're saying!"

Kusac! I'm up here on the hillside in a small cave with him, she sent.

Carrie! Are you all right? Kusac demanded.

"Tell him to come alone," he said.

She glared at him but did as she was told.

He has a gun and is threatening to shoot me. You're to come alone. Kusac, it's a . . .

Abruptly, she felt the damper field go on again.

"Good. Now we wait," he said, hauling her to the back of the cave and tying her ankles together.

"She's gone again," said Kusac, stopping.

"Then he has a damper unit," said Kaid. "You can't go up there alone."

"I have to," he said. "He's threatening to shoot her if I don't. She's up there by that outcrop of rocks, in a cave. Look how open the land is—there's no cover. He can tell if anyone else follows me. I have to do this alone, Kaid. Wait here for me," he ordered, beginning to walk again.

Kaid stood mutely watching him. There was nothing he could say. There was some cover, but against the grass, his brown pelt would stand out clearly. Had it been a few weeks later, when it would be seared by the heat of summer that would have been another matter.

"Captain, we can get up there unseen," said J'korrash. "We need to back up to the last clump of bushes, though."

Kaid turned to look at her. "How?"

Without our uniforms, our hides will blend in with the ᴜss. He won't be expecting us."

He stared at her then began walking slowly backward. Let's do it," he said. "My gut tells me this is another assassin. We've nothing to lose."

Her captor crouched at the cave entrance, his attention fixed outside, leaving Carrie ignored at the rear in semidarkness. She shifted slightly, trying to make as little noise as possible as she reached behind her, feeling at the rocks in hopes of finding one sharp enough to saw at her wrist bonds. Meanwhile, she was praying Kusac would at least keep to what little cover there was until he was nearly at the cave.

The ground behind her had a few scattered rocks on it, most of them underneath her, but her searching hands did find some larger ones. Again, she shifted her weight, edging up against the rear wall.

A shot zinged off the wall a few inches from her head, spraying chips of hot rock around her. She yelped in pain as one hit her bare thigh.

"Stay still. Next time, I won't miss," he growled.

"I'm lying on rocks. They're hurting me," she whined, pulling her legs up to her body as if in fear.

"Not for long," he laughed, turning back to the cave mouth. "I'll demand double the pay for killing both of you!"

He was an assassin, and the most dangerous so far, she reckoned. He was neither high on drugs nor a fool, unlike the others. Again she shifted, very slowly this time, until her ankles were close to her hands. She had no intention of letting this krolla kill her and Kusac without putting up a fight!

Slowly, keeping low, Kusac advanced toward the cave, gun ready. He'd already come to the same conclusion as Carrie. Mentally he was reading the area immediately around and within the cave. If ever there was a time to try out his enhanced skills, it was now.

He could sense Carrie and her captor. They were only about ten feet apart. Narrowing his mental probe, he focused in on the Sholan, trying to read his exact location and weapons from the position of the damper field. A faint flicker at the side of his vision almost distracted him, but he kept his senses trained on his target.

"I see you, Captain Aldatan!" the Sholan called out. "↑ here fast if you want your little alien mate to survive!"

"I'm coming!" he called out. "Send her out first!"

Laughter echoed in the cave. "I think not! I want you first!"

Movement, right there! He had the weapon and the damper pinpointed now, but he could only concentrate on one of them. Rising slowly to his feet, he braced himself for an incoming shot, ready to try to dodge it. Nothing happened; the entrance remained empty.

"Throw down your gun and come here!" yelled the Sholan, keeping behind the cover of the rocks flanking the entrance.

As his arm arced out to throw the gun, he struck with his mind, targeting the damper. Several things suddenly happened at once.

The damper unit on the assassin's wrist exploded, making him shriek out in pain and take his attention off Kusac.

Carrie, having managed to untie her ankles, propelled herself forward, shoulder ramming into him and sending him flying out of the entrance just as a hand appeared from nowhere to grab her as she fell. Then a single shot rang out.

Hearing the shot, Kusac dove for his gun and, leaping up, ran for the cave entrance, suddenly finding himself flanked by two naked commandos. He took in the body of the downed assassin, lying on the ground, clutching the bleeding stump of his wrist and gestured them to take control of him. But his attention was fully focused on who—or what—was holding a struggling Carrie in midair.

"Show yourself!" he snarled, hackles rising and ears falling as he faced the invisible person.

"Easy, Liege. I'm one of your Clan," said the disembodied voice as Carrie was gently lowered to the ground.

She ran to Kusac, standing partially behind him as, keeping his gun trained on the space where she'd been, he pulled his knife and sliced through her remaining bonds. Taking his knife, she held herself ready to fight if need be.

The air shimmered slightly, then before them stood a black-pelted Sholan holstering his gun, his gray eyes regarding Kusac calmly. Around his neck, the silver coin of Vartra glinted.

"He's the last of them," he said, pointing slowly to the injured assassin beyond them. "We think they were hired by the

Chemerian Ambassador Taira in retaliation for your foiling their plot to kidnap Kate and Taynar."

"Who's we?" demanded Carrie, wiping her forearm across her cut lip.

"I was placed on K'oish'ik by the *Watchers*," he said with a slight smile. "I've been here from the first, the night you landed in fact. My name's Chayak."

Kusac nodded slowly, keeping his weapon trained on him. "Your damper is still on."

"Oh, sorry." Chayak reached up and switched it off. Instantly his eye ridges creased in pain.

"He's telling the truth," said Carrie, mentally releasing his mind.

"I know," said Kusac. "That's a chameleon suit you're wearing."

"Still experimental," said Chayak, reaching up to massage his temples. "The Touibans are working on them, and we requested a couple to test. I was given one for this mission. There was another assassin by the way—he didn't get through to you, though. The others I couldn't get close enough to do that much about, except for the first one in the city."

"Why didn't you warn us?" Kusac demanded, finally holstering his own gun and accepting his knife back from Carrie.

"I needed to draw them out."

"So you let me and Carrie be the bait. I'm not impressed by that."

"I had my orders, Captain," Chayak said. "We need to pin this on the Ambassador, and I can't do that if all the assassins are dead."

Kaid's shadow fell across them. "I know you," he said, stopping beside Kusac and Carrie.

"Brother Chayak," he said, saluting him. "I was stationed at the Clan estate till I was seconded to the *Watcher* ships."

"I remember that. What's your involvement in this?"

"He was sent to protect me, by using me as bait to draw out the assassins," growled Kusac.

Chayak had the grace to look embarrassed. "I was to protect our Liege and take out the assassins."

"At least you were here when it mattered," grunted Kaid. "Lijou shouldn't be reassigning our people without our knowledge. I'll have to have words with him about this."

"How did you manage to be here right now?" Carrie asked sharply, obviously still suspicious.

"Your security was too good even for me after the last attempt," Chayak said. "I had to hide out. The plan was for Tirak to take me to Kij'ik, but Annuur had other ideas, apparently, so I had to hide outside the City. When I saw the Liegena and your son going for a swim, I realized the best way for an assassin to draw you out, Liege, was to capture your wife. So I followed her."

"What happens to him now?" asked Kaid, turning to look at where the injured assassin was being hauled to his feet by the commandos.

"With your permission, I'll take him to Shola for interrogation. As I said, we've been after Ambassador Taira for some time now, and he'll help us put him away for a very long time."

"Take him," said Kusac, reaching out to pull Carrie close to his side. She was shivering convulsively now that the danger was over, a mixture of being chilled because she was wearing only a swimsuit and the reaction to her ordeal.

"You're hurt," he said with concern, looking from her face to the cut on her thigh where a trickle of blood had coursed down her leg.

"It's not serious," she said, "but I'm cold. I'd like to get out of here into the sun."

"Thank you, Chayak," Kusac said. "I never even suspected your presence."

"Neither did I," said Kaid, shaking his head. "And I should have."

"I did have the damper and chameleon suit," said Chayak, moving past them to take charge of his prisoner. "It was essential you not know I was here."

"Shall we pick up the fragments of the gun?" asked J'korrash.

"Just check there's nothing large enough to be dangerous," said Chayak.

"Who was your handler?" asked Kusac, following him out. "Tirak or Annuur?"

"Captain Tirak. As far as I know, Annuur was unaware of me," he replied, taking the prisoner from J'korrash.

"You can ride back with us," said Kaid. "We've a flitter waiting by the river."

"So Raiban had nothing to do with it at all," said Carrie, trying to stop her teeth from chattering as they began to walk down the hillside.

"Apparently not," said Kusac, stopping to undo his belt and take off his sleeveless jacket to throw around her shoulders. "That should help you warm up," he said.

She pulled it close around her and smiled her thanks.

"Why would General Raiban have anything to do with the assassins?" asked Chayak.

"Old history. Forget I mentioned it," muttered Carrie. "The cubs? Are they safe?"

"They're back at the Palace," said Kusac. "We sent them back with Tanjo before we came after you."

"Are the attacks really over now, Chayak?" she asked tiredly.

"Yes, Liegena, they're over now. While I've been working undercover, all the Sholans in this system and the Ch'almuthian one have been double-checked. There's no one here who shouldn't be."

"Thank goodness for that."

"Let's get back to the Palace," said Kusac. "I want to call Shola and have a word with Lijou myself."

Comm room in the Palace

"Who better to protect you than one of your own?" asked Lijou. "Remember, you owe your allegiance as a Clan to me. I have the right to assign missions to your people. Besides," he added, his tone and face softening a little, "I did clear it with your Regent at the estate. We have the last assassin now, thankfully, and you are all safe. And I have my evidence against the Chemerian Ambassador."

Kusac grunted noncommittally but they both knew he was satisfied with the answer. "Is my father in the Palace?" he asked.

"He is, but he's in an Alliance Council meeting right now. I would be there myself if you hadn't caught me just before I was due to leave my office here."

"Please pass on my best to him, and tell him I'll be calling him at home soon," he said.

"I'll do that, and now I really have to go, Kusac. You look well, by the way. I had heard of your injuries. It seems you've recovered well from them."

"We're all well. A lot that's strange has happened here, Lijou. When I get home, I'll have to tell you about it."

Lijou looked curiously at him. "Maybe a report would be in order?"

Kusac grinned. "You know me and reports. I'll try."

"Stay safe," said Lijou, reaching out to cut their connection.

CHAPTER 17

KUSAC'S eyes opened scant seconds before ZSADHI'S alarm went off. Almost without thinking, he shook Carrie, and they were both up and diving into their clothes before they were properly awake.

Ch'almuth? asked Carrie, still struggling into her one-piece flight suit.

Yes. Make sure the others are roused while I see to Shaidan, he sent, pausing only long enough to grab his weapons before leaving the bedroom at a full run. *Bring our packs, please. I'll meet you in the nursery.*

Collapsing back on the bed, she pulled on her boots while sending out a roll call to the telepaths on their team. All answered and received her terse command.

Report to the shuttle bay in the main garage for immediate evac to the Couana. *This is not a drill.*

That done, she grabbed her own weapons and their backpacks—lying ready for several days now—and left.

Prepping the Couana *now we are, Carrie,* sent Toueesut.

He sounded far too alert to her mind as she glanced at her wrist comm and saw it was still an hour short of first hour, and the sky was only just beginning to lighten.

MUTAC being loaded, and our chef is cooking breakfast for us all for when we take off as I speak, he added.

As she ran along the corridor to the nursery, she saw Rezac and Kaid heading the same way to say good-bye to their cubs.

* * *

Kusac was crouched down in the corridor outside the nursery, holding their son as tightly as the cub was holding him. "We'll be back, I promise," he was saying. "You know we have to go and rescue Zhalmo."

"I know, Pappa," he said, obviously fighting back tears. "Zhalmo's a friend, and friends are special too."

"We'll stay in touch. I'll try to send to you every few nights."

Shaidan's head bobbed in agreement as Carrie went over to them.

"We'll be back before you know it," she said gently, stroking his hair. "Aunty Kitra and Uncle Dzaka will look after you for us. You like them."

Shaidan pulled away from Kusac to envelope her in a huge hug. "Yes, Mamma. Please take care, and hurry back!"

"We will, I promise!" she said, kissing his cheek.

We have to go, sent Kaid, coming out or the nursery, Rezac behind him.

Good-bye, kitling, we love you! sent Kusac as they both gave him a last, crushing hug.

The small fleet of shuttles was still landing in the bays adjacent to the *Couana* as theirs set down.

Kusac leaped out, Carrie, Kaid, T'Chebbi, Rezac, Jo, and Jurrel behind him as he headed over to the Touiban ship to monitor their team as they boarded.

"Check that the MUTAC is well secured," he ordered Banner and Jurrel then turned to Kaid. "Have the canisters of that anesthetic been delivered yet?"

Kaid's eyes took on a distant look before he replied. "Toueesut says they were loaded up last night."

Nodding, Kusac headed up the *Couana's* ramp only to stop halfway. "Carrie," he began.

She reached out to touch his cheek. "I'm your Second, aren't I? I'll take our stuff up to the cabin and get J'korrash to see to our Fire Team's ammo and weapons while I make sure our supplies are all in order."

He handed her his pack. "Thank you," he said, turning to watch her as she disappeared into the brightly lit interior of the ship.

Kaid exchanged a nod with him as he walked past.

*   *   *

"This mission will be nothing like the one you were on in your far past," Kaid reassured Rezac.

"It has its similarities," Rezac said, flashing a smile at his son. "At least this time I can fight without puking my guts up!"

"And we're properly trained," added Jo.

"There is that," Rezac agreed.

"Huh," T'Chebbi snorted, flicking one of her braids out of the way as they piled onto the elevator up to the cabins. "That makes a huge difference, you'll see."

The upper-level cabins had been drastically altered to fit in all of the twenty assorted Sholans, Primes, and Ch'almuthians. Only the double occupancy rooms for the three main team leaders remained unaltered, as they needed access to the private computing terminals.

Carrie opened the door to their cabin with mixed feelings as the others headed off at right angles past the mess room to their quarters. This room was full of their past, and not all of it had been pleasant. They'd discussed whether or not to ask for another cabin but had decided to face down the ghosts of the past.

Here it was that Kusac had tried to commit suicide on that ill-fated return trip after the Jalna mission. She put their packs on the bed and sat down, reaching with her mind to feel if there was any echo of that time.

Don't, sent Kusac. *Let the past lie, Carrie. It was a dark time for me, and I bitterly regret what I did then and the suffering I caused you all. I love life too much now to ever go there again.*

I hear you, she replied, taking a deep breath and getting up to wait by the door for the rest of their team to arrive. *You're right. Let's live for today, not the past.*

Kusac, wearing a headset now, was waiting for a report from Jurrel on the spare power cells in the MUTAC as well as making sure it was properly stowed. No one wanted that coming loose in midflight.

All their people had boarded, and the cargo hold and the forward lab were a hive of activity as, their personal kit stowed, they checked through the assigned supply packs they'd carry on their drop to the mountains after the rescue mission. The Fire Team Seconds were busy in the makeshift armory in the lab, checking the weapons that would presently be issued to them.

He was also deep in conversation with Toueesut and Captain Shaayiyisis, one of their two resident Sumaan crew. He stopped in midsentence, replying to Jurrel's report as he watched King Zsurtul, followed by a thunderous-looking Kezule, heading directly for them. He noticed the young King was wearing military fatigues and groaned aloud.

"Captain—Kusac—I am coming with you," said Zsurtul, advancing up the ramp. "Nothing you can say will make me change my mind. General Kezule has already tried."

With an effort of will, Kusac refrained from looking at Kezule. "Is this wise, Majesty? What if . . ."

"Life is full of what-ifs," the youth said. "I would never forgive myself if I didn't come. I want Zhalmo to see me as soon as she's rescued, to know that my feelings for her haven't changed."

"That might not be wise, King Zsurtul," he said. "She'll take some time to get used to being free again. It took me a long time to recover. She might not want you to see her in that state."

"I told him that," hissed Kezule. "Think of her, not yourself!"

"On the other hand," said Kaid, coming down the ramp to join them, "the one thing that really helped me was knowing that those I cared about were there from the get-go. Their presence alone helped heal my mind and spirit."

As Kezule gave a loud hiss of anger, Zsurtul turned to him with a wide smile. "Thank you! You understand exactly why I need to be with you."

Thanks a lot, Kusac sent to Kaid, who smiled benignly.

"It isn't safe, Majesty," said Kusac.

"If it's safe enough for them, then how is it not safe enough for me?" Zsurtul countered.

"Combat zone," said Kusac.

"And I wasn't in one when we retook the City and Palace? As I understand it, the *Couana* shouldn't be engaged in combat at all."

"True, but it's also our backup if things get tough. We may need its firepower either on the planet's surface or as we escape. It certainly has to dock with the M'zullian craft in order to take off those returning with it, and Zhalmo, before it can enter hyperspace!"

"We were just discussing this maneuver, if you remember, Clan Leader," said Toueesut. "A version of Prime attractor beam have we installed and been testing, and it is advanced enough for us to pull the M'zull ship close enough for people to transfer in flight. Then we enter hyperspace. No need being to slow down, less danger to ship and to us on it," he beamed up at Kusac, his whiskers bristling with obvious pride.

Zsurtul regarded Kusac calmly. "Then I see no reason I cannot come," he said. "It isn't as if I can't handle myself. If you remember, I was involved in firefights with K'hedduk's people in my mother's suite."

"And almost died when you followed him to his hidden ship. I will not be there to save your life a second time, King Zsurtul," Kusac reminded him harshly.

The young King's eyes darkened at the reminder. "I will follow all orders," he said quietly.

"Dammit, you can't take his request seriously," said Kezule as Kusac hesitated. "I can't be there to protect him either! Someone has to stay behind here!"

If it were me, would you stay behind? asked Carrie. *Did I when you were taken? Did we when Kaid was, and I was heavily pregnant at the time!*

Kusac gave a stiff nod. "Get boarded, Zsurtul," he said. "Report to J'korrash on the living deck to be allocated quarters."

"Aye, Captain," Zsurtul said, sketching a salute and bounding up the ramp before he could be stopped.

Kezule turned on Kusac, who merely lifted an eye ridge and regarded him calmly. "Ashay!" he called.

"Yes, Captain!" came a booming voice, followed by the ramp vibrating under them as loud footsteps were heard rushing toward them from the bowels of the ship.

Kezule forgot what he was going to say as he watched Ashay come trotting down to join them.

His head appeared first, at the end of a foot-long mobile neck; then the rest came into sight. He stood just over six feet tall at the shoulders with a tail as long as he was tall waving behind him. Coming to a halt beside Kusac, he settled his tail down, balancing on it and his well-muscled back legs. His muzzle-like mouth opened in a smile to reveal large teeth.

"Ashay, remember how you looked after Carrie when we retook the Palace?"

The head snaked down level with theirs, then nodded up and down. "Yes, I watch her well. When danger too near, I pick her up and run," he said proudly. "And I shoot enemies nearby too!"

"I have another job for you like that, Ashay," said Kusac. "King Zsurtul is coming with us. I want you to guard him well. He's not to be allowed near any danger, hear me?"

The huge head bobbed up and down again, and Ashay's tongue lolled out over the edge of his tombstone-like teeth as a gust of sweet breath blew in their faces.

"I hear, Captain! I good bodyguard! I look after little King well!"

"Thank you, Ashay. You may return to your duties."

Ashay started to turn away, but then the huge head swung back to Kusac. "Where Carrie? I not said hello to her yet."

"In the forward lab at the armory," he said.

"Then I go looking for her! Ashay pleased to see her again!" With that, he swung around, his tail narrowly missing them all as he took the ramp at an enthusiastic run.

"Satisfied, General?" asked Kusac, grasping hold of the ramp strut to keep his balance as the ramp once more vibrated under their feet.

Kezule had a strange expression on his face. "I have a feeling our young King may regret going with you," he said.

Carrie's shriek carried out to them. "Ashay! Watch your tail! And no! Don't slobber over me!"

Kaid coughed, hiding a huge grin behind his hand as Kezule looked at them in surprise.

"Think of Ashay as a large and enthusiastic pet," said Kusac. "Carrie says he reminds her of a young dog, a puppy."

"He will be safe enough with us, I be assuring you of that, General Kezule," said Toueesut seriously. "Ashay is very dutiful and will watch him most carefully."

"Biggest danger is getting swiped off his feet by tail," said Shaayiyisis mournfully. "Ashay still a youngster and hasn't yet reached full growth yet. Clumsy they are at his age." His huge head swung from side to side. "Very clumsy."

Kusac excused himself and drew Kezule down the ramp away from the others.

"Zsurtul being there may be the one way to save Zhalmo's

sanity, even her life," he said quietly. "You and I have no illusions as to how she'll have been treated, but has Zsurtul?"

"He saw the survivors from the cells and his mother," said Kezule tersely. "He may say little, but he knows what to expect."

"Good, because K'hedduk will have had her for about six weeks by the time we get there. She'll have fought him until he broke her, and he will have. The first thing he'll have done is made her pregnant. She'll have attempted suicide at least once." Even he could hear the bleak quality seeping into his voice, and mentally he shook himself. "When she's free, she'll try again. I did." He held Kezule's gaze with his own, seeing the shock written on the General's face.

"You attempted suicide? I never thought of you as ever giving in to anything."

"I wasn't. It was more complex than that, as it will be for her. K'hedduk maimed me. He took my Link to Carrie and Kaid away, and I wrongly decided they would be better off without me. Zhalmo will feel the same, Kezule."

"I know." For once, Kezule's face clearly showed his emotions. At his sides, his hands clenched into fists. "I have no right to ask . . . With your telepathic skills, can you- -will you help her?" His voice was barely audible.

"My time will be short, but I'll do what I can. I can erase, permanently, her memories of the worst of her captivity."

"Do it. Maybe that will be enough to keep her from trying to end her life."

"At best, it will be a rough and ready treatment," he warned. "Kitra, my sister, is remaining, as you know. Get her and Dzaka, her Leska, to work on Zhalmo. Conner too. Don't leave her alone when she returns; make sure she always has unobtrusive company."

"This will be a debt I can never repay."

"Deal straight with us and the Alliance, Kezule, that's all I ask of you," he said, moving back up the ramp. "I owe this to your daughter anyway. She went out of her way to look out for me and befriend me on Kij'ik."

As they'd get to Ch'almuth four days ahead of the M'zullians, Kusac was determined that their final checks before they left would not be rushed. Knowing this, Kitra, Dzaka, and Garras had waited till the last to say their good-byes.

Kitra found Carrie in the cargo hold with Zsurtul, stowing his battle armor, which had been sent on from the Palace.

"Carrie!" she said, bouncing over to her, tail swaying in pleasure.

"Hey, Kitra," Carrie said, hugging her, delighted to have the chance to see her bond-sister before they left. "I was afraid we wouldn't see you."

"No chance of that," said the young female, hugging her back. "They told me Kusac's around here somewhere."

"He's in the sick bay, going over the meds for us and the Primes with Toueesut and Doctor Zayshul."

"Take us there," said Kitra, linking an arm through hers.

Carrie balked, taking refuge in giving Dzaka, Kitra's mate, a hug. "Hi, Dzaka," she said. "You keep a good eye on our little sister for us, you hear?"

"Oh, I will," he smiled. "We have plenty to do here preparing to defend the planet."

"C'mon, Carrie," said Kitra, tugging her arm. "You can't keep avoiding her you know."

"I'm not avoiding Zayshul. I'm just giving them some space," she mumbled.

"Rubbish! Now which way to the sick bay?"

She sighed, knowing that when the youngster was this determined, nothing would stop her. "Zsurtul, go back up to your quarters and report to J'korrash," she ordered, letting Kitra drag her back to the main cargo area.

Garras was standing waiting for them near the ramp. When he saw them, he came over.

"You take care on this mission," he said in her ear as he bent down to envelop her in a hug. "Keep those husbands of yours under control."

"I'll try," she laughed, wrapping her arms around his neck and kissing his cheek. "You take care here. You're going to be facing enough danger yourself. I don't want to have to tell Vanna I lost you!"

"No fear of that," he laughed. "I have every intention of watching our children grow up."

"Ca-ree," said Kitra, almost dancing with impatience. "I want to see Kusac."

"The sick bay is over there," said Dzaka, pointing off to their right.

"Come on, then," sighed Carrie, letting go of Garras to lead the way.

The door was wide open, and she saw T'Chebbi first, going through the cupboards, checking items off on a comp pad. Kusac stood by the nurse's station with Toueesut and Zayshul, checking the drug cabinets there.

He swung around before they even entered, his face lightening as he saw the blonde cannonball heading for him at a run.

"Kitra!" he exclaimed, catching her as she leaped at him. "I hoped you'd come to say good-bye."

"Think I'd let you leave without seeing you?" she asked, clinging around his neck as he hugged her close.

"Oof! You're getting too big for this, you know," he said, bending to set her down. "Stop worrying, kitling," he said, stroking his hand across her cheek. "We'll be fine, I promise."

"How can you be sure?" she asked, her face crumpling. "You'll be stranded on that world with no way to escape!" She rubbed her eyes with one hand, obviously blinking back tears

He knelt down beside her and took hold of her other hand. "We have to go, Kitra. If we don't, we're leaving a lovely person in the hands of a monster. And there will be war between M'zull and the Alliance. We have to stop that, or billions of people will die."

"I know, but why does it always have to be *you*? Why can't someone else do it for a change?" Her voice sounded suspiciously close to breaking.

"Because we've been involved from the start," said Carrie, coming up behind her to wrap her arms around the young female. "Would you trust your safety to anyone else?"

"Yes! No," she said unhappily. "But I don't have to like it."

"Neither do we," said Carrie dryly, reaching up to tweak her ear. "Come on, love, this is no way to say good-bye to us. You're a Sister now, one of the Brotherhood. We don't send our people off with sniffles and tears, do we? Be brave for our sakes."

Kitra rubbed her hands across her face and straightened up, forcing a smile. "You're right," she said, turning to kiss Carrie's cheek. "I'm behaving like a cub, and I'm an adult now!"

"You are indeed," said Carrie, kissing her back. "You've got a most important task ahead of you when Zhalmo returns. We need you two look after her, make sure that what healing Kusac and I've done to help her is as it should be."

Kitra looked from one to the other of them. "You want me to finish healing Zhalmo?"

Kusac nodded. "You and Dzaka," he said, glancing up to where his bond-brother stood by the door. "Plus, I need you to keep an eye on Shaidan. He'll be very lonely without us and will need your company. You're so very good with cubs, you know that."

She nodded, lifting her chin in determination. "I can do those things."

"I know you can, kitling," said Kusac, standing up and running his hand across the myriad of tiny braids covering her head. "Dzaka, take care of each other. Kezule will be depending on you and Garras to lead the commandos in our absence."

"I know, Captain," he said, reaching out to clasp Kusac's forearm in the warrior handshake. "Be careful on M'zull. Don't scare them too much—I hear they're terrified of Sholans."

Kusac laughed as he returned the handshake before turning to Garras. "Take it easy, Garras. No heroics, please."

"As if," snorted the older male, embracing him. "Remember, the same applies to you. There're no prizes for nearly succeeding."

"I'll be careful. I've a new son and daughter to meet on Shola yet! Have you seen Kaid? He was here a few minutes ago."

"I've seen him," confirmed Garras, stepping back. "And the others. Time for us to go now and let you finish up your checks and be off."

"I should be going too," said Zayshul. "We've finished here. Be safe, all of you," she added, turning to squeeze out past the Sholans.

"Good-bye, Zayshul," said Carrie, reaching out to touch her arm as she passed her.

Startled, Zayshul stopped. "Good luck," she said before hurrying out.

A few minutes later, Carrie and Kusac were alone, Toueesut and T'Chebbi having escorted the others off the ship.

"Well, that's it for here," said Kusac. "We have everything we need to treat any of us, and the two cryo units check out too."

"Will two be enough?" she asked, moving over to lean against him.

"I hope we don't need even one," he said, resting his chin on the top of her head.

"Kusac?"

"Mm?"

"How are we going to get off M'zull?"

"If we're successful, we shouldn't need to. Once we've neutralized their fleet and their top military installations and people, then the Touibans will come to police the planet until a combined Alliance force takes over."

"But if we need to."

"We'll steal a ship or a shuttle and send a signal to Toueesut, who'll rendezvous with us and pick us up in the *Tooshu.*"

So you have contingency plans.

Did you doubt it? he murmured as the signal to get to takeoff positions sounded throughout the ship and the ramp began to rise.

"Did I tell you Toueesut has been experimenting with the chameleon coating on our battle suits?" he asked as they made their way across the now empty cargo bay for the elevator. "Thinks he's gotten it to where we'll be virtually invisible except in the strongest sunlight."

"No, you hadn't. That's great. What about those suits that Chayak wore?"

"We have several of those too. It was good of you to speak to Zayshul. She's not had an easy time of it, you know, being blamed for something she didn't do."

"I suddenly felt sorry for her," she said as the elevator began to rise. "Because we're together again."

He cast a sidelong look in her direction. "I was never in love with her," he said carefully. "I cared about her, but that was all. It's you and my family I love."

"I know," she said, smiling up at him. "I know that, Kusac."

The *Couana*, Zhal-Ch'Ioka, 13th day (April)

The three days were spent running everyone, especially Zsurtul, through drills. The young King, reduced now to the rank of a common Brother, was learning everything he had missed when he joined them at the last minute for the mission through the tunnels.

"Remaining on the *Couana*, you won't be going anywhere near combat," said Kaid, "but I prefer to have you as well prepared as possible for any eventuality."

Those designated as the tithe civilians practiced wearing lighter-weight armor under voluminous Ch'almuthian clothes. Kusac still wasn't happy.

"They're far too vulnerable," he grumbled to Kaid as they sat in the mess area late on their last night. "Let's not pretend we won't see heavy fighting, because most likely we will. One good shot, and they're dead."

"What else can we do?" demanded Kaid, sipping his c'shar. "If we put them in full battle armor, it'll be obvious they're concealing something."

"They have to be in full armor," said Kusac, tapping his claw tips impatiently on the table. "We haven't the numbers to see to any wounded, and I'll leave no one behind, dead or not."

"Creating an illusion over six people while fighting is beyond us," said Rezac. "And there aren't enough of us to protect one person doing that full time. However, Kusac, what if one of us sensed ahead for anyone we're likely to pass and made them see what they expected to see? Create the illusion in their minds only when necessary?"

"Risky," said Kaid, pulling a pack of stim twigs out of his pocket and offering Rezac one.

"Especially when I'll be sensing any electronic security and shorting it out," said Kusac. "That means two of us otherwise occupied, doubling our risk and dependence on everyone else."

"It's not that difficult," said Rezac, accepting a twig and sticking it in his mouth. "Zashou and I did that a lot. She was good at it, and you and I planned on using more or less the same technique to hide us from the M'zullians anyway. Both of us will be working like long-range scanners, only tightening our senses in when we're following something coming close. And it's not as if we can't deal with them instantly."

When Kusac looked at him sharply, Rezac shrugged. "What? I have no qualms about mind-killing. Have you? We use what skills we have. Not like you haven't done it before."

"I haven't forgotten what's at stake," Kusac said testily. He didn't like being reminded about blasting J'koshuk.

"You're also forgetting that, very quickly, we'll be twenty warriors, not fourteen with vulnerable prisoners," reminded Kaid.

Kusac nodded slowly. "We might be able to do it at that. We were only going to affect minds if wearing cloaks around our armor didn't fool the guards we passed. Treat the drones and females gently," he warned. "The Warriors are another matter. We don't need a trail of dead or unconscious bodies on the way in, though. Kaid, you can kill mentally, can't you?"

"Never tried," he said.

"It's quieter and quicker than shooting them," said Dzaka. "You just take control of the mind and send a large surge of energy through it."

Kaid nodded. "I can do that."

"Make sure you stop them from yelling, though," said Rezac. "What about our mates? They're more than capable of doing this too."

"I don't want their attention divided," said Kusac. "If they keep their senses trained on our immediate vicinity, they should have plenty of warning to react. We'll all be loosely Linked, after all, so that warnings are instantaneous."

"As Sholans, we're the bigger risk, in actual fact," said Kaid. "I'm not convinced a cloak will be enough concealment. The armor on our tails isn't flexible enough to keep them up out of sight."

Kusac sighed and pushed himself to his feet, picking up his empty mug. "We've been over this a dozen times. There is nothing else we can do, and as the most experienced warriors, we have to be there. We'll just have to wing it and pray it goes our way. At least we have the MUTAC to call on if the going gets rough."

He edged out from behind the table and went over to the small sink to rinse out the mug, then stowed it away in a cupboard.

"I'm going to bed, and I suggest you two don't stay up too long agonizing over what could go wrong because what actually will happen, we probably haven't foreseen."

Kaid laughed and began to rise. "You sound just like me. Good night, Rezac."

"You're not leaving me here alone," said Rezac, climbing off the bench seat. "I've neglected Jo long enough tonight. It's our last night in real beds, and I plan to enjoy it."

Chuckling, Kusac made his way down the corridor to his own room. Sounds of quiet laughter came from the rec area where some of the others were still up. He hesitated then decided to let them enjoy their last evening of relative freedom. Once they made landfall on Ch'almuth, there'd be little time for leisure.

Carrie was curled up on the bed, smelling fresh from the shower, reading. She looked up when he entered.

"Solved all our problems yet?" she asked with a smile, though she knew he hadn't.

"Some," he said, sitting down beside her. "We've decided our prisoners will wear full armor. We can't afford any injuries, and they're just too vulnerable in anything less." He reached out to play with a lock of her damp hair. "Rezac will make those we pass see what we want them to see, just as he was going to do to conceal us."

"Good. They'll be full combatants, then, rather than have to be protected by us. Means they can help us protect you and Rezac when you're working."

"So much of this is being left to chance," he sighed, winding the lock absently around his fingers. "But I can't see any other way to do it."

"You know what they say, no plan survives contact with the enemy. So we'd be altering it as we go anyway."

"True," he murmured.

She stretched out a leg and kicked him gently. "Go get a shower now," she said. "I know that dreamy look you've got on your face, and you're not getting into bed with me smelling of oil and sweat!"

He grinned, capturing her foot and lifting it up to his mouth. "You sure you want me to take a shower right now?" he asked, starting to lick her instep.

She giggled, trying to pull her foot free, but he was nibbling at her toes now, making her laugh even harder and try to squirm away from him. "Shower! Now!"

"If you insist," he said, rasping his tongue slowly across the sole of her foot before releasing her and heading off for their tiny bathroom.

When he emerged, still slightly damp, the lights were out, and she was waiting for him.

"At least you don't smell of that awful flea repellent," she said, wrapping her arms around him as he climbed in beside her.

"Neither do you," he said, pulling her across till she lay stretched out along him. He buried his nose between her shoulder and neck, breathing in her scent and that of her damp hair.

"This will likely be our last night of privacy for a long while," he said, moving his head so he could slowly lick along the line of her jaw.

"Do you think we'll ever have a quiet life?" she asked, playing with the small braids in his hair.

"I hope so, but I'm afraid we might find life just too quiet now," he murmured, letting his hands slide down her sides until they rested on her hips.

You could be right, she sent, biting at his cheek gently, feeling his shiver of pleasure run the length of his body.

I don't know how you had the courage to fight for me when I left you like that, he sent, his mouth hungrily searching for hers.

I knew there had to be a reason, especially when Lijou finally gave me your message cube and the bracelets for the cubs.

What did I do to deserve you? he asked, holding her closer still as they kissed frantically.

What other father would have given himself up to his deadliest enemy to rescue his son?

There was nothing else I could do, he sent, rolling over so she lay beneath him. Easing his knees between her legs, he raised himself up on his elbows, taking his weight off her. *How could I leave Shaidan there?*

You couldn't. That's just one of the reasons why I love you so much, she sent, her hands going up to grasp his head as his kisses grew deeper and more urgent.

He reared up, slowly breaking the kiss, his tongue caressing her neck. When she raised her chin and arched her body up against his, making low Sholan sounds of pleasure, he closed his jaws on her throat, pressing gently with his teeth as he felt the electricity begin to surge through them both.

Releasing her, he leaned back, his tongue and teeth nipping their way down her body, playing with her nipples until she was shuddering and moaning in pleasure, her hands kneading his shoulders then his sides. He tensed briefly as his genitals dropped—into her waiting hand. Then it was his turn to moan in pleasure as she began to stroke and gentle him until he was fully aroused.

He could wait no longer, and pushing himself up onto his haunches, he grasped her around the waist and pulled her toward him, letting her guide him into her warmth.

No one, no one has ever touched me the way you do, he sent as he moved slowly into her. He leaned forward again; her mouth closed over his and their minds began to merge. Shared sensations rippled through their bodies as every sensation of their lovemaking was amplified until he couldn't tell where he began and she ended. Each moment of ecstasy seemed to last forever, until suddenly they reached their climax and began the slow descent into a replete exhaustion of body and mind.

As they became aware of the world around them again, Kusac realized that Kaid and T'Chebbi had joined them.

Good to have you back at last, sent Kaid.

Been too long, Kusac agreed, wrapping his arms around Carrie and easing them, still joined, onto their sides. He felt T'Chebbi curl up against his back and, through his still sensitive Link to Carrie, Kaid stretch himself out behind her.

Not good to be without family for so long, came T'Chebbi's halting thought as her arm slid across his side and tucked close against his belly.

Carrie's lips brushed his, lingering there till he caught them with his own, feeling the magic they shared start to waken again. This time, though, Kaid and T'Chebbi were there too, their minds merging with his and Carrie's. He sensed the shiver of pleasure Carrie felt as Kaid began to nibble gently at her shoulders and his own as T'Chebbi's hand began to stroke his hip.

Surrounded by his family, in the velvety darkness, he felt

the stresses and tensions he'd lived with for so long begin to drop away as though he'd shed his winter pelt. He felt healed and knew he was where he belonged once more.

The next morning, Kusac suggested they call home while they still had the chance.

"You almost sound as though you think this is a suicide mission," said Banner when Kusac told him. "Only, if it were, you wouldn't have Carrie with you."

Kusac avoided his gaze.

"You think it is," said Banner in a hushed voice.

"Not the rescue," Kusac said quickly. "Whatever the risk, I do need my best people with me when we remain on M'zull. My worry is only a natural one, nothing more."

"I think all of us feel it is," said Banner, "but no one thought you did!"

"Keep that to yourself. Let's not talk up trouble, eh?" he grinned, slapping Banner on the shoulder before leaving the mess.

He let the others talk to their families or friends on Shola first, then finally it was his and Carrie's turn.

His parents were overjoyed to hear from him and proudly showed off his new twin brothers. Then it was time to talk to Taizia and to see Kashini and her twin brother and sister, his new son and daughter.

They both came away emotionally drained, yet pleased to have talked to their children again after so long. Carrie fought hard to keep back her tears, aware she was missing so much of their childhood yet knowing that unless they completed this mission, they might not live to grow older.

Kusac had timed the calls well because as soon as they were each finished, they had to go and prep for landing on Ch'almuth. That meant getting into their armor, collecting their weapons, and making sure their packs were ready to be picked up as they debarked.

The equipment they'd need for remaining on M'zull, plus the powered backpacks that would allow them to land safely, were still packed in containers and wouldn't be unloaded from the *Couana* until it returned after they had gained control of the tithe ship.

Toueesut was due to drop them off on the surface then rendezvous with L'Seuli on the far side of the moon, ready to come to their aid if need be.

"Long-range scans be showing no sign of M'zull craft in system," said Toueesut over the intercom. "Ch'almuth weather station contacted us and saying we cleared for landing."

"Copy that," said Kusac in his mic from his position by the MUTAC. Of all the team members, only he and Rezac were unarmored. As Sholans, they couldn't get into their Prime battle suits.

"Send the message to Commander L'Seuli now," he continued.

There was a slight delay, then, "Message sent. Answer we'll bring when we return for you."

"Acknowledged."

"Please be preparing for entry and landing."

There was a slight slowing of the *Couana* and an increase in their weight, and then they were in the planetary envelope.

"Lovely piece of engineering, and flying," murmured Kaid's voice through his headset on the Command channel.

"Aye," he replied, his eyes going from person to person, checking them over, making sure their visible weapons were held safely.

It hardly seemed any time at all before, with a slight jolt, the *Couana* landed, and the engines began to power down to an idle.

"Opening dorsal bay doors and loading ramp. Please be standing clear," came Toueesut's voice.

With barely a sound, the clamshell doors slid back, and the ramp began to lower and extend.

"We be wishing you good luck," said Toueesut, "but we know you will not be needing it. Safe to debark now, Captain Aldatan."

"Thank you, Toueesut. We'll see you in a few days," Kusac replied before giving the order for team leaders to exit.

Kaid led the exit, and through his Link to him, Kusac was aware of him ordering his unit to fan out to form a defensive pattern that the other teams joined.

"All clear," said Kaid once they were all in position outside. "You're clear to exit now."

Kusac gestured to Rezac, and together they guided the

floater containing their Prime combat suits down the ramp and onto Ch'almuth.

"Let's get under cover now," said Kaid, gesturing toward the nearby warehouse with his rifle. "I can see a dust cloud heading toward us."

"M'zayash," said Kusac succinctly using the Command channel. "The Elder of the village near here."

"How can you be sure?" Kaid asked as he watched their troops head off in an orderly unit.

"She just contacted me mentally," he replied dryly. "It's a welcoming group."

As they entered the warehouse, they heard the *Couana's* engines rising in pitch then accelerate as it took off.

Kaid reached up to release his helmet, telling the rest over the comm that they could remove theirs. Then he waited with Kusac at the open doorway as the two flatbed transporters drew closer.

Carrie joined them. "So who is this Elder M'zayash?"

"One of the village leaders. Think Noni with even more attitude and you'll be close," he said, flashing a smile at her. "And as powerful a telepath," he added.

The transports slowed as they approached the entrance, then floated slowly past them to come to a halt just inside. Kusac turned and, reaching out to take Carrie's gloved hand, led her over to the one on which an elderly Ch'almuthian female sat.

"M'zaynal," he said, inclining his head to her.

"So here you are again," she said. "As good as your word and that of your General Kezule."

"Of course. Did you doubt us?" he asked, feeling her cool mental probe and easily deflecting it this time.

"Not once the Touibans arrived to fix our shuttles and the weather station," she said, a faint smile on her lips as she turned her attention to Carrie. "Who's this with you? I haven't seen your kind before, child."

"My wife," said Kusac. "Also with me are my brother and his brother, and my best Prime warriors. We'll put an end to the tithe the M'zullians are exacting from you."

She nodded. "And so the war begins."

"Would you rather let them continue to take your young ones?" asked Carrie, raising her chin in defiance as she returned the Elder's stare.

"My, you're a feisty one," chuckled M'zaynal. "I like your mind-mate," she said, looking back at Kusac. "Good to know you have one more than your equal. No male should get too complaisant! Now load your people up; you're guests at our village for tonight. Tomorrow you can rough it here on the warehouse floor, but tonight, we welcome you all."

"Thank you for your hospitality. Load 'em up," he said to Kaid, pointing to the other, empty transport.

As he turned to walk toward it, M'zaynal stopped him. "No, you and your wife will join me on this one. You remember Nishon and Shikoh?" she said, gesturing to her companions.

"Indeed. You were expecting a child, weren't you?"

"We have a lovely young son," said Shikoh with a smile. "I'm surprised you remembered."

"And how is your son Shaidan?" asked M'zaynal as Kusac passed Carrie up into the transport.

"Our son is well," said Carrie, her tone slightly stiff as she sat down on one of the bench seats. "As are our other three children."

"You have four children?" said Shikoh, a tinge of awe in her voice. "Rashuk is our first. You don't look old enough to have that many children."

"I had twins," said Carrie, unbending a little as Shikoh got up and joined her.

"You did? You're so different from your husband, though. Are they like you or him?"

"Mothers always find something to talk about," observed M'zaynal as Kusac leaped on board. "So whom do your children look like? You or her?"

"Us," said Kusac, sitting opposite her.

"That's no answer."

He sighed. "Like me, but she is as Sholan as me where it matters, and I as Human as her."

"Hm," she said as the transporter started to move. "You're looking better than you did last time. Your mind is healed now."

He felt a light touch on his knee and looked up to find Shikoh leaning toward him. "We've had beds made up in the meeting hall for you and your people. After you break fast in the morning, we'll bring you back here, as we know you have much to do to prepare for the arrival of the tithe ship."

"Thank you, and yes, we have a lot still to do. I need to

hear details from you of what happens after the craft lands so we can finalize our plans tomorrow. One thing, though," said Kusac, glancing at Carrie. "Once we have our troops settled, Rezac and I have to assume a disguise." He suddenly realized that by changing, he was playing right into the heart of their legend. There was no option, though; he and Rezac had to change as soon as possible so they could get used to wearing alien bodies.

Carrie made a small growling noise, drawing all eyes to her.

"Your wife seems not to like the idea," observed M'zaynal.

"She has suffered much at the hands of the M'zullians," said Kusac.

"They killed my twin sister," Carrie said. "The thought of Kusac looking like one of them for the foreseeable future is not a pleasing one."

"We'll need a quiet place to do it. One with a floor of stone or wood, and protected from your telepaths. It takes a lot of concentration, and if our minds are touched while we change, I don't know what could happen."

"This sounds like a lot more than a disguise," she said, narrowing her eyes as she looked from him to Carrie. "I wonder if you are the Zsadhi of our legends."

"Don't tell me you have that legend too," he growled, frowning.

"Of course we do!" she said sharply. "It belongs to the Valtegan people, not one caste."

"How did you find out they think it's me?" he demanded, still keeping his voice low. "Have you been reading my people?"

She hissed softly in amusement. "I don't need to do that. You wear your geas like a second skin! You might well be him, we'll see."

"The gullible will always see what they want," he muttered.

"And you're depending on that," she said tartly. "Just remember, the M'zullians will have the same legend. You may be able to use that to your advantage when you stay behind!"

Kusac glared balefully at her. "You're as bad as our Noni!" he said.

"It's not my job to give you platitudes," she said, moderating her tone. "It's to make you face uncomfortable truths, to think again, to look from a different perspective. To help you understand the legend."

"Right," he said, lapsing into silence.

Cots had been set up in one end of one of the larger meeting rooms, leaving plenty of room for the suits of armor to stand overnight. Washrooms and toilets were nearby.

Once a guard roster had been set up to watch the room at all times and monitor the radio connection to the weather station for any advance news of the early arrival of the tithe ship, it had been agreed by Kusac and his team leaders that the troops could relax with the locals that evening.

That done, Kusac requested the shielded room for him and Rezac. With Carrie, Jo, and Kaid accompanying them, Nishon led them to another building that proved to be a chapel to their agricultural deities.

"It's very like the one in the Palace," said Carrie, looking around the painted murals on the walls.

"This way, please," said Nishon, leading them past the altar and down a corridor to a side chapel.

Kusac took one step into the chapel and stopped. As the scent of the flowers there filled his nostrils, a sense of prescience settled like a mantle on his shoulders. He knew he was stepping out of his life into the one chosen for him by the Entities. It was as if he could feel Ghyakulla standing on one side of him and L'Shoh on the other.

Rezac bumped into him, jostling him forward.

"You're blocking the door," he said, pushing past him.

He turned to one side, leaning against the door as the others filed in. Carrie stopped beside him, taking his hand in hers.

"You'll still be my Kusac," she whispered, leaning against him. "And I will still love you, even as a Valtegan."

He held her hand tightly, aware of the sense of expectancy in the very air. The choice was his alone to make. This was the final test. He must choose of his own free will to enter and become the Cleadh Mor, the Caliburn, or refuse and let war ravage their worlds. He stepped into to the room, Carrie close by his side. Under his feet, the flagstones felt cool.

"What deity is this?" Rezac was asking as he walked over to what was obviously the central image. "I thought you were a peaceful community here—this is a warriors' chapel!"

"It's the Chapel of the Deliverer, isn't it, Nishon?" said Kusac, looking at the walls and their vivid paintings.

"M'zaynal thought it fitting," said Nishon. "It is indeed the Chapel of the Zsadhi."

As he looked, he saw beyond the paintings and imagery, to the times Conner had recounted. There was painted the City of Discord and the warring castes, dominated by the Warrior M'zullians; yet overlaid on it were the warring clans of the Scots lowlands, fighting over land and herds. He saw the deities calling forth a Champion, arming him with a sword of magic, sending him forth to gather allies so they could ride against those who brought discord and famine to the land.

A shudder ran through him as he forced himself to look away from the murals. "Let's do this," he said, his voice rough with emotion.

Kaid nodded. "Rezac first, as you decided," he said.

"I've been asked to stay, if I may," said Nishon.

"Why?" demanded Rezac, beginning to undress.

"They need a witness," said Kusac, letting go of Carrie's hand so he could undo his belt and remove his jacket and tunic.

"A witness to what?" asked Kaid, swinging around to look at him. "And why this chapel? Are you trying to Link them to the Zsadhi legend?"

Nishon looked shocked. "No! We would never fabricate that! If he is the Zsadhi, it will be obvious."

"Shut the door, Nishon," said Kusac, handing his belt to Carrie, then his jacket. "Forget the legend, Kaid. Let's just do what we came here to do and get it over with."

"Aye," said Kaid, sitting down on the floor as Jo took the last of Rezac's clothes from him, putting them down by the door in a tidy pile.

Carrie did the same with Kusac's clothes then joined him and Kaid as Rezac sat down on the floor beside them.

Kneeling beside him, Jo and Rezac exchanged a kiss; then she moved back to sit with Banner, completing the circle around Rezac as he lay back on the floor.

They'd practiced changing several times in the intervening weeks. Each time it had been easier and less painful. Experiments had proved that they could only change their own bodies; however, they could affect the skin tones of the Primes.

"We'll monitor you as before," said Kusac, again taking Carrie's hand. "Just relax and draw the energy from the earth, then change."

Rezac slowed his breathing and closed his eyes. For several minutes, nothing happened; then, gradually, his body began to alter. Limbs straightened as his pelt began to disappear. A second body seemed overlaid on his, shimmering slightly as his tail began to shrink and his skin took on a greenish hue. His face was the last to change; as his features flattened, the ears appeared to move downward, level with his newly shaped nose and eyes. He let out a mewl of pain as the image of a M'zullian appeared to sink into his altered body, and the change was complete.

Kaid and Banner helped him to his feet and out of the circle. Jo handed him the khaki uniform trousers that the M'zullians wore and helped him into them as the two males returned to their places, reassured Rezac was fine.

He staggered slightly, holding onto his son for support, and drew in a shuddering breath. "I don't want to do that again soon," he croaked, his voice roughened by his new vocal chords. "Everything all right?"

"Yes," said Kusac, getting to his feet. "You made the change safely." He pulled Carrie into his arms, kissing her deeply before pushing her away and lying down where Rezac had been.

I love you, and I'm so sorry I have to do this to us, he sent to her as he began to try to control his uneven breathing and draw energy from the stones beneath him. He was afraid of how she would react to living with him as a Valtegan.

And I love you!

Carefully, he formed the image of how he wanted to appear then triggered the change. It still hurt like hell, but the alterations flowed throughout his body like a wave, changing him swiftly. He lay there, letting the pain subside, getting used to his new form.

"Damn, but that was fast," muttered Kaid. "I'd barely enough time to monitor you."

"I'm fine," he said, pushing himself into a sitting position and opening his eyes. The world looked subtly different, with colors a bit brighter.

"What's with the tattoo?" asked Banner as Nishon let out a muffled hiss of surprise.

"What tattoo?" asked Kusac as Kaid helped him to his feet.

"On your chest," said Carrie, looking not at him but at the wall behind.

Almost overbalancing, he swung around to look. In front of him was a painting of the Zsadhi, a glowing sword tattooed on his chest.

Kusac looked down as his own chest, relieved to see that his tattoo was small in comparison, only a few inches across. Then realization hit him. He pulled away from Kaid, reaching up to feel the top of his hairless head as he stared again at the painting. Under his fingers, he could feel the ridge of bone running down to the base of his neck. But it was more than just bone on top of his head: He could feel the skin there that he could raise to become a crest like Kezule's—and that of the figure in the painting.

"This is not what I visualized," he said, his hand going to the center of his chest, feeling the raised edges of the tattoo.

"Zsadhi," said Nishon, drawing the word out as he backed away to the door.

"Don't call me that," hissed Kusac, turning to look at him as the pale-faced Ch'almuthian wrenched the door open and fled.

"Dammit, Ghyakulla! I never agreed to this!" he cried out angrily.

"Kusac!" said Carrie, running forward to hold him as he staggered again. "Kusac, don't get angry over this. No one will see it under your clothes."

"They had no right to do this to me! I never agreed to be their legend!"

Kaid grabbed him and swung him around to face him. "Kusac, it's done now. Forget it. You never know, this may be to our advantage. Look how Nishon reacted."

"They've marked me! I wanted anonymity, to be able to go anywhere. Instead I'm one of their elite throwbacks, like Kezule!"

"Leave it for now, Kusac," said Kaid, taking hold of his head and forcing him to look him in the eyes. "It may work to our advantage. You could always try to alter it yourself later."

He took a deep breath then rested his forehead on Kaid's.

"You're right," he said. "Rezac and I both changed safely.

This is not important right now." He began to shiver, suddenly aware he was cold. "Where're those clothes, Carrie?"

Silence fell as he entered the room where the evening meal was being served.

"So you are the Zsadhi," said M'zaynal.

"No."

"Nishon says you have the mark."

He hesitated then began walking toward her table and the empty seats, the others behind him. "There is a tattoo," he admitted.

"Show it to us," demanded a male, standing up, one he recognized from his previous trip. Shaalgo, that was his name.

"No. It means nothing," he said, sitting down as far from her as he could.

"We've waited a long time for the Zsadhi, Captain," said M'zayash. "You have no idea how deeply it touches the psyche of all our people. He's the end to repression, hope for the hopeless. Just the knowledge you are on M'zull will bring you aid—if you bear the tattoo."

"Show it to them," said Kaid. "We need to know if it's the real thing."

"Oh, it is," he said grimly.

"Then show them."

Angrily he stood up, pulling the front of his shirt open, revealing the small tattoo in the center of his chest.

"You want me to be your Zsadhi, but a tattoo doesn't make me him! He's a concept, not a reality. You want a deliverer, someone to do your fighting for you; well it isn't going to be my people or me! We'll help you, but you need to get off your butts and be counted, learn to defend yourselves, fight for what you believe in rather than letting anyone with a weapon walk all over you!" He glared around the room at the silent and shocked faces. "I'm not even one of your people," he said, more quietly. "I'm no savior or deliverer, and I don't even have a sword with me. I'm only a Sholan, with a wife and children like you, and all I want is this war to be averted so I can live in peace with them."

A door opened, drawing all eyes toward it.

"He shall wear the form of one who was an enemy, then take yours as his own," quoted the black-robed Sholan walking toward them. Held across his hands was a glowing sword.

"Justice and retribution shall he bring to the unworthy and oppressors. Destroyer and deliverer you shall call him as he shakes the foundations of your worlds."

"Vartra!" said Kaid, his voice so low only those beside him could hear.

The Sholan stopped in front of Kusac. "Your sword, Avatar," he said, bowing and holding it out to him. "The Gods are with you, but remember well that a sword has two edges. Be not too quick to destroy."

It was the sword from his vision. Double-edged, with a two-handed grip beyond the golden colored quillons, the pommel a glowing multicolored gem. He hesitated, watching as the glow began to fade and the sword became his own, the one Kaid had gifted him. A single-edged, slightly curved blade, quillons now a disc of metal, the grip straight and elegantly bound in colored leathers.

"I left that on K'oish'ik," he said, instinctively reaching for it.

"And I was sent to bring it to you," said Vartra, looking up at him.

His hand closed on the hilt, and as it did, Vartra faded from view.

"Zsadhi." The name whispered around the room as, with an exclamation of anger and annoyance, Kusac pushed his chair back and left, still gripping his sword.

Kaid and Carrie found him in the sleeping room, lying stretched out on his cot, his sword beside him.

"We brought you some food," said Carrie as they threaded their way between the cots and the backpacks to him. She sat down on her cot, the one beside his. "You need to eat. Changing shape has depleted your energy levels, even if you did draw from the earth."

"He tricked me into taking my sword," said Kusac, staring at the ceiling. "Isn't it enough that we're doing this? Why do I have to be seen as Their agent?"

"Because They've given you abilities beyond those of a normal Sholan telepath," said Kaid, sitting on the foot of his cot. "Because being an Avatar of both the Sholans and the Valtegans tells our enemies you're not one person waging a vendetta but a force to be reckoned with. One that will unnerve the enemy," said Kaid. "Again, it may work to our advantage. Imagine the effect on K'hedduk and the Court if we broke into, say, the Royal Chapel, scrawled Zsadhi all over it, and drew swords like your tattoo one?"

"I don't want to talk about it," said Kusac, closing his eyes.

"You said it yourself, we're going to be doing this anyway, so why not use whatever extra we've been given?"

"Do you remember hauling down the banners in the Temple of Vartra at Stronghold and knocking over the braziers?" Kusac asked, putting his forearm across his eyes. "Well, I feel as betrayed right now as you did then."

"You're leading this mission," said Kaid harshly. "You don't have the leisure to cut yourself off from us! You're needed to talk to the Elders and get the information we need on what happens once the tithe ship lands."

"I'm delegating you to do it. Brief me in the morning."

With a snarl, Kaid got up and left, slamming the door behind him.

"Kusac, sit up and eat something," said Carrie. "The bowl of stew is going cold."

"I'm not hungry," he lied.

"You will sit up and eat now!" she said firmly. "Eighteen other people, me included, are depending on you to lead us! Be as angry at the Entities as you want, but stop endangering our lives because you're sulking! Now I know who Kashini gets it from!"

"I am not sulking!" he said angrily, removing his arm and glaring up at her.

"You are, too! You have to see the positive side to this."

He sat up. "Name one!"

She thrust the bowl into his unresisting hands. "Eat!" she ordered. "You want one positive thing? I'm sitting here beside you, despite you looking like a M'zullian, instead of either beating you to death or running screaming in the opposite direction."

"I had noticed," he said, crossing his legs and automatically lifting the spoon and beginning to eat.

"We all know you're mad at the Entities, but you're taking it out on us," she said quietly. "What's impressing most people is that despite how you look, you don't want to be seen as the Zsadhi. Your speech about standing up and being counted affected the young Ch'almuthians, you know. Don't undo that good by staying in here."

He finished shoveling the cold stew into his mouth, then handed her the empty bowl. "I need foot coverings," he said, inspecting the sole of one foot before uncrossing his legs and getting up. "These are far too soft to be walking on without them."

She sighed. "We have some for you somewhere, I'm sure."

He held his hand out to her, unsure if she'd take it. "Shall we go back to the others? As you said, I shouldn't send Kaid to do my work."

Slowly she reached out her hand and laid it in his, trying not to look away from him when he closed it around hers and helped her to her feet. "Let's go," she said, forcing a small smile onto her face.

Kaid glanced up as Kusac and Carrie entered, the frown on his face easing as he saw them. Without stopping what he was saying to the two senior Elders, he got up and moved along a couple of seats, making room for them.

"Double vision and headache better?" he asked Kusac as they took their seats.

"Just needed some quiet time," Kusac said, mentally thanking him for the excuse.

"M'zaynal told me the Elders meet the soldiers from the tithe ship," said Kaid. "Usually there are eight soldiers. They inspect the tithe, then take them on board."

Szayakk nodded. "Then they order our people to load the produce that they take."

"How many stay out to see the produce loaded?" asked Kusac.

"At first four, then the other four return once they've settled our people."

"Likely they lock them in a cabin, or cells," said Carrie, unconsciously pulling Kusac's hand onto her lap.

"Any idea how many soldiers total?"

Szayakk spread his hands. "We know of eight, that's all. There may be more that we never see."

M'zayash nodded. "I have only ever sensed eight."

"Let them load the prisoners, then take them down as they load the cargo," said Kaid. "That's assuming they are also the flight crew."

"My thought too. We'd have to use real Ch'almuthians, though, to leave our people free to fight."

"How will you get on the ship in armor?" asked Carrie.

"We won't, but I'm hoping K'hedduk will send them in armor this time," said Kusac. "We can take them one at a time if need be, if we males are the cargo handlers."

"One at a time, if unarmored," said Kaid. "We want those suits whole until we know if our armor is the same. We might just need them ourselves."

"Agreed. Then we'll need to have half our force armored, the others in stealth suits in case there's a flight crew and we need to take them out first. We can get into those suits in under five minutes."

"We need to rearrange the crates in the warehouse so we can conceal ourselves and our armor among them," said Kusac

"For that, we now have the forklift trucks working," said Szayakk.

"We'll also need an excuse to get them into the warehouse, out of sight of the others," said Kusac. From the corner of his eye, he saw Nishon cautiously approaching them.

"I've brought sandals, Elder," he said, bowing nervously to M'zaynal and him.

"Good," said Kusac, reaching out for a pair. "My feet are freezing on this floor!" He looked at them, turning them over in his hands then put them down on the floor. "Carrie?"

She knelt down and lifted up one sandal, then slipped the thong between his toes. "Like that," she said, her hand shaking slightly as she did it.

"You know, only the outside has changed, child," said M'zaynal softly. "If you've enough courage to fight by his side, surely you have enough to deal with this?"

She glanced at him briefly before whispering, "We'll find our own way."

"Don't take too long. This hurts you all."

"Enough," said Kusac, shoving his foot into the other sandal. "You don't know what she suffered at the hands of the M'zullians."

"But I do," said M'zaynal. "Her pain touches us all."

"Let's just continue with the planning," interrupted Kaid.

"I think we've covered it," said Kusac, sharply, getting up and walking to the door. "I need some fresh air."

"It is getting late," said Kaid.

Carrie rose. "I'll join him," she said.

"Well, time for me to sleep, then," said M'zaynal, rising stiffly to her feet. "You can break your fast here in the morning."

"Thank you for your hospitality," said Kaid, getting up as she left.

The night was dark, with barely any moonlight. What little there was reflected off the water fountain in the central courtyard. Kusac went over to it and sat on the edge, listening to the sound of the water. Why did this all have to come to a head now, when he and Carrie had just gotten together again? He was getting used to how his new body moved, and he'd managed to avoid looking in a mirror so far, but it wasn't easy for him either.

He heard her soft footsteps and looked up as she joined him on the rim of the fountain.

"I understand how you feel," he said. "So long as we can work together ..."

"You don't understand. I want to hold you so much it hurts, but you don't look like my Kusac anymore."

Reaching out, he laid his hand on her shoulder. When she didn't flinch away from him, he moved a little closer.

"Lean against me," he said. "It's so dark we can barely see each other. Forget how I look, just see me."

Her body was stiff and unyielding as she leaned against him. In the silence, the sound of the water falling into the catch pool made a cheerful chuckling sound at odds with how they both felt, and around them, they could hear the chirping of cicada-like insects.

He rested his chin on the top of her head, moving it gently from side to side in his usual caress.

Do you remember that first night I held you on Keiss? he sent. *There were insects chirping in the grass then.*

I could never forget it. I felt so safe with you.

And I felt so scared of how we'd Linked minds, he chuckled mentally. *You felt so small and vulnerable to me, but not alien—you never seemed that. But when I saw my hands against your smooth skin ...*

You're saying that's where I am again, she sent.

I'm asking if you can see me, not our enemy.

I see you, mostly.

We have to get past this, cub, unless you plan to leave me to sleep alone for the whole of this mission.

No! I wouldn't do that!

"Then we solve this, tonight," he whispered in her ear.

"I don't know if I can," she said.

"You can," he said, nuzzling at her ear. "Because you're my life-mate, my love, my Leska. You have more strength of will and determination in your little finger than any Sholan female I know."

"You think that of me?" she asked, her body losing its rigidity as she finally relaxed against him.

"I know it," he said, wrapping his arms around her. "The M'zullians depend on our fear of them to control us. I'm afraid of this body pushing you away from me, more afraid of that than our missions."

So am I. She was right, the old Ch'almuthian. If I can't give you the support you need, who can?

If you weren't by my side, life wouldn't be worth living, he said, trying to lick her neck, discovering his bifurcated tongue was only flicking it.

"That tickles," she said, pushing up her shoulder to stop him, but there was warmth in her voice now.

"Hmm. I can see I'm going to have to learn new tricks," he murmured.

A loud and obvious cough drew their attention, and he looked over to see a dark figure approaching them.

"Yes, Nishon?" Kusac said.

"I've come to show you to the guesthouse, Captain." He stopped a little way off and bowed deeply.

"I thought we were sleeping in the hall," Kusac said, surprised.

"Oh, no! You're married!" he said, obviously horrified. "We've had your personal bags taken there. I've already shown the other couple the way. We've even found boots to fit you, ones like the M'zullians soldiers wear. Captain Kaid took your sword over for you. None of us wanted to touch it."

"Thank you, Nishon," he said, reluctantly letting go of Carrie.

"Very kind of you," she added, getting up.

They followed him to a small building just off the main square. Lights were on in the main room, and Nishon pointed to a corridor off to one side.

"Your bedroom is the first one," he said, "and the bathroom is at the end." He indicated the door to their right. "The kitchen and dining area is through there. We'll bring your morning meal, so no need to rise early," he added, bowing as he backed out of the open door, leaving them alone.

They looked at each other, and it was Carrie who spoke first. "At least we get tonight alone to get used to each other."

He smiled. "I was thinking the same thing."

When he saw them leave with Nishon, Kaid stepped out of the shadows and took their place by the fountain. He was deeply troubled by Vartra's appearance earlier with Kusac's sword. Not just that, the Ch'almuthians had not seen a Sholan, they had seen him as one of their deities, a messenger of their Gods.

Vartra! he sent, trying to find the God's presence. *What the hell are You doing? You usually use me for Your dirty work! What's changed? Why Kusac? He has too much to lose now, dammit!*

I didn't choose him, came the quiet thought. *In this, I am only the Entities' messenger. Your role is to guard him well, as always.*

He's not resilient enough mentally for this, you know he isn't.

He's changed a great deal from the youth you knew on Shola, Kaid. Don't be blind to that. Besides, the Entities walk with him.

That's what frightens me, Kaid growled, sitting down on the fountain's edge.

He has resources you can't yet imagine to call on. See that your own fears for him don't make him doubt his abilities. The last was stern, a forceful admonition.

When have I ever done that? he demanded. *I'm still new to these mental abilities; he's spent his lifetime learning them.*

Be his strength, as Carrie is. Nothing more is needed, said the voice growing fainter as a hand touched his shoulder.

His hand automatically went to his knife as he swiveled around to face whoever had touched him. It was M'zayash.

"Peace, Sholan Brother," she said. "It's hard to watch one's pupil take the lead on a dangerous path, but this is what you trained him for, isn't it?"

"Indeed," he said, letting his hand rest on his thigh.

"Be content that he has such good companions as you and

his wife on this path," she said. "I sense that both of you were led to him by powers beyond you for just this day."

He looked sharply at her. "How would you know?"

She shrugged. "All Entities are the same; their forms just differ on each world. We all have our part to play with them. You three have been touched by them, I know that."

"Touched, and burned," said Kaid harshly getting up.

"Ah, but wasn't the salve worth the burning?" she asked cocking her head to one side in a very Sholan way.

He took a deep breath, sensing more here than what appeared on the surface. "Yes," he said softly.

"Then be content that this is what must be. I wish you a peaceful night, Kaid Tallinu," she said, bowing her head and slowly walking off.

He stood for a few moments longer, watching her retreating figure, not sure if she vanished as soon as she reached the shadows.

Bedtime, sent T'Chebbi sternly from inside the sleeping room. *Ease worries with me.*

Aye, he sent, feeling his mood suddenly lighten as he headed for the main building. *In a room full of others, I think not.*

Hah, a Challenge! You forget my skills! she replied.

Zhal-Ch'Ioka, 14th day (April)

Morning came, and Kusac woke to find Carrie curled across his body in one of her usual positions. They'd both been nervous of each other, but the darkness had helped them remember only who they were, not what. He hadn't rushed, and in the end, they had both enjoyed the sensations his new body aroused in them.

He moved slightly, easing her head off his shoulder and onto his chest, making her stir and utter small sounds of protest. At his waist, her hand unfurled and tucked itself around him.

Satisfied, he had just closed his eyes and begun to drift back to sleep again when Rezac began pounding on the door.

"Rise and shine, you two! First meal's here and it's hot. Fresh baked bread, eggs, and fried meat."

Go away, you evil person, said Carrie, burrowing deeper under the blankets and holding him tightly.

That's not nice, Rezac sent back. *I was just warning you before Jo drank all the coffee!*

There's coffee? Why didn't you say so at once! She threw back the blankets and bounced out of bed, searching on the floor for her clothes while Kusac groaned about his bruised ribs.

Their meal over, they traveled back to the warehouse and set up their base there, moving crates around until they had a small area at the center, concealed from casual eyes, where they could keep their armor and the radio to contact the weather station.

Kaid was talking to them now, telling them to turn on the automatic systems and evacuate the station at nightfall. There was no point in risking the M'zullians finding out they had access to working shuttles and were capable of reaching the weather station again.

While he was doing that, Kusac and Rezac were training in hand-to-hand combat with J'korrash and Schiya at the far end of the warehouse. They were taking a short water break, and Rezac was leaning on a crate, breathing heavily as he sucked up the water from a widemouthed cup.

"You certainly trained them well," he gasped. "I'm having a job keeping up with them."

Kusac was busy pouring water over his head then lifting it to let it run down his chest. He grinned, mouth wide. "Teach you to keep in shape," he said.

"You're doing very well," said J'korrash, dipping her cup in the water barrel that had been brought for them from the village. "I'd say you have the same level of fitness in these bodies as you had before."

"Makes sense," nodded Kusac.

"You're certainly getting more used to them," said Schiya, sitting down on a crate. "You're improving by leaps and bounds. You, Captain, are having less problem with the extra speed than Rezac."

"That's because I already have the extra speed, thanks to

the changes that K'hedduk made to me," he said dryly. "Slow down, Rezac, the speed will come with confidence and feeling at ease with your new body."

"We shouldn't be doing much hand-to-hand, though," said Rezac.

"We're training to get used to how our bodies move now, I told you that. Besides, you and I are likely to be at the front more often than the others because we're both male and telepaths. We can't risk you females being discovered. K'hedduk will torture the truth out of you one way or another."

"Point taken," said Rezac.

J'korrash and Schiya exchanged a look. "Our father gave us poison to take if need be," said Schiya quietly.

Kusac looked bleakly at them. "I can't advise you on that," he said. "I can only promise that if you're taken, we'll get you back as soon as possible."

"We know that, Captain," said J'korrash. "We'll just make sure it doesn't happen."

Kaid walked over to them. "That's the weather station staff prepped," he said. "How're you doing?"

Rezac pulled a face. "Getting there. Remind me to train every day in future."

Kaid laughed, slapping him on the shoulder. "Time you changed focus," he said. "I want you breaking down weapons and getting into your battle armor. You need to practice other forms of dexterity to make sure you have full control of those new bodies. How are you coping with the heat?"

"I don't have much of a problem," said Kusac. "Maybe because I'm fitter. I don't sweat, but there must be a point at which it gets too hot even for you," he added, looking over to J'korrash.

"We radiate heat," said J'korrash. "When it gets too much, we have to stop and seek the shade or water, but our tolerance is higher than yours."

"Heat isn't going to be the problem," said Kaid. "Cold is. Unfortunately we don't have a way to train you two for that, so you'll have to let J'korrash and Schiya monitor you when we're on M'zull."

Kusac nodded. "Will do. Meanwhile, if we're going to be stripping and reassembling weapons, I need these nails shortened." He held his hands out for Kaid to see. "The nails are too long."

J'korrash took a hand and inspected them. "Only by a little," she said, letting him go. "We put together a set of toilet needs for you, Captain, and Rezac, which included nail clippers and files. It should be in your personal bags. If your fingernails need doing, you better check your feet as well. Nothing more uncomfortable than having your nails hit the end of your boots."

"Yours could do with trimming, too, Rezac," said Schiya.

A distant look crossed Kusac's face as he sent to Carrie. "Carrie's fetching them for us," he said, relaxing. "She also says she sees a transport coming with second meal for us."

Kaid raised an eye ridge. "They are looking after us remarkably well," he murmured.

"Considering what we're doing for them . . ." began Schiya.

"No," said Kusac. "We're doing this for Zhalmo and to stop the war, they know that. This is a courtesy on their part. They owe us nothing, remember that."

"Yes, Captain," she said, accepting the reprimand.

CHAPTER 18

Ch'almuth Warehouse, Zhal-Ch'Ioka, 17th day (April)

THEY were in place well before dawn, waiting for the automated signal from the weather station that would let them know the M'zullian ship had reached the inner system. Rezac was leading his unarmored team of four posing as villagers for loading the cargo. He and his people wore rough Ch'almuthian clothes over their uniforms and had altered their appearances to make them look older so they wouldn't attract the guards' interest as potential breeding stock. Kusac and his team were wearing the lightweight chameleon armor that the Touibans had come up with for them. The remaining ten were in full battle armor.

The signal finally came in through Kaid's headset. "They've emerged from jump space," he said quietly over the comm sets they all wore. "And they're sending a message to the village, demanding the tithe. We've got about thirty minutes, so settle down everyone. Radio silence until I say otherwise."

The armored members were in the center of the crates arranged to one side of the warehouse, so they had a view through the open warehouse doors. Near the entrance, but out of sight of it, the crates of produce had been stacked, ready to be loaded.

The village transporter arrived first so that Rezac's people could join their number. M'zayash and Szayakk stood with the small group of eight youths who were to be the tithe. They looked suitably terrified, huddled together, clutching each other. As ordered, they each carried a cloth bundle containing extra clothing and a few personal effects. This would be where Kusac's people would conceal their helmets when they landed on M'zull.

They heard the distant boom as the ship broke the sound barrier, then the gradually increasing whine of the engines as it approached. Those among the crates finally saw it come slowly into view as it landed.

Gradually the engine noise decreased, settling into an idle. Metal grated on metal as the doors opened and the cargo ramp began to lower.

Kaid was monitoring the radio frequencies for the one the M'zullians were using, and when he found it, he raised his hand, sending mentally to those who could receive, which channel they were using.

The word was quietly passed to the nontelepaths, and they all adjusted their headsets.

"Eight outside in armor," said Kaid.

"Copy," said Kusac.

I can only sense their positions, too much electrical interference, sent Carrie. *One gunner has forward missiles trained on us. Flight crew of three remaining on deck. Turret not manned. Twelve in all.*

"Copy that," said Kaid.

M'zayash and Szayakk remained where they were, visible in the warehouse doorway with their charges, waiting to be summoned. They could all hear the heavy tread of armored feet coming down the ramp.

Our armor matches theirs, sent Rezac, sending the image of eight battle-clad soldiers fanning out facing the warehouse doorway.

"Bring the captives," ordered the one in charge, gesturing to M'zayash.

Delay them a little, M'zayash, sent Kaid. *Get your people to scream and refuse to go.*

On cue, several of the young females began to sob loudly and cling to M'zayash.

The Elder made soothing noises, patting their backs while Szayakk spoke firmly to them, ordering them to go with the soldiers for the good of their families.

"Stop their wailing," said the soldier, gesturing at them with his gun. "I want them on board now!"

Go now, sent Kaid. *I wanted the soldiers on edge.*

M'zayash and Szayakk spoke firmly to the small group and began shepherding them out onto the landing area. The five females were still openly sobbing and clutching each other, while the three young males looked suitably sullen.

"Where're the rest of the youngsters?" demanded the soldier who was obviously in charge as four of his comrades roughly rounded the youths up and led them into the ship.

"We had early summer fires— homes and crops were threatened, everyone helped. We lost several . . ."

"Then we'll want double the food and goods this time to make up the lack," said the officer, cutting her short.

"Double? We can't afford double," wailed M'zayash, wringing her hands. "Our people will go hungry and naked!"

The leader laughed. "What do we care? Punishment for missing the last tithe."

"Your ship never came!"

"Not your concern. Just get your folk to fetch the loading sleds out of the cargo hold now!" he said, pointing his rifle at her.

Rezac trotted out with the other nine, joining the five locals going around to the rear of the craft, getting his first good look at it, which he sent back to the others. It was a strictly utilitarian design, being basically wedge shaped with outthrust wings. A triple dorsal turret sat on top, an offensive plasma cannon with a standard sandcaster on either side of it. Missile launchers on either side of the hull augmented this.

Thug ship, sent Carrie. *Like the last one.*

Aye, Rezac laughed. *No finesse.*

Our show, then. Carrie, stay here as we agreed, please. We'll neutralize the Bridge crew first, sent Kusac, putting on his helmet and gesturing to his team to get ready. *We need a diversion.*

Accident with the crates? Kaid sent to Rezac as the other disappeared from sight.

Yeah, most likely scenario, he replied, passing the command on to the others of his team in the warehouse, waiting for them to return.

"If the suits are controlled from the ship," said Kaid, "you have that virus the Touibans gave us."

"Cheelar can see to that," said Kusac.

A few minutes later, Rezac and the others reappeared around the side of the craft towing three antigrav cargo loaders and headed for the warehouse, followed by the four soldiers who had taken the youths inside.

"Power the suits and move to the exit from here," said Kusac on their team channel, as he hit the control inside his helmet with his tongue. His HUD sprang to life, giving him the positions of all his team and those of the M'zullian soldiers as he led them to the small corridor out of the crates.

Rezac and his partner worked slowly, still loading when the other two units had left.

"Get a move on!" yelled the leader, moving closer to the warehouse and watching them. "I want to be off this mudball before nightfall!"

"Yessir!" shouted his companion, putting on a spurt of speed while Rezac managed to look up and stumble into him. Back they both staggered into the pile of crates, knocking them over in every direction. If some tumbled a little too close to the central pile, no one noticed.

Rezac let out a piercing yell and managed to fall away from the doorway with a crate partially on top of him.

"Go see what those clumsy louts have done to the cargo," ordered the leader, gesturing to two of the other soldiers.

"Yes, Lieutenant."

"You imbecile!" hissed one soldier, aiming a kick at Rezac. "I hope you haven't damaged the cargo! Get it off him," he ordered the other loaders as he backed away from Rezac and the crate apparently pinning him to the ground.

As those inside the protective ring of crates watched, all the other soldiers moved closer to see what was happening.

Kaid turned around to tell Kusac to head out only to find he and his team were already gone. He looked out the gap between the crates and was barely able to see the faint flicker that was them heading at a lope across the landing strip behind the soldiers to the rear of the ship.

Freed, and dodging a kick from the armored foot, Rezac scuttled back to the loader and began helping them to finish loading.

Kusac led his team silently into the almost empty cargo hold. They hugged the sides, darting behind the few cargo crates there while Kusac once again checked where the rest of the crew were.

He spared a moment to look around the hold, making sure

it was big enough to take the MUTAC. There was plenty of space; height might be a problem—it looked high enough, but it would be tight.

Waving them on, he headed for the ship's air lock, which the soldiers had left open. Immediately on their left was a locked door. On their right, the hum of the engines.

The prisoners, sent Kusac, gesturing to his left. *We'll get them later, when we're done.*

The air lock ahead was closed, but the corridor beyond it was clear. Motioning J'korrash to open it, he and the rest plastered themselves against the corridor wall.

It slid back silently, opening onto an empty and low-lit corridor that stretched straight ahead to a T-junction. Kusac scented a faint odor of laalquoi in the air.

"Breathers on," he said, switching on his own.

Like shadows, they slipped past the doors set into the walls on either side, stopping before each of the other two junctions while Kusac checked that the way was clear. At last they reached the T-junction.

There was a doorway to their left and another on the right along the T.

He pointed to their right, signaling to them to keep radio silence. From where they stood, they could see the air lock that led to the Bridge.

With hand signals, he ordered J'korrash to ready a gas grenade as he removed a stun grenade from the pouch at his waist. Back against the wall, he loosened the throwing knives strapped across his chest, waiting for her to take up position on the other side of the air lock. Thumbing the control, he opened the 'lock and threw in the stun grenade.

Even with his head turned away, he could still see the flare of light. J'korrash threw her grenade in as the flare died down.

He gave it a count of three, then, pulling two knives, charged in. His first knife found the chest of the comms operator as he jumped to his feet, eyes streaming. The next landed in the throat of the Captain.

Behind him, J'korrash's knife flashed past to the gunner, while Cheelar leaped across the room to get the remaining crewmember. The sharp crack as the Prime commando broke the male's neck was audible in the now silent Bridge.

The gunner had rushed at J'korrash and taken the knife in

the shoulder instead of the throat. As he grappled with her, Zsaya, their Ch'almuthian recruit, ran forward and sank her knife deep into the side of his neck. He stiffened, blood suddenly gushing out of his mouth, then fell to the deck, dead.

"Thanks," said J'korrash, kicking the body and retrieving her knife.

"Well done," said Kusac, nodding at Zsaya as he retrieved his own knives, wiping them off on their uniforms before slipping them back into his harness. Of the few Ch'almuthian recruits they'd had, she was the most promising. Right now she was closing the air lock door and taking up a post there as arranged.

Now they had the leisure to look around the Bridge, they could see eight lit screens among a bank of sixteen, each showing the view from a soldier's helmet cam.

He stilled his mind, doing another sweep of the ship, finding only the minds of the eight captives.

"Clear," he said to his team. "Power down the chameleon effect but keep the breathers on till your gauge shows the air clear. Cheelar, the com is all yours."

"Aye, sir," the youth said, pulling the dead body of the Captain out of his chair, then sitting down in it. Taking off his gloves, he began checking the system and uploading the virus from the data crystal the Touibans had given them.

Ship's clear, Kusac sent to Kaid. *Suits have cam feed to the Bridge. Cheelar checking if the Bridge comm controls them.*

Good work, sent Kaid. *Keep us posted.*

It took him a few minutes, during which time the air cleared, and they were able to turn off the breathers and breathe the ship air. The smell of laalquoi was absent from the Bridge, he noticed.

"They really don't trust each other, do they?" muttered Cheelar. "Got it. Yes, the Captain can control them from here."

"I assume it's in case of a mutiny," said Kusac, taking one of the freed command seats himself.

"Uploading the virus now," Cheelar said. "This should only take a couple of minutes. They'll query the Bridge. What should I do?"

"Send a static filled message saying you are experiencing problems," said Kusac.

"How do I do that?"

Leaning forward, Kusac put his hand on the Captain's control panel. "I'll create it when you need it," he said.

"Alpha One to Command. My suit's acting up again. Please stabilize the environmental controls."

Kusac nodded when Cheelar looked over to him.

"Command to Alpha One. You're breaking up. I have problems of my own here, deal with it." The youth's voice was transmitted with a large amount of background hissing and crackling.

They heard muttered cursing from the soldier; then he fell silent.

"Alpha Three. Command, my suit's medicating me!" There was a note of panic in the soldier's voice.

"Stop panicking, Alpha Three! The computer has a glitch right now. I can do nothing," said Cheelar.

"Turn off the suits' override then," hissed the first soldier.

"Negative, Alpha One. You know the regulations. It will be solved shortly, we're working on it."

"Three's fallen over," said J'korrash pointing to the third screen, which was now showing a close-up view of the landing pad surface.

"Look at the main screen," said Zsaya, pointing.

Seven of the soldiers were turning toward the ship, trying to get back on board before the problems they were experiencing became too great. They all began to talk at once, babbling their complaints over the comm as their suits went into odd gyrations of movement, then suddenly froze.

"I think we got them," said Kusac, sitting up. "Don't bother replying to them anymore, Cheelar. Can you shut the suits down from the Bridge?"

"No, I'm afraid not. I can medicate them, though," he said, his fingers flying over the key controls.

"Then you remain here while we go and disarm them. Any signs of movement, hit them with a strong sedative."

"Wait, I've just found a poison I can use," he said, his voice hushed. "Dammit, I hadn't realized how bad the M'zullian command was till now."

"Use it," ordered Kusac. "Power up your suits," he said as he put his helmet back on. "I don't want them to see us in case any of them are playing dead. Cheelar, warn us if anything changes."

"Aye, sir," he said as the others followed him back out into the corridor.

"On our way out, Kaid. We'll disarm them. Be prepared to cover us."

"Will do," replied Kaid.

They jogged down the corridor this time, slowing down only as they entered the cargo hold and crossed it to the open bay doors.

"Cheelar?" he asked.

"You're good to go, Captain," the youth said. "I've deployed the poison."

"Exiting now, Kaid," he said on their own Command channel.

"Copy. We're standing by to cover you."

He felt the touch of Kaid and Carrie's minds monitoring his position as they left the safety of the hold and made their way slowly around the side of the ship, this time keeping close to it and ducking under the wings.

The soldiers hadn't gotten far, but all were turned toward the ship to some degree, save the one that had fallen over.

Kusac scanned their minds swiftly first, sensing that they were all dead or unconscious.

"Take the nearest ones first," said Kusac. "Their suits check out as genuinely frozen."

He headed for the Lieutenant himself, quickly wrenching the energy rifle from the soldier's gloved hands.

"It's safe," he said to Kaid. "They're all dead."

The others came pouring out of the warehouse toward them, surrounding the nearest soldiers.

Kusac had turned away from the Lieutenant and almost missed the sudden movement toward him as Cheelar's warning sounded in his ears. There was a parting of the air beside him as the heavy suit arm just missed his head. He leaped to one side, swinging the rifle up and aiming for the helmet's faceplate. The range was almost point-blank, and he backed off, continuing to shoot at the same spot. There was a sudden low explosion, and as the blast sent him flying along the concrete surface, the enemy suit was lifted up into the air. Its remains crashed down motionless a few feet from him.

"Sorry," said Carrie apologetically, lowering her grenade launcher. "I wanted to be sure he was dead."

Kusac's laugh was slightly hysterical. "Oh, he's that for sure," he said, getting to his feet. "Next time, warn me."

Sorry, love, she sent. *I was frightened for you.*

"You all right?" demanded Kaid.

"Yeah, just bruised. This armor is definitely lightweight," he said, turning off the chameleon camouflage.

Yell incoming or something next time, Carrie, sent Kaid sternly as they began to open the suits of the nearest two soldiers. *You could have killed him!*

"I don't know how he survived that long, Captain," said Cheelar over the Command channel. "I poisoned them all as you ordered."

"Understood," said Kusac, walking stiffly over to help them.

"Saves us having to slaughter them later," said Kaid. "I never did like that part of the job."

"Shut the ship down, please, Cheelar and join us outside," said Kusac. "Let the kids out on your way past."

"Yes, Captain."

"Signal sent to the *Couana*," said Rezac from inside the warehouse. "They'll be here in half an hour."

"Do you need the suits?" asked M'zayash, ever practical.

"No," said Kaid. "No point now we know that ours are identical. Thankfully ours are far more advanced in design where it matters, and they can't be controlled externally!"

"Then we'll keep the suits. As you said the other night, it is time our young learned how to defend us themselves. This will be a start at least."

"Suits alone won't make warriors," said Kusac.

"No, but we can ask General Kezule for some people to train our young," Szayakk replied. "Today I have seen for myself that even in their suits, they are vulnerable. I just trust you are not equally at risk."

"There's always risk in war," said Kaid. "Our job is to minimize it in our favor."

The rest of their armored teams were stacking the now empty battle armor on one of two extra loaders sent specially by the village. The other one held the bodies of the dead soldiers for the villagers to dispose of.

"We've given your people a crate of dried meats and vegetables to help your food situation during the journey," said M'zayash as they prepared to leave with the still shocked, but relieved youngsters. "I heard how bad the food aboard the ship was so we left one of the crates we were taking back for you."

"Thank you," said Kaid. "You've been more than kind to us during our short stay."

"It's little enough to help you in your war effort," she said. "I wish we could do more."

"Your hospitality has been a wonderful boost to our spirits," said Kusac. "As is the food. Trust me, it is really appreciated."

"Take care on that savage world," she said as Kusac helped her up the steps into the loader. "Perhaps some day you and your family can come visit us and relax."

Kusac exchanged a glance with Carrie, who smiled and nodded. "We'd like that."

When they'd left, they turned back to the job of loading their personal effects onto the ship.

"I've had them clean up the Bridge," said Carrie, adjusting her rifle over her suit as it threatened to fall off. "There wasn't a lot of blood, but it's clean now."

"Thanks," said Kusac. "Cheelar, will that virus affect any other part of the ship's computer?"

"No, sir," the youth replied. "The Touibans gave us a means to remove it, so if you'll excuse me, I'll go do it now."

"Change out of that suit first," he said. "No need to risk its electronics when we don't need to."

"Aye, sir," he said. "Shall I put on my battle armor?"

"Might as well. We have to load it into their morgue anyway, and it weighs nothing if we're wearing it. Tell the others to do the same, please. And once again, you did a good job there."

"Thank you, sir," the youth said grinning widely before he left.

"I think I hear the *Couana*," said Kaid, looking up into the summer sky. He pointed up at a tiny glowing speck. "Yes, there it is."

"Right on time," murmured Kusac. "Carrie, did you by any chance check the rest of the ship?"

"Yes. There are plenty of berths for us, twenty-two to be exact," she said, counting items off on her gloved fingers. "The bedding is a little ripe, but there are washing facilities for clothing, so we can clean it. The morgue is empty of suits, so there's room for ours. The turret is controlled from inside it, and the missile launchers from inside the Bridge by one crewman. The kitchens are clean, but the food is laced heavily with laalquoi as you already suspected, so I'm having it unloaded. Those supplies from M'zayash will be very welcome. There's a basic sick bay—one autodoc and equipment, basic meds and dressings only. They obviously don't put much effort into keeping their people alive." she said, pulling a face. "There're showers and toilets, obviously, but the threc officer's cabins have their own shower facilities."

"You've been busy," said Kaid, raising his eye ridges. "I'm impressed."

"If you can let Jo, Noolgoi, and me go, we'll see to getting enough bedding cleaned for us. We can use our sleeping bags, but it would be nicer to save them for when we need to use them. Oh, and you need to get the cargo loaded off to one side of the bay to leave room for the MUTAC," she added. "Can we store our armor? We'll be a lot faster if we're not wearing it."

"Go, and thank you," said Kusac, reaching toward her to kiss her cheek. "Yes, put the armor in the morgue. We'll see to arranging it all later."

"How is it that females seem to be able to turn the most unappetizing surroundings into a comfortable den?" asked Kaid.

"It's their inbuilt Talent," said Kusac with a half smile as he watched her call for Jo and Noolgoi and clump off into the ship.

"Some somber news have I for you," said Toueesut as he and his swarm came dancing over to them once the *Couana* had landed. "The M'zullians attacked K'oish'ik at dawn. The battle still rages, but the City and Palace are safe. Do not worry," he said, forestalling Kusac's exclamation of shock. "They told us the cubs are safe underground with the General and his young daughter in the Command Center there."

"Thank the Gods for that," said Kusac in relief.

"How's the battle going?" asked Kaid.

"We are winning, but it is not being easy. There are many smaller ships and fighters to be reckoned with. Their surprise attack was not such a surprise as they hoped," he chuckled, his mustaches quivering with amusement. "The force fields around the City and the weather station are holding, and they

are keeping the battle from the planet surface. Only a few
fighters have gotten through, but they were shot down very
quickly. M'zullian casualties are being high, ours not so, thankfully due to our larger ships and more fighters."

"I'm betting that the only reason that the tithe ship is here
is because the females are promised to some Generals who
demanded them now," said Kusac thoughtfully.

"That is what I am thinking too," nodded Toueesut. "What
will he be doing when he learns that they have failed in the
battle at K'oish'ik?"

"He'll be angry and even more determined to destroy the
Prime world," said Kaid. "He assumed it would be an easy
target, that they'd have no allies, or none that would be there
when he attacked. He won't make that mistake twice."

"He'll surely face censure from his Generals for underesti-
mating Kezule," said Kusac. "The next attack will be an all-out
one."

"That's if his Generals agree to another in the near future,"
said Kaid. "Now they know the Alliance is aiding Kezule, they
may be less willing to go against it too soon. If not for us taking their tithe ship, they'd lick their wounds and, when ready,
go for Ch'almuth. It's a closer base to wage what may be a
sustained war on K'oish'ik. But knowing we took this ship and
then rescued Zhalmo from the heart of his Palace, who knows
what he'll do. It will certainly enrage him even more, and it
will weaken his standing with the Generals."

"Whatever he does, I think the sooner we leave for M'zull,
the better," said Kusac. "Before the news of his defeat reaches
them. Once we're based there, our actions will have to be
taken into account by K'hedduk and his Generals. We can
play on his defeat in our insurgent activities."

"Definitely," nodded Kaid, hearing the sound of the
MUTAC being started up and turning to watch.

Slowly at first, like a giant metal feline, it stalked down
the *Couana's* ramp and onto Ch'almuth. Picking up speed, it
began to lope the distance between it and the M'zullian ship.
It moved gracefully, like a feral feline, its tail curling and arching to provide balance as it moved.

"Damn, but that's a beautiful sight," said Kusac, staring at
it. "It's moving so much more . . . naturally now. Look at the
effect it's having on the Ch'almuthians!"

The locals were backing off, looks of apprehension and fear

on their faces as the nearest members of their unit tried to reassure them.

"I see," said Kaid. "You say that you fitted handholds onto the legs?" he asked Toueesut.

The Touiban nodded enthusiastically. "Yes, indeed. Hand- and footholds, but we also added an antipersonnel field to the legs so no one but your people can be climbing onto them. The pilot has cameras feeding images of the underside, and if he is seeing such people, he can also send a charge through the body to repel them. We also adapted cargo area inside for one injured person to be stowed. It is cramped but better than being roughly carried off a battlefield."

"I seem to remember Jurrel mentioning that," said Kaid.

"Jurrel," said Kusac over his mic. "Do you need time to practice?"

"I'm fine, but I wouldn't mind putting her through her paces," Jurrel replied.

"You have fifteen minutes," said Kusac, watching as the lope increased to a run. "They attacked K'oish'ik this morning. We're winning, but I want to leave as soon as possible so we get there before their fleet returns to M'zull. We don't want to run into an angry returning army when we land on or leave M'zull."

"Damn, that's going to make it tight for us," Jurrel muttered. "Fifteen minutes it is."

With the help of the loaders from both the *Couana* and the M'zullian ship—called *Aggressor*—they were loaded up within the hour, their supplies nestled at the sides of the bay with the MUTAC tied down safely in the center. Battle suits were taken off in the morgue and checked over before being fully shut down and rigged to fit to the ship's recharging units.

Meanwhile, Toueesut's swarm mates had been busy with the communications system, patching in one of their own that would allow them the luxury of communicating with the *Couana* in jump space as well as when they exited at M'zull.

The *Couana* planned to follow them but hide some distance out from M'zull, ready to come to their aid if necessary. Another addition was a self-destruct mechanism to prevent both the *Aggressor* and the MUTAC from falling into the M'zullians' hands.

Kusac took the Captain's chair to pilot their takeoff and entry into jump space with J'korrash on nav and screens, Kushool on engineering, Schiya manning the missiles with comms routed to her board, and Cheelar up in the turret. The rest of the unit were in the cabins, their safety webbing engaged.

Takeoff went smoothly; as did their entry into jump space. Once there, Kusac spoke to Toueesut and then signed off. Over the ship's comm, he gave the order to remove safety webbing and permission to move freely about the ship.

"Bridge crew, stand down," he said, releasing his own seat restraints and standing up. "We'll maintain an eight-hour watch. J'korrash, arrange it please, and you have the Bridge."

"Aye, sir," she said, getting up and taking his chair as he headed off the Bridge.

He made his way to the mess room, the only common area the ship had. He found Carrie, Kaid, and T'Chebbi already there and coffee and maush being brewed.

"Where's everyone else?" he asked, taking a seat with them.

"Sorting out the quarters," said Kaid. "It's going to be a bit cramped for us—we've been given the single officers' rooms."

"Cozy," said T'Chebbi from the brewing units she was watching.

"One way of putting it," said Kusac.

"They're working out a way to have one of the rooms as a rec room," said Carrie. "Apparently several of them have brought playing cards and readers with them."

"Damn," said Kusac, frowning. "I should have thought of that. We're going to need some form of relaxation."

"Don't worry, we brought a few things too," said T'Chebbi. "You had more to think of."

"Even so."

"Hey, you got us here," said Kaid. "You ran this show, you know, not me."

"We all did," he said. "As for entertainment, we need to keep up our training during the flight."

"I'll work out a schedule and routines," said Kaid.

"I'm worried we won't have enough time back on this ship before we have to jump to the surface," he said. "We've a lot to do in a very little time. I need to see to Zhalmo. We need to get the jump packs on, grab our backpacks, and actually jump at the right position, as well as throw down those three crates. Then there's the worry that they'll try to move the ship when we'll only have Jurrel and the MUTAC left in it. It's essential that it's there for us to leave in."

"You're worrying too much," said Kaid, relaxing back in his seat as T'Chebbi brought the two jugs of steaming drinks over on a tray with cups. "There should be no reason for them to move it if we land where they tell us. Do you want to leave someone else on the ship?"

"I'm considering at least having someone prepared to remain behind at the last minute if need be," he said as Carrie got up to fetch creamer and sweetener.

"That's reasonable. We'll still have nineteen of us. Who're you thinking of leaving?"

"One of the females, probably Schiya since I've worked with the others before, and they can almost anticipate my commands. I'm not happy with having to take females in the first place, but we need them."

"There is an alternative," said Carrie, stirring her coffee. "We could do what we did when we landed on Jalna—fake engine trouble so they assume it can't be moved."

"So long as they don't send a repair crew to it before we return," said Kusac.

"In case you've forgotten, pretty quickly it will be obvious that we're not the normal bunch of soldiers delivering captives," said Kaid. "They're going to be running around after us, not worrying about the ship, until someone works out we intend to leave."

"That's what's got me worried," said Kusac, spooning sweetener into his coffee. "I know we'll have a chameleon suit for Zhalmo and that I'll be carrying her out, but . . ."

"On a mission like this," interrupted Kaid, "planning can go only so far. We can't possibly infiltrate for more information first and then get her safely off planet, so we'll have to go in hot. If I'd seen a way around this, believe me, I'd have told you. Leaving an extra person on the ship is a good idea, and I'd have suggested it myself if you hadn't. Beyond that, there's little else we can do."

"Pity Ashay isn't with us," said Carrie. "He'd be great in that turret if they try to board the *Aggressor*."

Kaid laughed. "You couldn't get him up into the turret, Dzinae! But from what I've seen of Schiya, she's more than capable of keeping them back with the weapons. I believe the turret, as well as the missile launchers, can be controlled from the Bridge. Not just that, but also she's female, and they'll recognize that from her voice. That alone will make them extra cautious."

Kusac grinned. "I had factored that in when I suggested her."

"Let's leave this for now. We can go over and over this every day till we get there and not come up with anything better," said Kaid. "Besides, we can't be seen to be having doubts in front of our teams."

"Who's on kitchen duty?" asked T'Chebbi. "I'm hungry."

The others looked blankly at her.

She sighed and got up, still holding her mug. "S'pose I arrange crew details," she said. "Since you lot did not think of that."

"I have J'korrash sorting out eight-hour Bridge duties," said Kusac. "You'll need to coordinate with her."

"Carrie, come too. You need to know this," said T'Chebbi as she headed out of the mess.

"I do?" asked Carrie, dutifully getting up.

Kaid nodded. "Part of our training at the Brotherhood," he said. "Logistics."

"Right," she said, giving him an old-fashioned look as she hurried after T'Chebbi.

The *Aggressor*, Zhal-Zhalwae, Month of the Sun, 7th day (May)

The boredom of the trip was lessened by discovering some entertainment units stowed in lockers in one of the unused rooms, as well as a selection of games and martial-themed dramas. Daily training sessions taught the Primes and Ch'almuthians new combat skills, and the Bridge rotation, new technical ones. However, after the first week, because everyone wanted edible food, certain members of the unit were excused from the cooking roster and instead picked up the extra cleanup duties.

Early on, more news had come through from the *Couana* about the battle at K'oish'ik. Casualties had been light on their side, but the M'zullians had suffered badly, and barely a dozen from their armada of fifty ships had managed to escape into jump space. They were at least twenty-four hours behind them.

Kusac and Rezac trained hard in their new Valtegan bodies, Rezac particularly appreciating the extra strength and speed. For Kusac, he found little difference, but it did bring home to him just how much he had changed. It was with a kind of relief that the last day arrived. While those not on duty helped sort the packs they'd each need into easily reached crates, Kusac joined Kaid on the Bridge for the last conversation with the *Couana* before they returned to normal space.

Kaid, who had command of the Bridge, flicked on the ship's comm. "All crew to the morgue room now, and suit up before reentry to normal space," he said. "Schiya, report to the Bridge."

"We have been changing our plans," said Toueesut. "We will be exiting in your wake and using you to hide us. Our cloaking device from the Primes is superior to any sensors these M'zullians have. We'll be closer to come and cause a diversion to allow you to escape M'zull and jump to the surface at the right time."

"This is not what was agreed," said Kusac angrily. "You're endangering King Zsurtul."

"Clan Leader, do you think we are wanting to endanger ourselves? I not wanting blast marks defacing the lovely paint on the *Couana*. We will be most careful," reassured Toueesut.

"You intended this all along, didn't you?" said Kaid.

"No, no!" The Touiban shook his head for emphasis. "We are realizing that nothing on M'zull can match us for speed and maneuverability, but you continue to be vulnerable to them if they have craft in orbit or in space. We have tractor beam, and we will be locking onto your ship as planned, and it will travel with us and outrun them easily."

"Dammit, you'll be leaving us on the surface not knowing if you got to safely!" swore Kusac.

"We will let you know. Once *Aggressor* locked close enough, we use cloak and disappear, then open jump and we are gone. We send signal to you before we leave, you have our promises."

Kaid growled his disapproval deep in his throat, and when Kusac tried to do the same, he found himself hissing.

"You will be carrying the future of the Prime people on your ship, Toueesut," said Kusac. "Their only hope to become one peaceful people again! See you do guard them with your lives."

"Your honor is ours, Clan Leader," said Toueesut seriously. "Our sacred duty this is to see them both safe home to K'oish'ik."

"Take care, Toueesut," said Kaid.

"Good luck, and your Gods be with you, Captains," said Toueesut, signing off.

Kusac picked up his helmet and got up to leave, but Kaid stopped him with a gesture. "No, you'd better stay here in case their flight control asks me anything I don't have an answer for. Can you take over the gunner's board?"

"Sure," he said, sitting down again and storing his helmet in the side locker of the seat.

"Permission to come on the Bridge, sir?" said Schiya, standing in the open air lock doorway.

"Granted," said Kaid. "Time to get up in the turret, Schiya."

"Aye, sir." She hesitated at the foot of the spiral stairs. "Shall I stay there while you're on the ground?"

"No, you'll take the Bridge," said Kaid. "Take what action you think necessary if you have to deal with them, but keep us informed. Route all weapons to your boards and use them if need be. We need you and the *Aggressor* to get off M'zull."

"Understood, sir," she said, sketching a salute before heading up the stairs.

"All personnel suited up and secured to morgue bulkheads," said Carrie over her suit comm on their Command channel.

"Copy that," murmured Kaid, watching the readings.

"Computing jump exit vectors," said J'korrash, her ungloved hands rapidly keying in the parameters and double-checking them against the computer.

"Copy."

"Approaching exit point in five on my mark," she said. "Five, four, three, two, one. Mark."

Space wrenched briefly around them, and then they suddenly burst into normal space with its velvet black sky and the tiny glowing lights of distant stars. Signals from the main buoy began to register on the boards, and ahead they could see the M'zullian home world.

"Plotting a course to M'zull, Captain," she said.

"Transmitting our ID to the buoy," said Kaid.

"Incoming message from M'zull traffic control," said Noolgoi. "Welcoming us back and telling us to proceed to the Palace landing site."

"Have you the location, J'korrash?" asked Kaid.

"Aye, Captain," she said. "Sending it to your board now."

Kusac tuned the usual chatter of approach and landing out and began to quiet his mind, sending it out to the planet ahead, looking for the flight controller, searching through his thoughts for any that might affect them.

"They haven't heard from the fleet they sent to K'oish'ik yet," he said quietly.

"Acknowledged," said Kaid, sparing a moment's thought for him.

He let his mind roam farther, looking now for the Palace and the controller there, getting a mental picture from him of the landing area and the craft docked there.

"We're to land on the platform that will take us down to the lower levels. Once there, we taxi off the platform to one of the nearby bays."

"Is the platform the only way out?" asked Kaid, all attention now that they were locked onto the automatic landing pattern.

"No, there is an old tunnel," said Kusac. "Unused for decades, but the exit itself is clear. That's all the controller knows."

"Likely an emergency one for their Emperor. How busy is it?"

"Most there are maintenance crews, not soldiers, though there is a token guard at the entrance to the Palace. They're informing the Chief Drone of the seraglio, Keshti. He'll meet us and lead us there."

"Good. We won't have to find our own way then. Prisoners gear up in Ch'almuthian clothing," he said over the ship's com. "Jurrel, board the MUTAC. Approaching landing site in five minutes."

Kusac pushed his mind deeper into the Palace, looking for

the mental pattern that was Zhalmo, being even more careful to screen himself from detection. Abruptly he broke his concentration and turned to Kaid.

"I can sense her mind. She's in a bad way, half drugged and in no condition to contact till we get there. I'll need to look for her exact location when we're closer."

"Understood," said Kaid.

He looked out the tinted screen and blinked at what he saw—a rock wall slowly moving past them. "Where are we?"

"Going down on the platform," said Kaid. "You were gone a long time."

He reached up to rub his eyes, forgetting his hands were encased in the suit gloves and stopped just in time.

"You better get your helmet on," he said. "And the cloak."

"I will, don't worry," said Kaid, flashing him a grin. "Schiya, get down to the Bridge ready to take over."

"On my way, Captain," she said.

Once the platform stopped, Kaid taxied the *Aggressor* in the direction indicated by the flight controller waving his lit batons. By luck, they were guided to a bay opposite where Kusac said the tunnel exit lay. At the last moment, Kaid ignored instructions to back into the bay and parked the ship at an angle that would allow the MUTAC free exit if needed.

As he cut the engines to an idle, he could see the official gesticulating in rage at them. He laughed as he got up and put on his helmet and picked up the voluminous cloak that had been lying across his chair.

"You have the Bridge, Schiya," he said.

"Aye, Captain. Good luck," she said, taking his seat and stowing her helmet under the chair.

"Routing weapons systems and comms to my board," she added.

"All personnel to the starboard air lock," said Kusac as he fitted his own helmet in place. "Prisoners, make sure your suits are well concealed. You too, T'Chebbi and Banner."

Carrie, stay close by me, he sent. *Kaid, you and T'Chebbi take care, Banner too,* he sent to them.

You too, sent Kaid, clasping him by the shoulder as they left the Bridge and headed for the air lock, followed by J'korrash and Noolgoi.

Cheelar was waiting for them with their rifles. When everyone was assembled, Kusac took a deep breath, opened the air lock and began walking down the narrow ramp. At the bottom, he stopped, waiting for the others to descend and form up as guards around the prisoners.

Stay in the center, he signed to the Sholans in their cloaks as he watched a M'zullian in an overly elaborate embroidered robe hustle over to them. He was followed by two other drones wearing kilts and fancy wide collars made of beadwork.

Just like we wore, sent Rezac dryly. *Harem attendants.*

"Lieutenant Lioshu, you took your time," said the drone, coming to a stop before him. "I've been waiting here for you for over half an hour!"

"You exaggerate, Keshti, as always." Kusac said, ostentatiously pulling his rifle off his shoulder and into a ready position.

Keshti sniffed loudly. "Well, show me my new acquisitions. Let me see if they are worth my time or not!"

Kusac barred his way with the rifle. "You can examine them at your leisure in the seraglio. I haven't time to waste while you paw the females—or is it young males you prefer?"

"Insolence!" hissed Keshti, spinning on his heel and beginning to walk away. "Well, what are you waiting for?" he asked over his shoulder. "You're the one who said you were busy!"

Kusac gestured to his troop, and they began to follow the drone toward the other side of the vast cavern. Ahead he could see a small forest of poles, each with a grisly trophy on the top. Glancing at Keshti, he saw him pull a cloth from his pocket and hold it over his face.

"Looks like we found the previous Emperor and his followers," said Banner.

"Glad we can't smell them," said Cheelar.

"Keep focused," snapped Kaid. "Or that will be us!"

Kusac slowed, letting his team go in front of him and form the planned protective barrier. Now beside Rezac, he let his mind roam ahead of them, looking for electronic security measures. He found what they'd expected—cameras, controlled from a security station just inside the blast doors, focused on the roadway they were on and leading up the corridor immediately inside. Without thinking, he bypassed the natural mental shielding of the main guard there and made him feel bored. He sensed him look away, making some coarse comment about the female captives to his companion in the office. Beside him, he could feel Rezac creating a need to not look closely at their group.

They passed through unchallenged, and now he reached out to find Zhalmo again. Keeping a portion of his mind tuned to her presence, he returned to take notice of his own surroundings.

"Found her," he said briefly over their Command channel as they passed another doorway on their left. "Guard station. Twenty guards in there."

"Copy," said Kaid. "Security?"

"Minimal—cameras and comms linked to the first room we passed."

The walls on either side of them were fused rock, likely drilled out by some form of laser. It was around midmorning local time, and the broad corridor was virtually empty. Lighting too was basic and almost as harsh as that in the main cavern.

There had been a faint nagging at the back of his mind since they'd landed, but until now, he'd been able to ignore it. The nagging had now become an itch, a demand to be noticed. He spared a moment to examine it, found nothing to do with their current situation, and pushed it aside.

Keshti and his attendants kept up their pace as they stepped out of the utilitarian area and into a less brightly lit cross junction. Straight across the junction they went, down a corridor now painted with the distinctive brightly colored figures they all knew from the Prime Palace.

"Still only cameras," said Kusac, doing another check.

It took them several minutes to reach the junction at the far end and the elevator there, and in that time, only two people passed them. Again, Rezac made sure they were intent on their own business.

"This is going too well," growled Banner.

"Why shouldn't it?" asked Carrie. "We're meant to be here, and we have an escort."

"Getting out will be the problem," said Kaid.

They reached the junction, and Keshti headed down it. "I don't know why you all had to come," the drone grumbled. "How many of you does it take to deliver eight captives? We'll have to take the troop elevator."

"Trouble ahead. About fifty soldiers in the area," said Kusac.

A short way down, the corridor widened out into a small cavern where soldiers in various uniforms were milling about, taking other exits. It was obviously a major junction that serviced the military stationed within the Palace.

Immediately, Kusac joined his mind to Rezac's as they projected an aura of normality around them, one that concealed the Sholans in their midst from any unwanted attention.

Keshti and the two harem guards had stopped in front of a large elevator door that was just opening. They stepped in, moving to the side by the controls and waited for them to enter.

Quickly they filed in, and the door was shut. With a loud clang, they began their descent.

"We'll need the MUTAC," said Kusac.

"Aye," said Kaid.

They could hear Carrie cursing softly just under her breath.

Focus, sent Kusac. *There'll be trouble enough when it comes.*

The mental itch had become demanding again as soon as they'd entered the cavern. Now it was dominating his attention, drawing even his eyes to the elevator door and the level they'd left.

Go back! it whispered. *You must go back!*

He shook his head, making Kaid turn to look at him.

What's up? he sent.

Nothing, he replied, trying to block out the alien whisper.

Go back to the cavern! You must locate it.

Enough, he snarled, reaching out to it on the same mental wavelength and forcing it to silence. *You do not control me! I will rescue Zhalmo!*

Kusac, what is it? What's wrong? demanded Carrie.

He reached up and slapped the side of his helmet, then shook his head. "Comm malfunction," he said audibly. "Fixed now."

It seemed a lot more than that, said Carrie as the elevator slowed.

I'm fine, honestly, he reassured her, but he wasn't reassured. This was almost the same voice that had tried to stop him from saving Zsurtul's life. How in all the hells could it be here too?

The elevator shuddered, then ground to a halt and the door opened, focusing his attention back on their mission.

Keshti squeezed past them, muttering imprecations under his breath, and waited for them to exit so his guards could join him.

The drone led them along the corridor to their left, then turned right into one that was carpeted, the walls bearing incised carvings not of battles, but of scenes of the Emperor's might over his enemies.

"Security post ahead," said Kusac. "Four soldiers, but panic button to alert more in the cavern. Extensive camera networks and one to release gas into certain rooms. This leads to the Emperor's private living quarters and Throne Room."

The guards didn't bat an eye as they passed through the room and out into what was obviously a large waiting room for audiences with the Emperor. Already there was a fairly large sized group of people clustered together at the far end.

They marched through, their metal-clad feet ringing on the tiled floor, and exited into a grand cavern laid out to resemble the courtyard on K'oish'ik, minus the cafes.

"Have you sent to Zhalmo?" asked Kaid.

"No. She's in a bad way," he said shortly. "She won't want us there."

"Ah," said Kaid, understanding.

"These people are burrowers, not Valtegans," muttered Noolgoi as they took a diagonal route across the open courtyard to yet another corridor.

"Get ready," snapped Kusac, moving to the front again. "This is harem territory. She's very close now." Mentally he searched for the camera network and sent a surge of energy along it, knocking out the cameras in their area. "Cams neutralized. We need to be out of here in ten minutes."

Keshti stopped and drew a chain off his neck, using the key on it to open the door in front of him.

"Room's clear," said Kusac.

"Just put them in there," Keshti began, only to find himself being roughly pushed into the room by Kusac. He opened his mouth to yell out only to discover he couldn't make a sound.

Rezac and Kaid grabbed the two guards and dragged them in with them, each mentally knocking his unconscious as the rest of the team piled in.

As last in, Kho'ikk shut the door and taking the key that was passed back to him, locked it.

Striding over to the door on the right, Kusac positioned

himself there, rifle at the ready. "Helmets on," he ordered, but there was no need as the "prisoners" had already pulled off their voluminous clothing and dragged their helmets out of the bundles they'd been carrying.

Na'qui pulled her hypo gun from her thigh compartment and quickly sedated Keshti and his guards. "No point in taking chances," she said.

"Zsaya, Cheelar, guard the main door," Kusac ordered. "M'yikku and Jo, take the far one. Stun civilians if you can, kill if need be."

As he spoke, the door in question opened and a female in white stood framed in the doorway, looking at them in shock. A charged shot rang out, and she crumpled to the floor, stunned. Jo and M'yikku ran over, Jo dragging her into their room as M'yikku checked out the other.

"Clear," he said, closing the door and taking up a guard position by it.

"Room ahead is a pool room with four women and one male. We go through it and the next room—empty—to get to Zhalmo," said Kusac.

"Gas grenade," said Kaid, getting one ready as he approached Kusac at the door. "One guard?"

"Aye," said Kusac, throwing the door open and aiming his gun at the male ahead of them as Kaid threw in the grenade.

Shrieks filled the air as gas began to billow out and fill the room. The drone, a giant of a male, began to run toward them. A shot took him in the shoulder, but he kept coming.

With a curse, Kusac flicked his rifle off stun and shot him again, this time in the leg. He fell as though poleaxed.

The females had run to the far end of the room, huddling together in a knot, but the gas was having its effect on them and they were already beginning to collapse on the tiled floor.

Kusac ran for the next door. It was locked, but a swift kick from his boot had it exploding inward in a shower of splinters. The rest of the team following, he ran across what was obviously the Emperor's bedroom to the door leading to the room where Zhalmo was.

He tried the door. It was locked.

Zhalmo, he sent. *Zhalmo!* More insistently when she didn't answer.

He felt her mind stir out of the stupor it was in.

Zhalmo, it's me, Kusac. We've come for you. Don't be afraid, he sent as he raised his foot to kick down the door. "Stay back," he ordered the others. "I'll go in alone."

Kusac? The thought was faint and slow.

She was lying on the bed, naked, and had raised herself up on one elbow as the door burst open. Instantly she cowered back, almost trying to climb up the wall away from him in sheer terror.

Carrie, I need you here! he sent.

She came in at a run, stopping dead when she saw the terrified female.

Zhalmo? she sent, moving slowly closer to her. *I'm Carrie, Kusac's mate. We're here to take you home.*

"Home?" she said. "I'll never leave here. You're not real, not here! Leave me alone!"

"Clock's ticking," said Kaid from the next room. "I sent for the MUTAC."

"I know," snapped Kusac, pulling the lightweight chameleon suit out of his suit's thigh compartment.

Carrie reached up and unlatched her helmet, taking it off. "Zhalmo," she said, going over to the cowering female. "We're real. This rescue is real. You have to come with us now, or we'll all get caught. Do you understand?"

She relaxed a fraction, letting herself down onto the bed again. "Kusac?"

"Yes, Zhalmo. I'm here," he said, coming over. He held out the suit to her. "I need you to put this on. It will make you almost impossible to see."

She began to rock backward and forward, clasping her arms around her legs, tears streaming down her face. "I can't. You don't know what he'll do if he catches me."

"He won't catch you, I promise," said Kusac. *Get her off the bed, Carrie, and then we can get her into the suit.*

Carrie put her helmet on the bed and reached out to take Zhalmo by one thin, bruised arm. "Come to me, Zhalmo," she said gently.

"No! Oh, Gods! Home. I want to believe you, but it isn't true! It's just another of his tricks."

"Noolgoi, sedate her, but not fully," snapped Kaid from the doorway. "We haven't time for this."

"Aye, sir," she said.

"No!" said Kusac. "I'll handle her." He strengthened his

Link to her, taking control of her mind. It took only a moment before she was blinking her eyes slowly and beginning to droop back onto the bed.

"So tired," she murmured. "I knew it wasn't real. Just a dream."

Leaning forward, Kusac scooped her up into his arms and sat her on the edge of the bed. Between him and Carrie, they managed to get her cut and bruised body into the suit. Once it was sealed, her body heat immediately activated it, and she all but disappeared.

Carrie, meanwhile, grabbed her helmet and put it back on.

Picking Zhalmo up, Kusac left the room and joined the others, Carrie behind him.

"Let's go," he said, heading for the main door out. "Kaid, take command."

"Get rid of the cloaks," Kaid said. "T'Chebbi, Kushool, M'yikku, you have point. Kusac's team, guard him closely. Rezac, with me. Report on enemy locations. Banner, take rearguard."

The unit re-formed and they moved off.

"Kusac, take out the electronics at the security post," said Kaid.

Kusac reached mentally for the electrical system and, finding it, isolated those controlling the alarms. A surge of energy shot through them, burning the wiring out, rendering it useless. "Done."

"Go left," said Rezac. "They're waiting at the other exit. Four soldiers, another five on their way."

They stopped at the door to the courtyard, waiting for those on point to open it and clear the way. Unarmored as the guards were, their main danger to them would be in overwhelming numbers.

Rifles whined, then T'Chebbi gave the all clear. At a brisk run, they headed diagonally for the waiting room as T'Chebbi and M'yikku, already there, lobbed gas grenades in the open doorway. A few screeches were heard, trailing off into the distance.

"Clear," said Rezac as they entered. "They ran for the security post."

T'Chebbi gestured to M'yikku who ran forward with a stun grenade. The flare lit up even the room they were in.

Shots sounded, but they were quickly silenced; then T'Chebbi waved them onward.

Four bodies lay draped over the consoles or in untidy heaps on the floor as they quickly passed through and on into the empty corridor.

"Where'd they all go?" muttered Kushool.

"Other elevator, or down the corridor," said T'Chebbi.

At Kaid's signal, they stopped just short of the junction to their right, those at the front and rear standing guard.

Kusac took advantage of their stop to Link his mind to Zhalmo's and search for the memories of what had happened to her since her capture. Finding them, he began to erase them as carefully as he could in the short time he knew he had. She began to whimper and stir in his arms, and with a portion of his mind, he began to soothe and reassure her.

"Jurrel, report," said Kaid.

"Almost there," Jurrel said. "Where's the elevator from my entrance point?"

"On your right."

"Copy that. All right, here I go!"

"Move out," said Kaid, gesturing down the corridor. "Make every shot count. They outnumber us even if they can't hurt us."

"Wait," said Carrie urgently. "Just a minute longer and Kusac will be done."

"We haven't the time," began Kaid just as Kusac lifted his head.

"Finished."

"Go," said Kaid, starting forward. "You know the plan, stick to it. If anyone falls, go to their aid, but protect Kusac and Zhalmo at all costs."

There was a subdued chorus of "Aye," as they headed for the elevator.

The elevator opened onto a scene of utter chaos as the MUTAC, crouched in the center of the cavern, sprayed an arc of fire from the beam weapon mounted between its shoulders. Behind it, the tail scythed back and forth, cutting down anyone who came too near.

A group of soldiers armed with missile launchers ran toward it. The MUTAC crouched, then launched itself at them, landing on top of several of them and scattering the rest with a swipe of one forepaw. Its own launchers spat into action, missiles howling down the adjacent corridors to explode violently, sending showers of rock fragments back into the cavern to hit those nearby.

Almost unnoticed, they left the elevator and began running for their exit corridor.

"Incoming!" said Jurrel as they heard the whine of a missile heading their way. As one, they plastered themselves to the walls, watching it approach. Kusac turned himself so his body protected Zhalmo. Twenty feet from them, one of the MUTAC's antimissile shots hit it, and it exploded. Shards of rock and debris rattled off their suits.

"Go!" yelled Kaid, peeling himself off the wall.

As they neared the halfway mark, he halted them and called Jurrel.

"Break off combat and join us," he said.

"On my way," came the reply.

They heard him before they saw him, loping down the corridor at almost a full run. "I love this beast!" he said, slowing to a walk to pass them.

"Clear a route for us to the ship," ordered Kaid. "Schiya, lower the ramp!"

"Aye, Captain," she said. "But they have guards around me."

"They'll be dealt with. Call the *Couana* and tell them we're leaving."

The MUTAC sped up again and they ran to keep up with it. The guardroom was a smoking ruin as they passed it, as was the security point by the blast doors. Into the cavern the MUTAC exploded, cannon raking everything around it with burst after burst of plasma. Jurrel lobbed missiles at the other two ships sitting berthed there. As they exploded in balls of fire, he loped over to the *Aggressor*, again raking anything that moved with his cannon, keeping his shots short range.

They followed in his wake, shooting at anything that shot back at them, but the shock tactics of the MUTAC had bought them the time they needed.

The ramp was down, and crouching the MUTAC, Jurrel leaped inside, turning so his weapons were pointing outward, giving them cover as they raced up the ramp into the hold. Kaid stayed by the entrance, hitting the door control as the last of them ran inside. Whining, the ramp began to retract.

"Take off!" he ordered Schiya.

The ship's engines rose to a high-pitched whine, then it lifted from the ground and began moving toward their exit.

Chy'tu raced to the air lock, punched the controls, and headed up the corridor to the Bridge at full speed to take his place at the nav board, unfastening his helmet as he went. Kho'ikk and Shirzak followed him, heading for the turret and the gunner's board.

Kusac and Na'qui ran for the sick bay while the others began breaking open the crates and grabbing their packs. Five were staying with the ship, and the rest of them were jumping down to the surface to remain on M'zull.

Laying Zhalmo down on the exam bed, Kusac had one last thing to do before he headed back to the hold. When he was done, he turned to the medic as the ship rocked from side to side on its breakneck trip down the cavern tunnel.

"Do what you can to clean her up and make her look good for Zsurtul," he said. "And yes, it really does matter. Give her a uniform to put on. I've erased what memories I can. Tell Zsurtul that but not her, and remind him my sister Kitra will finish the healing. She's no longer pregnant, but keep a watch on her—I don't know how her body will react to what I've done."

She nodded, and he turned to leave. "Don't leave her alone, Na'qui, and watch she doesn't get suicidal, please."

"I will, Captain," she said. "Good luck with the rest of your mission."

"On second thought, may I put a message for Kitra in your mind? One advising her on Zhalmo's treatment?"

She paled a little but nodded.

"Thanks." He pulled off one glove and reached out to touch her forehead lightly. Marshaling his thoughts, he braced himself as the ship banked to the right. He needed to let Kitra know what had happened to Zhalmo since she had no memory of it now. Encapsulating it in a locked mode, he sent the thoughts to Na'qui, adding an apology for exposing Kitra to the cruelty that had been inflicted on Zhalmo.

The ship rocked again as he heard the guns go off.

Only a blockage in the tunnel, sent Schiya.

Back in the hold, Kusac found Jurrel had parked the MUTAC at the back, well out of their way. Carrie was waiting to hand him his pack and help him on with it.

"Gods, Kusac, what had he done to her? The poor girl was in a real mess," she said.

"You don't want to know," he answered grimly, putting on the backpack and locking it in place, then fastening on the jet pack. "I've had to leave a mental message for Kitra so she knows, and I wish I hadn't needed to do it."

"Poor cub," she said sympathetically.

"She's going to have to learn to be strong in our Clan," said Kusac, turning to let Carrie check that his fastenings were secure.

"I know, but she's still so young." She slapped him on the back. "You're good," she said.

Along the wide tunnel the *Aggressor* screamed, its lights picking out the rockfalls and other obstructions that Schiya swerved to avoid.

Once more Kho'ikk had to blast a large rockfall ahead. It exploded in a cloud of pulverized rock that the *Aggressor* shot through before the dust even had time to fall. Finally a circle of light appeared ahead of them, rapidly growing closer. Like a cork from a bottle, they shot out into the open and began to climb.

For now, there was no sign of pursuit on the sensor boards. Then points of light flickered onto the edge of her screen.

"Six fighters, ten o'clock," said Shirzak.

"Hailing us," said Chy'tu.

"What they saying?" demanded Schiya.

"Usual," said Chy'tu laconically. "Surrender and your lives will be spared."

Schiya hissed in derision. "Ignore them. Now would be a great time for the *Couana* to appear," she muttered.

"Five minutes we being there," said Toueesut, his voice suddenly coming over their comm. "Stay alive till then!"

"Dammit, that made me jump! Tell the Captain," said Schiya shortly, taking evasive action and heading out toward the mountain ranges to the north of the city.

She ignored Chy'tu's quiet voice as he relayed the information and concentrated on flying. She'd reached the start of the main range now, and she prayed that the reality of flying between the mountains would be the same as the simulations she'd practiced on the *Tooshu*.

Toggling the ship intercom, she said, "Hang on, could be a bumpy ride."

"And it hasn't been so far?" asked Chy'tu.

She cast a brief but scathing look at her brother. As she began a steep descent toward the range, she hoped the Captain had chosen her because of her superior flying scores.

A ravine was coming up, and she dipped down into it, flying low, almost grazing the tops of the trees.

In the hold, Jurrel was frantically tying the MUTAC down as it had begun to slide toward the outer hatch with Schiya's maneuverings. J'korrash and Cheelar ran to help.

"Dammit, they got blood and guts all over the MUTAC's claws." Jurrel complained. "Going to be hell cleaning that lot off after three weeks in jump space!"

I remember a flight like this, Kusac sent to Kaid with a hint of humor in his mental voice.

Aye, chuckled Kaid. *When you visited my place in the mountains.*

"Fighters still on our tail but falling back," said Chy'tu. "Waiting for us to crash, I guess."

"You want to take the helm?" Schiya demanded.

"No, you're doing a fine job—a very fine one—of just missing the trees," her brother reassured her.

She snorted and flipped an obscene gesture at him.

"New message," he said after a short silence. "If we don't return immediately, they'll open fire in one minute."

"You tracking them, Kho'ikk?" she asked, banking to the left and rising sharply as the ravine ended in a wall of solid rock. The ship's engines screamed as she accelerated, but they made it with inches to spare.

"Aye, but keep it more level if you want me to hit them."

A current caught them, sucking them down into the next ravine. She fought it, rising up again to level out just above the razor-sharp crest of the next ridge, then turned abruptly, heading straight toward the following group of fighters.

"Fire at will as we pass," she snapped. "How long till the *Couana* gets here?"

"Any time now," said Chy'tu, shutting his eyes briefly and uttering a prayer to any Gods that were listening as he saw them heading at a suicidal speed straight for the fighters.

At the last possible minute, the fighters broke away, and

Shirzak and Kho'ikk opened fire on them. Explosions rocked their craft as the two brothers scored hits.

A flash in the sky near them, and suddenly the *Couana* showed up on Chy'tu's nav screen.

"You some wild pilot! Good shooting too," said Toueesut's voice over the Bridge comm. "We get the others and fly aggravation for you to drop site, keep your path clear. Slow down, though, be giving us time to do this for you."

"Aye, Captain Toueesut," said Schiya, throttling back a little and lifting the *Aggressor* higher above the rocky landscape.

"Captain Kusac," said Chy'tu over the ship's comm, "the *Couana* has arrived and is escorting us to your drop site. Please make ready for your jump."

"Acknowledged," said Kusac. "Good flying, Schiya. We'll have to take you to Stronghold and the mountains there. You'd enjoy it. Good teamwork, all of you."

"Thank you, sir," said Chy'tu, glancing at the others with a wide grin on his face.

"We still gotta drop them yet," said Schiya. "It isn't over till that's done and the *Couana* has us locked on. I want the course to that drop point now, Nav!"

"Yessir!" said her brother turning rapidly back to his board and calling up the chart. "Sending to your station now," he said, punching it through.

A shadow fell over them as the *Couana* overtook them and then shot forward as their advance wave.

They saw a blossom of flame as one of its guns fired at a blip on their screens. Moments later there was an almighty explosion ahead of them.

"It's got some range," said Chy'tu, awe in his voice. "That ship had only just appeared on my screens."

"Coming up on drop point, Captain," said Schiya. "Hold tight. Opening bay doors now."

The clamshell doors began to rumble and fold outward as they all held onto the moorings fixed to the sides of the hold.

"Turn on the magnetics in your boots," ordered Kusac from the front by the open bay doors. "Keep them on till you jump. Remember, count to three, then jets on. Off at ten feet, then shields on! Remember to throw out the crates!"

"Coming up on jump site in five seconds from my mark," said Schiya. "Five, four, three, two, one. Mark!"

Kusac flicked his magnetics off and ran forward, leaping into the open space. He fell like a brick for the count of three, and then turned on his jets. The gyros on them forced him into an upright position, and he began a controlled descent.

Carrie, I'll be waiting for you on the ground, he sent, seeing her telltale appear on his HUD as she jumped.

I'm okay, she replied.

Within ten minutes, they'd gathered under the nearby trees, their three crates in their antigrav cradles recovered. Kusac had sent a party out with broken branches to sweep away every trace of their passage.

"Move out," Kaid said, calling up the map on his HUD when they returned. "We need to be well away from here before they send out ships looking for survivors."

CHAPTER 19

SCHIYA hailed the *Couana*. "Cargo deployed," she said.

"Returning to you now," said Toueesut.

Through the front viewscreen they could see the *Couana* approaching, slowing as it came closer. Its shadow fell over them and stayed.

"Deploying traction beam."

The *Aggressor* seemed to shudder slightly.

"Please be keeping speed steady as we pull you up," said Toueesut. "We will tell you when to cut engines."

"Acknowledged, *Couana*," said Schiya.

"Incoming vessels," said Chy'tu suddenly. "Ten fighters, closing fast!"

"Hold your fire. We will deal with them," said Toueesut.

A sound like a boom of thunder came from overhead and they saw a pulse of plasma shoot out toward the approaching fighters. It was swiftly followed by four more shots and a cloud of particles as the *Couana* fired off her sandcasters to interrupt the enemy tracking system.

The tug on the *Aggressor* increased and they saw the outline of the *Couana* begin to appear above them in their viewscreen.

Explosive flares showed in the distance, and four of the fighters winked out of existence on Schiya's board.

"Incoming!" said Shirzak seconds before their ship was jolted as a missile hit her wing.

"Shields holding," said Chy'tu.

The next missile exploded above them, making the *Aggressor* shudder as the *Couana's* shields took the damage. Once again, the plasma cannon sent off a volley of shots at the fighters.

"Standby to cut engines," said Toueesut as another, larger, shudder ran through their ship.

"Deploying shield around you—now. Cut engine!" said the Touiban Captain.

"Engines off," said Schiya, cutting the power.

They heard a series of loud clangs, then silence.

"*Aggressor* locked on. Please secure for rapid leaving of M'zull," said Toueesut.

"Acknowledged," said Schiya. "Relay the message to the sick bay, Chy'tu."

"Aye."

The *Couana* swung around and accelerated rapidly, the force of it pushing them hard against their seats. Schiya gripped the arms of her chair tightly and stared at her screen, watching the remaining fighters disappear.

"Engaging stealth mode," said Toueesut. "We be off M'zull in a few minutes," he reassured her.

Suddenly the pressure on them lifted, and the sky around them was the welcoming black of space.

"Please be transferring all personnel to *Couana*," said Toueesut. "Your emergency hatch in roof of cargo hold is below our empty pinnace bay. Our hatch is open. Ladders we will drop for you to secure and climb up."

"Understood, *Couana*. Closing down the Bridge now. You can reach us on Channel 8 on our suit comms. Kho'ikk, return to the Bridge," she said to her brother up in the turret.

"Acknowledged, *Aggressor*."

Schiya relayed Toueesut's commands to the sick bay, then closed down all ship systems except for the emergency ones. Turning on the magnetics in her boots, she released herself from the command chair's restraints, grabbed her helmet, and gestured to the others to leave, following them out into the dimly lit corridor.

They met Na'qui, Zhalmo, and Jurrel in the corridor by the sick bay. Zhalmo was now dressed in black fatigues, but she still looked dazed and ill.

Schiya took her by the arm. "We need to get you into a space suit, Zhalmo. We have to transfer to the *Couana*."

"The *Couana?* Where are we?" she asked.

"Leaving M'zull," said Schiya, drawing her sister down the corridor, silently thanking Na'qui for putting magnetic boots on her. "You were a prisoner. We came to rescue you," she said, sticking to what Kusac had told her to tell Zhalmo.

"I was?" she asked, her free hand going up to rub her eyes. "I think I remember. Everything's a bit hazy right now."

"Don't worry about it. You were drugged in the prison, but it's wearing off now."

They had almost reached the morgue.

"Shirzak, get up to that hatch and wait for us," Schiya said as Jurrel opened the morgue door.

It was like dressing a doll as they pushed and pulled her into a suit, then sealed her inside, and it made Schiya's heart ache to see her sister, usually so vibrant, like this.

Zhalmo seen to, she donned her own helmet, and after checking that everyone else was ready, she gave Shirzak the order to open the hatch. Sealing the morgue door behind them, they made their way to the hold.

The ladder had already been lowered, and Schiya sent Shirzak and Na'qui up first, and then helped her sister up. A pair of giant Sumaan hands reached down and lifted Zhalmo gently up the last few rungs. When she reached the top, Ashay had already taken her sister off into the cargo bay.

She waited for Jurrel to exit then watched as two suited Touibans swarmed over the *Aggressor's* hull, fixing a temporary hatch in place before retracting the ladder completely. That done, they all exited to the *Couana's* hold.

Their armor left near the elevator, Schiya headed for the sick bay while the rest of her small crew were escorted upstairs to their cabins.

Na'qui had been running tests on Zhalmo and was almost finished.

"She can bunk with me," said Na'qui, looking up at her as she entered.

"No, I want to be with my sister," said Zhalmo, surprising them both.

"That's fine by me," said Schiya. "You can be next door, can't you, Na'qui?"

"Of course. Well, there's no reason for you to stay here, Zhalmo. I can do what I need to do up in your cabin."

Zhalmo nodded slowly and got off the examination bed. "I'm very tired," she said, staggering slightly until Na'qui supported her. "I'd like to sleep now."

Na'qui let Schiya take her and stepped back. "A good idea. Lots of rest and plenty of good food and you'll be better in no time."

There was a knock at the door, and she turned around to see Zsurtul standing there.

"I came to see how Zhalmo is," he said.

"Prince Zsurtul?" Zhalmo said, blinking at him. "I thought you were on K'oish'ik."

"No, I came with the rescue mission," he said, keeping his face carefully neutral as he obviously saw how thin and ill she looked.

"Oh." She fell silent, her eyes almost closing. "I remember you were injured," she said. "I tried to save you, but . . ." Her voice trailed off again.

"You got captured when I was shot," Zsurtul finished for her.

"Ah. That's why you came to rescue me?"

"Part of the reason," he said, coming into the room and over to her.

"I'm so tired," she said, smiling slightly at him. "They were going to show me up to my cabin."

"Let me take you," he said, holding out his hand to her.

Almost hesitantly, she reached out and took it. "That's kind of you."

"She's weak, and still drugged," said Na'qui quietly.

"Then, if she permits it, I'll carry her up," said Zsurtul, drawing her slowly closer.

Schiya looked away, unable to bear seeing the naked emotion in his eyes.

When Zhalmo nodded, he swung her up into his arms, holding her close for a moment. "Shall we go upstairs?" he asked her gently as she relaxed against him.

"Please," she murmured, closing her eyes. "You know, I have a feeling I should be looking after you."

"It's my turn to look after you, Zhalmo," said Zsurtul gently as they walked away.

"It's going to be all right," murmured Schiya to herself, feeling her heart begin to lighten. "It's going to be all right."

* * *

"There's been a lot of changes at the Palace since you were captured," Zsurtul said.

"Mm?"

"A lot of the main facade was destroyed in the fighting. That's all being repaired. And the Temple has been completely redone. It's been dedicated to La'shol now."

"No Emperor worship?" she asked as he stepped onto the elevator.

"No Emperor now, only a King," he said

"King Zsurtul," she said as the elevator began to move upward. "It has a nice sound to it."

M'zull

Kusac had gladly handed command of this part of the mission to Kaid, who had far more experience than he in hostile conditions. Their current heading would take them, under cover of the trees, into the next ravine, where they'd detected a cave system on their way in. The plan was to make their base in there.

The *Aggressor's* wild flight had actually returned them to the mountain range that backed onto the capital city, as this would be an ideal point from which to mount various missions of insurrection. The aim was to increase the paranoia of not only the upper echelon of command but of the ordinary soldiers as well.

While he'd been busy scoping out the city mentally, Schiya had been electronically scanning the area surrounding the capital for them and had downloaded the map files to his and Kaid's suits. It was these they were using now.

A trilling riff of sound suddenly burst out on Channel 8, startling all but Kusac, who began to laugh gently.

"What the hell was that?" asked Kaid.

"Toueesut telling us all is well," he said. "Specifically, he said, "Leaving the mudrakers to you. Introduce them to the Sholan hell they deserve."

"All that in one trill," said Rezac. "No wonder they talk nonstop!"

There was a ripple of general laughter on the channel, and Kusac felt everyone's mood ease a little.

They went back to trudging through the snow in silence.

At least we're not wet or cold, sent Carrie from beside him. *It could be a lot worse. And the armor takes the work out of walking.*

True, he agreed. *I'll be happier when we've reached those caves, though.*

It was a good three hours before they did. When they got there, Kusac checked them out mentally for any life-forms and found them empty.

The entrance was narrow, opening up into a wider cave that led in turn to a large cavern with no other exits.

Setting a guard at the entrance, they started making camp. The tents, again courtesy of the Touibans, were self-expanding, with anchor loops and guy ropes if needed. They were modular, each for two people, and could be fitted together to form larger units. Each also had its own AC and security system built in, this a Sholan feature that had been added.

Kaid and Kusac let the group pair off as they wished, but they had the tents set up in a semicircle facing the entrance. They each carried their own eating and cooking utensils and a small stove with several battery packs, but there was a larger, communal one in one of the crates.

The crates held winter clothing for them all, vacuum packed to save space, and chameleon suits made of wind- and weatherproof material. There was more—weapon packs, other ammunition, a charger for the armor batteries, and a small generator, flashlights, and other assorted gear they had packed on K'oish'ik, including some instant hot meals and drinks.

T'Chebbi took charge of handing out the supplies as soon as the tents were up. Meanwhile, Carrie supervised them getting out of their armor at the back of the cave, where it was stored out of sight behind a large pile of loose rocks they'd stacked there for that purpose.

Cheelar was at the entrance setting up the force field across it to keep out wild beasts and the flakes of snow that had begun to fall. He set it far enough in to stop the snow piling against it but not so far that the guards could not see out without being seen. Kushool, still in her armor, was taking first watch. It was

too cold to wear anything else when on guard duty. They se
up a second force field across the entrance to the main cavern
to keep the heat in. As they each had an identity chip in their
uniforms, they could pass through the fields, but nothing else
could.

They gathered around the central area where J'korrash
had set up one of the larger stoves for warmth and heating
water. Sitting on the lightweight foil blankets that would line
their tents, they ate and chatted, drinking the hot maush that
J'korrash had brewed for them all in several of the pans. The
snow outside had thankfully tested pure enough to use for
drinking and cooking.

Kusac excused himself to go over to the group of four tents
that had been linked together. His people had decided the
team leaders should be in the center of the semicircle, with
the rest of them on either side. The tents weren't tall enough
to stand up in, but they were long enough and wide enough for
two people to sleep in with a crawl space between. At the back
there was a small section large enough for two backpacks.

Sleeping bags had already been spread out for him and
Carrie and their backpacks stored at the rear. Circuits giving
off heat or cool air, as needed, were built into the struts and
turned on automatically as he entered.

He needed to deal with the voice that had tried to force
him back into the cavern. It didn't matter that it had failed or
that he'd been able to silence it; what mattered was that it had
happened.

Stretching out on his sleeping bag, he clasped his hands behind his head and tried to relax. He was utterly convinced that
the voice had to be linked to the Cabbarans and the TeLaxaudin, specifically Annuur, and probably Giyarishis as he'd been
the one on Kij'ik. Their network was an integral part of the
puzzle. He knew that the Cabbarans had telepaths, but he had
assumed that only Naacha, in Annuur's group, was one. They
all had to be at least receptive to him. What if Naacha was
capable of linking them into a telepathic unit?

The TeLaxaudin, he knew, were technophiles and scientists.
Were they using the network to simulate a form of telepathy? They certainly used tech to work on building the adobe
houses with the Cabbarans. Or maybe they both made use
of it to enhance their mental abilities? He did know the network wasn't made only of inert materials. There had been a

biological component about it too—and the TeLaxaudin ships were made of a semiliving material that had been grown, not manufactured.

All the bits were part of the same jigsaw, but he couldn't see clearly where they belonged yet. The voice, or compulsion, was always demanding he do something against his nature— Link mentally to Zayshul, let Zsurtul die, and, finally, search the cavern for something rather than rescue Zhalmo. Unconsciously, he began to rub a faint itch on the inside of his wrist.

Or had it this time? It hadn't tried to prevent him from rescuing Zhalmo, but it had wanted him to go somewhere else first. When he'd shut the voice up, it hadn't come back, not even when he was in the cavern again. It was as if it knew he had to rescue her, and that once he had, he had to return her to their ship and get her safely off M'zull.

He sighed. Perhaps he was reading too much into all this. But how deep did the Cabbaran and TeLaxaudin involvement in their affairs go? Were they present on this world too? Were they manipulating the M'zullians, making them aggressive and bent on dominating every race they met?

Almost as he thought it, he knew, as clearly as if a voice in his mind had said it, that they weren't. He pounced on the thought, finding it was on the same frequency as the one earlier that day. He followed it, only to find that he was suddenly the prey as his mind was seized and held. Then darkness swept over him.

Ghioass, Unity's core

He regained consciousness in an alien place of nothingness. A pale shimmering light, like the inside of a frosted bubble, surrounded him. Sitting up slowly, he took stock of himself first. Interestingly, he was Sholan now, and wearing his black tunic. Reaching out with his mind, he could sense only as far as the edges of the bubble, but he knew there were beings out there.

Answers you want, Hunter, said a voice inside his mind. *Cannot give them to you yet.*

Who are you? he demanded, getting up into a crouch, ready to fight.

Not your enemy. Our imperative we silenced when we realized you would endanger yourself and Sand-dweller female. Important is she to the future.

We encouraged you to take the mission, a second voice said.

It was my decision alone! he snapped, turning around, trying to see through the pale glow, to find out who was out there.

Was it? asked the first. *Or did we . . . encourage you?*

The memory of how he'd impulsively offered to rescue Zhalmo played back in his mind. "Stop that," he said, standing up. "Get out of my mind! You have no right to be there!" He pushed at the presences, putting all his energy behind it, and expelled them. "If you have something to say, then do it in person! Don't steal into my mind like thieves!"

Silence fell, then gradually the pearly light faded to darkness and two figures appeared, one TeLaxaudin, and one Cabbaran.

"Annuur," he said. "I knew you were up to your fuzzy butt in this. Who's the TeLaxaudin?"

Annuur's long nose wrinkled as he reared up on his haunches.

The TeLaxaudin was different from those he'd met before, Kusac realized. This one was older, the body rounder, the bronzed flesh slightly more golden in places, and it was dressed in voluminous strips of blue and lilac draperies that rippled as if in a breeze.

A low humming came from it, and then the speech became Sholan.

"Khassis. I am a female and Elder of my people."

He walked toward them only to be stopped by the boundary of the bubble.

"It is not prison," said Khassis, in response to his mounting anger. "A place for your mind and ours to talk in safety only. You are not on our world so have to be in there."

Placing his hand on the smooth surface, he looked out at them. "Why have you called me here?" he demanded, quietly letting his mind drift into the fabric of the bubble, sense its composition. "What do you want of me?"

"Urgently must you go back to the cavern," said Khassis.

"Why should I do anything you demand of me? You tried

to make me let Zsurtul die, forced me apart from my family, tried to make me Link mentally with Zayshul," he said with mounting anger.

Khassis held up one small hand. "No," she said with finality. "We do not. We risk all to call you here."

Annuur stirred, his ears flicking as the whiskers on his long nose twitched. "Did we not help you on Shola? Your Talent returned to you with no asking for anything in return? How we be your enemy, Hunter?"

His hand closed into a near fist, claws coming out to sink deep into the fabric of the bubble. With a sudden ripping sound, he tore its fabric open and stepped out into their reality.

"Hunter?" he said, pelt and hair bushing out until he was almost twice his size. "You have that right," he purred, pacing slowly toward them, tail flicking in short, jerky motions.

Khassis looked up at him, her hands returning to their usual position in front of her body. "Your nature we know, Hunter, but your prey now is M'zull, not us," she said calmly.

"Maybe, but when your time comes . . ."

"Answer you we will," interrupted Annuur. "M'zull will win unless you return to Palace cavern."

"And how am I supposed to do that?" he asked, pacing around them, intrigued that they ignored his presence and the threat he obviously presented. "You know so much, yet you ignore the fact that we left it like an anthill that had been kicked over!"

"Not ignore," said Annuur. "Help be given you."

He stopped in front of them. "Help? Like you gave Vartra?" he asked, suddenly knowing where the Entity had been when he disappeared.

Annuur winced. "Not us."

"You say *not us* too often," snarled Kusac, lunging forward to cuff Annuur hard on the side of the head, trying not to fall over when his hand went right through him.

"Not us," said Khassis. "Three factions there are; we are not in ascendency now. We risk much calling you here."

"You risk nothing compared to us!" Kusac roared in anger, arms, hands, and claws extended.

"I will take you," said Annuur, looking sideways at Khassis, then back to him.

"I will not go! I'm not your puppet!" he snarled, turning away and reaching mentally for his own body and world.

"Come, and I will tell you much you wish to know," said Annuur's voice, fading into silence as he found himself falling, falling into nothingness.

He was still fighting as he returned to consciousness in his tent, with Kaid and Carrie trying to hold him down.

As soon as they saw he was conscious, they let him go and he sat up.

"What happened?" Carrie asked. "You were gone, just not here at all."

He shivered and rubbed his face with his hands, noticing with part of his mind that he was a Valtegan again. "A nightmare," he said, his voice cracking.

"Water," said Kaid, leaning back out of the tent. Moments later, he handed a canteen to Kusac who took it and drank thirstily.

"I had a nightmare," he whispered when he'd drunk his fill. He handed the bottle back to Kaid.

"You were gone, Kusac. We couldn't sense your mind at all," said Carrie, reaching out to wipe his face with a damp cloth.

"I don't remember," he said honestly, taking the cloth from her. Whatever had happened to him, the memory was gone. "I was probably just deeply asleep."

"Do you remember anything?" asked Kaid. "When you returned, you were flailing like you were fighting someone or something."

"I remember it had something to do with Vartra," he said at last.

Kaid growled. "What's He up to now?"

"No, not like that," said Kusac, shaking his head. "It was something about Him, not something He did."

"Are you all right now?" Kaid asked.

He nodded, reaching out again for the water. "I'm fine."

"If you're up for it, we're having a planning session now, working out the best way to approach this. What we really need is some good intel, which means sending a team into the city."

"What do we need to know?" he asked.

"How we can move among them without causing suspicion,

for a start," said Kaid. "If there are any civilians at all, we can pose as them; we'd be a lot safer. The military need to report into their units, be assigned quarters, things that would expose us too easily to pose as ordinary soldiers. Plus, we have no uniforms. We need disguises as well."

"Rezac and I can find that out for you."

"I want people out there actually seeing what it's like, Kusac. Mentally knowing is one thing, experiencing it first-hand is another. We're about ten miles from the city limits here, and about another ten from the center and the Palace. We also need at least one vehicle, not stolen if possible. We don't even know if they own any personal property or if it is all military owned."

"Point taken," said Kusac, getting up. "However, let Rezac and me see what we can find out before we send a team in there. It's a long way to walk."

"Agreed," said Kaid, backing out of the tent.

Kusac reached out to touch Carrie's face, then handed her back the cloth. "I'm fine, really," he said, smiling.

"Hm," she said, obviously not convinced. "Remember what happened on Kij'ik, and don't try to keep everything to yourself. We're a team, remember?"

"How could I forget? I won't keep things to myself, you have my word on that."

Ghioass

In the room that housed Unity's main physical interface, one restricted to the Elders, Khassis sat down abruptly on the cushion behind her as the Hunter disappeared.

"What have we created?" she asked, hands fluttering. "He escaped the force field as easily as if it were made of gossamer!"

"He did more," said Annuur, also sitting down. "He left us! Returned to his body before we were finished with him! Now the Isolationists' folly is exposed, to Unity and us. Alienated him they have with their personal agendas and machinations."

"If we release this transcript," said Khassis, shuddering. "His reckoning could destroy us all."

Annuur made a negative sound. "Mindless, he is not. Reasoning brought him this far. It will bring truth to him also."

"Nanites must be delivered to matter transformer now," said Khassis. "Takes time to manufacture and program those we need from control ones he carries. Naacha did alter the first ones, did he not? That Giyarishis put there?"

He bobbed his head in assent. "Matter transformer destruct when enough constructed to replicate on own. While it follows our program, will not accept Sand-dweller commands. Is safe from moment Hunter programs it by releasing his nanites."

"You will take him?" she asked.

"Must. He needs to trust us at least, or all are at risk here. Lweeu breeding—infants we have soon," he added with obvious pride. "More reasons to risk aiding him."

Khassis put her head on one side, eyes swirling. "You have sired young?"

Annuur's snout wrinkled in a grin. "This enforced break good time for family matters. All sept wished it. You first to know."

She inclined her head. "Offspring always a blessing," she said. "Honored to be first told."

Annuur spread his spatulate hoofed hands. "Early days yet."

"How will you help the Hunter?" she asked, returning to the business at hand.

"Has been here now. Unity can lock onto him again, take me there. He has been to cavern. With translocator, I send him. He return same way."

"None of your kind therc. You draw attention to yourself and Hunter," she objected.

"I go to their cave only. Talk to him, give translocator."

"May attack you again."

"Not going there physically. Hunter does not scare me," he said. "I have some four hours to wait before their night. I go then, when he sleeps."

M'zull, late evening

It had been decided that Cheelar and M'yikku would leave that night for the city and do some basic intel gathering. Also on their agenda was getting hold of some uniforms they could use, and possibly transport. A route had been plotted for them, and basic maps drawn that would bring them out into the open only a mile from the outer limits of the city, near some farmhouses. The snowline extended only for a few miles in that direction, then became a kind of tundra through which they could travel more rapidly. They'd soon reach the more temperate chaparral zone and could remove their winter clothing.

They would be wearing civilian clothes, passing as farmers or land workers. They'd carry their communicators and call in every four hours. If it looked as though they were going to be apprehended, they'd set off a signal concealed in a small homing device in their boots and destroy the comms.

Both carried small packs into which they would put their winter gear to make it easier to conceal. For currency, they'd have a handful of the coins they'd found on the soldiers on Ch'almuth.

Everyone turned in early to conserve the power. The guard on duty would wake Cheelar and M'yikku several hours before dawn.

Still in his Valtegan form, curled around Carrie, Kusac had fallen asleep almost at once. He'd only been sleeping for a couple of hours when he woke suddenly. He lay there for a while, staring at the inside of the tent; then, unable to quiet the restlessness that filled him, he slipped out of their sleeping bags and pulled on his clothes, remembering to shove his pistol into its holster on his belt. Picking up his jacket at the entrance, he crawled out into the cave and made his way over to the central area.

They'd left a few low-level emergency lights on, so he was able to see the jug of maush sitting by the stove. It was icy cold, but he poured himself a cup anyway. Checking his wrist comm, he saw it was still another two hours before Cheelar and M'yikku were due to leave. Deciding to see who was on sentry duty, he'd strolled through the force field into the smaller chamber when he heard the noise.

He stopped dead, cursing inwardly at the poor eyesight

he had in his Valtegan body, and slowly pulling out his pistol, he waited. The noise came again, off to his right. Silently, he turned around to face it.

I said I come to you, said Annuur's voice in his mind. Just as he realized he could smell no scent, the Cabbaran came trotting quietly toward him.

"You again!"

"That you, Captain?" Noolgoi called out from the cave entrance.

Annuur reared up on his haunches, gesturing for silence.

"Yes," said Kusac, gun trained on the Cabbaran. "Couldn't sleep. Nothing to worry about."

"Aye, sir."

How the hell did you get here? he demanded.

Not important, sent Annuur. *No need for gun. I come to send you to cavern.*

Why is that cavern so damned important? You're not manipulating me any more, Annuur! I know what you've been doing to Kezule and me!

Can't talk here. Later, sent the Cabbaran, slowly coming closer.

Stay right where you are, warned Kusac.

What, you shoot me? When I never offered you any violence, only tried to help?

You tried to stop me from saving Zsurtul!

Not me. Others.

A sense of déjà vu swept over him, and he began to remember the confrontation of a few hours earlier. *We've had this conversation before,* he said as Annuur took advantage of his distraction to move closer again.

Yes. You want war with M'zull? Then leave and go back to bed, the Cabbaran sent disdainfully. *You want to stop war then you go to cavern.*

Kusac stared at him, letting the barrel of his gun drop. *You're not here, are you? You're a dream.*

Not dream, I am here, but in mind and spirit only.

I remember now. You pulled me to your world, but I left it of my own free will.

Stronger than we anticipated, are you, agreed Annuur. *Enough talk. Time to go to cavern.*

Holstering his gun, Kusac turned away, still keeping an eye

on him, and took a drink of the cold maush. *Forget it, I'm going nowhere for you or your stick-insect friends!*

With an exasperated sound, Annuur knocked the cup from his hand and grasped him by the wrist, forcing a small object into his hand. *You will go, Hunter!*

His mind reeled, filling with Annuur's imperative. He knew he had to go to the cavern, and he knew what he had to do when he got there. Then suddenly, space wrenched and distorted, bending around him, sucking him into blackness.

The *Couana*

Zhalmo had slept off and on for most of the day, and now she was awake and filled with a restlessness she couldn't explain. Shadows of what could be nightmares seemed to pursue her, and she needed to be alone. Awake or asleep, since she'd boarded the *Couana*, Na'qui or her sisters had been at her side.

Grabbing her uniform, she padded silently to the small internal bathroom and shut the door. Putting the light on, she examined her body to find out why there were so many tender spots on it. Here and there she could see what looked like thin scars, and on her arms were a few patches of yellow, tender skin—bruises not quite healed. There were more of the scars around her wrists. Where had they come from? She knew they hadn't been there before. Were they marks from being bound when she was a prisoner? She couldn't remember. Finally she gave up trying to figure it out and got dressed.

Slipping quietly out of the bathroom on bare feet, she padded to the door, opening it only enough to let her leave the room. In the corridor, she made her way to the rec room, sure there would be no one there at this late hour.

She stopped dead in the doorway and tried to back away without disturbing Zsurtul.

The young King looked up instantly and half rose from the sofa on which he was sitting.

"Don't go on my account," he said. "I couldn't sleep either."

She hesitated.

"Please, join me," he said, gesturing. "I don't like sitting here alone. Besides, I'm losing this game of cards."

"How can you be losing when you're playing against yourself?" she asked, intrigued, as she stepped into the room and walked over to see what he was doing.

"It's a game called Patience. You play against yourself and try to match runs of cards," he said, gesturing at the cards lying on the low table. "Carrie taught me."

She sat down. "You'll have to explain it to me sometime. I can't really keep my mind on anything for long right now."

He nodded and sat down beside her. "I understand. You've been through an awful experience; you need time to relax and get over it."

"That's just it," she said hesitantly. "I can't remember much about it. It's like there're holes in my memory."

She saw understanding dawn in Zsurtul's eyes before he quickly looked away.

"I was going to make some maush to help me sleep. Would you like some?" he asked.

"Do you know something about this?" she asked sharply.

"No," he said, looking back at her. "I honestly don't know anything about any missing memories. Perhaps they'll come back to you in time."

"I have marks on me, scars," she said, pulling back her sleeve and showing him her wrist. "What caused these?" she demanded.

He took her wrist in his hand, looking at it, then her. "I don't know," he said gently. "I only know you were taken prisoner, Zhalmo. K'hedduk was known for his brutality when he was on K'oish'ik, so it's not surprising you have injuries." He raised her wrist and pressed it gently to his lips, never taking his eyes from her face. "I think it's a blessing your mind has chosen to forget what happened to you there," he said, returning her arm to her lap but letting his fingers slip down to her hand to hold it. "Do you remember anything from before your capture?"

Her eyes took on a faraway look for a moment. "Yes. I remember seeing you get shot," she said, taking her hand away from his and reaching out to touch his chest, feeling the bandage still there.

A look of horror crossed her face, and she began to pull at

his shirt, ripping it open till she saw for herself how small the dressing was. Not content, she pushed him this way and that, examining his side, seeing the pale new skin above and below the bandage.

"I saw him shoot you in the side, saw your suit damaged, the foam sealant covering the part of your suit that his shot blew away. You should be dead!" She was trembling all over, her face almost chalk white.

Amused at her till now, Zsurtul turned serious again and grasped hold of her hands, holding them still. "I'm all right, Zhalmo. Kusac saved me," he said. "Without him, I would have died."

"I thought you were dead!" she said, tears running down her face. "That there was nothing left for me to live for!"

"Zhalmo . . ." He pulled her into his arms, holding her close. "When I heard you'd been captured, I thought there was nothing to live for either," he whispered, covering her cheek with small kisses as her hands clutched at his sides frantically. "But I had to go on for the sake of my people. Then Kusac said he'd go to M'zull and bring you back . . . I had to come, had to see you as soon as you were recovered."

"You're here because of me?" she asked, raising her face to his.

"Why else would I be here?" He stroked her cheeks, wiping away the tears. "Now I have you back, I swear I won't let you out of my sight again."

"I don't think I'll be fit to be your bodyguard for a while yet," she said uncertainly.

"I had hoped you'd play a different role in my life."

A look of confusion came over her face.

"I began to fall in love with you as a soldier," he said, "but the female you are right now is even more lovely. I love you, Zhalmo, and I want to marry you."

She looked down at his chest, her fingers tracing what showed of his Royal tattoo above the bandage circling his ribs. "But you're King now."

"Not right now. Right at this moment I'm just the male who loves you and who thought he'd lost you forever," he said, tilting her face up to his and gently kissing her.

She hesitated then responded, her hands slipping under his shirt to caress him.

After a few minutes, he gently pushed her back. "You

should go back to bed and rest, Zhalmo," he said, his voice not quite steady. "I love you, and I don't want this to go further tonight when you're still not well."

"I don't want to sleep alone," she whispered, laying her head on his chest. "There are things I don't understand haunting my sleep."

"You need to rest and get well," he said, stroking her head.

"Then I'll sleep with you. You'll keep me safe from the shadows," she said, turning her head and kissing his skin just above the bandage.

He shuddered with pleasure. "You don't know how much I want that, but it's too soon for you. I need you to be sure it's what you want."

"If I promise to sleep?" she asked, her tongue flicking across him. "I don't want to sleep alone, Zsurtul. Please."

"Better there than here," he murmured, reaching down to pull her face up to kiss her again. "Only sleep, nothing else," he said.

She slid back to her place on the sofa, letting him get up and try to tuck his shirt back into his trousers. He gave up on buttoning it again and reached out to help her to her feet.

His room was next to the mess, and though it boasted a double bed like her room, it had no private shower and bathroom. The bedside lamp cast a gentle glow on the room as he pulled back the bedding for her.

"I'll sleep in the chair," he said, turning back to her. "You have the bed."

She shook her head, staying near the door. "I don't want to sleep alone. I want to be with you."

"Zhalmo . . ."

"Please. I need you," she said, folding her arms across her body and beginning to shiver. "I'm afraid to sleep alone."

He was at her side in an instant, drawing her over to the bed. "You'll be the undoing of me, you know," he whispered, pulling her into his arms and holding her tightly until her shivering stopped. When it did, he let her go.

"You first," he said, gesturing to the bed.

She reached out and tugged at his shirt. "Take it off," she said. "I need to feel you, not your clothes."

He groaned inwardly. This was more than male flesh could stand, but he began to shrug himself out of his shirt, wincing as he pulled his almost healed wound. She helped him, and, somehow, it was just natural for him to help her take off her shirt and pants. He did it slowly, with kisses, drinking in the sight of her for the first time.

"You are so beautiful," he whispered, his hands barely touching her shoulders as she pressed herself against him and then slipped into the bed.

Reaching for the light, he turned it off before shedding his own pants, aware she'd find out soon enough just how much he wanted her. He slid in beside her, pulling the covers over them, waiting for her to move closer. She curled up against his side, one leg going across him as he slipped an arm under her neck and drew her close. Cushioning her head just below his shoulder, she tucked her arm across his chest and sighed contentedly.

"You haven't said you'll marry me," he said, trying to keep his tone light as his tongue flicked over her ear. He wanted her so much it hurt, but he wanted even more not to scare her, to bring back the awful memories that he knew Kusac had taken from her.

"I love you, Zsurtul," she whispered. "We belong together. Yes, I'll marry you."

"I'm glad, because I told your father I would marry you."

"You did? What did he say?" she asked, astonished.

"He didn't object," he said, trying hard to stop his hand from straying down to her back. "Now sleep, Zhalmo," he said, kissing her forehead. "It's been a very long day for both of us."

"You sure you want to sleep?" she murmured, letting her leg move lower till it was touching his erection.

"No, but we're going to," he said firmly, pulling her leg back up across his belly. "I told you, I love you. I want our first time together to be special, even if we wait till our wedding night." He tried to not think what could happen to them if her memories of being raped surfaced this early in their new relationship.

"You, my King, are special," she said, reaching up to kiss him. "I've never met anyone as honorable as you." She turned around so her back was to him. "I think I'll be able to sleep now," she said, reaching her hand back to touch him.

"I'm glad," he said, turning around himself to curl up against her and draw her close. He knew that he'd also be able to sleep, knowing he held what was most dear to him in his arms. "Sleep well, my love. I'll be here when you wake, I promise."

K'hedduk's Palace

Kusac was plunged into a world of chaos, of raised voices and the sound of construction vehicles. He was back in the underground Palace. Staying against the wall of the side tunnel he was in, he looked out into the cavern and saw just how much damage the MUTAC had caused.

There were craters of various sizes all over the floor. Rubble was being dragged from the tunnel entrances and piled there for the earthmovers to collect and dump into low trucks. Males in every kind of uniform, his included, were scurrying about, intent on their own business.

Hurriedly he began to take off his padded jacket, only to find he was clutching a small device in one hand. About the size of a pack of stim twigs, it had two recessed buttons and a dial on the face. Unbidden, the information that it was the translocater that had brought him here came to his mind, as did the knowledge of how to use it to return to their mountain cave.

Thrusting it into the thigh pocket of his pants, he folded his jacket up and began to walk briskly into the cavern, toward an exit on the far side.

He was aware of the compulsion driving him onward in that direction, but he was also curious to find out why it was so important to Annuur and his TeLaxaudin allies that he come here.

No one stopped him or even queried his presence, though one or two ordinary soldiers suddenly ground to a halt in front of him and threw him a salute before scurrying off. Obviously his uniform color meant he was a high-ranking officer.

The tunnel he was approaching was clear of rubble; in fact, it was set back enough from the main cavern that it wouldn't have been seen by the MUTAC. Driven though he was, he was still in control of his own actions and was able to keep all his senses extended watching for trouble.

He headed down the tunnel, stopping at the first doorway to look inside. It was a lab of some kind, with workbenches and various machines and equipment whose uses he couldn't even guess. Closing the door, he continued down the corridor, picking another empty room at random and glancing in there. Once again, it was a laboratory of some kind.

He sensed the room he needed was just around the bend in the corridor—where two guards stood on duty. Slowing briefly, he slipped his knife out of its sheath and held it blade upward, concealed against his forearm as he turned the corridor.

The guards snapped to attention, rifles going down to the floor and hands up to to salute him.

"Commander," they said.

Kusac sketched a salute back at them and held out his hand imperiously. "Key," he said.

"You can't go in there, sir," said one nervously, keeping his eyes trained straight in front of him. "If you was entitled to go in, you'd have your own key."

"I left it in my quarters," he said. "Open the door and be quick about it! I haven't got all night, even if you have!"

The second guard risked a glance at his companion. "We can't, sir. Be more than our lives was worth if we let anyone in without their own key."

"Your caution is commendable, but you're being a damned nuisance to me right now," he said, right hand flashing out and slicing the throat of the first guard in a move almost too fast to see, while his left punched the other in the throat over the larynx. That guard dropped his rifle, clutching his throat and gasping for air as his companion slumped bonelessly to the floor.

Bending down, he searched the gasping one's pockets for the key card. Straightening up, he slipped it through the reader. The door open, and he hauled both guards inside, ripping the shirt off one to swab the blood off the dirty stone floor outside.

Closing the door, he wiped his knife off on the rag before slipping it back in its sheath and taking stock of this room.

The doorway here was a lot wider than the ones into the other labs, and this was echoed in the broad passageway leading toward the benches and a metal door at the far end. There were drag marks, scored deep into the concrete floor, and he bent down to examine them. He could sense particles of metal there that had been scraped off the heavy object that had been brought in here—a metal unlike any they had come across the M'zullians using so far. In fact, it was unlike any he knew.

Standing up, he walked around the benches, pausing to look at the control panels and screens that seemed to predominate here. What was so important that it necessitated a locked door and guards? Moving on, he approached the wide metal door at the other end of the room. Whatever it was he sought, it was behind this door.

Hesitating briefly before it, he brought up the key and slid it through the reader again. This time, he heard the hiss of hydraulics before the door slid to one side.

The air smelled of ozone and hot metal, and huge power cables were looped across the floor and walls. Banks of control desks with screens were arranged in an octagonal arrangement all facing inward with wide passageways between them. In the center, amid the nest of cables, squatted what he had been sent to find.

"Vartra's bones," he whispered, staring at it.

It was organic, resembling some giant insect, all its lines flowing into each other as if it had grown in that shape. The outer surface was black with greenish tinges here and there that glowed. Fine filaments linked one area to another, webs that sparkled and shone off and on in different colors in seemingly random sequences. It topped seven feet tall and was about five wide; each of its six sides had two spindly legs extending from it onto a base framework. It looked unfinished, as if part of it was missing. He walked around it, sensing it, feeling the thinking part of it sitting there waiting for new commands. It was TeLaxaudin, there was no doubt about that.

Mindful of where he was, he returned to the door and sealed it on the inside, then put his jacket down on the nearest console.

He walked around it again, resisting the mounting compulsion to touch it, finishing his circuit before coming to a stop. Now he did reach out toward it, briefly laying a finger one of the leg struts. It felt warm, and it yielded under his fingertip, like flesh. Repulsed, he hurriedly snatched his finger away. The flashing on the webs increased, as if messages were suddenly being sent along them.

It called to him, as if by touching it, he had awakened it to his presence. A low humming began to fill the room, and his head began to ache with the effort of ignoring the imperative Annuur had planted in him. As the humming increased, so did the pressure in his mind, until he fell to his knees in agony. Against his will, his hand reached out for the front where, as he watched, the fabric of the machine was flowing and changing, forming an aperture for him.

Terror filled him as, inexorably, he was pulled closer and closer. His hand, hovering above the aperture, was sucked down onto the surface as if by a magnet. The pain in his head vanished, and he watched in horror as the skin over his wrist seemed to split, releasing a flow of silver liquid that spread over the surface before being instantly absorbed.

You wanted answers, Hunter, said Annuur's voice inside his head. *Those are nanites, manufactured by us to program the transformer to construct more of them. We needed you to carry them. They will multiply then be released onto M'zull, where they will continue to multiply. When that has happened, the matter transformer will self-destruct. You carried those commands within you too. The nanites will spread to every M'zullian, and when they have reached the whole population, they will activate, destroying all their racial memories. They will forget there ever was an Empire, that they wished to enslave all other species, and that they hate the Sholans. On that day, you can conquer them easily and without bloodshed, if you so wish.*

His hand was suddenly released, and he fell backward onto the floor. The humming changed pitch then stopped as the aperture disappeared, flowing back into a featureless surface. He scrambled away from the machine, lifting up his wrist to examine it. All he could see was a small line of blood that vanished when he rubbed it. The flesh beneath was smooth and unmarked.

At the edges of his mind, he could feel Carrie, frantic to know where he was and that he was safe. He spared a moment to reassure her then shut off his Link.

He could hear voices in the distance and feared they had noticed the missing guards. In moments, they'd be entering this room.

"Get me out of here, Annuur," he croaked, pulling himself shakily to his feet and leaning on the nearest console.

Use the translocator, came the reply.

Grabbing his jacket, he fumbled in his pants pocket for the device, almost dropping it in his haste to reset and activate it. As the door slid back, he hid behind one of the consoles. A dry, leathery scent filled the room, and he heard the humming of a TeLaxaudin. The door hissed closed as its translator took over.

"Long enough you took to arrive," it said testily, the emotion perfectly translated into the tone of voice. "Bodies have I moved elsewhere, Hunter. Come out now, it is safe."

Kusac hesitated, weighing his need to know more against escape. Curiosity and anger won. Still clutching the reset translocator in one hand, he stood up and stepped out into the open.

"Lassimiss, I am," the TeLaxaudin said, stalking closer to Kusac, his crimson drapery strips moving sluggishly around his spindly legs.

"You work for K'hedduk." It wasn't a question.

"He thinks it. Several years have I been here. To destroy them I work." His head was turned to look at the device, ignoring Kusac.

"So you're responsible for them having that," he said, pointing at the device crouched beside him.

"No. His brother ruled when it found. I knew its nature. Transforms planets it does, creates life on barren worlds, repairs damaged ecologies. A weapon it is not, though they used it as one."

Kusac stared at him, his mind reeling at the thought that this might not be a weapon after all. "You helped them destroy two of our colonies and one of their worlds!"

Lassimiss' head turned, large eyes whirling as he focused on him properly for the first time. "They work out themselves how to use this. I not help them. Expect you I was told, with new command nanites to reprogram this unit. Destruction of them is what we wish."

Say nothing of me or we are all lost! came Annuur's agonized thought. *We not know our opposition had meddled so deeply!*

"I know nothing about this," said Kusac. "I'm finished with

you people for now! Whatever else you want done, forget it. I
will not be your puppet any longer!"

"Have what I need," said Lassimiss, gesturing toward the
device with one slim hand. "You remain here, I know. Help I
offer you in your plans to destroy them."

Consider it you will, say that, ordered Annuur. *Him we will
deal with, but no suspicion of you must he have.*

Kusac hesitated. If Annuur was being honest, there were
warring factions at work here, one as ruthless as the M'zullians
themselves, the other . . . Well, that remained to be seen. So far,
all he knew for sure about Annuur was that he hadn't done
anything directly to harm him despite the many opportunities
he'd had to do so.

"I shall consider it," he said, activating the translocator.
Again, he felt the wrenching sensation as space around him
altered, sending him hurtling into darkness.

He materialized back in the outer cavern in the exact spot
from which he'd left. Now, however, it was lit, and people were
standing nearby arguing. His sudden appearance silenced
them.

"He's back," J'korrash called out into the inner cavern.

Kaid reached him before Carrie and grabbed him by the
shoulders. "What happened?" he demanded. "You just vanished, leaving only your cup on the cavern floor."

Carrie flung herself into his arms a moment later, her mind
full of relief.

"I need something for a headache," he said, hugging her
lightly. "I'll tell you everything when I've had that."

J'korrash ran off to get him something from the med stores
as he walked back into the main cavern with the others.

Sipping hot maush, he told them everything he knew. "It
was definitely a TeLaxaudin machine," he said. "How they got
hold of it, I don't know."

"Nanites programmed to eat metal could explain the destruction of the J'kirtikkian fleet," said Kaid thoughtfully.

"The presence of such a machine on M'zull, and Annuur
saying it will self-destruct, definitely supports his claim of two
factions among his people and the TeLaxaudin," said Carrie.
"And it seems he is on our side."

"I'm positive he put those nanites in me that day I fought

him on K'oish'ik," said Kusac. "As far as I'm concerned, I don't think we should depend on this nanite plan. We go ahead with our own."

"Agreed," said Kaid. "If the M'zullians manage to turn that machine off, then none of that will happen."

"I got the feeling they couldn't do that," said Kusac. "That the nanites I carried also prevented them, or anyone, from accessing the controls of the thing again. It will produce the nanites, and it will self -destruct as soon as it has enough ready and has released them. Those will replicate themselves, cutting down on the time it takes before they can destroy the transformer."

"Do you still have that translocation device?" asked Kaid.

Kusac reached into his pocket and pulled it out, holding it in his palm for Kaid to see.

"Mind if I take a look at it? It might be damned useful to us."

"Knock yourself out," said Kusac, handing it to him. "Just don't try to use it tonight. I'll try to explain how it works tomorrow. I'm going to head back to bed. I'm exhausted, and this time, now that I've delivered Annuur's package, I know I'll be able to sleep."

"Good idea," said Carrie, getting up when he did.

K'hedduk's Palace

K'hedduk stormed into his office. He'd been at a meeting on the eastern seaboard when the message about Zhalmo's disappearance and the attack on the Palace had come in, and he had returned immediately. He was furious when he heard about and saw the carnage wreaked by the walking tank that had come with the attackers.

His staff trailed after him as he settled himself at his desk, flanked by his black-clad bodyguards. The sounds of carpenters hammering and sawing as they replaced the doors shattered by the attackers was still audible, even in here.

"Get me the people responsible for letting them into the Palace and the seraglio," he demanded.

"They're all dead, Majesty," said the Head of Security.

"Then get me Keshti and his staff!"

"They're in the sick bay, recovering from injuries or the drugs they were given. No one could've anticipate such a rescue, Sire," he added hurriedly. "They had all the passwords, everything. Even the prisoners looked genuine."

"Then fetch me any recordings of what happened," hissed K'hedduk, balked of his prey. "I want to see for myself what the walking tank looked like!"

His aides looked at each other, reluctant to speak.

"Let me guess," said K'hedduk sarcastically. "There are no recordings."

"No, Majesty. But we do have several soldiers outside who saw what happened. Some from the junction, others from the Palace landing area."

"Bring them in," snapped K'hedduk, getting up and going around to the other side of his desk.

A sergeant marched them in briskly and stood them to attention.

"I take it you've questioned them, Sergeant. Summarize their information for me."

"There were about twenty of them—eight prisoners and approximately twelve guards. Keshti met them as usual and escorted them to the seraglio. As all the guards were in battle armor, he took them down on the troop elevator."

"And no one thought it strange that all twelve were in full armor?"

"They said no, Majesty, because the guards said they were in a hurry to leave on another mission."

"Continue," said K'hedduk, his voice still deceptively mild as he leaned back against his desk and crossed his arms.

"None of the soldiers on your level survived, Majesty. We can only surmise that the prisoners were also armored soldiers who, when they took the Empress, threw off their disguises."

"Did no one try to stop them when they saw the Empress?"

"If you pardon, Majesty, they didn't see her," said the Sergeant uncomfortably. "All those that were seen were in full battle armor, and there was no way they could have brought an extra suit."

"They could have left someone behind in her place. A spy."

"Yes . . . Majesty," admitted the Sergeant.

K'hedduk looked at his security aide. "And have you started a search for this spy?"

"No, Majesty. We didn't think . . ."

"That is obvious! Continue," he said, turning back to the Sergeant. "Do we know who they were, how they got hold of the *Aggressor*?"

"It could only have happened on Ch'almuth, Majesty. It's obvious the tithe youths were, in fact, soldiers. And some of these men say there were aliens among them."

K'hedduk frowned. "How would they know that?"

"Some of the suits were made for beings with tails, and legs different from ours, they said."

Straightening up, K'hedduk stared at the soldiers beyond the Sergeant. "Who saw this vehicle that walked?"

Two soldiers stepped forward. "It didn't as much walk as run and jump, Your Majesty," said one. "It had a tail that was sharper than a knife. I saw it cut a Lieutenant in two with one swipe!"

"They did a sketch of it, Majesty," said the Sergeant, taking a piece of paper out of his pocket and unfolding it.

K'hedduk leaned forward and snatched it from him.

"These alien suits," he asked, his voice tight with rage, "Did their legs have joints that went backward where our knee would be?"

"Yes, Majesty!" the other soldier blurted out. "And tails, just like the machine. Their weapons are more powerful than ours, and their armor! Nothing we had seemed to penetrate it. We had no chance against them."

Crushing the drawing into a ball, he turned his back on them. "Leave, and fetch me General Geddash!" he hissed in anger.

Sholans! The damned Sholans and Primes had staged a rescue and taken his wife from the very heart of his Palace! On top of that, for a second time, they'd lost their tithe of breeders and goods!

He knew who was behind it—Kusac and Kezule! This was the Sholan's revenge for what had been done to him on the *Kz'adul*. He should've killed the creature when he had him in his hands, the same with Kezule.

His personal servant came in quietly and stopped beside him.

"I've brought you a hot drink, Your Majesty," he said quietly.

He toyed with the idea of sending the tray and servant both flying across the room as a way to assuage some of his anger, but the aroma from the hot shokka was heightening his hunger. As soon as he'd received the news of the attack and that the Empress was missing, he'd rushed back to the Palace without stopping to eat.

Taking the cup, he nodded and sipped the creamy drink. "Fetch me some food," he ordered. "Something quick to eat for now."

"Yes, Your Majesty." The servant left as silently as he'd arrived.

K'hedduk returned to his desk to wait for the General. Spreading out the crumpled drawing, he studied it carefully this time. Although crude, it was the shape of a Sholan. He'd seen the males assume just that four-legged stance in defense of their mates. First the Primes and the Sholans had joined forces, and now the Ch'almuthians! He was losing control, bit by bit, of the Empire he'd hoped to create.

A knock on the door broke his concentration, and he looked up to find the servant returning with a tray of sandwiches. The smell of the warm spiced meat was mouthwatering.

As the plate was set on his desk, he gave the servant a rare smile and thanked him.

"It is my pleasure to serve you, Majesty," the servant murmured before leaving.

He was halfway through his meal when his secretary showed General Geddash in.

"More bad news, Majesty," said Geddash, striding up to his desk. "The fleet has just emerged from jump space. They took dreadful losses at K'oish'ik. There were ships belonging to three other species berthed in their system, waiting for us. If I didn't know better, I'd call it a trap." He held out a sheaf of photographs.

His appetite abruptly gone, K'hedduk took the photos and spread them out on his desk.

"Those," said the General, pointing to a brightly painted blue and gold warship, "are a species currently unknown to us. Those," he indicated the photos of ships typified by their dart shapes and smooth lines, "are Sholan, and the rest are Prime ships. Our force was outnumbered and outgunned."

"How many returned?" he asked, picking up his shokka and sipping it to wash the taste of ashes from his mouth.

"A mere handful. Twelve, I believe," he said, sitting down in the chair opposite K'hedduk.

"The Ch'almuthians are now allied with the Primes and Sholans. They left one of their number behind when they stole the Empress. A Prime, I'll wager, since the Ch'almuthians are not soldiers. Find him," he ordered.

"They did?" Geddash's eye-ridges raised in surprise.

"No one saw them take the Empress from the seraglio onto the *Aggressor*. Therefore, they must've put her in battle armor," said K'hedduk. He was beyond anger now, just exhausted.

"I'll get my people on it right away," said Geddash.

"See our security here is increased immediately. When we find this spy, I'll know what we should do next. Meanwhile, make sure our fleets are prepared in case they retaliate and attack us here."

"They won't do that," said the General. "There were too few ships there to mount an attack on us, and they know it. Their visit to kidnap the Empress has given them that information! They'll have seen the size of our fleets."

"Even so, everyone on full alert, and no one lands without new codes that are changed daily."

"As you command, Majesty," said Geddash, getting up and bowing before leaving.

"Find me a female that looks as close to the Empress as possible," he said, dropping his voice so only Zerdish could hear him as he also got to his feet. "With all that's happened today, my people need some positive news. Keep your search secret from everyone, and when you find her, bring her to me. We'll let it be known that we recovered her, and we'll have her appear in public at my side. And have my News Officer bring me a positive way of presenting all this mess first thing tomorrow! Geddash wasn't far wrong when he pointed out that the rebels have seen the size of our fleets and that will make them think twice about attacking us here, on M'zull."

"Yes, Majesty," murmured Zerdish, following him out into the corridor, then across it to the Emperor's lounge. "Actually, I know of a female already. She's the wife of one of the older members of your Court, Lord Nayash."

"That old fossil? He's still alive? Is she one of the Ch'almuthian females?" K'hedduk asked, opening the door.

"Yes, and as like to the Empress as if they were sisters from the same brood."

He waited for Zerdish to send in the other guard to check out the room, and his bedroom beyond, despite the fact that there were guards outside the doors at all times.

"Come in with me, and we'll continue this discussion in private," he said, leading the way in.

He waited till Zerdish closed the door.

"The oldster won't give up his wife without screeching about it to everyone who'll listen," said Zerdish.

K'hedduk looked at him shrewdly. "And how do you know that, and what his young wife looks like, for that matter?"

Zerdish shrugged. "Like some of the other lords, he's brought her to the seraglio to meet with her countryfolk. Your late brother allowed the females to mingle together one day a week. It kept them from getting homesick, he said. I saw Nayash's wife on one of those visits."

"Has he heirs?" asked K'hedduk thoughtfully, walking over to his sofa and taking a seat.

"One son, from an earlier marriage. He's in the fleet, a Lieutenant, I believe. He's out with his ship right now."

"Excellent. Then his elderly father has just had a tragic accident in my service, and as his grateful Emperor, I have decided to provide for his young widow, personally, in my seraglio."

Zerdish smiled slightly. "I understand, Sire. I shall see to it immediately."

"If Resho's half capable, get her out of the hospital and have her see to getting this female ready to take on the role of my Empress."

Zerdish bowed and left.

Ghioass, Unity's core

"What insanity possessed Hkairass?" asked Khassis, pacing stiffly back and forth in the small chamber. "Sending one of his people to the M'zullians? Cannot believe they worked to make this war with Hunter Alliance happen!"

"Believe it," said Annuur tiredly, reaching for the fruit drink that had been left ready for him. His hoof-tipped fingers closed around the wide glass with surprising dexterity, and he lifted it up to his snout to lap thirstily.

"You left the translocator with the Hunter," said Khassis, sitting down on the cushions beside him.

"Purposely. It take him there to deal with Lassimiss, nowhere else. Nothing can we do with him for now. Reveal our own interference we will."

Khassis bowed her head thoughtfully. "No difference between our interference and theirs," she sighed after a few minutes silence. "They will argue this point."

Annuur gave a derisive snort. "They worked to destroy Sand-dwellers, never forget that! They Spoke in Council for poisoning them all. We do not. We work to preserve their lives, Hunters, Sand-dwellers, our Child race, all of them. Never forget this, Khassis."

Khassis uncurled herself and rose to her feet. "You speak wisely, Annuur. Must not let their arguments make us lose sight of our main differences. Must leave now before we are discovered. Unity, return us to our homes."

"As you command, Elder Khassis," said Unity.

As the Elder faded before his eyes, Annuur sighed. He hated traveling like this. Then with a wrench, he was home, being welcomed by his sept.

CHAPTER 20

The *Couana*, Zhal-Zhalwae, 8th day (May)

ZSURTUL woke to the sound of the door opening quietly and saw Na'qui's head poking through the gap.

"How could you?" she demanded angrily in disbelief, pushing the door wider and standing in the doorway. "We've been looking all over for her, worried she'd gone off to harm herself! You know what she's been through! You're no better than that monster, K'hedduk!"

The bed exploded as Zhalmo launched herself at the medic, grabbing her tightly by the throat and slamming her against the doorframe.

"How dare you enter our room like this! And never speak Zsurtul's name and that animal's in the same breath again! I asked him to sleep with me, and that's all we did! Had we done anything else, it would have been none of your damned business. Now get out of here!" With that, she flung Na'qui bodily out of the door, into the group of her brothers and sisters, and Jurrel that had gathered there.

She glowered at them all, hand on the door, ready to close it. "Yes, I'm back," she hissed, "He's *mine*, and don't you forget it!" Banging the door shut, she promptly burst into tears.

"Zhalmo, what it is?" Zsurtul asked, scrambling out of the wrecked bed and running to her side.

"I was your bodyguard," she sobbed, covering her face with her hands and leaning against the door. "The best of us all, and I failed you!"

"No, you didn't," he said, wrapping his arms around her.

"You didn't! It was my own fault that I got shot. I ran off on my own, leaving you behind."

"I failed! I'm not fit to be your wife!" The storm of emotions that had been building, not just since she'd been rescued but in the weeks she'd been a captive, suddenly broke. All the anger and the helplessness swept over her, as well as other emotions she couldn't name but that had still left their mark on her.

Zsurtul didn't know what to do, how to help her. Holding her close only seemed to make her weep even more. He did the only thing he could think of, he tried to send his feelings to her, to let her know how much he loved her and how proud he was of her courage and strength.

Her crying slowed as, at first tentatively, then more surely, her mind reached out to touch his, astonished that they could sense each other.

I thought you were dead, she sent to him.

And I thought I would never get the chance to tell you I loved you, he replied.

But I let you get shot! How can you love me?

I told you, it really was my fault, not yours. You did save my life. If K'hedduk hadn't been so focused on capturing you, he'd have made sure I was dead. I have many bodyguards, but only one you. Who could guard our children better than you?

"Children?" she asked, rubbing her hands across her eyes in confusion and looking at him.

"I meant it when I said I want to marry you, Zhalmo," he said, kissing the last of her tears away. "In fact, let's do it now. Toueesut is the Captain, and Captains can perform marriages."

He reached past her and opened the door. Everyone still stood there, unsure what to do—this was their King, and their sister.

"Tell Captain Toueesut he has a wedding to perform," said Zsurtul. "Your sister's agreed to be my wife."

They stood there, openmouthed, looking at him, too surprised to do anything.

"Well?" he demanded. "Didn't I make myself clear?"

"Yes, sir!" said Chy'tu, taking off at a run for the ladder up to the Bridge.

Zsurtul closed the door and turned his attention back to Zhalmo.

"Are you sure this is what you want?" she asked him. "We haven't known each other very long, and I can't remember what happened to me on M'zull . . ."

"Hush," he said, putting a finger across her lips. "The past is done with. I don't care what you can or can't remember. It's your future I want. We'll make our own memories, good ones, for the rest of our lives."

She smiled, a small one, but the first one since she'd been rescued.

"That's better," he said. "You know, I've never before had a female lay down the law to her family that I was hers," he said thoughtfully, resting his chin on her shoulder. "I like it."

She chuckled and held him close.

There was a polite knock on the door, and Zsurtul opened it.

Toueesut stood there, his swarm dancing in and out and around each other behind him in their usual fashion. The Touiban grinned, his mustaches bristling with pleasure.

"I am informed there is to be a wedding," he said. "Most joyful news this is! Many congratulations, King Zsurtul and soon-to-be Queen Zhalmo! But first there are ceremonies, important ones, which must be conducted to propitiate the good favor of all the Gods so they are smiling on your union. Yes, indeed there are! Come, come," he gestured to them as his swarm mates darted into the room and surrounded them, sweeping them out into the corridor amid the scent of fresh baked bread and flowers.

"Bathing there must be first and many beautiful oils and unguents have we with us. Lucky we have a fellow Sholan Clan member with us who be knowing the wedding ceremony as we have not yet experienced it ourselves."

"Don't look at me," said Jurrel, backing off. "I've never really been involved in the priestly side of the Brotherhood!"

"Then be going to the comm and calling Brother Garras to find out," said Toueesut, pointing in the direction of the Bridge.

As the Touiban turned to follow his happily trilling swarm and the couple they surrounded, he looked at Schiya. "You be organizing who is cooking the food. There must be a feast for a wedding! We will be getting the happy couple ready."

Schiya watched them dart off down the corridor toward their own private quarters then turned to her siblings. "Isn't

this all too sudden and too soon for her, or am I the only one
worrying?"

"Not if it's what she wants," said Chy'tu. "And from the
look on her face, I'd say it is." He linked arms with his sister,
drawing her toward the mess. "Come on, Schiya, I'll help you
organize the catering."

The actual service was to be a short version of the Sholan
one, including the ritual of sharing blood, except they would
exchange rings, not bracelets.

Bathed together in scented, steaming water that smelled to
them of almost every scent in the rainbow—Touiban scents
wakened other senses, they discovered—Zhalmo had balked
totally at wearing any of the Touiban female clothing that was
stored on the *Couana*.

"They're way too short for me, and too bright," she said.
"They clash badly with my skin color."

"It's all right for you," she grumbled at Zsurtul as they sat
on cushions wrapped in huge warmed towels in the Touibans'
private quarters, waiting for them to come out of the huddle
they'd formed to discuss clothing. "You get to wear your uniform! They refuse to let me wear mine."

"Think of it like this," said Zsurtul, grinning. "Imagine
what we're missing at home by getting married here: a State
Wedding."

She looked at him in horror. "Oh, no! My father won't let
us get away with this! We'll have to have one as well!"

"We'll have to give the people something," he agreed. "But
we should be able to get away with just a blessing and the
signing of the Royal Register. Oh, and I insist on you having a
coronation. You will be Queen, you know, in your own right."

She groaned and pulled the towel over her face.

"Regretting this already?" he joked.

Her head popped out again with a look of consternation on
it. "No, never! I forgot I'm marrying a dynasty, not just you."

"We'll start a new dynasty, of Kings, not Emperors," he said,
reaching out from the folds of the heated towel to touch her
cheek as the Touiban huddle broke up.

Two of them disappeared into the adjacent female quarters
to return with armfuls of soft gauzy drapes in gold and pastel
colors.

"Solution we have," said Toueesut. "Dress you wear as

tunic, but over these scarves tucked into a band to make a long skirt. Beautiful and floaty you will look." He nodded vigorously. "Yes, this will do. Jewelry we have too, rings for exchanging and earrings and necklaces. You choose from them. All we have is yours to choose," he bowed.

Whisked off to the adjacent female quarters to be dressed, with Schiya accompanying her, Zhalmo finally emerged for the ceremony looking like a formal vision of the Prime Earth Goddess, La'shol, in gold spun pastels that drifted and swayed with her every movement. She'd chosen only a pair of bright blue ear studs for jewelry.

The main Touiban room had been draped in more of the gauzy materials. Incense burners had been lit, filling the room with the scent of oranges. Lighting had been reduced to a gentle glow from the colored glass lamps that hung down low from the ceiling.

It was like stepping into the opulence of a nomadic tent, and Zhalmo only had eyes for her surroundings when she entered. Chy'tu had to take her by the arm and call her name.

"We're ready now, Zhalmo," he said gently. "Are you sure this is what you want?"

She smiled. "Yes."

Toueesut stood beside a small table with a bowl of incense, a knife, and two matching gold and gemmed rings sitting on it. To his other side was a small stand holding a brazier with glowing charcoal.

Chy'tu led her forward to kneel on the cushions beside Zsurtul. Behind them, the rest of the Primes and Jurrel were gathered. Ashay and Shaayiyisis hovered by the open doorway, their bulk preventing them from actually entering the crowded room.

"A wedding we celebrate today," said Toueesut, resplendent in a fresh turquoise blue jacket edged in gold braid, as his swarm fell silent and still behind him. "Always joyous this is but more so since the bride was lost to us, and now we have her safely back among her family again. This wedding important for peace as King Zsurtul and Zhalmo one day will rule over beginning of unified Valtegan people. Will no longer be castes, but all combined as one." He stopped, hearing exclamations of surprise from around him. "Legends of your people I hear," he said, looking at Zsurtul. "When Zsadhi comes, so does end of castes."

"Zsadhi?" asked Zsurtul.

"Jurrel be knowing," nodded Toueesut, his mustaches wriggling from side to side. "Captain Kusac is your Zsadhi. He has the mark."

Zsurtul swung around to look at Jurrel, who spread his hands.

"I only know what we all saw," he said. "When he changed into a M'zullian Valtegan, he had a tattoo of a sword on his chest. The Ch'almuthians called him the Zsadhi."

"Later, later. Wedding now!" said Toueesut as his swarm began to trill impatiently.

When he had their attention again, he continued. "This wedding unifies your people, King Zsurtul. Do you wish to have Zhalmo as your wife and share your life with her?"

"Yes, I do," said Zsurtul, looking at her in such a way that she felt her heart skip several beats.

"Zhalmo, do you wish to be married to Zsurtul and share your life with him?"

She tried to say the words but couldn't find her voice, so she nodded.

"You have to say it, love," said Zsurtul quietly, reaching for her hand.

"No hands yet!" said one of the other Touibans, darting forward and smacking Zsurtul's hand away, then darting back behind Toueesut.

Zsurtul grimaced and rubbed the top of his hand.

"Yes, I do," she said in a rush, suddenly finding her voice.

"Good, good," beamed Toueesut, picking up the knife and waving it about. "Many peoples, ours all included, are believing blood is life, so they share blood when they marry. Now you will share blood." He handed it to Zsurtul, who looked apprehensively at it.

"Make a small cut in your palm," hissed Jurrel from behind.

Zsurtul turned his other hand over, looking at the palm, then rapidly made a small cut in it. As the blood began to pool in his palm, he handed the blade to Zhalmo.

Without even looking at her hand, she made the small incision and handed the knife back to Toueesut.

He took the knife from her and then took hold of their hands, pressing them together. "The bowl," he said to his swarm brothers.

The bowl was snatched up and held under their hands as Toueesut pressed them firmly together. Blood slowly trickled from between their palms and fell into the incense.

"Blood is mingled, so is life and love," said Toueesut, letting their hands go and taking the bowl.

Na'qui swiftly handed small pads of absorbent material to them.

As Zhalmo pressed hers to the cut, she turned to look at the medic. "I'm sorry for earlier," she whispered.

Na'qui smiled and shook her head. "Forget it," she whispered back.

"Now we offer this to the Deities we all worship," said Toueesut, tipping the resinous incense over the hot charcoal.

It sputtered for a moment then flared up in a bright flame before settling down to send out calming and uplifting scents, some of which Zsurtul remembered from Shola.

"Ahh," said Toueesut, breathing in deeply. "A good omen, that flame, I am told. Now the rings. They shall be an outward sign that you two have exchanged vows to each other."

He picked up the rings, and handed the larger to Zhalmo and the smaller one to Zsurtul.

Zsurtul reached for her hand and eased the ring onto her index finger, his eyes glowing with an inner light as he watched her face. "You look so lovely," he said, "that I wonder at my good fortune every time I see you."

Her color rose in a blush as she took his hand and placed the ring on his finger, her hands trembling slightly. "And I marvel at the love that caused you and your friends to come so far to rescue me," she said.

"As Captain of the *Couana*, I now say you are legally married," said Toueesut, clapping his hands, mustaches bristling in pleasure. "Let no one ever come between you from today."

Zsurtul leaned forward to kiss her, loving the way she met his lips with a passion he'd guessed at but not yet explored.

The Touibans trilled in songs that rose and fell in pitch, weaving a magic of music about them as they got to their feet and turned around to face the others.

"Majesties," said Jurrel, bowing to them. Then, "May I hug the bride?" he asked Zsurtul.

"Just a hug," the young King grinned, wagging a finger at the Sholan amid laughter.

M'zull, Zhal-Zhalwae, 9th day (May)

It wasn't until after dark that Cheelar and M'yikku returned. They were ushered to the center of the cave to get warm, helped out of their damp clothing, and given hot drinks and instant hot meal rations to eat.

Around them, the team leaders and their Seconds gathered to hear their reports.

"It isn't nearly as far in the snow as we thought," said Cheelar as he shoveled the food into his mouth, alternating with gulps of the hot maush. "Only about an hour's walk, and most of it is among the trees."

M'yikku nodded, eating more slowly. "We were able to walk in animal tracks most of the way. Some kind of hoofed herd beast like those we hunted on that other world—the time the M'zullian half-breeds attacked us."

"I remember," said Kusac. "What did you find out about them?"

"They're not all soldiers," said Cheelar, scraping his spoon around the plastic container for the last scraps. "There's a farming community outside the city, some five miles from here. They allocate the less able to farm. We saw people who were mainly older, and some who seemed less mentally alert, which was strange. They seem to be unable to ensure they breed healthy sons, perhaps too much inbreeding. There were some able-bodied farmers too, but not many. It was a market day when we were there." He stopped to drain his cup, then reached out for more from the pot nearest to him.

"Seems they're allowed to keep some of what they farm, and they sell or trade it for other goods," said M'yikku. "There are also people in mountain settlements, though not as high up as we are. They're more self-sufficient in that they have females of their own. Sounds like they actually live as families. Only the males come to trade, though. Everyone else looks down on them as decadent. There were a couple in the village."

"Did you go to the city?" asked Carrie, pouring more maush for herself and Kusac from the other jug. She offered some to Kaid, but he shook his head.

"Yes, there's a transport system to the city from the farms. A train runs twice a day. We caught it there and back," Cheelar said. "There're huge interactive maps at the main station where you can find the location of various buildings, from shopping areas to government offices."

"The money we took from the soldiers on Ch'almuth is worth very little," said M'yikku. "Bought us the train trips and that's all. We found out that they do use the old Empire coins that we use on our world, though, and they are more valuable here."

"Were they suspicious of you?" asked Kaid.

"Strangely, no. They assumed we were mountain folk because of our coloring," said Cheelar. "The city, now, it was quite different. More modern, full of soldiers, though the stores were a mix of civilian and military. They do earn enough to eat at restaurants and buy personal goods, so it isn't a completely repressive lifestyle. We saw a few drones about on errands. They're a much lighter color than any of us or the Primes, but we'll fit right in as far as everyone else goes."

M'yikku nodded. "There's a variety of skin colors around, though the darker ones like General Kezule did seem to be mostly officers. We didn't have too long there, though. Their money system is based on actual coins, so we were lucky we did bring some of our own with us. Outside the city they have massive metalworks for making their ships and war vehicles. You could see and smell the clouds of smoke. The workers do come into the city to spend their money. Owning covered vehicles seems to be the prerogative of the upper ranks. The most common private transport was a sort of hoverbike for one or two riders, or covered vehicles similar to our aircars that travel a couple of feet off the ground."

"We did hear the Court gossip," said Cheelar. "There are huge viewscreens on the sides of all the tall buildings. They broadcast the news according to the Emperor, and according to him, they recovered Zhalmo. Sure looked like her, up on that huge screen."

"What?" said Kusac in astonishment.

"It can't be her," said Kaid dismissively.

"What was the gossip—the real truth?" asked Carrie.

"Ah, well. That's another story," grinned Cheelar. "Seems some old lord had a fatal stroke and died, and K'hedduk kindly took his young widow under his protection into his seraglio."

"And she just happened to look a lot like Zhalmo," added M'yikku.

"The main gossip on the streets is they're looking for the spy left behind by the armed soldiers who tried to kidnap Zhalmo. They think she was taken out in battle armor, so one of us stayed behind," said Cheelar.

"Apparently K'hedduk is really twitchy about that."

Carrie began to laugh as Kaid and Kusac smiled. "So we started his paranoia without even trying!"

"Better, with him killing one of his courtiers to get his wife, all of them will be wondering who's next," said Kaid.

"Perhaps we should rescue Zhalmo's double," said Kusac thoughtfully.

"No," said Banner. "We don't have the MUTAC now as backup."

"Maybe getting in touch with the old lord's son as a potential ally would be useful," suggested Cheelar. "Mind you, they say he's on his ship in the fleet."

"Perhaps. We'll keep it in mind," said Kaid. "He'll have to come back for the funeral, so it is a possibility."

"So we know we can mingle freely with the M'zullians in the city," said Kusac. "They can own property like the hoverbikes, and not everyone is a soldier as we thought. What about clothing? Were many in uniform?"

"A mix," said Cheelar. "They do seem to wear off-duty clothing too. Black is to be avoided—just like back home, it's the exclusive uniform of the Emperor's bodyguards. According to those we spoke to, we should stay away from them; they're vicious for the fun of it, and no one bothers to control them except K'hedduk. Our khaki color is for the special ops people. Most of those in uniform wore a form of camouflage—mainly gray with random patches of darker gray and some black."

"Urban camo," said Kaid, nodding.

"We also found out that the lords own the soldiers. They provide them from the nurseries on their land and promise them to their Emperor's service in return for various favors and money. The Emperor has his own units, of course."

"That's worth knowing," said Kusac thoughtfully. "We need a couple of you to go up and investigate the mountain villages at some point. Ideally, I'd like to split us up into units of three or four and spread us over several major cities. I wish we could get some of us up into the fleet, but that seems an impossibility at the moment."

"Maybe not," said Kaid. "If we did pursue that young lord—what's his name, by the way?—then he could get us access to their fleet."

"But why would he?" asked Carrie. "Unless you plan to make him get us access?"

"Lord Nayash was the name," said M'yikku, smothering a yawn. "The funeral and burial services should be in two days' time on his estate. It'll likely be a State one, with K'hedduk supposedly taking in the widow like that. Interestingly, Nayash has land, or at least trade agreements, up in the mountains too."

"If K'hedduk's there, it would be a one-in-a-million opportunity to kill him," said Kaid. "Create confusion everywhere while the elite fight it out to see who takes power. A great atmosphere for us to create even more unrest and set them against each other."

"It would," said Kusac thoughtfully. "Were there cargo areas on the trains? If there are, we can at least use them to get the non-Primes into the city."

"There were," said Cheelar. "If you're carrying luggage or produce, they expect you to go there rather than the regular seating areas."

"You two can turn in now," ordered Kaid. "Good work, both of you. There's nothing you've told us you need to keep to yourselves," he grinned, looking pointedly at the other team members waiting in a patient group.

They nodded, and rising, headed off toward the tents and their impatiently waiting siblings.

"What now?" asked T'Chebbi, who had been her usual quiet self.

"Rezac, what were their funerals like back in your day?" Kaid asked.

"The Emperor didn't go to any in our time," said Rezac. "And obviously as slaves, we weren't free to leave the seraglio level alone."

"I expect it's the same as the funeral Kezule held after we retook the Palace and City," said Kusac.

Kaid grunted assent. "We need a base nearer the capital," he said. "And we need at least one of the females in the capital itself. I don't want to risk using comms. They'll be monitoring every frequency there if K'hedduk's as twitchy as they say. I must admit I didn't quite expect this paranoia so soon. I expected anger and retaliation from him. It means he isn't feeling as secure on his throne as he'd like to be."

"We want them all paranoid, thinking there are rebels after them, so we can orchestrate the illusion of a civil war. Killing K'hedduk would go a long way to helping that. We need to strike at a different section of society afterward."

"In which case, this Lord Nayash's son is a good idea," said Kaid. "We have two options—we capture him, then you try to alter yourself to impersonate him, or you control his mind and use him as a puppet. Either way, it will give us access to at least part of the fleet and will allow you to talk up some trouble with the other lords. It also gives us his soldiers at our disposal."

"On K'oish'ik, the lords lived on estates at the edge of the city but had apartments in the Palace on the level below the Emperor. I expect they do get buried in a graveyard on their estates," said Rezac.

"So if we can locate Nayash's estate, we can lie in wait for K'hedduk by the graveyard," continued Kaid. "That's one hell of a good starting point."

"It is," agreed Kusac. "If the mountain folk are as independent as Cheelar and M'yikku suggest, they may be of more use to us than anyone. I'm really going to have to find out more about their Zsadhi legend," he sighed. "I may need to make use of it after all."

"J'korrash was compiling information on it before we left K'oish'ik, and on Ch'almuth," said Banner.

"Good idea. We need to use every advantage we have over them," said Kaid. "Playing on their superstitions and fears is always a good way to unsettle any group of people."

Kusac nodded to Kaid, then looked at Banner shrewdly. "If you know she's been studying it, I bet you know about as much as she does."

"I know a fair bit," grinned Banner.

"So tell us about it," said Carrie, leaning against Kusac, and moving closer when he put his arm around her.

"It's an ancient legend, back from the days before they were able to leave their planet and journey into space," began Banner. "A time when both males and females fought, but the females ruled. Queen Ishardia was good and wise, but she had a jealous sister who wanted her throne. The sister plotted and finally made her move with the help of the chief of the guards, whom she had seduced. They burst in on the Queen and her husband as they slept . . ."

"You tell it with no passion," complained J'korrash from behind him. "A tale like this, full of hate and jealousy and revenge, needs passion, Lieutenant Banner."

Banner shrugged and grinned at the others. "Then you tell it, J'korrash."

"The Captain sent for me," said J'korrash, seeing Kaid's questioning look as she stepped into their small circle and joined Kusac and Carrie on the padded blanket they were using.

She sensed my need, Kusac sent to Kaid and Carrie.

T'Chebbi leaned forward, holding out a wide mug and the jug of still warm maush to her. J'korrash accepted them, pouring herself a drink, then passing the jug on to Carrie.

When they had all gotten fresh drinks, she began.

"In the dawn of our people, there was a time that stood out in its turbulent history for its peace and prosperity. Trade agreements were sealed and marriages arranged. The lands of the Queen and King knew only plenty and prosperity, as did their neighbors. Down the river, trade boats sailed, bringing ambassadors with spices and exotic foods from afar, each wanting to be part of the new age of peace. The Queen's name was Ishardia, and her husband, for she broke with tradition and not only made him King to rule with her but also listened to his counsel, was Zsadhi. But the seeds of trouble were sprouting in her own garden. Her sister, Tashraka, was jealous of her standing among the tribes and of her sister's husband. She had no patience for this time of peace, believing they were stronger than the other tribes and should take what they wanted." She stopped to sip her drink.

"Was this story set where the capital is now?" asked Kaid.

She nodded. "Indeed it was. Their lands contained the Holy Pool, and because of that, they were considered first among the tribes. Tashraka approached Zsadhi, offering him not only herself, but goods and possessions no male had ever owned if he would help her overthrow her sister. Zsadhi made the mistake of laughing at her before refusing her offer because of his love for Ishardia. Mortally offended, Tashraka vowed vengeance on him and her sister. When told, Ishardia refused to take her sister's threat seriously, making excuses for her behavior, unable to believe her beloved sister could wish them ill."

"No one wants to think ill of their family," murmured Kaid, resting his head against T'Chebbi's shoulder, watching as the rest of the Primes and Ch'almuthians drew closer to hear the story.

"Tashraka took the head of the Queen's guards as her lover, and together they plotted. He knew of a powerful sorceress in the town who would help them—for a terrible price. Together, one night they stole through the silent streets to the hovel where the sorceress lived. In return for their newly born egg, Tashraka obtained a spell that changed her into the likeness of her sister and the guard into the likeness of Zsadhi. Wrapped in cloaks to conceal their new shapes, they returned to the Palace. There they revealed themselves to the guards, claiming that they were the real Ishardia and Zsadhi and that her sister Tashraka and the chief guard had trafficked with a sorceress for shape-changing spells and were even now impersonating them."

"Magic?" murmured Banner skeptically.

J'korrash glanced at him. "Who knows?" she smiled. "The guards burst in on the Royal couple in their bedchamber and dragged them out into the Throne Room, where the false Tashraka and her lover sat on the thrones. They were sentenced to death, Ishardia to be burned at the stake and Zsadhi, who was only a male after all, to be taken deep into the desert and left there without food or water after he had witnessed his wife's execution."

"Some sister," muttered T'Chebbi.

"Almost destroyed by grief, Zsadhi was dragged to the desert and left, and for ten years, nothing was heard of him. It was assumed he'd perished. For ten years, the country groaned under the cruel hand of Tashraka, still in the shape of Ishardia. An army she'd raised, sending it out to kill all the females and children in the neighboring tribes. The males became her slaves, toiling for her or tortured for her amusement, so that none dared stand against her. Meanwhile, she studied magic with the sorceress, who demanded a place at her Court." She stopped to look around her circle of listeners, smiling slightly at the looks on their faces.

"Then the rumors started. At first it was whispers of a

desert holy person, a follower of the Goddess La'shol, who preached against Queen Ishardia, calling her a false Queen, one who trafficked with a sorceress of evil. Tashraka ignored them as beneath her notice. But one by one, her best female officers were picked off in their villas, and the whispers of this desert prophet became louder until the wailing of the males and children left bereft could be heard outside her Palace." She stopped, raising her cup to her lips, taking a drink. Over the rim, she regarded them all, eyes flicking around the rapt circle of her listeners.

"It was said the avenger was a giant of a male," she continued, lowering her cup to the ground again. "His skin burned almost black from the heat of the desert, dressed in only a loin cloth and weapon belt, he carried a great sword of precious steel that cleaved through the guilty as if cutting a water-rich melon. On his chest was blazoned the sword of the Goddess, with two edges, one to destroy, the other to heal. The innocent and worthy had nothing to fear from him; it was only those who cleaved to the false Queen who need fear his and La'shol's wrath."

Kusac shifted uneasily until Carrie took his hand and squeezed it comfortingly.

"Tashraka was no coward. She dressed in full regal attire, including the headdress of the Queen, and stood, surrounded by her guards, on the Palace steps. "Let this desert lunatic come before me with his claims that I am a false Queen," she said to her people. "I will prove that he is false by challenging him in mortal combat! The Goddess knows I am the true Queen!" "

Stopping briefly for effect, she waited a moment or two before continuing.

"As she spoke, one of the moons began to slide across the face of the sun, blotting out its light. When its disc reached the center, fire blazed forth across the sky, turning everything as red as freshly spilled blood. The wailing crowds parted in terror to let a lone male walk through them to stand in front of the false Queen. All who looked on his face saw that of the chief guard who had disappeared when Ishardia had been executed.

"I, the true Zsadhi, challenge you, in the name of the Goddess," he said, drawing his sword and holding it aloft. As he did, the moon passed away from the face of the sun, and the fire in the sky shot like a lightning bolt to his raised sword, bathing him in flames. When they died, light returned to the land, and Zsadhi had resumed his true form, and the people saw that there were two of him."

"So the Entities took a hand," murmured Kusac.

"Tashraka cast off her crown and her robes. Beneath them she wore armor made of glittering links of bronze that glowed like a banked fire. Drawing her own sword, she stepped forth to meet Zsadhi in combat," said J'korrash. "The fight was terrible, for Tashraka was no mean warrior. Anger and fear fueled her, for she knew the Goddess had kept her sister's husband alive and had hidden his true form in that of her lover. She flung her evil magics at him, but each time Zsadhi countered it with one of his own, one learned from the Goddess. Till dusk they fought, each taking grievous wounds, until at last Zsadhi's sword pierced Tashraka's evil heart, killing her. As she died, her own shape returned, and all could see she was indeed Tashraka and not Ishardia. At the same moment, her lover once more became the guard, and with a cry of rage, he flung himself at Zsadhi. Before he had taken three steps, the Royal guards turned on him and cut him down."

"What of Zsadhi?" asked Kaid.

"Zsadhi was wounded to death," J'korrash said. "He fell to his knees, his crimson blood spilling over the sand. But before he could die, the Goddess herself appeared, a bowl of water in her hands. She bade him drink, and miraculously he was healed. She told the people that he was their King, and he would rule over them justly until the time there was one worthy to take his place. For the first time ever, a male ruled alone in our land. His first acts were to condemn the sorceress to death by fire and to expose all of Tashraka's supporters and give them to the people to toil on their behalf in improving the lives they had ruined. He ruled for many years, fathering daughters to succeed him, though never marrying again. It was said he could see into the hearts and minds of people just by looking at them, but he was a good and just ruler. The tomb he built to honor his murdered Queen stands to this day by the Summer Palace. On it is inscribed this story."

"It sounds as though he had telepathic abilities," said Carrie.

"Well told, J'korrash," said Kaid. "I would never have sus-

…ed that there was such a legend among your people, given
…w male oriented it is now."

"That was the doing of another Queen, who chose to make
…ne males her warriors rather than risk her telepathic females,"
said J'korrash, sitting back and sipping her maush. "She was
the one who divided our people into castes. Our father has
memories of her and what she did. When the males rebelled
against her cruelty, she died horribly at their hands. They apparently slaughtered nearly every female, and those they did
allow to live, they put in harems and sedated them heavily so
they couldn't communicate mentally with each other."

"And so the Valtegans we know were born," said Kusac.
"What happened to Zsadhi?"

"It's said that Zsadhi didn't die," said J'korrash. "That when
his end was near, the Goddess came for him and took him to
her Realm. The people believe he sleeps still in her kingdom,
waiting for their time of dire need. Then, with fire and thunder and lightning, the Goddess will wake him once more. His
name has become legendary for truth and justice."

"Very similar to the Arthurian legends," said Carrie. "Arthur fought against his sister Morgause and their illegitimate
son. He killed Mordred but was mortally wounded. The Lady
of the Lake, a kind of Earth, or Mother Goddess, had him
taken to her Realm of Avalon to sleep until his country's hour
of greatest need."

"I don't care what happened to Arthur or Zsadhi, I have no
intention of dying like them," Kusac said, frowning. "Or waiting around for centuries like Vartra."

"Thank you for telling the story so well, J'korrash," said
Carrie, elbowing Kusac in the ribs.

"Yes, thank you," he added hastily, rising to his feet. "If
we're going to track down this new Lord Nayash, we'll have
to leave early in the morning, so I'm turning in now. All the
males will come with me. I'll take some of the females in their
scout masking suits and the chameleon ones, but I'll decide
who tomorrow. We'll dress in a mix of our khaki uniforms
and more casual clothing for now until we can get hold of
their regular uniforms. Kaid, Banner, and T'Chebbi will, of
course, remain, and Kaid will be our handler, as we'll constantly be broadcasting images from small cameras back to
him. Good night, everyone, and make sure you get a good
night's sleep."

"I've had enough of being a Valtegan," muttered Kusac he crawled into their tent after Carrie. "I want my own bo back."

"Can you do that inside the tent?" Carrie asked dubiously sitting on her sleeping bag and beginning to pull off some of her layers of clothing.

"Changing back is easier," he said, collapsing on his bag and hauling on his bootlaces. Taking the boots off, he tossed them to the rear of the tent and began stripping. When he was naked and shivering, he lay down on the bag and began to slow his breathing and concentrate.

He let the change flow through him, not fighting the pain when it came, letting it just wash over him. Then it was done, and he was Sholan—and warm—again.

"Come here," he purred, reaching out to help her undress and pulling her into his arms. "I need to remember who, and what, I am."

"You're the man I love," she murmured, using the Human word as she sank her fingers into his pelt, pushing her hands through the luxurious soft fur on his chest and belly. "It's so good to have you back as you."

He rolled her over onto her back, supporting his weight on his knees and one forearm as he pulled her sleeping bag over them both. Lowering himself gently on top of her, he eased her thighs apart gently with one knee then sighed as he matched his body to hers.

"We fit so well like this," he murmured, nibbling on her earlobe. "It never feels this right when I'm a Valtegan."

"Mmm," she said, eyes half closed in pleasure. "We can't do anything about it, though, with everyone else so close by."

"Says who?" he asked grinning at her, ears tilted toward her.

"Kusac," she said warningly.

"A Challenge!" he said happily. "I like Challenges like this. When I'm done, you'll not care how close the others are!"

"Kusac, no!" she whispered, trying to squirm out from under him as his hands caressed her and he began to lick and nibble his way across her jaw and down her throat.

The first tinges of light could be seen among the trees as he and Carrie ran through the snow, their hands and feet paws now, barely touching the surface as they seemed to skim over it. He angled closer to her, glancing briefly at her golden-pelted form before launching himself at her and bringing her down so they tumbled over and over in the powdery snow. They finally rolled to a stop under a tree, she lying on her back and he crouched possessively over her, his tail swaying gently from side to side.

"I never dreamed it would be like this," she said, her warm breath making clouds in the frosty air as he lowered his head to run his tongue along her jaw.

"Snow can be fun," he said, extending his right hand to scoop some up and rub it in her face.

She laughed, a deep purr underlying it as she batted at his offending hand with both of hers.

"The other dreams were never this vivid," she said.

He stopped, his body going rigid as he raised his head and sniffed the cold, crisp air. "This isn't a shared dream," he said quietly, bending his head to nuzzle her. "This is real."

"It can't be," she whispered, looking down at her golden Sholan body. "How can it possibly be real?"

"I have no idea, but it is," he said, stepping off her and sitting down on his haunches. "Look at us. We're different than we've imagined ourselves. Before, you looked as I visualized you would in Sholan form, but Gods, Carrie, you're far more beautiful than I could ever have imagined."

He reached out to take her hand and help her up. "I must look different to you."

She accepted his hand, settling herself on her own haunches, the last foot or so of her tail gently rising and falling as an indication of her confusion.

"You are different," she said slowly. "I see you with all my senses—your scent tells me more about you now, and there's another dimension to reading your body signals." She smiled, a Sholan smile as she lowered her jaw, teeth covered, yet the edges of her lips curled up. Leaning forward, she put her hand around his neck and kissed him.

"You do yourself an injustice," she murmured, drawing him closer, responding to subtle shifts in his scent. "You're far more beautiful than the youth you portray yourself as. The. a maturity about you that I love. Now I know what Tasia mea about the broken hearts our marriage would cause. How wɛ I so lucky to have you fall in love with me?"

I'm the lucky one, he sent as their kiss deepened and his hands slid down her sides, claws just extended, sending shivers through her.

She arched herself toward him, head back, throat exposed, submitting to him in the age-old mating ritual.

He growled deep in his throat, taking her gift, his teeth closing over her larynx and holding her there. He could feel her heart beating against his lips and tongue, smell her scent— intoxicating him now, driving common sense from his mind.

We should be worrying about how this happened, he sent, releasing her only to start gently nipping and licking his way down the side of her neck and along her shoulder.

"When we Linked last night—you showed me then. Right now," she whispered, "I only want to be your Sholan wife, be loved like a Sholan!"

I will—I am, he sent, raising his head to lick her ear briefly before sliding his arms behind her back to lay her down on the ground. Straddling her, his tail whipping from side to side, he threw back his head and let loose a growl that rose to a challenging roar that bounced off the trees around them.

Mine! he sent as they both felt Kaid's presence demanding to know where they were and what was happening. Even as Kaid backed off, he shut him out with a *Later* and lowered his head to bite and lick his way down her body, his claws raking through her fur, drawing sharp gasps of pleasure from her as her hands kneaded his shoulders before she drew her claws down his back, less gently.

There was no time for thought, only raw emotion. He moved lower, his nips less gentle, his tongue more searching, until her cry of need for him rang out in the forest.

Flipping her over, he pulled her up onto all fours then parted her long hair, his teeth closing on her scruff, and then he entered her, instantly swelling to his full arousal. Their minds, already Linked, spiraled around each other, taking them higher and higher until release came in an explosion of senses that left them clutching each other and gasping for breath.

They lay in the snow, bodies still shuddering as they began

turn to normal again. Around them, dawn was breaking, tinting the sky with rose, pink, and turquoise.

"That was . . . unprecedented," Kusac murmured, licking her cheek gently. "It's never been like that before."

Sated, Carrie could only muster a faint purr.

"We should get back to the caves. The Gods alone know how far we've come."

Kaid's still trying to reach us, she sent.

"I know." He sighed and moved, gently letting himself slide out of her despite her whimpers of protest. He licked her nose, chuckling. "You are a delightful Sholan, you know. Come on, we've a long day ahead of us, we need to get back."

"But I'm still Sholan," she said, sitting up to watch him rolling in the snow.

He stopped to grin at her, ears and tail twitching high in pleasure. "Yes, you are." He pounced on her, rolling her into the snow until she was alert and yowling her complaints. "Come on," he said, nudging her with his nose as they started to lope off back along their trail.

They were only ten minutes from the caves, and before they came in sight of the entrance, they reared up into an upright stance.

Nezaidu was on guard duty, and though she didn't bat an eyelid at Kusac, she did a double take when she saw Carrie.

"You know Carrie," he said, taking his wife's hand and pulling her to his side as he walked past her.

"Oh, Gods, what are they going to say?" murmured Carrie as they walked along the short tunnel into the main cavern.

"I have a rough idea," said Kusac, squeezing her hand as every head turned to look at them.

He knew exactly what impact she'd have on the Sholan males there. In Sholan form, she had a delicacy of body and movement that was belied by the reality of those who knew her. She was, quite literally, stunning to look at with her golden pelt and long hair. The color was rare among Sholans, only belonging to a few families, Kusac's being one of them. Several jaws dropped in shock as they saw her.

"Carrie?" said Kaid, blinking.

"Yep," she said brightly. "Don't ask how it happened because we woke up outside in the snow like this."

"We heard you," said Kaid dryly, putting his empty down.

T'Chebbi cuffed his ear. "You'd have done same," she chided him. "Not every day Carrie is Sholan!"

Kaid glared briefly at her, then looked back at them. "You must have changed her," he said to Kusac.

"Not necessarily," said Rezac, grabbing some hot food from the pans on the stove. "He showed me how to do it. She could have picked it up from him when they paired last night."

"I believe I did," she said, tail swaying slightly as she accepted a hot drink from T'Chebbi. *Tallinu, don't be mad at us. You have no idea how much I've wanted to be Sholan.*

He smiled at her. *Actually, I have, and I'm not really angry, just concerned.* "Can you change back, Carrie?" he asked. "That's more important, to be honest. We don't have armor and clothing for you as a Sholan."

"You're golden," said J'korrash, reaching out to touch Carrie's arm. "Just like the Captain's young sister."

"I thought I might be," she said. "A couple of years ago, I once nearly changed into a Sholan."

"Let's get you changed back," said Kusac reluctantly. "I think you're safer here as a Human. J'korrash, you're coming with us. Kushool, you, too. Get ready."

"Yes, Captain!"

"Save us some food, please," said Carrie over her shoulder.

Kusac, be careful. I don't want anything happening to Carrie by her trying to change again, sent Kaid.

Do you think I do? he asked as he and Carrie walked over to the tents. *Neither of us remembers anything. As she said, we were out running in the snow when we realized what had happened. You saw her almost change on the* Khalossa; *you know that. Every now and then, I do a kind of shared meditation with her, where we're both Sholan. We thought it was one of those.*

Be careful, please.

Of course, sent Carrie.

In the tent, Carrie sat on their sleeping bags, turning her hands first one way, then the other. "I remember looking at your hands for the first time," she said, letting them drop into her lap.

"It must seem strange to suddenly find yourself in a Sholan body," he said, sitting opposite her.

"Not really. I've felt myself at least a large part Sholan for

ong now that it seems as comfortable as my Human shape."
eside her, her tail thumped on the ground a couple of times
nd she grinned widely. "I like my tail, though."

He laughed, reaching out to touch her face. "And I like it
on you." He hesitated briefly. "I love you in this form, Carrie.
I've always wanted to run and hunt with you, but we couldn't,
till now. It doesn't mean I don't love your Human form . . ."

"I do understand," she said, covering his hand with hers. "I
don't have a problem with it, either, so long as I can change
again when I want to. At least I know how handsome you are
as a Sholan now," she grinned.

"Minx," he said, flicking her nearest ear. "Now lie down
and relax. Think of yourself back in your own shape and reach
for the energy of the earth beneath us; then just change back.
I'll be here monitoring you, and to help if need be."

She lay back, looking up at him. "Did you ever wonder how
I would look as a Sholan?"

"I suppose I did, even though I had a fair idea from the way
not only the Human males reacted to you, but also the Sholan
ones on the *Khalossa*. If you remember, I had to give you my
torc to keep them away from you," he said with a rueful grin.
"Now concentrate, or they'll have eaten all the food by the
time you're done!"

Her change, when it happened, was as fast as his last one had
been. One minute she was Sholan, the next, she was Human, shivering violently with the cold and the energy she'd expended.

"Oh, Gods, I feel awful, Kusac," she said, sitting up and
clutching one of the sleeping bags around her. "I think I'm
going to throw up."

He'd barely time to yell for a bowl for her and have one
thrust into the tent by T'Chebbi when she did. T'Chebbi also
had a bowl of water and a cloth and threw Kusac out to take
over looking after her.

I'm fine, really I am. I'm just exhausted, she sent to him as
he went over to the others around the stove. *It took more out
of me than I thought.*

You need to eat, he replied, grabbing plates and food for
them both. *Get some clothes on and join me.*

Once she'd eaten, she did feel better and was able to help
him with his clothes and boots when he changed back into a
Valtegan.

They moved out as soon as he was ready, the three fema
Carrie, J'korrash, and Kushool wearing the scent-maski.
one pieces under the chameleon suits, the others wearing un.
forms or off-duty clothing. The plan was for only Cheelar and
M'yikku to go into the village and buy local carry packs for
them all while the rest of them waited near the station. When
they rejoined, they'd all transfer their outer winter clothing
into them and find one of the luggage trucks on the train. That
way, those in the chameleon camouflage wouldn't run the
risk of being walked into by the locals and giving themselves
away.

There were several luggage cars attached to their train
when it arrived. They took over the end one, the seven of them
standing near the entrance glaring menacingly at anyone who
came near. The plan worked well, and as they began to approach the station some thirty minutes later, Kusac reminded
the females to keep in the center of their group at all times
until they reached the estate of the late Lord Nayash.

Despite the early hour, the station was fairly crowded, with
uniformed soldiers moving about in units, and farming folk
from various outlying estates and villages interspersed with
workers heading out of town to the factories.

They formed a tight knot around the three females, and
under Cheelar's lead, they made their way off to one side,
where one of the large maps stood.

I can see the map, Kaid sent to Kusac. *Taking an image of
it now so we have it for our own use later. Have you found
Nayash's estate?*

Yes, we need to get another train——one goes right to it.

What about the news vids?

*M'yikku has gone to check the nearest one out, and get us
tickets,* Kusac replied. *Should give us the time of the funeral.*

At that moment, M'yikku came jogging back to them.
"We've four hours," he said. "It said that the son, Shuzak
Nayash, arrived last night at his estate."

I heard, sent Kaid. *Better get going.*

Kusac gestured for them to move off toward the platform
where their train was waiting. They were doing fine until a
large civilian barged through the center of the group only to
walk straight into apparently nothing. He bounced back with
a cry of surprise on his lips, but not a sound came out as Kusac
swiftly grasped hold of his mind.

ith perfect timing, Rezac suddenly turned around, his
e bag swinging out to the side and neatly clipping the male
l in the body.

Reeling, the M'zullian stumbled and fell over, saved at the
last moment by Cheelar. What no one else saw was Rezac hit
him precisely behind the ear and knock him out.

With much fuss, Rezac and Cheelar escorted him over
to one of the nearby bench seats that lined the station and
helped him to sit down. Propping him up carefully, they left
him sitting there as if napping and swiftly rejoined the group
that had continued to make its way to their next train.

"That was almost fatal," muttered Kusac, frowning. "We
need our own transport!"

We'll have it when you take over this estate, sent Kaid.

This time, there were no empty luggage cars, and they had
to share it with two farm workers.

They put their bags in the corner, against the wall farthest
from the other males, then stood in front of them chatting
while Carrie and the other two females crouched down behind their luggage. Once they were concealed, Kusac and the
others settled themselves on the floor with the two workers.

"You heading to the Nayash estate?" asked the younger of
the two farm hands.

"Yes. Thought we better show ourselves at the funeral,"
said Cheelar. "You going there?"

The older one laughed. "Yeah, all his people gotta be there
to mourn him."

"Won't be much mourning going on, though," said the
younger. "Just hope his son's better'n he was. Didn't even give
us a holiday or a feast on the new Emperor's coronation like
he was supposed to do."

"Heard a rumor his death wasn't natural like they said,"
Cheelar said.

The two looked at each other, then the younger one began
digging in his pack.

"You better be keeping them kind of stories to yourself,"
said the older one, accepting the fruit that his companion
brought out of the pack. "I heard it ain't healthy to be spreading rumors about this new Emperor. You just down from the
mountains, then?"

Cheelar nodded.

Kusac had been passively reading their minds, and now he

spoke up. "Yes. Been up there a couple of years. Working the shokka crops up there."

The oldster nodded. "Only a few take to the mountain li. Most only last a season, two at tops, then ask for a transfe. down to the villages instead. Mountain folk are mighty close communities, but I reckon you know that."

"We like it well enough up there," said Kusac.

He cackled, biting into the fruit. "Aye, I'll bet you do! But I bet you never see hide nor scent of their females!"

"Get closer to them than we would down here!" Kusac leered.

"That's the truth! Ah, well, just be watching what you say at the funeral. There'll be plenty of them crimson robes about to pick up on the slightest hint of treason."

Damn! I forgot there'd be Inquisitors here, he sent to Kaid. *We'll need to be extremely careful.*

"Thanks for the warning," he said.

The trip only took them twenty minutes, and then they were pulling in at the local station. They took their time getting up and gathering their bags, wanting to leave after the two farm workers.

The elder stopped at the doorway and looked back at them. "Watch yourselves out there," he said. "Remember what I told you."

"We will, thanks," said Kusac.

They climbed out of the truck and joined the tail end of the crowd slowly making its way off the platform and down the access road to the estate. It was full daylight now, and the day's heat was beginning to build. As they got closer to the wall, they saw it wasn't a main entrance, it was one for goods, servants, and estate workers only. Two guards in dark green uniforms stood at either side of the metal gates, watching everyone as they filed in.

Sensing them notice their unfamiliar faces, Kusac sent to Rezac, telling him to divert the one on the left while he did likewise to the one on the right. As they drew level, both guards grew slightly restless, looking away from them.

He forgot he even saw us, sent Rezac,

Good, replied Kusac as they passed through into the estate grounds. *Make the workers forget us now.*

They hung back, waiting for the rest of the workforce to pass them so they could dive into cover as soon as they saw a suitable place.

mixture of trees marched up to the dirt road where they re—palmate and deciduous ones mixed. Ahead they could e them peter out to give way to fields of waist-high crops. In the distance, a large square building, two stories high, could be seen. Kusac signaled to them, and one at a time, they faded into the trees before they reached the fields.

A plan had been forming in his mind, and as they gathered together and headed deeper into the woodland, he explained it to them.

"We'll take Nayash after the burial. There are just too many ways I could slip up in an impersonation of him before then. Taking him later means I get more time to read him and absorb all the information I can."

"I take it we're killing him," said Carrie's voice quietly from beside him.

"Yes," said Rezac before he could answer. "He's too dangerous to leave alive."

"I know. I only asked because originally we said we might try to recruit him."

"We can't do that," said Kusac. "One look at a Sholan and he'll likely go into a killing frenzy."

"What about killing K'hedduk?" asked Kaid through the comm link.

"I'll create a diversion," said Kusac. "Rezac and J'korrash will be ready with sniper rifles. If Rezac misses, then J'korrash will take him out. Hopefully the distraction should keep their attention elsewhere, and we'll be gone when they notice he's dead."

"This is a good spot," said Rezac, stopping by a small clearing filled with bushes and the spiked runners of some wild fruiting plant. "We can hide our gear in the center of these bushes. No one in their right mind is going to look there."

"Do I hear a note of personal experience, Rezac?" asked Carrie.

"Yeah," he said with a wry laugh. "I was hiding a truck and trying to impress Zashou, only I got the thorny suckers caught in my clothing and on my legs instead. Very painful, to both ego and skin."

The three females chuckled gently and waited while the males got their weapons out of the bags, then stripped out of their uniforms and stowed them away. With much swearing and sucked fingers and hands, they thrust the bags into the center of the thorniest bushes and pulled branches ␣ them.

The camouflage suits, being made of slightly heavier mate␣ rials, had panels of blast-proofing in strategic chest, back, and groin areas to give them some kind of protection from energy weapons. It wasn't much, but it was better than nothing.

Kusac was the last to finish settling his throwing knives into their harnesses across his chest and down his thighs. Since they'd had no room to take the lightweight helmets on this mission, they had hoods with a fine mesh scarf they could fasten across their faces. Mics at their throats responded to subvocal speech; small earpieces completed their comm equipment. Toueesut had assured them that this system worked on a wavelength not available to the M'zullians, but they intended to use it only as a last resort, relying instead on the telepathic abilities of the females and them passing on instructions verbally to the nearby males.

The suits activated, they all vanished from sight.

"I'm going to use the Zsadhi legend at the funeral," said Kusac. "I'll need to call on you for energy, Carrie, as well as you, Kushool. Carrie, you gather from them and send it to me."

"You're going to trigger the gestalt to create the illusion of fire and lightning?"

"Hopefully the fire at least," he said. "For their bodies to be burned is the worst fate that can happen to a M'zullian or a Prime, so that will certainly have some effect. Just how localized it will be, we won't know till I try. What we need to do now is make our way to the graveyard and set up somewhere safe there so I can see the actual burial site. Remember to leave as few traces of our passage as possible."

They moved off, following Rezac and Kusac, who were picking their way carefully through the undergrowth.

We've managed to pick up one of the transmissions from the Palace newsroom, sent Kaid. *Cheelar was right—the young widow looks almost exactly like Zhalmo now.*

What's happening? he asked.

Very dramatic, was Kaid's dry reply. *Scenes of a black-draped female sobbing over the coffin and the Emperor looking magnanimous with his wife by his side; then she took the grieving widow away, and the coffin was placed on a gun car-*

*·iage before the procession headed off to the Emperor's chapel
in the main square.*

Above or below ground?

*Above. You should have a good three hours at least to get
into position before they finish the service and reach the estate.
I think they plan to fly the coffin and party out there. I'll keep
you posted.*

How are you picking this up? On the portable comm? sent
Kusac.

Yes. Glad T'Chebbi packed it.

Aye, he sent, and then passed on the news to Carrie to dis-
seminate to the others.

They took their time, moving slowly and carefully, with
Kaid updating them at regular intervals. Finally, with about
thirty minutes to spare, they came out on a low ridge over-
looking the outbuildings not far from the main house. Lying
flat in the long grass and crawling to the edge, they could see
a crowd gathering some distance away by a fenced area that
enclosed half a dozen elaborate small low buildings. Here and
there were dotted dark shapes that looked to be gravestones.

Pulling his binoculars from one of his leg pockets, he studied the area through them.

"That's the graveyard," said Kusac, handing the binoculars
to Rezac.

Are there many mourners? he asked Kaid.

*Some, but I reckon most are there for show, not out of friend-
ship. They should leave after the interment.*

"Is it the custom for them to have a meal at the house after
the funeral?" Kusac asked Cheelar.

"I don't know, Captain," he said. "We haven't exactly had
any experience of funerals on our world, let alone here."

"Rezac," he began.

"Seeing to it now," muttered Rezac. "Ah! Yes, there will be
some kind of food for the mourners. Even the workers will be
given something to eat to remember their old lord."

"In which case, we'll need to lie low until they're all gone,"
said Kusac.

"It'll make getting into the house easier if we don't," said
Rezac. "With so many of them coming and going, the doors
will be left open, even if they have guards all over."

"Too much risk of running into someone," said Kusac.
"We'll wait for nightfall."

They settled down to wait, pulling nutrition bars from their pockets to snack on.

"It's beginning to cloud over," said Carrie. "You might be able to call real lightning if this keeps up."

Kusac rolled over to look up at the sky. It was indeed clouding over in an ominous way. He rolled back and returned his attention to some movement off to one side of the estate.

They're on their way to you now, sent Kaid. *You should see them in a few minutes.*

"While I'm trying to create these illusions," Kusac said, "I don't want any of you watching them. Watch the funeral party for any sign they've spotted us or think the illusion is coming from this area. Warn me in plenty of time. Get those weapons ready just in case. Carrie knows the energy transfer drill, so, Kushool, just concentrate on what she tells you to do. The rest of you, remember, we telepaths will be dead on our feet when we finish, particularly me. Rezac, choose your vantage point. You too, J'korrash."

"Aye, Captain," they replied, moving stealthily up to the ridge.

Draw from the earth, came the quiet thought from right beside him.

Startled, he lifted his head and looked around. There was nothing to see, only the very faint mottling of the air, if you knew where to look, where his team members were lying in the grass.

He looked back down at the graveyard, seeing the funeral procession now as it wound its way along a tree-lined roadway to the graveyard entrance. He saw only one red-robed Inquisitor. A gentle breeze fanned his face, penetrating the mesh of his mask, bringing with it the scent of blossoms not of that world.

"The earth it is," he muttered.

"What?" asked Carrie from beside him.

"Nothing," he said, pulling off his gloves and handing them to her. "Thinking aloud."

He concentrated on the scene below him, wishing for the huntersight of his own body, surprised when it suddenly flicked on, giving him a much closer, though narrower view of the proceedings.

"Crap," he muttered. "You're unnerving me, stop it!"

"Me?" asked Carrie, hurt.

'No, Ghyakulla. Hush!"

"Abort assassination," said Kaid suddenly in his comm link. "K'hedduk's not there. He's sent some General instead!"

"Dammit!" muttered Kusac, sending the update to Rezac and J'korrash, who slithered hurriedly back down beside them. "We continue with the rest of the plan."

J'korrash swore volubly. "Bastard has more lives than is natural!"

"Silence!" hissed Rezac.

Kusac spread his fingers, digging them into the soil beside him, feeling his way into the earth, sensing the living creatures moving about in it, then the slumbering strength of the rock beneath. Taking a deep breath, he began to draw on the energy within it, to pull it into himself while at the same time Linking in to Carrie. Through her he felt the new surge of feminine energy as she brought in Kushool. Rezac joined their small circle, and he felt the gestalt spring to life, magnifying the power. It was like holding a live electric cable that spat and writhed around, trying to escape. Carefully, he began to weave the power and pull it within himself.

He imagined scarlet and yellow flames licking at the coffin, and then growing taller and taller, forming a pillar. Peripherally aware of the sound of distant cries of fear and terror, he opened his eyes as a peal of thunder rang out overhead. A pillar of twisting flames appeared to reach from the ground to the base of the low-lying clouds. Moments later, a flash of lightning rent the sky above it, arching down to the earth to hit the coffin. With a crack like the splitting of a great tree, the coffin exploded in a shower of sparks and shards of wood; then the heavens opened.

One minute the energy was being sucked out of him, leaving him empty and almost unable to move with exhaustion, the next, when the lightning struck the coffin and the ground, it surged back into him, leaving him gasping for breath as the rain sluiced over them all.

"Gloves first," said Carrie, grabbing hold of his hands and forcing them into the gloves. Then he was dragged down from the ridge top and under the cover of the nearby bushes.

"Cheelar, get up there with the binoculars and find out what's happening," ordered Carrie.

Moments later, the youth came sliding back down the soaking grass. "The party's broken up," he said. "There's a 'copter

overhead for the General, and most of the rest are headir
back to the house at a run. Wasn't safe to stay up there."

"Where's the drink for him?" demanded Carrie, pulling his
mask aside and rubbing his face. "Kusac, you all right? Talk
to me!"

He reached up to take hold of her wrist. "I'll survive," he
said, hearing the exhaustion in his voice. "That wasn't all me,
you know. Ghyakulla did the storm."

"I thought I smelled nung flowers," Carrie said, taking the
offered can of protein drink and breaking the heating seal.
"Here, drink this." she said, passing it to him. "Give Kushool
and Rezac one too."

"Everyone else all right?" he asked, waiting a moment or
two before raising the can to his lips.

"Feel like I've been hit with a sledgehammer," said Rezac,
taking the can J'korrash held out to him and gulping it down.

"We're all fine," said Carrie, taking her can gratefully from
J'korrash. "Seems to have taken more from you two than us."

"That was some light show," said Cheelar, carefully securing his binoculars back in his pocket. "The rain was a good
touch. It drove them all away with no chance of them coming
looking for anyone up here, even if they suspected someone
had caused it."

"Did the rain put out the illusory flames?" he asked, down-
ing the drink now it had cooled enough for him.

"What illusion? They were real," said Cheelar. "And no, it
didn't. The coffin was still burning."

The rain was lessening now, as if it had just been a sudden
summer storm.

"Check again, please," he said.

Cheelar was back within a couple of minutes. "The rain's
stopped now, and the flames too. The coffin is burned to a pile
of ashes, and there's no sign of anyone there."

"That certainly sent a message to everyone, loud and clear,"
said J'korrash. "I'd say that the locals will spread the rumor
about the Zsadhi no matter what spin K'hedduk puts on it."

"Let's get out of here," said Kusac, stumbling to his feet and
closing the mask over his face. He crushed the can and shoved
it in his thigh pouch. "Try to leave no traces behind. K'hedduk
is going to know that it wasn't completely a divine intervention and will have the area searched as soon as he regains his
wits and courage."

What do you mean not completely a divine intervention?"
ed J'korrash.

"He didn't cause the storm or the rain," said Carrie, giv-
ng Kusac a hand. "It was one of the Entities, Ghyakulla, the
Earth Goddess."

"Oh," said J'korrash in a quiet voice.

"The Zsadhi, the original one," said M'yikku, "was helped
by La'shol, our Earth Goddess."

I take it everyone is all right, and it went well, sent Kaid.

You could say that, replied Carrie. *One trashed and burned
coffin, a fifty-foot pillar of flames, and a storm, with lightning,
then a torrential and short rainfall to finally drive them all away
or indoors. Yeah, it went well.*

*Ghyakulla made sure our people know their legend was re-
sponsible and that I'm it,* sent Kusac unhappily as they made
their way carefully along a narrow animal track back down
the ridge.

Isn't that what we want? asked Kaid compassionately.

I wasn't expecting Her help, Kusac muttered.

A wind was blowing, a warm one, laden with the scents of
summer—damp grass and blossoms—and the heat was rising.
It wouldn't be long until the ground underfoot was dry again.

Are you and Rezac recovered enough to go on? Kaid asked.

Aye, sent Rezac.

Yes, Kusac said.

*Be careful, and good luck. I'll let you know what news the
Palace puts out, but I think you can be certain they'll say nothing until the rumors start to grow loud in a few days' time.*

Stay safe yourselves, he sent.

They cut across the grounds, still sticking to the margins
where there was cover from trees and bushes, heading toward
the main building.

M'zull, the Palace

"How high was the pillar of flame?" demanded K'hedduk.

"We only have ground observers' word for it, but they say
about two thousand feet," said Zerdish.

K'hedduk slowly lowered himself into the chair behind desk. "How many were killed?"

"None, Majesty. Only the coffin of the late Lord Naya. was burned. The local people are saying the pillar was no natural."

"Of course it wasn't natural," snapped K'hedduk, recovering his composure.

"I meant they are attributing it to divine action," said Zerdish carefully.

The TeLaxaudin sitting on the cushions near the desk stirred and began to hum. "I told you wiser not to go," Lassimiss said through his translator.

K'hedduk ignored the small alien. "And just who do they attribute it to?"

"To the Zsadhi," said his aide reluctantly.

"Superstitious peasants," muttered K'hedduk. "Get the propaganda department to come up with a rational reason for it, and get it broadcast on all the news stations as soon as possible!"

"Yes, Majesty," said Zerdish, bowing.

Lassimiss unfolded himself and got to his feet. "I go now. This you deal with, not me." He stalked off to his enclosed carrier and disappeared inside it.

K'hedduk turned his thoughts back to the pillar of flame as the TeLaxaudin left his office. He had to ensure that this rumor was snuffed out as quickly as possible. Leaning forward, he thumbed his comm unit.

"Get me Inquisitor Ziosh," he said.

CHAPTER 21

THOUGH the front of the house was square with an imposing pillared facade and long driveway, the rear had seen several additions over the years. Behind the high wooden fence, it sprawled out to either side of the main building, bracketing a heated swimming pool. Set to one side of it was the obligatory island.

"I remember hearing that they only considered open water as holy," murmured J'korrash as they concealed themselves amid the thick bushes and trees.

The large pool dominated the garden. Beyond it was a tiled area that led up to the rear of the house and the three covered lanais, or porticos, where the new Lord Nayash was entertaining the remaining funeral guests.

Tables covered with a variety of food stood against the walls of the largest lanai, and sandy-skinned servants, obviously drones, moved among the guests with trays of drinks. Counting the two guards at the front entrance, Kusac could see another four, each wearing a green armband, presumably for mourning. There were twenty guests, including Nayash, and four servants as well as a couple of kitchen staff inside.

"They're trying to work out what happened," whispered Carrie from beside him. "They seem to be convinced it was sabotage by a rival House. Their tempers are high, mainly to hide their fear."

"I can't sense anyone even thinking about the Zsadhi legend," he said as an altercation broke out among a small group of males.

Saboteurs are good, sent Kaid. *Who are they blaming?*

No one person yet, Kusac replied, watching as a male dre
in dark green fatigues moved over to calm them down.

*These courtiers won't know the Zsadhi legend well, if th
know it at all,* came Rezac's thought. *If he's a savior of th
downtrodden, then the workers and servants will think of him
soon enough.*

Find out who the elite blame, Kaid sent. *We may hit them
next, or one of their allies.*

Well, we have a fair idea of who their allies are today, Kusac
replied. *Which one's the new lord?* he sent to J'korrash.

The one by himself near the fountain, she replied, drawing
his attention to the figure out on the tiled area, dressed in dark
green with an abundance of gold braid. *Looks like an under-
dressed Touiban. Don't feel sorry for him—he hated his father
for taking a much younger wife that he himself wanted.*

Kusac smothered a laugh at her description. *No brothers
or sisters?*

One older brother who died in a ship out at J'kirtikk.

We'll wait till nightfall, Kusac decided. *There are just too
many people about right now. Pass the word on; I want everyone staying alert. No food until they all go inside. You can
drink, though—stay hydrated at all costs, but be silent. Carrie,
you three females keep an eye on our rear, please, see no one
approaches. We males will watch the building.*

Right, she sent.

It was a long day for them. Thankfully the reception broke
up just after noon; then Nayash sent his guards down to the
workers' dormitory building to take some laborers with them
to the graveyard to investigate his father's remains. Apart from
the servants clearing up, the rear of the house was deserted.

"Eat now while you can," Kusac said quietly, rolling on his
side to get the empty can that he'd been lying on for several
hours out of his pocket. He crushed it, then put it in a sealed
pack and stowed it in one of his side belt pouches and pulled
out an instant paste meal and a nutrition bar.

I hate field rations, sent Carrie, reluctantly sucking on her
paste. *What you having, Tallinu?*

Stew, sent Kaid, with a laugh in his voice. *Banner caught a
rabbitlike beast this morning when he went out to scout around
the area.*

Bastard, she sent good humoredly.

Think of me when you get settled in there and are eating cordon bleu cooking!

Might not be that good on this world with their restricted diet, she replied, pulling a face as Kusac grinned at their interchange.

So long as it isn't laced with laalquoi, I'll be happy, he sent, stowing the remains from his meal in his garbage bag and returning it to the pouch.

They settled down again to wait, as the day got hotter.

The sound of laughter from inside the house roused them from their heat-induced stupor.

It's Nayash, sent Kusac, reaching out for the young lord. *He's heard that his father's remains have been burned almost to ashes. Nice son.*

A series of orders to have what was left put into the grave anyway, and have it covered over, were sent over a comm unit.

He's coming out! warned Carrie.

Flanked by two of his guards, Nayash, wearing only swimming shorts with a towel thrown over his shoulder, came out from the far right onto the lanai. Cutting across to his left, he made for the steps down to the pool and the loungers by a table set under some palm trees off to their right. As he threw his towel over the lounger and headed for the pool, the guards took up positions at opposite ends of the garden.

"It's all right for some folk," muttered Jo quietly as Nayash began swimming across the pool.

I'm going to have to find a way to cover up that damned tattoo, Kusac sent to Carrie, Kaid, and Rezac. *At least until I need it, if I do. Looks like this guy is the outdoors type, given a chance. Plus, I have a feeling water is more than just social here.*

I'd love a swim, sent Carrie wistfully. *These suits don't keep us completely cool. I feel like I'm being broiled here.*

I'll see that all you females at least get a shower as soon as I can, he promised, patting her arm.

Perhaps it was a mistake taking them with you, sent Kaid.

Rubbish. They are the start of my harem, sent Kusac with a laugh.

Start? said Carrie ominously.

Maybe I should rephrase that, he sent, backtracking.

I think you better, sent Carrie, ignoring muffled chuckles from J'korrash and Kushool.

Nayash got out on the small island and wandered about there for a while, shifting various pieces of furniture and uprooting the odd small ornamental flowering tree, which he tossed to one side near the water's edge.

Seems the females get to swim here too, sent Kusac, surprised. *He's getting rid of things his stepmother liked. You may get your swim yet, Carrie, if you can sustain an illusion long enough, and if we dispense with the guards.*

Sounds good to me.

Nayash dove back into the pool and swam a few more circuits before going to relax in the jet pool at the far end.

He'd only been there a few minutes when one of the guards he'd sent to the graveyard came out to make a report in person.

"We've done as you asked, Lord Nayash. While we were there, an officer from the Palace arrived to check over the scene. He was not pleased we were burying the remains."

"It's none of their business," said Nayash. "What else did he want?"

"He poked about in the dirt and ashes looking for signs of how the pillar of flames was generated. Then, when he found nothing, he took three of the workers and began to search around the area for signs of intruders."

"Did he find anything?"

"The workers said no, but he was using a comm link to report to the head of the Emperor's Security at the place. He said the incident had posed a threat to the Emperor and had to be thoroughly investigated."

"If they found nothing, there's nothing they can do. What were your impressions?"

The guard hesitated. "I think he may believe you arranged it, Lord Nayash. However, the workers, superstitious as ever, are saying it was the Zsadhi."

"They're superstitious fools, as you said. Tell the foreman that if I hear any more of this Zsadhi nonsense, there will be repercussions. As for the authorities thinking it was me, even I wouldn't do something quite so obvious, and they know that. Give them all the help they need if they come back, but keep me posted. Dismissed."

The guard saluted and left.

Seems our lordling is known to be something of a rebel, sent Kusac. *And we have the Zsadhi rumor starting now.*

Let's hope they don't try to pin the blame on Nayash, Rezac
nt. *It could make life here difficult for us.*

We'll deal with it later, came Kaid's thought. *If they can't
find any evidence against him, or a motive, then they can't really
do anything about it.*

Something to take into consideration, though, sent Kusac.

The sun was finally beginning to sink in the sky, and welcome shadows were falling across the garden when the young
M'zullian finally got out of the pool. Grabbing his towel, he
headed indoors again, followed by his two guards.

He hasn't plans to leave for the city tonight, has he? asked
Kaid.

*No. He intends to stay home, and he's calling his unit billeted
in the city. He wants them replacing his father's guards,* sent
Rezac.

*And as the new lord, he's putting in an application for a wife
as well as a promotion commensurate with his new rank,* added
Kusac.

Wise. He's surrounding himself with his own people, said
Kaid. *You'll have to reassign a few, or at least replace them with
some of ours.*

I can't spare more than two, sent Kusac. *We need people in
other locations than the capital.*

Not if they can move about freely.

*Too risky. I want Rezac to take over another House, a mili-
tary one and not an ally to me, and set up there.*

Let's get you well established first, sent Kaid. *You should be
able to win some of your people over to your side, and then we
can see about placing Rezac.*

Don't I get a say in this? asked Rezac plaintively.

No, sent Kaid.

Yes, said Kusac.

We'll see, temporized Kaid.

Night had fallen several hours before when finally a car
drew up at the front of the house.

The new guards, sent Rezac quietly, it being his turn on
telepathic guard duty.

Kusac rolled over and mentally latched onto where Rezac
was scanning. "Four of them, not personal friends, but trusted,"
he said.

"The six inside are getting ready to leave," Rezac said. "The

replacements will report in, then go to their quarters abo̅
the garage. Two will go on patrol outside the building for t̅
next six hours, then change over with the other two."

"Let's move this along," muttered Kusac. ""We've waited
long enough."

Mentally he reached out for the young lord, finding him
in the downstairs family room. Swiftly pushing past the natural mental barrier into his mind, he began to make Nayash
feel drowsy. When the steward announced the Sergeant of
the Guard, Nayash stood up, smothering a yawn, and greeted
him.

Nayash gave him a password for the night, and the Sergeant
left to escort the six guards off the premises before joining the
other three in their quarters and allocating guard duties.

Nayash, now yawning deeply, made his way upstairs to his
old room above the master suite in the west wing.

Within half an hour, the house had settled down for the
night, and the two guards were doing their rounds. Kusac
waited long enough to be able to time their appearance before moving out.

"I'll take point with Cheelar. J'korrash and Rezac take the
rear," he said.

Quiet as shadows, they slipped across the tiles and into the
main lanai. The easiest way into the house from the rear was
through the outdoor kitchen.

They stopped by the door into the main building, making
sure none of the servants was stirring, then opening the door
silently, Kusac led them in.

On their right, the family room was a large open space with
no walls or doors. Opposite it were the two entrances to the
main kitchen. Darting across to a pair of square pillars, Kusac
signaled the others to follow.

There was a small bar on their right, and next to it, a curved
staircase leading to the floor above. Cheelar slipped forward
to the next pillar, stopping briefly before going on to the one
beyond it. Now that he had a clear view of the staircase, he
gestured them to join him.

Hugging the wall, they took the stairs two at a time. Again,
much of this floor was open plan. Ahead was an entertainment
room, with wall-mounted screens and consoles. To their right
was a narrow curved corridor with a view down to the living
room below on one side and the foyer on the other. It led to

two bedrooms in the west wing. Nayash, fast asleep, was in one on the right.

Rezac joined Kusac at the front of the group as they quietly made their way to the door. Signaling for Cheelar to accompany them into the room and for the rest to remain on guard outside, Kusac reached again for the M'zullian's mind. This time, he knocked him out cold.

Once inside, Rezac dug out the rope he carried. He swiftly tied the youth up and taped his mouth shut. Cheelar grabbed a chair, bringing it over so they could tie him to it.

Kusac sat down on the bed while the other two positioned the chair opposite him. Taking a deep breath, he powered off his chameleon suit and ordered Rezac and Cheelar to do the same. Then, reaching forward to take the M'zullian's head in his hands, he began matching the frequency of his mind to the young lord's. Slowly he began gathering enough information to change into the other's likeness.

Inside the house, there was no earth to use as an energy source, so calling on Carrie to help, he began to visualize the features in front of him as his own.

There was less for him to alter in this change than in a full body one from Sholan to Prime. Instead, the changes were subtle; Nayash was a tad shorter, not quite so athletic in build, and his face was rounder.

How does that look? he sent to Rezac when he'd completed it.

Rezac studied them both carefully. *Good,* he sent. *I wouldn't be able to tell you apart from looks alone.*

Cheelar handed him a glass of water taken from the night table by the bed. He drank it gratefully.

"Wake him, please," he whispered, handing the glass back.

A couple of slaps to the face and Nayash's eyes flew open. Struggling against the bonds, he took one look at Kusac and tried to yell for help before realizing his mouth was taped shut.

Kusac seized control of his mind again, rendering him still and speechless, and began probing, this time for all that made Nayash an individual, all his memories, all his hopes and allegiances—everything.

The youth sat there as if frozen, his face paling as Kusac meticulously worked his way through every thought pattern he could find, absorbing them into his own mind, making them his.

Pale and shaking himself, Kusac finally let Nayash go. "G
you are a piece of work," he said, looking at the M'zulliaɲ
contempt. "You're only twenty, and you've backstabbed aɹ
lied your way to Lieutenant Commander on your ship already
It's going to be a pleasure to replace you. Oh, and you're going
to have an epiphany because of your father's funeral. From
now on, you're going to deal honorably with your men!"

He laid his hand against the youth's chest, feeling the beating of his heart, then sent a short surge of energy through it.
Nayash stiffened, his eyes rolling back in his head before he
slumped against Cheelar and Rezac.

"Get a sheet or a large towel and lay him on it," Kusac said
tiredly.

"He's dead?" asked Cheelar, looking from him to their
prisoner.

"Yes," said Rezac shortly, letting the dead youth go and
heading for the en suite bathroom to fetch a large towel.

"Call the others in," said Kusac. "We can base ourselves
here for the time being. There are walk-in closets large enough
for us to hide in until I can get some of you officially installed
here."

"What about the body? In this heat, he'll get ripe very
quickly, and there's nowhere we can really bury him safely."

"We'll bury him on the island. Go get the others," he repeated, lying back on the bed.

When Rezac returned with the towel, the others had come
in and fanned out to explore the room, finding the closets on
either side of the bathroom.

Kusac sat up as Rezac and Cheelar placed the body on the
spread out towel. "He was digging up plants, so with any luck,
there should be some holes deep enough."

"Leave it to us," said Cheelar, gesturing to M'yikku to help
him.

"Take J'korrash. She can sense if the guards are coming,"
said Kusac, beginning to unseal his chameleon suit. "I need to
get out of this and into his clothes."

"You need food badly. Any chance you can get some sent
up here?" asked Carrie. "I think we're all ready for something
real to eat."

He laughed gently as he stood up and stripped off the suit.
"Yeah, I could do with something to eat. I feel sick and shaky
right now."

only did what you had to do, she sent. "I'll go get you
thing of his to wear. What did he have on?"

"Shorts and a T-shirt," said Kusac, sitting down on the bed
again.

Carrie reached out to squeeze his shoulder. "You'll be glad
to know your tattoo is gone," she said softly.

"Really?" he asked, looking down at his bare chest, then
feeling it to be sure. "I can feel it, but only just," he said." I was
worried how I was going to cope with it."

"I'll go get a shirt and shorts," she said, going over to the
dresser by the bed and opening drawers. Moments later she
came back with them.

Cheelar and M'yikku were gone about half an hour, but
J'korrash kept them up to date with a running commentary.
There had indeed been a hole deep enough for the body, and
they'd been able to bury it easily there.

"I'll try to do something more permanent with it tomorrow," he said when they returned.

"Someone's coming," said Rezac suddenly, grabbing
J'korrash. "An aircar, landing outside!"

They scattered to the closets, taking Kusac's gear with them,
leaving him standing alone in the bedroom.

It's an Inquisitor, sent Rezac as they heard the doorbell
sound.

"Crap!" muttered Kusac, diving into the bed and throwing
the covers over himself. At this time of night, an Inquisitor
could only be here because K'hedduk had sent him. He prayed
that his experiences on Keiss would help him keep his act together long enough to not make the Inquisitor suspicious.

Trying to relax, he began to access all the memories he'd
taken from Nayash. How did he view Inquisitors? Did they
intimidate him? Did he have anything to hide? Was he even
perhaps in league with them? All these questions and more
were tumbling through his mind, preventing him from concentrating on actually being Shuzak Nayash.

A tapping sounded at his door, and his name was called out
in a low voice.

"Enter," he said, sitting up.

The door opened and his steward stood there nervously in
a dressing gown. "Lord Nayash, it's Inquisitor Ziosh. He's in
the study."

"Thank you, Laazif," he said, getting up. "When he's gone,

bring some sandwiches and shokka up here. I can't slee[ ]
haps a snack will help."

"Yes, sir, of course."

Trying to collect his scattered thoughts, Kusac grabbed t[ ]
robe thrust out of the closet at him by Carrie and made h[ ]
way downstairs to the study. He knew Nayash had a problem
with authority and an overinflated view of his own abilities
as a leader, but how did he relate to the Inquisitors? Did he
know this Inquisitor Ziosh?

As he entered the room and the carmine-robed Inquisitor
turned around, he suddenly knew this was K'hedduk's High
Priest—and head of the Order on M'zull.

His heart began to beat faster even though he knew that his
team was only a thought away.

"Inquisitor Ziosh," he said, walking over to the desk to lean
negligently against it. "To what do I owe the pleasure of your
late visit?"

Ziosh regarded him for a moment, and then removed his hands
from where they were tucked into his wide sleeves. "Congratulations on your inheritance, Lord Nayash. His Majesty hopes you
will find your new status more to your liking."

Kusac blinked, surprised, and hastily searched for anything
in Nayash's memories to give him a clue as to what Ziosh was
inferring. There was nothing.

"Thank you, but I'm afraid I don't follow your . . ."

"It's well known," interrupted Ziosh, "how little in common you and your father had, especially after his latest marriage. His Majesty bade me inform you that he will look after
your former stepmother and that you need not concern yourself over her."

"I have no doubt of that," he said dryly. He did know that
Nayash had wanted the female for himself. "As the head of the
house, that was my responsibility."

"You were on deployment at the time. The need to act
quickly lest one of your rivals took her for himself was para-
mount," said Ziosh smoothly.

Nayash would not let this go unchallenged.

"I see. And should I wish to take on the responsibilities of
a dutiful stepson?" He arched an eye ridge.

"Unnecessary. His Majesty provides for all his subjects."

"But it is my duty."

Ziosh moved closer, his robes making a slight susurration

as they brushed across the polished wooden floor. "Then I would, regrettably, be forced to look more closely at certain—irregularities in your past. And that brings me to the purpose of my visit. Your father's funeral."

Kusac straightened up, looking uncomfortable. "Ah, yes. The pillar of flame."

"Indeed. Do you have any knowledge of what caused it?"

"Knowledge, no. I was as shocked as anyone when it appeared. I sent my guards down to search for clues, then workers to bury what was left of my father and his coffin. Some officials from Palace Security have already been to inspect the scene. "

"What did they find?"

"Nothing beyond his charred remains."

Ziosh moved closer still, till he stood almost toe-to-toe with Kusac. "Sabotage!" he hissed.

"Excuse me?" He assumed a puzzled expression.

"It was an act of sabotage, maybe even an assassination attempt against His Majesty! If affairs of state hadn't demanded his attention, I fear he would be lying dead, along with your father, in that blasted hole!"

He dropped the nonchalant pose, suddenly extremely concerned. "You can't think I would want to assassinate the Emperor, or sabotage my father's funeral?"

"That is indeed the question. I would hate to think your enmity for your father would allow you to commit such a blasphemous act," said Ziosh, taking a step back. "You know the penalty for blasphemy and attempted regicide?"

"Why would I risk everything by committing such a crime?" he demanded. "I now own everything I wished for!"

Ziosh let a small silence fall. "Apart from your stepmother." His voice fell like pebbles in a still pool.

Kusac hurriedly raised his hand to touch his heart then his lips in the age-old sign of obeisance to the Emperor. "From my heart to my words, may the Emperor live forever! He protects her now, you have reassured me of that. My duty as a son is fulfilled." He forced his mind to stillness, then gently opened it, hoping to pick up at least the surface thoughts of the priest.

Ziosh studied him carefully before nodding his head, once, slowly. "Indeed. To burn your father's body would be to condemn his soul to the eternal fires and prevent him from taking his rightful place at the feet of the Emperor."

"If he has a soul." The words were said before Kusac could stop them.

The High Priest's mood changed abruptly, and he chuckled. "As you say, the late Lord Nayash was not known for his piety. I trust you will remember your duties to the Holy Church," he said, folding his hands once again inside the sleeves of his robe and turning away. "I will send Church soldiers tomorrow to collect your father's remains for examination. I want to know what caused that pillar of fire. Good night, Nayash. I'm glad we had this little chat. I will see myself out."

Kusac mumbled a good-bye, leaning back in relief as he watched the carmine-robed priest stride out of the room. He sent a brief reassuring thought to a frantic Carrie and Kaid, letting them know all was well.

What the hell had the younger Nayash been up to, or was this just Ziosh's attempt to assert his power over the new lord? He examined what little he'd managed to pick up from the Inquisitor—Ziosh had been the power behind the throne on M'zull, ruling through K'hedduk's brother. Had he been able to muster the support, K'hedduk would not be ruling here today. Now he was building his own power base, and he was looking to Nayash to be part of it. He groaned, quickly stifling it as his steward returned.

"Shall I bring the food to your room, sir?" Laazif asked.

Kusac stirred and looked over at him. "Yes. Bring it now," he said, pushing himself away from the desk. "And make that a large pot of shokka!" he added, heading back upstairs.

Laazif placed the large tray of sandwiches and the insulated jug of shokka on the desk near the door. "Will there be anything else, sir?" he asked, edging backward toward the door.

"No. You may retire for the night," said Kusac, waving him away as he got to his feet and headed for the food like a starveling.

As you said, what a piece of work that Nayash was, sent Carrie, cautiously emerging from the closet. *Even the staff was terrified of him!*

Only one mug? sent Rezac plaintively as they all silently emerged and clustered around the food.

I could hardly ask for more, sent Kusac, pouring a generous amount into the bowl then taking a large gulp before handing it to Carrie.

J'korrash waved a plastic beaker at them and grabbed for the shokka. *From the bathroom,* she sent. *You just need to be inventive, Rezac.*

Grabbing several sandwiches, Kusac headed back to the bed and sat down, taking the time to mentally answer all Kaid's anxious questions while he ate, and update him on what he'd learned from the Inquisitor.

"There's a power play going on here," he said very quietly to the others. "That was the Head Inquisitor. He manipulated the last Emperor and is displeased K'hedduk isn't such an easy puppet. He's looking to Nayash to support him against K'hedduk."

"As Kaid says, we'll have to get more intel on that," said Carrie. "Was Nayash aware of all this?"

"No. I'll need to get up to speed as soon as I can on the politics here. There's nothing I can do right now."

You'll likely have one of K'hedduk's people making an overture to you too, sent Kaid.

Probably.

There's a comm unit here, Kusac, sent J'korrash, still over at the desk. *And it's linked into a network at the Palace. Have you the password? I'll see what I can access from here.*

Kusac sent it to her, widening their telepathic channel so all the telepaths could "hear" each other.

See if you can access your troop records, sent Kaid. *Maybe J'korrash can hack into them and add in our people. Make it easier to have them assigned to you personally.*

I can do that, J'korrash replied, snatching the plastic beaker from her brother as she worked on the comm. *Interesting. You have lands on the mountains adjacent to the one where our base is. Several settlements and farms, one of them quite large.*

Military, J'korrash, sent Kaid gently. *Concentrate. I know it's late and you're all tired.*

I want to contact them, interrupted Kusac. *You know, they seem to be more like the Ch'almuthians. We may find allies there.*

Make yourself secure first, sent Kaid.

Got it! interrupted J'korrash. *The ground troops are in the barracks near the main city right now, waiting further deployment orders from the Palace, and some of the naval ones are based there on leave for a few days because of the funeral. Where do you want them? Military or Naval?*

Military, sent Kusac. *That'll explain their skills.* Then to Kaid on a private channel, *I am making us secure, I'm just looking ahead as well.*

How many names do you want added to the roster? J'korrash asked. *And what names shall I use? My brothers' names seem to be common here, as they all appear on the lists somewhere.*

Put down five. Find a name for Rezac, Kusac replied. *Might as well make sure you're on it for now to explain your presence here.*

Rezac nodded in agreement.

Done, she said, typing quickly. *Rezac is Rezikk. It's as near as I can get. I'm adding retroactive orders, matching the time Nayash sent his guards, for them to report here tomorrow. Exiting now. Trick is not to stay on too long and draw attention to myself,* she sent, turning back to join them by the bed where they all sprawled or sat.

Can we get them to send out kit separately? Say it went missing in transit somewhere? asked Rezac. *We need the extra bedding and stuff for the females.*

You can just call them up normally for that, sent Kushool. *If their bureaucracy is anything like ours was, the right hand won't know what the left hand is doing.*

Don't they need paper orders or something? asked Carrie.

"Your orders are being delivered by courier tomorrow first thing," J'korrash whispered to her brothers. "If you leave just before dawn and hide out in the garden, you can arrive as soon as the courier has left."

"Well done, J'korrash," whispered Kusac, hearing Kaid echo him mentally. "For now, go settle down in the closets. It'll be light in another six hours, so let's get some sleep. I want one telepath on with one of us males . . ."

"I'll sort that," J'korrash whispered quietly. "You and Rezac get bedded down, you've expended the most energy. You too, Carrie. Cheelar and Kushool, you take the first two hours, M'yikku and I will go next, and Carrie and Rezac can take the last watch."

Time we all slept, Kaid sent as their group broke up silently to find comfortable spots to sleep. *Be safe, my kin.*

You, too, Tallinu, replied Carrie as Kusac reached out to pull her close.

Sleep well, Brother, sent Kusac.

Prime world, same day

The day was beautiful, thought Conner. The sky was that deep summer blue bordering on cerulean, and the courtyard sparkled in the sunlight as it glinted off the newly repaired white marble buildings. A warm breeze sighed through the palm trees, keeping the temperature from climbing too high. Straightening up, he looked around to check on his charges. All were busily replanting flowering plants, raised in the Palace greenhouses, into the decorative containers that lined the fronts of the main buildings.

"Good day, Brother Conner," said a lilting Sholan voice from behind him.

"Good day to you, Sister Kitra," he said, turning with a smile to face her. "Have you come for Shaidan?"

"Yes. Dzaka and I are taking him to the market for second meal today," she said, mouth dropping in a wide grin. "He's gone ahead to order for us."

"He'll enjoy that," said Conner as Kitra, seeing Shaidan at the other end of the courtyard, began waving enthusiastically to him.

"So will I. Dzaka has been promising to take me for weeks now."

"It's very good of you to share your treat with Shaidan."

She laughed. "It's twice the treat with him along," she said as the cub ran over to her and skidded to a halt beside them.

"Hello Aunt Kitra," he said. "Is it time to eat?" He was barely able to stand still, and his tail was twitching in suppressed excitement.

"Yes, kitling, it is," she said, reaching out to hug him. "Give Brother Conner your trowel, then go and wash your hands and we'll be off."

"Where are we going?" he asked, almost dropping the trowel in his rush to get rid of it. "Are we going to the market?"

"Thank you, Shaidan," said Conner, trying not to smile as he accepted the earth-covered garden implement.

"Yup, Dzaka's there now. Shoo! Hurry up! I'll wait for you at the fountain," she said, flapping her hands at him as his face

broke into a huge widemouthed Human grin and he ran ⊂
into the temple.

"He really looks forward to these outings," said Conner,
walking with her over to the central fountain. "I was worried he'd feel totally bereft with his parents going off on the
M'zullian mission."

"He did," said Kitra, glancing up at him as she smoothed
down her off-duty tunic before sitting on the edge of the fountain. "He was beside himself with grief when they left. We
didn't dare leave him alone all that day. Even took him to bed
with us that night."

"I had no idea," murmured Conner. "He hid it very well."

"He's just like my brother," she said wryly. "Torn apart inside, and you'd never know it. But a couple of days later, he
changed, suddenly became more positive about everything."

"I'm sure you and Dzaka were responsible for that."

"Some," she said. "Doctor Zayshul makes a point of seeing him every couple of days too, but it's more than just what
we're doing. I have a feeling he can sense my brother somehow. They are very closely bonded, you know."

"I hope that's not a bad thing," said Conner. "If anything
should happen to him . . ."

"Nothing will happen to Kusac, or Carrie," said Kitra
fiercely. "It can't. They've been through too much already. And
if it did, he'd make sure none of it leaked out to Shaidan."

"You're right, I'm sure," Conner agreed, seeing Shaidan in
his slightly grubby white tunic emerging again from the temple. "Well, time for me to gather up the others for their lunch,"
he said, getting up. "Enjoy your meal, Kitra. Whatever it is that
you are doing, keep it up because Shaidan has finally become
a normal ten-year-old cub."

"Can we go now?" Shaidan asked breathlessly, reaching for
Kitra's hand as she got to her feet. "We shouldn't keep Uncle
Dzaka waiting, should we?"

"Absolutely not, Shaidan," she laughed.

Shaidan had never been to the marketplace outside the
Palace. Though still inside the City walls, it wasn't considered
a safe place for the cubs, or the Prime children, to go alone.
With all the damage that had been done to the Palace recap-
turing it from K'hedduk, no one had had the time to take
them there.

...aidan's ears were perked wide as they made their way
...wn the slope toward the tented village that sprawled around
...e of the larger tree-lined wells. In the middle of the encamp-
...ient was one large tent where much of the formal commerce
was conducted. Around it were the living tents of the nomads,
and in the outermost ring were the market stalls and food
tents that the locals frequented.

The air was full of a fascinating array of scents, most of
which Shaidan couldn't identify. With almost every step, something caught his eye. A bright splash of material here, the glint
of metalwork there, the scent of spiced, broiling meat, or the
tang of ripe fruits cut open for sale. The nomads in their long
robes and head wrappings were no less colorful as they called
out their wares to the passersby.

"Ooh!" said Kitra, suddenly stopping and dragging Shaidan
over to a stall displaying exotic beaded collars and pendants.
"I have to see these! Have you ever seen anything like them,
Shaidan?"

He stood dutifully beside her, eyeing the vibrantly colored
broad collars that the stallholder was now showing to them,
listening to him reel off their beauty and their value.

"Not those, Aunt Kitra," he said, tugging on her hand.
"Those are cheap ones that will break easily. You want one of
those over there." He pointed to a small stand at the back of
the tent awning where more modest collars were displayed.
"Those are better quality ones, ones the Court females wear.
And they don't even cost what he's asking for the others."

Kitra arched an eye ridge at the merchant, who began to
exclaim that the child was mistaken, those were far inferior to
what he was offering her.

Kitra, our meal is ready, came Dzaka's gentle thought to
both of them. *We can go shopping after we eat.*

"I'll think about it," said Kitra, interrupting the merchant's
flow of chatter and handing him back the collar she'd been
looking at.

"He's trying to sell you cheap necklaces," said Shaidan as
they left his stall and hurried down the tent alley to the restaurant where Dzaka was waiting for them. "I heard him, Aunt.
You'd be better doing what Doctor Zayshul and the others do,
buy from the merchants that come to the Palace to trade. You
won't get cheated then."

"How did you get to be so wise?" she murmured, giving

his hand a loving squeeze before letting him go to gree.
mate.

Shaidan surveyed the mounds of cushions set around t.
low table where his uncle had been waiting. "We sit on them"?
he asked, grinning. "No chairs?"

"Hello there, kitling," said Dzaka, reaching out to ruffle his
hair before helping Kitra to settle herself on the cushions. "No
chairs. Is that a problem?"

Shaidan shook his head. "Nope," he said, dropping to his
knees, then squirming into a comfortable position. "This is fine
by me. Wait till the others hear about this!"

Dzaka laughed and gestured to a waiter standing nearby.
"We're ready to eat."

There had been a sweet white drink, made from fermented
milk, Aunt Kitra had told him, and rice and spicy vegetables,
but the best part had been when the waiter had brought out
the meat on a stick that was on fire.

And it had tasted as good as it looked, too. It had been a
bit spicy-hot at first, but the white drink had cooled his mouth
down, and he'd quickly gotten used to the taste. Even the
bread had been different. It was flat, and he could fork rice
and meat into it, and vegetables, and even one of the sauces
too, then fold it up to eat, almost like a sandwich. It had drib-
bled out the other end, but Aunt Kitra and Uncle Dzaka had
only laughed as the same had happened to them. The waiter
had kindly brought them all lots of paper napkins to make
sure they didn't get it on their clothes and faces. He hadn't
needed his, though—he'd just leaned over his plate while eating so it fell there.

Almost full to the brim, he leaned back on the cushions as
the empty plates were taken away.

"That's what I call a feast," he said, satisfied.

"Oh, there's more to come," said Dzaka with a grin.

Kitra groaned, rubbing her belly. "I don't think I could eat
another morsel! What about you, Shaidan?"

"Dessert," said Dzaka succinctly.

Shaidan screwed his face up in thought. "I could make
room," he offered. "For dessert. Be a shame to waste it."

"It would," agreed Dzaka solemnly. "It's quite special.
Something they call iced sherbet, with fruit."

This surprised him. "They have ice here?"

I'm told the dish was invented by the nomads," said Dzaka. "They come down from the mountains, after all, where there snow on the peaks in the winter, though I have no idea how they keep it frozen here."

Shaidan sat up and waited impatiently for the desserts to arrive. When they did, he stared in disbelief at the three large dishes piled high with layers of colored ice, topped by bright red and yellow berries.

"Ooh . . ." he said, reaching out to touch the frosted side of the glass dish that was put in front of him. "It really is cold! How do you do it?" he demanded of the waiter before he could leave. "How do you make the ice and keep it cold when it's so hot outside?"

The Prime flashed him a toothy grin. "Same way they do in the Palace, young sir. We have our own generators to provide us with the power."

"Oh," he said, slightly disappointed at the prosaic answer. He'd hoped it was something more exotic.

The waiter hesitated. "Actually, I tell a lie, may the good Goddess of the Fields forgive me," he said. "But you must not tell anyone, young Sholan," he said, his voice dropping to a whisper as he leaned closer. "It is magic, and a secret. In the large tent in the center of our village, we keep a great barrel of steel in which we place the fruit juices and fruit that make our sherbet."

Shaidan's eyes grew larger, and his ears pricked forward to better hear the low whisper.

"Each night we make a new batch, and our holy men say the special prayers and light the incense and candles. Then they dance around it, calling on the spirits of winter and snow to give their blessings to our confection. If the Gods will it, by morning, we have the magic of sherbet to serve to our most special customers."

He bowed, and slowly backed away from the table, leaving Shaidan not quite sure whether to believe him or not.

"Now you know," said Kitra, picking up her spoon and taking a taste. "Oh, Dzaka, Shaidan, this is amazing! I have never tasted anything as good as this!"

It was good. The cold of the ice dissolved on his tongue, leaving behind the sharp, yet sweet taste of the fruit to cool his mouth after the spicy heat of the main meal.

* * *

After they'd eaten, they took a slow stroll back thro the market, stopping at several of the stalls. They spent so time at one with a wide selection of swords and daggers of a shapes and sizes.

"Shaidan," said Dzaka, gesturing him over to join him. "It's about time you had a knife of your own. Your pappa will get you a proper one when he gets back, but until then, how would you like this one?"

It was a real knife not a toy one, he saw that instantly. The eight-inch curved metal scabbard was embossed with the shapes of all manner of beasts leaping along its length. The pattern was echoed on the hilt, which ended in a plain round boss. Slowly, he drew the blade out. It was like a claw, both the curved edges honed to the point he knew it could cut a hair.

"I know you'll be careful with it," said Kitra. "Back on Shola, you would have your first knife by now, so Dzaka and I thought it only right to get you one."

"It's beautiful," he breathed, handing her the scabbard so he could run a claw tip along the blade and feel the heart of the steel.

"Don't draw it unless you need to use it," said Dzaka. "And if you do, be prepared to use it as I've trained you."

"I will, Uncle Dzaka," he said, automatically reaching out with his mind to check for danger even as he looked around them alertly.

There's no present danger, Shaidan, sent his uncle. *But now you can defend yourself if need be.*

Understood, Uncle Dzaka, he replied, taking the scabbard back from his aunt and sheathing his knife.

"Here, let me fix it to your belt," said Kitra, leaning forward.

Lying in bed that night in his own room in the Palace, freshly showered and his hair braided, he reached his hand under his pillow to touch the knife. He couldn't quite believe it was his, it was so beautiful and unexpected a gift. It made him feel more grown up, less helpless, as he'd been when they'd been prisoners of the Directorate. Now he could defend them all if danger threatened them.

He could sense his aunt and uncle in the main room— they'd taken over his parents' suite while they were away. They were settling down for the evening with some friends to

a board game. Faint thoughts came from his brothers and
sisters as they all wished each other good night. He joined in,
sending his special one to Gaylla, who was cuddled up with
her favorite doll.

As he began to drift off to sleep, he sensed that he wasn't
alone and turned around to look off into the shadows by the
window.

"Vartra," he said sleepily.

"Yes, youngling," the Sholan replied, stepping out of the
shadows and over to his bed. "Are you too tired to take a trip
with me tonight?"

Shaidan sat up, suddenly wide awake. "A trip? To see
Pappa? We won't be long, will we? 'Cos I don't want to worry
Aunt Kitra and Uncle Dzaka."

Vartra smiled. "Yes, to see your pappa, and your aunt and
uncle won't even know you're gone." He held out his hand
and stood up. "Come with me."

Shaidan threw back the covers and got out of bed. Just before his hand touched Vartra's, he exclaimed and darted back
to the bed, reaching under his pillow for his knife. Clutching it
tightly, he turned back to Vartra.

"I'm ready," he said, holding out his hand.

As their hands met, Shaidan turned around to look at the
bed. With a shock, he saw himself still lying there.

Vartra's hand tightened on his reassuringly. "It's all right,
little one. We're pathwalking to meet your father. Your body
will remain here, but we'll be elsewhere."

"But . . ." he began, but anything else he intended to say
was lost as they plunged into a darkness more absolute than
any he'd ever known. He gasped for air, biting down on the
terror that surged through him.

We're safe, Vartra sent to him. *A moment only and we'll be
there.*

Suddenly he was blinking in the sunlight, standing in a neat
garden edged with a wild array of flowers of all colors and
sizes. Insects buzzed among them and he was sure he could
hear birds singing, though he'd never yet seen one.

"Shaidan!"

It was his pappa's voice! Turning around, he saw him standing there, arms held open for him.

"Pappa!" He ran to him, wrapping his legs around him as
he was lifted up into his arms. "Pappa," he said again, burying

his face against his father's neck, smelling his scent, and ~~~ ing his warmth. "It really is you! I have missed you so muc~

"So have I, korrai," said his father, hugging him tight~ before setting him down. "What's that you're holding?" he asked.

"Uncle Dzaka and Aunt Kitra got me a knife today. One to last me till you give me one, they said." He held it out to show Kusac.

"That's beautiful," he said, pulling it out of the scabbard to look at it. "I know you'll look after it well and use it only if you need to."

"Yes, Pappa," Shaidan said.

"I can only stay for a short while, I'm afraid, Shaidan," his father said, handing back the knife and resting his hands on his son's shoulders and looking deep into his eyes. "Vartra says he can bring us together now and then, when we need to see each other. Can you keep being brave for your mother and me?"

Shaidan straightened up, standing as tall as he could. "I can do that," he said, his bottom lip only quivering a little.

His father smiled, reaching out to press his fingers against his lips. "That's my son," he said softly. Kneeling down, he pulled him into an embrace again, resting his cheek against Shaidan's. "We'll be back as soon as we can, never doubt that, Shaidan."

"I know, Pappa," he said, feeling his father's tongue rasp gently against his cheek.

"I love you." The words sounded faint, and as he looked up, he felt his father's arms around him begin to loosen.

"No! Don't go!" he cried out.

Remember, I'm only a thought away, korrai, sent his father as darkness gently surrounded him.

Lisanne Norman

The *Sholan Alliance* Series

"Will hold you spellbound"
—*Romantic Times*

"This is fun escapist fare, entertaining...."   -—*Locus*

To Order Call: 1-800-788-6262
www.dawbooks.com

RM Meluch

The Tour of the Merrimack

C.S. Friedman

The Best in Science Fiction

THIS ALIEN SHORE 0-88677-799-2
A *New York Times* Notable Book of the Year
"Breathlessly plotted, emotionally savvy. A potent
metaphor for the toleration of diversity"
—*The New York Times*

THE MADNESS SEASON 0-88677-444-6
"Exceptionally imaginative and compelling"
—*Publishers Weekly*

IN CONQUEST BORN 0-7564-0043-0
"Space opera in the best sense: high stakes adventure
with a strong focus on ideas, and characters an
intelligent reader can care about."—*Newsday*

THE WILDING 0-7564-0164-X
The long-awaited follow-up to *In Conquest Born*.

To Order Call: 1-800-788-6262
www.dawbooks.com

CJ Cherryh

Complete Classic Novels in Omnibus Editions

To Order Call: 1-800-788-6262
www.dawbooks.com

OTHERLAND
Tad Williams

"The Otherland books are a major
accomplishment."–*Publishers Weekly*

"It will captivate you."
   –*Cinescape*

In many ways it is humankind's most stunning achievement.
This most exclusive of places is also one of the world's
best-kept secrets, but somehow, bit by bit, it is claiming
Earth's most valuable resource: its children.

CITY OF GOLDEN SHADOW (Vol. One)
978-0-88677-763-0

RIVER OF BLUE FIRE (Vol. Two)
978-0-88677-844-6

MOUNTAIN OF BLACK GLASS (Vol. Three)
978-0-88677-906-1

SEA OF SILVER LIGHT (Vol. Four)
978-0-75640-0030-9

To Order Call: 1-800-788-6262
www.dawbooks.com